Neath Port Talbot
Libraries
Llyfrgelloedd
Castell-Nedd
Port Talbot

Books should be returned or renewed by the last date
stamped above.
Dylid dychwelyd llyfrau neu eu hadnewyddu erbyn y dyddiad
olaf a nodir uchod

Boyd, Damien
Heads or Tails

0 9 MAY 2022   1 3 JUL 2023
- 6 APR 2022   - 4 MAY 2023
1 1 DEC 2021   2 8 AUG 2018   1 3 SEP 2023
2 0 AUG 2018
0 2 JUL 2021   0 9 MAR 2023
- 9 AUG 2018
0 6 APR 2020   0 2 JUN 2021   - 5 JAN 2022
2 6 JUL 2018
2 5 OCT 2019   0 3 NOV 2022
1 4 JUL 2018
0 5 MAR 2019   1 SEP 2022
1 5 MAY 2018
3 1 JAN 2018
1 5 SEP 2018   1 0 JAN 2018

ALSO BY DAMIEN BOYD

As the Crow Flies
Head in the Sand
Kickback
Swansong
Dead Level
Death Sentence

HEADS OR TAILS

DAMIEN BOYD

THOMAS & MERCER

Text copyright © 2017 by Damien Boyd

Published by Thomas & Mercer, Seattle

www.apub.com

Amazon, the Amazon logo, and Thomas & Mercer are trademarks of Amazon.com, Inc., or its affiliates.

ISBN-13: 9781542046619
ISBN-10: 1542046610

Cover design by @blacksheep-uk.com

Printed in the United States of America

For my father, Michael

Prologue

Manchester City Council
Social Services

Dr S Beckwith CPsychol FBPsS
75 Harley Street
London
W1G 8QL

21 May 1977

Dear Solomon,
Re: Child A
I refer to our telephone conversation earlier today and should be grateful for your assistance, please, with Child A.

As discussed, he is twelve years of age and is currently placed with a foster family in Oldham. For reasons that I hope are self-explanatory, we thought it sensible if the placement was made outside the immediate Manchester area.

Child A is very withdrawn and yet displays outbursts of violence that his foster family are currently able to manage. Having said that, the violent episodes are becoming more extreme and more frequent, and it is not known at this stage how long this situation can continue. Removal to a specialist children's home may be the only option, but I am anxious to avoid that if we can.

By way of background, Child A's mother died of cancer when he was seven years old, leaving him an only child living with his father. Physical examination (a medical report is available) reveals evidence of prolonged sexual abuse, which Child A says began soon after his mother died and continued until his father's murder on Good Friday.

I will not go into detail here about the precise nature of the abuse Child A suffered at the hands of his father, suffice it to say that it has taken some time and patient coaxing to extract any detailed information. What has become clear is that it was sexual, physical and mental abuse of the utmost violence and severity, suffered over a prolonged period.

Child A believes that his mother's death was his fault and that the abuse was his punishment. He remains convinced that he deserved it, and no amount of assurances to the contrary appear able to persuade him otherwise.

To complicate matters, his father met his death at the hands of Child A's best friend, a fifteen year old boy who has since confessed to the murder. He was, he says, acting to protect Child A. He has pleaded guilty to one count of murder and is due to be sentenced next month.

Needless to say, the murder has had a profound effect on Child A, who witnessed it at close quarters. His father was stabbed in the neck on answering the front door and fell at Child A's feet, his jugular vein severed. Child A then watched as his father was shot in the head at close range. When police arrived on the scene, they found him covered in blood and cradling his father's head in his hands.

Child A is currently under the care of Dr James McDonald, and it is at his suggestion that I am writing to you now. Dr McDonald's view is that more specialist assistance will be required if Child A is to avoid being institutionalised for much of his life.

His foster family can, of course, bring him down to your consulting rooms at your convenience, and I very much hope you are able to assist.

I look forward to hearing from you as soon as possible, please.

Yours sincerely,

Steven Grey
Senior Social Worker
Children's Services

Chapter One

Rotting seaweed. It was more of a stench than a smell. Nick Dixon grimaced. Being downwind of the sewage treatment works wasn't helping either, although it was keeping him awake. That, and the cold.

He was standing on top of a concrete sluice gate looking down at the tidal section of the River Huntspill, where it snaked out a short distance to join the River Parrett. The thick grey mud below the high tide mark shimmered in the moonlight, revealing the outline of a net shaped like a huge funnel and suspended on a long pole just above the waterline.

Several sheep grazing along the base of a steep grass embankment off to the right were just visible, and beyond them the River Parrett, the incoming tide bringing with it yet more seaweed. And elvers, millions of elvers.

'We don't usually get a detective inspector when we're out catching poachers.'

'How *is* your colleague?' asked Dixon, turning to Keith Bates, the Environment Agency officer shivering next to him.

'Still in an induced coma.'

'You nick 'em for elver poaching and I'll nick 'em for grievous bodily harm, all right?'

'Point taken.'

'What time's high tide?'

'Just after eight, but they'll be here well before sunrise. They'll come for them while the tide is still coming in, otherwise the elvers will get swept back out of the net. It was pure luck we spotted it, really.'

'How long have we got, then?'

'An hour or so, maybe. The net'll be under water in ten or fifteen minutes, then it's just a case of how long they want to leave it. Too long and they won't be able to get to it until the tide goes out again.'

Dixon nodded and turned up the collar of his coat. It had been a long night, stuck in the middle of nowhere, and he'd lost all track of time several hours ago. The will to live had followed soon after.

The call from the Environment Agency had come in just before last orders and Dixon had left his girlfriend, Detective Sergeant Jane Winter, and his Staffordshire terrier, Monty, sitting by the fire in the Red Cow. Then he'd left the new Bridgwater Police Centre at Express Park just before 2 a.m. and had spent the rest of the night lying in the bushes, losing all feeling in his legs until Bates had suggested checking on the net. Running any distance, and at speed, would be out of the question, but the dog handlers were on hand to deal with a chase, if it came to it.

The streetlights along the Esplanade at Burnham-on-Sea were visible a couple of miles away to the north, as was the marker buoy on Stert Island, but apart from that, light pollution was non-existent. The night sky offered some small consolation, not that he could identify many of the stars he was looking at.

'What will you do with the elvers?' he asked.

'They'll be released further up, beyond the tidal reach.'

'How many will there be?'

'Thousands. At Dunball, where it's narrower, maybe fifteen kilograms. That's about three grand's worth. Not bad for an hour's work.'

'And here?'

'Half that, probably. But they know we're after them at Dunball.'

'They'll know we're after them here soon if we don't get back under cover.'

Dixon followed Bates down to an area of dense undergrowth on the edge of the service road that followed the River Parrett behind the embankment. He glanced up at the old sign on the edge of the bushes, NATIONAL RIVERS AUTHORITY, **PRIVATE ROAD, NO UNAUTHORISED ACCESS**, and wondered who had been using it for target practice. There were several bullet holes in it, and it had taken at least four shotgun blasts at point blank range.

Armed Response?

No thanks. It's just a couple of fishermen.

He ducked under the wire fence and then crawled under the bushes until he was alongside PC Cole.

'Everyone in position?'

'Yes, Sir. The vans are ready to block either end of the service road, and both dogs are still here.'

'Better make sure they're awake.'

Dixon tipped his head to the left and right, trying to work out what was lying on top of the embankment in front of him while he listened to Cole whispering into his radio. A Christmas tree; it must be a Christmas tree, its dead branches obscuring different stars as he moved his head from side to side. He was killing time, which was not something he had ever been very good at. Watching the dew forming on the sleeve of his coat was next on the list.

'Bats.'

'Eh?'

'Can you see 'em?'

'This isn't bloody *Springwatch*, Cole.'

'No, Sir.'

Dixon turned when he heard movement behind him and watched Bates crawl alongside them, his bobble hat catching on the brambles.

'Did you say bats?'

Dixon rolled his eyes.

'I did,' whispered Cole, lying next to Dixon.

'There are bat boxes in the roof of the pumping station over there.'

'You'd have thought they'd still be hibernating,' said Cole.

'The days have been mild and it is late March. The clocks go forward on Sunday, don't forget.'

Dixon smiled, thinking of evenings after work and walks on the beach with Monty.

'You haven't got your waders on, Sir.' Cole grinned, his teeth glinting in the moonlight.

'If you think I'm going anywhere near that mud, you're very much mistaken,' replied Dixon.

'It's not too bad, provided you don't panic,' said Bates. 'Just keep still.'

'How deep is it?' asked Cole.

'Deep enough.'

'Deep enough for what?' muttered Dixon.

◆ ◆ ◆

'It'll take them, what, twenty minutes to get the elvers out of the net and boxed up?'

'About that,' replied Bates.

'And they'll want to be well clear before dawn,' continued Dixon, squinting at his watch in the darkness, 'which is less than an hour away.'

'Yes.'

He started crawling backwards out from under the bushes.

'Where are you going, Sir?' whispered Cole.

'Check the net.'

'But, we've had no reports of—'

'Boat, Cole,' replied Dixon. 'They must've come by boat.'

He crawled to the top of the embankment and peered into the darkness beyond. The water was still several yards below the top of the mud bank, although the line of seaweed that marked last night's high tide was much higher, on the grass, which explained the manmade embankment to catch the spring tides.

Away to Dixon's left, two men were emptying the contents of the flow net into two large plastic crates filled with seawater. One was gathering the net and tipping it, the other trying to guide the wriggling mass of baby eels into the crate with his hands. The elvers glistened in the light of the men's head torches, a handful escaping over the side of the crate and sending the second man scrabbling in the grass.

Dixon scanned the waterline, spotting the outline of a small boat out on the bank of the River Parrett, perhaps fifty yards away. Then he crawled back down the embankment to where Cole and Bates were waiting for him.

'They're here,' he whispered. 'There's a boat out on the Parrett. Get the dogs and tell the vans to close in. I'll circle round and go for the boat. Quick as you can.'

'Yes, Sir.'

'I'll get the net,' said Bates.

Dixon nodded, then turned and ran a few paces along the base of the embankment, before crawling up and over it. Once below the skyline on the seaward side he was up and running again, tiptoeing along the waterline, crouching as low as he could. He arrived at the boat just as the silence was broken by voices in the darkness.

'Police! Stay where you are!'

'Shit!'

Then a dog barking, closely followed by a scream.

'You get the other one. He went that way.'

Dixon sat down in the boat and listened to the footsteps coming towards him, the beam of light from a head torch bouncing around as it approached. A large bearded figure wearing a dark green one piece waterproof suit loomed out of the darkness and stopped abruptly when he saw him.

'Nice boat.' Dixon smiled.

The man turned and ran past him, a police dog handler not far behind being pulled along by a large German shepherd. Dixon watched the handler release the dog and waited for the scream.

One, two, three . . .

'We've got him, Sir.'

◆　◆　◆

'Where do they end up?' asked Dixon, watching Bates shaking the last elver from the net.

'They're sold to the Continent. A bit of a delicacy in certain parts, apparently.'

Dixon shook his head.

'Never fancied jellied eels, myself.'

'Me neither.'

Several police vans had arrived, lighting up the scene with their headlights. The eel poachers were handcuffed and sitting in separate vans, each arrested on suspicion of causing grievous bodily harm. A flatbed lorry was on its way to collect the boat.

'I wonder where they put it in the water,' said Cole.

'Stolford, possibly,' replied Bates. 'Or Combwich.'

'Let's get those places checked for a vehicle and trailer, Cole.'

'Yes, Sir.'

'Any weapons?'

'There's a crowbar in the boat. I've bagged it up for forensics.'

'Good.'

Dixon looked down at the water and watched it lapping against the concrete sluice gates at the end of the River Huntspill. The tide had come in another six inches in the time it had taken to make the arrests, the tide line just visible in the half light of dawn.

'I wonder what's holding them up.' Cole pointed north along the River Parrett at a police van parked half a mile away on the concrete service road, beyond where it crossed over the embankment and followed the high waterline. 'They were blocking the Highbridge end.' Both officers were out of the van and appeared to be looking down at something in the water.

'Get 'em on the radio,' said Dixon.

Cole turned away, speaking into his radio.

'D'you think it's them?' asked Bates. 'The two who hit Colin?'

'We won't know till we get the forensics,' replied Dixon. 'Unless they confess. It's either that or we've got to hope Colin wakes up.'

'Well, we'll—'

'Excuse me, Sir,' interrupted Cole.

'What is it?'

'A van, Sir. Stuck in the mud. And there's a body in it.'

Chapter Two

Dixon fastened his seatbelt as Cole accelerated along the service road. They followed the concrete track that veered up and over the embankment opposite the entrance to the West Huntspill Sewage Treatment Works, before screeching to a halt in front of the police van.

'Get those two back to Express Park and booked in,' said Dixon, climbing out of the patrol car.

'I've got everyone keeping an eye out for a vehicle and trailer.'

'Good. And we'd better get the rest of the team out of bed. Louise, Mark and Dave.'

'Yes, Sir.'

'Tell Louise to get herself over here and get Dave to ring me.'

'Will do.'

Dixon turned to the uniformed officers standing by the van.

'Coastguard?'

'On the way, Sir,' replied an officer with thick grey mud plastered halfway up his thighs. A set of footprints led no more than a few paces out into the mud.

'You didn't get very far, I see.'

'No, Sir. We'll need the hovercraft. It's been paged.'

Dixon nodded.

'Where's the body?' he asked, looking down at the van.

'Driver's seat, Sir,' replied the other officer. 'If you walk along a bit and look back you can see him.'

'Him?'

'Yes, Sir. IC1 male, approximately forty years of age. Short dark hair. Slumped forward over the steering wheel. That's about all we can get from here.'

'And you're sure he's dead?'

'Looks it, Sir. He hasn't moved the whole time we've been here. We've tried shouting to him, but the driver's window is shut.'

The mud bank shelved away steeply towards the water beyond a band of rocks covered in thick black seaweed. The rocks were small and looked like quarry debris, probably dumped along the bank to act as makeshift tidal defences. A set of tyre tracks ran from the top of the embankment behind Dixon, across the concrete and the rocks, and into the mud. The van had then slid down to its present position, no more than a foot above the waterline, before the suction had brought it to a halt.

A silver Ford Transit. Too low in the mud to see the registration number, or the wheels for that matter, but it looked new. 'Pest Erase UK, the pest eradication specialists' and an 0800 number were emblazoned on the side of the van. 'Members of the BPCA' too, whatever that was.

Dixon walked along the concrete track and looked back at the driver's seat. Several days of stubble was all he could add to the description he had already been given. That and a trickle of blood down the right side of the driver's nose. Perhaps he had hit his forehead on the steering wheel? But was that before or after he had driven down the embankment? Or was he pushed? Lots of questions coming thick and fast, but no answers. Yet.

Sirens in the distance began to drown out the skylarks in the fields behind him. Then a trailer appeared, reversing on to the jetty at Burnham, the bright orange hovercraft on the back visible even from over a mile away. Dixon looked back to the van. The water was now lapping at the front bumper, and it would not be long before the passenger compartment was swamped. He checked his watch. There were still almost two hours to go before high tide, which would submerge the whole van.

He took out his iPhone and took several photos of the scene, zooming in on the driver. The trickle of blood was clearer now, if anything. Odd that. Dixon scrambled down over the rocks, slipping on the seaweed, trying to get as close as he could to the van. He looked again, squinting into the sunrise reflecting off the window. Then it hit him. The driver had turned his head.

He's alive!

Dixon ran back up to the two uniformed officers standing on the concrete track.

'Get on to the Coastguard and tell them the casualty is alive.'

'Yes, Sir.'

'What've you got in the boot?'

'A stinger and a couple of accident warning signs, Sir. There's some cones too, and a broom, but that's about it.'

'Give me the stinger and the signs,' replied Dixon, handing the officer his phone. 'Here, look after this for me.'

'You're not going out there?'

'He's alive, and I don't intend to let him drown.'

'The Coastguard will be here in a minute, Sir.'

'And how long d'you think he's got before he drowns?'

'Yes, Sir.'

'Have you ever deployed a stinger before, Sir?' asked the other officer, handing Dixon the road signs.

'No.'

'I'd better do it then. There's a knack to it. I'll need to make sure it lands fully extended as well, because there's no way it'll slide across the mud.'

'Just make sure you do it the wrong way up; I don't want holes in my shoes.'

'No, Sir.'

Dixon followed the officer down to the edge of the mud and watched him deploy the stinger. The steel lattice frame extended out from the bank, landing a couple of paces short of the van, with the spikes that would usually deflate car tyres facing down into the mud. Then it sank from view, the mud closing over it and leaving little more than a faint outline where it had been.

'That'll have to do,' muttered Dixon. Then he tucked the road signs under his arm and ran straight along the line where the stinger had been.

Any hope that the van would have compressed the mud behind it was soon dashed. It was like treacle. Wading through deep snow in the Alps had been much easier. He had gone less than halfway before the mud was up to his waist, but the stinger was beneath him, taking at least some of his weight and stopping him sinking even further. When he reached the end, he threw the road signs on to the mud in front of him and crawled across them. They soon disappeared, but not before he had reached the back of the van, grabbing the handle at full stretch and pulling himself across.

'I've lost my bloody shoe,' he muttered as he tried to pull himself up on the roof rack.

'Can you get up on the roof, Sir?' shouted one of the officers on the bank.

Dixon tried to get one foot up on to the bumper and step up, but the suction was immense. Not just holding him, but pulling him down.

He grimaced. 'There goes the other shoe.'

Then he was clear of the mud and on the roof of the van, scrambling over the ladders towards the front.

'Throw me the broom.'

'Yes, Sir.'

Dixon caught it and, standing above the driver's door, swung it like an axe at the window, shattering it with the first hit. Then, holding on to the roof rack, he lowered himself into the mud adjacent to the driver, sinking up to his waist. He held on to the wing mirror and looked in the passenger compartment.

'What's your name?'

No reply.

Blood was pouring down the left side of the man's chest, coming from wounds to that side of his neck. He was wearing a black polo shirt and fleece, embroidered with the Pest Erase UK logo, the white stitching saturated with blood. Dixon leaned in. There were several wounds, each an inch long. Stab wounds, surely?

'What's your name?'

The man turned his head, slowly, revealing a hole in his forehead. Dixon had seen one before, jagged and made by a bullet, but this was different. A perfect circular incision half an inch or so in diameter, which accounted for the trickle of blood running down the man's nose, a piece of skull the size of a penny missing.

'Help . . . me . . .'

The voice was low, almost a whisper, the eyes wide and fixed on Dixon.

'What's your name?'

'Ha . . . Harry . . .' His voice tailed off.

'Stay with me, Harry. All right? Stay with me.'

Water surged into the footwell, reaching Harry's knees, just as the first wave hit Dixon. He gasped.

Shit, that's cold.

It could have been worse. There was very little wind, and the waves were lapping gently around his chest rather than crashing over him, but creeping ever higher all the same.

Then he spotted Harry's left wrist, handcuffed to the steering wheel.

'Shift this van out of the way.'

The voice came from the concrete track. Dixon looked up. The first HM Coastguard vehicle had arrived, and a man in blue overalls was speaking into a radio. One of the police officers was moving their van and the other was pointing out into the River Parrett. Dixon turned to see the hovercraft heading straight towards him.

'Help's here, Harry. They're gonna get you out.' Dixon was shouting, trying to make himself heard over the noise of the hovercraft's engines as it edged ever closer.

He tried the driver's door, but the mud was halfway up the side of the van. Then he heard a woman's voice.

'Are you the police officer?'

The hovercraft was behind him now, its bow sitting on the mud. Two Coastguard officers, a man and a woman wearing yellow dry suits and red lifejackets, slid over the side, their special boots acting like snow shoes and holding them on top of the mud.

'Detective Inspector Dixon. This is Harry. He's conscious, but unresponsive. He has injuries to his neck and head. And he's handcuffed to the steering wheel. The door won't budge, so you'll have to bring him out through the window.'

'I'm Bev,' said the woman. 'Let's get you clear first. Can you climb in?'

'Yes, I'm fine,' replied Dixon. 'Just get Harry out.'

He took hold of the side of the hovercraft, managing to pull his legs out of the mud. Then he rolled over the side, landing in a muddy heap on the floor.

'Shall we take you back to Burnham?' asked the pilot.

'No, just over there will do.'

Dixon looked up at the bank from the hovercraft. A second Coastguard vehicle had arrived, and an ambulance. A third Coastguard officer was getting ready to walk out to the van, pulling a stretcher with a rope paying out behind it. He had on the same mud boots and was carrying a long walking stick with a flat bottom. More useful than a road sign, no doubt. The hovercraft settled on the mud adjacent to the seaweed covered stones along the shoreline.

'Inspector Dixon?'

He glanced up at the hand outstretched towards him. 'Here, let me help you.' The man was stocky and bearded, with dark curly hair, thinning on top and greying at the sides.

'Thank you,' replied Dixon, stepping over the side of the hovercraft on to the seaweed.

'Steve Yelland. Officer in Charge. I'm in touch with the Watch Officer at Milford Haven.' His moustache was a mixture of grey and nicotine stain. Dixon noticed a radio in his left hand and another dangling from his right wrist.

'He's handcuffed to the steering wheel.'

'We've got a set of bolt cutters in the truck, and the fire brigade are on the way with their cutting equipment.'

'How long have we got?'

'Ten or fifteen minutes. Plenty of time. We've established a safety zone, so if you could just stand over th—'

The look on Dixon's face stopped Yelland mid-sentence.

'Fair enough.'

Yelland turned away and shouted across to another Coastguard officer standing by the large four wheel drive truck.

'Get the bolt cutters, Phil.'

Dixon looked back to the van. The water was halfway up the driver's door, at least up to Harry's waist in the passenger compartment. A Coastguard officer was leaning in the window.

'The bolt cutters aren't here, Steve,' shouted Phil, leaning in the back of the truck.

'Where the hell are they?'

'Must be back at the station, in the drying room. We used them on the last training exercise, didn't we?'

Yelland ran over and began rummaging in the back of the truck. 'Who was on the last exercise?'

'I was. And Bev and Toby.'

'Well, why didn't you put the bloody bolt cutters back?'

Phil shrugged his shoulders. 'I thought we did.'

'They'll have to break the steering wheel with a holdfast stake,' said Yelland, handing him a long metal bar.

'Right.'

Phil ran down to the edge of the mud and handed the metal bar to the officer about to walk out to the van.

His progress was slow. Painfully slow. His mud boots stopped him sinking to more than knee deep and the wading stick ensured that he kept his balance, but he was still taking too long. Far too long. Dixon watched the water level creeping up the side of the van, each wave taking it higher.

'Is that the bloody sewage works?' asked Dixon, turning away, his hand over his nose and mouth.

'It's right behind us,' replied Yelland, gesturing over his shoulder to a large concrete plinth at the foot of the embankment behind them. There was a viewing platform on top and a large yellow sign: OUTFALL, 70 METRES, NO ANCHORS.

Dixon scraped some mud off his trousers and held it to his nose. He winced. Drowning was bad enough, but at a sewage outfall? It was too horrible to contemplate. At least Harry was drifting in and out of consciousness.

A voice crackled over one of Yelland's radios. 'We've broken the steering wheel, but we can't get him out. It's his left foot. It's stuck. Over.'

'Stand by,' replied Yelland. Then he spoke into the second radio. 'Watch, this is OIC Burnham. Casualty's foot is stuck in the footwell of the van. Now a confined space due to water ingress. Please advise. Over.'

'Await further instructions. Over.'

'I didn't see anything, but then his feet were already underwater when I got there,' said Dixon. 'Can't someone get in the passenger side?'

'It's too dangerous,' replied Yelland. 'What if the van slides into the water?'

'Burnham, this is Watch. Return to place of safety and await the fire brigade. They are on the way. ETA ten minutes. Over.'

'Watch, this is Burnham. That will be too late. Over.'

'Stand by.'

'Burnham, this is Watch Manager. You have permission to sever the leg. Do not enter the vehicle. Over.'

'As if the poor bugger hasn't suffered enough,' muttered Dixon, shaking his head.

'Phil, see what we've got in the truck to cut off his leg.'

'Right.'

'Oh shit,' said Yelland, putting the radio to his mouth. 'Watch, this is Burnham. Get a message to the *Arco Dart* and tell her to slow down. Over.'

'Roger that.'

'What's the *Arco Dart*?' asked Dixon.

'A dredger, coming out of Dunball Wharf,' said Yelland, pointing to the south where a huge ship with a crane on the front was steaming out into Bridgwater Bay. It was low in the water, heavily laden, with a small pilot boat in front leading the way.

'We've got nothing, Steve, except this,' said Phil, holding up a small knife.

'Try the ambulance.'

'The *Arco Dart* isn't slowing down,' said Dixon.

'It'll take a minute,' replied Yelland, rubbing the back of his neck.

'All they've got is a thing for cutting seatbelts and clothes,' shouted Phil. 'They said they're an ambulance, not an operating theatre.'

'Right, that's it,' said Yelland. 'Everyone back to shore.'

'What? You can't just leave him there!'

'It's my jurisdiction below the high tide mark, and we're not taking any chances with the bow wave. We can go back out when it's passed.'

The Coastguard officers down at the van began climbing into the hovercraft. One of them leaned back into the passenger compartment and said something, but it was lost in the noise of the hovercraft engines. Then he climbed in and it flew them back to the shore.

Dixon watched the *Arco Dart*, which slowed down as it went past them, but too late to reduce the bow wave that was already racing towards the van. It was at least two feet high and would surely wash right over it.

'What about pulling the van out?' asked Dixon, turning to Yelland as the bow wave approached.

'There's no time now.'

'Is that it?'

'We'll go back out when the wave has passed and see what we can do, but I can't risk—'

'Here it comes, Steve,' shouted Phil.

The water hit the side of the van with a crash, sending spray high into the air. The van rocked under the impact and slid forwards, then the wave raced up the exposed mud and the seaweed covered rocks at Dixon's feet. The hovercraft, a few yards away, bounced on to the rocks as the wave passed under it, before the pilot turned back out towards the van.

The tide was up to Harry's neck now; that much was visible from the shore. His head was tipped back, his mouth open, and he was fighting to keep his chin above the water with his last gasp. His eyes were wide open, tears mixing with the seawater. Harry was conscious enough to know what was happening to him. Dixon shook his head. He was watching a man's life ebbing away on a flood tide and there was nothing he could do to stop it.

A Coastguard officer on board the hovercraft leaned into the passenger compartment. He held Harry's chin clear of the water and was talking to him, but Dixon couldn't hear what was being said.

'What about an oxygen mask from the ambulance?' asked Dixon.

'Not watertight. We'd need scuba gear,' replied Yelland, shrugging his shoulders. 'The fire brigade have breathing apparatus, but there's no time.'

The hovercraft pilot grimaced and drew his index finger across his throat. Only Harry's forehead was visible above the waterline now, the blood mixing with the murky grey seawater. The Coastguard officer slumped back into the hovercraft and shook his head.

'Watch, this is OIC Burnham. We've been unable to recover the casualty. Vehicle is now submerged. Over.'

'Await further instructions. Over.'

The first waves reached Dixon's feet, standing on the edge of the rocks on the rotting seaweed. He watched the back of the van, the rear windows still visible, and the ladders on the roof. Not quite burial at sea, and not quite a gravestone, but near enough.

'Crew back to place of safety, Burnham. Stand down. Repeat, stand down.'

Chapter Three

'What happens now?'

'It's a police matter from here,' replied Yelland. 'We're all volunteers and have jobs to go to, but we'll be back with a tractor when the tide goes out to recover the vehicle.'

'And the body,' muttered Dixon.

'Yes, and the body.'

The mud on Dixon's clothes had dried to a light grey crust, which crumbled when he sat down on the edge of the concrete track. He started brushing it off, watching the Coastguard officers packing their dirty kit into the back of their truck. The hovercraft turned out to sea and sped off towards the jetty at Burnham, leaving the ladders sticking out of the water with a red flag tied to them, the only sign of the van and Harry's resting place.

'Here's your phone, Sir.'

'This is a crime scene,' said Dixon. 'I want a fingertip search of the whole area, once this lot have gone.'

'Yes, Sir,' replied the uniformed officer who had been looking after his phone.

'Here comes the fire brigade,' said the other officer.

'Too bloody late.' Dixon watched Steve Yelland walking along the concrete track towards the fire engine. He was waving his arms above his head. A short conversation with the driver followed and then the engine began reversing back along the track.

'D'you need a lift back to Express Park, Sir?'

'No, thank you.'

◆　◆　◆

'What the bloody hell happened to you?'

'He was alive when I got to him,' said Dixon, without looking up at Detective Chief Inspector Lewis. 'He had a hole in his forehead, and he was still alive.'

'And the Coastguard couldn't get him out?'

'No, Sir,' said Dixon, getting to his feet to face Lewis and Detective Constable Louise Willmott, who was standing behind him.

'Who was he?'

'The local rat catcher, handcuffed to the steering wheel.'

'What happened?'

'God knows. But I'm sure as bloody hell going to find out.'

'You want the case then?'

'I looked into the man's eyes, Sir, and then I watched him die. It's my case.'

Lewis nodded. 'What about the poachers?'

'They're connected unless and until I know otherwise. Can we put Dave and Mark on it?'

'I already have.'

'We need to find their vehicle and trailer and search their homes. I can interview them later.'

'I've organised a search of the area.'

'Thank you, Sir.'

'Anything else?'

Dixon shook his head. He was watching the flag tied to the end of the ladder on top of the van disappearing under the waves.

'Well, I'll head back then. I assume you can make your own way back?'

No reply.

'We'll be fine, Sir,' said Louise.

She waited until Lewis had gone and then turned to Dixon, who had sat back down on the edge of the concrete track, facing out to sea.

'Are you all right, Sir?'

Silence.

'What d'you want me to do?'

'Get on to Pest Erase UK and see if they can tell us who he is,' replied Dixon. 'Harry. His name's Harry.'

'Yes, Sir.'

'And try the West Huntspill Sewage Treatment Works. It's behind us, over the embankment. See if anyone saw anything, and if they've got any CCTV.'

'What about you?'

'I'll be here.'

Dixon was flicking the mud off his trousers when he heard footsteps behind him.

'You still here, Sir?'

'You should be in bed, Cole. You were on duty all night.'

'So were you. Anyway, it's a nice little bit of overtime. I've got to watch the van until the tide goes back out.'

'I'll do that. You help with the search.'

'Are you sure?'

'Yes. I'm sure.'

'We found an old Range Rover with a boat trailer over at Stolford. Registered to a Martin White. Lives in Highbridge.'

'Address?'

'Can't remember off hand, Sir, but Dave Harding and Mark Pearce are over there now.'

'Good.'

'I'll leave you to it.'

'There's no one answering at Pest Erase, Sir,' said Louise, dropping her phone into her handbag. 'And the sewage treatment works is all locked up. I'll try again at nine.'

'What time is it?' asked Dixon.

'Nearly eight.'

The tide was washing over the rocks at the base of the concrete track now. Another few minutes or so and it would turn, if it hadn't already.

Dixon reached into his pocket and took out a Mars bar.

'Breakfast,' he muttered. He wiped the mud off the wrapper and then tore it open.

'When did you last eat?' asked Louise.

'Last night.'

'What about your blood sugar levels?'

'I'll be fine. Really.'

'Did he say anything? Y'know, before he . . .' Louise's voice tailed off.

'Not to me,' replied Dixon, shaking his head. 'Track down the Coastguard officer who had his head inside the passenger compartment, will you? See if he said anything to them.'

'Yes, Sir.'

'So, you think it's murder?'

'I'm going to do you a favour, Louise, and pretend you didn't ask that question.'

'I'll try Pest Erase again.'

'Thank you.'

Louise walked along the track with her phone clamped to her ear and had gone less than ten yards before Dixon could no longer hear her over the cries of the seagulls. Behind her a line of three uniformed police officers were walking along the top of the embankment, each with a metal detector. Another line of three, including PC Cole, followed behind, their eyes fixed on the ground in front of their feet.

Dixon looked up when Louise sat down next to him. 'Get anything?' he asked.

'His name's Harry Lucas, Sir.'

Dixon sighed. A name to the face.

'Have you got an address?'

'Yes, he lives over at East Huntspill.'

'Family?'

'A wife and two children.'

'Better get family liaison over there.'

'Will do.'

'What about the sewage works?'

'It's run by Wessex Water. They're sending someone over now.'

Dixon nodded. The flag tied to the end of the ladder was emerging from the water in front of him as the tide receded. It was hanging limply, saturated, the red material covered with a thin film of mud and sediment.

'What about the search?'

'They've found some tyre tracks and a couple of footprints. That's it though. Scenes of Crime are on the way to take a look. They'll need to be here anyway when the Coastguard get the van out.'

'We'd better get a pathologist out here too,' said Dixon.

'Yes, Sir.'

'And make sure it's Roger Poland.'

Dixon was watching a large concrete block emerging from the waves ten yards or so below the van. The sewage outfall, no doubt, which explained the smell getting stronger. Three ducks were swimming hard to hold their position in the outgoing tide just behind it.

'You'd have thought they could find a nice quiet pond somewhere, wouldn't you,' said Louise, fishing her phone out of her coat pocket again.

A blue four wheel drive was parking on top of the embankment behind them. The driver was tall, dressed in a shirt and tie, with a blue HM Coastguard waterproof coat. Moustaches were popular with the Coastguard; this one grey with a goatee to match.

'Inspector Dixon?' he asked, striding across the grass towards them.

'Yes,' replied Dixon, standing up.

'Geoff Garrett, Senior Coastal Operations Officer. Sorry, I couldn't get here earlier.'

'There's not a lot you could've done.'

'No. It does happen sometimes, sadly. You been here all morning?'

'And all night,' replied Dixon. 'We were out after elver poachers down at the Huntspill outfall. He must've been here the whole time.'

'He wouldn't have known much about it, by all accounts.'

'We'll need to keep the precise nature of his injuries under wraps for the time being.'

'We always do, Inspector.'

Dixon nodded.

'We are on the same side,' said Garrett.

'Roger will be here at midday,' said Louise. 'He's just finishing up a post mortem now.'

'Good.'

'I've lined up the tractor for midday too,' said Garrett. 'One of the local farmers. There's some pretty nasty stuff in the van, but it's all in sealed containers, so it shouldn't leak.'

'Nasty stuff?'

'Rat poison. Phostoxin pellets and bromadiolone blocks.'

'Nice to know it *shouldn't* leak?'

'That's what Pest Erase said.'

Dixon sat back down on the edge of the concrete path to watch the tide going out.

'I'll be back at midday,' said Garrett.

'Can you give Louise a lift back to Express Park?'

'Yes, of course.'

'Find out how Dave and Mark are getting on, then come back in my Land Rover. It's on the top floor of the car park.'

'What about Wessex Water?' asked Louise.

'You can speak to them when you get back. Just make sure you're back by midday.'

'Yes, Sir,' replied Louise, catching the keys that Dixon had thrown to her. 'Will you be all right?'

'Fine.'

◆ ◆ ◆

'Louise said I'd find you here.' Jane sat down next to Dixon on the edge of the concrete road. 'I brought your wellies.'

'Thanks.' Dixon took his socks off and wrung them out, grey sludge dripping on to the seaweed in front of him.

'Those can go in the bin,' Jane said, smiling. 'Are you staying here all day?'

'What time is it?'

'Eleven thirty.'

'I'll stay till we've got him out.' Dixon was sliding his feet into his boots.

'You don't have to.'

'I want to.'

'I brought you these too.' She handed him a bacon and egg sandwich and a bottle of Diet Coke.

He smiled, took his insulin pen out of his pocket and began wiping the mud off it. Then he opened it, allowing the seawater to drain out of the cap.

'You can't use that. Here.' Jane handed him his spare insulin.

'You've thought of everything.'

'Lou said you'd been in the mud.'

'Where's Monty?'

'In the car behind the embankment. I wasn't sure where you'd got to with the search.'

'It's fine. He can come out.'

'I'll go and get him.'

Dixon was halfway through his sandwich when Monty arrived and he had to fend him off.

'What's he got?' asked Jane, frowning.

'A bit of bacon.'

'That's all right. I thought for a minute he was eating seaweed.'

'We'd better keep him away from the water. The van's full of pesticides. Probably won't leak, but . . .'

'You got the poachers?'

'Crafty buggers turned up by boat.'

Jane smiled. 'And then you found the van?'

'Must've been here all the time.' Dixon shook his head.

'Coincidence?'

'I don't know yet.'

'They do exist.'

'I hate to say it, but you may be right this time. Anyway, Dave and Mark are on it, so we'll see what they come up with.'

'Has somebody been over to the treatment works? Only there was a man there opening up when I arrived.'

'I'll send Louise over there when she gets back.'

The water was lapping against the side of the van now, the flag hanging down from the end of the ladder now clear of the water, fluttering in the breeze, such as it was.

'Another few minutes and the passenger compartment will be visible.'

'You're not going back down there, are you?'

'No,' replied Dixon, shaking his head. 'He can't tell me anything now, can he?'

'So, we just sit here then?'

'We do.'

◆ ◆ ◆

The sound of engines was coming from behind the embankment. Several of them. Then Roger Poland appeared on the top, carrying his bag and a large silver case.

'Tractor's here, and a fire engine. They're waiting for the Coastguard.'

Dixon was looking at his watch. 'They said they'd be here at midday.'

'You've had quite a night of it,' continued Poland.

'You could say that.'

'I'd better head back,' said Jane. 'I took an early lunch. Shall I leave Monty?'

'Yes, you can do.'

The dog's lead was looped around her neck, so she took it off and handed it to Dixon. Then she kissed him on the cheek and walked off in the direction of her car.

'In there, is he?' asked Poland, gesturing in the direction of the van. The water was now below the level of the windows, front and back.

'Yes.'

'Tell me about his injuries,' said Poland. He dropped the case on the ground and sat down on it.

'He had a hole just here,' said Dixon, drawing a circle in the middle of his forehead with his right index finger.

'A bullet hole?'

'Couldn't have been. He was still alive, Roger.'

'Anything else?'

'Stab wounds in his neck.'

'Missed the arteries then, if he was alive.' Poland frowned. 'It all sounds vaguely familiar, you know.'

'Really?'

'I read about a case years ago,' continued Poland. 'I'm sure I did. The victim had a hole in the centre of his forehead made by a trephine.'

'A what?'

'Trephine. It's a cylindrical saw with a handle on the end. Looks a bit like a corkscrew. You turn it and it cuts a circle. It used to be used for cranial surgery. Still is, actually. Vets use them too.'

'Were there any other injuries?'

'I can't remember,' replied Poland, his eyes closed. 'I seem to recall the victims suffocated though.'

'Suffocated?'

'They were buried alive.'

'You said *victims*?'

'Nine or ten, from memory.'

Dixon took a deep breath and exhaled slowly, allowing his cheeks to puff out as he did so.

'Keep it under your hat for the time being, will you?'

'What?'

'Just until you do the PM. I need twenty-four hours to get a head start, that's all.'

'A head start on what?'

'Connections with old cases always bring people crawling out of the woodwork; you know how it is. All wanting to stick their noses in.'

'People will wonder why I never said anything,' said Poland.

'You did say something. To the Senior Investigating Officer. To me.'

'All right, all right.' Poland leaned forwards, his elbows resting on his knees. 'Whatever you say. I'll see if I can find the reference. I've got a feeling I've still got the book at home.'

'You will let me know when you're doing the PM?'

'Always do, don't I?'

◆　◆　◆

'We'll try the back axle first, but if we can't get a cable around that, we'll have to run it through the passenger compartment.'

Dixon was listening to the conversation between Steve Yelland and his superior, Geoff Garrett.

'Hovercraft standing by?'

'They're on the way. And the "D" Class lifeboat.'

'Good.'

'Two mud techs will go out. Phil and Bev. It's not far, but I'll get the hovercraft to drop them by the van.'

Garrett nodded.

'Shall we try to remove the casualty first?' asked Yelland.

'Better leave him where he is,' said Dixon. 'It's a crime scene.'

'But—'

'No buts. He stays where he is.'

'All right,' said Yelland. 'We can work around him.'

Dixon looked along the concrete service road. There were three Coastguard vehicles, a fire engine, two police cars and an ambulance. Waiting behind the embankment was the mortuary van, Roger Poland's Volvo and his own Land Rover, with Monty curled up on his bed inside. The tractor was waiting on the road ready to pull the van out of the mud, once the cable had been attached.

Further along the embankment two dog walkers were being turned back by a uniformed police officer.

33

Dixon turned when he felt a tap on his shoulder. 'There's no CCTV,' shouted Louise over the noise of the hovercraft engines. 'The sign on the gate says there is, but there isn't. He said we can try Wessex Security. They may have been out here last night for a routine check.'

'Had he heard of Pest Erase?' Dixon was leaning over and shouting into Louise's ear.

'Yes. They do the pest control on site, so they have keys to the gates.'

They turned to watch the hovercraft when the engines revved up to take the mud technicians out to the van, any attempt at further conversation abandoned for the time being.

The hovercraft stopped at the back of the van and the two Coastguard officers dropped a mud stretcher over the side and then climbed into it. The hovercraft then moved off, waiting on the mud only a few yards away with its engines idling.

Both Coastguard officers were leaning over the side of the stretcher, trying to reach the back axle of the van.

'It's no good, Steve,' shouted Phil. 'The mud's closing over as fast as we can dig. We're not getting anywhere.'

'Passenger compartment it is then,' replied Yelland.

Phil gave a 'thumbs up' sign and stepped over the side of the stretcher into the mud. Once at the driver's window, he leaned in and passed the cable to Bev, who had smashed the window on the passenger side. They both then returned to the mud stretcher where they were picked up by the hovercraft and flown back to the shore.

'Stand clear,' shouted Yelland.

'The cable might snap, I suppose,' said Dixon, turning to Poland.

'It would take your head off if it did.'

The tractor began inching back towards the embankment, dragging the van and bringing with it a wave of mud that reared up behind it like a bow wave. Then the van began to rise up as it reached the rocks, water trickling out from under the doors that were now clear of the mud. It bumped and clattered across the rocks, slewing from side to side on the seaweed, before its wheels hit the concrete at the side of the track.

'Right, it's over to you, Inspector,' said Yelland.

'Thank you,' replied Dixon, waving to Donald Watson, the senior scenes of crime officer waiting by the Scientific Services vans.

'Screens first,' said Watson to his colleagues, all of them wearing white overalls.

Dixon walked over to the driver's window and looked in. Harry was slumped forwards, his forehead resting on the steering wheel. Seawater was dribbling from his nose and mouth, and from the hole in his forehead. His eyes were open, staring blankly at the papers that had been on the dashboard and were now floating all around him. The dashboard was covered in a thin film of grey slime.

'You'd better have a look, Louise.'

'Yes, Sir.'

She turned away sharply, her face pale. 'Why would anyone do that?'

'There'll be a reason,' replied Dixon, stepping aside to allow the photographer through.

'Ready?' asked Watson.

Dixon nodded. Then Watson opened the driver's door, allowing the water in the passenger compartment to gush out. The handcuff on Harry's left wrist was visible now, freed from the broken steering wheel. Then the water reached his left ankle, revealing another handcuff that secured his foot to the clutch pedal.

'There's the reason they couldn't get him out.'

'It's no one's fault,' said Poland.

'Oh yes it bloody well is. And I'm going to find out whose,' replied Dixon.

'No, I meant . . . never mind.'

Chapter Four

The stench of rotting seaweed and mud lingered in Dixon's nostrils as he sped south on the M5. Ten minutes in the shower was all he'd had time for, and besides, he could always have another later. A quick shower and a change of clothes; he felt human again, which was more than could be said for Harry.

It was just after 3 p.m. and the team would be waiting for him in meeting room 2. Still, he had been up all night and was rarely late. They could wait.

He parked on the top floor of the staff car park at Express Park and walked along the landing to the Safeguarding Coordination Unit, their office the only one enclosed with soundproof partitioning.

'I've left Monty at home,' he said, leaning around the door. 'It'll be another late one, I'm afraid.'

'I might nip over and see my folks,' replied Jane. 'Did you feed him?'

'No, it was too early.'

'All right. See you later.'

Meeting room 2 sounded grand but it was just a glass cubicle on the landing opposite the open plan CID area. Detective Constable Dave Harding looked asleep, his head back, eyes closed and brown suede shoes resting against the partition. DC Mark Pearce was talking to Louise, who seemed to be shrugging her shoulders at regular intervals, but stopped when he saw Dixon walking along the landing.

'Dave, he's coming!' A kick under the table had Harding sitting bolt upright by the time Dixon walked in.

'Tell me about the poachers then,' said Dixon, pulling a chair out from under the table.

'Martin and Owen White,' replied Harding, reading from his notebook. 'They're brothers. Martin lives in Highbridge and Owen lives with their mother in Bridgwater. She's cooling off downstairs.'

'What happened?

'Let's just say she objected strongly to the search.'

'Did you find anything?' asked Dixon.

'Martin had some cash and a small amount of cannabis. Personal use. But that's it.'

'How much?'

'About an eighth.'

'The cash.' Dixon sighed.

'Oh, just over a grand.'

'Any previous?'

'Martin's got form for affray, but it was ten years ago: a punch up in the Somerset and Dorset. Owen has several dishonesty convictions, burglary non-res, theft from employer, that sort of stuff; nothing recent and nothing violent.'

'What about the Range Rover and trailer?'

'That's Martin's. And the boat. He's the brain cell behind the operation, if you can call it that. There was a rounders bat—'

'Baseball,' interrupted Pearce.

'Whatever,' continued Harding. 'There was a bat in the back, which has gone off to forensics with the crowbar.'

Dixon nodded. 'When will we get a result?'

'Later on today, but if not, first thing tomorrow.'

'Let's get the tyres on the Range Rover checked against the tracks from Dunball the night of the assault too.'

'That's being done now, Sir.'

'Have they said anything?'

'Nothing,' said Pearce.

'I reckon they just got greedy,' said Harding. 'They've got elver fishing licences, and there were legal dip nets in the shed at Martin's place.'

'What's a dip net?' asked Louise.

'It's just a big square net on the end of a stick. There are strict size limits on them to preserve stocks. You just stand in the water and catch what you can, but the real money is made with the flow nets.'

'Anything to connect them with Pest Erase or Harry Lucas?' asked Dixon.

'Nothing,' said Pearce.

'They're just a couple of local lads out doing a bit of poaching,' said Harding. 'If you ask me, they panicked, hit the Environment Agency bloke and scarpered.'

'Hit him a bit too hard, as it turned out,' said Dixon.

'Yes, Sir.'

'Have they got solicitors?'

'With them now,' said Pearce.

'What about the rat catcher?' asked Harding.

'Harry Lucas,' replied Dixon. 'He was found handcuffed to the steering wheel and clutch pedal. The Coastguard couldn't get him out before the tide came in and he drowned in his van. Roger Poland will be doing the PM tomorrow morning. The van's been recovered and has gone for forensics.'

'Didn't he have—?' Pearce was pointing at the middle of his forehead.

'There were other injuries,' interrupted Dixon. 'Stab wounds, if anybody asks. That's all anyone needs to know for now.'

'Yes, Sir.'

'He's got family over at East Huntspill. Karen Marsden is there now, and I'll be going over after this. I'll be back to interview the brothers later. In the meantime, Dave, can you see what comes up on the traffic cameras in Highbridge and on the A38 at Dunball?'

Harding sighed. 'Why is it always me?' he muttered.

'He may have gone cross country,' said Pearce.

'He may, but then again he may not,' replied Dixon, 'so we check.'

'Yes, Sir.'

'What am I looking for?' asked Harding.

'Mark, get on to Pest Erase and find out what you can about Harry,' said Dixon, ignoring Harding's huffing and puffing. 'I had a look at their website and they look like a franchise to me.'

'Yes, Sir.'

'My phone's buzzing,' said Dixon, reaching into his jacket pocket.

Looks clean cut, cylindrical saw, definitely a trephine, see you at the PM Roger

'Give me a second.' Dixon tapped out a reply.

What about when the widow does the ID?

Then he put his phone on the table in front of him.

'Right, Mark, let's check Harry's social media profile too. Whatever you can find. Previous convictions. Anything.'

'Yes, Sir.'

Dixon's phone buzzed again and he leaned forward to read the text message.

I can cover it R

'Louise, did you get hold of the Coastguard officer talking to Harry before he died?'

'Not yet, Sir. I've rung the Station Manager, but he hasn't returned my call.'

'Chase him up and fix up a meeting.'

Louise nodded.

'Right, that's it for now. Let's go and see Mrs Lucas.'

◆　◆　◆

There were only ten houses in Nut Tree Close, which was set back from and parallel to the main road through East Huntspill, a wide grass verge separating the two. The houses were semi-detached and arranged in five pairs, with open gardens and concrete drives at the front of each property leading to a built-in garage, chicken wire fencing marking the boundaries. Number 10 was at the far end.

Dixon parked his Land Rover across the drive and turned to Louise.

'Try to avoid giving any details.'

'I know.'

'If she asks, just duck the question. All right?'

Louise nodded.

The front door was answered by Police Sergeant Karen Marsden, the family liaison officer. She stepped out into the porch and closed the inner door behind her.

'She's taking it quite well, Sir, all things considered,' she whispered. 'But her sister's being a right pain in the arse.'

'What have you told her?'

'Just that he'd been stabbed and the Coastguard couldn't get him out of the van before he drowned.'

'What about the children?' asked Dixon.

'I arranged for her mother to collect them from school. She's taken them back to her place in Pawlett.'

'Names?'

'There's Kyle, aged eight, and Zara, who's twelve.'

'And Mrs Lucas?'

'Sharon. She's thirty-four. The sister lives locally and is here now. Her name's Linda.'

'What's her problem?'

'Doesn't seem to have a lot of time for the police. I didn't ask why.'

'See if you can get her out of the room while I speak to Sharon, will you?'

'I'll do my best.'

'Lead on then,' said Dixon, gesturing to the door.

They followed Karen into the lounge at the front of the house, where two women were sitting on the sofa, the older woman with her arm around the younger.

'Sharon, this is Detective Inspector Dixon,' Karen said. 'He's leading the investigation into Harry's death.'

'When can we see him?' asked the older woman, standing up sharply.

'Sit down, Linda,' said the younger woman, tears running down her cheeks. She was wearing jeans and a white sweatshirt, her dark hair held back in a band. What make up she had on was streaked down her face. 'Anyone would think it was Luke who'd been murdered.'

'How about some tea?' asked Dixon. 'Linda will give you a hand, Karen.'

'I blood—'

'That'd be great, Linda, thank you,' said Karen, holding open the glass door through to the open plan kitchen diner at the back of the house.

'Oh for God's sake,' Linda muttered.

Dixon watched Louise close the door behind them, then waited until she sat down at the computer table in the corner and took out her notebook.

'Sharon, I want you to know that we will find Harry's killer. All right?'

She nodded.

'I need to ask you some questions about him,' continued Dixon, sitting down on the edge of the sofa next to her. 'Will that be OK?'

'Did he know what was happening to him, at the end?'

'No, I don't believe he did.' It was a lie, told for the right reasons, and Dixon would live with it.

'Were you there?' asked Sharon.

'I was. And I want you to know the Coastguard did everything they could to get him out. There just wasn't enough time.'

'Did he say anything?'

'Not that I'm aware of. But if he did, I will find out, and I will tell you what it was.'

'Thank you.'

'How long have you been married?'

'Fifteen years.'

'What was he like?'

'A big softie, really. We always used to say he wouldn't harm a fly, and then he ends up in pest control. He hated it, but needs must and it was all he could get. He had a squirrel job once, in a roof they were, so he trapped them all and released them in the woods miles away.' She smiled. 'He must've been the worst pest controller in the world.'

'Why did he buy the franchise then?' asked Dixon.

'It seemed like a good opportunity. There wasn't much competition around here, just a few single operators, you know, a man and a van. The idea was that it would become a management thing. He'd run a fleet of vans from an office. But you have to start out doing it yourself until it grows.'

'And was it?'

'Oh, yes. I did the books for him. We're doing well . . . were doing well.' Sharon shrugged her shoulders.

'What area did he buy?'

42

'They call them territories. Sometimes it's by postcode or by county, depending on the number of people and businesses. We got the whole TA postcode, and it's a huge area. Taunton, Bridgwater, and right over to Minehead and Somerton.'

'Why Pest Erase then? Why not set up on his own?'

'It's an established brand, with support, training, billing, and all the professional accreditations you need for the business clients. There was national advertising, and it came with some existing contracts too, so he'd get the work in Somerset.'

'Like what?'

'Wessex Water was one. And a couple of housing associations, garage chains too. Plus, they acted for several local authorities and the hope was that he could get into Somerset County Council. He got Sedgemoor District.'

'How much did the franchise cost?'

'Seventy thousand pounds, but that included all his training and the van. Then it's fifteen percent of earnings.'

Sharon lit a cigarette.

'Did he have an office?' asked Dixon, passing her an ashtray from the mantelpiece.

'Not yet. All the chemicals and stuff are in the garage.'

'How long had he been doing it?'

'Twelve months.'

'And what did he do before?'

'He worked at the furniture place in Highbridge, the one that went bust, Bailey and Whyte.'

'So he lost his job when the company went into administration?'

Sharon nodded. 'Before, but it was on the way.' She took a long drag on her cigarette. 'He ended up going back to do the pest control on the site. That was after it went bust though.'

'How did he afford it then, the franchise?'

'We took out a small mortgage on this place and the rest came from a bank loan.'

'Tea's coming,' said Louise, opening the inner glazed door behind Dixon.

Karen Marsden and Linda walked in, each carrying two mugs. Linda handed one to Sharon and then sat down in the armchair next to the fireplace. Karen handed a mug each to Dixon and Louise and then walked back over to the door.

'Linda, shall we—'

'I'm staying here. I wanna make sure these two don't fob her off with some crap.'

'They're not, Linda,' snapped Sharon. 'Now, will you leave us to it.'

Linda stood up. 'Don't let them bullshit you.'

'I won't,' replied Sharon. She waited for Linda to close the door behind her. 'I'm sorry about her, Inspector. She's got a bit of a chip on her shoulder.'

'Why?'

'Her husband was a key holder at the cricket club and there was a break-in one night. Anyway, when the police rang him he jumped in his car, raced over there and the first thing they did was breathalyse him for his trouble. Failed, didn't he. Useless tosser.' Sharon stubbed her cigarette out. 'I feel a bit sorry for him because he lost his job too. He was a lorry driver.'

'They should've reminded him not to drink and drive when they made the call,' said Dixon. 'And offered to send a car for him.'

'Well, they didn't. Eighteen month ban he got.'

'Did he fight it?'

'Tried to but got nowhere.'

'Was Harry ever in trouble with the police?'

'Surely, you can check that yourself?'

'I'm asking you.'

'Not that I know of.'

'Does the name Martin White mean anything to you?'

'No.'

'How about Owen White?'

'No,' replied Sharon, frowning. 'Who are they?'

'Did Harry ever go fishing?'

'Occasionally. Like, once in a blue moon. He did a lot when he was younger, before we had the kids.'

'What did he fish for?'

'Carp.'

'What about sea fishing? By boat?'

'No, never.'

'Ever use nets?'

'No.'

'Has Karen mentioned the identification?' asked Dixon.

'No, but I've seen enough telly programmes to know it was coming. When d'you want me to do it?'

'As soon as you feel up to it, really. Harry is over at Musgrove Park Hospital. Karen can take you over there.'

'Can Linda come?'

'If you want her to.'

Sharon nodded. 'Isn't this where you ask me if I know of anyone who might want to kill him?'

'I was getting round to that,' replied Dixon.

'Well, I don't.' Tears began trickling down Sharon's cheeks. 'I really don't.'

'What about local pest controllers, when he started his new business?'

'Not that I'm aware of,' replied Sharon, shaking her head. 'He never said he'd had any trouble.'

'Would he have told you?'

'Yes. We never had any secrets.' She took a deep breath. 'I even knew he was shagging my sister.'

'Linda?'

'She doesn't know I know.'

Dixon looked at Louise and raised his eyebrows.

'I lost interest in that side of things after the kids were born. She doesn't have to know I know, does she?' asked Sharon.

'What about her husband, Luke wasn't it? Could he have found out and—'

'Killed Harry? No way. He's not capable of it.'

'What does he do now?'

'He's on incapacity benefit, or whatever it is these days. ESA or something like that. It's his back. He was working as a shopfitter at the time and lifted something . . .' Her voice tailed off.

'I'm gonna have to speak to them both at some point, Sharon, given what you've said. But if I have to let on I know about this I won't tell them it came from you. All right?'

'Thank you,' she replied. 'I've got enough to deal with now without opening that can of worms.'

'Quite.'

'Can we do the identification now? Then I'd better go and tell the kids.'

Chapter Five

Martin White was well over six feet tall and made a point of glaring at Dave Harding and clenching his fists. Not a good move, thought Dixon, threatening the conducting officer in your police interview. White had short dark hair with patches of grey in it and a beard that would soon get him a job sitting in a grotto at Christmas, although he might struggle with the cheerful disposition.

The interview suite had been busy at Express Park and the only room available had a table in it, the traditional layout with the officers sitting opposite the suspect and his solicitor. Dixon made a mental note to request this room in future, rather than the others where the interviewing officer was expected to sit next to the suspect and opposite the tape machine. He never had understood the new less adversarial concept in police interview technique. Bollocks. It was clearly designed by someone who had never sat opposite a man like Martin White.

Dave Harding made the introductions and then reminded White that he was under caution.

'Do you understand, Martin?'

'Yes.'

'Grievous bodily harm,' continued Harding. 'Carries a possible life sentence, does that.'

'I have advised my client of the sentencing options open to a judge in the event of a conviction.'

'Thank you, Mr Griffin,' replied Harding. 'And if Mr Stafford dies then it will be a murder charge. You've advised him of that too?'

White glanced at his solicitor, who nodded.

'Got greedy, did you?' asked Harding.

'What?'

'Fishing with a dip net not lucrative enough?'

'Look, I lost my job and couldn't get benefits. What else was I supposed to do? It was either that or thieving.'

'Elver poaching is thieving.'

'Not really. I mean, who's losing out? Who am I stealing from?'

'Where were you working?'

'On the taxis. Webb Cars.'

'And why did you lose your job?'

'No comment.' White was shifting in his seat, from time to time tugging at his beard.

'Fingers in the till, was it?' asked Harding, raising his eyebrows.

'Just the odd cash job. They found out and . . .'

'So, you started on the elvers?'

'Yeah.'

'Where did you get the net?'

'Owen made it.'

'And who did you sell them to?'

'There's a wholesaler over at Barnstaple. He does scallops and exports to the Continent. Takes the elvers on the side.'

'What's his name?'

'Does it matter?' asked White. 'He didn't know we were using a flow net.'

'Yes it does.'

'No comment then.' White smirked.

'How much does he pay you?'

'Three hundred quid a kilo.'

'Nice work if you can get it.' Harding's eyes narrowed. 'But you have to watch out for the Environment Agency, don't you?'

White was pulling at his beard again.

'The night of the twelfth of March, Colin Stafford, an Environment Agency officer was assaulted at Dunball and we've got tyre tracks placing your Range Rover at the scene, so you tell me, where were you?'

White sighed. 'We had the net out, just above the King's Sedgemoor Drain sluice.'

'What time did you put the net out?'

'About sixish.'

'What did you do then?'

'We had a few beers in the Scarlet Pimpernel.'

'What time did you go back for the net?'

'Eleven or so.'

'And what happened?'

'We got the net in, and then Owen says he thought he heard something and went back to the car. Next thing I know there's this bailiff shining a torch in my face. Then wham, Owen smacks him on the back of the head.'

'Nice that, blaming your brother. I wonder if he'll blame you,' said Harding.

'Fuck off.'

'Close, are you?'

White closed his eyes and gritted his teeth.

'What'd he hit him with then?' asked Harding.

'I dunno.'

'Did you try to stop him?'

'I didn't have the chance. It was dark and I was looking straight into the bailiff's torch. There was no way I could see Owen behind him.'

'What happened then?'

'We finished loading up the elvers and got the hell out of there.'

'You just left him?'

'I didn't know how hard Owen hit him. We thought he'd wake up with a bit of a headache and that'd be that.'

'Whose car were you in that night?'

'My Range Rover.'

'And Owen got the weapon from your car?'

'I dunno.'

'Well, it's either going to have been the baseball bat or the crowbar. We're having both tested so we'll soon know.'

'It was the baseball bat. All right? It was the bloody baseball bat.'

'Whose baseball bat?'

'Mine.'

'You carry a baseball bat in your car?'

'Yes.'

'Don't tell me, you're a big fan of the Boston Red Sox?'

'Protection; it's for protection.'

'So, that's an offensive weapon,' said Harding, nodding. He turned to White's solicitor. 'You've explained joint enterprise to him as well, I suppose, Mr Griffin?'

Griffin leaned over and whispered into White's ear.

'The baseball bat is for banging the stakes in to hold the net in place,' said White. 'That's all.'

'Really.' Harding went for maximum sarcasm. Dixon was impressed.

'Yes.'

'There's hardly a mark on it.'

'There's been a lot of rain lately and ground's soft. Plus, it's washed by the tide.'

Harding pursed his lips.

'I had no idea Owen was going to use it for that,' continued White, 'and no way of stopping him.'

'Of course you didn't.'

'Let's talk about last night, Martin,' said Dixon, leaning forward and placing a plastic cup on the table. 'What time did you put the net out?'

'About tenish,' said White, frowning.

'By boat?'

'No, we drove round.'

'Why recover it by boat then?'

'We thought we'd been seen. And it was a calm night, moonlit.'

'Where were you seen?'

'At the gate at Sloway Lane.'

'Well, that's right. You *were* seen.'

'I know that now.'

'You weren't seen dumping the van in the mud though.'

'What van?'

'Now hold on a minute,' said Griffin. 'What's this all about?'

Dixon placed a photograph of Harry Lucas on the table in front of White. Harry was sitting at a table outside a restaurant, smiling at the camera.

'Have you seen this man before, Martin?'

White picked up the photograph and looked at it, before passing it to Griffin.

'No.'

'Look again.'

'I've never seen him before.'

'His name's Harry,' said Dixon. 'Harry Lucas.'

White was staring at the table in front of him, avoiding Dixon's stare.

'I've never heard of him.'

'He was found in his van at dawn this morning. He had multiple stab wounds in his neck and had been handcuffed to the steering wheel. The Coastguard couldn't get him out before the tide came in.'

White sat up. 'What's this got to do with me?'

'The van was found a few hundred yards from your net, Martin.'

'My client hasn't been arrested for any offence in connection with this,' said Griffin.

'That's right. He's just helping us with our enquiries at this stage. Aren't you, Martin?'

'I didn't kill him and neither did Owen. We never even saw a van.'

'D'you know what a trephine is?' Dixon noticed Harding frowning.

'No,' replied White.

'OK, so when you were placing the net, did you see anything further along the River Parrett, north towards the sewage treatment works?'

'No, we were down on the Huntspill and the embankment's in the way.'

'No lights?'

'Nothing. All right.'

'Where did you park?'

'We left the Range Rover on Sloway Lane and carried the net along the Huntspill to the end.'

'And you saw no other vehicles?'

'No.'

'Was the gate locked?'

'Yes. We'd have driven down there if it had been open.'

'What about when you came back in your boat?'

White shook his head.

'For the tape, Mr White shook his head,' said Dixon. 'You must have motored along the River Parrett from Stolford, and you're saying you saw nothing?'

'That's right.'

'Did you hear anything?'

'No.'

'Inspector, I think my client has made his position clear, and unless you have anything to connect him to the van . . .'

'Have you ever worked in pest control, Martin?'

'No,' replied White, frowning.

'Inspector—'

'Not yet, Mr Griffin,' replied Dixon. 'Not yet.'

◆ ◆ ◆

The interview with Owen White had followed much the same pattern. He admitted hitting Colin Stafford, the Environment Agency bailiff, although he said it had been Martin who had heard the noise and ordered him – he was quite clear that Martin gave the orders – to fetch the baseball bat from the Range Rover.

When confronted by Stafford, Martin had shouted, 'For fuck's sake; hit him, Owen,' and Owen had simply done as he was told.

Owen's solicitor, Frank Clarke, was well beyond retirement age and had looked asleep for much of the interview, but he sat up sharply when Dixon took over the questioning.

'So, was it Martin who ordered you to kill Harry Lucas?'

'No. Who's—'

'Yes, who's Harry Lucas?' interrupted Clarke.

'He was found handcuffed to the steering wheel of a van stuck in the mud not five hundred yards from your net, Owen,' replied Dixon. 'What can you tell me about that?'

'Nothing,' replied Owen, rubbing the stubble on his chin.

'I'm not sure I like where this is going, Inspector,' said Clarke. 'This is not a line of questioning we were expecting, and I've not had the chance to discuss it with my client.'

'Let's proceed on the basis that Owen is just helping us with our enquiries then, shall we?'

Clarke leaned over and whispered in Owen's ear. Owen shrugged his shoulders.

'All right then,' said Clarke.

'Where did you leave the Range Rover last night?'

'Stolford,' replied Owen. He took off his glasses and began cleaning them on his shirttail.

'When you set the net?'

'Oh, in a lay-by on Sloway Lane.'

'What did you do then?'

'We climbed over the gate and walked along the Huntspill to the sluice.'

'Did anyone see you?'

'A dog walker. That was on the way back. She got her phone out, which is why we decided to collect the net by boat.'

'Did you see anyone?'

'What do you mean?'

'Apart from the dog walker.'

'No.'

'What about when you were out by the River Parrett? Any lights?'

'No.'

'Did you hear anything?'

'I thought I heard a banging sound in the distance.'

'Banging what?'

'I don't know. It sounded metallic, maybe.'

'And this was when you were setting the net?'

'Yes.'

'What time was that?'

'Ten fifteen, maybe a bit later. Something like that anyway.'

'Did you say anything to Martin about it?'

'No.'

'How many times did you hear it?'

'Three, I think, but it was faint. It sounded miles away.'

'Did you see anything when you came back by boat?'

'There was something on the mud, maybe. Near the concrete thing that marks the sewage pipe.'

'What did you see?'

'A reflection. Just for a second. If you're telling me there was a van in the mud, then it could have been the windscreen, but I wasn't really looking around to be honest. I can't swim and hate the bloody boat.'

'You weren't wearing a lifejacket when you were arrested,' said Dixon.

'Martin says they're for poofs,' replied Owen, folding his arms.

'So, you think you saw something in the mud near the sewage outfall?'

'Yes.'

'But you said nothing to anyone.'

'I had no idea what it was, did I?'

'Would you have done, if you'd known?'

'Anonymously probably, but yes, I'd have made the call.'

Dixon nodded.

'And, when he wakes up, please tell Mr Stafford I'm sorry I hit him.'

◆ ◆ ◆

'Fuck it,' muttered Dixon as he kicked a chair out from under a vacant workstation in the open plan CID area. 'Did you see that?'

'Mark and I were watching on the monitor,' replied Louise.

'If Owen is right about the banging, then it was Harry trying to get help, which means he was in the mud all night, conscious and just waiting for the tide.'

'You can't be sure. He's not sure.'

'The whole bloody time we were there.'

'It's not your fault, Sir.'

'I know that.' Dixon dropped on to the swivel chair. 'Check with SOCO and see if the horn on the van had been disabled.'

'Yes, Sir.'

'Where does it leave us with the murder though, Sir?' asked Pearce.

'Nowhere,' muttered Dixon. 'Let's get 'em charged with GBH. They'll be remanded in custody, and that will give us more time.'

'What about the Environment Agency?'

'See if they want to do them for the poaching too.'

'And the offensive weapon?'

'Yes.'

'The ID's been done, Sir. It is Harry Lucas,' said Louise.

'Roger covered up the forehead?'

'Yes. She didn't ask about it either.'

Dixon checked the time: 8 p.m. That made it over thirty-six hours since he'd got out of bed the day before, and he suddenly found himself stifling a yawn.

'Do you want what I've got so far, Sir?' asked Pearce.

'Tomorrow will do, Mark. I'll be in for eight.'

'Oh, and this arrived for you,' said Pearce, handing him a padded envelope.

Dixon tore it open and pulled out a paperback book. *Cause of Death: Diaries of a Home Office Pathologist* by Dr Geoffrey Burkett. A piece of paper was sticking out of the top, with a handwritten note: 'Read this! RP.'

Dixon exhaled slowly. Maybe he wasn't going to get much sleep tonight after all, he thought as he opened the book at the start of chapter 9, 'Moss Side'.

Chapter Six

The cottage was dark. Dixon put his key in the lock. And quiet. Jane must have taken Monty with her. It must be serious if Monty is doing what Jane tells him, thought Dixon, smiling as he stepped into the darkness. Maybe he'd need a pre-nuptial agreement to clarify that Monty was his? He shook his head. Once a solicitor, always a solicitor. And he hadn't even asked her yet.

A beer in the Red Cow was tempting, but then so was his bed, and it was touch and go whether he'd be able to stay awake long enough to microwave a curry, let alone eat it. A small drop of blood appeared on his shirt when he pulled out the needle. He'd lost count of the number of times Roger had told him not to inject his insulin through his clothes. He sighed. Being diabetic was a bloody nuisance sometimes.

The smell of chicken tikka masala followed by the ping of the microwave woke him, but then he'd never been good at sleeping standing up, even when leaning against a kitchen worktop. He dragged the plastic container out on to a tray and slumped down on to the sofa, switching on the TV while he waited for the sauce to stop bubbling.

He clicked 'play' on the DVD without looking up and smiled when he recognised Gordon Jackson's voice.

'Good luck.'

'Thank you.'

The Great Escape had always been a favourite.

He managed to stay awake long enough to eat his curry, but was asleep before the machine gun fire started.

◆　◆　◆

'Isn't that the football song?'

Jane sounded miles away.

Then the sound of a plastic container being pushed around a wooden dinner tray. Much closer. Dixon opened his eyes to find Monty standing on the sofa next to him, licking the last of the masala sauce from the tray.

'Isn't that the football song?'

'No, it bloody well isn't.'

'What is it then?' asked Jane, appearing in the doorway of the kitchen holding a jar of coffee.

'*The Great Escape*,' replied Dixon. 'One of the finest war films ever made.' He picked up the remote control and switched off the TV.

'Really?'

'Well, top five.'

'Tea or coffee?'

'Tea, please. And you can hop it.' Dixon pushed Monty off the sofa, dropped the plastic tray on the floor and watched him pushing it across the carpet with his tongue. The last trace of any sauce was long gone before it reached the TV stand, but that didn't stop him pushing it underneath. 'What time is it?'

'Eleven.'

'How were your parents?'

'Fine.'

'What did they say?'

'What about?'

'You know what about.' Dixon was propping himself up on the door frame.

Jane had met her birth mother, Sonia, for the first time only a few weeks before. Dixon had gone with her, but kept his distance, ready to pick up the pieces although there had been none to pick up. 'Expect nothing and you'll not be disappointed, whatever else happens' had been his advice, and Jane had taken it, coming out of the meeting relatively unscathed.

The half empty bottle of wine on the table at an early evening reunion had turned out to be more than just Dutch courage, Jane ordering a coffee for herself and another bottle of Pinot Grigio for Sonia.

There had been lots of tears, from Sonia, but Jane had remained calm and distant throughout, which had surprised Dixon, watching from the bar, although he couldn't begin to imagine what it must be like to find out that you were adopted and then to come face to face with the person who had given you up. It was either that or Sonia's admission that she didn't know who Jane's father was.

Dixon felt responsible too, having been the one who found Sonia. Maybe Jane would have been better off never meeting her? She would certainly have been better off never knowing, even she said that, but once she knew, she had to meet her mother.

'They don't want to meet her.'

'Really?'

'They said it didn't feel right.'

'Did you tell them about—?'

'No,' replied Jane. 'They don't need to know she's an alcoholic. What good would it do?'

'None at all.'

'Specially if they're not going to meet.' Jane handed a mug of tea to Dixon. 'Did you get the van out all right?'

'Yes. Roger's doing the PM in the morning. He sent me that book on the side there. Open it at the yellow sticker.'

Dixon watched Jane's facial expression as she scanned the pages.

'Have you read this?' she asked, her eyes widening.

'Not yet.'

'What's the connection?'

'It's the use of the trephine, the cylindrical saw.'

'Really?'

Dixon nodded.

'Take my advice and read it in the morning,' said Jane, snapping the book shut. 'If you want to sleep, that is.'

◆ ◆ ◆

Dixon had woken early, even for him, and spent an hour or so reading *Cause of Death* by the light of his iPhone. Neither Jane nor Monty had stirred, although Monty was probably just pretending to be asleep – rain hammering on the cottage window often had that effect.

Chapter 9 had made grim reading. The author's last case before retirement, unsolved, his bitterness that his career was ending in failure shining through much like a footballer retiring after a Cup Final that ended in a 6–0 defeat.

A killer on the loose in Manchester, linked to at least four murders and suspected of several more, although the victims had never been found. 'The Vet', as he had been christened by the local press, liked to torture his victims with surgical instruments more often found in a veterinary surgery or a museum of veterinary science.

A fleam had been used to bleed the victims, the veins in the neck opened up with an unusual measure of precision. Then a trephine had been used to remove a piece of skull the size of a penny, right in the middle of the forehead. Cause of death was always the same: asphyxiation. The victims had been buried alive and suffocated before they bled to death.

No other injuries had been found on any of them. Burkett had found no evidence of a blow to the back of the head to incapacitate the victim, nor had any drug been administered, leading him to conclude that the victims had been held down by a person or persons unknown.

The murders had taken place over a period of four years, ending with the killing of Derek Hervey, a snooker hall owner in his early forties. He had been buried in a shallow grave on a building site near Old Trafford and children playing had unearthed his decomposing body after a period of heavy rain. According to Burkett, it was not a pretty 'site'. Dixon frowned. No doubt the pun was intentional. Hervey had been found on 18th January 1996, giving a date of death on or about Christmas Eve the previous year. This coincided with a missing persons report filed by his wife two days earlier.

Hervey had complained of coming under pressure to pay protection money to a gang, although, not surprisingly, Burkett had not identified the criminals involved. 'The word on the street' was that a new enforcer was operating in the city, while rival gangs fought over turf. Writing in 2001, Burkett said that two informers were among the missing and suspected victims of The Vet.

A rival gang member, unidentified by Burkett, a drug dealer and a police officer from the Greater Manchester Police Tactical Vehicle Crime Unit completed the list of known victims. Police Constable Brian Hocking, the first victim, was found buried in a flower bed in Alexandra Park, Manchester, by a gardener on 14th June 1992.

Dixon sat down on the corner of the desk in the anteroom in the Pathology Department at Musgrove Park Hospital and watched Roger Poland through the glass. He was mumbling into a Dictaphone and leaning over the body of Harry Lucas laid out on the slab. Better still, he had his back to the window.

Timing was everything. Too early and Dixon would have to endure 'the internals', as Poland insisted on calling them. Too late and he would miss the post mortem altogether. It was a fine line, but one that it was vital to get right. Watching a brain being weighed was 'too much information' for anyone, let alone first thing in the morning. He grimaced when the laboratory assistant spotted him and tapped Poland on the shoulder.

The lab was clearly not soundproofed.

'Don't just sit there,' shouted Poland, waving at Dixon.

He opened the door to the lab and peered in.

'You been to Express Park yet?' asked Poland.

'Not yet. I texted Louise and told her I was coming straight here. Why?'

'You'll find out. Did you read the book?'

'You never mentioned it'd been signed by the author,' replied Dixon. He opened the book at the flyleaf and read aloud, 'To Roger, God Help You! With best wishes, Geoff.'

'My old tutor. Nice old boy. Knocking on a bit these days. He sent that to me when I got the Home Office job.'

'Well?'

'There are striking similarities. The use of a trephine, although it's off-centre and missing the venous sinus.'

'What's the significance of that?'

'The Vet always made the incision dead centre, right between the eyes,' replied Poland, 'cutting the vein behind the skull on the midline.' He was running the tip of his index finger from the bridge of his nose, up his forehead and into his hairline. 'This one's missed it, although the first incision was central—'

'He had more than one go at it?'

'Several. You can see them clearly now he's been cleaned up.' Poland turned back the green sheet that had been covering Harry's head. 'My guess is he was wriggling.'

'Wouldn't you?'

'And the injuries to the neck were made by a fleam. There were several goes at that too.'

'What about the blood loss?' asked Dixon, dropping the book on the side. 'There didn't seem to be that much when I got to him.'

'There wasn't,' replied Poland. 'He missed the jugular. Several attempts, but they all missed. See here . . .'

Dixon looked at the left side of Harry's neck.

'I can see four—'

'There are five,' interrupted Poland. 'Mind you, it's not easy. Here.' He passed Dixon a set of different sized steel blades on a metal ring, each with a bulge in it near the tip. 'This is a fleam. Pick a blade, line it up with the blood vessel and then hit it with your other hand, or possibly a small mallet. It opens the vein with a nice neat cut, or it's supposed to.'

'Where on earth did you get them?'

'eBay,' replied Poland, grinning. 'I had to pay extra for next day delivery.'

'What's it used for?'

'Nothing these days. They're antiques. Vets used them for laminitis in horses, I think. Toxins in the blood, so they'd open a blood vessel in the neck and drain some off. The same principle applied to people, but then we really are going back in time. Leeches and all that.'

'And the trephine?'

'Vets use them too. Opening up the sinuses and draining an abscess is one thing I can think of. Horses again. You'd use the trephine to drill a hole in the front of the skull. And cranial surgery in humans, of course. They're still used for that sometimes.'

'Is it the same killer?'

'I'll need to check the old post mortem reports before I can—'

'What about Dr Burkett?' interrupted Dixon. 'Will he be able to help?'

'Oh yes, I'll speak to him too.'

'Any other injuries?'

'There's a blow to the back of the head. Blunt object. Should have been sufficient to incapacitate, but maybe it didn't . . .' Poland's voice tailed off. 'Here we go.'

'Eh?'

'Behind you,' said Poland, nodding.

Two men were standing in the anteroom, looking at them through the glass. Dixon recognised neither of them.

'Who are they?'

'Major Investigation Team,' replied Poland, whispering.

'Oh shit.'

Poland turned to his lab assistant. 'Better see what they want, Alex.'

'Can I help?' she asked, opening the door. She stepped back sharply as the men walked in, brushing past her.

'Dr Poland?'

'Yes.'

'Detective Superintendent Wainwright. This is DI Hamlin. Avon and Somerset MIT. We're taking over this investigation.'

'I was expecting you.'

'And you'll be Dixon?'

A dark pinstripe suit under a green waxed coat. Wainwright thrust his hands into his trouser pockets, revealing red braces stretched over a beer belly. The braces matched his tie.

'Yes, Sir.'

'Sling your hook then,' he said, grinning. 'There's a good lad.'

'This is my case.'

'It was,' snapped Wainwright. 'DCI Lewis will fill you in.'

Dixon counted to ten, breathing slowly through his nose. Wainwright turned to Poland.

'Is it The Vet?'

'It's too early to say.' Poland glanced at Dixon and nodded towards the door.

'Are you still here, boy?' Wainwright let out an exaggerated sigh, still looking at Poland.

Dixon picked up Poland's book from the side and turned towards the door.

'He wasn't buried alive though, was he?' continued Wainwright.

'Er, no—' replied Poland.

'Yes, he was,' muttered Dixon, raising his voice as he stalked out of the lab. 'He was buried at sea.'

Chapter Seven

It was a half hour drive from Musgrove Park Hospital to the Bridgwater Police Centre at Express Park, but it took Dixon little more than twenty minutes, even in his old Land Rover. He left his car parked across the entrance, rather than waiting for the huge steel gates of the staff car park to open, and ran in the front door. The two receptionists looked at each other and shrugged their shoulders as he raced past, one of them pressing the buzzer to open the security door just as he reached it. He arrived at the top of the stairs before the door swung shut at the bottom.

Meeting room 2 was full. Dave Harding, Mark Pearce, Louise and DCI Lewis were all sitting at the table.

Dixon wrenched open the door. 'What the bloody hell—?'

'Wind your neck in,' interrupted Lewis. 'You know about The Vet?'

'Roger told me.'

'That explains the Major Investigation Team then, doesn't it?' Lewis fixed Dixon with a glare, eyebrows raised. 'Doesn't it?'

'Yes, Sir.'

'Make yourself a coffee. We'll be finished here in a few minutes.'

Dixon sat down at a workstation in the CID area. He switched on the computer and then swivelled round in his chair to look out of the floor to ceiling windows, watching meeting room 2 in the reflection. Dave, Mark and Louise were sitting in silence, shaking their heads at regular intervals, their arms folded.

The meeting appeared to be dragging on so Dixon amused himself deleting his emails, mostly newsletters and junk, all bar three that came from Mark and attached company search results for Pest Erase UK, a copy of Harry's franchise agreement and his management accounts. He looked up when he heard the meeting room door open and watched Dave, Mark and Louise file out, muttering to each other. Lewis was standing behind them in the doorway, waving him in.

'Sit down.'

'If you've—'

'And shut up,' continued Lewis.

'Yes, Sir.' Dixon slumped on to a chair opposite Lewis at the head of the table.

'There's going to be close liaison with the Manchester lot on this one. That's the reason for the MIT,' said Lewis. 'All right?'

Dixon nodded.

'Four murders that we know about, one a copper, five others missing and suspected victims. Disappears off the radar in 1996 and then he turns up here, of all places.'

'Or someone does, using the same—'

'Isn't it The Vet?' interrupted Lewis.

'Roger didn't know. He's got to look at the old PM records and speak to the original pathologist.'

'Well, you've got your work cut out.'

'I have?'

'Get up to HQ and report to Detective Chief Superintendent Potter.'

'I'm on the MIT?' asked Dixon, from behind a wry smile.

'You are,' replied Lewis. 'And watch your back.'

'What's that supposed to mean?'

'DCI Chard is staffing.'

'It just gets better and better,' replied Dixon, puffing out his cheeks. 'What about the others?'

'Janice Courtenay is taking over the elver poaching case and they'll work with her.'

'What if it's connected?'

'It's not.'

'Says who?'

'Deborah Potter.'

'She's probably right,' said Dixon, nodding. 'Anything else?'

'Pack an overnight bag.'

◆　◆　◆

Jane had been full of good advice when he poked his head around the door of the Safeguarding Coordination Unit on the second floor.

'Remember, you're part of a team. And you're not in charge.'

Then came the one that was occupying his mind as he sped north on the M5.

'Keep out of Chard's way.'

Detective Chief Inspector Simon Chard had been responsible for Dixon's recent brush with the Professional Standards Unit. He had escaped with the lowest sanction available: management advice. But there was still a blot on his record and a letter on his personnel file confirming it. He had 'failed to meet the requisite Standards of Professional Behaviour'; those were the words used at the disciplinary hearing, and the fact that Chard had mishandled the investigation from the start had been irrelevant. Dixon had failed to disclose his personal involvement, and that was that. But it had been worth it, and Chard was still a twat.

Dixon had visited the Avon and Somerset Police Headquarters at Portishead a couple of times before. Once when he transferred from the Met. Then again when attached to the Cold Case Unit pending his disciplinary hearing. And most recently on a flying visit to the High Tech Unit with a computer memory stick. But he still marvelled at the medals on the guardhouse officer's uniform. At least eight of them, all silver, they swung forwards as he leaned over to speak to the driver of the car in front, the jangling just carrying over the rattle of Dixon's diesel engine.

The officer returned to the guardhouse and picked up the phone, so Dixon took the opportunity to send a text message.

I let Monty out and left the telly on for him. Nx

Jane's reply arrived just as the officer lifted the barrier for the car in front.

Be careful xx

A wave of his warrant card failed to get Dixon past the barrier without further scrutiny. It hadn't worked last time either, or the time before that.

'Name.'

'Detective Inspector Dixon.'

He waited while his name was scribbled on the list.

'Visiting?'

'DCS Potter, MIT.'

'OK, carry on, Sir. You know where to go?'

'Yes, thank you.'

Clipboard tucked under his arm, the officer raised the barrier and waved Dixon through.

◆　◆　◆

'Well, thank fuck for that.'

'Eh?'

'The cavalry's here. We can all go home.'

Dixon resisted the temptation to turn around. A forced smile, held long enough for the laughter to subside, was all he could muster. He glanced around the room: large, open plan, with a crowd gathered around a whiteboard against the far wall and two people standing behind him, one of whom he could identify.

A woman stood up at the front of the group, streaks of grey in dark shoulder length hair matching her pinstripe suit.

'Back to work, everyone,' she said as she weaved her way between the empty desks. 'And you should know better,' pointing to the source of the sarcasm behind Dixon.

'Yes, Guv.'

Twat.

'Dixon?'

He nodded.

'Deborah Potter. Your reputation precedes you,' she said, shaking his hand.

'I bet it does.'

'This way.'

He followed her along a short corridor to a glass partitioned office with her name on the door.

'I read your file,' she said, closing the door. 'Don't make the mistake of thinking I listen to the likes of Simon Chard. He's not in your league. You've got something that makes the rest of us nervous.'

'A disciplinary record?'

'You're here, aren't you?'

'Yes, Guv.'

'And you can drop the "Guv". It's Deborah.'

'Nick.'

'You've got the George Medal too.'

'That was all a bit of a mix up, really.'

'Bollocks.' She poured herself a coffee from a Thermos flask. 'Want one?'

'No, thank you.'

'I can't stand that crap you get from the machine,' she said, taking a sip of coffee. 'Sit down and tell me about the school.'

'I failed to disclose—'

'I know that bit. It took guts, real guts, to save his life like that. Most of us would've let the bugger die.'

'I wanted answers. And he'll die in prison. That's the way it should be.'

'What about the mud then?' She closed a file on the desk in front of her and locked it in the bottom drawer. 'Did you do a risk assessment before you went swimming in it?'

Dixon frowned. 'He was still alive and the tide was coming in.'

'I'm joking.' Potter smiled. 'Did he say anything?'

'Not to me. But he may have spoken to the Coastguard crew. I had asked my team to track them down.'

'I'll pass it on to Superintendent Wainwright. You've met, I gather?'

'Yes.'

'Go easy on him. He's a good copper, but his wife's having chemo at the moment, so he's a bit . . .'

Dixon nodded.

'He's setting up a Major Incident Room at Express Park.'

'You've ruled out a connection with the poachers?' asked Dixon.

'For the time being,' replied Potter. 'But we'll keep an eye on it. You hadn't found any connection?'

'No. I was working on the basis that if it had been them, they'd hardly come back later to collect the eels.'

'Good, so we'll call it a coincidence.'

Dixon frowned.

'Did you bring an overnight bag?'

'Yes.'

'We're sending a team to Manchester to liaise with GMP,' said Potter. 'The senior investigating officer from the original team is coming out of retirement. Your job is to brief them on what we've got. All right?'

'Is that it?'

'I doubt it very much.'

'What's that supposed to mean?'

'There are glaring holes in what they're telling us, statements missing, names redacted. Read this on the train.' Potter leaned forward and handed Dixon a red box file. 'We need to know what's not in the statements. So, I thought I'd throw a fox in the chicken coop.'

'It's a cat amongst the pigeons, isn't it?'

'I really don't give a shit, so long as you ruffle some feathers. Lewis tells me you're good at that.'

Dixon smiled.

'Good. Just don't ruffle mine,' continued Potter. 'And remember, you'll be representing Avon and Somerset Police, so don't muck it up.'

'I won't.'

Dixon stood up to leave.

'You mentioned a team?' he asked.

'A DS from Bristol is going with you. Jonny Sexton.'

'Where is he?'

'He'll be around somewhere.'

Dixon allowed the office door to close behind him and then tapped out a text message to Jane.

If I ever apply for promotion remind me to get a pinstripe suit :-) Nx

'Inspector Dixon?'

An Irish accent behind him, soft and quietly spoken.

Dixon spun round. 'Yes.'

'Jonny Sexton, Sir.' A hand outstretched, Dixon reached out to take it just as his phone bleeped.

And braces? xx

'Excuse me a minute, I've just got to tell someone to piss off.' He slid his phone back into his pocket, message sent, and shook Sexton's hand.

'There's a car waiting to take us to Temple Meads, Sir,' said Sexton.

'You read this?' asked Dixon, holding up the box file.

'I just flicked through it, Sir.'

'Well, it'll keep us busy on the train.'

◆ ◆ ◆

'You're having a fling with a fellow officer?'

Dixon was staring out of the window as the train pulled out of Bristol Parkway. 'It's a bit more than a fling, but thank you for asking,' he replied, resisting the temptation to tell Sexton to mind his own business.

'Me too.'

'Really?'

'He's a firearms officer,' replied Sexton. 'It's how we met.'

'You were in Armed Response?' Dixon turned back to Sexton sitting opposite him.

'Originally.'

'Why did you leave?'

'I suppose I might as well tell you before someone else does. I killed an eighty year old man.'

Dixon frowned. 'What happened?'

'He pulled a gun on a colleague. Turned out it was plastic, but there was no way of telling. It was dark; it all happened so fast. And he had dementia.' Sexton sighed. 'That's what the enquiry found. Anyway, it was politely suggested I might not be suitable for firearms duty. There'd been protests, and because of what happened to my brother—'

Dixon raised his eyebrows.

'He was the officer shot and killed a couple of years ago in Montpelier.'

'I remember that.'

'He was unarmed.' Sexton was shaking his head. 'He didn't stand a chance. Anyway, they thought it might make me trigger happy.'

'And did it?'

Sexton hesitated. 'No.'

'So you switched to CID,' said Dixon.

'Was switched. Back to uniform first though.'

'Tell me about your partner.'

'Husband. We got married just over a year ago. He's on leave at the moment. There was an incident.'

'Did he have to shoot someone?'

'He did. Up on the Mendips,' said Sexton, raising his eyebrows. 'Near Priddy.'

'Is he all right?' asked Dixon, shifting in his seat.

'He'll be fine. Your statement helped, apparently.'

'He did what he had to do.'

'Thanks.'

'You didn't tell me his name.'

'Jayden Blake.'

'What did you make of this stuff?' asked Dixon, opening the red box file on the table in front of him.

'Some names have been blanked out from the police statements, informers probably. And they had someone undercover by the looks of things. This can't be all of them either. There are none from the Tactical Vehicle Crime Unit, Brian Hocking's colleagues. You'd expect something from them, surely?'

Dixon nodded. Then he took a handful of statements from the box file and began flicking through them. He glanced at Sexton. Tall, short blond hair, a DIY job with clippers probably, an old ear piercing, and a striking resemblance to the Tunnel King in *The Great Escape*. He'd have to google the actor's name later.

'I'll leave you in peace to read that,' said Sexton, putting in a set of earphones. 'I'm going to . . .'

'You carry on,' said Dixon.

He watched Sexton: eyes closed, head nodding up and down. Dixon smiled and turned back to the statements: a selection from the investigation into each murder, all of them with sections or names blanked out. He frowned. It was to be expected in what the manual would classify as an 'intelligence led' operation, the need to protect the identity of the witnesses obvious, and the officers involved in – he glanced at the lid – Operation Bowood would have known who they were anyway. But it made it difficult for those looking back over twenty years later.

In the bottom of the box, in a clear plastic wallet all on its own, was a report from a chartered clinical psychologist, Dr Steven Pearson. Dixon turned to the final paragraph.

'To conclude, therefore, in my opinion the likely killer is a young (mid-thirties) white male suffering from an antisocial personality disorder (psychopath). He is highly intelligent, likely to have a history of violence in the family, either domestic and/or professional, and is likely to have witnessed and/or suffered extreme violence as a child. He will be prone to violent mood swings and be fastidious to the point of obsession. He is likely to have difficulty forming relationships and will, therefore, live alone, probably in an upmarket flat. He is likely to be familiar with the local area.'

A description wide enough to cover just about everyone involved in organised crime Dixon had ever encountered. Even the Albanians. He dropped the statements back into the box and closed the lid just as a figure appeared standing by the table.

'Tickets, please.'

Chapter Eight

A tropical fish tank. That was it. Dixon frowned.

'You're not a fan of modern architecture, then?' asked Sexton.

'That's not architecture. It's just a square box with a blue light. Where's the imagination, the invention in that?'

'No idea.'

'I'm in the wrong business.'

Dixon looked up. Arranged over six floors, the Greater Manchester Police headquarters building was more glass than anything else, some of it blue – that must be the imaginative bit, he thought. Plastic and glass over a steel frame probably; at least Express Park had some concrete to hold it up in a strong wind. A bright blue light illuminated the GMP crest and more blue glass in the atrium, which extended the full height of the building at the front. No strip lights swinging in the breeze, though, so that was one improvement on Express Park perhaps.

Sexton had paid the taxi driver and was stuffing the receipt in his wallet.

'C'mon, let's get in there,' said Dixon, looking at his watch. 'It's gone six already.'

'DI Dixon and DS Sexton for Chief Superintendent Douglas.'

'Take a seat,' replied the receptionist. 'I'll let someone know you're here.'

Dixon dropped his overnight bag on the floor and pulled a copy of the *Manchester Daily Post* out from under the glossy magazines on the glass table. He spotted the coffee machine only seconds after Sexton.

'Want one?'

'Better put a sugar in mine,' replied Dixon. 'Oh, for—'

'What is it?'

He held up the front page of the newspaper.

'*He's back*,' said Sexton, reading aloud.

Dixon threw the paper down on the table. 'Looks like GMP have a leak.'

'We're looking into it. But it's big news around here and impossible to keep under wraps.'

He spun round.

'You'll be Dixon?'

'Yes.'

'Chief Superintendent Douglas.' They shook hands.

'This is DS Sexton.'

Douglas nodded, then turned back to Dixon. 'If it was me, I'd send a troublemaker or the best I'd got. Which are you?'

'Both, Sir.'

'Good answer,' said Douglas, grinning. 'This way.'

They were standing in the lift before he spoke again.

'You got to him before he drowned, I gather?'

'Yes, Sir,' replied Dixon.

'Did he say anything?'

'Just his name. He wasn't really in a fit state . . .'

'And the post mortem?' asked Douglas, nodding.

'It was a trephine. And a fleam. But the pathologist will need to check the records to see if it's the same killer. He's going to speak to Geoffrey Burkett too.'

'He knows him, does he?'

'Dr Poland is an old student of his.'

'Small world.'

'He was going to fax up a copy of his report.'

'Not seen it yet,' replied Douglas, shaking his head.

Dixon watched Douglas in the mirror, straightening his tie. An unusually thick head of hair for a man in his fifties. And artificially dark: not even a single grey at the sides. Trousers slightly too long, pockets too full. Still, at least it wasn't a pinstripe suit. He smiled. Jane would never let him out of the house looking like that, not now people knew they were living together.

Once out on to the fourth floor it was a familiar sight: open plan, workstations, glass partitioned meeting rooms and a handful of offices along the far wall.

'I know what you're thinking,' said Douglas. 'I bet it's not like this down your way.'

'You'd be surprised,' muttered Dixon.

'We're just waiting for a couple more, and then you can brief the team. We've only put six on it for the time being, till we know more. You see the old boy over there?'

Dixon nodded.

'That's Ray Hargreaves. He was the original SIO. Seventy-nine he is now.'

'I'm expecting to learn more from you than you will from me,' said Dixon.

'We'll see.'

◆ ◆ ◆

'Is that it?'

'For heaven's sake, Manesh,' snapped Douglas. 'You'll have to excuse him, Nick. DI Pandey gets a bit ahead of himself sometimes.'

Dixon sighed. It had taken him no more than twenty minutes to brief the Manchester team on developments so far, the finding of Harry Lucas and what was known about him and his background.

'I don't think it's that bad.' Hargreaves was cleaning his reading glasses with the end of his tie. 'Considering it only happened yesterday morning and you've spent most of today travelling.'

'Thank you, Sir,' replied Dixon.

'The last police officer who called me "sir" gave me a speeding ticket, young man. Ray will do.'

'So is it the same killer or not?'

'DS Rufus Chapman,' Douglas frowned. 'Straight to the point as always.'

'The short answer is we don't know yet,' replied Dixon.

'What d'you know about Operation Bowood?' asked Douglas.

'Precious little. We've got copies of some of the statements from each murder with bits blanked out—'

'There was far more to it than that. I'm guessing you don't get much in the way of organised crime down in the West Country . . .' said Hargreaves, eyebrows raised.

'Easy mistake to make.'

'This was a major operation that ran for the best part of a decade,' said Douglas. 'Where the hell d'you start?'

Hargreaves drained his coffee, leaned back in the chair and dropped the plastic cup into a bin behind him.

'It was fairly quiet in the late eighties,' he said. 'Usual stuff. The mafia had a small presence here; the triads used to charge around Chinatown as if they owned it—'

'Which they did,' interrupted Pandey.

'There were a couple of smaller outfits trafficking heroin, street gangs really. Guns were everywhere, but that was about it. Then the Carters appeared from nowhere.'

'The Carters?' asked Dixon.

Jonny Sexton was making notes next to him.

'Michael and Kenny. Brothers. Michael Carter was an evil son of a . . .' Hargreaves shook his head. 'Killed a man at the age of fifteen.'

'How?'

'Shot him in the head.'

'Any other previous convictions?'

'No.'

'It was a turf war on a scale not seen before or since. Certainly not in Manchester,' said Douglas. 'I was training at the time and remember it well.'

'I was still at school and I remember it,' said Chapman.

'They took the pubs, the clubs, protection, gambling, drugs. Within a very short space of time they pretty much cleared everyone out,' continued Hargreaves. 'They left Chinatown to the triads though. They weren't that stupid.'

'When was this?'

'The early nineties. We beefed up the organised crime team in response, but the flow of information dried up. Informers were disappearing as fast as we could cultivate them. We shut down a nightclub they were using as their HQ in late ninety-five, then they took over a snooker club.'

'Did the Carters have someone on the inside?' asked Dixon.

'You don't muck about, do you?' Pandey shook his head.

'Yes, they did,' said Hargreaves. 'It's another aspect of this we're not particularly proud of.'

'Who was it?'

'That doesn't matter now. He died in prison in 2005. Natural causes, before you ask.'

Dixon nodded.

'Michael Carter was smart. We got someone undercover on the fringes and picked off some of the smaller fry, but we never got close to Carter himself.'

'Those are the redacted bits in the statements?'

'Just in the versions we sent out. You never know where they might end up,' said Douglas. 'We blanked out the names of the informers who are still around too. You can see the originals though.'

'Is the undercover officer still around?' asked Dixon.

'His identity is classified,' replied Douglas. 'He's a serving officer and it's just too dangerous.'

'I never knew that,' said Chapman. 'Who is it?'

Douglas glared at Chapman, his brow furrowed.

'How did he get in?' asked Dixon.

'We knew they were targeting a snooker club, so we got him a job behind the bar before the Carters bought it.' Hargreaves shrugged his shoulders. 'And they kept him on.'

'Bought it?' Dixon frowned.

'Off Hervey's widow.'

'What about Carter's family?'

'There was a father and the brother, but we never really got close to either of them . . .' Hargreaves's voice tailed off.

'Why not?'

'The father was serving fifteen years for armed robbery and there was never any real evidence the brother was involved. He popped up on the surveillance from time to time, but then so did all sorts of different people.'

'Where are they now?'

'The father's dead. The brother, Kenny, disappeared.'

'And where does The Vet fit into all of this?'

'Around about late ninety-one the violence stopped. Up to that point it had been the usual, you know, sawn-off shotguns, knives, beatings; the occasional murder of a competitor and then intimidation of the rest. Then it all went quiet.'

'And that's when The Vet arrived?'

'We didn't know it at the time. The first we knew was when Brian Hocking turned up dead,' said Hargreaves, shaking his head. 'He'd got a kid too.'

'Did you see his body?'

'Yes. There were two injuries. That's it, just two. Hardly Carter's beat-them-to-a-pulp style. A single incision to the neck opening up the jugular vein and then the forehead.'

'There were rumours that Hocking had been on the take,' said Douglas. 'They were stealing high end cars to order and he was making sure Tactical Vehicle Crime were out of the way each time. Got greedy, we reckon.'

'So he was killed in a way that would strike fear into anyone else thinking of defying the Carters,' said Dixon.

'Several others had gone missing before that, including two inform-ers,' said Hargreaves. 'We've got nine disappearances in total between 1990 and the end of 1996.'

Douglas gestured to four piles of document archive boxes, each four boxes high, leaning against adjacent workstations. 'All yours.'

'And you never saw The Vet?'

'No one did,' said Douglas. 'That was the whole problem.'

'Where does the name come from, "The Vet"?' asked Dixon.

'We have the *Manchester Daily Post* to thank for that,' said Hargreaves. 'It came from the implements used and the surgical preci-sion. GMP used to leak like a sieve.'

'Used to?'

Douglas gritted his teeth.

'The public were fairly relaxed about it,' said Hargreaves. 'It was perceived as villains killing villains, with the exception of Hocking, of course.'

'And Hervey, surely?'

'He ran a snooker club,' said Douglas. 'Drugs were changing hands and—'

'Nothing was ever proven,' interrupted Hargreaves.

'His case runs to several box files.'

'So, what happened to the Carters?'

'The Shannons did,' said Hargreaves. 'Irish. They'd moved in and were squeezing them. They took over, basically, when the Carters disappeared.'

'They just disappeared?' asked Sexton.

'Michael and Kenny Carter did and the rest of the gang just melted away. The Vet too.'

'What happened?' asked Dixon.

'We don't know,' replied Douglas.

Dixon looked at Sexton and back to Douglas.

'That's it? You don't know?'

'No, we don't,' replied Douglas.

'What d'you think happened?' asked Dixon, turning to Hargreaves.

'You have to remember we'd lost our informers, those with any knowledge of the Carters anyway. We were blind.'

'What about the undercover officer?'

'He'd been pulled out by then,' said Douglas.

'So, the Carters could've been killed by the Shannons?'

'We'd have known about that.'

'How?'

'The Shannons were different. Old school. You could have a conversation with them, off the record. We'd have known.'

'Are the Shannons still around?'

Douglas nodded.

'What information was withheld from the public about the murders?' asked Dixon.

'They knew about the trephine, but not that the injury was to the forehead,' replied Hargreaves. 'We also managed to keep it out of the press that the victims had been buried alive. It took some doing, but we managed to persuade the editors.'

'That's all in Burkett's book though, isn't it? So it's out there now. Anything else?'

'Handcuffs,' said Douglas. 'Each victim had been handcuffed. Burkett agreed to leave that out when he wrote his book.'

'What about the PM reports and photos?'

'In the boxes.'

'And surveillance?'

'In the boxes.'

'What about the profiler? Pearson. Is he still around?'

'Useless tosser,' said Pandey. 'It's so general it could apply to anyone.'

'Yes, he's still around,' said Douglas. 'Profiling has become far more sophisticated over the years. Back then it was—'

'Worthless,' muttered Hargreaves.

'Was there anyone who fitted the profile?' asked Dixon.

'Several,' replied Hargreaves. 'That was the problem. I was sceptical, to be honest, but Pearson said he might be of some use and managed to persuade the SIO at the time. The best that can be said is it didn't do any harm. He just wasted his time and our money.'

'You ignored his report?'

'Pretty much.'

'Is there anything else?' asked Dixon.

'Just this,' replied Pandey, sliding a thin green file across the table. 'We had the evidence re-tested in 2011 as part of a cold case review, and the set of handcuffs on PC Hocking gave us a partial DNA trace, probably from a spot of saliva. The report's in the file.'

'There's no database match, before you ask,' said Douglas.

◆ ◆ ◆

'I need something to eat,' said Dixon.

'We passed a Premier Inn in the taxi. It was a couple of hundred yards back that way,' replied Sexton, waving his arm in the wrong direction.

'That way,' said Dixon.

'Right.'

'See if you can get a couple of rooms and if they've got a restaurant.'

'How long for?'

'Two nights.'

'Will do.' Sexton picked up the phone. 'Is it nine for an outside line?'

Dixon began turning the archive boxes around to read the index of each. He would start with the last murder and work backwards, if only because he found Derek Hervey's files first. He dragged the first box across from the top of the pile on to the vacant workstation and sat down on the swivel chair.

'Two twin rooms and the restaurant closes in half an hour,' said Sexton.

'Tell them we're on our way.'

'I did.'

'Mind if I join you?' asked Hargreaves. 'I've not eaten all day and Mrs Hargreaves bailed out on me.'

'Divorced?' asked Sexton.

'She died.'

'Oh, sorry.'

'Don't be. She was divorcing me at the time.' Hargreaves grinned as they walked over to the lift.

'When did you take over Bowood?' asked Dixon, watching Hargreaves jabbing the button to close the lift doors.

'I took it over from Paul Butler in 1994.'

'And he authorised the profiling?'

'Yes.'

'What about the surveillance?'

'There's hours of it. Stills and video. They put it all on disc in 2011. Just watch the stuff from 1995 and ignore the rest. Everyone who's anyone is there.'

'Thank you.' Dixon nodded.

'Anything else we need to know?'

'Not here,' said Hargreaves, stepping out of the lift.

◆ ◆ ◆

'Three coffees, please.'

'Yes, Sir.'

It had been an interesting meal. Dixon had opted for the safe bet: fish and chips with mushy peas. But he had to admire Sexton's courage. Beef Madras anywhere but a curry house showed a real sense of adventure. He watched Hargreaves weaving his way across the restaurant towards the gents.

'When he gets back, finish your coffee and make your excuses. All right?'

Sexton frowned.

'He's got more to say,' continued Dixon, eyebrows raised.

'Oh, right. Yes, of course.'

Sexton did as he was told when Hargreaves returned to the table.

'Subtle,' said Hargreaves, taking a large swig of coffee. 'How's your history?'

'Not bad, why?'

'What happened on the fifteenth of June, 1996?'

'In Manchester?'

Hargreaves nodded.

'I was still at school,' said Dixon.

'I'll give you a clue: there was a loud bang.'

'A bomb?'

'That's right. The IRA planted a one and half ton bomb outside the—'

'Arndale Centre,' interrupted Dixon.

'Well done. They gave a warning an hour before it went off and we evacuated the whole area. Eighty thousand people and no fatalities, thank God. Some casualties, but no fatalities.'

'And the Shannons are Irish.'

'They are.'

'What about the Carters?'

'No.'

'What's the connection then?'

Hargreaves leaned forwards across the table, his voice hushed. 'About a month after the bomb went off, Special Branch told us to leave the Carters alone.'

'Why?' Dixon watched him twiddling his cufflinks so the Manchester United crest was the right way up.

'Your guess is as good as mine. We were already pulling our under-cover officer out by then anyway.'

A waiter began collecting the coffee cups.

'A double scotch and a taxi, please,' said Hargreaves. 'In that order, preferably.'

'I'll get the bill,' said Dixon.

'I know.'

'Did you ever find out what was going on?'

'Not really. We had our suspicions, but we never had them confirmed.'

'And?'

'The word on what was left of the street was that Carter knew who was behind the bomb and had been talking to the anti-terror lot. Then he disappeared. He was never heard of, or from, again.' Hargreaves pointed at the chocolate in front of Dixon.

'Do you want that?'

'You have it,' replied Dixon, sliding it across the table. 'I'm diabetic.'

'The information we had was that either the Shannons or the IRA had him killed.'

'And?'

'It was the IRA, with the Shannons pointing them in the right direction. That's the most likely explanation,' continued Hargreaves. 'And it cleared the way for the Shannons.'

'So, either Carter really was talking to Special Branch,' said Dixon. 'Or the Shannons just spread the rumour that he was so the IRA would step in and do their dirty work for them.'

Hargreaves snatched the glass from the waiter and drained the whisky in one gulp. 'No one's ever been prosecuted for the attack, except a GMP officer who was leaking stuff to the press.'

'Really?'

'The journalist was sent down for contempt for refusing to reveal his source and the officer was acquitted.'

'What was the information?'

'Names of suspects, from memory. None of it was ever printed.'

'What happened after that?'

'Operation Bowood was closed down and we turned our attention to the Shannons.'

'And The Vet?'

'If the Irish didn't kill him then he's still out there. Somewhere. And coming out of retirement too, by the sound of things.'

'Your taxi's here, Sir.'

'Will you be back tomorrow?' asked Dixon, standing up.

'No fear. There's a Champions League game against Barcelona.'

'Home or away?'

'Away,' replied Hargreaves, grinning. 'You're on your own.'

Chapter Nine

Two rings. He smiled. She must have been waiting for his call.

'What's up?' Jane asked.

Dixon pressed the 'mute' button on the TV remote and slumped back into his pillows.

'Not a lot. You?'

'Same shit, different day. How's Manchester?'

'Cold.'

'And the case?'

'Looks like a copycat to me, but I've not said so yet. I want to keep this lot interested as long as I can.'

'How d'you know?'

'There's no precision to Harry's murder. I saw the injuries to his neck. Whoever did it was hacking away with the fleam. Five goes at it, according to Roger. And he had at least two goes with the trephine. The Vet knew what he was doing.'

'There must be a connection though, surely?' asked Jane.

'There must. Particularly as there's stuff that was never released to the public.'

'Like what?'

'The handcuffs, for a start. How did the copycat know about them?'

'They're not in Burkett's book?'

'No. The IRA are involved too.'

'What? You be bloody careful.'

'I know, I know.'

'How long are you staying up there?'

'Tonight and tomorrow night probably. Unless I can get away any sooner,' said Dixon. 'Have you spoken to Sonia?'

'Not today.'

'How's Monty?'

'Fast asleep.'

'Typical.'

◆ ◆ ◆

'What'd he have to say then?' asked Sexton, through a mouthful of cornflakes at breakfast the next morning. Dixon was pushing a piece of bacon around his plate, deep in thought.

'Hargreaves. What'd he say?'

'The IRA killed Michael Carter in 1996 and the rest of the gang disappeared.'

'Including The Vet?'

Dixon nodded.

'What were the IRA doing here?'

'Just google "Arndale Centre 1996" when you get a minute.'

'A bomb?'

'One and a half tons of it.'

'And they know that for sure?' asked Sexton.

'That was the information they had at the time.'

'If that's right, then this must be a copycat, surely?'

'Yes, but where is he getting his information from?'

'About the handcuffs?'

'Yes.'

'Stuff like that is bound to creep out over time,' said Sexton. 'On internet forums and stuff like that. It's been twenty years, don't forget.'

'Maybe,' replied Dixon. 'Let's keep it to ourselves for as long as we can, though. Roger Poland will confirm it soon enough, I expect.'

'OK.'

Twenty minutes later they were back on the fourth floor of the GMP headquarters building staring at the huge pile of archive boxes. Douglas had signed them in and was hovering.

'Get anything useful from Ray Hargreaves?'

'Just gossip about the IRA,' replied Dixon.

'It was never proven.' Douglas shook his head. 'It could just as easily have been the Shannons.'

'Or both.'

'Well, I'll leave you to it. I've got everyone out trying to find out what they can.'

'Thank you, Sir.'

Dixon turned back to the box on the workstation in front of him. He dropped the lid on the floor and then pulled out a handful of files. It felt a bit like a lucky dip.

The post mortem report on Derek Hervey made interesting reading. Handcuffs again, and a single clean incision with a fleam to open up the jugular vein in the neck. A thirteen millimetre hole had been drilled in his forehead, then he had been buried in a shallow grave beneath a pile of sand on a building site. Time and trouble had been taken to replace the sand, which seemed odd given that the discovery of the body was inevitable. Dixon frowned.

'Who have you got?' he asked.

'Lee Henry,' replied Sexton. 'A small time drug dealer.'

'What about the fleam?'

'A single cut to the external jugular vein.'

'And where was he found?'

'Cypress Street Allotments, buried in some poor sod's vegetable patch.'

'Is it overlooked?'

'There are some terraced cottages opposite, but no one saw or heard anything.'

'How long was he there?'

'Only a few days. The bloke was going to plant some brassicas, whatever they are.' Sexton shrugged his shoulders.

'They're not being buried with any real intent to hide the bodies, are they,' said Dixon. 'Hervey was buried under a pile of sand on a building site and Hocking in a flower bed in a public park.'

'The burial is almost the murder weapon,' said Sexton.

'And a statement. A murder isn't going to intimidate anyone if the body isn't found, is it?'

Dixon pulled another folder from the box and began flicking through the witness statements in it, comparing them with the copies in the red box file. He found the original versions of the edited statements and cross-checked each redaction.

'You getting the same names redacted?' asked Dixon, peering over the computer in front of him.

'Yes,' replied Sexton. 'Just the informers. There's reference to a barman here called Rick Wheaton. Maybe that's the undercover officer?'

'If it is, it's not his real name.'

'You learning anything new?'

'Lots. I'm just not sure it's stuff I need to know,' replied Dixon, shaking his head.

He put the lid back on Hervey's box and fished a pile of witness statements out of another on the floor next to his workstation. They came from Brian Hocking's colleagues in the Tactical Vehicle Crime Unit. It was a specialist unit targeting vehicle crime in Manchester and they had just started filming *X Cars*, a fly-on-the-wall documentary for the BBC. They had been investigating a spate of thefts of very high value cars, having been told that the vehicles were being stolen to order.

Hocking, a trained pursuit driver, received a radio call just before midnight to join in the pursuit of a silver Porsche 911 Turbo that had been reported stolen minutes earlier. The high speed pursuit had lasted eleven minutes when Hocking took a wrong turning, allowing the vehicle to escape.

His partner and passenger throughout the chase, PC Potter, confirmed that the Porsche had been out of sight for a matter of seconds. Dixon smiled. PC Deborah Potter had seen it turn right at a crossroads, but Hocking had turned left. When questioned, Hocking had said he had made a simple mistake. His shift ended at 2 a.m. He left the police station just after that and never arrived home. His body was found two days later.

Dixon spotted Douglas at the coffee machine.

'Is it an Anti-Corruption or a Counter Corruption Unit?'

'Counter,' replied Douglas.

'I'm guessing they've got a file on Brian Hocking. Can I see it?'

'Is it relevant?'

'I won't know that till I've seen it, Sir.' Matter of fact.

'Leave it with me,' said Douglas, with a loud sigh.

'And the officer who was sent down?'

'Baker.'

'His too.'

Dixon placed a coffee on the desk in front of Sexton. He had made no effort to stir in the powdered milk, which was floating on the top.

'Er, thanks,' said Sexton.

'You looked at the other murder?'

'An associate of the Shannons, apparently. The post mortem is almost identical. You could change the names and not notice any difference.'

'Where was he found?'

'In the middle of a local football pitch. They'd even cut out the turf and replaced it over him. The groundsman got a bit of a shock when he was marking out the pitch.'

'Make a start on the disappearances then and see if anything leaps out at you.'

'That's the rest of the boxes!'

'Apart from the surveillance. I'll look at that.'

'Will do,' replied Sexton, puffing out his cheeks.

'Jane said you were up here.'

Dixon looked up to find Roger Poland standing next to his workstation.

'What're you doing here?'

'Flying visit. I've got a two o'clock with Geoffrey Burkett. Then I'm briefing this lot before the train home at sevenish.'

'Can I come with you to see Dr Burkett?'

'Yes, of course,' replied Poland. 'They're laying on a car.'

'Have you got your PM report?'

'Here's your copy.' Poland dropped a large brown envelope on to the desk in front of Dixon. 'It's in your email too.'

'Thanks.'

'How's life on the Major Investigation Team?'

'Different.'

'You're not really a "small cog" kind of chap.'

Dixon was flicking through the post mortem report.

'Are you?' said Poland, smiling.

'Am I what?'

'Never mind.'

Dixon was still reading Poland's report in the back seat of the patrol car.

'How far is it?' asked Poland.

'Half an hour or so,' replied the uniformed officer sitting in the driver's seat. 'Depending on the traffic.'

'It's not him, is it?' asked Dixon, sliding the report back into the envelope.

'Not as far as I can see,' replied Poland. 'I've looked at the original PM reports, X-rays and the photographs. Leaving aside the amateurish attempt to find the jugular vein with the fleam, the force applied to the trephine is very different.'

'More or less?'

'More. The best that can be said is that they're both right handed.'

'Is that it?'

'As far as similarities go, yes.'

Dixon glanced at the road signs as the car sped down the slip road, southbound on to the M60. 'Where does he live?'

'A little place called Marple,' said Poland, smiling. 'Rather apt, I have to say.'

'Do you?'

The rest of the journey was spent in silence, only the crunch of gravel bringing Dixon back to the present.

'Is this it?'

'Yes, Sir,' replied the driver.

Dixon looked up at the large double fronted detached property. Paint was peeling off the old metal window frames, condensation forming on the single glazed panes. The lawn had long since been replaced with parking and the single garage door was ajar, obviously too small for whatever was parked inside.

'It's a Bentley,' said Poland. 'He bought it when his wife died.'

'Whose is that?' asked Dixon, pointing to a red Nissan Micra parked against the overgrown hedge.

'The carer's, probably.'

Poland rang the doorbell and turned to Dixon. 'You'll like Geoff.'

'Rachel' it said on the badge pinned on to the white uniform just beneath the EK Care Services logo.

'Roger Poland and Detective Inspector Dixon to see Dr Burkett.'

'Come in. He's expecting you.'

They followed Rachel through to a conservatory at the back of the house where Dr Burkett was sitting. Patches of rust on the window frames and red streaks running down the wall underneath. Odd, the things that catch your eye, thought Dixon as he watched a narrowboat motoring past the end of the garden.

'The Peak Forest Canal, if you're wondering, young man,' said Burkett. He reached down and pulled a lever on the side of his reclining chair, which sprang forward, sitting him bolt upright. His glasses fell off the end of his nose into his lap.

'I was, Sir, thank you,' replied Dixon.

'This is the police officer I told you about, Geoff.'

'You're going to catch The Vet when the whole of Greater Manchester Police failed, is that right?'

'I think you're going to tell me I'm after a copycat, Sir,' replied Dixon, turning away from the window and shaking Burkett's cold and frail hand. He was dressed in a shirt and tie under his dressing gown, but would have needed help for that, the tartan blanket over his legs probably hiding pyjama bottoms.

'How are you, Geoff?' asked Poland, pulling up a chair.

'Old and bored, but I mustn't grumble, I suppose. I can still see to read and watch the TV, so that's something to be grateful for. And my marbles are all still lined up.'

'Pleased to hear it.'

'What about you? Still in Somerset is it?'

'Musgrove Park Hospital, plus the police work, of course.'

'Let's have a look at it then,' said Burkett, pulling a set of reading glasses from the top pocket of his dressing gown.

Poland handed a copy of the post mortem report to Burkett, letting him read it while he powered up his laptop.

'I made tea,' said Rachel, placing a tray on the table. 'I hope that's right?'

'Yes, thank you,' replied Poland.

'Help yourself to the biscuits, but he mustn't have any.' Rachel gestured to Burkett, who was still reading.

'I heard that.'

'He's diabetic.'

'Really?' asked Poland.

'Type 2,' said Burkett, shrugging his shoulders. 'Last couple of years.'

'Well, he's Type 1, so I'd better have them,' said Poland, picking up the plate.

Dixon had watched three narrowboats motor past along the canal before Burkett dropped the report on to the coffee table and shook his head.

'Amateur.'

'Who, me or the killer?' asked Poland.

'What about photos?'

'Here, said Poland, placing his computer on Burkett's lap. 'You know how to—?'

'Of course, I do.' Burkett began scrolling through the photographs, peering over his reading glasses. 'It's definitely a fleam, but he's missed the vein entirely. There's a faint nick in it on one of the incisions, this one here, but that would have closed up on its own, I expect.'

'It's certainly not enough for the victim to bleed out, is it?' asked Poland.

'Definitely not,' replied Burkett. 'But then he didn't, did he?'

'No.'

'And he's made a right hash of the trephine.'

'What's the significance of the fleam?' asked Dixon.

'It opens up the blood vessel with a clean incision about an inch long, depending on the size of the blade,' said Burkett. 'And it won't close without intervention. Pressure alone won't do it. This is a vein, remember, so it's taking blood back to the heart and lungs. It's not pumping like an artery. Hit one of those with a fleam and it's like a fountain!'

'How long would it take to bleed out then?'

'Half an hour or so. It happens in minutes with an artery, so they're buried deeper in the tissue for that very reason.'

'This is the external jugular vein, Nick,' said Poland. 'There's an internal one, which is bigger, but you'd have to go through muscle to get to it.'

'There's one on either side,' said Burkett, holding his hands to the sides of his neck. 'Not the pulse you can feel on your left hand. That's the carotid artery.'

'And The Vet hit the jugular every time.'

'Every time, first time,' replied Burkett. 'And he went through the venous sinus with the trephine too. With surgical precision. He really could've been a vet.'

'Could it be The Vet operating on his own, perhaps, with no one to hold the victim down?'

'What d'you mean?' asked Poland.

'He's twenty years older now, maybe even an alcoholic, his hand shaking, victim struggling. I'm clutching at straws here—'

'No, it's not him,' said Burkett. 'These marks here . . .'

Poland leaned over and looked at the laptop screen.

'Bruises?'

'There's no finesse,' said Burkett. 'The Vet never went deeper than he had to, hit it with just the right amount of oomph. This guy's got no idea. And he's hitting the fleam so hard he's leaving bruising around the wound. Even drunk, The Vet would do better than that.'

'And the trephine?'

Burkett smiled. 'The Vet used to take his time. Not too much pressure, plenty of turns of the handle. You can see the marks on the skull in my original photographs. This chap's pushing too hard and it's taking fewer turns of the handle. Roger?'

Poland nodded. 'He's even gone through the dura into the surface of the brain. The Vet never did that.'

'Never.'

'What about the original burials then?' asked Dixon.

'The sequence was always the same,' said Burkett. 'The fleam was used, and the victim allowed to bleed to the point of almost losing consciousness. That much was evident from the blood on their clothes. Then, and only then, was the trephine used, at the point when the victim was beyond screaming.'

'Why, though?'

'You'd need to ask the profiler. That's his department,' replied Burkett.

Dixon glanced at Poland and rolled his eyes.

'We never found a specific reason,' continued Burkett. 'And you won't without finding The Vet. I don't know that there was one anyway. This was gang warfare, don't forget. The triads hack you to death with meat cleavers and machetes, so the Carters came up with this. For the fear factor.'

'Did it work?'

'For a few years.' Burkett nodded. 'The photos helped, of course. They added to the drama of it all.'

'What photos?'

Burkett sat up. 'Didn't anyone tell you about the Polaroids?'

'No they bloody well didn't.'

'The Vet used to take a Polaroid photo of each victim. You know the old instant camera? Press the button and the picture pops out the bottom. Collectors' items they are, these days, I shouldn't wonder.'

'What happened to these Polaroids?'

'I never saw them, and it's just a rumour, really. But if they're out there somewhere, I doubt they're in anyone's family album.'

Chapter Ten

Dixon used the patrol car to take him back to GMP headquarters, Poland staying behind and calling a taxi. It would give him an extra half an hour with Dr Burkett to chat about the good old days, as Roger had put it.

'How'd you get on?' asked Sexton as Dixon switched on the computer at the adjacent workstation.

'Don't ask.'

'Not the same killer?'

'No.'

'We can go home then.'

'All in good time,' said Dixon, dragging the box of surveillance evidence on to his desk. He counted twenty-four photograph albums, arranged in date order, and four compact discs, one for each year until 1996. Just watch the stuff from 1995 and 'ignore the rest'. That's what Hargreaves had said. Dixon frowned. He'd start with 1996 and work back.

Photograph albums first. Grainy, some black and white and some in full colour. Faces, groups of faces, the same ones coming and going.

Hervey's snooker club, a betting shop, pubs. He was staring at a photograph of Michael Carter standing on the pavement outside the club, smoking, when he heard footsteps behind him.

'Big lad, isn't he,' said Douglas.

'Who's that standing next to him?' asked Dixon, handing him the photograph album. 'It just says "unidentified" on the back.'

'Devindra Kohli. Carter caught him with his fingers in the till and he disappeared.'

'Are there others of Carter?'

'There are some from 1994 certainly,' replied Douglas. 'Pass me the albums.' He began flicking through the photographs, before handing an open album to Dixon. 'Here he is, in the middle.'

The picture had been taken from a distance using a zoom lens. Clean shaven, dark hair, tall and stocky, sharp suit. That was about the best Dixon could get from it, no matter how hard he squinted at it.

'Who's that he's with?'

'That's his brother, Kenny, on his left. I don't know who the other one is.'

'Pull up a chair, Sir,' said Dixon, gesturing to the empty swivel chair at the workstation behind him. 'Tell me about the brother.'

'He was younger,' replied Douglas, sitting down.

'Michael and Kenny Carter. Manchester's answer to Ronnie and Reggie.'

'Michael was. Kenny wasn't a villain by nature. It was Michael's operation.'

'What did Kenny do?'

'The books, possibly. We never saw him taking any sort of active role.'

'You never mentioned the Polaroids either,' said Dixon, fixing Douglas with a stare.

'We've never seen any of them. That's if they exist at all. It was just a journalist from the *Post* spreading gossip.'

'So, how did Rick Wheaton get in?'

'You ever been undercover?' asked Douglas.

'Two weeks as a trainee teacher in a boarding school,' replied Dixon. 'Does that count?'

'No.' Douglas laughed. 'This was deep undercover. You don't just drop in and out of it, you live it. He became one of them. Only on the fringes, mind you. The snooker club was theirs, and he worked behind the bar.'

'Where is he now?'

'I really can't say.'

'And he volunteered?'

Douglas nodded.

'And they never suspected him?'

'He wouldn't be here today if they had. Others tried and failed.'

'Are there any photos of him in these albums?'

'No.'

'So, how did he do it?'

'He witnessed some things he shouldn't have, told no one, and they began to trust that he'd keep his mouth shut. Beatings, mainly. You'd be surprised what someone can achieve with a snooker cue and bit of determination.'

Dixon winced.

'There was a bit of drugs too. He'd been in six months before he started feeding stuff back.'

'Risky, if they had someone on the inside.'

'I'm not convinced they ever did,' said Douglas. 'Despite Baker's conviction. He went to his grave swearing blind he'd been framed.'

'And was he?'

'We'll never know now. But I've seen no evidence they had anyone on the inside.'

'The first time then . . .' said Dixon.

'There was a killing at the snooker hall. A beating . . .' Douglas shook his head. 'And the bloke died. There must have been at least fifteen people in that night, and they all saw it, so he had cover. Then there were a couple of drug deals. It got easier when the Shannons turned up because Carter thought it was them.'

'But he never got close to Carter?'

'Never got beyond the snooker hall, really,' replied Douglas. 'He tried, but never broke into the inner circle.'

'Why not?'

'It was close knit. All extended family.'

'Really, who else?'

'A couple of cousins. They're all in the albums.'

'Where are they now?'

'Spain, last I heard.'

Dixon nodded.

'How did Wheaton get out?' he asked.

'Ray Hargreaves had him arrested. When the bomb went off, Michael got very jumpy and started accusing those close to him of all sorts. It was the safest way. A month in a safe house, then the Carters disappeared. After that it was ten years with the Met before he came back to Manchester.'

'Whereabouts in London?'

'The East End. Bow, I think.'

'I was at Wimbledon for seven years.'

'Soft out west.'

'Of course it is,' said Dixon, smiling.

Douglas stood up. 'Looks like the pathologist's back.'

'It's not the same killer,' said Poland.

'You're sure?' asked Douglas.

'Definitely. And Geoff Burkett agrees.'

The GMP officers sitting in front of Dixon started murmuring amongst themselves, Chapman and Pandey included. Much of what was said was lost in the general chatter, but Dixon picked out 'wasting our fucking time', although he couldn't be sure whether it was Chapman or Pandey who had said it.

He turned when there was a knock at the door behind him, leaned over and opened it.

'Excuse me, Sir.'

'What?' replied Douglas.

'There's been another body,' said the uniformed officer leaning on the door frame. 'In Somerset.'

Poland looked at his watch.

'I'd better get back,' he said. 'Is there an earlier train?'

'There will be if you change at Birmingham,' said Chapman.

'Thanks.'

'Get a car lined up to take Dr Poland to Piccadilly,' said Douglas.

'Via the Premier Inn,' said Dixon.

'You coming too?' asked Poland.

Dixon nodded.

'Hadn't you better check with—?'

'No.'

Once back at his workstation, Dixon put the lid on the surveillance box and dropped it by the pile. He handed the CDs to Douglas.

'Can you get these copied and sent down to me, please, Sir?'

'Manny can do that,' he replied, passing them to Pandey.

'Are we going?' asked Sexton.

'There's been another body.'

'Where?'

'Buried in the sand on Dunster Beach,' said Douglas, smirking. 'It sounds idyllic.'

Dixon ignored the sarcasm. 'Can you leave this stuff out, Sir?' he asked, gesturing to the boxes.

'If we must.'

'I may need to have another look at it at some point.'

'Really?'

Half an hour later they were sitting on a train at Manchester Piccadilly, Dixon staring out of the window at another as it pulled away from the adjacent platform.

'Are you sure we're not supposed to be on that one?'

'You can if you like,' replied Poland. 'But you'll end up in London.'

'It'll be dark in twenty minutes.' Sexton was looking at his watch.

'Clocks go forward the day after tomorrow, don't forget,' replied Poland.

'Did you speak to your assistant?' Dixon shifted in his seat and glanced across at the commuters sitting on the other side of the aisle: one staring at a laptop screen, the other a copy of the *Manchester Daily Post*.

'When you were in the hotel. He's arrived at Musgrove.'

'Same injuries?'

Poland nodded. 'He's getting better at it too. He got the jugular vein this time and—'

'I can imagine.'

'Is there an ID?' asked Sexton.

'Not yet.'

'What time was it?'

'First thing this morning. A dog walker found him just behind a groyne at the far end of the beach.'

'I'll bet you a tenner the dog found him,' muttered Dixon.

'How are we gonna explain this to Potter?' asked Sexton.

'You let me worry about that,' replied Dixon. 'GMP will probably stand down once Roger confirms it's the copycat, and we were due back tomorrow anyway.'

'She's not going to be happy.'

'She'll get over it.'

◆　◆　◆

It was cold and dark when Dixon joined the back of the taxi queue just after 10 p.m., an abandoned copy of the *Manchester Daily Post* tucked under his arm. Roger Poland had stayed on the train to Taunton, where his car was waiting for him, and Sexton had decided to walk home. It was not far, apparently, and he would get a lift out to Portishead in the morning.

Dixon stamped his feet. There were three people in front of him in the queue, but only two taxis, although his angst proved short lived when a third drew up.

'Portishead, please,' he said, opening the back door.

'Whereabouts?'

'The police HQ.'

'Oh, right.'

On way don't wait up Nx

He slid his phone back into his pocket and closed his eyes, the buzzing in his breast pocket the only thing that stopped him nodding off.

Where r u? Jx

On way to fetch car Nx

We're watching The Lavender Hill Mob Jxx

Apt ;-)

Waiting up :-)

Dixon smiled. Jane's taste in films was improving, only a couple of rogue DVDs finding their way on to the shelf. *Robin Hood: Prince of Thieves* had been one. He shook his head. Great fun, maybe, but Robin of the Hood did not have an American accent. Even Alan Rickman couldn't save that one. *The Money Pit* had been another, although after *Saving Private Ryan* he could forgive Tom Hanks pretty much anything.

'Will this do?'

'Yes, fine,' replied Dixon, climbing out of the taxi at the front entrance. The lights were off in the gatehouse, so he ducked under the barrier and walked along the access road to the car park, glancing up at the second floor of the headquarters building. Detective Chief Superintendent Potter was standing in the window of her office, watching him.

'You're supposed to be in Manchester,' she said as he dropped the red box file on to a workstation. The reflection in the window had given him advanced warning.

'They're winding down now. Roger's told them it's a copycat.'

'And Burkett confirmed that?'

'He did.'

'They'll probably stand the whole team down now.'

'What about this latest body?' asked Dixon, sitting on the corner of the workstation.

'There's no ID yet. Is Poland back?'

'He will be, by now,' replied Dixon, looking at his watch.

'Did you ruffle any feathers?'

'I don't think so. I didn't find many that needed ruffling.'

'What did you find?'

'The Carters—'

'We know about them.' Potter nodded, then took a swig from a plastic cup, the smell of scotch reaching Dixon where he was sitting.

'They disappeared after the Arndale Centre bomb,' he said. 'Michael Carter was turning supergrass, so the IRA killed him.'

'We didn't know that.'

'It's not official. Just what informers could find out. The rest of the gang melted away, leaving Manchester to the Shannons. Can you check with Special Branch?'

'I can try,' replied Potter. 'Did we get anyone on the inside?'

'A barman at the snooker club. Went by the name of Rick Wheaton. You may remember the name?'

'I don't.' Potter frowned.

'You never mentioned you were Brian Hocking's partner.'

'You don't miss much.'

Dixon waited.

'I was young, just out of training,' continued Potter. She turned the swivel chair to face Dixon and then sat down on it. 'I didn't know he was in it up to his neck. How was I supposed to know that?'

'What happened?'

'When he was killed I was moved out of the Tactical Vehicle Crime Unit to VO15 – that was gun crime. Then I applied for a transfer.'

'To Avon and Somerset?'

'To anywhere I could get one. This is where I ended up.' Potter drained the plastic cup. 'Better rinse that out before I bin it,' she said, raising her eyebrows.

'Rick Wheaton got a job behind the bar in one of their clubs,' Dixon said. 'Never got in beyond that though.'

'Did he turn up anything useful?'

'A bit of drugs and a couple of thugs who beat someone to death right in front of him. He got nothing on Carter himself though.'

'How long was he in for?'

'Over a year.'

'And he never saw The Vet?'

'No.'

'How'd he get out?'

'He was arrested after the bomb went off.'

'And they've heard nothing about what's going on now?'

'Nothing at all,' replied Dixon, folding his arms. 'They had a small team on it trying to find out.'

'What about the redacted statements?'

'Just informers. I've seen the originals.'

'And the surveillance?'

'Four discs. They're copying them and sending them down.'

'All right,' said Potter, frowning. 'I'll speak to Douglas in the morning, when Poland's done the PM. You'd better go.'

'What about Wainwright?'

'Resources are tight. I'll be taking him off it and reducing the team to six. You can take it from here.'

Dixon nodded.

'But remember, you report to me. All right?'

'Fine.'

'The Incident Room can stay at Express Park and you can use local officers as and when.'

Dixon smiled.

'Let me know what Poland says in the morning,' continued Potter. 'I'll send Jonny Sexton down when he gets here too.'

'Thanks.'

'And don't muck it up.'

◆ ◆ ◆

'You're early,' shouted Jane as Dixon stepped in through the back door of the cottage just before midnight. 'I wasn't expecting you till tomorrow.'

'There was a second murder.' He dropped his bag on the floor and knelt down to scratch Monty behind the ears.

'Where?'

'Dunster Beach. It's a copycat though. Roger's confirmed it from the first body, so the Manchester lot are leaving us to it.'

'Is the MIT being wound up?'

'Not yet.'

Jane appeared in the doorway of the kitchen, looking down at Dixon on the floor with Monty. 'You eaten?'

'We got something on the train.'

'A beer then?'

'Thanks,' replied Dixon, standing up. 'Spoken to Sonia?'

Jane took a deep breath and exhaled, puffing out her cheeks.

'What?'

'Four times this evening,' she said, shaking her head. 'I think she's had a few too many.'

'Doesn't she always?'

'Not this bad. Anyway, I told her I'd try and see her at the weekend. Will you come?'

'Yes, if I can.'

'Are you back at Portishead?'

'The Incident Room at Express Park,' replied Dixon. 'The team's being scaled back.'

'At least I can keep an eye on you,' said Jane, smiling. She put her arms round him and kissed him.

'You can.'

Jane reached over and picked up the newspaper that Dixon had left on the worktop.

'"The Vet strikes again!" They don't muck about, do they?'

'They don't let accuracy get in the way of a good headline either.'

'Did Roger find you?'

'We came back on the train together,' replied Dixon, taking a swig of beer.

'So, what happens now?'

'We could watch the end of *The Lavender Hill Mob* again?'

Chapter Eleven

Dixon turned right off the A39 and drove down through Dunster. He looked over his shoulder at Monty, sitting in the back of the Land Rover, whining as the reek of salt in the air grew stronger. Even Dixon could smell it now.

'Smells like the tide's in, old son,' he said.

A walk on Dunster Beach would be a first for both of them, although the circumstances could have been better. He flicked the windscreen wipers to intermittent. Investigating a murder too. Still, at least one of them would enjoy it.

Monty had his feet up on the front seats now and started barking at the patrol car blocking Sea Lane.

'Access to Haven Close only, Sir,' shouted the uniformed officer walking towards the Land Rover. 'The beach is closed.'

Dixon wound down the window and held out his warrant card.

'Sorry, Sir,' said the officer.

'Surely, Scenes of Crime have finished?'

'Yes, Sir. We're just trying to keep the ghouls away. There's nothing to see. The tide's been in and out twice since he was found.'

'There's been a full search?'

'Yesterday afternoon.'

'Is there anyone on the beach?'

'No, Sir.'

'What's to stop people walking along from Blue Anchor then?'

'Er, nothing, Sir.'

'Please tell me you haven't been here all night.'

'Since dawn, Sir,' replied the officer, looking at his watch. 'Half an hour at most.'

'I suggest you find something else to do,' said Dixon, glancing in his rear view mirror at a car waiting behind him. 'Where was he found?'

'He was buried on the other side of the last groyne. About halfway along.'

'Which way?'

'Towards Blue Anchor. Right next to the groyne. There was some blue tape on the posts. I'm not sure if it's still there.'

'What about the tide?'

'It'll be on its way out now.'

'Thank you. Now can you—?'

'Of course, Sir.'

The officer ran back to the patrol car and reversed it out of the way, reaching for his radio as Dixon drove past.

He pulled up next to an old World War Two pillbox that looked like it had been rendered with stones from the beach. Miserable places at the best of times: cold and damp, even in high summer, at least this one had a sea view. He checked the ticket machine, which was blocking the entrance. Then he checked his pockets and the glovebox. Putting the blue light on top of his Land Rover would have to do.

He drove to the far end of the car park and stopped with the last groyne directly in front of him. Off to his right the concrete outfall took a freshwater stream out to sea. What was left of a line of blue and white police tape trailed in the wind like the tail of a kite from one of the huge timbers that made up the groyne: a line of logs pile-driven into the beach and forming a barrier out towards the sea, designed to stop the shingle washing away. It had stopped the body washing away – a body with no name yet. Dixon grimaced. Time enough for that.

He let Monty out of the back of the Land Rover.

'C'mon then, old chap.'

He fished Monty's ball out of a wellington boot under the bench seat and set off after him across the shingle towards the wet sand. He threw the ball and watched it rolling towards the sea, Monty reaching it just before the waves swept it away.

Not a footprint in sand freshly washed by the tide; a few paw prints, but Dixon knew who was responsible for those. He looked along the groyne to his left, the sand smooth, offering no sign whatsoever of a grave dug and then dug up.

He took his phone out of his pocket and rang Sexton.

'Where are you?'

'Express Park, Sir.'

'Already?'

'Yes. Where are you?'

'Dunster Beach. Check and see if house to house is planned for today and, if not, organise it. Dunster north of the A39, and make sure they include the chalets west of here. We'll need someone on the beach speaking to dog walkers too. I can see some in the distance already.'

'Leave it with me, Sir.'

'Have we got a name yet?'

'David Cobb. He only retired last year, poor sod.'

'What'd he do?'

'He worked for the council.'

'Find out which one and what he did.'

'Yes, Sir.'

'I'll be over at Musgrove for the PM.'

Dixon rang off and kicked at the sand in front of him. Monty ran over, thinking it was a game, and started digging, sending a spray of sand behind him.

'You won't find anything, matey; they've been over it with metal detectors,' he said, kicking the ball along the beach.

Dixon watched the hole filling with water and wondered whether David Cobb had suffocated or drowned in his shallow grave in the sand. And whether he'd been conscious when the hole had been cut in his forehead.

◆ ◆ ◆

'You're early,' said Poland, looking up when Dixon walked into the pathology lab.

'Time and tide, if you'll pardon the pun.'

'Well, you're just in time for the internals.' Poland was pulling on a pair of latex gloves.

'Have you got a cause of death?' asked Dixon.

'I'll need to have a look at his lungs. It wasn't blood loss, so he either suffocated or drowned when the tide came in. If his lungs are full of water—'

'I get it,' interrupted Dixon, peering at the side of Cobb's neck. 'You said he got the jugular this time?'

'Not completely, but he's improving.'

'Not enough to kill him?'

'Not on its own. You could apply a bit of pressure and stop the bleeding. It may have looked like he'd done the job to begin with. He got the venous sinus this time though, and together that would've been enough. He's not in The Vet's league. He was opening up the vein—'

'You carry on. I'll wait in your office,' said Dixon, making for the door.

He was sitting back in the chair with his feet on the radiator when Poland walked in.

'He suffocated. The lungs are dry. And it's the same killer who murdered Harry Lucas. Not The Vet as we know.'

'Can I come back in?'

'You're quite safe.'

David Cobb was lying on the slab, a green sheet covering him up to his shoulders. A bit of a paunch perhaps, but nothing much. A thin grey beard hiding pockmarks, and a receding hairline accentuated by the hole in his forehead.

'Tell me about him,' said Dixon.

'His wife identified him last night, so there's a lot we know for sure,' replied Poland, glancing down at his notepad. 'He's sixty, married with three children. He has angina and is on the waiting list for a triple heart bypass. Looking at the heart it was a bit more urgent than anyone realised.'

'But it wasn't a heart attack?'

'No. Six feet tall and fourteen stone, so a bit overweight. On a diet, apparently.'

'Still too heavy for one person to carry.'

'You could drag him from the car park at Dunster Beach.'

'Across the shingle?' asked Dixon.

'It's not far,' replied Poland.

'Any incapacitating injury?'

'A blow to the back of the head. Blunt object, just like Harry Lucas.'

'Handcuffs?'

'His hands were in front of him.' Poland picked up a plastic evidence bag from the side, a set of handcuffs clearly visible behind the white label.

'Anything from SOCO about where he was killed?'

'Nothing,' replied Poland. 'The tide had been in and out again, so any evidence would have been washed away.'

'How long would it take?'

'What?'

'All of it.'

'The blow to the head.' Poland acted out the arm movement. 'Roll him on his side and line up the fleam, or try to.'

'What about light?' asked Dixon.

'That's your department,' replied Poland. 'Then the trephine. He's pushing hard with that so he'd be through the skull in maybe five minutes.'

'That long?'

'Yes. The skull's thickest at the front. Why d'you think you head-butt people?'

'I don't.'

'You know what I mean.' Poland sighed. 'Right in the middle this time too, so he got the venous sinus. Blood loss would have got him eventually, if he hadn't suffocated first.'

Dixon swallowed hard.

'Then he's just got to bury him,' continued Poland. 'A shallow grave in soft sand. Ten minutes tops. Less if he'd already got Cobb to dig it.'

'It all points to him being in a hurry,' said Dixon. 'He didn't even bother to bury Harry; he just rolled the van into the mud.' He reached into his pocket. 'My phone's buzzing.'

Poland waited.

'Manchester MIT standing down. We're on our own. DP,' said Dixon, reading aloud.

'That's just the way you like it,' said Poland, grinning.

Dixon smiled. 'Is he working alone?'

'There's no sign of anyone else.'

'I wonder if he hung around.'

'No idea.'

'I would,' said Dixon. 'After all, you wouldn't want your victim coming round and climbing out. Would you?'

'I suppose not.'

'In soft sand, you'd just have to sit up. Do we know how deep he was buried?'

'About a foot,' said Poland, flicking through his notes. 'But he wouldn't have needed to hang around for long.'

'When? You never said when.'

'My colleague, Davison, reckoned he'd been dead about twelve hours when he got to him yesterday morning. And he'd have suffocated straightaway under a foot of wet sand.'

'The night before then.'

Poland nodded. 'We're no nearer finding out why he's copycatting though, are we?'

'I'm more interested in where he's getting his information from. We can worry about "why" when we've got him,' replied Dixon, turning towards the door. He stopped when he had opened it.

'D'you think he had to dig his own grave?'

'No idea. Why?'

'You want to kill me and bury me in a shallow grave, you'll have to dig the bloody thing yourself.'

'I'll remember that,' said Poland, smiling.

◆ ◆ ◆

Meeting room 2 was familiar, although the same could not be said for the officers sitting around the table, apart from Jonny Sexton. And name badges would have been useful, he thought as he listened to the officers introducing themselves. A small team was one thing, but a small team he didn't know was quite another. He'd have been better off if Potter had stood down the MIT and returned the case to Bridgwater CID. Still, he could call on Dave, Mark and Louise when and if he needed to.

'Let's start with Harry Lucas,' said Dixon. 'Have we spoken to the Coastguard officers?'

'Not yet, Sir.' Glasses, sitting at the far end of the table.

'Let's chase that up, shall we?'

'Yes, Sir.'

'What about the house to house?'

'We've done either end of the coast path. Clyce Road in Highbridge and Sloway Lane in East Huntspill.' Short dark hair, too much perfume. Must be Tracey somebody, the house to house manager, thought Dixon.

'Anything?'

'Nothing, Sir.'

'Work colleagues?'

'We've got statements from his area franchise manager, and Superintendent Wainwright went to their head office yesterday. The statements are being typed up now.'

'What do they say?'

'Not a lot, really.' Leaning back in his chair, arms folded.

'Traffic cameras then. Anything there?' asked Dixon.

'A few cars that we've ruled out. Otherwise nothing.'

'There are lots of country lanes he could've used to avoid them.' The shrugging shoulders almost reached her earrings.

'I'm well aware of that.' Dixon took a deep breath. There were some days he would have taken the bait. But this was not one of them. 'The staff at the sewage treatment works,' he said. 'Has anyone spoken to them?'

'There's a statement from the manager. Someone took it the day he was found.'

'And you've not been back?'

'No, Sir.'

'Let's do that, shall we? Speak to everyone who works there or has reason to visit. All right?'

'Yes, Sir.'

'What about his family and friends.'

'I'm still doing that, Sir.' Tracey again.

'Social media and phone records?'

'We're doing that as well.'

'Is there a copy of his customer list?' asked Dixon.

'I'm working through it, Sir.' Sitting at the back, black leather jacket. 'I've spoken to some of them by phone and visited others. I can let you have copies of the statements.'

'Have you spoken to all of them?'

'Not yet. It'll take me another day or so.'

'Keep at it.'

'Yes, Sir.'

'Any connection with the eel poachers?'

'None.'

'Anything on the van?'

'The horn had been disconnected.'

'It seems he thought of everything.' Dixon sighed. 'David Cobb then.'

'Superintendent Wainwright went to see Cobb's widow yesterday, but she was too upset to see him.'

'House to house?' asked Dixon, looking at Sexton.

'Starts at ten. There's a roadblock on Sea Lane too and officers on the beach talking to dog walkers. I'll be heading over there in a minute.'

'You said he worked for the council?'

'Yeah, he retired a year ago. Head of Environmental Services at Sedgemoor District Council.'

'OK,' said Dixon. 'I'll try the widow again and then catch you up.'

It was a schoolboy mistake, sitting with his back to the door. He took a deep breath as DCI Lewis sat down next to him in the canteen.

'Potter's put you in charge then?'

Dixon dropped a sugar cube into his coffee and stirred it.

'I thought you were diabetic?' continued Lewis.

'I've been up since six,' muttered Dixon in reply. 'And I'd rather she disbanded the MIT. Manchester have stood their team down, so there's no liaison to worry about.'

'It's a double murder,' said Lewis. 'And the press would have a field day if she did that.'

'What's happened with the Whites?'

'They've been remanded in custody and Janice is gathering evidence. There's nothing to connect them to Harry Lucas.'

'Except they heard him banging and did nothing. The bastard had even disabled the horn on the van, would you believe it?'

Lewis shrugged his shoulders.

'Did you bump into Chard?' he asked.

'He was lurking behind me, ready to insert the knife.'

'Deborah Potter won't take any notice of him.'

'I hope you're right, Sir.'

'Tell me about David Cobb.'

'Same killer, according to Roger. He was found buried in the sand on Dunster Beach. I'm going over to speak to his widow now.'

'What'd he do for a living?'

'He retired a year ago, apparently. He was the Head of Environmental Services at Sedgemoor District Council.'

'There's your connection,' said Lewis, nodding.

'Eh?'

'You never had to phone the council about a wasps' nest or rats?'

'No,' replied Dixon.

'Lucky you. Well, when you do, you phone Environmental Services.'

'Really?'

'It used to be Environmental Health,' replied Lewis, standing up. 'I'm not sure if it's the same these days, with all the cuts.'

Dixon glanced into the back of the Land Rover before he inserted his key in the lock to find Monty curled up on his bed, fast asleep. It had been an early start followed by a walk on the beach, so he could be forgiven for that, perhaps. He started growling when Dixon opened the door, but soon stopped when he realised it was him.

'You weren't asleep at all, were you, you crafty bugger,' said Dixon, climbing into the driver's seat.

He switched on the engine and then opened a web browser on his phone. He typed in 'Sedgemoor pest control' and hit 'enter'. He ignored the adverts from pest control firms and looked at the first search result.

'Sedgemoor District Council – Pest Control; The Pest Control Service at Sedgemoor District Council aims to guard against the diseases and damage caused by pests.'

He clicked on it and read aloud.

'Pest Treatment Services. Councils do not have a duty to provide a pest control service. However, a pest service can be obtained through the Council's preferred provider, Pest Erase UK Ltd.'

◆ ◆ ◆

Dixon recognised Karen Marsden's old Audi parked in the drive of Castle Cottage, a small pink house at the bottom of Castle Hill, Nether Stowey. The cottage backed on to the road, with net curtains at leaded windows, and room for only one car in front of the garage.

He parked as tight as he could to the neighbour's garden wall, his nearside wing mirror lost in the branches of an overhanging fir tree. There was enough room for a car to get past, just, and they could always knock on the door. He turned in the driver's wing mirror to be on the safe side.

Dixon admired Karen Marsden. The work of a police family liaison officer was far from easy, dealing with the grief and anger of victims and their relatives day in and day out. And then came the frustration at lack of progress in the police investigation, always directed at her even when she was just the messenger.

'I was expecting Superintendent Wainwright,' said Karen, opening the door at the side of the cottage before Dixon had rung the bell.

'Change of plan.'

'There's still a Major Investigation Team?' Her voice was hushed, her hand holding the inner door closed behind her.

'Yes. It's confirmed as a copycat though, so Manchester have dropped out,' replied Dixon. 'How is she?'

'Not good, but she wants to speak to someone now, which is progress.'

He followed Karen along a corridor to the living room at the far end. It overlooked the garden at the back, or was it the front of the cottage?

'Mary, this is Detective Inspector Dixon,' said Karen. 'I'm sure he won't mind me saying so, but he's the best we've got. He'll find out what happened to David.'

'I hope so, Inspector.' Mary Cobb looked up at him, her eyes full of tears.

'I'll do my best, Mrs Cobb.'

She held a tissue to her eyes. 'He'd only just retired. It was supposed to be the start of the rest of our lives . . .'

'What sort of man was David?' asked Dixon, sitting down on the sofa next to Mrs Cobb.

'Quiet, unassuming, a good husband and father.' She closed her eyes. 'I don't know what else to say.'

'And your children?'

'Claire is in America. She's flying back tomorrow, and Mark is driving down from London tonight. They're both married. Mark has children, but Claire doesn't.'

'He retired early?'

'Yes.'

'Was there any particular reason? Was he having any trouble at work, perhaps?'

Mary Cobb shook her head.

'Did he ever say that he was concerned about his safety?' continued Dixon.

'At Sedgemoor District Council?'

'About twelve months ago, perhaps?'

Karen Marsden looked at Dixon, her eyes wide.

Dixon waited.

'He never had any trouble with anyone he worked with, but . . .'

Silence.

'Go on.'

'You're right. There was something troubling him, a few months before he retired, so that's a year ago, isn't it?'

'Can you remember what?' asked Karen.

'He'd had someone come into his office, shouting the odds. It really shook him.'

'Were the police called?' asked Dixon.

'Yes, but the man had gone by the time they got there.'

'Did he mention a name?'

'No. Look, he was fine the next day.' Tears started to roll down her cheeks. 'You don't think it's connected, do you?'

'I don't know for—'

Dixon was interrupted by a car horn out in the lane.

'I'd better move my car. I'll leave you to it, but I will be back, Mrs Cobb. All right?'

'Yes.'

Karen Marsden leaned on the door of the cottage, watching Dixon squeezing down the side of her car.

'You know who killed him, don't you?' she asked.

'Nice spot this,' said Dixon. 'Is there a castle?'

'Up there,' replied Karen, looking up the hill on the other side of the road. 'There's nothing left except earthworks, according to M—'

Dixon was out in the road by the time she finished her sentence.

'Tosser,' she muttered as he climbed into his Land Rover.

Chapter Twelve

On the pavement would have to do. Dixon left the blue light on top of his Land Rover, the hazard lights on and a business card on the dashboard. It would be a brave traffic warden who gave him a parking ticket.

The reception area at the Sedgemoor District Council Offices in Bridgwater was a hive of activity. There were queues for the Council Tax and Business Rates and the Housing Benefit Enquiry Desks, but only one person behind the Housing Advice and Homelessness Desk, and no one to advise. She looked asleep. Quite an achievement that, with all the background noise. At least two children were crying. It must have been two, thought Dixon, glancing around the room; one child couldn't cry in stereo, surely?

'Who is the Head of Environmental Services?' he asked the receptionist at the General Enquiries Desk.

'That'll be Mr Jones.'

'I'd like to see him, please.'

'Well, he—'

'Detective Inspector Dixon, Avon and Somerset Police,' said Dixon, brandishing his warrant card.

'Oh right. Hang on,' said the receptionist, reaching for the phone.

He was flicking through a leaflet about Dunster Castle when the door opened behind the reception desk.

'Is someone looking for me?'

'That's him over there.' The receptionist's finger was pointing at Dixon, so he walked over.

'Police?'

'Are you Mr Jones?' asked Dixon.

'Simon, yes.'

'Is there somewhere we can talk?'

'Yes, of course. Follow me.'

'How long have you been Head of Environmental Services?' asked Dixon, following Jones along a narrow corridor.

'Nine months.'

'You took over from David Cobb?'

'Yes.'

'Did you work here before that?'

'I was his assistant.' Jones stopped to peer through a frosted window. 'This one'll do,' he said, opening the door to a small interview room: two chairs and a round table. 'Is David all right?'

'I'm afraid he's dead, Mr Jones,' replied Dixon, sitting down. 'He was found buried in a shallow grave on Dunster Beach yesterday morning.'

'Oh God.'

'D'you remember an incident about twelve months ago when the police were called?'

'Here?'

'Yes.'

Jones mopped beads of sweat from his forehead with a tissue. 'I heard about it later. David didn't pursue a complaint so it wasn't taken any further, if I remember rightly. He said he was just letting off steam.'

'Who was?'

'Toby Horan.'

'And he was a pest controller?'

'Er, yes. How could you . . . ?' Jones looked quizzically at Dixon. 'He runs Westcountry Pest Services. He was our preferred provider until Pest Erase UK opened up.'

'Why did you switch to them?'

'Toby was a one man band: a man and a van operation. Pest Erase came with BPCA membership, that's the British Pest Control Association, Constructionline certification and they were accredited by CHAS, I think.'

'What's that?'

'The Contractors Health and Safety Assessment Scheme. Toby had none of those accreditations.'

'So, what happened?'

'He came in and had a go at David. There was a lot of shouting and that was about it, I think.'

'Were any threats made?'

'Just general "I'll get you for this", "You don't know who you're dealing with", sort of stuff,' said Jones, shaking his head. 'The pane of glass in David's office door was broken too, I think.'

'What was the effect on Horan's business?' asked Dixon.

'It hit him hard. He went bust six months later, so I heard. It was unfortunate.'

Dixon stood up.

'D'you have Horan's address?' he asked.

Dixon was watching the traffic warden on the other side of King Square while he waited for Louise to answer her phone.

'Hello, Sir,' she said, just before her voicemail cut in.

'You interviewed the bloke from Wessex Water at the sewage treatment works?'

'Yes.'

'And he said Harry was their pest controller?'

'That's right,' replied Louise. 'He'd been doing it for about a year. Pest Erase do all their rat catching where they've got a franchisee.'

'And where they haven't?'

'They just get someone local to do it.'

'Who did it before Harry?'

'I didn't ask.'

'Find out and text me, will you?'

'Er, yes, Sir.'

Dixon rang off and sent Sexton a text message.

Express Park quick as you can

The reply came as he was turning out of King Square, so he pulled over on the pavement and reached for his phone, watching the traffic warden in his rear view mirror scribbling down a note of his registration number.

What about the house to house?

He hit 'reply'.

Leave them to it

Another text arrived just as he was sliding his phone into his jacket pocket.

Toby Horan, Westcountry Pest Services

He tapped out a reply – *Thanks Louise* – and then slid his phone back into his pocket.

'Who's the rat catcher now?' he muttered as he pulled away, the front wheels of his Land Rover dropping off the kerb with a clunk.

◆　　◆　　◆

'Which one is it?'

'That one straight in front of you,' replied Sexton. 'The one with the double garage and the boat outside.'

They were in a cul-de-sac of newish red brick houses, all of a similar design, some with columns either side of a grand entrance porch, some with a single garage, some with a car port, but only one with a double garage: the house on the corner where Marlborough Court forked, perhaps a hundred yards away. The double garage had a new roof, either that or the garages themselves were new; a small fibreglass speed boat on a rusting trailer, a half-hearted attempt to hide it behind a box hedge; and no sign of a van.

'Is everybody in position?'

'Armed Response are going in with us, and there's another car behind the house.'

Dixon frowned.

'What's the matter?' asked Sexton.

'It's too easy,' replied Dixon, grimacing. 'Too easy by far.'

'What d'you mean?'

'There's nobody in. You can see that from here.'

He looked at his watch: 4.30 p.m.

'She could be collecting the kids from school,' said Sexton.

'How old are they?'

'Thirteen and fifteen.'

'There's no Toby Horan on the electoral roll, is there?'

'No, Sir. Just Anna Turnbull, his ex-wife presumably. He's got a mobile phone registered to this address though, a bank account and a van.'

Dixon had checked the Land Registry records. The property had been transferred from the joint names of Tobias and Anna Horan into the sole name of Anna Turnbull six months earlier. A sure sign of divorce and an ex-wife reverting to her maiden name.

'And you don't think this is too easy?'

'Well, it's—'

'Let's just get it over with,' said Dixon.

Sexton rang the doorbell and waited. Dixon squatted down and pushed open the letter box.

'Police. Open up,' he shouted.

Silence.

'Over to you,' he said, turning to the Armed Response team waiting behind him.

'Armed police. Open this door,' shouted the uniformed sergeant, stepping forward. He shook his head. 'Ready, on three.' He took the battering ram from the officer standing behind him. 'One, two . . .' The 'three' was lost in the crash of the battering ram hitting the door just above the lock. A second blow and the door swung open.

Dixon stepped back and watched the armed officers run into the hall, the first following the corridor to the back, the second entering the open plan living room on the right. The third and fourth headed up the stairs.

He counted four shouts of 'clear' before he had even stepped into the hall.

'Let the other Armed Response team go,' he said, turning to Sexton.

'Yes, Sir.'

A cursory glance at the photographs on the mantelpiece in the living room, and in the clip frames on the walls either side, told the story of a relationship breakdown; the photomontages cut with precision to remove an adult male, a tattooed arm around a small boy holding a carp the only trace of him. That left Anna, the children and the occasional grandparent; Anna's mother and father no doubt. There would be photographs of Toby somewhere, unless the divorce had been so traumatic that they had been incinerated or shredded, all trace of him expunged from the former matrimonial home.

Dixon felt the side of the kettle.

'Somebody was here within the last half an hour.'

'Is it warm?' asked Sexton.

'They had a cuppa,' replied Dixon, gesturing towards the sink where a mug was lying on its side in the washing up bowl.

He glanced back down the corridor where four uniformed officers were waiting just inside the front door.

'Let's get on with it then. You know what to look for.'

'Yes, Sir.'

'And make sure you check the loft.'

Toby Horan hadn't been living at the property last October when the electoral roll had been updated, if that was to be believed, but it was still possible they might find something with his DNA on it. Better still something, or someone, who could give Dixon a forwarding address.

A car horn sounded outside, followed by a door slamming and raised voices.

'What the bloody hell is going on? And what have you done to my front door?'

'Mrs Turnbull, Sir,' said the officer following a woman into the hall.

She threw her handbag on the table. 'It's Ms!'

'Ms Turnbull, Sir.'

'You'd better have a warrant.'

'Technically, we don't need one, Ms Turnbull,' said Dixon, with his best disarming smile. 'But I got one anyway.'

'Well you'll be paying for that door.' She snatched the piece of paper from his hand. 'What are you looking for?'

'Not what, who. We're looking for your ex-husband.'

'What's he done now?' she asked, sweeping her long dark hair back as she glanced down at the warrant.

Dixon ignored the question.

'D'you know where he is?'

'No. I wish I did. Useless tosser. He signed over the house and then buggered off. Left me with the kids, not that I mind that, of course.'

'D'you have any idea where he might be?'

'No. My solicitor's been trying to find him too. And the Child Support Agency.'

Dixon followed her into the living room and watched her drop into an armchair.

'Sam will be home from school soon,' she said. 'How long's this gonna take?'

'He has a bank account registered to this address?'

'I send the statements back. Every single one. "Addressee gone away" scribbled all over them, but they still keep sending 'em.'

'Do you read them?'

'Wouldn't you?' She lit a cigarette.

'He doesn't seem to have a lot of money, does he?' asked Dixon.

'He's got money.'

'Where?'

'If I knew that, I'd tell my solicitor, wouldn't I?'

'Who is your solicitor?'

'Fiona Lees at Cobbetts in Bridgwater.'

'Are you happy for us to talk to her?'

'If you must.'

'He has a mobile registered to this address?'

Anna stood up and walked over to the sideboard. She opened the top drawer, took out a phone and threw it to Dixon. 'Here. The battery's dead.'

He caught it and dropped it into an evidence bag held open for him by a uniformed officer.

'Sam's been playing with it.'

'D'you need to go and get him?'

'No, he gets a lift home with Kim, three doors down. I take them, she fetches them.'

'Is Sam the fisherman?' asked Dixon, pointing at the photomontage on the wall.

'He used to go with his dad.'

'Do you have a picture of Toby?'

'I burnt them.'

'All of them?'

'Yes.'

'Then we'll take that one, if we may?'

'He's not in it.'

'His arm is, and it gives us a partial of the tattoo on his left forearm.'

'You must be really desperate to find him,' replied Anna, with a wry smile. 'Go ahead. Take it.'

'We'll leave the rest,' said Dixon, turning to the uniformed officer standing behind him.

'What about your daughter?'

'Layla. She goes to a friend's house after school usually.'

'May I?' asked Dixon, gesturing to the sofa.

Anna shrugged her shoulders.

'When did you meet Toby?' Dixon sat down.

'Sixteen years ago. Layla's fifteen so . . .'

'And how did you meet?'

'At the Clarence. There was live music one night and we met at the bar.'

'What did he do for a living?'

'He was a pest controller. Always has been.'

'Working for himself?'

'Yes.'

'How old was he when you met?'

'Thirty-six.' Sharon stubbed her cigarette out in an already over-flowing ashtray. 'Do I need a solicitor present for this?'

'No, you don't, but you can have one if you wish,' replied Dixon.

'Just get on with it.'

'Does it pay well, rat catching?'

'It's all right. He worked long hours and he liked the freedom of working for himself. He's not one for taking orders.'

'Is he still working?'

'How do I know?'

'Did he like his job?'

'That's an odd question to ask about a pest controller.'

'I've met one who hated killing things.'

'He never had any problem with that,' said Anna, smiling. 'I used to say he liked it a bit too much.'

'Did he have a computer?'

'He took it with him.'

'What about the books, accounts, customer lists, that sort of stuff?'

'On the computer. He had a notebook too, but he always kept that with him.'

'Who was his accountant?'

'John Wheeler, in Burnham.' Dixon turned round to check that Sexton was making notes.

'Do the kids have computers?'

'Yes. What's this got to do with them?'

'Are they in touch with their father?'

'No. Look, this is getting out of—'

'We're going to have to take their computers, Anna. Yours too, but you will get them back. All right?'

'You still haven't said what Toby's done.'

'We'd also like to take, with your permission, a DNA sample from Sam. Just a swab from inside his cheek. That's all.'

'Why?'

'It'll give us a familial match with his father,' replied Dixon. 'There's no suggestion that Sam has done anything wrong at all.'

'You still haven't said what Toby's done.'

'Possibly nothing, Anna. It is OK to call you Anna?'

She nodded.

'But he's wanted for questioning in connection with the deaths of two men.'

'Murders?'

'Yes,' replied Dixon, nodding.

'He always said he'd . . .' Her voice tailed off.

'What, Anna?'

She lit another cigarette, blowing the smoke out through her nose.

'There was a national franchise outfit and they opened up in the area. Big advertising budget, national contracts. He lost the local hospital work, the council, Wessex Water, several garage chains. And all of it practically overnight.'

'He went bust?'

'He ceased trading, if that's what you mean. He was just left with a bit of domestic work, old biddies and their wasps. So he started drinking instead. He'd always liked a few beers, but this was different. "Something to fill the day," he used to say.'

'And he always said he'd what?'

'Kill them.' She shook her head. 'But I never thought he meant it, that he'd actually go through with it.'

Dixon glanced at Sexton, who was standing behind the sofa scribbling in his notebook.

'And that was the cause of the divorce?'

'That was the start of it, I suppose, although we'd had some problems for a while.'

Dixon waited.

'He'd always been a bit . . . volatile. That was the word my mother used. She stopped coming here in the end. "Walking on egg shells" was another of her pearls of wisdom.' Anna shook her head. 'She'd be saying I told you so, if she was here now.'

'Where is she?'

'Dead.' Matter of fact. 'She never liked him. She thought he wasn't good enough for her precious little daughter.'

'What did you think?' asked Dixon.

'He was a good father, and it was good to begin with, I suppose. He had . . .' Anna hesitated, '. . . issues.'

Dixon raised his eyebrows.

'Let's just say things were fine while he was taking his pills,' continued Anna, with a heavy sigh. 'When he'd been drinking, he'd forget to take them, and all hell would break loose.'

'Was he always taking medication?'

'Not to begin with. It started after Sam was born, maybe a couple of years after. Manic depression, I think, but he never had a formal diagnosis.'

'What about treatment?'

'He refused to get any. Then the panic attacks started, and he got some Prozac off a mate of his.'

'He didn't go to the doctor?'

'No. A friend of mine is a psychiatric nurse, and she said he might be bipolar, but I couldn't get him to a doctor.'

'What about medication?'

'He was getting if off this mate. God knows where he was getting it from. Prozac usually, but sometimes it was diazepam. Whatever he could get his hands on, basically.'

'Did he say why he wouldn't go to a doctor?'

'No, and he got nasty if I pushed it, so I thought, sod it.'

'Nasty?'

'It's all in the divorce papers,' said Anna. 'And both times he put me in hospital. I had to get an injunction in the end to get him out of the bloody house. Things were pretty bad by then. He'd started on illegal drugs, as opposed to illegal prescription stuff.'

'What?'

'I found some cocaine. Not much. Then when he hit Sam, that was the last straw.'

'When was this?'

'A year or so ago.' Anna was biting her lip. 'Look are you gonna be much longer?'

Dixon ignored the question. 'What about his family? Did he have any brothers or sisters, parents still alive, perhaps?'

'I need a drink.' Anna stood up and walked over to the sideboard. Dixon watched her pour herself a large neat vodka.

'Family, Anna?' he asked.

'No. Just us.'

'What about a connection with Manchester?'

'Not that I know of,' replied Anna, frowning. 'That's an odd question.'

'Has he ever been there?'

'No.'

'What football team did he support?'

'He didn't.' She drank the vodka in one and then slammed the glass down on the top of the sideboard. 'Look, he loves his kids, his booze and the precious bloody Coastguard. That's it.'

'He's a Coastguard volunteer?'

'He never answered a shout drunk. Never did that. Not in all the time I've known him anyway.'

'When did he join?'

'Just before we met. He was starting his training, I think.'

'And he's still a member?'

'Yes. Loved it he did. It kept him going, really. And he never missed training. They were the only days he was sober. Never missed a single one.' Anna sighed. 'Couldn't stay sober for us, but he could for his precious bloody Coastguard.'

'D'you know why he joined?'

'There were two girls down at the end of the jetty. They were cut off by the tide, clinging on to the flag pole down there, and he managed to get out to them and keep their heads above water until the Coastguard arrived. He got some award for it, I think. I'd read about it in the local rag. It was part of the attraction, to be honest. Local hero and all that.'

'The current's pretty strong down there,' said Dixon.

'They only just got to him in time.' Anna smiled. 'I remember he didn't want all the fuss, though, seemed embarrassed by it. He even refused a TV interview.'

'Did you keep any newspaper cuttings, anything like that?'

'No.'

'Are you happy for us to take a swab from Sam then?'

Anna nodded, releasing the tears from the corners of her eyes. 'The silly fucking sod,' she muttered.

Dixon sat in his Land Rover watching through the front windows as the uniformed officers searched Anna's living room. Lights on, curtains open, it seemed like the whole neighbourhood had come out to watch too. He slid his phone out of his pocket and sent Louise a text message.

Did you get the names of the coastguard officers?

Chapter Thirteen

'What've you got then?'

'A photo of the tattoo on his left arm – a dragon, by the looks of things – and a detailed description from Anna Turnbull that matches what Simon Jones told us at the council,' replied Dixon. 'The passport office has got nothing and we're waiting to hear from DVLA.'

DCS Potter sat down on the corner of Dixon's workstation at Express Park.

'Social media?'

'Nothing,' he replied. 'Anna and the kids have Facebook accounts, but there are no photos.'

'An e-fit then?'

'They're working on it now.'

'What about DNA?'

'A swab from the son.'

'She was all right with that?'

Dixon nodded. 'We found some fishing tackle in the garage loft, but apart from that there was no trace of him at the house.'

'What about his van?'

'It's a white Ford Transit.'

'Aren't they all?'

'With "Westcountry Pest Services" written in green on both sides and on the back doors. There's an 0800 number too, but it's dead.'

'He's probably living in it,' said Potter.

'Anna gave us a list of known associates and friends. We're checking them now. He was a Coastguard volunteer too.'

'Coastguard?'

'I'm waiting to hear if he was there when Harry drowned.'

'Maybe they know where he is?'

'They just have pagers, sadly. Anna's solicitor has been trying to find him for three months. She's even had an enquiry agent after him.'

'And they've got nothing?'

'No.'

'What's he living on, I wonder?' asked Potter.

'Cash,' replied Dixon. 'All those cash in hand jobs.'

'And there's no phone number for him?'

'We're checking with the networks now, but he's bound to be using an unregistered pay-as-you-go.'

'Computer?'

'We're looking at the kids' laptops, but he took his with him. High Tech have got his old iPhone too, but it's at least two years since he used it.'

'And David Cobb was the same killer?'

'Definitely, according to Roger Poland.'

'Good, well we've got enough to go public with the e-fit. Good work.'

'Thank you.'

'Vicky Thomas has scheduled a press conference for six o'clock. You want to sit in?'

'No, thanks.'

'We'll put his face on every TV screen between here and Bristol,' said Potter. 'See if that flushes him out.'

◆ ◆ ◆

'How'd you get on?'

'Can you flip it to the local news?'

'What's on?' asked Jane.

'Deborah Potter taking the credit.' Dixon closed the back door of the cottage behind him. 'D'you want a cup of tea?'

'Yes, pl— Shit, he looks a nasty piece of work.'

'Are they showing the e-fit?' Dixon was shouting over the kettle. 'Yes.'

'And that's before you know what he's been doing.'

'Is he your prime suspect?' asked Jane.

'He's our only suspect,' replied Dixon, appearing in the doorway. 'Have you fed Monty?'

'I fed him when I got in. I thought he was with you.'

'I dropped him off on the way to Burnham.'

'To see the ex-wife?'

'Very helpful she was too. Been looking for him for months.'

'So, what's it all about?'

'Revenge. He's going after the people who put him out of business. His competitor and some poor sod at the council.'

'Who's next?'

'No one if we can find him first. We've got everyone and their dog out looking for him.'

'Why the trephine and the—?'

'No idea yet. We'll find out when we catch up with him.'

Jane switched off the TV.

'What did Potter say?' asked Dixon, handing Jane a mug of tea.

'Usual stuff. You eaten?'

'Not yet.'

'D'you want to pop over to the Red Cow?'

'I'd better not. My blood sugars have been a bit high lately.' Dixon sat down next to Jane, closed his eyes and rested his head on her shoulder. 'Is there anything in the freezer?'

'A chicken pie.'

'That'll do,' he said, getting up.

'You want one?'

'Better had.'

'I'll bung a few oven chips in too.' He fished Jane's phone out of her handbag on the kitchen table and dropped it into her lap. 'This just buzzed.'

'Thanks.'

'Who is it?' asked Dixon, switching on the oven.

'Sonia. Oh God. She's in the Red Cow and wants to see me,' said Jane.

'She's driven all the way down from Carlisle?'

'Yes.'

'What does she want?'

'Doesn't say.'

'Are you going?'

'I can't very well not go, can I? It's only over the road.'

'And she never said she was coming?'

'Nope,' replied Jane, her brow furrowed.

On the phone four or five times a day and now turning up on the doorstep. Dixon sighed. It did not bode well.

'D'you want me to come?'

'No need.'

'I'll wait outside then.'

Dixon watched from the upstairs window as Jane walked across the road to the pub. Then he put Monty on his lead and wandered over to the car park. He let himself into the beer garden and peered through the back window into the lounge bar.

Jane was sitting by the fire, opposite a tearful Sonia. Waterproof mascara might be in order, thought Dixon, not that he was an expert on make up. Her eyes were dark and puffy, her nose running, her earrings and nose stud glinting in the lights from the bar. The blue stripe in her hair was new, but apart from that she looked the same and was dressed in the same dark blue jeans and padded coat.

Dixon was no lip reader either, although if he had to guess, Sonia was asking for something and Jane was saying no. And a resolute 'no' at that. That much came from the body language more than anything else. Lots of head shaking, more tears, a wine glass knocked over. Then Sonia stood up and made a less than straight line for the door.

He watched her stagger across the car park towards an old Ford Sierra parked in the corner. The one with the hubcaps missing and the man sitting in it. Not an altogether unusual sight in a pub car park. Waiting for someone, Dixon had thought, and he'd been right.

Sonia opened the door and climbed into the passenger seat. Dixon glanced back to the bar where Jane was ordering a gin and tonic, then back to the Sierra. The engine had still not come on, which was odd, so he stepped back behind the corner of the pub and watched.

Arms waving, muffled shouts – male and female – followed by a scream. Then the driver's door of the car flew open, hitting the car parked next to it. The man climbed out, walked around to the passenger side, wrenched open the door and dragged Sonia out on to the tarmac.

'Just get back in there and get the bloody money.'

A sharp kick as she was lying on the ground was the last straw. Dixon hooked Monty's lead over a fence post.

'What d'you think you're doing?' he shouted as he marched across the car park.

The man came towards him, several inches taller, looming over him, but at least twenty years older.

'Who the fuck are you?'

'Police,' replied Dixon, ducking under the fist looping towards his head. 'Now wind your neck in. Unless you want to add assaulting a police officer to the list.'

Sonia stood up and grabbed hold of the man to stop herself swaying.

'Why don't you just sod off and leave him alone?'

'What's your name?' asked Dixon.

'Sonia Beckett.'

'Not you, him,' said Dixon, pointing at the man.

'John Smith.'

'Really.' Loaded with sarcasm.

'I'm not making a com . . . a complaint,' muttered Sonia.

'You don't have to,' replied Dixon. 'I witnessed the assault. John Smith, I am arresting you on suspicion of common assault. You do not have to say anything but—'

'What's going on?' asked Jane, appearing beside Dixon. She was holding Monty on his lead.

'Just leave us alone!' screamed Sonia.

'He was assaulting her,' said Dixon. 'So, I was just arresting him.'

'Let them go, Nick,' said Jane.

'Are you two together?' asked Sonia, trying to focus on Dixon.

'Yes,' replied Jane.

'So, you're going out with a copper?'

'I *am* a copper.'

'You?' Sonia fell across the boot of the car. 'You never said you were a fucking copper.'

'Well, I am.'

'A pig. Of all the . . .' Sonia shook her head, slid along the side of the car and slumped back into the passenger seat.

'D'you know this man?' asked Dixon, turning to Jane.

'He's her partner, Tony.'

'Abusive partner,' muttered Dixon.

Jane's eyes widened. 'I don't want everyone to know.'

They watched the Sierra, with Sonia slumped in the passenger seat, pull out of the pub car park and turn south towards the motorway.

'That chicken pie's still in the oven.'

'Good.'

'She wanted money?' asked Dixon.

'Five grand.'

'What for?'

'Gambling debts, she said,' replied Jane, looping her arm though Dixon's.

'His probably,' he said. 'He was behind it.'

'I thought as much.'

'Drugs is more likely anyway,' said Dixon. 'She dropped this.' He handed Jane a small plastic bag, white powder residue stuck to the sides.

'D'you know what? I really don't care. I can't. I had to know and now I do. So, let's just forget it, shall we?'

'You'll need to block her phone number.'

'I already have.'

Chapter Fourteen

A chicken pie and *The Great Escape*, curled up on the sofa with Monty and Dixon, seemed to do the trick. He knew a brave face when he saw one though, and Jane had been doing her best. She was no worse off than she was before, she knew that, or said she did. And she still had her adopted parents in Worle. Sonia had never been a part of her life and now never would be. Nothing lost, perhaps, but it still hurt, that much was obvious. Nobody cries when Steve McQueen is in the cooler, surely?

Dixon woke several times during the night to check his phone. An odd impulse, given that he hadn't even switched it to silent mode. The last time was just before 6 a.m., and Monty got a run in the field behind the cottage while the kettle boiled. Then Dixon checked his phone, again, the local TV news and the internet. Nothing. It was the largest manhunt in the history of Avon and Somerset Police, according to ITV Westcountry, and so far, it had drawn a blank. DCS Potter was clearly prone to exaggeration.

'Got anything?' asked Jane, leaning over the bannister.

'Not yet.'

'It's early days.'

'I'd better get in,' said Dixon. 'Will you be all right?'

'Yeah, fine.'

'What've you got on today?'

'I'll go over to Worle.'

'I'll take Monty. Clocks go forward tonight don't forget.' Dixon smiled.

He watched Jane turn back towards the bedroom, her half-hearted smile gone before she reached the door. She'd been better off as a detective constable in CID. At least they got to work together then, although that had been unofficial once their relationship had become public knowledge. Her promotion to sergeant had resulted in a transfer to the Safeguarding Coordination Unit and several child protection training courses. Dixon frowned. His old joke about never working with children and animals was starting to wear a bit thin.

He arrived at Express Park twenty minutes later, just before 7 a.m. Jonny Sexton was slumped over a workstation, fast asleep, so Dixon made a coffee and placed it on the desk in front of him. Then he dug him in the ribs.

'You been here all night?' he asked.

'Yes, Sir,' replied Sexton, yawning.

'Anything come in?'

'The odd phone call. A few sightings. I've got uniform following them up.'

'What?'

'A couple of the van. Or at least a white Transit with faded sign writing. Another with it scrubbed out. And we've got a couple of sightings of Horan, one giving another name.'

Dixon raised his eyebrows.

'Joe Boardman,' continued Sexton.

'Any photos?'

'We've got his driving licence photo from DVLA. It's in your email.'

'How does it compare to the e-fit?'

'Not bad.'

'Let's get it out there,' said Dixon, 'in time for the morning news.'

'Yes, Sir.'

'Email it over to Vicky Thomas and she can earn her money for a change.'

Sexton grinned. 'I take it you two don't—'

'No, we don't,' interrupted Dixon. 'Get it up to Manchester too. See if anyone there recognises it. What about known associates?'

'Jackie and Doug were going through them. They'll be back in in an hour or so.'

'Who was chasing up the Coastguard?'

'Tracey.'

'Well, tell her to get on with it, will you?'

'Yes, Sir.'

Dixon shook his head. Jackie and Doug sounded familiar, but he couldn't put faces to the names. A Major Investigation Team sounded good in theory: the best detectives on the force working together on the highest profile cases, but in practice it threw together officers who had never worked with each other before, giving the SIO no real idea of the team members' strengths and weaknesses. It was different in the Met and Manchester perhaps, where the force was large enough for the MIT to be a permanent fixture, but in Somerset, when it only assembled when needed, it was counterproductive. That was Dixon's two pence anyway, and he'd share it with anyone who would listen when he got the chance.

He sat down at a workstation by the large windows at the front of the building, switched on a computer and swivelled around on his chair to look out of the window while it booted up. Louise was waiting at the entrance to the staff car park, music on by the looks of things. Dixon smiled. In-car karaoke. It was one advantage of an old diesel Land Rover

– the engine was too loud for music. Then she was gone, up the ramp and on to the top floor of the car park.

The photograph from DVLA did bear a striking resemblance to the e-fit, thought Dixon as he clicked 'print'. The faintest of smiles, more of a smirk, although why anyone would smirk when they were having their driving licence picture taken was beyond him. No facial hair, but that could change in a matter of days. And probably would if he was living rough. No visible tattoos or scars on his face and neck either, which was a shame, although the nose looked as if it had been broken at some point. Eyes like a shark – black and dead – he was not someone to spill your beer over.

Dixon looked up when a printer on the other side of the room began spewing out the photograph and noticed PC Cole walking towards him. An old fashioned bobby-on-the-beat, that was Cole. And a few months ago he'd jumped into an ice cold river to pull Dixon out.

'Excuse me, Sir.'

'What is it, Cole?'

'There's a friend of mine in reception asking to see you.'

'A friend of yours?'

'We were at school together.'

'What does he want?'

'He's seen something he thinks you might be interested in.'

Dixon followed Cole down to reception where a man was sitting with his back to the window. He was dressed in a one piece fishing suit.

'Dave, this is Inspector Dixon, the one I told you about. Just tell him what you told me. All right?'

'I was out fishing on the Langacre Rhyne,' said Dave, taking off his bobble hat. 'The other side of Middlezoy.'

'It's closed season, Sir,' said Cole, shrugging his shoulders.

'It was just an hour or two. Fly fishing for pike.'

'Let's assume you were fly fishing for trout then, shall we?' said Dixon. 'The trout season's open.'

'There aren't any trout in the Langacre,' replied Dave.

'Just spit it out, Dave.' Cole nudged his elbow.

'East of Middlezoy, there's an old barn.' Dave hunched over and started whispering even though the reception area was deserted. 'Right out in the fields it is. Anyway, there was smoke coming out of it this morning. Just a wisp, mind you. Then it was gone.'

'And?'

'I went over and had a look. There's an old caravan in there. And a white Transit van.'

Dixon straightened up and looked at Cole. Then back to Dave.

'What time was this?'

'Just after dawn.'

'Was there a light?'

'No.'

'Where is this place?'

'Just behind Bere Aller there's a lane called Beer Drove. Follow that west and when it turns sharp left you turn sharp right down a farm track. Then you're heading right out across the fields north towards where the River Cary meets Eighteen Feet Rhyne. Across the field on your right is a line of trees. It's behind that.'

'D'you know it?'

'I know the lane he's talking about, Sir,' replied Cole.

'You can go, Dave,' said Dixon. 'We'll need a statement from you at some point. All right?'

'Fine.'

'Did you catch any trout?'

'Not a bloody thing,' replied Dave, grinning.

Dixon waited until the door had swung shut and then turned to the receptionist. 'Get DS Sexton down here as quick as you can, will you?'

'Yes, Sir,' replied the receptionist, picking up the phone.

'You doing anything for the next couple of hours, Cole?'

'Checking on a barn the other side of Bere Aller?'

Dixon smiled. 'You said you know where it is.'

Cole nodded. 'You coming too, Sir?'

'Yes.' Dixon turned when the security door at the side of reception swung open and Sexton appeared, pulling on his jacket.

'Where are we going?' he asked.

'We've had a report from a fisherman of smoke coming from a remote barn on the levels beyond Bere Aller,' said Dixon. 'And there's a van in there too.'

'Can't we just send uniform?' asked Sexton. 'I haven't had breakfast yet.'

Cole frowned.

'What did we find in Horan's garage loft?' asked Dixon.

'Fishing tackle,' replied Sexton, nodding.

'We'll take uniform with us.'

◆ ◆ ◆

Dixon turned into a farm gateway on the edge of Bere Aller, wrenched on the handbrake and walked back to the patrol car following him.

'Leave this here and come with me in the Land Rover. Hats off too.'

'Yes, Sir.'

The farm track was narrow with deep ruts, the grass in the middle brushing the underside of Dixon's Land Rover as it bounced along.

'D'you reckon you'd get a Transit along here?' he asked.

'Yes, Sir,' replied Cole. He was sitting on the bench seat behind Dixon, opposite another uniformed officer. Sexton was in the passenger seat.

'Maybe we should approach on foot?' asked Sexton.

'We may need the vehicle if there's a pursuit,' said Cole.

'Is there backup?' asked Dixon.

'There are two cars within ten minutes of us, Sir,' replied Cole. 'And I put Armed Response on standby.'

Dixon nodded, although the gesture was lost as the Land Rover lurched along the track.

'Looks like there's another way out to the east,' said Sexton, trying to follow the map on his phone.

'Bound to be,' said Dixon. 'Who would hole up anywhere there was only one way in and out?'

He stopped behind a gate, a hedge screening them from the line of trees off to their right, the top of the barn just visible through the foliage. The field beyond the gate opened out, offering nothing to cover their approach.

'At least they're evergreens,' muttered Cole.

'What are?'

'Those trees.'

Dixon slid out of the front seat and peered over the gate into the field beyond. A few yards ahead the track forked, the right fork leading straight to an open gate in the hedge adjacent to the barn. The left fork led to another gate in the far hedge line and the next field.

'All right, you two, lie down in the back,' said Dixon, climbing back into the Land Rover.

Cole looked at Monty and hesitated.

'He won't bite you,' said Dixon. 'I'm going straight across into the far field. If you two hop out there you can get around the back of the barn on foot.'

'What about us?' asked Sexton.

'We'll drive straight up to the front door. Is your stab vest under that coat?'

'Yes, Sir,' replied Sexton.

'Ready?' asked Dixon, looking over his shoulder at Cole and the other officer lying in the back of the Land Rover.

'Very cosy,' mumbled Cole.

Dixon accelerated across the field, stopping once he was through the gate on the far side. Cole and the other officer slid out of the back door and began running along the hedge line towards the back of the barn. Then Dixon spun the Land Rover around and drove back towards the barn, stopping in the gateway directly in front of it.

Sexton jumped down from the passenger seat and ran into the barn, Dixon close behind him. He wrenched open the back door of a white Ford Transit van parked against the right hand wall.

'Clear.'

Sexton ran over and opened the door of a small caravan in the far corner.

'Clear.'

'There's no one here,' muttered Dixon, looking up. What had once been a hayloft above had collapsed, and there was no easy way up to what was left of it anyway.

'Someone's definitely been living here,' said Sexton.

'I can vouch for that,' said Cole, peering in through a gap in the wall. 'We found the toilet behind the hedge.'

Dixon winced. Then he took a step back and looked at the side of the van.

'Westcountry Pest Services,' he said, reading aloud. 'Let's get forensics out here as quick as we can. Better warn them about the track. And I want to speak to the landowner too.'

'Yes, Sir.' Sexton reached into his pocket for his phone.

'Have a look around outside will you, Cole? See if you can find anything else apart from the latrine.'

'Yes, Sir.'

'There ought to be tyre tracks, at least. He must have another vehicle of some sort.'

The earth floor was strewn with damp straw and bits of wood from the collapsed hayloft. A handy source of fire wood, at least. Dixon squatted down and held his hand close to the remains of a fire on the floor; then he picked up a piece of charred wood. Stone cold. A small hole in the roof provided a makeshift chimney, although the corrugated iron along one sidewall had fallen out, so ventilation was hardly an issue.

Blankets had been pinned up at the windows of the caravan. Dixon peered in the door, using the light on his phone. Cold and damp, much like a World War Two pillbox. The smell was much the same too, with the addition of wet carpet, from the condensation no doubt, water running down the inside of the windows.

He put on a pair of rubber gloves and stood up on the metal step. A pile of clothes on the bed and an old sleeping bag – a disgusting prospect for most, but a good source of DNA for Dixon, not that he would get his hands dirty collecting it. There was even a toothbrush sticking out of the bathroom sink.

'You are spoiling us,' he muttered, stepping back out on to the earth floor.

'Anything?' asked Sexton.

'Some clothes and a toothbrush,' replied Dixon.

'We don't need DNA, do we? We know who he is.'

'We think we do,' said Dixon, looking in the back of the van.

The shelves that had once housed rat poison were empty, apart from some tins of food, a few bottles of water, a roll of bin bags and a box of firelighters.

'We know he's a smoker but there are no fag butts,' said Sexton.

'Probably flicked them on the fire.'

Sexton nodded. 'Scientific Services are on the way.'

'Good.'

'You'd better come and see this, Sir.' Cole was shouting from outside the barn.

Dixon and Sexton walked outside to find Cole ten yards or so out into the field on the far side of the trees, staring at a narrow track in the grass that led diagonally across the field to a gate in the far corner.

'What is it?'

'A single tyre track.'

'Motorbike?'

'Yes, Sir.'

'Get on to Anna,' said Dixon, turning to Sexton, 'and find out if Toby had a bike.'

'Yes, Sir.'

'And let me know when SOCO get here.'

'Where are you going?'

Dixon opened the back door of the Land Rover and Monty jumped out.

'I'll be back in ten minutes.'

Dixon was walking back towards the barn when the first of the Scientific Services vans crept through the gateway on the far side of the field. He flagged it down and leaned in the passenger window.

'Is Donald Watson coming?'

'Yes, Sir. He was on another job over Taunton way, but he's coming now.'

'Good. You got a ladder in there?'

'There's one on the roof of Don's van.'

'How long's he going to be?'

'He was ten minutes behind us.'

'Park through there,' said Dixon, pointing to the gate in front of the barn. He followed the van through the gate and then bundled Monty into the back of the Land Rover.

'Concentrate on the van and the caravan.'

'We'll get set up and wait for Don, if it's all the same to you, Sir.'

'There's a latrine around the back and some motorcycle tyre tracks in the field behind those trees.'

'What d'you need the ladder for?'

'Up there,' replied Dixon, pointing to the remains of the hayloft; an area the size of a pool table where a few floorboards had survived the collapse.

'There's no way up.'

'Not now there isn't, but what if he moved the van? He could just stand on the roof.'

'Good point.'

'Find anything else?' asked Dixon, turning to Sexton.

'No, Sir, just bags of rubbish. I didn't go in the caravan though.'

'Or the van, I hope,' said the scenes of crime officer.

'Or the van,' said Sexton.

Dixon turned to PC Cole. 'Can you check the other way out of here? We'll never get the caravan out down that track.'

'Yes, Sir.'

'If we put it on a flatbed lorry, it won't stay on it for long,' said the scenes of crime officer, smiling.

'The other van's here, Sir,' said Sexton.

'Let's have the ladder off the roof.'

'Are you going up, Sir?'

'I'll hold it, you climb it.'

'I thought you were supposed to be the climber?'

'Ladders are far too dangerous.'

Sexton lifted the ladder off the roof rack while Watson and his team got to work, and carried it into the barn, setting it up under the loft. Dixon placed his foot on the bottom rung and watched Sexton climb up until his head was level with the hayloft.

'Can you see anything?'

'Hang on.' Sexton leaned forward across the floorboards. He took hold of a blanket and dragged it off the hayloft, dropping it on the floor next to Dixon.

'What is it?'

'A desktop computer,' replied Sexton, grinning. 'And a laptop.'

'Leave them where they are, Jonny. SOCO can get them down.'

'Yes, Sir.'

Watson appeared from inside the caravan, leaning out the door. 'Have you been in here yet?'

'No.'

'You'd better come and have a look.' Watson grimaced and ducked back inside.

'I looked in, but it was pretty dark,' said Dixon, from the step.

'Put these on, please, Sir,' said another scenes of crime officer standing behind him. Dixon ripped open the bag and began putting on a pair of white overalls. 'And these.' A pair of blue latex overshoes.

'We took the blanket down and got some light in here,' said Watson as Dixon stepped inside, blinking furiously in the light from two arc lamps, one set up inside the caravan and one shining in the front window.

'What the bloody hell's that?' Dixon turned away from the kitchen worktop.

'Just blood. There's lots in the shower too.' Watson pointed to the small bathroom. 'And take a look in the kitchen sink.'

Dixon took a deep breath and leaned over the sink, peering into the washing up bowl. The water, perhaps an inch or so, was light pink; three old fashioned razor blades lying in the bottom.

'There's more on the mattress and the sleeping bag too. Even on the TV remote control,' said Watson.

'Is there an aerial?'

'He watches DVDs.' Watson swallowed hard. 'And look on the table.'

Dixon turned towards the dinette at the front of the caravan, squinting into the light from the arc lamp that was shining through the large window behind it. He held his hand up in front of his eyes. A small flat screen TV was sitting on the table, in front of it a green plastic box.

'Is that a first aid kit?'

'It is,' replied Watson.

'What d'you think?'

'We'll know more when we know whose blood it is.'

'And how many people's,' said Dixon. 'There's no sign of a struggle though is there?'

'Not really.'

Dixon spun round. 'I mean it's cold and damp and covered in blood, but apart from that, it's actually quite tidy.'

'He hasn't made his bed,' said Watson.

'You know what I mean. If there'd been a struggle in a confined space like this, it'd look like—'

'A bomb hit it,' interrupted Watson.

'Yes.'

'So, what are you thinking?'

'Razor blades and a first aid kit,' replied Dixon. 'Looks like self-harming to me.'

Watson puffed out his cheeks. 'And then some, judging by the blood,' he muttered.

'He's hardly squeamish, is he?'

'I suppose not.'

'What else is there?'

'His film collection is up there,' said Watson, pointing to a small cupboard above the window.

Dixon opened it and glanced along the array of films. He sighed. Not one would have made its way into his own collection.

'Likes his horror films, doesn't he?' muttered Watson.

'Those aren't horror films.' Dixon let the cupboard door slam shut. 'We'll catalogue them.'

'Just as long as I don't have to watch them.'

Watson smiled. 'Not exactly *Goodbye, Mr. Chips*, is it?'

'There's no Boris Karloff. No Peter Cushing.'

'Look under the seat,' said Watson, sneering.

'What is it?'

'Paperbacks and scrapbooks of some sort. I haven't made a start on them yet.'

Dixon lifted the cushion and then the seat. There was a small box of books, all of them biographies of serial killers, and several lever arch files. He leaned over and lifted the flap of the top one to reveal newspaper clippings, each carefully cut from the paper and placed in a clear plastic wallet. It took him a moment to focus on the headline – 'He's Back!' – from the *Manchester Daily Post*.

'This top one's only two days old,' he said.

'I noticed that,' replied Watson.

'I'll need to have a look through this lot when you've done your bit.'

'Of course you will.'

Dixon dropped the dinette seat back down and turned towards the door.

'I'll leave you to it.'

'Wait a minute, there's more.'

'What?'

'Open the top drawer.'

A cutlery drawer should have cutlery in it, thought Dixon, holding his breath as he pulled it open. And this one did, counting the two charred dessert spoons. The crack pipe definitely wasn't cutlery though.

'And what are these?' He pointed to a white and blue box. 'What's Sycrest when it's at home?'

'An antipsychotic,' replied Watson.

'I bet that mixes well with crack cocaine.' Dixon scowled.

'The best bit is he's gone off without them, hasn't he?'

'Let's hope he had another box in his pocket,' muttered Dixon, stepping back out into the barn.

'Anything interesting?' asked Sexton.

'You'd better go in and have a look.'

'Yes, Sir.'

'Have we had his medical records yet?'

'I'll get someone to chase it up.'

'What about the computers?' asked Dixon.

'You'll get nothing from them,' said the scenes of crime officer. 'The hard drives have been removed.'

Dixon sighed. 'Let's get a search team out here with metal detectors.'

'They're on the way, Sir,' said Sexton.

'Get them to check the fire. And the latrine. Let's have the dive team too. The Langacre Rhyne is only a couple of fields away.'

Chapter Fifteen

'What's his name?'

'Ken Cardew, Sir,' replied the uniformed officer. 'He lives in the farm on the other side of the rhyne.'

'I'm assuming there's a bridge . . .'

'Yes, Sir. Over the Sowy River and the rhyne. It's just a concrete thing that takes the farm track over.'

Dixon looked up at the driver of the antique tractor in front of him. Woolly hat, pipe held between his gums, grubby tweed, baler twine for a belt and holes in his trousers and his wellies. He looked like something off *Last of the Summer Wine*.

'Mr Cardew is it?'

'Aye.'

'And this is your land?'

'Aye.'

'Would you mind stepping down off your tractor?'

'If I must.'

Dixon waited, listening to the huffing and puffing and the creaking of bones, all of it audible over the noise of the tractor engine that Cardew had left running.

'When was the last time you came over here?'

'Christmas, I suppose. The land's been under water since then.'

'It flooded?'

'This whole area between the Langacre and the Eighteen Foot. We was all right on t'other side.'

'When you came over at Christmas, did you go in the barn?'

'No.'

'What did you do?'

'Dropped some hay for the livestock. Then I was back a couple of days later to fetch the buggers in.'

'Do you use the land much?'

'I winter some animals over here. Apart from that, not really.'

'Why not?'

'The grass is terrible. Marsh grass it is. And it'll be even worse now. Good for bullocks, if I had any.'

'When did the floods recede?'

'About a month ago. But the barn was clear maybe a month afore that.'

'Did you see any lights, or smoke coming from the barn?'

'No. And if I had, there'd have been the devil to pay.'

There would.

'And you saw no one suspicious?'

'There were a couple of fishermen going along the rhyne a few weeks ago. Then another this morning. Then you lot turned up.'

'Do you usually see anglers along here?'

'A few. Not during the floods though.'

'Can you see the barn from your house?'

'No.'

'When did you last go in it?'

'November, maybe.'

'And was the hayloft intact then?'

'It's not collapsed, has it?'

'I'm afraid it has.'

'Bugger,' muttered Cardew.

'Was there a van in the barn when you went in?'

'No, there bloody well wasn't.'

'What about a caravan?'

'That old thing?' Cardew smiled. 'My wife and I used to go off for weekends in it. Then the old bugger upped and died. Not had much use for it since then.'

'So, you left it in the barn?'

'Didn't have the heart to dump it. And it would've cost more to get rid of it than it was worth.'

'Does anyone else use the land?'

'I get the odd dog walker, but I soon move 'em on.'

'We're going to need to take the caravan, Mr Cardew, for forensic examination.'

'Be my guest. Just don't bring the bloody thing back.'

Dixon smiled.

'Somebody been living in it, have they?' asked Cardew.

'It looks like it.'

'Bloody good job I didn't see 'em.'

'Well, if you do see anything suspicious . . .'

'I know, I know.'

Dixon watched Cardew reversing his tractor back along the track, turning on to the field halfway along to allow a flatbed lorry to pass. Dixon looked away when it bounced over the ruts.

'It's all right, Sir,' said PC Cole, appearing behind him. 'It's longer the other way, but much flatter. Either west to the A361 or east. That way it comes out round the back of Henley.'

'Will we get the van and caravan on the back of that?' asked Dixon, pointing at the lorry.

'It'll be fine, Sir,' replied Cole.

'Your pocket's buzzing, Sir.' Sexton grinned.

Dixon pulled out his phone. 'Hi, Louise. What's up?'

'I've just had Steve Yelland on from the Coastguard, Sir. He's given me the list of names. You're not gonna believe this.'

'Go on.'

'Yelland was there, with Philip Brewin on the shore. The mud techs were Beverley Milner, Matthew Wale and . . . wait for it . . . Toby Horan.'

'He was there?'

'He was the one with his head in the van talking to Harry when he drowned, Sir.'

Dixon arrived at the Coastguard station on Burnham seafront just after midday, having left Jonny Sexton and PC Cole to make their own way back with the search team. He had left before the dive team had arrived too, but the search of the area around the barn was underway with metal detectors and sniffer dogs.

The caravan had been emptied of its contents, which had been catalogued and bagged up for examination back at the lab, and Donald Watson had now turned his attention to the van.

There would be no shortage of DNA, but it would only be of interest if it turned up a second profile. The blood was Horan's. Dixon felt sure of that.

He parked on the forecourt and looked up at the station: a long, single storey building with two blue garage doors on either side of the Coastguard office. The doors on the right were open, the two hovercraft sitting on their trailers inside. The two garages on the left were closed, but 'Coastguard Search and Rescue' was emblazoned on both in bright orange lettering, presumably to deter parking in front of them.

Steve Yelland had sighed loudly down the phone, but had promised he was on his way. Dixon would give him another five minutes before he rang him again.

On another day, Monty might have got ten or fifteen minutes on the beach. But not today. The vision of Harry Lucas drowning in his van had been bad enough when he thought the Coastguard officer had been offering words of comfort. Now he knew that officer had been his killer. Dixon thumped the steering wheel. And all the time he had been only a few yards away, watching Harry's torment unfold.

He got out of his Land Rover and stood leaning into the wind, staring along the Esplanade.

'About time,' he muttered, when he spotted a dark blue Land Rover with a yellow roof driving towards him. It parked next to him, and Steve Yelland climbed out, a large bunch of keys jangling in his hand.

'Coffee?' he asked. 'There's a kettle in the office.'

'Thank you.'

Dixon followed him through the side door.

'I gave the list of names to your colleague.' Yelland was filling the kettle.

'Tell me about Toby Horan.'

'He's a volunteer. They're all volunteers. He's been here fifteen years or so, maybe longer. Always been reliable, until the last few months. He used to respond to every shout, but then he started turning out less and less, then stopped altogether. That was the first time I'd seen him for, I dunno, a couple of months.'

'Are there records?'

'Yes.'

'Who decides who responds and who doesn't?'

'It doesn't work like that.' Yelland flicked on the kettle. 'There are twelve volunteers in Burnham and all of them get paged for every shout. When enough turn up, off we go.'

'And how d'you become a Coastguard officer?' asked Dixon.

'You volunteer. There's an informal interview with Senior Coastal Ops, that's Geoff Garrett. After that it's basic competences and fitness. Some train for cliff rescue, others as mud technicians. Toby's a mud tech.'

'No background checks? Criminal Records Bureau?'

'No. Why, has he got one?'

'He's the prime suspect in Harry Lucas's murder,' replied Dixon, matter of fact.

'Oh, shit, no.' Yelland sat down on a swivel chair. 'And he was . . .' His voice tailed off.

'Talk to me about the bolt cutters.'

'Oh God.' Yelland closed his eyes and sighed, his chin dropping on to his chest. 'He . . .'

Dixon nodded.

'The bastard.' Yelland sat up. 'The bolt cutters are always in the truck. Always. Unless they've been used, I suppose. Then they'll be washed off and left in the drying room, but if that happens, a note should be left on the steering wheel.'

'Where were they that morning?'

'We found them in the drying room when we got back. There was no note in the truck though.'

'Or, if there was, Horan took it.'

Yelland nodded.

'What can you tell me about him?'

'Not a lot, really. I only know him through HMC, and he was never that social. He's divorcing, I heard. A pest controller too, I think, but that's it.'

'Did anyone notice anything unusual about his behaviour at the scene, or hear anything he said to Harry perhaps?'

'Not that I know of. It's difficult to hear anything over the hovercraft engines. I can ask around though, if you like?'

'We'll do that.'

◆ ◆ ◆

Dixon hadn't bargained for the conference call with DCI Chard when he rang DCS Potter to bring her up-to-date with developments, but he had managed to get through it without incident. And now he was sitting in the corner of the canteen at Express Park topping up his blood sugar with a sandwich and a mug of tea.

'Ah, there you are.'

'Yes, Sir.'

'Busy morning, I gather,' said DCI Lewis, sitting down next to Dixon.

'We got lucky.'

'D'you think he might go back to the barn?'

'We'll be watching.' Dixon gritted his teeth. 'He's a Coastguard officer, and I found out this morning he was the one talking to Harry when he drowned.'

'He was there?'

'He was. Which explains the missing bolt cutters, doesn't it?'

Lewis grimaced. 'Makes you wonder what he was saying to him.'

'I can imagine.'

'Dunkery Beacon,' said Lewis, changing the subject. 'Farmers were up there yesterday burning off the gorse and—'

'Swaling they call it, Sir.'

'That's right, swaling. On the side of Dunkery Beacon. Anyway, some fuckwit managed to cremate a body lying in the heather.'

'A body?'

'Female, dead before the fire started, according to Roger Poland. He's up there now.'

'Is there a—?'

'There's no injury to the forehead, no, so it's probably not connected. I thought you ought to check it out all the same. Just in case.'

'I will, Sir.'

'I've given it to Janice Courtenay. She's taken Louise with her.'

Dixon drained his tea.

'Don't tell her I sent you, for God's sake,' said Lewis. 'I don't want Janice thinking I don't trust her.'

'I won't, Sir,' replied Dixon, through the last mouthful of sandwich.

◆ ◆ ◆

'Maybe on the way back, old son, all right?' Dixon glanced in his rear view mirror at Monty, paws up at the back window, barking at the Exmoor ponies up to their bellies in the heather.

On a clear day Dixon would have had a grandstand view across the Bristol Channel to Wales, but today the summit cairn on Dunkery Beacon was only just visible a few hundred yards off to his left, up through the low cloud.

The police officer at the Dunkery Gate roadblock had assured him that the way along the side of the Beacon was passable and he 'should be all right' on the track down to Hanny Combe too, but only one police Land Rover appeared to have ventured down towards the Combe. The remaining cars and Scientific Services vans were blocking the road ahead at the junction.

A large white tent was visible further down the slope, beyond the Land Rover off to Dixon's right, several figures in white overalls milling around outside it. He spotted Janice Courtenay too, standing on the road by Roger Poland's Volvo, yelling into her mobile phone.

They had previously shared an office at Bridgwater Police Station, before the move to the new Police Centre at Express Park, and had always got on well. Or so Dixon thought. Maybe he was being overly sensitive, but he got the distinct impression that Janice had been avoiding him since the Perry investigation had unravelled. She had taken the fall for the lab mucking up the DNA samples. And it was hardly her fault that the crime scene had flooded. Then she had been sent on a training course and Dixon had taken over as SIO, his disciplinary process rushed through. He'd probably still be languishing on suspension were it not for that.

He parked on the grass verge behind Poland's Volvo.

'What are you doing here?' snapped Janice as Dixon slammed the door of his Land Rover.

'Hi, Jan,' replied Dixon. 'Just thought I'd check to see if it had anything to do with—'

'I'd tell you if it had.'

'Of course you would. Are you heading back down?'

'Yes.'

They walked side by side down the track towards the Land Rover.

'What've you got then?' asked Dixon.

'A female, aged seventyish. Dead before the fire started, apparently. That's it, really.'

'Clothes?'

'Burnt off,' said Janice.

'What about a handbag? ID? Car keys?'

'Nothing.'

'Jewellery?'

'Nope.'

Thick gorse and heather on the right as they walked down the track gave an indication of what it had been like on Dixon's left before the fire. Now it was a barren, charred landscape, the odd sprig of blackened gorse all that was left of the dense undergrowth. Occasional islands of light brown or green in the scorched earth marked out bushes that had somehow survived the inferno.

'Stinks, doesn't it,' he said.

'Some of the farmers are licensed by the National Park Authority,' said Janice. 'They burn off the heather and gorse to allow new grass to grow. It's supposed to improve the grazing. And there's a beetle of some sort, Heather Beetle or something, that they're trying to kill off.'

An area the size of two rugby pitches on the slopes above Hanny Combe had been torched, some of it still smouldering on the far side.

'Who found the body?'

'We've got a statement from him,' replied Janice. 'He's a local farmer with a grazing licence up here. Louise has his details.'

Dixon followed Janice across the charred landscape towards the tent.

'Don't they check the area before they set it alight?'

'They're supposed to, but it's a large area and thick heather, to be fair to them.'

'And she was already dead?'

'She was.'

'How long? Do we know?'

'Not yet.'

'Hello, Sir,' said Louise. 'What're you doing up here?'

'Checking up on us,' muttered Janice.

Poland poked his head out of the tent.

'I thought I heard your voice,' he said. 'What're you doing here?'

Dixon cleared his throat.

'It's got nothing to do with your case,' said Poland.

'I think you'll find that's my department,' said Dixon, with his best disarming smile.

'Touché.' Poland winked at him before, disappearing back inside the tent.

'Can I come in?'

'Put these on.' A set of overalls flew out of the tent and landed at Dixon's feet.

'What did the farmer say?' asked Dixon, leaning on Louise's shoulder while he wrestled his way into the overalls.

'They came up yesterday morning, gave the area a quick once over and then set it alight. They use accelerant around the edges to get it going and then watch from a distance. They've got a water bowser in case it gets out of hand.'

'They just leave it to burn?'

'The hotter the better, apparently. It kills the heather and the beetles and some rough grass called . . . hang on . . .' She was flicking through her notebook. '*Molinia.*'

'How do they put it out?'

'They don't. It burns out, more often than not. They only put it out if it's going too far or getting near anything.'

'How long does it burn?'

'All day sometimes. This one burnt out about fourish yesterday afternoon. Then they came back up today to check it, before starting another one. That's when they found her.'

'What's the farmer's name?'

'It's Eric Stokes, and his son, Frank. Eric must be in his eighties, at least.'

'You have told him he didn't kill her?'

'Not yet, Sir,' replied Louise.

'Better do that,' said Janice. 'Now it's been confirmed by Dr Poland.'

'Can I come in?' asked Dixon.

'Yes.'

'Thanks,' he said, ducking under the tent flaps being held open for him by Poland.

He looked down at the body and swallowed hard.

'Why are her eyes so wide open?'

'The eyelids have burnt away,' replied Poland.

'And the fingerprints?'

'Yes.'

Her hands were clawed and reaching for the sky.

'The muscles contract,' said Poland. 'Then the skin splits. That's why she's . . .' He waved his hands in the air.

Dixon turned away.

'Teeth?'

'Dentures,' replied Poland. 'They've melted.'

'You'll get some DNA off her though?'

'Yes, lots of that. Not much use if there's no database match, though, is it?'

'No.'

'Not a lot else to say, really. Not until I get her back to Musgrove Park.'

'How long's she been dead?'

'Two or three days. Not long, but I'll know more when I've done the post mortem.'

'Cause of death?' Dixon took a deep breath, squatted down and peered at the side of her neck.

Poland stood up and pulled off his mask. 'I'll need to run some tests. Toxicology, for starters.'

'If you had to guess?'

'An overdose of some sort.'

Dixon frowned. 'So, she comes up here, lies down in the heather and takes an overdose? No ID, nothing.'

'That's right.'

'Why?'

'That's your department,' said Poland, grinning.

'Actually, it's Janice's,' replied Dixon.

Chapter Sixteen

The low cloud had lifted by the time Dixon left the tent at the top of Hanny Combe, revealing a huge plume of smoke coming from the west. He looked across the lower slopes of the Beacon as he drove back down to Dunkery Gate, stopping at the police roadblock.

'Are they burning another area?'

'Yes, Sir. That's Codsend Moors, the southern slope of Rowbarrow,' replied the uniformed officer standing in the middle of the cattle grid.

'Did they check it first?'

'We checked it with them, Sir. If you keep turning right down the lane you can almost get over there.'

'Is it Stokes?'

'Yes, Sir. And his son.'

'Let's have a closer look then, shall we,' said Dixon, glancing over his shoulder at Monty in the back of the Land Rover.

He parked at the end of the lane at Codsend and followed a farm track across the fields leading up towards the fire, letting Monty off his lead.

The smell was unmistakeable, even though the wind was taking the smoke away from him to the north. And the flames, an intense red and orange he'd only seen before in a wood burning stove, clawing thirty feet or more into the sky. A figure was just visible through the inferno, walking along the edge, spraying the heather and gorse with something from a can; accelerant probably.

Never play with fire, Dixon's father had told him. Clearly, Stokes's father had never imparted the same wisdom.

The fire was still over a hundred yards away when Dixon reached the gate at the top of the field, but he stopped to put Monty on his lead anyway before heading across the open moor towards the quad bike towing the water bowser, parked a safe distance off to the right.

An old man came limping through the heather towards him, slowing when he saw Dixon's warrant card in his outstretched hand.

'Eric Stokes?' shouted Dixon, trying to make himself heard over the crackling of the fire.

'We checked this area afore we lit it.'

'I know that, Sir.'

'Oh.'

'I wanted to ask you about this morning.'

'I gave a statement already.'

'Where's your farm?'

'That's us over yonder,' said Stokes. 'Higher Codsend.'

'Has someone told you the woman was already dead?'

'Yes. We thought it'd be all right to get another going after that. The season closes on the fifteenth so there's not much time.'

'Season?'

'Can't burn after that. Nesting birds.'

'And you always check the land before you start the fire?' asked Dixon.

'We run the dogs through, but that's more to flush out any wildlife to be truthful with you.'

'What d'you farm?'

'Sheep, mainly. We'll be moving 'em up here when the new shoots start to come through. They're on the lower pastures at the moment.'

'Did you see anything unusual in the days before the fire?' Dixon was watching the flames behind Stokes. They were thirty yards away, but not getting any closer.

'It's all right, the wind'll take it that way,' said Stokes, gesturing up the hill to the north. 'See anything when?'

'Yesterday or the day before.'

'They already asked me that. Like what, you mean?'

'Cars where you don't usually see them. People doing things they don't usually do. People you've not seen before.'

'Where?'

'Anywhere.'

Stokes frowned. 'Now you put it like that . . .'

Dixon waited.

'There was a woman in the post office at Wheddon Cross.'

'When?'

'The day afore yesterday, about lunchtime.'

'What was she wearing?'

'A red bobble hat, grey raincoat. She had grey straggly hair too.'

'Did you see any facial features, marks?'

'She was leaving as I walked in, so I didn't really . . . I didn't think anything of it to be truthful with you. Could've been anybody, couldn't it?'

'Can you remember anything else?'

'Nope,' replied Stokes, sucking his teeth.

'Have you got the contact details of the detective you spoke to?' asked Dixon.

Stokes fished a business card out of his pocket. 'Detective Constable Louise Willmott?' he asked, squinting at it.

'Give her a ring and tell her what you just told me.'

'Of course.'

'But do me a favour, don't tell her we had this conversation.'

Stokes smiled.

'My old man always told me never to play with fire,' said Dixon.

'Mine taught me how to do it,' said Stokes, grinning. 'Just keep your wits about you, Eric, he said, and an eyebrow pencil handy.'

◆   ◆   ◆

Dixon hated fire and had done so ever since his tent had gone up in flames on a campsite in the Llanberis Pass. Climbing trips had gone wrong before, usually involving falls and broken bones, but that was something different. And he'd had to put up with his climbing partner, Jake, pissing himself laughing. Dixon had had the last laugh though, sharing Jake's tent, clothes and money for the rest of the trip.

It had been worth the walk up to Codsend Moors to get a closer look at the swaling and give Monty a run. He'd only questioned Stokes to make it look like he was there for some other reason than walking his dog, but he appeared to have got away with it.

He dropped Monty at home and arrived back at Express Park to find the Major Incident Room on the second floor all but deserted. Jonny Sexton was sitting at a workstation, his eyes fixed on the screen in front of him.

'Where is everyone?' asked Dixon.

'Watching the barn. We've got teams watching the three ways in and out.'

'There are four.'

'Eh?'

'Including Cardew's farm.'

'He's not going to go through there, is he?'

'Why not?'

Dixon listened to Sexton's phone call while he put the kettle on. Then he picked up a copy of the call record off the printer. The public had been vigilant, judging by the number of calls; sightings of the van at regular intervals throughout the day, even though it was already at the lab, several sightings of Horan himself, which were being followed up by uniform, and several more alternative names for him. Dixon sighed. The reality was that Horan almost certainly knew they were on to him, had abandoned the barn and gone to ground somewhere. The callers were well intentioned, of course they were, but it was a colossal waste of police time and resources.

He spent the rest of the afternoon and evening reading the statements that had accumulated over the last forty-eight hours, each meticulously handwritten by the investigating officer and signed by the witness. Just one of them might contain the snippet of information needed to unlock the case, and each had been typed up and entered on the computer system by a small army of civilian clerks, where they could be catalogued and cross-referenced at the touch of a button. The software was a bloody marvel, but it hadn't helped in any of the investigations Dixon had been involved with. Not since he'd moved to Somerset anyway.

Horan would get stopped for jumping a red light or speeding, or something crass like that. That was the way these things usually ended.

A Matter of Life and Death was starting on TCM at 9 p.m. He looked at his watch. He had time to get home, but then he had it on DVD anyway, so what was the rush? And it would be starting again on +1 at 10 p.m.

Fed Monty. Gone to see parents. Jx

Dixon screwed up the note and dropped it in the bin. He left the back door of the cottage open, but Monty sat by the dog food cupboard, wagging his tail.

'You're wasting your time, old son,' he said, shaking his head.

A beer cracked open, TV on, and his dog curled up on the sofa next to him. Dixon was asleep before Monty.

'What's this rubbish?'

'Eh?'

'What's this?'

Dixon opened his eyes to find Jane standing in front of the TV, pointing the remote control at it.

'*A Matter of Life and Death.*'

'It's black and white!'

'Not all of it.'

'You and your old films,' she said, shaking her head. 'What else is there?'

'*The Great Escape*'s in the machine.'

Jane dropped the remote control into his lap.

'How were your folks?' he asked, following her into the kitchen.

'Fine.'

'Did you tell them about Sonia?'

'Yeah.'

'What'd they say?'

'What could they say?'

'Not a lot, I suppose,' replied Dixon, shrugging his shoulders. 'Anyway, what's done is done, so let's just forget it, shall we?'

'So, which d'you want?' he said, turning back to the TV.

'Eh?'

'*A Matter of Life and Death* or *The Great Escape*?'

'The one with the football song.'

Dixon took a sharp breath and spun round to find Jane grinning at him.

'Every time,' she said, planting a kiss on his lips. 'You fall for it every time.'

◆ ◆ ◆

A late night and a deep sleep interrupted by a telephone call just after 3 a.m. It could have been better. Dixon had tiptoed out on to the landing to take the call, but had woken Monty, who had trodden on Jane when he jumped up.

'What is it?' he had asked.

'A motorbike, Sir. He saw us and was gone before we could get going. Could've gone anywhere.'

'What sort of bike?'

'No idea, Sir. We just saw the single headlight.'

'What time was this?'

'Just now.'

'Where were you?'

'Round the back of Henley, Sir.'

It was not the best start to a Sunday, although he had managed to get back to sleep, albeit only for a couple of hours. Now, it was just gone 9 a.m. and he was sitting at a workstation on the second floor at Express Park, on his third coffee already. He leaned back in his chair and watched Jane's approach in the reflection of his computer screen.

'We don't often get visitors up here.'

'We had one this morning.' Jane perched on the corner of Dixon's desk, leaned over and whispered in his ear. 'Not long after you left.'

'At home?'

'It was Louise. You'd better speak to her.'

'What did she want?'

'She wouldn't tell me anything.'

'Where is she?'

'Downstairs. She doesn't want Janice to know, apparently.'

Dixon leaned back in his chair. 'Where's Jan?'

'Gone to the post mortem.'

'Roger's doing it today?'

'Just to rule out foul play.'

'Leave it with me,' muttered Dixon, reaching for his phone. He tapped out a text message to Louise while he listened to Jane's footsteps walking back along the landing towards the lift.

Car park five minutes by my land rover ND

Dixon walked out to the top deck of the car park, opened the back door of his Land Rover, and let Monty out for a sniff around the cars.

'Not that one!'

Too late. Still, DCI Lewis would be none the wiser. One alloy wheel would just be cleaner than the others.

'Everything all right, Sir?' asked Louise, peering around the back door of the Land Rover.

'Monty just cocked his leg on Lewis's car.'

Louise smiled.

'What's up?' asked Dixon. 'You came to the cottage this morning.'

'Thanks to you jogging Stokes's memory, we got a description of the woman, and we were able to pick her up on the CCTV arriving at Taunton station.'

'When?'

'The day before yesterday.'

Dixon nodded.

'Then we checked all the stations the train had called at,' continued Louise, 'and we found her again. Getting on this time.'

'Where?'

'Manchester.'

Roger Poland spotted him first, standing in the anteroom glaring through the window into the pathology lab at Musgrove Park Hospital, and jabbed the scalpel in his direction. Dixon's lip reading was clearly getting better too.

'Janice, you'd better—'

'Oh shit.'

'When were you going to tell me, Jan?' asked Dixon as she opened the door into the anteroom.

'When I was sure.'

'When you were sure about what?'

'It might be a coincidence.' Janice folded her arms.

'I still needed to know straightaway.'

'We only found out last night. Anyway, who told you?'

'That doesn't matter. What matters is I know now. So, what've you got?'

'An unidentified female, late seventies, early eighties, gets on the 0807 train from Manchester Piccadilly arriving Taunton at 1158 the day before yesterday. Then she walks out of Taunton station and isn't seen again until early afternoon at Wheddon Cross Post Office. That's the last sighting of her too. You know the rest.'

'How did she pay for her ticket?'

'Cash. There's no card transaction recorded anyway.'

'What about buses and taxis?'

'Dave and Mark are on it now.'

'Is there a bus?'

'Yes.'

'And we've still got no ID?'

Janice shook her head.

'What's the CCTV like?'

'We're working on enhancing the image now. And I've been on to the Centre for Anatomy and Human whatever to see if they can help.'

'Facial reconstruction will take far too long,' said Dixon, grimacing.

'It's the best we've got at the moment.'

'What's Roger found?'

'See for yourself,' replied Janice, holding the door to the lab open.

'Lead on,' said Dixon. 'It's still your investigation.'

Poland looked up and raised his eyebrows. 'Everything all right?' he asked.

'Fine,' replied Janice.

'Toxicology?' asked Dixon.

'Tomorrow,' replied Poland.

'Any needle marks?'

'If there were, they've been destroyed. As you can see.'

Dixon took a scented dog bag out of his pocket and clamped it over his nose and mouth.

'D'you want a mask?' asked Poland.

'No, thanks, I'll be fine.'

'There's no DNA match either,' said Janice. 'Nothing coming up on the database.'

'There's evidence of muscle and intestinal spasms and her pupils are constricted. There's no sign of regular use, but I'm thinking heroin overdose,' said Poland.

'Injected?'

'Yes.'

'Suicide then?' asked Janice.

'Probably,' replied Poland. 'There's no sign of a struggle.'

'Why though?' asked Dixon.

'And she's had spinal surgery at some point,' continued Poland, ignoring the question.

'Really?'

Poland nodded. 'There are some photographs if you want to see it.'

'No, I don't,' said Dixon. 'Thank you.' He turned to Janice and raised his eyebrows.

'I'll get Louise checking with Manchester doctors,' she said.

'Start with the hospital,' said Poland. 'Might be quicker. Within the last five years, I'd say.'

'Would it have affected her mobility?'

'Probably not,' replied Poland. 'I'll write down exactly what it is.'

'So, an elderly woman goes out without any form of ID, gets on a train paying cash for her ticket, travels all the way to Taunton and then out on to Exmoor where she lies down in the heather and commits suicide.'

'That's about it,' said Poland.

'Is there any evidence of dementia? Alzheimer's perhaps?' asked Dixon.

'No.'

'And nothing anywhere that might have identified her if it hadn't been burnt. No melted cards or anything like that?'

'No.'

'Jewellery?'

'No.'

'She could just've forgotten them,' said Janice.

'Not even any keys?'

'Nope,' said Poland.

'Which tells us she wasn't going home,' said Janice.

'You'll let us know when you get the toxicology results, Roger?'

'Straightaway.'

'I'll leave you to it, then,' said Dixon, heading for the door. He had got halfway across the car park when Janice caught up with him.

'Look, I was going to tell you, Nick.'

'It doesn't matter, Jan. Really,' replied Dixon, opening the door of his Land Rover. 'Just let me know if you get a name.'

'Of course.'

'And can you get Louise to email me the CCTV footage?'

Janice's reply was lost in the slam of Dixon's car door. He took his phone out of his pocket and sent Sexton a text.

On way now. Get us on a train to Manchester. 2ish today.

Chapter Seventeen

Dixon had been sitting on Platform 1 at Bristol Temple Meads, staring at the still from the CCTV footage, for nearly ten minutes when Jonny Sexton sat down next to him. It was another five minutes before he noticed.

'What d'you make of it?' he said, handing Sexton the photograph.

'No idea.'

'Leaving aside who she is, you have to ask yourself why,' said Dixon, shaking his head.

'It could be a coincid—'

'Not you as well.'

'Well, I've not seen her before.' Sexton handed the photograph back to Dixon.

'Janice is going to text me the name of the ticket office clerk she spoke to at Piccadilly, so that will be our first job.'

'And after that?'

'We throw a few stones in the water and watch the ripples.'

Sexton grinned.

'Have you told Potter?' he asked.

'Not yet,' replied Dixon. 'Any sign of the motorbike?'

'No.'

'And the DNA in the caravan?'

'We'll know tomorrow morning. Toxicology should be available then too.'

Dixon was thinking about Jane as the train pulled out of the station. Sexton was sitting opposite him, earphones in, head nodding up and down. It was an overnighter he could have done without. Why couldn't her bloody mother have turned up a week or two earlier when he was twiddling his thumbs, preparing witness statements and dying of boredom? Then he would have had time for it. For Jane.

She understood, but that made it worse not better. And two weeks ago she had been right in the middle of her worst case yet in the SCU, one that kept her awake at night, sobbing into her pillow. Dixon had asked about it, but talking just made it worse, so he had made her a gin and tonic and put something light-hearted on the TV. *I'm All Right Jack* had done the trick that night. A few days later and not even Peter Sellers could help. Then it was up to Monty, and he had done his best, sitting on her lap, licking the tears from her cheeks.

If they hadn't got together, then Jane wouldn't have ended up doing child protection work. Someone had to do it, of course, but Dixon felt it was down to him that it was Jane. His fault. Should he do something about it? And, if so, what? He watched the fields and hedges flashing by. Cows. Sheep. Solar panels. More cows. At least he'd remembered to put the clocks forward that morning.

Interfering, she'd call it. He knew that. And she sure as hell wouldn't thank him for it.

'Fancy a beer?' asked Sexton. 'There's a buffet car.'

'I'll go,' said Dixon, hoping it would take his mind off it all.

His phone buzzed in his pocket just as he was paying for the beers.

'I've had a text message,' he said, placing the cans on the table in front of Sexton.

Ticket office Muriel Chatterjee, waiting for name for guard on train

'It's Janice. She's got a name for the person who sold the woman the ticket south.'

Sexton nodded, looked at Dixon and then began putting his earphones back in. This time the music was louder, the bass beat carrying over the clackety-clack of the train. Still, Dixon was up-to-date with the investigation and he wasn't in the mood for small talk.

He was closing in on the copycat, Horan, but the 'why' and the 'how' still eluded him. Why bother copycatting at all when it was unlikely anyone would believe it to be the work of The Vet? And where was Horan, the local rat catcher, getting his information from?

Catch Horan and the case was closed, Potter had said.

Bollocks.

◆ ◆ ◆

'Where's the ticket office?' asked Dixon, yawning, as they got off the train in Manchester several hours later.

'Over there,' replied Sexton, throwing his bag over his shoulder.

'We're looking for Muriel Chatterjee.' Dixon was pressing his warrant card against the glass in the ticket office.

'She's not in till Tuesday.'

'Can you give me an address for her?'

'I'd need to check with my manager.'

'Well?'

'He's not in till the morning.'

Dixon sighed, took out his phone and sent Janice a text message.

◆

Need address for muriel chatt asap ta

'Same hotel?' he asked, turning to Sexton.

'Yeah, I rang them earlier.'

After a short taxi ride to the hotel, and a visit to a local curry house, Dixon was lying on his bed, flicking through the channels on the TV. First he tried TCM, then Film4, before jabbing the 'off' button in disgust and discarding the remote control. He was about to ring Jane when a text message arrived.

27 byron avenue droylsden

Sexton must have been asleep. Either that or he still had his headphones in. Whatever the reason, he didn't answer his door, so Dixon decided to go alone. The house was a standard red brick three-bed semi-detached, but the front had been painted brown and the garage door black. An odd choice, he thought, what with the white uPVC front door. The net curtain twitched while he waited for a receipt from the taxi driver.

He stepped over the low front wall and rang the doorbell.

'Yes?'

A woman was visible behind the frosted glass, but making no effort to unlock the door.

'Police,' replied Dixon. 'I'd like to have a word with Muriel Chatterjee, please.'

'I've already told you I cannot remember the woman.'

Dixon's eyes widened.

'Can I come in, please, Mrs Chatterjee?'

First the chain, then the locks. Three of them.

Once inside the porch, he turned and looked at the locks on the inside of the door.

'You can't be too careful, a woman on your own,' said Muriel.

'Very sensible,' replied Dixon.

'What d'you want?'

'You work in the ticket office at Manchester Piccadilly?'

'Yes. Look, I've already spoken to the police about this.'

'Who did you speak to?'

'I don't know his name. He asked me whether I remembered selling a single to Taunton to a woman three days ago. Of course I don't,' said Muriel, shrugging her shoulders. 'D'you know how many tickets I sell in a day?'

'A lot.'

'Hundreds.'

'What did he look like, this man?'

'I didn't see him. He telephoned. He sounded Indian, maybe, I don't know.'

'And what did he say when you said you didn't remember?'

'Nothing. He rang off.'

'And he specifically said a single to Taunton?'

'Yes.'

Dixon was unfolding two pieces of paper he had taken from his jacket pocket. He handed one to Muriel. 'This is the woman.'

Muriel reached up and switched on a light. Then she squinted at the picture.

'No, I'm sorry, I really don't remember her.'

'And here she is standing at your counter,' said Dixon, handing Muriel the second piece of paper. 'That's you behind the glass, isn't it?'

'Yes.'

'She was going to Taunton.'

Muriel shook her head.

'Paid cash . . .'

'No, it really doesn't ring any bells. I'm sorry.'

'OK,' said Dixon, folding up the piece of paper. 'I'm sorry to have wasted your time.'

Back out on the pavement he sent Janice a text message.

Anyone tried to ring muriel chatt yet?

Then he rang for a taxi.

Janice's reply came when he was sheltering in the bus stop at the end of the road.

No

◆ ◆ ◆

'Good morning, Sir.' Dixon glanced over to the workstation on the far side of the CID area at the GMP headquarters. The boxes of files were still there.

Douglas sighed. 'I thought it had been established you were after a copycat?'

'We are. But I need to know why, and where he's getting his information from.'

Dixon had had a surprisingly good night's sleep, despite keeping Jane up talking on the phone until gone midnight. The strange and empty bed hadn't helped either, and he'd got used to sleeping with his dog curled up by his feet. Breakfast had been rushed, although there was time to fill Sexton in on his visit to Muriel Chatterjee.

'For fuck's sake,' muttered Chapman.

'You sort them out, Manny,' said Douglas, turning back to the coffee machine.

'Well, what can we do for you?' asked Pandey.

'You were going to let me have copies of the surveillance.'

Douglas looked at Pandey and raised his eyebrows.

Pandey looked embarrassed. 'I'll organise that now. Sorry, Guv.'

'And the files on the officer who died in prison?'

'Counter Corruption. I submitted a request,' said Douglas. 'Chase it up will you, Manny?'

'Yes, Guv.'

'Thank you, Sir,' said Dixon.

'Anything else?' asked Pandey.

'An address for the profiler, Dr Steven Pearson, please.'

Dixon sat down at a workstation next to Sexton and began turning the various boxes piled up next to him so that he could see the index on the side of each.

'Here's Pearson's address and phone number,' said Pandey, dropping a yellow Post-it note on to the desk in front of Dixon.

'Thank you.'

'What d'you hope to find? I mean, it's not as if we haven't been over this stuff thousands of times.'

'Is DCS Butler still around? asked Dixon. 'He was running the case before Hargreaves.'

'Very sad that,' replied Pandey. 'He disappeared in 2011. He'd been suffering from depression for some time, apparently, and the thinking was he killed himself.'

'You never found a body?'

'Never did, no.'

Dixon passed the note to Sexton. 'See if you can fix us up with Dr Pearson this morning, Jonny.'

'Yes, Sir.'

Dixon turned back to the file in front of him, watching Pandey in the reflection of the computer screen. He hesitated, shrugged his shoulders, and then walked away.

'Stone Mead Avenue, Hale Barns,' said Sexton as they climbed into the back of the taxi. 'It's over near the airport according to Google Maps.'

'I know it,' the taxi driver muttered.

'Douglas didn't seem too pleased to see us,' said Sexton, putting on his seatbelt.

'I have some sympathy for him.'

'He probably thinks we're checking up on them.'

'Then he'd be right.'

'Sometimes all it takes is a fresh pair of eyes.'

Dixon nodded, glancing across at the industrial estate as the taxi sped down the slip road on to the M56.

The rest of the short journey was spent in silence.

'I'm in the wrong business,' muttered Dixon, looking up from the passenger window of the taxi at the large house with a double garage and a Maserati parked outside. 'Yet another reminder.'

Sexton smiled. 'You could do a psychology course with the Open University.'

The doorbell was one of those irritating ones that left you wondering whether it had rung or not. Dixon looked at Sexton and raised his eyebrows.

'Shall I . . . ?'

Dixon nodded.

This time a dog started barking.

'Dr Pearson?'

'You'll be Dixon.'

'Yes, Sir.'

'Steve will do.' He stepped back to let them in, his hand outstretched. A white polo shirt with a Pringle sweater draped over his shoulders, the telltale diamond pattern visible in the mirror behind him. At least the trousers were a sensible navy blue.

'Did we drag you off the golf course?'

'I'm sneaking out for nine holes this afternoon, now the clocks have gone forward.' Pearson grinned.

'This is DS Sexton,' said Dixon.

'We spoke on the phone.'

More shaking of hands.

'Let's go through to the conservatory.'

Dixon was impressed. You could fit his entire cottage into the conservatory. There was even a putting green in the back garden, flags and all.

'What's your handicap?'

'Plus two.'

'You should turn pro.'

'Never had the temperament for it.' Pearson grinned. 'Shrink, heal thyself. One bad shot and I'm all over the place. Clubs in the pond.'

'That was the reason I never took it up,' said Dixon.

'D'you play?' Pearson asked, turning to Sexton.

'No, Sir.'

'I have to content myself playing for the seniors these days.'

Dixon sat down on a bamboo two-seater sofa with his back to the garden. Sexton pulled a chair out from under a smoked glass table, took his notebook out of his pocket and sat down.

'I read your profile on The Vet,' said Dixon.

'What did you think?'

'D'you want me to be honest?'

'Go ahead.'

'It seemed a bit wide.'

Pearson smiled. 'Could've been anybody, you mean?'

'I wasn't going to put it quite like that.'

'You're right. It was. But I stand by it. The fact that it fitted several people in the Carters' circle wasn't my fault.'

'Who?'

'Michael himself, possibly. And his brother, Kenny, although neither were well educated as far as we knew. There were several others too.'

'Tell me about Michael Carter.'

'Paul Butler pulled him in several times, but never got anything on him. You've seen his previous convictions?'

'Yes.' Dixon nodded.

'Anyone fill in the blanks?'

'We know he shot and killed a man,' said Dixon.

'Right there.' Pearson was pointing to the centre of his forehead with his right index finger.

Dixon sat up. 'In the centre of the forehead?'

'He stabbed him first though.'

'In the neck?'

Pearson nodded, slowly. 'He was fifteen years old at the time.'

Dixon let out a long, drawn out sigh. 'And Butler never got anything on him?'

'No. Although he never believed he was The Vet anyway. Hargreaves tried too and never got anywhere.'

'Who did Butler think it was then?'

'He never knew. He was convinced Kenny was the brains of the outfit, but that theory retired with him. Hargreaves was always focused on Michael and there was no real evidence Kenny had any involvement, to be fair to him.'

'What did you think?'

'I didn't. That was their problem,' replied Pearson. 'I prepared the profile to the best of my ability, and the rest was up to the police. And when Hargreaves took over, I was shut out.'

'What d'you think now?'

'The closest I got was watching an interview with Michael on a monitor.'

'Could he have been The Vet?'

'Could've been, but probably not. He fitted some, but not all, of the criteria. And, yes, they all did, before you say it.'

'And Kenny?'

'I never had any real contact with Kenny, so it's difficult for me to say.'

'Try.'

'The Vet was well educated, as I said. Ordered. Obsessive compulsive even. That much was obvious to me, and Kenny didn't come across as well educated from what I could gather.' .

'What happened to Paul Butler?' asked Dixon, shifting in his seat.

'He retired in 1994 and battled with depression for a long time. Then he just disappeared. That was five or six years ago, I think.'

'What did you make of that?'

'I'd not seen him for years. I thought it odd, but people change and retirement hits some hard. Your time will come,' said Pearson, smiling at Dixon.

'Maybe I'll take up golf,' replied Dixon. 'What about the DNA sample?'

'That was thought to be from The Vet, but it was never confirmed. It was only partial and never gave a match. The science was nothing like as advanced back then, don't forget.'

'Was it checked against Michael?'

'We got a covert sample of Michael's DNA.'

'By covert, you mean illegal?'

'Yes, but there was no match. It's been checked and double checked several times over the years. Scumbags, yes, but The Vet, I don't think so, no.' Pearson stood up. 'I never offered you a cup of tea.'

'We're fine, thank you,' said Dixon. 'Were you ever told what happened to the Carters?'

'Not really. I heard some rumours they'd been killed by the IRA. Michael was going to turn informer after the bombing and the Shannons are supposed to have tipped them off.'

'And both were killed?'

'Yes. That's the version I heard anyway.' Pearson shrugged his shoulders. 'I've no idea what happened to the rest of them.' He looked at his watch and then sat back down.

'So, what d'you make of the murders we've got down in Somerset?'

'It's a copycat, isn't it?'

'Why do people do that?'

'Paying homage, possibly. Or trying to disguise a killing as someone else's handiwork. It could also be some form of compulsion, or the killer's setting it up so he can claim diminished responsibility if he's ever caught. I had thought The Vet might have been doing that. The old 'not guilty by reason of insanity' routine. I couldn't really tell without taking a closer look.'

'Would you be willing to do that?' asked Dixon. Sexton looked up.

'Er, yes, I suppose so, if you'd like me to.'

'I'll need to get clearance for your fee,' said Dixon, standing up. 'I'll get back to you.'

'I'd need to come down to Somerset for a few days,' said Pearson.

'Yes, of course. We have hotels and golf courses.'

'Potter'll never go for that,' said Sexton as they walked down the gravel drive to the road.

'I've got no intention of asking her,' replied Dixon. 'I just wanted to see how he'd react.'

'And why the bloody hell didn't anyone tell us Michael Carter had shot his victim in the forehead?'

'Why indeed.'

They waited for the taxi in silence, sheltering under a tree, although it didn't last long.

'If it wasn't Michael or Kenny, who was The Vet?' asked Sexton, kicking a stone across the road.

'*Is* The Vet.'

'Eh?'

'There's no evidence that Michael or Kenny or The Vet are dead. Just rumours.'

'Who *is* then?'

'Have the schools broken up for Easter yet?'

'I don't think so.'

'How come that lot are playing football?' asked Dixon, gesturing to the park on the other side of the road.

'You never played truant then?'

'It was never really an option at my school.'

The arrival of the taxi saved Dixon from further questioning. An inquisitive soul was Sexton. A good quality in a detective, but a pain in the neck when you're stuck sheltering under a tree waiting for a taxi.

Sexton opened the passenger door. 'GMP headquarters, please.'

'Wait a minute,' said Dixon, fumbling in the pocket of his coat. He pulled out a piece of paper and read the address out loud. 'Ellesmere Drive, Cheadle.'

'What number?' asked the taxi driver.

'We'll worry about that when we get there.'

'You're the boss.'

'What's at Ellesmere Drive?' asked Sexton, when the taxi pulled away.

'Detective Chief Superintendent Paul Butler's widow,' replied Dixon.

Chapter Eighteen

Number 27, Ellesmere Drive was the last property on the right of the short cul-de-sac. It ended at a low brick wall with a high hedge on top, more football pitches beyond just visible through gaps.

'Popular in Manchester, football,' said Dixon.

Sexton smiled.

They had paid the taxi driver at the top of Ellesmere Drive and walked the rest of the way. The driveway of number 27 was all but blocked by green, brown and blue wheelie bins, a high net along the hedge protecting the house from flying footballs.

The other side of the semi had a new roof, and number 27 looked like it could do with one too. Perhaps Mrs Butler was struggling to get by on a widow's pension?

Dixon rang the doorbell under the watchful eye of a large black cat sitting on the window ledge to his right.

'Mrs Butler?'

'Yes.'

She looked young for seventy-six. And fit. That much was evident from the bicycle leaning up against the wall in the porch, one of the old fashioned ones with a wicker basket on the front. A large collie was standing behind her.

'Detective Inspector Dixon, Avon and Somerset Police. Might we have a word?'

'Come in.'

She closed the door behind them and opened the living room door on her left. 'In here. We'd better not let the cat out. They don't get on.'

'Is this your husband?' asked Dixon, picking up a photograph from the mantelpiece.

'That's Paul, yes.'

'What happened to him?'

'He was murdered.'

Dixon waited, ignoring the fidgeting from Sexton sitting to his left on the sofa.

'Oh, look, they never found a body and, yes, he'd been depressed, but that was because nobody believed him.'

'About what?'

'The Carters.'

'Did he leave a note?'

'No. He just walked out one day and was never seen again.'

'Where was he going?'

'He had a doctor's appointment but never got there. I was at work, came home and there was no sign of him.'

'Was he on medication for depression?'

Mrs Butler nodded. 'They looked for him, of course they did. But they never found a trace. And that was that. No inquest, nothing. In the end I applied to the High Court and had him declared dead. That was more for the children, really, to give them closure.'

'So, who d'you think murdered him?'

'The Vet.'

'And this was in 2011?'

'Yes. I have no doubt about it at all. Never have had. But no one would listen. The Carters and The Vet were long gone by then, and people were just grateful for that, I think. They certainly didn't want me rocking the boat.'

'Why kill your husband, though?' asked Dixon. 'He was retired by then.'

Mrs Butler smiled and shook her head. 'He was like a dog with a bone, Inspector. Come with me.'

They followed her up the stairs and into what had once been used as a spare bedroom. A small desk in the window overlooking the back garden was just visible under piles of paper and box files, all of it leaning against an old computer monitor. More files were piled up on the floor and on the swivel chair. Mrs Butler switched on the light.

'Did anyone have a look through all this when your husband disappeared?' asked Dixon.

'A quick look. It doesn't take long to get the gist of it.'

'Did they take anything?'

'Some papers he shouldn't have had, apparently. They said he must've taken them when he left.'

'And did he?'

Mrs Butler shrugged her shoulders. 'I expect so.'

'Has anyone else been in here?'

'I was burgled about five years ago.'

'I'm sorry to hear that.'

'It happens.'

'Was anything taken?'

'My jewellery.'

'What about from this room?'

'I really would have no idea about that. The papers were all on the floor though. I know that much.'

'Did local police attend?'

'Yes. They dusted for fingerprints in the living room and my bedroom, but didn't find anything.'

Dixon hesitated. 'Not this room?' he asked.

'No.'

'When were these taken?' He was staring at the left wall, above the bed, almost every inch of it covered with photographs. Some had fallen off, leaving small lumps of Blu Tack in each corner and a glimpse of the green and gold striped wallpaper behind.

'After he retired. I told you – a dog with a bone. It was in the days before the bomb and just after. The Carters disappeared then.'

'Are any photos missing?'

'I don't know.'

'Jonny, see if you can match the photos lying on the bed to gaps on the wall.'

'Yes, Sir.'

'And who are these people?' asked Dixon, turning to the opposite wall, above the chest of drawers.

'The Shannons.'

Dixon recognised Snooker City, Hervey's old club and renamed in the picture, where Rick Wheaton had worked behind the bar, whoever he was.

'What was he working on?'

'He was convinced Kenny Carter was the leader, the driving force behind it all. But he never found any evidence of it, and he never persuaded anyone else about it either. Then, when he retired, the focus shifted to Michael Carter, and that was that. But he refused to let it drop, as you can see.'

'Did he find anything?'

'No. I always knew someone would come, though. That's why I left it. I always knew you'd come. Paul was never wrong.'

Dixon smiled.

'Then when the killings started again it was just a matter of time,' continued Mrs Butler.

'Can I sit here for a while and go through these papers?'

'Yes, of course.'

'Jonny, go back to Central Park and chase up those files and the surveillance, will you?'

'Yes, Sir.'

'What time's our train home?'

'There's one at six and another at seven.'

'I'll catch you up.'

'Would you like a cup of tea, dear?' asked Mrs Butler.

'And a biscuit if you've got one, please.' Dixon picked up the papers on the swivel chair and put them on the bed. Then he sat down in front of the computer. 'Does it work?'

'No one's touched it since 2011, but you're welcome to have a look.'

'Thank you.'

He reached down and switched it on, noticing several pieces of paper on the floor under the desk: a photograph of a car, an old Ford Sierra registration number P316 PYU; two emails from Ray Hargreaves; and a note that looked as though it had been Sellotaped to the wall above the printer on the right. The Sellotape was brown and brittle to the touch, the glue long gone, with a corresponding brown stain on the wallpaper.

Dixon stared at what looked like a list of codes, each a series of letters and numbers, all but the last one on the list crossed out.

He turned back to the computer and frowned at the blank screen.

'Here you are, dear.'

Mrs Butler placed a mug of tea and a plate piled high with digestive biscuits on the desk next to Dixon.

'D'you know what this is?' he asked, holding up the list of codes.

'It used to be on the wall there,' she said, pointing above the printer. 'Where did you find it?'

'On the floor.'

'I just assumed it was his passwords. As you get older you have to write them down, you know.'

Dixon switched the monitor off and on again. Then he tried the same with the computer. Still the same blank screen. He sighed, put on a pair of latex gloves, leaned over and dragged the tower out from under the desk. He tipped it forwards and shone the light on his phone at the screws in the back.

'Bollocks,' he muttered.

'What is it, dear?'

'I'm sorry, Mrs Butler, I thought you'd gone.'

'It's all right. You get used to it as a copper's wife.'

'You see these screw heads?'

'Yes.'

'They've been tampered with. I'm guessing in that burglary some-one took the hard drive out of the computer.'

'What does that do?'

'Well, it's got the memory, the documents, photographs, every-thing. It's like taking the brain out.'

'I've never lost any money or anything like that,' Mrs Butler said, shaking her head.

'I'm guessing they weren't after your bank details.'

'Can it be restored or whatever it is you do?'

'I'm afraid not,' said Dixon, pushing the box back under the desk. 'Can I take some of these photographs, please? And this note?'

'Take the lot, if you like, dear. I've got a bag somewhere.'

'Thank you.'

Dixon slid the note with the list of codes on it into his pocket and packed the rest of the papers and photographs into an old holdall handed to him by Mrs Butler. He looked up at the wall above the bed: a patchwork of photographs he'd left behind, bright and faded wallpaper, and Blu Tack stains.

'It's about time I redecorated in here.' Mrs Butler smiled. 'You will let me know if he was right all along, won't you?' A small tear appeared in the corner of her eye. 'It would be nice to know.'

'I will,' replied Dixon.

◆　◆　◆

The taxi waited for Dixon while he put the holdall with his overnight bag in the left luggage at the Premier Inn. Then he ran back out to the cab and jumped in the back.

'D'you know a club called Snooker City?'

'Yeah, mate.'

'Take me there, please.'

'Are you sure?'

'Why d'you ask?'

'Well, you're a copper, ain't ya?'

'When you're ready,' said Dixon.

'Your funeral.'

A single storey red brick building in an otherwise residential area, the only indication of Irish ownership the small shamrock dotting the 'i' of 'City' on the fluorescent sign. Dixon walked in and stood at the bar, listening to the click of the snooker balls behind him. Four of the tables were being used; the other eight empty. Arranged in four rows of three, they covered an area the size of two tennis courts.

'I'm looking for Paddy Shannon,' said Dixon to the barman, watching two burly figures appearing either side of him in the mirror behind the bar.

'Who wants him?' A broad Irish accent was to be expected.

'My name is Detective Inspector Dixon.'

'No Manchester copper would come in here looking for Paddy.'

'I'm not from round here.'

'What d'you want?'

'A chat.'

'What about?' the barman asked, lining the beer mats up on the top of the bar.

'I'm investigating the murders in Somerset. The copycat. And there's a rumour he had Michael Carter killed.'

'And you think he's going to confess to you?'

'Look, I'm not interested in Paddy Shannon or Michael Carter, I just want to catch this copycat. And The Vet, if I can. He's still out there, isn't he?'

The man behind the bar looked at the men either side of Dixon and nodded. They stepped back and returned to the nearest snooker table. Dixon waited for the familiar click before he spoke again.

'You're Paddy Shannon?'

'I am.'

'Are the rumours true?'

'You want me to tell you if I had Michael Carter killed?'

'I reckon you'll tell me if you didn't and throw me out on my ear if you did,' said Dixon, smiling.

'You've got a bloody cheek, so you have.' Shannon pushed a glass up under the Bushmills optic and placed it on the bar in front of Dixon.

'Drink.'

Dixon did as he was told.

'And what happens if you just disappear then? I've got enough on my payroll not to see the inside of a cell.'

'I'm guessing the officers on your payroll don't include any from Avon and Somerset?'

'No.'

Dixon smiled. 'There you are then.'

'And I suppose they all know you're here.'

'One does. That's all it takes.'

Shannon poured himself a Bushmills and downed it in one.

'We lost a man to The Vet,' he said, sucking his teeth. 'A friend of mine, so he was.'

'What was his name?'

'Dermot McGann.'

'He's listed as disappeared. A possible victim of The Vet.'

'He was a victim all right. The bastard sent me a feckin' Polaroid of it.'

Dixon drained his Bushmills and placed the empty glass on a beer mat. 'Have you still got it?'

Shannon stared at him, then picked up the empty glass and refilled it. 'Wait here,' he said, disappearing through a door at the end of the bar.

Dixon listened to the click of the balls on the snooker tables, and the score: eighty, eighty-one, eighty-eight. There must be some good players at Snooker City, he thought, resisting the temptation to turn around to watch.

'I kept it,' said Shannon, closing the door behind him, 'so one day I could give it back to the bastard, before I killed him.' He handed Dixon the Polaroid photograph. 'I reckon you'll be finding him first.'

Dixon looked down at the picture of Dermot McGann, eyes wide, nostrils flared, teeth gritted; his hands reaching out towards the camera, the flash glinting on the handcuffs.

'Why "Heads or Tails"?' asked Dixon, pointing to a message scrawled on the bottom of the photograph.

'Heads I kill you, tails I don't.' Shannon flicked an imaginary coin into the air with his right hand. 'With a piece of skull.'

'Can I keep this?'

'You can.'

Dixon slid the photograph into his jacket pocket and picked up his glass.

'And now you've got a copycat on the loose,' said Shannon, nodding.

'Killing innocent people.'

'Are you wearing a wire?'

'No.' Dixon held open his jacket.

'We didn't kill Carter,' said Shannon. 'But we bloody well would've done if we'd got our hands on him.'

'Which Carter?'

Shannon picked up a towel and began drying beer tankards, hanging each in turn above his head. 'Both.'

'Did the IRA kill them?'

'No.'

'So, they're still out there?'

'I suppose.'

'No rumours about where they might've gone?'

'Spain or Cyprus, I expect. Where would you go?'

'I'd go home,' said Dixon.

'I suggest you do that, right now.'

'I will.'

Dixon stared into Shannon's eyes and then turned away.

'One last thing,' said Shannon. 'Call it a gesture of goodwill. That assistant of yours – the feckin' little poof,' he sneered. 'He's not who he says he is.'

'Who is he?'

'You'll have to ask him that.'

'And how would you know?'

'I make it my business to know about fellow countrymen on the wrong side of the law. You never know when you might need a friend.'

Dixon paused in the doorway and looked back at the bar. Shannon had gone, but the games of snooker were still going on, the click louder on one table as the player smashed into the pack, sending the cue ball bouncing off the table. Dixon looked down at the floor in front of the bar and imagined a man having his brains bashed in with a snooker cue. Then he stepped out into the rain, grateful to have avoided that fate. Or worse.

◆ ◆ ◆

Seventeen missed calls. Dixon had felt his phone buzzing in his pocket throughout his visit to Snooker City. It was the one Avon and Somerset officer he had told he was going to see the Shannons. Better call her back, he thought as he dialled the number.

'Are you all right?'

'Yes, fine.'

'You're doing my bloody head in,' Jane muttered. A mug slammed down on a desk in the background.

'I'm fine. Honestly.'

'What is it with you and gangsters? You can't just saunter in and fire questions at them!'

'That depends what you want to ask them about.'

'And a text? That's all I get?'

'I didn't have much time.'

'You're going to get yourself killed one day.'

'How's your day been?'

'Idiot.'

Dixon waited.

'Not too bad,' continued Jane, the loud sigh almost drowning out her reply. 'Where are you now?'

'At the hotel, picking up my bag. The cab's waiting to take me to the railway station.'

'What time d'you get in?'

'Just after ten.'

'I'll pick you up.'

'Thanks.'

'Just try to stay out of trouble until then.'

Dixon was about to give her his standard 'yes, Mother' reply when he noticed the dialling tone. Jane had put the phone down on him. That was a first. Still, four hours on the train would give her time to calm down. Whether he stayed out of trouble in the meantime would be up to Jonny Sexton.

Chapter Nineteen

Dixon dumped his bags on the table and dropped down on to the seat opposite Sexton. Then he dragged the bags on to the vacant window seat next to him, Mrs Butler's holdall underneath his own overnight bag.

'You made it then, Sir,' said Sexton, taking out his earphones.

'I did.'

'Find anything useful?'

'I don't know yet.'

'You were a long time at Mrs Butler's,' said Sexton.

'I went to see the Shannons.'

'You just walked in there?' Sexton's jaw dropped.

'Pretty much.'

'What did they say?'

'That they didn't kill Michael Carter and neither did the IRA.'

'What difference does that make to the copycat?'

'We need to know where he's getting his information from, don't we? And it means the Carters are still out there somewhere. The Vet as well. There must be a connection of some sort. Then we've got the old lady who travelled all the way from Manchester to kill herself.'

'Anything else?'

'Paddy Shannon gave me this.' Dixon dropped the Polaroid photograph on to the table in front of Sexton.

'Who is it?' asked Sexton, picking it up.

'Dermot McGann.'

'Heads or tails?'

'The toss of a very special type of coin,' muttered Dixon. 'Give me a minute.' He fished his phone out of his jacket pocket. 'I had a couple of texts that got lost in all the missed calls.'

'Who were the calls from?'

'Jane.' He navigated to Messages and scrolled down, ignoring the multitude from voicemail. 'Here's one from Roger – Heroin and fentanyl enough to kill a seasoned addict let alone an elderly lady not used to it – and another from Janice – *Manch Daily Post* running e-fit and CCTV still tonight.'

'Maybe we should have hung around for that?' asked Sexton.

'We need to get back,' said Dixon, watching the adjacent train creeping away from the platform. It took him a moment to realise that train was stationary and it was theirs that was moving.

'Fancy a beer?' asked Sexton, sliding the photograph across the table.

'Interesting fellow, Paddy Shannon,' said Dixon, ignoring the question. 'Likes to keep track of fellow Irishmen on the wrong side of the law, as he put it.'

'Really?'

'Follows their careers closely,' said Dixon, raising his eyebrows.

Sexton looked along the aisle, out of the window, anywhere to avoid Dixon's stare.

'Did he . . . er . . . did he say anything about . . . ?'

'You?'

'Yes.'

'Well, it's funny you should say that,' said Dixon, dropping his phone and the Polaroid back into his pocket.

Sexton took a deep breath. 'What did he say?'

'That you aren't who you say you are.'

'Is that it?'

'Leaves me thinking all sorts of things though, doesn't it?' Dixon scowled.

'It's not what you think.'

'For all I know you could be Carter's son and heir. Or a member of the IRA . . .'

'All right, all right.'

'Either way, I can't trust you.'

'Yes, you can.'

Dixon waited. Sexton was holding his train ticket between the thumb and index finger of his left hand and flicking it with his right, his eyes darting around the carriage.

'It's vital my cover isn't blown,' he said, looking back to Dixon.

'Go on.'

'I'm in the CCU.'

'And whose corruption are you countering?'

'Not yours.'

'From Bristol?'

'Yes.'

'Investigating who?'

'The Manchester MIT.'

'Does Deborah Potter know?'

'That's why she put me with you and sent us up here.' Sexton leaned forward across the table. 'Look, Manchester CCU have had their suspicions about the MIT for years. They've got people on the inside before, but it's never lasted, so this was a chance to have another look, from a different angle. The Carters had someone on the inside and the Shannons do too. It was a chance to—'

'I get it.'

'So, we're all right?' asked Sexton, nodding his head.

'I'll have that beer now,' Dixon muttered.

He was watching the fields flashing by when Sexton placed two cans of beer on the table in front of him.

'Did you get the file on the officer who died in prison?'

'The CCU wouldn't release it.' Sexton sat down.

'Why not?'

'Manny didn't say.'

'What about the surveillance?'

'I've got the discs here,' replied Sexton, tapping his bag on the seat next to him.

'Well, that's something at least.'

'What happens now?' asked Sexton.

'I try to catch up on some sleep,' said Dixon, closing his eyes. 'And you try to keep me awake with your music.'

◆ ◆ ◆

No hug, no kiss. Not even a smile. Dixon had received a frosty reception at Highbridge Railway Station and an almost silent drive home, his one question about Monty answered with a curt 'of course I have'. He thought it best not to inflame the situation and, after giving Monty a run in the field behind the cottage, he sat down next to Jane on the sofa and waited for her to start talking.

At least she was watching *The Great Escape* again. Richard Attenborough was outlining his plans to dig three tunnels when Jane hit the 'pause' button, freezing it just at the point he reveals how many prisoners of war will be escaping.

'*Two hundred and fifty—*'

'I'm not sure how much more of this I can . . .' Jane threw the remote control on the floor and stormed into the kitchen. Dixon followed. He turned her round to face him and put his arms around her waist. She turned away, staring out of the window into the darkness. 'I had a call from Sonia's probation officer. They had to break into her flat, and she found my number scribbled on the wall.'

'Is she dead?' Dixon asked, wiping a tear from Jane's cheek with his thumb.

She managed a nod before starting to sob, her face buried in his shoulder.

'I've only just found her, and now she's gone.'

'How?'

'They don't know yet. There's got to be a post mortem, but it looks like an overdose.'

Dixon sighed.

'Her probation officer said Sonia didn't turn up for a meeting, so she called round on her way home and saw her on the floor.'

'What about Tony?'

'No sign of him.'

Dixon reached over and flicked the switch on the kettle, his right arm still holding Jane tight.

'What happens now?'

'Social Services will organise a funeral and she's promised to let me know when it is. I stopped being her next of kin when I was adopted.'

'Will you go?'

'I dunno yet.'

Dixon tore off a piece of kitchen roll and handed it to Jane. 'Are there any other relatives?'

'Didn't say.' She pulled away from him and dabbed her eyes. 'And you. Taking all these bloody risks all the time. I can't lose you as well.'

'You won't.'

Jane looked up at him, her eyes full of tears.

'Tea?' he asked.

She smiled. 'That's your answer for everything, isn't it?'

'I'm sorry about Sonia.' Dixon tore off another piece of kitchen roll.

'Don't be. If it wasn't for you, I'd never have met her.'

'Yeah, I'm sorry about that too.' He shrugged his shoulders.

'And I'm sorry I shouted,' said Jane, snatching the second piece of kitchen roll from Dixon's hand. 'Did the Shannons give you anything useful?'

'Food for thought,' he replied. 'And a nice glass of Irish whisky.'

'What about the woman up at Dunkery Beacon?'

'Nothing yet. The ticket office clerk at Manchester didn't remember her, nor did the guard on the train. Janice got the Transport lot to track him down.'

Jane reached up for two mugs from the cupboard. 'I'll make it,' she said. 'You go and sit down. Have you eaten?'

'Some crap on the train.'

'D'you want anything?'

'No, thanks.'

Dixon sat down on the floor next to Monty and leaned back against the sofa. Then he pressed 'play' on the remote control.

'What's in that bag?' asked Jane, pointing to Mrs Butler's holdall by the bottom of the stairs.

'Papers and photos from a retired police officer who couldn't let go.'

'That'll be you, when your time comes.'

'I hope so.'

They were in bed before the Germans found 'Tom', the first tunnel, Dixon lying awake thinking about Dunkery Beacon and the flames spreading across the hillside. Why that hillside? And why that particular spot on that hillside? If she'd wanted open moorland, there was plenty of that around Manchester.

He picked up his phone and set the alarm for 5.30 a.m. Then he put his arm around Jane, closed his eyes and was asleep before Monty had jumped on the bed.

◆ ◆ ◆

'What time is it?' asked Jane, yawning as Dixon silenced the alarm.

'Five thirty.' He was trying to slide his legs out from underneath Monty without waking him up.

'Where are you going?'

'Fancy a nice walk on Exmoor?'

'Are you taking the pi—?'

Dixon leaned over and kissed Jane, silencing her mid-sentence. 'What've you got to lose?'

'Two hours' sleep.'

'Apart from two hours' sleep.'

She sighed.

'There you are then,' he said, grinning. 'And it's a lovely morning.' He opened the curtains and then snapped them shut.

'It's pissing down,' protested Jane.

'It's only water.'

'And it's still dark!'

Thirty minutes later they were speeding south on the M5 with the headlights on full beam. Dixon had needed a torch to find a spade in the outhouse behind his Land Rover, and he'd brought a trowel too, just in case.

'In case of what?' had been Jane's question, which he chose to ignore.

'I don't know why you keep all that crap. We haven't even got a garden,' said Jane, rolling her eyes.

'I don't go climbing any more but you have to admit my ice axe came in handy that time.'

'Yes, well . . . what are we looking for?'

'A wild goose.'

'Just what I need at the crack of bloody dawn. Another wild goose chase.'

'She travelled all the way from Manchester to die on that particular hillside. Why?'

'I don't know.'

'Neither do I,' replied Dixon, dipping the headlights as he turned off the M5. 'I don't know who she is, where she came from, anything about her, but I do know that she chose to die on that particular spot.'

'Then the spot must be significant,' said Jane, nodding.

'Right. So, we dig.'

◆ ◆ ◆

The sun was just creeping above the horizon as they turned south on the A396 towards Wheddon Cross, a faint plume of smoke climbing into the sky in the distance.

'They must've been out burning again yesterday,' said Dixon.

'Let's hope they don't do it again while we're up there.'

'Quite.'

The police roadblock was long gone and Dixon drove straight across the cattle grid at Dunkery Gate. He followed the road across the side of the Beacon and then turned down the track towards Hanny Combe.

'How will you find the exact spot?'

'We'll know it when we see it,' said Dixon.

He stopped on the track and wrenched on the handbrake. 'This looks like it.'

'Shall I let Monty out?' asked Jane, climbing out on the passenger side.

'Yeah, you can do, the adders'll still be hibernating.'

'Snakes?'

'Let's just get on with it, shall we?'

'Which way?'

'That way,' replied Dixon, pointing across the bonnet of the Land Rover.

They trudged across the charred ground, the wet branches of the burnt gorse and heather leaving black stripes where it brushed their trousers. The scorched earth was black, brown in places, but rarely green, except for a few patches that had survived. Jane stopped in her tracks.

'Is this it?'

Dixon ran over and looked down at the ground in front of Jane. An area of green grass marked where the body had been, just as if it been spray painted, the head, torso, legs and arms taking shape in the dried grass.

'The body protected the grass from the fire,' said Dixon.

'Seems a shame to dig it up now.' Jane was stamping her feet. 'Why don't you use the ground penetrating radar?'

'D'you know how much that costs? They'd never let me have it.'

'So, what do we do?'

'Dig, carefully, and stop the second we find anything.'

'Off you go then,' said Jane.

Dixon slid the leading edge of the spade under the turf and lifted clear a patch right in the middle of where the torso had been, revealing the soil underneath: dark brown and compacted. Then he knelt down and began scraping with the trowel.

'We'll be here all day if you do it like that,' muttered Jane, pulling up her collar and turning away from the rain that had started again.

Dixon picked up the spade and began clearing the earth away, going no more than an inch deeper each time. Then he stopped.

'What's that?' he asked, pointing into the hole, now nearly a foot deep.

Jane peered over his shoulder.

'A rib,' she said.

Chapter Twenty

It had taken Dixon what seemed like a lifetime to find a signal, and he was almost at the summit cairn before his phone connected to the network, and then it was '999 calls only'. Still, that had been enough.

Jonny Sexton was the first to arrive. Jane had left half an hour earlier, taking Monty with her in the Land Rover and leaving Dixon with her umbrella: small, navy blue and covered in penguins.

Sexton bounced down the track towards Hanny Combe in his shiny new BMW, swerving violently from side to side trying to avoid the worst of the ruts, and stopped opposite Dixon. He wound down the window on the passenger side and leaned across the seat. 'Janice Courtenay's on her way, Sir. And Roger Poland.'

'SOCO?'

'They were at a burglary in Bridgwater, but they're coming.'

'Good.'

'I've got uniform blocking the Beacon at either end too.' Sexton grinned. 'Nice brolly.'

'Piss off.'

The rain had washed the worst of the mud off the one exposed rib in the bottom of the small hole Dixon had dug. One thin grey bone poking out of the mud and marking a shallow grave on an exposed and bleak hillside, or so he hoped. He would know soon enough.

'Is that it?'

Dixon rolled his eyes. 'We'll let SOCO do the rest.'

'It could be a sheep carcass.'

'Behave yourself, Constable.' Dixon smiled. 'Or you can hold the brolly.'

'You should've got the radar up here, Sir.'

'I knew where to look.'

'How?'

'Ask yourself why she chose this spot to lie down and die?'

'And you decided to dig just because of that?'

'I'd been watching *The Great Escape*.' Dixon shrugged his shoulders.

The sound of vehicles clattering over a cattle grid in the distance just carried on the wind.

'Sounds like they're here,' said Sexton.

'Either that or Stokes is on his way with more firelighters,' muttered Dixon. 'Better walk up to the road and check.'

'Yes, Sir.'

The smell of the scorched earth and charred vegetation, now saturated by the rain, had long ago begun to catch in Dixon's throat. At least it masked the smell of the bodily fluids that had seeped into the ground during the fire. Kneeling over, trowel in hand, and at that time in the morning, had left Dixon grateful he'd had no breakfast. Medicinal fruit pastilles would have to keep his blood sugar levels topped up until lunchtime.

The small convoy stopped on the road above Hanny Combe: Roger Poland's Volvo in front, followed by a Scientific Services van. The car behind must be Janice, thought Dixon.

The moment of truth. Poland squatted down and peered at the bone. 'It's a human rib,' he said, straightening up. He drew a line in the blackened soil parallel to where the body lay with the toe of his boot. 'It'll be this way up, so let's have a trench along here. We can go across bit by bit from there.'

'Give us twenty minutes to get set up,' said Donald Watson, the senior scenes of crime officer. 'Keeping us busy, aren't you?' he said, frowning at Dixon.

'I didn't kill him.'

'How d'you know it's a "him"?'

'Just a wild guess.'

'I've got a Thermos of coffee and some biscuits in my car,' said Poland, watching Dixon unwrapping a packet of sweets. 'A man cannot live on fruit pastilles alone.'

'Who is it then?' asked Watson.

'That depends on who she is,' replied Dixon.

'We've had a few calls from yesterday's piece in the Manchester daily rag,' said Janice. 'Louise is following them up now.'

'Let's leave SOCO to it,' said Poland.

◆ ◆ ◆

'Who is it then?' asked Poland, handing Dixon a plastic cup of coffee.

'I haven't got a bloody clue, but I wasn't telling him that,' replied Dixon, through a mouthful of digestive biscuit.

'Really?' asked Sexton, sitting in the back of the car next to Janice.

'It could be Paul Butler, I suppose.'

'The retired DCS?'

'He disappeared in 2011. The assumption was it was suicide, but . . .'

'What about Michael Carter?' asked Sexton. 'Maybe Shannon lied to you and they did have him killed? It could be The Vet too. Maybe the Carters got rid of him?'

'We'll know the answer to that one when we see the skull,' replied Dixon.

'Well, it's not Horan, that's for sure,' said Poland. 'Whoever it is has been dead for years not days.'

'We've got a partial DNA profile from The Vet and there's a covert sample from Michael.'

'Covert?'

'Don't ask.' Dixon glanced over his shoulder at Janice. 'Will we get DNA off it, Roger?'

'There may be some hair left. If not, there's the tooth pulp. That should've survived, assuming they left the teeth when they buried him.'

Dixon winced.

Sexton tapped on the inside of the window. 'Tent's up. Shouldn't be long now.'

'I'd better get down there,' said Poland.

By the time Dixon had finished his coffee and poked his head inside the tent a trench had been dug to a foot deep along the side of the skeletal remains. Three scientific services officers were on their hands and knees, brushing soil away with a trowel in one hand and a paintbrush in the other.

One foot had been exposed, a right arm lying across more ribs and the right side of the pelvis. Watson was edging ever closer to the skull.

'Lying on his back,' said Poland, pointing at the hip joint.

'His?'

'Definitely a male.'

'He had rubber soled shoes on,' said Watson. 'The uppers have gone, but the sole is still there. They look like Doc Martens.'

'Anything else?'

'A couple of rusty zips.'

Dixon stepped back outside into the wind and rain, the smell overpowering in the confines of the tent, not helped by the arc lamps warming the stagnant air.

'Skull, Sir.' Sexton shouting from inside the tent.

Dixon took a deep breath and stepped back in to see Watson brushing the top of the skull with his paintbrush. It looked like a paintbrush anyway.

'Any hair?'

'Yes.'

Dixon smiled.

A delicate scratch at the earth with the tip of the trowel then a brush, the bristles flicking away the now loose soil. Dixon resisted the temptation to yell 'get on with it', but only just.

Watson sat back on his heels and reached for a smaller brush. Then he leaned forwards, right over the skull. Several flicks with the smaller brush, a blow, more flicks. Then he sat back. 'A perfect hole. Right in the middle,' he said, pointing at the forehead with the brush.

'Let me have a look,' said Poland, squatting down and peering at a dark brown circle in the centre of the grey bone. 'The skull is full of mud, but it's a clean cut. Almost certainly a trephine.'

'The work of The Vet?' asked Dixon.

'I'd say so, but I'll confirm it when I get him back to the lab.'

'Well done, Sir,' said Sexton.

Watson began scraping with the trowel and flicking with the brush again, gradually revealing more of the skull, first the eye sockets, then the nasal cavity.

'Let's get the DNA checked as quick as we can,' said Dixon. 'We can get a sample from Paul Butler's children so we can rule him out too.'

'Or in.'

'Do it without worrying his widow. I don't want to give her false hope.'

Sexton nodded.

'And I want a news blackout on it. At least until we've got Horan.'

'You go,' said Poland. 'We'll let you know if we find anything else here.'

◆ ◆ ◆

The rain had been replaced by low cloud by the time Dixon stepped back out on to the moor, flashes from the cameras inside the tent lighting up the surrounding area, despite the arc lamps.

'What about my team?' asked Janice as they trudged across to Sexton's car.

'I need to know who that woman is, Janice. Let's worry about it after that.'

'Leave it to me.'

'Where to now, Sir?' asked Sexton.

'Express Park, once you've dropped Janice back to her car.'

'I'll walk,' she replied. 'It'll be quicker.'

'You should get a proper car,' said Dixon, raising his voice over the noise of the exhaust pipe scraping along the top of a rut. He was watching Sexton fighting with the steering wheel as his car bounced along the rough track.

'It'll be fine,' Sexton replied, nervously glancing in his rear view mirror.

'Where are we with Horan?' Dixon asked as they sped over the cattle grid at the bottom of Dunkery Beacon.

'Lots of sightings, and they're all being followed up, but nothing yet.'

'We're still watching his ex-wife?'

'Twenty-four seven.'

Dixon closed his eyes and leaned back in the passenger seat, sitting up sharply at the sound of skidding tyres. 'An old Land Rover might slow you down a bit too.'

Sexton grinned.

They arrived back at Express Park a good ten minutes ahead of Janice, Dixon watching from the window as she drove up the ramp into the staff car park. He'd even had time to poke his head around the door of the SCU. Words hadn't proved necessary. He'd just pointed to the centre of his forehead. Jane had nodded, and then thrown him his car keys.

Twenty minutes reading the call log in the Major Incident Room and his emails, followed by another twenty minutes with those of the team who were not out and about, and he was up to speed with the hunt for Horan. And a major manhunt it was too.

'DCS Potter would like to see you, Sir.'

'In Portishead?'

'No, Sir. She's in with DCI Lewis downstairs.'

Dixon closed his eyes, took a deep breath and wandered over to the lift, hoping his phone would ring; Poland, perhaps, at the post mortem. That would sound urgent enough to dash off.

'Ah, there you are.'

A lift with glass sides. There really was no escape.

'Yes, Sir.'

'Deborah Potter's in here,' said Lewis, holding open the door of his office.

'You've found another one?' asked Potter, looking up at Dixon hovering in the doorway.

'Yes.'

'Who is it?'

'I don't know yet, Ma'am. There's enough hair to get a DNA sample. I left before the teeth had been uncovered, but we should get an ID.'

'Any ideas?'

'Not that I'd share yet.'

Lewis sat down behind his desk. 'You went to see the Shannons?'

'I did.'

'Get anything?'

'A Polaroid photograph, Sir,' replied Dixon. 'An assurance they didn't kill Michael Carter and some very interesting information about Jonny Sexton.' He glared at Potter.

'You didn't need to know,' she said.

'Which means the Carters, The Vet and Horan are all out there,' continued Dixon. He sighed. At least she hadn't said she 'didn't think'. And she was right. He didn't need to know about Sexton. Not really.

'What's the photograph of?' asked Lewis.

'One of The Vet's victims, Sir. Before he was killed.'

'And you don't want to go public with this latest body?' Potter folded her arms.

'Not until we've got Horan. I don't want to send him further underground.' Dixon winced. It was an uncomfortable pun, but then weren't they all?

'Where are you with that?'

'Lots of leads. Nothing yet, though. The team are on them.'

'What are you doing?'

'I'm coming at it from the other end,' replied Dixon. 'There's a connection between Horan and Manchester.'

'What connection?'

'You mean apart from the body we've just found on Dunkery Beacon?'

'Yes.'

'I don't know yet, but he's got information no one else has, and he must be getting it from somewhere.'

'Your job is to catch Horan,' said Potter, 'not The Vet. I don't give a shit what's going on in Manchester.'

'What's going on in Manchester will lead me to Horan.'

'Are you trying to catch Horan or The Vet?' asked Potter, standing up sharply.

'Both.'

'Really.' The sarcasm dripped from her voice.

'Horan because he's the prime suspect in two murders. The Vet because he will lead me to Horan.'

'And you know that for sure?'

'No.'

Potter frowned. 'Does this investigation end when you find Horan?'

'It ends when I say it ends.'

Lewis raised his eyebrows.

'Don't tell me, I just staked my future on it?' continued Dixon, from behind a wry smile.

'You did,' muttered Potter.

'Sounds familiar.'

He just caught the exchange between Lewis and Potter as he walked along the landing, before Lewis closed the door behind him.

'Good, isn't he?'

'Very, much as it pains me to say it.'

◆ ◆ ◆

Dixon was sitting in the staff canteen just after midday when Janice sat down next to him. She waited for him to finish his mouthful of sandwich.

'Well?' he asked, raising his eyebrows.

'We had a call from a care home in Cheadle. Denise Marks; fits the description. She walked out of the home four days ago and hasn't been seen since.'

'And they didn't report her missing?'

'She still has her own flat, and it's not altogether unusual. She comes and goes as she pleases, apparently.'

'What sort of care home is that?'

'Not dementia care,' replied Janice. 'She was still quite sprightly, apparently. I've given the details to Roger Poland.'

'What's her story then?' Dixon took another bite of his sandwich.

'Well, I'm not sure what you were expecting.'

'Nothing.'

'But this strikes me as one giant can of worms.'

Dixon stopped chewing.

'Denise Marks,' continued Janice. She leaned forwards across the table, and whispered, 'retired Police Sergeant Denise Marks.'

'Greater Manchester?'

'Yep.'

'What did she do?' Dixon dropped the last of his sandwich back into the box.

Janice took a deep breath and spoke as she exhaled.

'Witness protection.'

Chapter Twenty-One

'Green Tree Court,' said Sexton. 'I googled it. Not your ordinary care home by any stretch.'

'I'm starting to get bored with this bloody train journey.' Dixon was looking out of the window watching the Burnham lighthouse in the distance. 'What's the problem?'

'The price.' Sexton slid his phone across the table and shook his head.

'How much is it?'

'Sixteen hundred quid a week.'

'A week?' Dixon snatched the phone off the table. 'Proud to be five star, it says. It looks more like a posh hotel.'

'I'd love to be able to afford that,' Sexton muttered. 'I'd move in now.'

'And how does a retired police sergeant afford that, I wonder, without selling her flat?'

'Even with selling her flat. That's over six grand a month.'

Dixon nodded. 'Well, Janice won't notify the Manchester lot until she hears from us. That gives us a bit of time.'

'What for?'

'First dibs.'

◆   ◆   ◆

'Let's see if we can catch the last train home,' said Dixon as they stepped on to the platform at Manchester Piccadilly. He looked at his watch: 5.15 p.m.

'That's the 8.27,' replied Sexton, 'and it only goes as far as Temple Meads.'

'You can go straight home and I'll get a cab.'

'Where first then?'

'Green Tree Court.'

'Not the police station?'

'Sod that.'

The taxi dropped them outside an almost new care home on the outskirts of Cheadle. Light brown brickwork with green roof tiles and huge fish tanks in the entrance hall. Purpose built, certainly. They were even offered tea or coffee and a cake while they waited for the duty manager.

'Inspector Dixon?'

'Yes.'

'Sarah Evans, I'm the senior nurse on duty.' The dark blue uniform and name badge confirmed it.

'I understand that you were able to identify Denise Marks from the *Manchester Daily Post* yesterday?'

'Leanne, our receptionist, spotted it first. It's definitely her.'

'How well did you know her?'

'Quite well. She'd been living here since we opened.'

'When was that?'

'Two years ago. We're not fully occupied yet. She was one of our first residents.'

'Can we see her room?'

'Er, yes. Follow me.'

A long, wide corridor led past dining rooms, bathrooms, and open bedroom doors. 'She liked the privacy down this end,' said Sarah, stopping outside the last door on the right. 'And she had no mobility problems.'

'What problems did she have?' asked Dixon.

'None, to be honest.'

'Has anyone else been here?'

'No.'

It looked just like a room at the Premier Inn, were it not for the hospital bed and red alarm cord. A flat screen TV stood on built-in furniture, all of it brand new.

'Just clothes in the drawers and a few dresses in the wardrobe. That's all she had here, except make up and toiletries,' said Sarah.

'What about the bedside table?'

'That's private.'

Sexton stepped forward and opened the drawers.

'What's in here?' asked Dixon, pointing to a door on his left.

'The en suite.'

En suite was an understatement. Marble tiled wet room did it justice.

'It's like a five star hotel,' said Sexton, gazing in. He handed Dixon a small box with a flip top lid.

'What's this?' he asked.

'Spare dentures.'

'That's exactly what we are. A five star hotel, with care on hand,' said Sarah.

'Did you never wonder what she was doing here, if she was otherwise fit?' asked Dixon, opening the bathroom cupboards to reveal nothing more exciting than shampoo and toothpaste.

'Not really. Maybe it was the company. For some that's priceless.'

'What about these photographs?' asked Sexton.

'I don't know who they are. She had no family, as far as I'm aware.'

'Bring them,' said Dixon. 'And how did she afford it?'

'I never asked. It's not something you . . .' Sarah's voice tailed off. Dixon was sucking his teeth.

'Can we have the address of her flat, please?'

Eton Drive, Cheadle. Four blocks of modern, purpose built flats, each on three floors with bay windows and black and white timber gables. Victorian to the casual observer, and hidden by landscaped gardens and conifers.

'Nice.'

'Very,' said Dixon, looking up. 'It's the garden flat, so it must be that one. See if you can see anything.'

Sexton squeezed between the wall and the bushes along the front of the building, peering in the windows. 'The blinds are down.'

Dixon pressed the entry phone buzzer marked 'Deliveries' and waited. Nothing. Then he began pressing them all in turn until one crackled.

'Yes.'

'Police. Can you let us in, please?'

He got no reply, but the lock buzzed and he wrenched the door open.

'They're trusting,' said Sexton.

'Or stupid.'

The light in the entrance hall came on automatically. Flat 2 on Dixon's left had ignored the buzzer and the lights were off behind the frosted glass pane in the front door, so he gave them the benefit of the doubt. The rest of the flats, apart from Denise's, were up the stairs, which cast a shadow across her front door. Dixon only noticed that it was open when he was standing right in front of it. He looked at Sexton and pointed to the lock, the inner latch hanging off a large splinter of wooden door frame by one screw.

He put on a pair of latex gloves, turning to check that Sexton was doing the same. Then he pushed open the front door. He paused to give his eyes a chance to adjust to the gloom, before tiptoeing along the corridor into an open plan living room.

The torch on his iPhone was enough to confirm the room was clear. Sexton switched on the light.

'Furniture would be traditional,' muttered Dixon, sliding his phone back into his pocket.

'It's a sofa bed.'

'Which makes all the difference. Still, it's more than I had for a while.'

'No TV either.' Sexton pushed open a door to his right. 'The kitchen. Never touched by the looks of it.'

Dixon peered over his shoulder. 'There's no kettle, nothing.'

'Probably ate at the care home. I would. Did you see the menu?'

'Check the bedrooms.'

Dixon walked over to the window and fumbled for the cord behind the floor to ceiling curtains, pulling them open to reveal patio doors, the key still in the lock. 'More of a courtyard flat than a garden flat,' he said, listening to the click of Sexton's heels on the laminate flooring. They stopped when he reached the carpet in the hall outside the bedrooms, to be replaced by the opening of doors and the flicking of light switches.

'There's a bog roll in the loo. Nothing else. And no furniture at all in either bedroom,' said Sexton, walking back into the living room.

Dixon turned to the only other pieces of furniture in the flat: a small table up against the wall and one office chair.

'Must've been an iMac,' said Sexton. 'That's a wireless keyboard and a Magic Mouse.'

'Someone beat us to it.'

'Looks like it.'

Dixon leaned over and looked under the table. 'They didn't even bother to take the power cable.'

'And I thought my garden was low maintenance,' said Sexton, looking out of the window.

'She liked her conifers,' replied Dixon, on all fours now, under the table. He slid a small whiteboard out from between the table leg and the wall.

'What've you got?' asked Sexton.

One side of the whiteboard was blank, so he turned it over to reveal a sequence of letters and numbers. He passed it up to Sexton and then crawled out from under the table.

'It's just like the ones you found at Butler's place.'

Dixon took his phone out of his pocket, switched it to camera mode and then zoomed in on the code. 'Three should do it,' he said, checking the code was visible in the photographs. 'Butler had a list and crossed them out, all except the last one. Denise used a whiteboard and rubbed the others out. But, what the hell are they?'

'Passwords of some sort?'

'To what?'

Sexton shrugged his shoulders. 'Did they know each other then? Butler and Denise.'

'We'd better find out.' Dixon unfolded a piece of paper he had taken out of his pocket and held it next to the whiteboard. 'This is a copy of the Butler list. There's no match,' he said, shaking his head.

'It must be significant, though, mustn't it?'

'It isn't if we don't find out what it is.' Dixon gestured to the whiteboard in Sexton's right hand. 'Put that back, will you? Behind the rear leg, facing the wall, so it looks like it slid down the back.'

'Shall I call it in?' asked Sexton, straightening his coat as he followed Dixon towards the front door of the flat.

'We'll do it from a phone box on the way to the station. Anonymous tip off.'

'Eh?'

'I don't want them to know we've been here.'

'Who?'

'If I knew that . . .' Dixon rolled his eyes as he tapped out a text message to Janice.

OK to tell GMP now. On way to station. Will catch up with you tomorrow. ND

◆　◆　◆

It took a minute or so standing in the queue at the taxi rank outside Bristol Temple Meads for Dixon to realise that the flashing lights and hooting horn were coming from his own Land Rover on the far side of the short stay car park. He ran across, jumping over the puddles, and climbed in the passenger door. He leaned over to kiss Jane, sitting in the driver's seat, but pulled up short when he noticed the look on her face.

'What's the matter?'

'It was a drug overdose.'

'Oh shit, Jane.'

'I'm fine, really.' She switched the engine on.

'You don't look it.'

'I wish I'd never met her now.'

'No, you don't.'

'If I'd never gone looking for her . . .' She leaned forward, her forehead on the steering wheel.

Dixon put his arm around her, but said nothing. He just sat there, one arm round Jane and the other round Monty, who had jumped over into the front of the Land Rover.

'Does it make a difference?' she asked, turning her head towards him.

'To me?'

Jane nodded. 'To know my mother was a druggie.'

'No, it bloody well doesn't. And besides, Sonia was just the woman who gave birth to you. Your mother lives in Worle with your father and an overweight cat. They're your real family.'

Jane smiled. 'And you.'

'I think she's talking to you, old chap,' replied Dixon, turning to Monty.

'I'm talking to both of you.'

They kissed, sheltered from prying eyes by the rain pouring down the windscreen.

'Well, me certainly. I can't speak for him.' Dixon smiled. 'He's very particular.'

◆ ◆ ◆

A long day, a short night and an early start. Jane had wanted to talk and there was no way he was going to let her down, getting to bed just after two in the end. A small glass of Pinot Grigio – Jane had drunk the rest of the bottle – and a screening of *A Shot in the Dark*. Dixon had thought it might cheer her up, but Jane talked all the way through it until she finally fell asleep on the sofa, her feet resting on Monty.

Dixon had covered them both with a blanket, marvelling at the number of different ways Jane had been able to say the same thing over and over again, although it had become a bit slurred by the end. Then he crept upstairs to bed, spending ten minutes staring at the photograph of the code on his phone, before falling asleep himself.

The next thing he knew his alarm was going off. He tiptoed down the stairs to find Jane watching Monty from the kitchen window as he wandered along the hedge in the field behind the cottage.

'You all right?'

'Bit of a headache.' Jane rubbed her eyes and sighed. 'I've decided I'm glad I found her, just in time to meet her. But I've lost nothing, so that's an end of it.'

'At least you know.'

'It's satisfied my curiosity, if nothing else. And now I can forget it. Her.' Jane frowned. 'It.'

'Why don't you take the day off?' Dixon flicked the kettle on. 'Call it compassionate leave.'

'There's no need.'

'I'll authorise it.'

'You're not my line manager.'

'I'm your superior officer, Sergeant.'

Jane pulled him towards her and kissed him. 'I love it when you try to pull rank.'

'I'm not pulling—'

'You'd better let him in before he scratches a hole in that door,' interrupted Jane, picking up Monty's food bowl. 'I'll feed him while you make the coffee.'

Dixon sighed.

Jane put Monty's food bowl on the floor. 'Just one last thing, then I won't mention it again,' she said, raising her voice over the sound of the metal food bowl clattering on the tiles.

'What?'

'You will come to the funeral with me, won't you?'

Chapter Twenty-Two

'Where the hell have you been?'

'Manchester.'

DCI Lewis held open the door of his office. 'In here. Now.'

Dixon trudged in and pulled a chair out from in front of the desk.

'Don't sit down. You won't be staying.' Lewis threw the file he had been carrying on to his desk. 'What are you playing at?'

'You've lost me, Sir.'

'You're supposed to be leading the Major Investigation Team in the hunt for Horan, and instead you're racing about all over the place.'

'My time is better spent—'

'No, it isn't. You're leading the team. Let them do the legwork.'

Dixon closed his eyes and began counting to ten.

'Who are you trying to catch, Horan or The Vet?' snapped Lewis. He was standing with his back to Dixon, looking out of the window.

'We've had this conversation before.'

Lewis sat down and leaned back in his chair. 'This isn't about The Vet.'

'Yes, it is. He left a body on our patch, don't forget.'

Lewis sighed.

'And Horan is more than a copycat,' continued Dixon. 'He's getting inside information from somewhere.'

'What about the witness protection officer?'

'She led us to the body on Exmoor. And someone got to her flat before we did and pinched her computer.'

'Just like Butler.' Lewis was leaning forward now, both elbows on his desk with his chin resting on his hands. 'Sit down,' he muttered, shaking his head.

Dixon did as he was told.

'And you found nothing?'

'A six grand a month care home and a posh but empty flat. That and a password for something, but we're buggered without the computer.'

'So, a counter corruption officer wasn't a bad shout?'

'There must've been someone on the inside all along. That's the only way The Vet could've stayed hidden for so long. And got clean away.'

'I wonder what became of the Carters?' asked Lewis.

'There's never been a DNA match.'

'There's DNA?'

'A covert sample from Michael, apparently.'

'Have we cross-checked it with the samples from the barn?'

'You got any eggs?' asked Dixon.

'Eh?'

'You could teach me to suck them at the same time.'

'Sorry,' replied Lewis, smiling.

'They don't match.'

'Can't say I'm surprised.'

'It doesn't match with the partial sample thought to be from The Vet either.'

'Look, I know what you're like, how you work, but Deborah Potter doesn't.' Lewis was pointing at Dixon with a Bic biro. 'As far as she's concerned you're leading the MIT, so you'd better get on with it, sharp-ish, before she puts someone else in over your head.'

'Yes, Sir.'

'What about Janice?'

'Can you leave her on Denise Marks for the time being? I don't want Manchester thinking we're giving it a high priority.' Dixon winced. 'That sounds awful, doesn't it?'

'I know what you meant,' said Lewis. 'They'll know by now though, if they've been to the care home.'

'Maybe not.'

'Well, that's your problem. Just accept this bit of friendly advice: get up there and at least make it look as though you're leading that team.'

◆ ◆ ◆

Dixon spent the rest of the morning in meetings with the house to house team leader, the crime scene coordinator and the scientific support manager. Then he spent an hour reading the call logs and flicking through the various witness statements that had been taken. Multiple sightings by well intentioned members of the public, all of which had been followed up, statements taken and entered on the computer system by the civilian support staff.

Another hour had been spent updating the Policy Log and Investigation Plan, although he left out any reference to Denise Marks, other than a passing one when noting the body found in the shallow grave on Dunkery Beacon. The rest could go in Janice's records.

It was just the sort of administrative nightmare he hated and had always been determined to avoid, to the point of refusing promotion – or at least he would if and when it was offered. And now he found himself leading a Major Investigation Team, albeit a reduced one. He shook his head, reached over and took his mug off the copy of the Major Incident Room Standardised Administrative Procedures manual he had been using as a coaster. Then he spat on the cover and used a tissue to wipe away the coffee stains. A few well placed yellow Post-it notes would make it look the part too.

Roger Poland's post mortem report on the body on Exmoor had not been terribly enlightening, although that was hardly his fault. The injury was consistent with known victims of The Vet – the same number of turns of the trephine indicative of a man of similar strength, identical positioning of the trephine catching the venous sinus. Too much information, as usual, prompting a turn to the conclusions at the back of the report.

The crime scene report on the barn, van and caravan ran to over a hundred pages, plus colourful appendices, and confirmed what Dixon already knew. He tapped out an email to Sexton asking him to get Dr Pearson to look at it and clicked 'send'. Seconds later the computer on the other side of the workstation pinged and Sexton looked up.

'Just get him to give it the once over. Unofficially. Let us know if anything leaps out at him.'

Sexton reached for his phone. 'The self-harming should give him something to work on.'

Dixon managed to watch some of the surveillance footage before a meeting of the whole team around the conference table in the larger meeting room on the second floor. He had brought them up-to-date with developments on Exmoor and in Manchester and found himself wondering whether any of them would be leaking the information that night – not to the press, but to someone else. He sucked his teeth as he glanced around the table. Dave, Mark and Louise may not be MIT material in the eyes of the powers-that-be, but he trusted them with his life.

There were some interesting theories, the best coming from the leather jacket, leaning back in his chair, chewing gum.

'Maybe The Vet was going to grass on the IRA and went into witness protection?'

It would explain a lot.

The silence had been deafening when Dixon had showed them the codes found on the scrap of paper at Butler's house and on the whiteboard at Denise Marks's flat. Not surprising though; Dixon had no idea either.

It was the 4 p.m. conference call he had been dreading. The email had arrived the night before, but it was the list of attendees Dixon had trouble with: DCS Potter – *fine*, DCS Douglas – *if you must*, DCI Chard – *twat*.

He joined the call late and got off to a bad start, even before Chard had opened his mouth.

'How far have you got with Horan?' snapped Potter.

'We've had lots of sightings, but nothing substantive yet.'

'You've updated the Policy Log?'

'Yes.'

'I'll look at it tomorrow. I'm coming down to Bridgwater in the afternoon. Will you be there?'

Thanks for the warning. Not bloody likely.

'Yes.' Dixon managed to stifle a sigh.

'I gather you've been to Manchester again?'

'Who told you that?'

'I did,' said Douglas.

'Yes, we went back.'

'Why?' asked Potter.

Dixon was sitting in meeting room 2, the only option if he wanted a bit of privacy. And he did. He put his feet up on the chair opposite and leaned back. 'It turns out the charred body on Exmoor belonged to a retired witness protection officer. Police Sergeant Denise Marks.'

'Greater Manchester Police?'

'Yes,' said Douglas. 'And you can imagine our surprise when we get to her care home to find that officers from Avon and Somerset have already been there. I thought we were supposed to be cooperating on this, and instead we're made to look like a right bunch of bloody idiots.'

'What did you find?' Potter sounded unnaturally calm.

'Nothing.'

'And what did you find when you broke into her flat?' Douglas again.

'We didn't. Someone had beaten us to it and taken her computer.'

'And you expect us to believe that?' Chard this time, sticking his oar in.

'Yes, I bloody well do.' Dixon sat up. 'Just ask yourself who got there first, given that we didn't notify Greater Manchester Police until we were on the train home.'

Silence.

Potter blinked first. 'Who?'

'Someone who knew Denise Marks had bought a train ticket at Manchester Piccadilly and that she was dead.'

'And who's that?' asked Douglas.

'I don't know,' replied Dixon. 'Yet.'

'But, you still think The Vet and Horan are connected?' asked Potter.

'Yes, I do.'

'And I suppose you're gonna catch both of them.' Chard's sneer was obvious even down the phone line. 'GMP gets nowhere in twenty years and you're going to waltz in and—'

'I'm sorry,' interrupted Dixon, tapping on the desk. 'Someone's booked the meeting room. I'm going to have to go, I'm afraid.'

'I've emailed the report to Dr Pearson,' said Sexton as Dixon sat down at the workstation opposite. 'He's going to look at it overnight and get back to us tomorrow.'

'Have you looked at the surveillance yet?'

'Just the stills.'

'Anything?'

'Not really,' replied Sexton. 'None of the DNA is matching up either. We've checked Denise Marks and the body on the moor against Michael Carter and the partial from The Vet. Nothing. It's definitely Horan at the barn though; there's a familial match with his kids. And he has a history of mild self-harm. His GP records have come through, although they're pretty thin.'

'Where are they?'

'They're being scanned on to the system now.'

Dixon spent the rest of the afternoon watching the surveillance footage, the boredom broken only briefly by what turned out to be a false alarm. Multiple patrol cars were despatched to the cafe at Brean Down, the motorcyclist turning out to be the National Trust warden.

It was just before 5 p.m. when Jane sat down on the corner of Dixon's workstation. She waited for a few minutes and then waved her hand in front of the screen. 'I thought you were asleep.'

'Don't tempt me.'

'I'm off.'

Dixon looked at his watch. 'Yeah, me too, I think. Ring me if anything comes up, Jonny. All right?'

'Yes, Sir.'

'How have you been today?' asked Dixon, smiling at Jane.

'Fine.'

'Fancy a walk on the beach?'

'I was going to do Tesco's.'

'Sod that. We'll get a takeaway.'

◆ ◆ ◆

Dixon sat down on an old tree stump opposite the wreck of the SS *Nornen* and threw Monty's ball towards the waves that were rolling in no more than fifty yards away. Monty reached the ball before it got wet, but dropped it on the way back, distracted by some foul smelling seaweed or a rotting fish carcass.

'Any news on your mother?'

'Someone from Social Services rang. The funeral will probably be the end of next week or the following week even.'

'Who will organise it?'

'They will. There's no one else, apparently, and I don't count.'

Jane sat down next to him and Dixon put his arm around her. 'How was work?'

'Not too bad today.'

'Which counts as a good day?'

'You got it.' Jane forced a smile. 'How are you getting on with the MIT?'

'I got a friendly earwigging from Lewis about not doing it all myself.'

'What did I tell you? You're running a team.'

'Of people I don't know.'

'You haven't got the patience for all that management crap anyway, and you certainly can't delegate.'

'Thank you, Sergeant.'

'My pleasure.' Jane smiled, her first real smile for days. 'Let's walk along to the Sundowner for some chips. We've got time. It's open till nine and light till eightish now.'

'Yes, OK,' replied Dixon, turning up his nose. 'I think dogs have been pissing on this tree stump anyway.'

'Monty did.' Jane grinned.

'You could've said.'

'Why d'you think I sat this side?'

Two hours later they were sitting in the Red Cow, Dixon watching Jane ordering the drinks at the bar: a beer for him and a gin and tonic for her. The tide had come in while they were eating their fish and chips, so they'd had to walk back to Berrow Church along the road. He made a mental note to check the tide tables in future and was looking in the App Store on his iPhone when Jane sat down in front of him.

'What're you looking for?'

'Tide tables.'

'There's a free app,' replied Jane. 'I've got it on my phone.'

'Well, why didn't you—?'

'Why didn't I what?'

'Never mind.' Dixon took a large swig of beer. 'I tell you what then, clever clogs, tell me what this is.' He opened 'Photos' on his iPhone and showed Jane the picture of the code written on the whiteboard at Denise Marks's flat. 'And this.' He unfolded a piece of paper. 'I found this on the floor underneath DCS Butler's desk at his house.'

'Is he the one who disappeared?'

'Yes.'

Jane placed the phone on the table next to the piece of paper and compared the two. 'I know what they are,' she said, taking a large swig from her glass. 'Get another round in. And you can make mine a double.'

◆ ◆ ◆

'Well?' Dixon was holding Jane's gin and tonic just out of reach.

'D'you want the full version or the Noddy version for Luddites?'

'The Noddy version first.'

'What percentage of the internet d'you reckon is indexed in Google?'

'I dunno. Seventy?'

'Four.'

'Really?'

Jane nodded. 'That's the "surface web", the bit that's publicly available. The rest is known as the "deep web". Some of it is private networks, NHS, government, business, stuff like that. Then there's the "dark net". That's the stuff that's deliberately hidden because they're up to no good.'

'That's the course you went on: Child Protection and the Internet?'

'Welcome to my world.' Jane leaned forward and took the glass from Dixon's hand. 'The dark net is only accessible using a special web browser known as TOR and the URLs are hidden. The URL is the—'

'Web address?'

'That's right. The Uniform Resource Locator. Such and such dot com, that sort of thing. Only on the dark net they're a random mix of letters and numbers.'

'Just like these?'

'Cheers.' Jane took a swig of the drink Dixon had bought her. 'They're constantly changing too.'

'So they can't be found by the likes of you and me?'

'Right. Which explains why they've been crossed out as you go down the list.'

'Cross out the old one and write in the new one . . . or rub it out on a whiteboard.' Dixon smiled. 'And where d'you find the URL for a dark net site?'

'You don't. There's no search engine for dark net sites. No Google. You have to know where they are.'

Chapter Twenty-Three

Dixon folded up the piece of paper and put it in his pocket. Then he picked up his phone. 'This'll be the latest one, on the whiteboard.'

'Won't whoever it is just change it?' asked Jane.

'Let's hope they think there's no need. After all, they've got her computer.'

'What are we waiting for then?'

They stood up as one. Their empty glasses banged down on the table, waking Monty up with a start. Less than sixty seconds later Jane had switched on the kettle and Dixon his computer. It was one advantage of living opposite the pub.

'What now?' Dixon was sitting with his computer on the arm of the sofa and Monty curled up on his lap.

'Swap.' Jane sat down next to Dixon and passed him a mug of coffee. He placed the laptop on her knees.

She opened Internet Explorer and then placed the cursor in the address bar at the top.

'I thought you said you had to use a special browser?'

'There's a way you can access dark net sites from a normal one. Sometimes it works, sometimes it doesn't. D'you want me to explain it?'

'Don't bother.'

'What's the address?'

'2hr9458nv032ye23.' Dixon was reading aloud from the photograph on his phone while Jane typed in the letters and numbers. Then she added '.onion' on the end.

'What the bloody hell's dot onion?'

'It's the extension, the dark net equivalent of dot com.'

'Sorry I asked.'

'TOR is The Onion Router,' continued Jane. 'All of the internet traffic is routed through at least three different computers so it can never be traced. It's supposed to be like the layers of an onion, which is why it's called The Onion Router and the domains end with dot onion. Get it?'

'If you say so.'

Then she added '.to' in the address bar and hit 'enter'. 'Some dark net sites disable it, so we'll see.'

'What does that mean?'

'Bugger,' muttered Jane. 'Tor2web error: sorry we couldn't serve the page you requested,' she said, reading aloud. 'It may mean the site's offline or they've disabled Tor2web. At least we know your ISP isn't blocking access to Hidden Services.'

'Some do?'

Jane nodded. 'Nothing for it. We'll have to download the Tor Browser bundle.'

'Will I need a tin hat?' Dixon raised his eyebrows.

'No.'

'What about taping over the camera?'

'It's not all bad.' Jane rolled her eyes.

'Just most of it?'

'Certainly the bit I deal with.'

Once the site opened, she scrolled down to Tor Browser, clicked on it and then clicked 'download'.

'There's no going back now.'

'I needed a new laptop anyway.'

'It'll be fine,' Jane said, clicking 'run'. She crossed herself and began muttering the words of the Lord's Prayer.

'Now you're taking the piss, aren't you?'

Dixon tried to follow the clicks as Jane went through the set up sequence.

'D'you want your computer used as an exit relay?'

'What's that when it's at home?' he asked.

'Traffic goes into the onion network, bounces around various computers and then out again to the site you want to visit. That last computer is the exit relay. We can trace that one if we've got the site you visited.'

'So, other people will be visiting sites via my computer?'

'Yes. Once you join the network you're using other people's computers and they're using yours.'

'No bloody fear.'

'I thought not.'

'How many people are doing this then?'

'Millions are accessing the deep web every day without really realising it. Not so many use the dark net, but enough . . . Too many.'

'Can you uninstall it when we've got what we need?'

Jane smiled. 'Here we go.' She read aloud, 'Congratulations. This browser is configured to use TOR.'

'What now?'

'Give me that URL again.'

Jane tapped 2hr9458nv032ye23 into the address bar as Dixon read it to her from his phone. Then she added '.onion' on the end and hit 'enter'. 'It can be slow because you're being routed through the other computers.'

'This slow?'

'It's not unusual. It'd be faster in the big cities where there are more computers in the network.'

'Another advantage of living in the country,' muttered Dixon.

'Here we go,' said Jane. 'It's a forum. PhpBB. It's a free download, probably hosted on a virtual server, with the traffic routed through TOR.'

'You're showing off now, aren't you?'

Jane grinned.

'You'd have thought they'd hide it behind a login screen, at least, wouldn't you?' asked Dixon.

'They probably think there's no need. And there isn't, really. After all, who's going to find it?'

'You mean apart from us?'

'You know what I mean.'

'Look, look.' Dixon jabbed his finger at the bottom of the screen. 'In total there is one user online.'

'That's us. One guest, based on active users over the past five minutes.'

'They'll know we've been on the site though?'

'From the server logs,' replied Jane.

'The statistics are interesting,' said Dixon. 'Total posts 176; total topics 1; total members 3; our newest member: DeniseM. It doesn't say when she joined.'

'It'll be in her Member Profile, and it should tell you next to her posts as well,' replied Jane. 'Most users ever online was three on Thursday, March 22, 2.05 a.m. That's all of them.'

'And it's the night before she travelled down.' Dixon shook his head. 'And look at the last post. The early hours of this morning, by Siegfried.'

'Isn't he a character from Wagner?'

'He's also a character from *All Creatures Great and Small*.'

'About the vets?'

'That's it. Let's have a look then.'

Jane clicked on 'Your First Forum' to reveal the topic 'Shit Happens', started by author Tristan. She looked at Dixon. *'All Creatures Great and Small?'*

'Siegfried's brother.'

'What d'you want to do now?'

'Read it. Can you copy it first? Get a screenshot of every page?'

'I can download something that will copy the whole site.'

'Will it take long?'

'Shouldn't do.' Jane was scrolling down the forum thread. 'It's not a big site, and there aren't any photo . . . oh shit.' She turned the laptop towards Dixon. 'There are photographs.'

'That's Harry.' Dixon gritted his teeth. 'Before and after.' The look on Harry's face, the fear in his eyes, had haunted him since that morning in the mud. But this was different. Worse. Harry was fully conscious, his eyes wider, full of tears and focused on something behind the camera. The trephine, probably.

'There's another.' Jane scrolled down to reveal a photograph of a man lying in a shallow grave in the sand, his hands reaching out towards the cameraman. His head was tipped to the left, the trickle of blood dripping off the front of his temple on to the sand beneath him.

'David Cobb.'

'Still alive by the looks of things.'

'I've seen enough.' Dixon stood up. 'What can I do?'

'Make another coffee?'

'This is pretty grim stuff.' Jane grimaced as Dixon leaned over the back of the sofa a few minutes later and handed her a mug. 'It looks like Siegfried is The Vet and Tristan the copycat, reading between the lines.'

'What makes you say that?'

'This bit: "I did what I did and got away with it. I got lucky. But things are different now. There's DNA and no one on the payroll."'

'Do they know each other then?' Dixon was standing behind Jane, peering over her shoulder.

'Definitely. You need to read this.'

'How much longer to copy it?'

'Not long,' replied Jane. 'It reads like Tristan is taunting Siegfried. He tells him what he's going to do and when. Then posts him photographs of it.'

'The modern day equivalent of The Vet's Polaroids.' Dixon sighed. 'Scroll down to the bottom of the thread.'

Dixon was standing in front of her now, with his back to the television, watching her eyes darting from side to side as she read the forum posts. She looked up.

'There's going to be another murder.'

'When?'

'Today.' Jane's eyes widened. 'You get a mention.'

'Read it out.'

'"That wanker from the furniture factory is next. They need to know who they're fucking dealing with. They need to be taught a lesson." Then the next post is from Siegfried.'

'When?'

'Early hours of this morning. "Just leave it, will you? Denise is dead and they've found him. Dixon is getting too close, and we really don't need this. Just calm down. You need to get out. Spain or somewhere. Have you got money?"'

Jane went silent, her eyes still darting from side to side.

'Read it out,' snapped Dixon.

'"Too late. I've got him."' Jane looked up. 'It's timed just after six this evening: "Going to cremate this fucker in his own bloody factory. The furniture should do it" – then there's a smiley face – "What say you?" That's the last post. There's no reply from Siegfried.'

'Call it in,' said Dixon, putting on his coat. 'And finish copying that website.'

'Where are you going?'

'Bailey and Whyte on the Walrow Industrial Estate. It's the only furniture factory I can think of.'

'Didn't they go bust?'

'They went into administration, but they're trying to sell it. The Administrator took the contract away from Horan and gave it to Harry Lucas. Big one too, I shouldn't wonder.' Dixon checked his phone and snatched his car keys off the side.

Jane had dialled 999 and was holding her phone to her ear. 'Police, please.' She looked over her shoulder towards the kitchen. 'Be careful,' she shouted, but the back door had already slammed shut.

◆ ◆ ◆

Dixon accelerated hard along Brent Street, heading south towards the A38, his phone clamped to his ear.

'Yes, Sir.'

'Where are you, Jonny?'

'The chippie in Highbridge. I just stopped on my way home.'

'The code is a website address on the dark net. Horan's been posting photos of his murders online. He's in the Bailey and Whyte factory now with another victim.'

'I'm on my way.'

'Don't go in until I get there.'

Sexton had already rung off. Dixon dropped his phone on to the passenger seat as he turned across the central reservation and out on to the southbound A38. The car behind him braked sharply and flashed his lights. If he was hooting his horn too, Dixon couldn't hear it over the roar of his old diesel engine.

He allowed his speed to drop as he approached the motorway roundabout and then accelerated hard on the long straight towards the roundabout at the entrance to the industrial estate. Bailey and Whyte was on the far side, its huge units backing on to the River Brue.

He flicked his headlights to full beam as he raced along the quiet service road, all of the offices and warehouses on either side quiet and dark. An industrial estate at night was a grim place, but there would be few pedestrians to worry about, maybe just the odd boy racer burning rubber in a souped up Ford Fiesta. Dixon winced. Knowing his luck, he'd get pulled over himself.

He left tyre tracks in the soft grass verge of yet another round-about and sped along Commerce Way. The large factory loomed out of the darkness ahead, the entrance lit by streetlights and the roof by his headlights. He screeched to a halt in front of the large steel gates at the entrance, jumped out of his Land Rover and looked in the window of Sexton's BMW.

'Oh shit.'

'He said he was going in. Told me to wait here.'

Dixon spun round to see a small man in a blue raincoat holding a spaniel on a lead.

'We walk along the Brue.'

'Is there another way in?'

'At the far end of the complex,' replied the man. 'There's a side gate just there. That's where the young man went, through there and in that door.' He was pointing to a small door at the side of two huge steel doors, large enough for a lorry to back into the warehouse.

'Wait here.' Dixon opened the side gate and began walking across the car park, breaking into a run as he neared the open door.

A single gunshot was amplified by the steel fabricated units, the echo tinny but recognisable all the same.

Dixon sprinted back to his Land Rover.

'Have you got a phone?'

'Yes.'

'Dial 999 and tell them where you are; tell them you heard a gunshot.'

The man started fumbling in his pocket.

'Then get clear,' continued Dixon, climbing into his Land Rover. He started the engine, put on his seatbelt and then reversed along Commerce Way. Fifty yards should do it. The gates would be no match for a Land Rover.

He slipped it into first gear and stamped on the accelerator, crashing into the gates at almost thirty miles an hour. The chain snapped and the gates dropped off their hinges, crashing to the ground. Into second gear now, foot down hard on the accelerator, Dixon aimed at the middle of the large steel doors, his Land Rover smashing into them and punching a hole clean through.

Once inside the loading bay, Dixon swerved sharply to avoid a body lying on the concrete floor, hitting another man a glancing blow with the front wing of the Land Rover. The man fell down the side of the Land Rover as the front crashed into a stack of chairs, which fell across the bonnet and roof.

Dixon jumped out and ran over to the body lying on the ground, bending down and picking up a handgun as he did so. He rolled the body over. Jonny Sexton had a single bullet hole in the middle of his forehead, his body limp and lying in a puddle of his own blood.

It was then that Dixon spotted the second victim, slumped forwards with his hands tied behind him, a small pool of blood seeping into the concrete floor at his feet. The hole in his forehead had not been made by a bullet. More blood was pouring down his neck, turning his white shirt red to match the tie under his grey suit.

Footsteps behind him. Dixon spun round – too late.

'You see? And I'll have my gun back if you don't—'

The last word of the sentence was drowned out by a loud crack on the back of Dixon's skull, just behind his right ear. He saw nothing except perhaps a swinging arm. He couldn't tell, his vision blurred for a reason his mind was too slow to comprehend. A sharp pain hit him, but not in his head, in his ear. He tried to reach up.

'He's broken my fucking wrist!' A second voice behind him.

The word 'wrist' made it through the fog, but what came after that was muffled by another crack. No pain from this one though, only darkness.

Chapter Twenty-Four

Jane leaned back, allowing the water to wash the shampoo from her hair. Funny how things turn out. She always thought someone would be worrying about her when she went out to work, not the other way around.

Was that a knock at the door? She couldn't tell over the noise of the running water and Monty barking. It was either the door or something on the TV had set him off. Or perhaps he was sitting on the window ledge again and someone had walked past the cottage with a dog. She waited. More barking, a pause – Monty must have stopped to draw breath – then a knock and yet more barking.

She turned off the shower, thanking her lucky stars whoever it was hadn't knocked five minutes earlier, and reached for Dixon's bathrobe. Jehovah's Witnesses? An Avon lady? Dixon said he had left that catalogue out on the doorstep.

There's not another bloody election going on, is there?

Monty was standing at the front door, his paws up on the wire cage Dixon had fitted to catch the post, a figure visible through the frosted glass pane.

Jane opened the door. She noticed the tears streaming down Louise's face first, even before she realised who it was standing there in front of her.

'What's going on?'

'You'd better come.' Louise's car was behind her out in the road, the engine still running.

Jane braced herself for something bad. Something very bad. 'Tell me.'

'There's a fire.'

'Where?'

'Bailey and Whyte, the furniture place in Highbridge.'

'That's where Nick went.'

'Jonny Sexton went in. There was a gunshot and Nick went in after him.'

'What about the fire brigade?'

'It's too intense. The furniture's burning.'

'They haven't gone in?' Screaming now.

Louise shook her head. 'They can't.'

Jane turned and dashed up the stairs, reappearing less than a minute later in jeans and a pullover, her wet hair straggling behind her. She stamped her bare feet into a pair of trainers on the landing and ran down the stairs, ignoring the laces trailing in her wake. A coat, snatched off the back of the kitchen door. Phone. Door keys.

'Right, let's go.'

Once in the car she tied her shoelaces and then checked the time as Louise raced out towards the A38, following the exact same route Dixon would have taken less than an hour earlier. She should have gone with him. There's no way she'd have let him go into that factory. Not alone. And a gunshot?

'Who said there was a gun?'

'There was a dog walker there who heard it.'

Armed Response! You call for Armed Response for fuck's sake!

They crossed the motorway roundabout without slowing down, the child's booster seat in the back of Louise's car sliding across and slamming into one of the doors, the sky ahead lit up bright orange.

'That's not . . .' Jane's voice tailed off.

'It's full of furniture,' replied Louise. 'I heard one of the fire officers say it would burn for days.'

'Days?' Jane glanced along Burnham Moor Lane off to her left. A small crowd was gathered on the motorway bridge watching the flames in the distance.

'It gets worse as you get nearer,' muttered Louise, 'although we've got the whole of Walrow sealed off now.'

'Anyone would think it was bloody Bonfire Night.'

Louise stopped at the police cordon at the entrance to the Walrow Industrial Estate and spoke to PC Cole. He ducked down and glanced across at Jane sitting in the passenger seat, then waved them through.

They raced past a Sky News van, which was first on the scene, but it wouldn't be long before the other outside broadcast news crews arrived. The white belly of a helicopter hovering overhead glowed orange.

Jane wasn't counting, but there must have been at least six ambulances parked along Commerce Way. Then came the fire engines, lines of them parked on either side. Another large crowd was gathered on the railway bridge off to the right, watching the flames climbing into the sky.

'We won't get much further,' said Louise. She slowed a hundred yards from the entrance to the factory, turned right and parked on the forecourt of South West Tyres.

Jane looked up at the factory. A line of conifers obscured all but the flames towering above them and four fire fighters on long ladders directing hoses on to the roof. She watched them disappear behind clouds of acrid black smoke, before appearing again as the smoke was carried away on the wind.

'There's Lewis.' Louise climbed out of her car, went round to the passenger side and opened the door.

Jane sat motionless, watching the flames, not even noticing Lewis striding across to the car with the Chief Fire Officer in tow, the white helmet the sign of his senior rank.

Lewis squatted down beside the car and looked up at Jane. 'There are twelve fire appliances here already and more on the way.' He glanced up at the CFO and nodded.

'I'm John Stewart, Fire OIC. We're doing everything we can. The Environment Agency are keeping the sluice gates shut so we can pump water from the River Brue, and we're trying to contain it at this end of the factory so we can go in.'

'Is he still in there?' Jane turned her head slowly, revealing the tears cascading down her cheeks.

Lewis nodded.

'I want to see,' said Jane, taking off her seatbelt.

'That'll be up to Fire OIC,' replied Lewis.

'I can show you where he went in,' said Stewart. 'But I can't let you get too close. It could collapse at any time.'

Jane stood up, feeling the full blast of the heat for the first time, over a hundred yards away and yet scorching, the roar and crackle of the flames drowning out the helicopter hovering overhead.

Louise put her arm around Jane and walked with her, Lewis just in front, more to be on hand to stop her if she tried anything stupid. Jane knew that.

They got no further than the entrance gates, knocked off their hinges by Dixon's Land Rover now over an hour ago. A ring of fire engines circled the end units, two of them with long ladders pouring water from above.

'Sections of the roof have collapsed, so we can get water in that way,' shouted Stewart.

'How long's it going to take?' asked Louise.

'We'll know more in an hour or so.'

Louise was holding Jane up now. She gestured to Lewis and together they helped her back towards the car and sat her down on a low wall. She looked up at the flames, climbing even higher into the sky now, if anything.

'Stay with her,' said Lewis.

'Yes, Sir,' replied Louise.

'As soon as I know any more I'll let you know.'

'He was going to ask me to marry him,' Jane mumbled.

'Really?' Louise sat down on the wall next to her and put her arm around Jane.

'He was getting there. I know he was.'

'Look, we don't know he's—'

Louise was cut short by a huge explosion that sent sparks high into the air. Jane looked up sharply, the whites of her eyes a mixture of red and orange.

'It must have been an oil tank or something.' Louise held her tight.

'First my mother and now this.'

'Your mother?'

'My birth mother. We found her a few weeks ago, met her twice, and now she's dead.'

'How?'

'Drug overdose.'

Jane sat motionless, not that she could have moved if she wanted to, with Louise's arm clamped around her waist. She watched the flames above the conifers, and more ladders now as two more appliances got into position. Louise watched the fire in the reflection in Jane's eyes, waiting for more tears to come, but they never did. And together they sat in silence, listening to the fire, the sirens, the helicopter, the pumps, all of it punctuated by explosions as the flames reached another oil tank or a gas bottle. Then a huge roar as part of the roof caved in.

'Here comes Lewis,' said Louise, shaking Jane. She looked up.

'They think they've got it contained this end.' Lewis was leaning over and shouting at them. 'The chemicals are all at the far end and if the flames get there we're going to have to start evacuating houses.'

'What about this end?' asked Louise.

'They're going to let it burn out.'

Jane could see Lewis's lips moving, and she could hear what he was saying too, but understanding it was beyond her.

'But Nick's in there, Sir,' shouted Louise.

Lewis nodded. 'I know.'

'But—'

'It's going to be a day, possibly two until engineers can go in and make it safe. Another two before we can get the bodies out.'

Much of what Lewis had been saying was going in one ear and out the other, but the word 'bodies' hit Jane like a sledgehammer. She fell forwards on to her knees and it took both of them to get her up.

'You'd better get her out of here, Louise,' said Lewis. 'Take her home. I'll ring if there's any news.'

'Yes, Sir.'

'Has she got family you can ring?'

'Leave her with me, Sir.'

'All right.'

Louise squatted down in front of Jane, holding her hands. 'We need to go, Jane.'

'Just take me home, will you?' She was looking at Louise, but her eyes had glazed over. She was on the beach with Nick, holding his hand as they strolled along the sand and refusing to let go when he tried to kick Monty's tennis ball, almost pulling him over in the process. She could hear the laughter, loud and clear, over the flames that had receded now, at least in her head.

'Are you ready?'

'I could murder a cigarette.' Something felt odd about that sentence, but Jane wasn't sure what it was.

'Wait here,' said Louise. 'You won't do anything stupid?'

'No.' And besides, Nick would expect her to look after Monty now anyway.

'C'mon then. We'd best go.' Louise returned holding a lit cigarette between her thumb and index finger. 'Here,' she said, handing it to Jane.

'Thanks.' Jane exhaled the smoke through her nose. 'I'll have this first. I don't want to smoke in your car.' Funny the things you think of at a time like this, she thought.

I'm not his *next of kin either.*

She stubbed the cigarette out on the wall and then dropped the butt down a drain.

'Let's go then.'

Louise was directed out of the industrial estate on another road, Commerce Way, now blocked by fire engines that had come from Bristol and Taunton, and they were crossing the motorway roundabout before the putrid smell of smoke cleared, even with the windows open. The orange glow was still visible in the wing mirrors, but at least the smell had gone.

'I can stay with you for a while, if you like,' said Louise.

'Thanks.'

'D'you want me to ring your parents?'

'Not until we know for sure.'

'What about his parents?'

'Maybe later.'

Louise parked on the pavement outside the cottage and waited while Jane tried to open the front door, but her hands were shaking too much to get the key in the lock.

'Here, give it to me.'

Louise opened the door, allowing Monty to jump out. They watched him circling, looking behind the parked cars, then up and down the road, before running back into the cottage with his tail clamped down.

'He's looking for Nick,' said Jane.

Chapter Twenty-Five

The first thing he became aware of was the pain – sharp and coursing up the right side of his head. He tasted blood. Then the coughing started.

Smoke. That's fucking smoke.

Dixon tried to open his eyes, but couldn't. His eyelids felt stuck together – congealed blood, probably. At least the power of rational thought was coming back. He dropped the gun in his right hand and tried to roll on to his back, but something was lying across his legs. Whatever it was, it wasn't heavy and he could move them. Just.

He rubbed his eyes. Then he opened them, blinking furiously, the smoke stinging worse than CS gas.

Dropped the gun?

He turned his head.

A revolver? Where the hell did that come from?

Then he saw Sexton's body lying under a pile of tables and chairs a few feet away. A neat hole in his forehead, the back of his head missing.

What's that noise? And where's that orange light coming from?

Then he remembered – where he was and how he'd got there – and it didn't take long to work out why he was still there, trapped under a pile of furniture with a gun in his hand. The same gun used to kill Sexton, no doubt.

A strong smell of petrol hit him, even over the acrid smoke that was tearing at the back of his throat and his eyes. He brought his right arm up and buried his face in the sleeve of his coat – anything for even a moment's relief from the smoke – finding the source of the petrol as he did so. His coat was soaked in it.

The flames were edging ever closer, so he wriggled out of his coat, rolled it up and threw it as far away from him as he could get it.

He looked around, searching for a way out. Several pallets of large wooden boxes had been pushed across the steel doors, blocking the way he had come in, and they were well alight, some of the boxes having burnt away to reveal their contents – small chests of drawers – more wood to add fuel to the fire. Behind him more flames. The tyres of his Land Rover were burning too, the flames getting far too close to the fuel tank for comfort.

The large door to the factory floor itself was blocked by a forklift truck, the pallets sitting on the forks ablaze. More flames were visible behind it, devouring several huge stacks of half-finished tables and chairs. The lathes and other machines were burning too, the fire no doubt powered by the oil. And more petrol probably.

Flames were licking along the underside of the roof, seeking out anything flammable to help them on their way. Smoke was rolling along ahead of it, billowing down the walls and meeting the smoke coming up from the inferno below.

Offices on a mezzanine floor on the far side of the factory floor collapsed with a loud crash sending paper into the air to dance above the flames, before adding yet more fuel to the fire.

Sexton was dead, but what about the man in the chair? Dixon winced. A pile of chairs had fallen in between them, the fire racing along it. It had reached the man, burnt through his bonds, and he had fallen forwards into the flames. Behind him the pallets were catching fire one by one as the flames engulfed a metal staircase that led to another mezzanine floor above him, the offices not yet alight.

Using the staircase was out. The pallets beneath it were ablaze, sending flames roaring up through the treads, and it was glowing red already, but an office meant a window, surely? A way out.

Dying on a mountainside was one thing; he had accepted that risk, but a fire?

Fuck that.

Dixon rolled on to his front and pulled his legs up underneath him. Then he stood up, sending the chairs that had been lying across him crashing on to the concrete floor. There were not many – just enough to make it look as though they had fallen on him, knocking him unconscious.

Gits.

He snatched a red fire extinguisher off one of the steel columns holding up the mezzanine floor above him, pulled out the pin and turned the hose on himself. It was a powerful jet of water, but he didn't stop until his clothes and hair were saturated. He noticed a blue roller towel above a small sink against the wall behind his Land Rover, so he ripped out the towel, soaked it and wrapped it around his face and neck like a scarf.

Then he used the last of the water in the extinguisher to put out the fire on the Land Rover tyre directly below the fuel tank. That would buy him a bit of time.

He opened the driver's door, reached across and grabbed his phone from the passenger footwell. Then he jumped up on to the bonnet. From a standing position on the roof he would be able to jump up and reach the girders on the underside of the mezzanine floor, but he'd have only one go at it. Landing heavily back on the Land Rover roof rack might break an ankle. Or worse.

Balancing on the edge of the roof rack, he squatted down and looked up at the girders, focusing on the large beam that would take him hand over hand out to the front edge of the upper floor.

Shit!

He jumped down and ran across to the forklift truck, weaving in and out of the chairs and past his coat that was now alight on the floor. He was breathing through the wet towel over his nose and mouth and was crouching as low as he could. Dodging the flames, he snatched a pair of heavy duty gloves off the floor of the cab and then ran back to his Land Rover.

Back on the roof in a flash, he launched himself upwards, springing up as high as he could. He managed to catch hold of the girder with his right hand and hung on. A burning pain seared through his fingers, despite the gloves, but going back was no longer an option.

Moving hand over hand now along the girder, he made his way to the front of the mezzanine floor, dangling precariously above the burning remains of his Land Rover. Trying to ignore the pain from his hands, he pulled up and reached for the rail on the balustrade above.

Boxes of paper next to a photocopying machine on the mezzanine floor were alight, but his path to the door of the office was clear. Two loud bangs below startled him and he glanced to down to watch his Land Rover lurch to one side as the tyres blew out. The fuel tank would be next.

Time to go.

He pulled up again, reaching the next rail and getting his left foot on to the edge of the mezzanine floor. Then he climbed up and over the balustrade. He was directly above the inferno now and could feel the heat of the steel floor through the soles of his shoes. He pulled his wet sweater up over his head and ducked down to avoid the flames from the fire beneath him that were travelling up the walls and across the ceiling, seeking out electrical cables and air ducts, anything to help them on their way. Thick black smoke swirled in the air currents generated by the inferno.

One sharp kick and the office door flew open, then he sent the swivel chair through the window. The effect was immediate, the sudden rush of air fanning the fire. The carpet burst into flames, as did every piece of paper in the room. It wouldn't be long before the flame resistant sofa went too, and the fumes of that would kill him in seconds.

Only one thing for it.

The River Brue was below him now, but too far away to make the jump. He climbed up on to the window ledge and from a standing position was able to reach the flat roof. Smoke was billowing out of the window right in his face, so staying put and waiting for the fire brigade was not an option either. He took hold of the edge of the roof in both hands and pulled up, scrabbling up and over with his feet.

Factory roofs are dangerous places at the best of times. He knew that from his legal training, helping on two cases where employees had fallen through to their deaths. Stick to the edge: he remembered that from the inquests.

A large blast echoed in the unit beneath his feet. He heard the boom and felt the vibration, the last gasp of his old Land Rover, no doubt, the fuel tank having exploded. Then he saw his salvation at the corner of the building.

A drainpipe.

Seconds later he was on the ground, picking his way through the undergrowth along the River Brue behind the industrial estate, sirens competing with the roar of the fire and explosions, flickering blue lights with the orange glow. He turned at the sound of a sickening crash to watch part of the roof collapse, huge flames climbing into the night sky. Then ladders went up from fire engines in the car park at the back of the factory, spraying water on to the roof.

He arrived at a gap in the bushes and, leaving his gloves on, crawled down to the water's edge. He plunged his hands into the cold water and screamed – nothing could have prepared him for the pain that hit him. Then he turned and vomited into the water.

He stumbled on through the bushes, trying not to fall down the bank into the river. Having been saturated less than five minutes ago, his clothes were almost dry, but the water had done the trick. He had thrown the blue towel away, its job done, and could still feel the heat from the inferno behind him, even through the undergrowth.

He hesitated at a gap in the fence, slumping on to a tree stump in the undergrowth. Beyond it the car park, blue lights and sanctuary. He thought about Jonny Sexton lying dead on the concrete floor – the flames must have reached him by now. And the man who'd been tied to the chair – no name and yet already cremated.

No. The killers had thought he had been getting too close. Now they thought he was dead. And it would have to stay that way for the time being.

Then he passed out.

Chapter Twenty-Six

'I'd better ring his parents.'

'Lewis'll do it if you'd rather,' replied Louise.

Jane was sitting on the floor with Monty. He was licking the tears from her cheeks, but not keeping up with the stream cascading down. 'What time is it?'

'Ten.'

'They need to know tonight, before they see it on the news.' Jane was dialling the number when there was a knock at the door.

'I'll get it,' said Louise, jumping up. She stepped back to reveal DCI Lewis standing in the drizzle. He sighed.

'Well?' asked Jane, standing up.

'It's not good, I'm afraid.' Lewis stepped into the cottage. 'They still can't get in. Two tried from a side door on the factory floor, with breathing apparatus, but couldn't get into the loading bay past a forklift.'

'Could they see anything?'

Lewis thrust his hands deep into his pockets. He was staring at the floor. 'Two bodies.'

'Who?' screamed Jane.

'They couldn't see. They were burnt beyond . . .' Lewis's voice tailed off.

'Is that it?'

'They could only stay for a few seconds. The roof started falling in behind them.'

'What about the Land Rover?'

'Gone.' Lewis was shaking his head.

'What d'you mean gone?'

'Look, it's gone, Jane. All right?' He put his arms around her, turning his head to watch her sob into his shoulder. 'It's just gone.'

'Should we ring his parents?' whispered Louise.

'I'll do it,' mouthed Lewis, nodding his head, but making no sound.

'He shouldn't have gone in there,' gasped Jane, between sharp intakes of breath.

'His partner was in there and then a shot was fired. What would you have done?'

'The same.'

'It was Jonny Sexton who shouldn't have gone in there. But, once he had . . .'

'Nick had no choice,' said Louise.

'What were they doing there anyway?' asked Lewis.

Jane pulled away from him and picked up the laptop. 'You need to read this, Sir,' she said, opening the lid. 'Horan has been posting photos on a dark net bulletin board. Before and after each killing. He even gives the where and when before he does it. That's how Nick knew to go to the fac—' She took a deep breath. 'Sorry.' Then she ran upstairs, slamming the bedroom door behind her.

◆　◆　◆

A loud crash somewhere behind him; rain falling on his face. He opened his eyes and watched sparks climbing into the night sky. Then he got up and stumbled on along the river bank, the orange glow fading the further he got from the fire. He followed the fence until it became a brick wall at the bottom of some gardens. Just beyond that a path used by anglers opened up in front of him and, a few paces ahead, streetlights illuminated a tarmac path – the back entrance to Highbridge Railway Station.

He dropped on to a bench in the waiting area on Platform 2, sheltering from the drizzle – cold now, although that was almost a relief – and tried to take off the gloves. He grimaced. Just the right one would have to do, pulling it off slowly, bit by bit, and wincing with each small movement. Then, holding his phone in his gloved left hand, he tapped out a text message.

◆　◆　◆

Jane was lying on the bed, face down, sobbing into Dixon's pillow when her phone buzzed in her pocket. She rolled on to her back and pulled it out, staring in disbelief at the screen.

Under pavilion 20 mins Nx

She wiped the tears from her cheeks with her left hand, at the same time tapping out a reply with her right.

R u ok? Jx

She waited, her heart pounding in her ears and the back of her throat.

Fine. Got an eyebrow pencil I can borrow? Nx

She ran downstairs to find Lewis and Louise in the kitchen waiting for the kettle to boil. 'Look,' she screamed, holding her phone out towards them.

They both leaned forwards and peered at the screen, reading the exchange of text messages.

'Shit,' muttered Louise.

'How do we know they're from him?' asked Lewis.

'He's the only person I know who signs off his texts. Always does it, to me anyway,' replied Jane. 'I'm sure.'

'Yes, but someone would see that in your message centre.'

'Are you saying I shouldn't go?'

'No. Just that it might not be him.'

'I'll go with her, Sir,' said Louise.

'And you can watch from the seafront, Sir,' said Jane.

'All right.'

'There's someone else who can come too,' said Jane, picking up Monty's lead. 'He'll know straightaway if it's Nick.'

◆ ◆ ◆

Dixon cut through the car park at the back of the fishing tackle shop, then jogged along the lane opposite, bringing him out on the edge of Apex Park. He looked down at the lake as he ran past, remembering his days catching carp as a boy. Maybe he'd get his fishing rod out again when this was all over. He was sure he still had it somewhere, although holding it might be a bit of a problem.

He stopped under a streetlight, the sirens fading into the distance now, and looked at his right hand. No wonder the Touch ID on his iPhone had failed. His fingers were blistered, two of them having burst leaving the skin hanging off in strips, and the palm of his hand was glowing red.

'You could fry a bloody egg on it,' he muttered as he began inching the glove off his left hand, gently tugging at each fingertip in turn. 'Shit!' He breathed in sharply through gritted teeth. One last tug and the glove fell to the ground, revealing a left hand in much the same state as his right. The blisters were smaller and none had burst, so it was not quite as bad perhaps.

He flexed the fingers of both hands, slowly at first, his jaw clenched, breathing through his nose. Once they were moving it was not too bad.

Punching someone was definitely out, but he could pull a trigger if needs be, he thought.

He picked up the glove and stuffed it gingerly into his back pocket. A souvenir. He'd never have hung on to that steel girder without the gloves. A cold shiver ran down his spine. No point in dwelling on it, so he jogged on towards Marine Drive and then the jetty.

◆ ◆ ◆

The waves were lapping against the concrete pillars under the pavilion – on their way out: Jane had checked the app on her phone – and she had spent the last ten minutes trying to walk Monty around in circles on the small patch of wet sand left by the receding tide. It was no good though. He refused to move, just sitting there staring along the beach, first towards the lighthouse, then under the pavilion towards the jetty.

'He's doing the same as we are,' said Louise, staring at the top of the jetty.

Jane glanced up and saw DCI Lewis leaning over the sea wall, watching them.

The lights on the Esplanade were twinkling in the misty drizzle that was still falling, so they sheltered under the pavilion, at the base of the sea wall. Lewis disappeared, having stepped back into one of the covered seating areas along the seafront probably.

'What time is it?'

Louise held her watch up to the faint glow from the streetlights. The pavilion was closed, its flashing lights switched off for the night. The seafront was deserted too, thanks to the rain.

'Ten thirty,' she said.

'He's late.'

'Did he say where he was?'

'You saw the texts, Lou.'

'Yeah.'

They spun round when they heard someone running down the concrete steps behind them. A figure appeared at the bottom, leaning around the sea wall and pointing towards the jetty.

'Someone's coming,' whispered Lewis as loud as he dared.

A silhouette appeared on the jetty three hundred yards away, lit up by the streetlights behind him or her. Whoever it was, they were looking along the beach towards the pavilion. Waving. Then they jumped down on to the sand.

Jane felt the jerk of the lead, but had no time to react before it was wrenched from her hand. Monty went from a standing start to a sprint, sailed over the low concrete struts of the pier and set off along the beach, his lead trailing behind him.

A faint whistle carried to Jane on the wind – the first few notes of the theme to *The Vikings* – a whistle as familiar to her as it was to Monty.

'It's him,' she said. Then she started to run.

Dixon dropped to his knees and put his arms around Monty, the dog whining and licking his face at the same time. Then Jane arrived and threw her arms around both of them.

Louise, who was just behind Jane, picked up Monty's trailing lead and pulled him away. Not far, just enough. Jane had her arms around Dixon, her tears – of joy this time – washing the black smoke dust from his face.

'I thought you were dead.'

'So did I.'

They kissed and held each other tight, Dixon trying to keep his hands clear at the same time.

'What's the matter with your hands?' asked Lewis, who had run along the Esplanade and down another set of steps adjacent to Dixon.

'Let me see,' said Jane, flicking on the torch on her phone. 'Oh, shit!'

'It's not as bad as it looks.' Dixon closed his eyes. 'Feels it, mind you.'

'And you weren't joking about the eyebrow pencil either.' Jane was shining the torch in his face.

'I managed to soak a towel and wrap it around my head.'

'What about Sexton?' asked Lewis.

Dixon shook his head. 'He was dead before I got in there. They shot him in the head. Then I was hit from behind and—'

'They?'

'There were two of them. I heard voices, but never saw them.'

'What about the victim?'

'If he was alive when the fire started, he wasn't when I woke up.'

'Cremated then,' muttered Lewis.

'Who have you told that I'm alive?' asked Dixon, looking at Jane.

'No one, only . . .' She looked up at Louise and Lewis.

'Have you told anyone?'

'Not yet.'

'Me neither,' replied Louise.

'Let's keep it that way.' Dixon was helped to his feet by Jane and Lewis. 'If they know I'm alive, they'll disappear. As it is, they think we're both dead. And I'd like to keep it that way.'

'They'll see you've been on the bulletin board, though,' said Louise.

'They'll just move it.' Jane was holding Dixon up now. 'But I've got a copy on Nick's laptop.'

'What about the press?' asked Lewis.

'How long will it be before anyone can get into the loading bay and check?'

'The fire won't be out until tomorrow night probably; then engineers'll have to go in and make it safe. That'll take a couple of days.'

'There's our deadline, then. In the meantime, put out a press release saying three people are missing and presumed dead: one victim and two police officers. Release the names too. Give it the whole line of duty bit, which Jonny deserves.'

'Vicky Thomas won't like that. It's deliberately misleading the public.'

'That's just tough. And besides, she won't find out until it's too late.'

Lewis puffed out his cheeks. 'The Chief Con will want to be involved too.'

'He can't be.'

'You want me to lie to the Chief Constable?'

'We'll say you never knew. No one told you I was alive. All right?'

Lewis looked at Louise and raised his eyebrows.

'Never saw you, Sir,' she said, shrugging her shoulders.

'We'd better tell the Chief Fire Officer,' continued Dixon, 'but he'll need to keep it under his hat. Let him know there's no one left alive too. We don't want him sending anyone in there.'

'They tried once and only just got out,' said Lewis. 'They're containing the fire now at the loading bay end of the factory.'

'Who will take over the MIT?' asked Jane.

'That's Deborah Potter's problem,' replied Dixon.

'Yes, but if she thinks you're dead she'll have to appoint someone else.'

'That's the way it's got to be. No one can know I'm alive. We can't risk the news reaching Manchester.'

'So how do we—?'

'We don't. Janice and her team do. They're going to catch The Vet and Horan.' Dixon held out his hands, watching the rain falling on his palms and fingers. 'They've got a legitimate reason to be investigating, and all the enquiries will be related to Denise Marks on the face of it. So no one can object. And they won't suspect what's really going on either.'

'I can leave them on that for the time being,' said Lewis. 'I'll speak to Janice first thing in the morning.'

'Thank you, Sir.'

'And what will you be doing?'

'Helping out, from behind the scenes.'

'And me?' asked Jane.

'You're going on compassionate leave,' replied Dixon, smiling. 'After all, it's not every day you lose your fiancé, is it?'

◆ ◆ ◆

Jane pulled up across the drive of the large detached house on the outskirts of Taunton. The Volvo was in the drive, but all the lights were off and the upstairs curtains drawn.

'D'you think he's in?'

'He'll be watching telly, I expect.' Dixon was sitting in the passenger seat, his hands wrapped in wet towels. 'Can you pop my seatbelt?'

They squeezed between the Volvo and the hedge, turning their backs to the rose bushes overhanging the path. 'Doesn't he ever prune anything?' muttered Dixon.

Jane rang the doorbell and then checked the time on her phone. 'He's probably asleep. It's nearly midnight.'

An upstairs light came on, followed by the hall and porch lights. Dixon could definitely hear muttering over the footsteps stomping down the stairs.

'Who is it?' Keys rustling.

'Jane and Nick.'

'Nick?' Roger Poland opened the door. 'I was watching the local news. They said you were dead.'

'Close, but not quite,' replied Dixon, holding up his hands.

'Ouch.' Poland winced. 'You'd better come in.'

They followed Poland to the kitchen at the back of the house. 'Let's have a look at those hands then,' he said, switching on the light. He looked Dixon up and down. 'Has anyone looked at that ear?'

'Not yet.'

'I'll bathe it, but it looks split to me. You're going to need stitches in it.'

'I can't go to hospital, Roger. Can you fix it?'

'You'd better tell me what's going on.'

'Any chance of a cup of tea first?' Dixon raised what was left of his eyebrows.

'I'll do it,' said Jane.

'Well?' Poland reached into a cupboard and took out a first aid kit. 'Mugs, tea and sugar are above the kettle, Jane.'

'Thanks.'

'You eaten?' asked Poland, turning to Dixon.

'I had supper, but I threw it up.'

'Better put a sugar in his tea, Jane, and there are some biscuits in the cupboard.'

'We found a dark net bulletin board,' said Dixon. 'Horan, The Vet and Denise Marks were the only members. Horan was posting photos, before and after shots of each victim. He said he'd got his next victim at the furniture factory and by the time I got there, Jonny was already dead. Then I was knocked out, and when I woke up the place was on fire.'

Poland was wiping the dried blood from Dixon's ear with a medicated wet wipe. 'There's a one-inch laceration on the scalp above the right ear. Not through to the bone.'

'Can you be a bit less clinical? You're not doing my post mortem yet, y'know.'

Poland smiled. 'How did you get out?'

'I got up on to a mezzanine floor and out the office window.'

'He soaked a towel and wrapped it around his head and neck,' said Jane.

'Good thinking.'

'Paul Newman in *The Towering Inferno*.' Dixon shrugged his shoulders.

'So, why not the hospital?' asked Poland.

'They think I'm dead, and I want them to keep thinking that.'

'Well, you need stitches in that ear and antibiotic cream for those hands.'

'And some painkillers?'

'Head injury assessment first. I'll make a call.'

Dixon sat in the kitchen with Jane, eating biscuits and listening to Poland on the phone in the hall. He heard parts of the conversation: 'Police, yes . . . don't ask . . . there's a reason . . . trust me, he's one of the good ones . . . stitches . . . burns . . . both hands . . . blistered, yes . . . twenty minutes. Thanks, Paul. I owe you one.'

Dixon winked at Jane.

'A curry usually does the trick,' he said, when Poland walked back into the kitchen.

'You're paying.'

'Who was it?'

'Paul Arnold. An A&E consultant at Musgrove Park. He's a good lad.' Poland opened a cupboard and took out a bottle of scotch. 'We'll need that pullover off. There are some scissors in the drawer.'

'Cut it off?' asked Jane.

'And bag it up,' said Dixon.

'I've got an evidence bag in my briefcase.' Poland took a swig of whisky.

'Can I—?'

'No, you can't.'

◆　◆　◆

It was nearly 2 a.m. by the time Dixon climbed into his own bed, four stitches in his ear and five in the side of his head. All of it swathed in bandages.

'Are these really necessary?' he asked, holding up his hands, each in a clear plastic bag with an elastic band around the wrist.

'Just for tonight. It keeps the cream off the duvet.' Jane was sitting on the edge of the bed. 'The chemist opens at seven, so I'll go and get your prescription.'

'I don't pay, remember?' Dixon was struggling to keep his eyes open now. 'My exemption card's in my wallet.'

Jane nodded.

'You said you heard their voices?'

Dixon nodded his head on the pillow.

'Did you recognise them?'

Jane turned to watch Monty jump on the bed and curl up by Dixon's feet. When she looked back, he was sound asleep.

Chapter Twenty-Seven

Voices this time. Yes, voices. Much better than being woken up by smoke. And this time it was Monty lying across his legs, rather than chairs. But whose voices were these?

He lay in bed listening to the murmur coming from downstairs. Then the front door of the cottage opened and shut. Monty looked up, before returning to his vigil.

Dixon reached for his phone on the bedside table, only to find his hands still in the plastic bags. The cream underneath had gone, absorbed into what was left of his skin, probably, so he flicked the elastic bands off with his teeth and pulled off the bags. Much of the redness had gone from the palms, but his fingers were still in a bit of a state. He wondered whether to stick a pin in the blisters. Best not. The doctor had been quite specific about that. He tried clenching his fists.

Shit!

If he felt a bit drowsy before, he was wide awake now, so he sent Jane a text message – *Where r u Nx* – heard the bleep of it arriving, then footsteps coming up the stairs.

'Feeling better?'

'Yeah, a bit.'

'Everyone's here.' Jane was smiling at him from the doorway.

'Who?'

'Janice, Dave, Mark and Louise. Lewis is on his way too.'

'What time is it?'

'Just gone nine.'

'Is the fire out yet?'

'They're saying tomorrow now. And another couple of days before they can get in there. It's on the local news.' Jane closed the bedroom door behind her. 'The Chief Con's giving a press conference later.'

Dixon sat up.

'C'mon, you. Shift,' Jane said, pushing Monty on to the floor. 'These are your painkillers.' She handed Dixon a box. 'And this is the cream for your hands. Give me a shout if you need me to open it.'

'Thanks.'

'And I rang your parents. I thought someone better had before they saw it on the telly. I swore them to secrecy and said you'd ring them later.'

'I will.'

'D'you need help getting dressed?'

'No, I'll be fine.'

Once dressed, Dixon hesitated on the landing, looking down at the team sitting below. Janice was on a kitchen stool, Dave and Mark on the sofa and Louise on the windowsill in front of them. Jane was sitting behind the sofa on one of the two dining chairs that had come from her flat, the other empty and waiting for him. Or Lewis perhaps. Monty squeezed past him and ran down the stairs.

'Are you feeling better, Sir?' asked Louise, standing up.

'Yes, thanks.'

'Shit, look at your hands.'

'Thanks, Dave.'

Janice walked over and kissed him on the cheek when he reached the bottom of the stairs. 'It's good to see you. When the news came through we . . .' She shook her head. 'We all thought . . .'

'I didn't know until I got here,' said Pearce. 'Lewis never said anything.'

Jane pushed the vacant chair out from under the dining table with her foot.

'It was definitely one of my nine lives.'

'And you only had six left before,' muttered Jane.

'Thank you, Sergeant.'

'Has your Land Rover gone?' asked Louise.

'Every cloud.' Jane muttering again.

'I'm more worried about Jonny and the other man. Have we got an ID for him yet?'

'The MIT are working on it,' replied Janice. 'There's a missing persons report that looks promising. It's the factory manager employed by the Administrator.' She glanced down at her notebook. 'Andrew Barker. He'd been left in charge of a skeleton staff while they tried to sell it as a going concern. DCI Chard's following it up.'

'Chard?'

'Potter's put him in charge of the MIT.'

Dixon's frown was obvious, despite the bandage across his forehead.

'So, what's with the secrecy?' Harding shrugged his shoulders. 'Everyone still thinks you're dead, apart from us.'

'And, it's got to stay that way. Jonny Sexton was a counter corruption officer.'

'What?'

'Manchester CCU have been investigating their own MIT for years, ever since the Carters were on the streets, and they got nowhere. So it was another opportunity to get someone in there.'

'A GMP officer is on the take?'

'Yes, Dave. And if he knows I'm alive, he'll disappear.'

'The bulletin board's gone.' Jane snapped Dixon's laptop shut on the dining table.

'Can you email a copy of the file you downloaded to everyone, while you're there?'

'I've already done it.'

'What about our Major Investigation Team, then?' asked Harding. 'Why not involve them?'

'I don't know them. And I don't trust them,' said Dixon.

'There's a compliment in there somewhere,' said Pearce, grinning.

'Shut up, Mark.'

'Yes, Sir.'

'So, who was it in the factory?' asked Louise.

'The Vet and Horan.'

'The copycat?'

'Let's stop calling him a "copycat", shall we?' There's far more to Horan than just copying The Vet. We found a dark net forum or bulletin board or whatever you call them. That's the file Jane's emailed you. Three members: your Denise Marks, Horan and the third we think may be The Vet. Horan had been posting photos.' Dixon took a deep breath. 'Anyway, read it for yourselves, but they're connected, the two of them, and you're going to catch them both.'

'We are?' Janice looked at him quizzically.

'Think about it. You're investigating the death of Denise Marks, which is the perfect cover for making all the enquiries we need to make. You need to rule out foul play, find out whether there's a connection with the body in the shallow grave, identify the body in the shallow grave.'

'Chard won't like that.'

'Ignore him,' said Dixon. 'It works for me.'

Janice smiled.

Monty started barking when there was a knock at the back door.

'I'll get it,' said Jane, letting in DCI Lewis.

'I'm assuming you're happy with this, Sir?' asked Janice, before Jane had closed the back door behind him.

'We've got a few days until anyone can get in the factory, so it makes sense to me.' He threw his coat over the bannister. 'What have we got to lose?'

'Our jobs.'

'I'm authorising it, Janice. All right?'

'Yes, Sir.'

Lewis placed a file on the dining table. 'You wanted these?'

'Thank you, Sir.' Dixon smiled.

'How far have you got with Denise Marks then?' he asked, turning to Janice.

'We've established who she is, which you know, and that she died of an overdose of heroin and fentanyl,' she replied. 'I'm still waiting for details of her witness protection cases. They refused the first time I asked, so I resubmitted the request.'

Dixon looked at Lewis, his eyes wide.

'I'll see what I can do, but they're highly confidential, for obvious reasons.'

'Maybe if we give them the name we're looking for?' said Dixon.

'And what's that?'

'Carter.'

Jane took advantage of the silence. 'Coffee, anyone? Only I'm not sure we've got enough mugs.'

'Not for me,' said Lewis.

Jane waited for someone else to respond. She looked at Dixon and shrugged her shoulders. 'I'll go and put the kettle on.'

'Let's start with what we know,' said Dixon. 'A fifteen year old Michael Carter is sent to borstal in 1976 convicted of murder. He stabbed a man in the neck and then shot him in the head at point blank range. Right here.' He was pointing at the middle of his forehead with his index finger.

More silence.

'Sound familiar to anyone?'

'The fleam and the trephine,' said Janice.

'When was he released?' asked Lewis.

'1988,' replied Dixon. 'Then he pops up in Manchester, clearing out the street gangs on Moss Side, which is no mean feat.'

'How did he do that?' asked Louise.

'Fear.' Dixon stood up and walked to the middle of the room, standing with his back to the TV. 'Gun crime was endemic, so it was no good shooting people. It was an occupational hazard, a risk they accepted, and more would just pop up. You had to terrify them.'

'And so The Vet was born,' muttered Lewis.

'Born on the streets of Moss Side and christened by the *Manchester Daily Post*. Polaroid photographs of each victim taken on an old instant camera.'

'I remember them,' said Harding, turning to Pearce. 'Point and shoot and then the print comes out.'

'Before my time.'

'But we know Michael Carter's not involved because there was no match with the covert DNA sample,' said Louise.

'And where did that covert sample come from?'

'Er, I don't know.'

'Neither do I,' said Dixon. 'Check, will you? And see when it was last cross-checked against the national database. If it hasn't been done for a while, do it.'

'Yes, Sir.'

'If we get really lucky, it'll turn up a match now.'

'Who with?' asked Lewis.

'Probably some pisshead who used to play a bit of snooker. That's if there's any match at all.'

'You mean it didn't come from Michael Carter?'

'We don't know that it did, do we? And until we do, we assume it didn't.'

'So, it could be him on Dunkery Beacon?'

'It could.'

Janice nodded. 'Anything else?'

'I'd like to see the file from Carter's murder conviction. Anything you can find.'

'Mark?' asked Janice.

'Fine.'

'And retired Detective Chief Superintendent Paul Butler's missing persons file. If anyone asks, you're exploring the possibility the body in the shallow grave might be him.'

'And might it?' asked Lewis.

'Your guess is as good as mine.'

'You're not inspiring me with confidence,' said Lewis, shaking his head.

'We can get Roger to have a look at it when the file comes through, but it could be him, yes.'

'What else do we know?' asked Pearce.

'We know that Horan had inside information about The Vet's methods. And he had it before the bulletin board started. Read the file. They know each other. Of old. Then, when the killings begin again, Denise Marks starts posting that she can't live with it. Siegfried tries to placate her—'

'Who's Siegfried?'

'Just read the file, Dave.'

'Live with what?' asked Louise.

'Guilt. She knew about the body buried on Dunkery Beacon and did nothing about it. And then the killings start again.'

'Which is why she kills herself,' said Janice.

Dixon nodded. 'Probably.'

'You've got a theory. I know you have,' said Jane, standing in the kitchen doorway with five mugs of coffee on a tray.

'Let's hear it.' Lewis reached up and took a mug.

'This is a rumour, mind you, but after the Arndale Centre bomb in 1996, Michael Carter was going to turn supergrass. The story goes that he was killed by the IRA before he could do it, though, and that allowed the Shannons to take over the city. The Shannons deny any involvement.'

'You asked them?'

'Yes, I did, Dave.'

Jane scowled.

'So, what I think happened is this,' continued Dixon. 'Michael Carter is taken into witness protection with Denise Marks as his supervising officer. And ever since then he's been working as a pest controller in sleepy old Burnham-on-Sea. He even got married and had two kids.'

'Living right under our bloody noses,' said Lewis.

'And everyone else's. But how much do we really know about our neighbours? I bet even his wife doesn't know who he really is. And for twenty years it's fine. That is until Harry bought his Pest Erase franchise and put him out of business. Then all hell broke loose.'

'But there were no prosecutions after the Arndale bombing?'

'Maybe there wasn't enough other evidence. Who knows? But once Carter was in the system they couldn't just abandon him. The IRA would have known he was grassing on them.'

'So, Horan is Michael Carter?' asked Janice. 'Do they even look the same?'

'Possibly. With twenty years in between, remember. And maybe a touch of plastic surgery.'

She shook her head.

'What happened to The Vet then?' asked Louise.

'He's still out there somewhere. And remember, none of this would have been possible without someone in Greater Manchester Police knowing about it as well.'

'Who?'

Dixon tore a piece of paper off a notepad on the side and spoke as he scribbled on it. 'You get the difficult job, Jan. I want to know everything about this person. It's not going to be easy, but you need to do it without anyone knowing. Start when they were born and work forwards, not the other way around. All right?' He folded the piece of paper and handed it to her.

'All right.' She looked down and began unfolding the note. 'Shit!'

'We need to look at the CCTV on the Walrow Industrial Estate. I know the MIT will be doing it, but you need to do it too, Dave. All right?'

'Why me?'

'The footage in the factory will have gone, but the traffic cameras may throw up something. I went in there just before ten and the fire started not long after that. Then they'd have been on their toes.'

'They might have gone in on foot from Dorset Close.' Harding sighed. 'I know, I know. Check. But, what do I tell the MIT about the CCTV?'

'Tell them nothing.'

'And Deborah Potter?' asked Lewis.

'You know her, is that right, Sir?' asked Dixon.

'Yes.'

'Where was she before Avon and Somerset?'

Lewis hesitated.

'I'll give you a clue. It's a big city up north.' Dixon raised his eyebrows. 'With two football teams. United and—'

'She came down from Manchester. In the late nineties.'

'Tell her nothing.'

Chapter Twenty-Eight

'What do we do?' Jane waited until Dixon had closed the front door of the cottage behind DCI Lewis.

'Wait.'

'You're joking?'

Dixon sat down and picked up the TV remote control, quickly dropping it into his lap. 'There's the surveillance footage to watch. Pass me that file on the table.'

'So, we just sit here twiddling our thumbs watching telly?'

'I won't twiddle mine, if you don't mind.' Dixon smiled. 'You told me I was crap at delegating, so I delegated.' He opened the file while it was still in Jane's hand. 'Manchester surveillance photos from the nineties,' he said. 'Five years' worth, one binder per year. Pick one.'

'1995,' said Jane, sighing.

'I'll take 1996 then,' said Dixon. 'I'll put the 1995 DVD on in the background too.'

'There's something else we need to have a talk about.' Jane began flicking through the photos. 'What am I looking for?'

'Anything interesting.'

'When you were on the beach, you said you were my fiancé.'

'Would that be such a bad thing?'

Jane dropped the photo album on to the sofa. 'You're doing my head in, you really are. You go out sometimes and I never know whether you're coming back.' She puffed out her cheeks. 'I'm not sure I can do this any more.'

'I always come back.'

'You bloody nearly didn't this time. And what happens if we have a child?'

'Look, I—'

'It's not a bloody game, Nick. You just walked into the snooker club too. And then there was the mud.'

'The hovercraft was already on its way.'

'That's not the point.'

'You want me to change, is that it?'

'Just take care. I want to *know* you're coming home, not *hope* you're coming home.'

'Maybe we'll take some time off when this is over. Go away somewhere. What d'you think?'

Jane was shaking her head. 'Just don't leave it too long.'

Dixon glanced across at Jane, watching a single tear in the corner of her eye. She blinked and it was gone. She had a point, and he felt the same about her. He took a deep breath and looked down at his hands. He knew it would never happen to him, but it nearly had. And what did that tell him? Luck had played a part, certainly, but would it last? If we can just get this one over with, he thought, things will be different next time. Call for backup, do risk assessments. All that – he grimaced – crap.

Things would look different after the funerals.

'I need to see Jonny's family. He's got a husband in Bristol. He was the Armed Response Officer up at Priddy.'

'Really?'

'Yes. It'll have to wait though. I can't very well go there now.'

'What exactly are we looking for?' asked Jane, thumbing through the photograph album. 'They all the look the same to me. The same faces appearing over and over. Michael Carter. Someone called Jerry Gooch.'

'Terry Gooch. The leader of a rival gang. He disappeared not long after those photos were taken.'

'The other names have been redacted,' continued Jane.

'What are they doing?'

'Standing around outside a snooker club.'

'Keep looking.' Dixon glanced up at the television, a shot of a car pulling up outside the snooker club catching his eye.

'What year is that?' asked Jane.

'1995.'

'Pause it,' she said. 'Here, this is a still from that bit just then. Look.' She was holding the 1995 photograph album open in front of him.

Dixon looked at the photograph album, then the TV. 'So it is.'

'You never answered my question last night, before you fell asleep.'

'What question was that?'

'The voices in the factory.' Jane was watching him trying to turn the page in the photograph album with his fingernails. 'Here, let me.'

'What about them?'

'You recognised them, didn't you?'

'One. Now we just need evidence.'

'But he tried to kill you. Why not just arrest him?'

'He's going down for more than attempted murder, Jane. Much more.'

◆ ◆ ◆

'Can you fire up the laptop and put it on my knee?'

'What d'you want it for?' Jane yawned. 'There's something about surveillance videos. They just make me . . .'

'I noticed,' said Dixon, watching her yawning again. 'At least we're not stuck in a van all day filming the bloody things.'

'True. It could be worse.'

'I want to read that bulletin board again.'

Jane leaned over the back of the sofa and picked up the laptop from the dining table. She opened the lid, pressed the 'on' button and then left it on Dixon's knee. 'You've got time for a cup of tea before that thing's ready.'

'Thanks.'

'We could go over to the Red Cow for lunch too, if you like?'

'Love to, but it might blow my cover.'

'Good point.'

'Can you change the DVD for the 1996 footage too?'

'How're your hands?'

'Killing me.'

Jane was looking at her watch. 'You can have a couple more codeine if you need them.'

'Better had. If I nod off, you'll have to give me a prod.'

'It'll be my pleasure.'

Dixon watched the surveillance footage on the TV while he waited for his old laptop to start up. Every now and then he would hit the 'pause' button on the remote control and then flick through the album, looking for the corresponding photograph.

Jane handed him a mug of tea, glancing down at the laptop screen as she did so. 'It's ready to go. Let me find the bulletin board for you.' She sat down next to him, leaned over and began flicking at the touch-pad with her finger. Dixon put his arm around her.

'You will say "yes", won't you?'

'I don't know. I really don't know.'

Jane smiled and kissed him on the cheek. Then she looked down at his right hand. His arm was around her waist, with the palm and fingers turned away from her. 'I'll get the cream.'

'Thanks.'

'Rats always leave a trail,' muttered Dixon as he turned to the copy of the bulletin board thread on the screen: 'Shit Happens' started by Tristan the previous September.

'Why does it start in September? Butler must've been following it before he disappeared in 2011, surely?'

'It'll be a fresh installation every time they move it,' replied Jane. 'Here.' She handed him the tube of cream.

'So the earlier stuff is lost?'

'Yes.'

'Shame.'

Dixon turned back to the screen. It was a long post, although it contained nothing that he didn't already know, and identified Tristan to be Horan beyond doubt. He was being put out of business by '*some twat called Harry who's bought some useless bloody franchise*'. Tristan had lost the council contract, which included the local schools, and the hospitals – Taunton, Bridgwater and Burnham – and now he was losing Wessex Water too. And all because someone, who had no idea what he was doing, had had six weeks' training and then bought the franchise with its national contracts.

Siegfried's response had been less than sympathetic, which had added fuel to the fire.

Dixon winced.

Less of the fire metaphors in future.

It was a reasonable question though. '*Why didn't you buy the franchise first?*' Although it unleashed a tirade that ended with the news that Tristan's 'bitch of a wife' had started divorce proceedings. The response was timed less than two minutes later, which meant they had both been online at the same time, surely? Dixon scrolled down.

All of the posts came in a thirty minute window at the same time and almost always on a Monday, although sometimes weeks apart. Perhaps it was an agreed time. They'd both check, and if one was online, then they'd chat.

DeniseM had been a registered member from the start, but never joined in the discussion, instead just lurking in the background. That much was confirmed by Tristan's last post in the October exchange: '*I know you're reading this, Denise. Can't you do something about it? You useless piece of shit.*'

Nice.

The next set of posts came in November, Tristan becoming ever more animated now. Phrases such as '*Don't these bloody people know who I am?*' popped up several times, as did '*I'm going to teach them a lesson they won't forget*'. Always with Siegfried trying to talk him down.

'*It's not as if you need the money*' got a simple retort: '*That's not the fucking point*', by which time it was obvious even to the impartial observer that Tristan was 'losing it'. Dixon scrolled down a bit further and smiled when he read Siegfried's post at the start of the January exchange.

'*You're losing it, mate. You need to get a grip.*'

DeniseM chimed in at this point: '*You need to calm down. It's not going to be long before you attract attention to yourself and that will not end well for any of us. Least of all you.*'

Dixon raised his eyebrows. Tristan's response had been short and to the point as usual.

'*I don't give a shit.*'

The March exchange didn't fit the pattern at all. Tristan started it in the middle of the month, on a Wednesday, with the announcement that he'd bought a trephine on the internet and The Vet was coming out of retirement. Then came the post that identified Siegfried as The Vet more than any other, pleading with Tristan not to risk it, pointing out that he'd '*got lucky*', the advances in DNA profiling and, interestingly, reminding Tristan that there's '*no one on the payroll*'. The 'these days' was unspoken, but Dixon knew it was there.

Then came the photographs of Harry Lucas. Dixon scrolled past them, glancing up at the television screen as he did so. He'd seen enough death in the last twenty-four hours.

Dixon continued reading, Tristan strangely calm now. '*I could've done with your help. Some twats in a boat saw me, I'm sure they did. Anyway, hope you like the photos. Burial at sea was the best I could do. Bring back any memories? Heads or tails? The toss of a very special coin.*' Then a smiley face. '*I remember the looks on their fucking faces!*'

Twat.

Dixon swallowed hard.

'What's up?' asked Jane. She was sitting on the floor with her back to the sofa, watching the surveillance footage on the TV.

'It's what The Vet did with the bits of skull. Horan's revelling in it.'

'What?'

'He taunted his victims. "Heads I kill you, tails I don't." That's what Paddy Shannon said. See what you think.' He turned the laptop to face her.

'*The toss of a very special coin . . .*'

'Explains this photo, doesn't it?' Dixon scrolled down to the picture of David Cobb on Dunster Beach. 'And the Polaroid of Dermot McGann.'

'*The looks on their faces . . .*' muttered Jane, through a heavy sigh.

Then came DeniseM's first intervention. Pleading with Tristan to stop. '*I can't live with this. You have to stop or I will stop you. This is not what it was supposed to be about. I will stop you. You know that I will.*'

Tristan's response had been dismissive to say the least. '*Piss off, Denise. You've been well looked after and you can't turn me in without taking yourself down too. Live with it.*'

Denise had chosen not to. She was being paid for something. That must be what the phrase 'well looked after' meant. But what? Dixon had suspected as much from the posh care home and the flat. She knew about the body in the shallow grave on Dunkery Beacon all along. And had turned a blind eye to more criminality besides. That would usually bring witness protection to an end for an individual and his family. It made sense.

Dixon had read the final exchange before. Or rather the business end of it that had taken him to the furniture factory. But the beginning of it was no less enlightening.

'I need your help.'

'No way.'

'You owe me.'

'I owe you nothing. I've paid you back and more. It wasn't my fault it ended the way it did.'

'They'll think it's you anyway.'

'They don't actually. Don't you read the papers?'

'If I get caught it'll come out. The whole lot. Where will you be then? You won't last five minutes in prison. Just this last one, then it's over. It'll be just like the old days. Then I won't contact you again. Separate ways. I'll take the board offline and that will be that.'

And that had been that, thought Dixon, adjusting the bandage on the side of his head.

'Don't touch that,' said Jane.

'It itches.'

'Tough.'

'Give me the remote, will you?'

'What for?'

'I'm going to start 1996 again.'

'You're kidding? I've sat through half of it already.'

'Sorry,' said Dixon, pointing at the laptop screen. 'I was reading this.'

◆　◆　◆

'Cheese on toast?' asked Jane.

'That'll do for me.'

His eyes had almost glazed over watching the surveillance footage. And there were only nineteen hours still to watch. He'd be dreaming about the snooker club, although he'd rather that than the fire. He looked down at the palms of his hands, stretching his fingers as far as he could. His right hand had taken the brunt of it, but then he was right handed so that was to be expected, perhaps. The blisters on all but his little finger had burst and the skin beneath was beginning to dry out. The doctor had been right – they looked worse than they were. He had been far more concerned by the concussion, but even his headache had gone now.

'D'you want Lea and Perrins on yours?' Jane was shouting from the kitchen.

'Yes, pl—' Dixon froze. 'Where's the remote?' he screamed.

'Dunno,' replied Jane, poking her head around the door. 'Try under Monty.'

The dog was curled up on the sofa next to him, so Dixon pushed him on the floor. 'C'mon, shift, you dozy little sprite.' Then he snatched up the TV remote control and jabbed the 'pause' button, ignoring the pain in his fingers.

'You son of a . . .'

'What is it?' Jane was standing beside him now, watching him trying to press the buttons with his left hand. 'Here, give it to me.'

Dixon handed her the remote control. 'Just take it back a couple of minutes, then press "play".'

'What are we looking for?'

'Just watch and pause it when I say.'

'That's a Jag, isn't it?' Jane was tipping her head to one side. 'Could be a Daimler, I suppose. The Asian bloke in the sheepskin coat is in the way.'

A sheepskin coat, collar turned up, cowboy boots, sunglasses in winter; the man was standing outside the snooker club, the footage appearing to have been shot from an upstairs room in a building opposite. A step up from a surveillance van.

The conversation was animated, although both men had their hands in their pockets, presumably due to the cold. A thin layer of snow had settled on the top of the wall outside the club, and on the flat roof.

'Is that Michael Carter?' asked Jane.

Dixon nodded. 'Watch the car in the background.'

'Looks like an old VW Golf to me,' said Jane, watching the car back into a space on the far side of the car park, even though it was empty. A man and woman sat in the car talking for thirty seconds – Dixon timed it – then got out and walked across to the front door of the club.

'Pause it.' Dixon waited. 'What d'you notice about that?'

'They're holding hands?' Jane was shaking her head.

'They are. Press "play".'

The woman rummaged in her handbag, found a set of keys and opened the front door of the snooker club. Then they went in, closely followed by Michael Carter and the sheepskin coat.

'What's odd about that?' asked Jane.

'Several things.' Dixon handed Jane the 1996 photograph album. 'Find me the corresponding photo.'

Jane began flicking through the album. 'I can't. There's one of Carter talking to the Asian man, but none with the couple in the background.'

'Exactly.'

'D'you think it's deliberate?'

'Of course it is.'

'Why?'

'That's the undercover police officer. Rick Wheaton was his cover name. He worked there for twelve months and that's the only image of him we've found anywhere. Funny that, isn't it?'

Jane nodded.

'Not only that, but he's holding hands with Derek Hervey's widow.'

'That's her?'

'There's a photo of Hervey and his wife on the file in Manchester.' Dixon handed Jane his phone. 'Rewind it and take a photo of them standing together by the front door. Zoom in and get a couple of them.'

'If I zoom it'll go all grainy.'

'Stand nearer the telly.'

'Here.' Jane handed Dixon's phone back. 'Is that it?'

'One more thing.'

'What?'

'The toast's burning.'

Dixon listened to Jane's footsteps as she ran into the kitchen and then the clatter of the grill while he tapped out a text message to Louise.

Need address and tel for Derek Hervey's widow, Angela, soon as poss pls

'That was the last of the bread,' muttered Jane. She was standing in the doorway watching the smoke billowing from the grill.

'I've seen enough smoke to last me a lifetime.'

'Course you have. Sorry.' Jane tipped the toast into the bin. 'How about a mug of soup?'

'That's fine.' He was about to switch the surveillance DVD back on when his phone rang.

'Hi, Louise.'

'I've got the information you wanted about the covert DNA sample, Sir.'

'Fire away.' Dixon rolled his eyes.

Twit.

'The sample was logged by Detective Chief Superintendent Hargreaves on the third of March 1995. It's been tested against the database three times since: 1996, 2005 and 2011. Then again today.'

'And?'

'It throws up a match this time. Robin Ellis, aged fifty-five. He's an estate agent in Winchester. Got nicked for drink driving two years ago and received an eighteen month ban.'

'Which agent?'

'One of the posh ones. Wilton and Parker. They do the big million pound plus houses, looking at the internet.'

'Have you got an address for him?'

'And a phone number.'

'Text them to me, will you?'

'OK.'

'Is it a full match?'

'Yes.'

'Thanks, Louise. How's Janice getting on?'

'Not too good, I don't think. She had a run-in with Chard earlier too, but she can fill you in on that. Did you see the press conference on the local news?'

'No, I missed it.'

'The Chief Con seems to think the sun shines out of your arse.'

Dixon smiled. 'He won't when he finds out I'm still alive.'

Chapter Twenty-Nine

Dixon spent the rest of the day watching the surveillance, when he wasn't on the telephone or coating his hands in antibiotic cream, and went to bed just before midnight, halfway through the 1994 footage. They had stumbled on highlights of the Chief Constable's press conference on the local TV news when Dixon had been channel hopping, but the evening had taken a turn for the better when Louise dropped off a takeaway from the Zalshah.

Now the alarm on his phone was buzzing, taking it ever closer to the edge of his bedside table.

'What time is it?' Jane's voice was coming from under the duvet.

'Six.'

'How long have we got?'

'Half an hour. We need to drop Monty off at your folks' on the way.' Dixon sat up. 'You did ring them?'

'Not yet. They'll be fine.' Jane threw back the duvet. 'Where are we going?'

'Winchester first, then Surbiton. And we need to be back by six for Janice and the team.'

'I'm driving, I suppose.'

Dixon smiled. 'No Little Chef, I'm afraid. We'll have to make do with a bacon sarnie from a van.'

'You know just what to say.' Jane jumped out of bed and ran across to the bathroom.

'I'll let the dog out, shall I?' mumbled Dixon.

'He's your dog.'

They arrived in Arthur Road, Winchester, with plenty of time to spare before their 11 a.m. appointment with Robin Ellis. And that was despite breakfast sitting in a lay-by on the A303. Ellis had insisted on meeting them at home, rather than his office, for reasons he hadn't felt the need to spell out, although Dixon had understood. Ellis had only just hung on to his job after the drink driving incident, so he was no doubt anxious to avoid the police turning up at his office.

It was a large bow fronted Victorian property with a tiled front path and stained glass windows in the front door.

'Nice, isn't it,' said Jane, leaning over the steering wheel and looking up at the house.

'Spoilt by next door's loft conversion, if you ask me.'

'Hark at you.'

'It looks like a big square box has been dumped on the roof, or fallen off a plane or something.'

'Since when did you become an architect?' Jane smiled.

'Next door was sold two years ago for one point two million. I looked it up.'

'You've been watching daytime TV again, haven't you?'

'C'mon, he's in there. Let's get it over with. And remember, avoid giving my name unless he asks. I'm just your colleague.'

'I know, I know.'

Jane rang the doorbell. Dixon was standing behind her with his hands in his pockets. He made out a blue blazer and red tie approaching the front door from the inside, and the click of leather heels on a wooden floor. Ellis opened the door and stepped out into the porch, pulling the door shut behind him.

'Look, what's this all about?'

'Detective Sergeant Winter, Sir,' said Jane. 'And this is my colleague.' Dixon was standing behind her holding up his warrant card in his left hand with his finger over his name.

'May we come in?' continued Jane.

'My wife's in.' Ellis's eyes were wide, a look of panic on his face.

I wonder what you've been up to while the cat's away . . .

'This relates to an incident in Manchester twenty years ago, Sir. You're not suspected of having committed any offence, if that helps. We're just hoping you might be able to help us with our enquiries.'

Ellis breathed out. 'Can my wife sit in with us?' Eyes wide again.

'Yes, Sir,' replied Jane, with her best disarming smile. 'I'm sure she'll have no problem with any of it.'

'Follow me.'

The back of the property had been knocked through to make the whole area open plan, with floor to ceiling glass windows overlooking the garden, and two large sofas arranged around an open fire. There were built-in shelves on either side full of books and photographs.

A woman sitting with her back to the door stood up.

'You can stay, Clare, it's fine,' said Ellis, trying to sound matter of fact.

Dixon sat down on the end of the sofa nearest the photographs and took out his notebook and pen.

'Where were you in 1995, Mr Ellis?' asked Jane.

'We lived in Hale back then. We moved down here in 2002.'

'You'll remember The Vet then.'

'Doesn't everyone?'

'So, you'll know we're investigating the series of copycat killings in Somerset?'

'Yes. Look what's this got to do with me?'

'In 1995 a DNA sample was obtained. It came from saliva. It's been tested several times over the years and has never thrown up a match. Until now.'

'Who with?'

'You, Mr Ellis.'

'Me?'

'Let's be quite clear. We're not suggesting that you're The Vet.'

'Well, that's a relief,' muttered Mrs Ellis.

'But, a sample of your saliva was obtained,' continued Jane, 'almost certainly without your knowledge, and presented as if it came from a man called Michael Carter. Does that name mean anything to you?'

'I remember the Carters. Everyone in Manchester back then had heard of them.'

'Michael was the leader.'

'Bloody hell.'

'D'you know anyone who might have done that?'

'No, of course not.' Indignant now.

'Anyone who might have wished to hurt you?'

'No. Look, we lived in Hale. Had two young children in the local primary school. I was an estate agent. That's it.'

'Did you ever play snooker at a club in—'

'I've never played snooker,' interrupted Ellis, shrugging his shoulders. 'A couple of games of pool in the pub, but I never went to a snooker club.'

'Did you ever come into contact with the police at that time?'

'What's that supposed to mean?' Ellis was on his feet now, pacing up and down in front of the fire.

'Were you arrested, perhaps?'

'No, look—'

'Did you know any police officers? Friends, perhaps?'

'No.' Ellis looked at his wife. 'Did you?'

'One of the mums at the school was a police officer,' she replied, shaking her head. 'But that's it.'

'What was her name?' asked Jane.

Mrs Ellis grimaced. 'God, I can't . . . Debbie, possibly? Something like that.'

'Did you know her well?'

'Not really. Just to say "hello" to at the gate.'

'What about you, Mr Ellis, did you meet Debbie?'

'Not that I remember. It was rare for me to drop the kids off, to be honest.'

'And you never had any dealings with the police at any other time?'

'No.'

Dixon stood up and walked over to the built-in shelves. He picked up a framed ticket and handed it to Jane. She looked at it, then handed it to Ellis.

'Ah, the FA Cup final,' he said. 'The only one I went to and we bloody well lost one–nil.'

'Manchester United?' asked Jane.

'I was a season ticket holder. Never missed a home game and managed the occasional away match too. Even went to Milan once. Have to make do with the telly these days.'

'Who did you go with?'

'I used to go with my brother. Then when my son was old enough, he started coming too.'

Jane looked at Dixon and raised her eyebrows.

'Did you sit in the same seats?' he asked.

'Yes. Every game. In the South Stand we were. It's not the same these days, I don't think, but back then you had a designated seat, even if it was an unwritten rule.' Ellis smiled.

'And who did you sit next to?'

'Hugh, my brother, and then George sat in between us when he started coming. On my left it was . . .' He frowned. 'He was a copper, come to think of it. I'm sure he was.'

'What was his name?'

'Ray. I never knew his surname.'

◆ ◆ ◆

'Who's Ray then?' asked Jane, putting her key in the ignition.

'Detective Chief Superintendent Raymond Hargreaves. Retired now, but likes his football.'

'How d'you know?'

'Cufflinks.' Dixon smiled.

'Where to now?'

'Head out to the motorway, then follow the signs for London. I need to ring Lewis.'

Dixon was dialling the number when a text message arrived, his phone buzzing in his hand.

'Who is it?' Jane was watching the traffic lights.

'Louise – *Fire out, structural engineers inspecting this afternoon* – looks like they may go in tomorrow.'

'Is that enough time?'

'Depends what we find this afternoon.'

◆ ◆ ◆

'Is this it?' asked Jane as she parked across the drive of a three storey townhouse in Selsdon Close, Surbiton. She had spent the last hour trying to stick to 50 mph through the roadworks on the M3 whilst listening to Dixon on the phone to DCI Lewis. She left the engine running and waited.

'So, that's it then,' she said, when he rang off. 'We're going straight up to Manchester?'

'Janice and the team will meet us there.'

'It's a sod of a long drive.'

'We can leave your car and go on the train if you'd rather.'

'How do we get it back?'

'Well, we'd have to—'

'Sod it,' said Jane. 'It's easier to drive.'

'Better ring your folks and ask them to hang on to Monty.'

'I'll ring them later. I left them with a bag of his food in case we got back late, so it'll be fine.'

'Good,' said Dixon, looking up at the house from the passenger window, a small car parked in the drive. 'Leave it here. She's not going out, is she?'

'What about your night insulin?'

'Just in case.' Dixon smiled, tapping his breast pocket.

'Crafty sod,' muttered Jane. 'You knew.'

'Hoped.'

Jane rang the doorbell and turned to Dixon. 'Posh hotel?' she asked, smiling.

'Premier Inn.'

Jane sighed and turned back to the front door at the sound of a key turning in the lock.

'Angela Maxwell?'

'Yes.'

'Detective Sergeant Winter. And this is my colleague. You spoke on the phone?'

'We did. Come in,' she said, stepping back. 'The sitting room's upstairs.'

At the top of the stairs, Jane turned right into the living room and looked along the mantelpiece at the various framed photographs. 'It's why you never interview a witness on the phone,' she had heard Dixon say often enough. He was behind her, his eyes darting around the room.

'You're after the copycat?' asked Angela, appearing in the doorway behind them.

'Yes,' replied Jane.

'Sick bastard. I nearly threw up when I saw it on the news.' She gestured to the two armchairs opposite the fire as she sat down on the edge of the sofa. 'You'd better sit down.'

'We're now looking at events in Manchester, Mrs Maxwell, back in the nineties.' Jane took her phone out of her handbag.

'Oh.'

'What can you tell me about this man?' She leaned forwards and handed her the phone with the photograph on the screen.

'That's me and Rick outside the snooker club.'

Dixon was making notes, holding the pen between the tip of his index finger and thumb. Reading them later would be a challenge, he thought, but then it was really just for show.

'Tell us about Rick.'

'My husband, that's Derek, hired him in 1995. It was around about then anyway. He'd been there a while when Derek . . .' She took a deep breath. 'When Derek disappeared.'

'Take your time.'

'It was a lifetime ago. Feels it anyway,' said Angela, forcing a smile. 'And I've been married and divorced since then.'

'We understand.'

'Anyway, Rick was just the barman. He looked after the club when Derek wasn't there. Tried to keep order, not that there was ever that much trouble. The Carters saw to that. They'd sort of moved in by then.'

'We've read your statements about what happened in the run up to Derek's murder,' said Jane, 'but what we're interested in now is what happened afterwards.'

Angela nodded.

'With Rick,' continued Jane. 'You're holding hands in the photo.'

'He said he'd look after me. That he'd protect me. And he did. When Derek disappeared, I sold the club to the Carters.'

'Whose idea was that?'

'Rick's. I couldn't keep it anyway, not without Derek, and I got a good price.'

'And you were having a relationship with him?'

'Yes.'

'How about before Derek died?'

'That's a bit near the knuckle.'

'Humour me.'

'It started afterwards. We'd kissed before, I suppose, if I'm being honest. And flirted, but nothing had happened.'

'What about Derek, was he ever seeing anyone else, to your knowledge?'

'There was someone else, a couple of years before he died. The Carters said she was an undercover copper and that was the last I saw of her.'

'When was that?'

'Maybe 1994?'

'Going back to afterwards then, did Rick move in with you after Derek died?'

'Yes, he did.'

'And how was it?'

'Fine.'

'What did he say he'd done before he worked at the club?'

'He'd been in the police, but got thrown out for stealing.'

'Did the Carters know that?'

'I think so. Everyone did. He didn't exactly make a secret of it.'

'What about your children?'

'Oh God, he wasn't a—'

'No, that's not what this is about, Angela,' interrupted Jane, raising her hand.

'They liked him,' she said, blowing out her cheeks. 'They were only young, though, and don't really remember any of it. Not even their father.'

'And Rick stayed at the club when the Carters bought it?'

'Yes.'

'Was that part of the deal?'

'Not specifically. It just happened that way. They needed a barman, I suppose.' Angela shrugged her shoulders.

'How did it end?'

'He just disappeared one day. They all did. The Carters and everyone.'

'Did he ever get in touch again after that?'

'Never.'

'And what did you do?'

'I moved down here and met Jamie. I wanted to move anyway and had discussed it with Rick. He said he would come, but then . . .' Her voice tailed off.

'Did anything else happen?'

'Not really. I had a burglary about a year after moving here, but that's hardly relevant, is it?'

'It could be. What was taken?'

'Nothing. I had the back window fixed and that was that.'

Jane looked at Dixon. He nodded.

'Would it surprise you to learn that Rick was working for the Carters all along?' she asked.

Angela sighed. 'Not really. I knew they wanted the club and once Derek had gone they were welcome to it.' She stood up and walked over to the mantelpiece. 'Look, I was young, alone, my husband murdered, two young children, and Rick was offering to look after us. I did what I had to do, felt I had to do anyway. Hindsight is a wonderful thing.'

'What would you do differently?'

'Oh, I dunno. Maybe not believe all Rick's crap, I suppose. We were going to be together forever, and then one day he was gone without so much as a bloody note.'

'Do you have any photographs of him?'

'There's one.' She opened the door of the sideboard, reached in and pulled out a red photograph album. 'I only kept it because it was such a good picture of the girls.' Then she began leafing through the pages. 'Here it is,' she said, folding back the tissue paper.

Jane walked over and looked at it. 'May I?' she asked, taking the album from Angela.

'Of course.'

Jane placed the photograph album on Dixon's knee and pointed to the photograph; Rick Wheaton kneeling down with an arm around each of Angela's daughters, grinning at the camera.

The bottom inch or so of the picture was plain white, and it had been secured using self-adhesive corners, the two at the bottom stretching as if there was something behind it. Dixon smiled.

'Any chance of a cup of tea?' he asked, winking at Jane.

He waited until they were both in the kitchen, put his little finger nail behind the photograph and flicked it out of the adhesive corners. Then he turned it over.

The paper was thicker than usual and on the back at the bottom was a small pouch, now empty, but it would once have contained fixer or some other chemical used in the printing of Polaroid instant photographs.

Dixon quickly took photographs of the front and back of the picture with his iPhone and was holding it up when Angela walked back into the sitting room.

'You've taken it out,' said Angela. 'You could've asked.'

'It's a Polaroid,' said Dixon.

'So, what?'

'Whose camera was it?'

'Rick's. I've still got it somewhere.'

'What?'

'When he buggered off he left loads of stuff behind. I tipped most of it, took some to the charity shop, but there's a box in the loft. No idea why I kept it, really.'

'And the camera's in the box?'

'Yes.'

Dixon stood up. 'Can we see it, please?'

'You'll have to go up in the loft and get it. How are you with heights?'

◆ ◆ ◆

Dixon was able to stand up in the loft, which had been only partially boarded out for storage, and used the light on his iPhone as a torch.

'It's a small box, an old shoebox, I think, against the far wall. Red, possibly?' Angela was standing at the bottom of the ladder with Jane. 'It might be in another box, with some wallpaper.'

He squeezed past several picture frames leaning against a suitcase and headed towards an open box with several rolls of wallpaper sticking out of it. And there it was. A red shoebox sitting in the bottom of the larger box, holding the wallpaper upright. He lifted the lid.

'Is this it?' Dixon was holding the shoebox above the loft hatch.

'That's it.' Both Angela and Jane were looking up at him.

'How long has it been up here?'

'I moved in here late ninety-six. So, since then.'

'Can we take it with us?'

'Er, yes, I don't see why not. I certainly don't want it.'

Dixon tucked the box under his arm and climbed down the ladder. He passed the box to Jane and closed the loft hatch behind him.

'So, let's be quite clear,' he said, turning to Angela. 'Everything in this box belonged to Rick Wheaton and hasn't been touched since.'

'Not since I put it in the loft, no.'

'And no one's used the electric shaver?'

Jane's eyes widened.

'No.' Angela was shaking her head.

'One last thing, Mrs Maxwell,' said Dixon, sliding a photograph out of his pocket. 'Do you recognise this man?'

◆ ◆ ◆

'She's watching from the window,' muttered Dixon. 'Just drive around the corner and park.'

Seconds later, Jane pulled over and wrenched on the handbrake. 'Well?'

'The Polaroid camera, an electric shaver, an old Sony Walkman, several cassettes, an empty wallet, sunglasses and . . . wait for it . . . a hairbrush.' Dixon grinned. 'All of it safely in an evidence bag. And we've got a witness statement from Angela confirming it all belonged to Rick Wheaton.'

'D'you think that's what the burglar was looking for?'

'I'm guessing Rick Wheaton *was* her burglar. And I wonder how she's going to feel when she finds out he killed her husband and used the camera to take a snapshot of him dying.'

Chapter Thirty

The bar at the Premier Inn was small and crowded, although Dixon recognised the faces sitting at a table in the far corner: Janice Courtenay, Mark Pearce, Dave Harding and Louise Willmott.

'No Jane?' asked Louise.

'She's parking the car.'

'Have you eaten?' Janice was looking at her watch. 'Only they stop serving food at nine.'

'We stopped on the way, thanks.' Dixon spun round when he felt a tap on his shoulder.

'Detective Inspector Dixon?'

'Yes.'

'Simon Baxter, DCS, and this is DI Caroline Porritt. Manchester CCU. Lewis told me to look for a man with a sore head and burnt hands. He wasn't joking was he?'

'No, Sir. You'll forgive me if I don't . . .' Dixon glanced down at Baxter's outstretched hand.

'Er, no, of course not. Sorry.'

'Could I see your ID too, please, Sir.'

Baxter looked at Porritt and raised his eyebrows. Then they both took out their warrant cards and held them up.

'Thank you,' said Dixon.

'You were lucky to get out.' Caroline Porritt smiled. 'I saw it on the telly.'

'My partner wasn't quite so lucky, although he was dead before the fire started, mercifully.'

'We heard,' said Baxter. 'He was Bristol CCU?'

'He was.'

Baxter shook his head. 'I've lined up a firearms unit for tomorrow. How have you got on?'

'Good.' Dixon looked around the crowded bar. 'Let's take this upstairs, shall we? Jane'll know where to find us.'

'But I haven't finished my beer.'

'Bring it with you, Mark.'

'Yes, Sir.'

Dixon passed the keycard to Louise who opened the door. Room 239 was on the second floor and was identical to every other room in the hotel no doubt: a large double bed, two chairs and a stool in front of the long dressing table. Clean and comfortable certainly, but hardly an ideal venue for a briefing.

Dixon sat down on the bed, by the pillows. Baxter and Porritt took the chairs and Janice the stool. Mark and Dave perched on the edge of the dressing table and Louise took the window ledge, leaving the other side of the bed for Jane.

'Well, what have you got for me?' asked Dixon.

'Nothing on CCTV or the traffic cameras,' said Harding. 'Although I've not seen all of it yet. Chard wouldn't release it.'

Mark Pearce dropped a file on to the bed. 'That's the file on Michael Carter's murder conviction. The guts of it, anyway. Witness statements and interviews.'

'What about you, Janice?'

'Hit a brick wall at the age of twelve,' she replied, shaking her head. 'After that it was fine. Schools, university, police. No problem, I've got everything. But before that, nothing.'

'Did you try adoption agencies, Social Services, stuff like that?'

'I did.' She was smiling now. 'His father died when he was twelve years old. He had no one else, so he went into a foster home and they adopted him, so his name changed.'

'How did the father die?'

'He was murdered,' replied Janice, matter of fact. 'By Michael Carter.'

'What?'

'Wait a minute, you haven't heard the best bit yet.' She smiled. 'His father was a veterinary surgeon.'

'Who are we talking about?' asked Pearce.

'All in good time, Mark.' Dixon frowned, making time to process the information. 'His father was a vet?'

'Yep.'

'And he was murdered by a fifteen year old Michael Carter?'

'He saw it too. It's on the file. He was standing in the hall and it happened right in front of him. Bang, and down he went right at his feet. You need to read Michael's interviews too.'

Dixon was brought back to the present by a dull thudding sound low down on the door, as if someone was standing with their back to it, kicking it with their heel. Louise opened it to let Jane in, a beer in one hand and a gin and tonic in the other. A tube of toothpaste and two brushes were sticking out of her pocket and the evidence bag was tucked under her arm.

'Hi, Jane,' said Janice. She made the introductions to Baxter and Porritt.

'What was Carter's motive?' asked Dixon, smiling at Jane when she placed the beer on his bedside table.

'The father was abusing his own son and he was Michael's friend, so Michael put a stop to it,' replied Janice.

Dixon nodded.

'Who are we talking about?' asked Baxter, looking quizzically at Porritt. She shrugged her shoulders.

'Rick Wheaton,' replied Dixon. 'Every single previous attempt to get someone in undercover with the Carters fails until Hargreaves sends in Rick Wheaton. And he succeeds because he's a lifelong friend of the family. Michael Carter was protecting him when he killed his father and Rick was repaying the debt.'

'So, Rick Wheaton is The Vet?'

'He is.'

'A fucking police officer?'

'It explains the reference on the bulletin board too,' said Jane.

'It does,' said Dixon.

'And none of this would've come up on background checks back then either,' said Baxter, nodding. 'Even without the change of name.'

Dixon passed round his phone with the photograph of Rick Wheaton holding hands with Angela outside the snooker club. 'This is a still from the video footage, only it never appears in the corresponding photo album. You can see Wheaton and Angela are an item, and she admitted it when we saw her today.'

'But he killed her husband,' said Porritt.

'She doesn't know that.' Jane took a sip of gin and tonic.

'Yet,' continued Dixon. 'Anyway, when he disappeared, she moved to London. She tipped most of his stuff, but kept some of it in a box in the loft.'

'Has she still got it?' asked Baxter.

'No,' replied Dixon. 'We have.'

Jane held up the evidence bag.

'We've also got a statement confirming that these items belonged to Rick Wheaton and have not been touched since.' Dixon smiled. 'We've got the Polaroid camera, an electric shaver and a hairbrush.'

'We need to get them off to the lab.' Baxter stood up. 'A match with a partial sample is better than nothing.'

'I was hoping you'd say that, Sir. Can you get a DNA test done overnight?'

'Yes.'

'Good.' Dixon took a swig of beer. 'Then we can pick them up tomorrow.'

'Them?'

'The covert DNA sample is fake and it's finally thrown up a match with an estate agent from Winchester. He had a few too many at lunch one day and drove home from work. The important bit, though, is that he used to live in Hale and was a season ticket holder at Old Trafford.'

'What's that got to do with it?'

'He used to sit next to a copper, Sir,' said Dixon. 'Called Ray.'

Dixon set his alarm for 7 a.m. and left the ringer on in case DCS Baxter rang. He promised to do so as soon as the DNA result was available, whatever time it was. He had also agreed to delay the arrest of Hargreaves until the result was known. Better to take them together, Dixon had said, and Baxter had agreed.

Jane was fast asleep, which was hardly surprising given that she had spent over nine hours behind the wheel of her car. Still, it would be a nice mileage claim. At forty-two pence per mile, it might even be enough for a night in a posh hotel.

He opened the file on Michael Carter's murder conviction and turned first to the post mortem report, which was much as he had expected. A single stab wound to the left side of the neck had opened up the jugular vein and then the fatal shot to the head, at point blank range judging by the powder residue. Dixon skipped over the post mortem photographs, but the pictures taken at the scene confirmed the exit wound must have been sizeable. Blood and brain had been plastered up the white walls in the hall. It must have made quite an impression on a twelve year old.

Michael Carter had been interviewed at length by the investigating officers, Detective Inspector Daniel Smith and Detective Constable Raymond Hargreaves. Dixon sighed. Nothing wrong with that in the ordinary course of events, but these were not ordinary events, by any stretch of the imagination. Maybe Hargreaves had felt some grudging admiration for Carter, not surprising perhaps when the evidence pointed to his victim having been a paedophile abusing his own son. But it was still a murder, and Hargreaves was still a police officer.

The police surgeon had been called to certify Carter fit for interview, which he was, and he had been interviewed in the presence of his own father, Samuel Carter. He freely admitted the killing, saying that he knew what was being done to his friend and had decided to stop it. It seemed to have been generally accepted that the gun was his father's, but he denied that when asked in interview and refused to say where he had got it from.

When the front door opened, he opened fire immediately, hitting the man in the forehead, and then he stabbed him in the neck to make sure. Only then did he notice his twelve year old friend standing at the bottom of the stairs.

Psychiatric reports had been prepared, which were not on the file, and he had been sentenced to be detained at Her Majesty's pleasure. Next stop borstal, followed by a transfer to Strangeways at the age of eighteen. He had finally been released in 1988 – soon to be reunited with his childhood friend.

Dixon slid his phone off the bedside table and sent Louise a text message.

Need another dna test dunkery beacon body and toby horan asap, lewis will expedite, ta

Chapter Thirty-One

'You really shouldn't be having that.'

'Eh?'

'Orange juice is packed with sugar.'

'Yes, Mother.'

Jane sighed. 'Go ahead then. See if I care.'

Dixon picked up the glass of orange juice and put it on the corner of his breakfast tray. Then he turned to the coffee machine.

'DCI Lewis put the request for the DNA test in last night, Sir,' said Louise. 'So, we should get it back today.' She was standing by the hot plate holding two pieces of bacon in a pair of tongs.

'Thanks,' replied Dixon.

Jane used the distraction to snatch the glass of orange juice from Dixon's tray, down it in one, and then replace the empty glass.

Ten minutes later they had finished their cooked breakfasts, and Dixon was doing his best to ignore the empty orange juice glass when his phone buzzed. He smiled and held the phone out in front of him for Jane to read.

On way, good news

'Who's that from?' she asked.

'Baxter.'

'Janice is about to make the biggest arrest of your career,' muttered Jane.

'It's her investigation, and I'm dead, remember?'

'Yes, but—'

'That's the deal. And it doesn't really matter as long as we get the bastards.'

'I suppose not.'

'I keep wondering what Horan was saying to Harry at the end.'

'Maybe you'll get a chance to ask him.'

'Maybe I will.' Dixon turned to Louise sitting at the next table. 'Any news on the factory?'

'Not yet. The engineers will be trying to make it safe. God knows how long that'll take.'

'Keep an eye on it, will you?'

'Yes, Sir.'

He looked up to see Baxter and Porritt striding towards him across the restaurant.

'It's a match then?' he asked.

'As good as we'll get from the partial sample.'

'What was it?'

'They found a hair follicle in the shaver. Blunt blades, so it must've pulled it out. There was nothing on the hairbrush, oddly enough.'

Dixon nodded. 'Hargreaves first,' he said.

'There are six of you and six of us, plus I've got a firearms team meeting us there.'

'That should be enough.'

◆ ◆ ◆

'Perverting the course of justice hardly cuts it,' said Jane, 'bearing in mind what he's conspired in.'

'It'll do for starters,' replied Dixon, stepping back behind the bushes.

Joel Lane, Werneth Low, was outside the M60 and well on the way to the Peak District. Large gardens, with fields behind them, and trees – it was almost like being back at home. Even Hargreaves's small bungalow had a tree in the front garden, although Dixon had no real idea what it was without leaves to give it away.

The gravel drive swept in, past the tree, to the front of a bungalow that was dwarfed by the double garage attached to it.

Dixon watched two firearms officers, the lead one holding a battering ram, creeping along the front of the garage. Behind them Janice and Louise were tiptoeing along with Baxter and Porritt, all of them wearing their regulation stab vests. Two more firearms officers, with Dave Harding and Mark Pearce in tow, were moving silently down the path at the side of the garage.

Dixon and Jane crept forwards and ducked down behind a Ford Mondeo with a Manchester United sticker in the back window.

'What if he rings—?' whispered Jane.

'They won't give him the chance. They're going straight in. Front and back.'

Jane nodded and waited for the crash of the front door.

'What about that bay window?' asked Jane, peering through the windows of the car.

'It's the dining room,' replied Dixon. 'It's empty.'

In front of the garage and a narrow path along the front of the bungalow had been block paved, presumably so the postman could get in and out without waking them up, but it meant the firearms team arrived at the porch unseen.

Dixon watched the hand gestures, counting down from three, and then the swing of the battering ram. There was a loud crash, immediately followed by two more coming from the back of the bungalow.

'Armed police!'

'Stay where you are. Armed police!'

The second shout came from the back. Maybe someone had been in the kitchen.

Dixon ducked down behind the car and listened to the sounds all around him. Birds in the trees, splintering wood, a siren in the distance, dogs barking, glass crunching underfoot, the drone of traffic out on the main road, a scream.

'Armed police. Put down the—'

Then a gunshot.

'He's firing.'

'Not at us, Jane,' said Dixon, bowing his head. 'Not at us.'

Two paramedics ran past and in the front door.

Seconds later Louise and Porritt appeared at the front door leading an elderly lady out of the bungalow. They were holding her up and waited while a patrol car swung into the drive. Then they helped her into the back.

'He shot himself?' asked Jane.

'If you were his age, would you let them send you to prison?'

'I suppose not.'

'Me neither.'

Dixon stepped over the broken glass in the hall and followed the corridor to an open door. He saw the television first, a huge screen mounted on the wall to the left of the fireplace. Sitting directly in front of it was retired Detective Chief Superintendent Ray Hargreaves, his head back, mouth open, the back of his skull and most of his brain splattered up the wall behind him.

A red football shirt covered in signatures and mounted in a display case on the wall had not escaped, the glass shattered by the bullet before it embedded itself in the plaster.

A small drawer in the desk next to Hargreaves was open, presumably where the gun had been hidden, ready for just such an eventuality. Now it was in his lap, still with his finger on the trigger.

'What's the score?' asked Jane, glancing up at the television.

'It's just the highlights,' replied a firearms officer. 'It's last night's Premier League game. We won two–nil.'

◆　◆　◆

'Are you ready?'

Janice was pacing up and down in the bottom of the stairwell, beads of sweat forming on her forehead.

'Are you ready, Jan?' asked Dixon.

'Yes, yes, I'll be fine.'

'Here's the list. Name them all in the open, in front of everyone. Leave them in doubt who he is. And start with my attempted murder.' Dixon grinned. 'Let him know I'm still alive.'

Silence.

'All right?'

'It's just another arrest, Jan,' said Jane. 'You've done it hundreds of times before and you've got Armed Response right behind you.'

'Yes, but this is The Vet we're talking about.'

Dixon grinned. 'Feels good, doesn't it?'

Janice forced a smile, which soon disappeared when the double doors opened at the bottom of the stairs to reveal four firearms officers followed by Baxter and two more CCU officers in stab vests.

'Everyone in position?' asked Dixon.

'We've got two officers in the lift, and the back stairs are sealed off. That just leaves the fire escape.'

'We can cover that,' said one of the firearms officers.

'Everybody ready?' asked Baxter.

'Where is he?'

'He's sitting at a workstation on the far side. We've got an officer at the coffee machine.'

'Right, let's get on with it,' said Dixon.

Baxter spoke into his radio. 'On three. One. Two. Three. Go.' He pushed open the door and edged out into the CID area on the fourth floor of the Greater Manchester Police headquarters. The firearms officers fanned out on either side of him, the two on the right making for the fire exit. At the same time, the door on the far side of the CID area opened and two more firearms officers crept in, with Louise and another CCU officer behind them.

Dixon and Jane let the door close behind them and walked along the back wall of the open plan office.

'He's the one with his wrist in plaster,' whispered Dixon from behind a wry smile. 'Nice to know my old Land Rover made an impression.'

Janice and Baxter followed the two lead firearms officers across the office, weaving in and out of the workstations.

DI Manesh Pandey was the first to spot them coming. 'What the—?'

'Armed police! Stay where you are!'

Detective Chief Superintendent Warren Douglas spun round to find himself looking down the barrel of a machine pistol.

'Hands!'

'What the hell is going on?' he snapped, standing up with his arms in the air.

Janice stepped forwards. 'Detective Chief Superintendent Warren Douglas,' she said, her voice clear and loud. 'I am arresting you on suspicion of the attempted murder of Detective Inspector Nicholas Dixon.'

Douglas's eyes darted around the room, finding Dixon and fixing him with a cold stare.

'And the murders,' continued Janice, 'of Detective Sergeant Jonathan Sexton, Police Constable Brian Hocking, Derek John Hervey—'

'You're The Vet?' screamed Pandey. 'All this fucking time!'

He lunged at Douglas, but was restrained by two CCU officers.

'Where's Hargreaves?' demanded Douglas, still glaring at Dixon.

'He's dead,' muttered Baxter.

'Lee Henry,' continued Janice. 'And Detective Chief Superintendent Paul Butler.'

Douglas glanced at the back stairs and then the fire exit to find them both blocked, before turning back to stare at Dixon. A CCU officer stepped forwards and handcuffed himself to Douglas's good arm.

'You do not have to say anything, but it may harm your defence if you do not mention when questioned something that you later rely on in court.'

'I know the words.'

'Anything you do say may be given in evidence.'

Silence.

Dixon reached into his pocket, took out a ten pence piece and flicked it, sending it spinning into the air. The coin landed on the corner of a workstation, bounced on to the floor and rolled towards Douglas, falling on to its side and spinning to a standstill at his feet.

'Heads or tails?' muttered Dixon.

'Fuck you.'

◆　◆　◆

'What wouldn't you give to be in there now?' asked Jane, smiling at Dixon.

'I'll settle for being a fly on the wall. And besides, Janice gets to do all the paperwork.'

They were perched on the edge of a table watching Douglas's interview on a black and white monitor, the camera looking down on the scene from above. Janice and Baxter were sitting with their backs to it, Douglas sitting opposite them and next to his solicitor, Susan Allsopp. From time to time he glared up at the camera.

'That's for your benefit,' said Jane.

It would be the first of many interviews, but it would set the tone for those that followed.

Douglas had been abused by his father from the age of seven. It started not long after his mother died of cancer and continued right through until Michael Carter had ended it on the night of his twelfth birthday, which that year happened to fall on Good Friday. Of course, Douglas knew the Carters and, yes, he should have disclosed that before he went undercover.

He could not explain why Hargreaves had faked Michael Carter's DNA sample and denied any conspiracy with him. As for The Vet, he had always believed it was Michael Carter, although he had never been able to prove it. No one had.

'Let's talk about your own DNA then,' said Baxter, leaning back in his chair. 'The sample taken from you after your arrest is a match with the partial sample on the handcuffs used by The Vet. How do you explain that?'

'You said it yourself: it's a partial sample. That's hardly conclusive.' Douglas smirked.

'It's not a match, though, with the sample you gave in 2006 for police database elimination. Why is that?'

'I don't know.'

'Every police officer goes on the database,' said Baxter. 'And you knew your DNA would match, so you faked your sample, didn't you?'

'No.'

'He's lying,' said Dixon.

'What about?' asked Jane.

'All of it.'

A knock at the door stopped Douglas in the middle of yet more denials. Baxter stepped outside the interview room, reappearing a few moments later carrying three evidence bags.

'You may wish to take a moment to discuss these developments with your solicitor, Warren,' said Baxter.

'What developments?'

'This is a fleam.' Baxter placed an evidence bag on the table in front of Douglas. 'It was found under the loft insulation in the extension at the back of your house.'

Douglas leaned forward, his head in his hands.

'This,' Baxter allowed the second bag to drop on to the table with a bang, 'is a trephine. It was under the floorboards in your kitchen. Any thoughts on that, Warren?'

Dixon smiled. He was enjoying the irony in Baxter's voice. Or was it sarcasm?

'And this last one contains eleven circular pieces of skull,' continued Baxter. 'They've been identified as human remains.'

No reply.

'They were behind an air brick in your garage.'

'I don't . . . I . . .'

'I'll tell you what we've also got.'

'What?'

'The Polaroid camera.' Baxter smiled. 'D'you know, Angela had kept it all this time. She had your Walkman too, and your electric shaver complete with hair samples. But then you thought she might, which is why you went looking for it, isn't that right?'

'No.'

'And this is a photograph taken on that same camera.' Baxter dropped the photograph of Dermot McGann on to the table in front of Douglas. 'Isn't it?'

Silence.

'I tell you what we haven't found yet, but we will.'

'What?'

'The rest of the photographs. I'm assuming you took two and kept a set. There'll be ten more, won't there? If you add Paul Butler and the body on Exmoor to the nine victims we know about.'

Baxter waited.

'And what can you tell me about "heads or tails"?' he continued.

'No comment,' said Dixon.

'No comment,' mumbled Douglas.

'Are there any more victims we don't know about?'

'No comment.'

'I think I'd like to have a moment to discuss these new developments with my client,' said Douglas's solicitor.

'Tell us where the other bodies are, Warren.' Baxter leaned forwards. 'There are families who need closure. They need to bury their dead, to grieve.'

Douglas looked up and stared into the camera, giving it his best penetrating glare.

'Twat,' muttered Dixon.

'What about Paul Butler's widow, Warren?' continued Baxter. 'She thinks he committed suicide, but we know different, don't we?'

'No comment.'

'This interview is terminated at 3.24 p.m.' Baxter was looking at his watch. 'Take as long as you need, Miss Allsopp. Your client's not going anywhere.'

'We'll need a news blackout,' said Dixon, when Baxter and Janice walked into the anteroom.

'Hang on a minute.' Baxter dropped his papers on to the table. 'It'll be the biggest news story in Manchester for years. We catch The Vet and—'

'Wrong. *We* caught The Vet. Avon and Somerset, and he's a senior Manchester officer. I'd have thought you'd want to keep that quiet.'

'It'll have to come out at some point.' Baxter was shaking his head.

'Yes, but not before we've got Toby Horan.'

'Whoever he is . . .' Janice's voice tailed off.

'Oh, I know who he is,' said Dixon, with a wry smile. 'And how to find him.'

Chapter Thirty-Two

Dixon waited until they were out on to the M56 before he rang DCI Lewis.

'Well, have you got him?'

'Detective Chief Superintendent Warren Douglas is in custody.'

'You son of a—'

'Thank you, Sir.'

'What about the other one? Hargreaves?'

'He shot himself before he could be arrested.'

'Where are the others?'

'Janice and Louise are staying in Manchester to continue the interviews with Douglas. Dave and Mark are helping with the searches and will be travelling back tomorrow.'

'What about you?'

'We're on the way now.'

'Is there anything you need from me?'

'How far have they got at the factory?' asked Dixon.

'A search team are in there now.'

'We need to tell Horan what he wants to hear. Can you get a press release out saying that the search team have found three bodies? Or two and they're still looking for the third.'

'But, they'll only find two, surely?'

'That's right. It also needs to say that a firearm has been recovered from the scene and that we're not now looking for anyone else in connection with the recent murders.'

'You want me to get Vicky Thomas to lie again?'

'It's not really a lie, is it? We're not looking for anyone else. Just Horan.'

'That's a bit of a stretch, isn't it?'

'It's semantics, Sir,' replied Dixon. 'It just needs to be worded so that Horan will think he's in the clear.'

'What about the MIT?'

'We'll have to get Chard out of the way. Can you get Deborah Potter on board and ask her to summon him to a meeting at Portishead?'

'When?'

'Tomorrow.' Dixon looked at Jane driving the car and raised his eyebrows. 'If that doesn't work, tell him there's been a sighting of Horan on the Shetland Islands.'

'You're a cheeky sod. I'll see what I can do,' said Lewis. 'What's the plan then?'

'There's a joint training exercise tomorrow night, Sir. The RNLI, the BARB hovercraft and the Coastguard. If Horan thinks it's safe, he'll be there. And so will we.'

Dixon's phone buzzed as Jane parked behind the cottage. She wrenched on the handbrake and then switched off the engine. It was just before 9 p.m. and pitch dark, the light on his phone illuminating the passenger compartment of Jane's car. Monty sat up, having been curled up asleep in the passenger footwell since they picked him up from Jane's parents in Worle.

'Who is it?' she asked.

Dixon handed her the phone and she read the message aloud. 'Welcome back to the land of the living. You are a credit to A&S Police. Deborah Potter.'

'Looks like Lewis has done his bit,' said Dixon, opening the passenger door and moving his legs to allow Monty to jump out. 'Now we've just got to hope Horan turns up tomorrow night.'

'And if he doesn't?'

'We'll worry about that tomorrow.'

'What do we do until then?'

'Sleep,' replied Dixon, yawning.

He opened the back door of the cottage and switched on the lights.

'If you're quick, we'll catch the news,' said Jane, watching Monty sniffing along the hedge.

Dixon switched on the TV.

'Structural engineers spent the day at the scene of Thursday's fire at a furniture factory in Somerset. The building was finally made safe late this afternoon allowing fire officers to gain access to the loading bay for the first time since sections of the roof collapsed during a fire that raged for over twenty-four hours.'

'It's on,' shouted Dixon.

'Two bodies have been recovered from the scene so far and the search continues for a third. A firearm has also been recovered. Sapna Ghosh is at the scene.'

'That's Lewis on the left,' said Jane, from the doorway behind Dixon. 'I'm sure it is. You can see his arm.'

'Smoke is still rising from the embers of the old Bailey and Whyte furniture factory here in Highbridge, and you can see fire fighters behind me are still pouring water into the main building as efforts to dampen it down continue. Much of the roof has collapsed and those sections that remain were finally made safe late this afternoon. Three fire officers using breathing apparatus were then able to gain access to the loading bay via the factory floor. We've not been able to send cameras in there at this stage . . .'

'Bloody good job,' muttered Dixon.

'. . . but we are told that two bodies have so far been recovered, as well as a firearm. It has also been confirmed that the fire was started deliberately . . .'

'No shit.'

'. . . late on Wednesday night. In a separate development, police have confirmed that they are now not looking for anyone else in connection with the recent murders of David Cobb and Harry Lucas, bringing to an end the largest manhunt in Avon and Somerset Police history. I have with me Detective Chief Inspector Lewis of Bridgwater CID.'

'He's got his hand in his pocket,' said Jane.

'Probably got his fingers crossed.'

'What can you tell us, Chief Inspector?'

'We've been able to identify the two bodies recovered from the loading bay. We've also recovered a firearm and what we believe to be the murder weapon used in the murders of David Cobb and Harry Lucas. The search continues for a third body, but I can confirm that we are now not seeking anyone else in connection with the murders.'

'Thank you, Inspector.' She turned back to the camera. 'This is Sapna Ghosh for *BBC Points West* in Highbridge, Somerset.'

'I thought he did rather well.' Dixon was putting the kettle on.

'Me too.'

'And he didn't actually lie, did he?'

'No.'

'All we need now is the newspapers and internet news to run it too.'

'It's on the BBC website front page, not just the Somerset news.' Jane was looking at her phone. 'It's even on Burnham-on-Sea dot com.'

'And Horan to see it.'

'Where did that bit about the murder weapon come from?'

'No idea.'

They were watching a similar report on Sky News, recorded earlier, during daylight hours, when there was a knock at the front door.

'Thought you'd be back by now,' said Lewis.

'Come in, Sir,' said Dixon, stepping aside to let him in.

'Cup of tea, Sir?' asked Jane.

'Got anything stronger?'

'A beer?'

'That'll do.'

'We've just been watching you on the telly,' said Dixon, smiling.

'Was it all right?'

'Perfect. And you didn't lie, except for that bit about the murder weapon.'

'That was true.'

'Really?'

'We recovered a trephine from the remains of a coat on the floor in the loading bay.'

'That'll be Horan's. They've got Douglas's trephine in Manchester.'

'And the coat?'

'Mine. The crafty buggers must have put it in my pocket when they left the gun in my hand. Still, it all adds authenticity to the news report.'

Dixon pushed Monty off the sofa and Lewis sat down. 'What did The Vet have to say for himself then?'

'Denials. Then he switched to "no comment" when they presented him with his trephine and the bits of skull.'

'You really need some more furniture in here,' said Lewis. 'An armchair or something.'

Jane rolled her eyes as she handed him a can of beer and a glass.

'How did you get on with Deborah Potter?' asked Dixon.

'Fine. Quite a fan of yours, it seems. She's going to keep Chard out of the way tomorrow.'

'Good.'

'What time's the training exercise?'

'Seven. We'll need some more legs though,' replied Dixon. 'Dave and Mark should be back from Manchester. Janice and Louise possibly.'

'And me,' said Lewis, grinning. 'I'm not missing this.'

Chapter Thirty-Three

'What time is it?'

'Ten past eleven.'

Dixon noticed light streaming in through a gap in the curtains. 'In the morning?'

'I made you a coffee, but it'll be stone cold by now.'

'What time did we come to bed?'

'Elevenish. We were watching *The Shawshank Redemption*, and you fell asleep.'

Dixon yawned. 'Twelve hours?'

'Yep.'

'Well, I don't believe I fell asleep in front of *The Shawshank Redemption*.'

'You did.'

He shook his head. 'What about Monty?'

'He's been fed and been out,' replied Jane, sitting up. 'Dave and Mark are on their way back and will be here just after lunch. Janice and Louise are leaving at two and will be here by seven.'

'And Cole?'

'It's his day off, but he said he'd come.'

'Did you tell him what for?'

'No.'

Dixon sat up and picked up the mug on his bedside table. 'Any chance of a fresh coffee?' he asked.

◆ ◆ ◆

'What d'you want for breakfast?' Dixon was watching Monty from the kitchen window and eating a bowl of cornflakes.

'I had some earlier,' replied Jane. She opened the back door to let Monty in. 'So, what do we do for the rest of the day?'

'We wait.'

'Is that you or me?' asked Jane, when a phone started ringing in the bedroom.

Dixon delayed his answer until Jane was already halfway up the stairs. 'Mine,' he whispered.

'It's yours.'

'Is it?'

'Hi, Jan, how's it going?' Jane appeared on the landing. 'Yeah, he's fine. Hang on, I'll pass you over.'

Jane dropped Dixon's phone over the bannister and he caught it, wincing as he did so.

'Sorry,' said Jane. 'I forgot.'

'Hi, Jan.'

'The good news is Douglas is offering us a deal: the Carters in return for immunity.'

'Immunity?' Dixon laughed. 'That's not good news, Jan; that's taking the piss.'

'He knows where they are.'

'He's murdered ten people we know about.' Dixon was pacing up and down in front of the television. 'Eleven if you include Paul Butler.'

'He denied killing Butler.'

'I bet he did. He knows we haven't got any evidence.'

'Baxter's reluctant, but then he's Counter Corruption.'

'Look, Janice. Tell him no deal. All right?'

'But he says he knows where the Carters are.'

'So do I. You said that was the good news. What's the bad?'

'The *Manchester Daily Post* has got hold of the story. They're going to put it live on their website at midnight and it'll be on the front page of the paper tomorrow.'

'What story?'

'The arrest of The Vet.'

'Nothing else?'

'No. GMP must have a leak. Baxter's got the Chief Constable leaning on the editor, but it's such a big story . . .'

'Relax, Jan. If Horan does what I expect him to do, it'll all be over by then anyway.'

'So, it's no deal.'

'That's right.'

'Can I tell him you know where the Carters are?'

'Yes. Tell him I know where both of them are. And tell Louise I'm still waiting for the result of that last DNA test.'

Jane waited until Dixon rang off. 'So, where are they then?'

'Kettle's boiled,' replied Dixon, smiling. 'D'you want that coffee?'

◆　◆　◆

Dixon was in the shower when he heard voices downstairs. Then Jane tapped on the door.

'Who is it?' asked Dixon, wiping away the condensation on the glass and peering out.

'Dave and Mark. They've been in the pub for a bite to eat.'

'What's the time?'

'Nearly five. Lewis is on his way and Cole will be here soon too.'

'All right, I'm coming.'

By the time he was dressed, DCI Lewis had arrived. He was sitting at the dining table with a mug of tea, watching Dave Harding and Mark Pearce watching the local news on the TV.

Dixon was halfway down the stairs when there was a knock at the door, and Jane opened it.

'Holy shit,' said Cole, looking up. 'You're supposed to be . . . I thought you were . . .'

'You look like you've seen a ghost,' said Jane, smiling. 'I've always wanted to say that to someone.'

'Don't just stand there, Cole, come in,' said Dixon.

'And you lot knew all the time?'

'Yep,' said Pearce, without taking his eyes off the screen. 'Here we go; they're running it again.'

A different newsreader confirmed that the search for a third body continued, then switched to Sapna Ghosh at the factory. She interviewed Chief Fire Officer Stewart who said that huge piles of smouldering furniture were hampering the search team.

'He's a good lad, is John,' said Lewis.

'The Chief Fire Officer is in on it?' asked Cole.

'Yes.'

Then came an interview with Deborah Potter, who gave much the same information as DCI Lewis had the night before.

'So, we were after that Horan bloke for nothing then?' asked Cole.

'You know, this might just work,' said Lewis, smiling.

Janice and Louise arrived just as Jane was reversing out from behind the cottage.

'We hit the rush hour traffic at Bristol,' shouted Janice, leaning across the passenger seat of her car.

Louise had jumped out and was waiting while Dixon wound down the passenger window on Jane's car. She handed him an envelope.

'This is the DNA test result, Sir.'

'What does it say?'

'You were right.'

Dixon smiled. 'Tell Janice to follow us.'

'Yes, Sir.'

'Right about what?' asked Jane.

'You'll see,' replied Dixon. 'With a bit of luck.'

◆ ◆ ◆

The jetty was a hive of activity when Dixon and Jane drove along the sea front and turned into the short stay car park. Dixon was wearing a bobble hat to hide the dressing on the side of his head, and a pair of gloves. A couple of days' worth of stubble completed his disguise.

Jane parked facing the Esplanade and switched off the engine.

'We'd better wait for the others.'

Janice and Louise were parked next to them, but Dave, Mark, DCI Lewis and PC Cole had gone through the town to ensure they arrived separately rather than in convoy.

Dixon watched a huge blue tractor towing the inshore lifeboat on its trailer up Pier Street and then across to the jetty. Behind came the new 'D' Class lifeboat, *Burnham Reach*, that had recently replaced *Puffin*, the inflatable that had plucked him from the waves only a few weeks before. Three lifeboat crew in their bright yellow dry suits were running along behind.

'Don't fancy it on a night like this,' muttered Jane.

A strong onshore wind was whipping the bushes along the wall in front of the car, bending them right over on to the bonnet of Jane's car. Even the lamp posts on the promenade were moving in the gusts of wind.

'At least it's not raining,' said Dixon, watching the thick grey clouds above racing across the sky.

The large doors were open at the front of the Coastguard station, several Coastguard mud technicians climbing into their yellow mud suits in readiness for the training exercise. At the BARB station a Land Rover was being hitched up to the trailer, ready to tow the hovercraft out to the jetty.

'It'll take off in this wind.'

'They won't launch it, surely, if the wind's too strong?'

'Maybe not.'

'There they are,' said Jane, pointing to a car that passed in front of them before turning into the car park. 'They've all come in one car.'

Dixon climbed out of Jane's car, pulled up the collar on his coat and ran across to the sea wall. He leaned over and looked along to the jetty. A small crowd had gathered at the top, some pointing cameras at the lifeboats and the hovercraft that was now being reversed into position, and several Coastguard officers were standing at the water's edge, or as near to it as they dared. The wind was whipping the surf into foaming breakers that were crashing on to the jetty, perhaps thirty yards below the hovercraft.

On the beach the other side of the jetty, the inshore lifeboat, still on its trailer, was being reversed into the sea by the tractor. The water was up over the wheels of the tractor and the lifeboat was starting to bounce around in the surf, crashing into the netting on either side of the trailer. The waves were breaking over the cabin on the tractor when the lifeboat roared out through the surf, rearing up as it crested the waves, before dropping down on the far side, the noise of the impact drowning out even the two large outboard engines. Seconds later, and before the lifeboat had cleared the breakers, the tractor was back up on the beach, seawater pouring off it.

Once clear of the surf, the inshore lifeboat set off across the estuary towards the Hinkley Point power station, just visible in the distance.

Still on the beach, the smaller inflatable 'D' Class lifeboat was being towed by a tracked vehicle that was reversing into position, ready to launch, and beyond that, two HM Coastguard vehicles, a Land Rover and a pickup truck.

Dixon watched the hovercraft being manhandled off the trailer on to the jetty. He couldn't hear anything over the wind and the waves, but the propeller on the back was turning, the engine idling, judging by the exhaust fumes.

A figure wearing black trousers and a green coat left the crowd at the top of the jetty and walked down towards the Coastguard officers standing near the BARB Land Rover. His left hand was raised, holding up the hood of his coat in the wind, the sleeve riding up to reveal a wrist swathed in bandages.

Dixon smiled.

He waited.

The conversation seemed animated, but they were probably just shouting to make themselves heard over the wind and the waves. Heads were shaking and shoulders being shrugged, presumably the launch of the hovercraft aborted due to the weather conditions.

Let me see your face, you son of—

The figure turned into the wind and the hood snapped back.

Dixon turned and ran back across the road to the car park. 'It's him,' he said as the others climbed out of their cars.

'Where is he?' asked Lewis.

'On the jetty,' replied Dixon. 'There are steps either side at the top. Louise, you and Cole go down the steps on to the beach on the left. Dave and Mark, you take the right hand side.'

'Yes, Sir.'

'Janice, you're with me and Jane. It's your arrest, remember.'

'What about me?' asked Lewis.

'You go where you want, Sir,' replied Dixon.

Lewis grinned.

'Let me bring up the Armed Response team,' he said. 'They're waiting in Abingdon Street.'

They waited a few seconds for Lewis to make the call and then crossed the road to the top of the jetty. Horan was still standing by the BARB Land Rover, although he was not taking part in the conversation, just standing there, eavesdropping by the looks of it.

Louise and PC Cole went down the steps on to the beach to the left and walked towards the tide line. Dave Harding and Mark Pearce went down the steps on the right. Dixon stepped forwards, Jane and Janice either side of him and DCI Lewis behind. He turned at the sound of footsteps running up behind to see four firearms officers moving into position behind the sea wall, the small crowd having melted away.

The roar of the wind and the crash of the waves masked their approach, but Dixon still tiptoed down the jetty. He felt oddly calm and yet he was about to bring down the leader of Manchester's most violent crime gang of the nineties.

Who's the rat catcher now?

Dixon was standing no more than three feet behind him now. He stopped and took a deep breath.

'Hello, Kenny,' he said.

Carter spun round.

'You?' He backed away from Dixon, the Coastguard officers stepping aside. 'It said in the paper you were dead.'

'You surely don't believe what you read in the papers?'

Carter glanced down at the beach either side of the jetty.

'You're not supposed to be looking for anyone else?'

'We're not. Just you. And we've found you, haven't we, Kenny?'

'My name is Toby Horan.'

'It is now, but it was your brother's name first, wasn't it? After he went into witness protection. There's a familial match between your DNA – you left a plentiful supply in the caravan – and Michael's body in the shallow grave on Dunkery Beacon. You know, the one Denise Marks led us to.'

'He ruined everything.' Carter was backing away down the side of the BARB Land Rover now. Dixon and Jane followed, with Janice and Lewis taking the other side. 'We had Manchester sewn up. Then he gets all bloody patriotic when the IRA blew up the Arndale Centre. I told him what would happen. I fucking told him.'

'So, you killed him. Let me re-phrase that. You got The Vet to kill him. Then you took his place in witness protection, paid off Denise and lived happily ever after in Burnham-on-Sea.'

'Until that bastard . . .'

'Be fair, Kenny. They didn't know who they were dealing with, did they?' Dixon was following Carter as he backed away towards the BARB trailer. 'And how could they? Paul Butler was right all along, wasn't he?'

'I fucking showed them.'

'That's right, Kenny. You did.' Dixon shook his head.

'You'll never pin anything on me. Chief Superintendent Douglas will see to that.' Carter grinned.

'He may struggle with that from his cell, Kenny,' replied Dixon. 'Warren Douglas is in custody.'

'Fuck.'

'We found his trephine, and d'you know he'd even kept the little pieces of skull. Heads or tails and all that.' Dixon sneered. 'Tosser.'

Carter glanced down at the beach to his right, watching Louise and PC Cole following him as he staggered back along the jetty.

'Oh, and Hargreaves is dead. Shot himself when they went to arrest him.'

Carter was holding on to the empty trailer, the hovercraft behind him now, its engine still running.

'Stuck your neck out a bit,' continued Dixon, 'turning up to rescue Harry Lucas. What did you say to him as he was drowning?'

'I . . .'

'D'you know what, Kenny? I don't want to know. It's over.'

The beach on the other side of the jetty was crowded with Coastguard officers, lifeboat crew and police, all watching what was unfolding above them. And there was no way past Dixon and Jane on one side of the Land Rover and Janice and Lewis on the other.

Janice stepped forwards. 'Kenneth Carter, I am arresting you on suspicion of the murders of—'

Carter lunged at Janice, pushing her off the jetty on to the beach below. Then he turned and sprinted down the jetty. He jumped into the hovercraft and opened the throttle, sending it lurching towards the surf.

'He'll never make it,' shouted one of the Coastguard officers. 'We just aborted the launch due to the high winds. Anything more than fifteen miles an hour and it'll flip.'

The hovercraft hit the first wave and bounced, the front rising up. Carter threw his weight forwards, over the handle bars, sending it down again behind the wave, before it hit another wave and reared up again.

'The waves are smaller on the jetty,' said Dixon.

'The water's shallower,' replied the Coastguard officer.

'He's going to make it.'

Dixon and Jane jumped down on to the beach where Dave, Mark and DCI Lewis were kneeling over Janice. 'She's fine. Go!' shouted Lewis.

Then they sprinted across the sand to the Coastguard Land Rover. Dixon glanced across to Carter, who was now clear of the breakers and heading north just beyond the surf, the hovercraft bouncing across the waves. Carter was fighting with the handlebars, trying to hold it straight in the strong cross wind.

Dixon wrenched open the driver's door and looked in. 'No keys!'

'Here!' Steve Yelland was running towards them. 'I've got them. Get in.'

Yelland set off along the beach with Dixon and Jane in the passenger seat. Dixon watched the 'D' Class lifeboat being reversed out into the waves.

'The Beach Master is launching the "D",' said Yelland. 'And we've got a message to the inshore lifeboat too. Just to be on hand, if needed.' He glanced across at the hovercraft. 'That's Toby Horan, isn't it?'

'No, it isn't.'

'Who is it then?'

'Long story,' replied Dixon.

'Did he kill the pest control bloke?'

'Yes.'

'I thought you weren't looking for anyone else?'

'We needed to flush him out, and it worked.'

The tide had gone out beyond the end of the pavilion so Yelland was able to drive round it, finding the gap in the groyne in the shallow water. Then he sped off along the beach with his blue light flashing and siren wailing. Dixon watched the dog walkers putting their dogs on leads as the Land Rover raced towards them.

They had caught up with Carter by the time they reached the lighthouse and kept pace with him along the beach.

'Where's he going?' asked Jane.

Yelland grimaced. 'No idea. He'll never get round the end of Brean Down.'

'Why not?'

'It's the overfalls off Howe Rock. The currents on the Parrett and Axe meet up off the headland there. Huge waves, criss-crossing. It's bad enough in the inshore lifeboat. The "D" Class can't go in there.'

'What about the helicopter?

Yelland snatched his radio off the dashboard. 'Watch, this is OIC Burnham. We are in pursuit of a police suspect attempting to make his escape in the BARB hovercraft heading north towards Howe Rock. Despatch Rescue 187. Over.'

'Stand by, Burnham.'

'Only a couple of miles to go,' said Dixon. 'There's the SS *Nornen*.' He was pointing at the large yellow marker buoys bouncing around in the surf.

'Any sign of the lifeboats?' asked Jane.

'Yes.' Dixon was looking over his shoulder. 'They're still a way off though. Better tell them to stay back. He might be armed.'

'Which lifeboat is it?' asked Yelland.

'The inflatable.'

'Burnham 2, this is Coastguard. Better keep your distance; he may have a gun. Over.' Yelland glanced across at the hovercraft. 'He is. He's going to try and go round Brean Down.'

'Is there any chance he can make it?'

'None. He'll know that too.'

'If he does, he's got away because we can't go any further.'

'Really. He's not getting round it in this wind.'

'Let's give him a chance to land then,' said Dixon. 'Switch off your blue light and siren and get off the beach there.' He was pointing at the Berrow Beach access road.

'You're sure?'

'Yes. And stop once we're out of sight.'

Yelland turned on to the slip road and slid to a halt on the soft sand once he was hidden by the dunes. Dixon jumped out and ran back.

Seconds later he was back in the Land Rover. 'He's turned away from the beach, so he's definitely going for it.'

Yelland sped out to the main road, turned left and floored the accelerator, getting up to over 70 mph along Warren Road, his blue light flashing and siren wailing.

The National Trust car park at Brean Down was empty and the cafe closed.

'Head for the gate,' said Dixon, pointing beyond the 'No Vehicular Access' signs.

'It's all right. I've got a key.'

'We haven't got time for that.'

Yelland smashed into the five bar gate at over 30 mph, knocking it flat. The Land Rover bounced over it. Then he accelerated up the road that led diagonally on to the top of Brean Down, turned left and sped out towards the headland and the fort.

'Can you see him?' asked Yelland.

'Not now. He was still on the Burnham side though.'

'What about the lifeboats?'

'The inshore was closest when I lost sight of them,' replied Dixon. 'How much light have we got left?'

'Not long. Twenty minutes, something like that.'

Yelland stamped on the brakes when they reached the fort and they jumped out, sprinting down to an abandoned gun emplacement overlooking Howe Rock.

'He's going for it,' said Yelland. 'He must be bloody mad.'

'Or suicidal,' muttered Dixon.

They watched him wrestling with the controls, a handlebar and throttle just like a motorbike. The inshore lifeboat was coming up behind him, but he would reach the overfalls first. It formed a diamond pattern off the headland of waves going in different directions, some much bigger than Dixon had seen anywhere else in the Bristol Channel.

'It's a northwesterly.' Yelland grimaced. 'As soon as he gets round the point, it'll hit him.'

Carter was perhaps two hundred yards away now, sitting at the controls of the hovercraft as it bounced over the waves, the spray soaking him each time.

'There are two propellers,' shouted Yelland. 'One underneath the front to give it lift and the bigger one at the back to propel it forwards. If the wind gets under it, he's had it.'

'Here we go,' said Jane.

Dixon watched the hovercraft close in on the edge of the overfalls. The first wave turned it sideways, then another hit from the front. It reared up, the wind billowing under the skirt. It appeared to take off and do a half-somersault, before it landed upside down.

'Where is he?' asked Yelland.

'Underneath.' Dixon shook his head. 'Buried at sea.'

The hovercraft was being battered by waves hitting it from all angles now, some sending it spinning round, others crashing over it. Another rolled it over.

'Burnham 1, this is Coastguard,' Yelland was shouting into his radio. 'Expanding box search from last known position. Burnham 2, stand off. Rescue 187 has been requested.'

Dixon watched the larger of the two lifeboats, Burnham 1, rear up as it crested the huge waves surging in different directions.

'The hovercraft's empty,' said Yelland, watching through binoculars. 'There's no sign of him either.'

The hovercraft reared up and sank just as Burnham 1 reached it. The lifeboat began making a search in the overfalls, being tossed and bounced around as it raced backwards and forwards across the currents, the sound of its engines soon drowned out by a red and white Coastguard helicopter hovering overhead.

They watched in silence for ten minutes, until Yelland's radio crackled into life.

'Burnham 1, this is Milford Coastguard. Back to place of safety. Hovercraft is submerged. Rescue 187 will take it from here. Stand down. Repeat, stand down.'

Chapter Thirty-Four

'Here are your keys.'

'You're going to need a new car,' said Jane. She was lying on the sofa with her feet resting on Monty.

'I thought I might go for something a bit different this time.'

'Really?'

'Maybe the short wheelbase version. I liked that one the Coastguard have got.'

Jane sighed.

Dixon was standing in the kitchen doorway with a mug in his hand. 'Tea?'

'No, thanks.' Jane sat up. 'How'd you get on with the Chief Constable?'

'Not sure, really. I remember he used the word "subterfuge" and frowned a lot.'

'Is that it?'

'And I made him look like an idiot on the TV, apparently.'

'Anything else?'

'I wasn't listening.'

'What the—?' Jane spun round on the sofa, stopping mid-sentence when she noticed Dixon smiling at her. 'What?'

'I'm getting a commendation.'

'You jammy git.'

'Janice is too.'

'What for?'

'She was senior investigating officer, don't forget, and technically it was her team that made the arrests. The Environment Agency bloke woke up and identified Martin White, so she got the eel poachers too.'

'Was she there?'

'Yes.'

'How is she?'

'Fine. She was winded, that's all, and her ribs hurt for a day or two, but she's fine.' Dixon sat down on the arm of the sofa. 'Deborah Potter was there too. She offered me a transfer to Portishead.'

'What did you tell her?' Jane frowned.

'That I'd think about it and let her know. I rang Paul Butler's widow afterwards and said I'd call in on the way back from your mother's funeral.'

'Fine.'

'Then I went to see Jonny's family.'

'How were they?'

'Not good. His parents have lost both their sons now,' replied Dixon, shaking his head.

'And will you?'

'What?'

'Think about it.'

'Saved by the bell,' he said, smiling as he reached into his jacket pocket and took out his phone. 'It's from Janice.' Dixon dropped the phone into Jane's lap. 'You coming?'

She picked it up and read the text message aloud. '*West Huntspill Sewage Treatment Works, quick as you can.*' Then handed the phone back to Dixon. 'What's that all about?'

'My guess is Kenny Carter's put in another appearance.'

◆ ◆ ◆

The uniformed officer opened the gate on Sloway Lane and Jane drove out along the River Huntspill towards the outfall into the River Parrett.

'There's an odd sort of symmetry to this, don't you think?'

'It's called a coincidence,' replied Dixon, watching a heron on the far bank.

'I thought you said—'

'You're right. Let's stick with symmetry.'

Dixon ignored Jane's emphatic nod.

At the outfall she turned north along the service road that followed the River Parrett. A short wheelbase Land Rover was visible in the distance, on the top of the embankment.

'There it is again,' said Dixon. 'It's the Defender 90. Much quicker too. What d'you think?'

'Lovely.' Jane sighed.

An ambulance was parked on the embankment behind the Land Rover and beyond that a fire engine.

'Let's leave this here and walk the rest of the way,' said Dixon.

Jane pulled into a lay-by on the service road and Dixon let Monty out of the back of the car. Then they crossed the embankment and walked along the grass just above the high tide line. Two more Land Rovers were visible in the distance, on the concrete service road beyond where it crossed over the embankment. Three Coastguard mud technicians were climbing into bright yellow mud suits, while another carried a large orange stretcher to the edge of the mud.

Dixon stopped to put Monty on his lead as they approached the sewage outfall, marked by the huge concrete viewing platform and warning sign, not that he could imagine anyone dropping anchor along here. Janice spotted them and walked along the service road with Louise to meet them.

'Is it him?' asked Dixon.

'He's face down in the mud, but he's wearing a green coat and black trousers, so . . .' Janice's voice tailed off.

'You all right, Sir?' asked Louise.

'Fine, thanks. These are getting better anyway,' he said, holding out his hands.

'He's over there,' said Janice. 'The Coastguard are getting ready to go out and get him.'

'Well, he was one of theirs, wasn't he?'

'There's no hovercraft, unfortunately,' said Louise, raising her eyebrows.

Dixon handed Monty's lead to Jane and walked across to the stones at the edge of the mud. He looked at the body, perhaps twenty yards away down the slope towards the concrete outfall, the waterline a further five or so yards below that. At least the ducks had gone this time.

An orange fishing net appeared to be tangled around Carter's left wrist, hiding the bandages, and a mat of thick black seaweed covered his head, affording it some protection from the seagulls. Not that he had lain there for long.

'A dog walker found him,' said Janice. She was standing next to Dixon on the edge of the mud.

'Where would we be without dog walkers?'

Janice smiled. 'How did you know it was Kenny?'

'Denise Marks told me. And if you assume Paul Butler was right about the Carters then it all drops into place. That and Michael's interview.'

'What about it?'

'If I'd stabbed someone in the neck and then shot them at point blank range, I like to think I'd remember which way round I'd done it, even at the age of fifteen.'

'He didn't do it?'

'Kenny did and Michael protected him, but nobody cared. They'd got a confession and that was that.'

'And the DNA test?'

'Horan was related to the body on Dunkery Beacon. That made it either Kenny or Michael,' Dixon shrugged his shoulders. 'So I had a fifty-fifty chance either way. But Angela Maxwell confirmed it. She recognised him.'

He watched the mud technicians wading out across the mud, dragging the stretcher behind them. They were up to their waists by the time they reached the body, but somehow managed to manhandle it on to the stretcher, rolling Carter on to his back and tying him on. Then they turned and began wading back towards the safety of the stones.

Dixon stood over the stretcher and looked down at Carter, watching the seawater draining from his nose and mouth, leaving streaks in the wet mud on his face. The large mat of rotting seaweed tangled around his neck and arm had come with him on the stretcher and a paramedic began cutting it away.

'I'd leave that, if I were you,' said Dixon, grateful for the stench.

Chapter Thirty-Five

Two funerals in three days. It was enough for anyone.

Jonny Sexton's had been very different: a huge crowd of mourners, led by his family and the Chief Constable – who had not finished frowning at Dixon – past and present colleagues and friends, a guard of honour; Avon and Somerset Police had been out in force for a colleague killed in the line of duty. And rightly so.

And the TV cameras, of course. They had been there too.

Now Dixon was sitting outside Carlisle Crematorium watching the other mourners – both of them – admiring the daffodils and the rose garden, a few early buds on the way. Neighbours, apparently. They hadn't known Sonia well, they had told Dixon, but her probation officer had told them the funeral would not be well attended so they felt they ought to be there to make up the numbers. He shook his head. It sounded sad and it was.

Two more arrived as the hearse drew up to the front.

'That's Sonia's probation officer, I think,' said Jane. 'I'm not sure who the other one is.'

Dixon squeezed her hand.

That made six.

'We'd better go in.'

Carlisle Crematorium was identical to every other crematorium he had ever been in, but it did have a nice view. Dixon was looking out of the window at the spring flowers in the Garden of Remembrance, and beyond them Carlisle and the Solway Plain. It was as good a place as any to meet your maker, he thought as he put his arm around Jane.

She had felt fine before the service, or at least had said she had, but as soon as it started she had begun to cry. Still, she had come armed with a packet of tissues, so all Dixon had to do was be there.

It was an odd relationship, mother and daughter. Jane had only met her birth mother twice, but her death could still invoke this reaction. Maybe she was crying for what she'd lost?

He glanced around the crematorium. No sign of Tony, which was a relief. Still, it would have been a first, arresting someone at a funeral. *Twat.*

They were sitting in the front row, the only other mourners on the other side of the aisle. He noticed a middle-aged couple and a girl of fifteen or so sitting at the back. They must have crept in once the service had started.

The eulogy was short, and the vicar obviously hadn't known Sonia. A few prayers, two hymns and that was that. In and out in under twenty minutes. It wasn't much to show for fifty years of life.

Once the service was over, Dixon left Jane talking to the vicar and followed the late arrivals to their car on the far side of the car park.

'Excuse me, I didn't get a chance to ask you who you were,' he said, catching up with them just as the man was opening the car doors.

'Er, I—'

'Sonia was my mother,' said the girl, her jet black hair obviously dyed. 'These are my foster parents.'

'What's your name?'

'Lucy.'

'Who are you?' asked the man.

'My name's Nick,' replied Dixon, smiling. 'Would you mind waiting here a minute?'

'Well, we—'

'Why?' asked the girl.

'There's someone I think you'd like to meet.'

The girl nodded.

Dixon ran back over to Jane, who was sitting on a bench staring at the spring daisies. She looked up, her eyes full of tears. He sat down next to her, took her hand and smiled.

'Come and meet your sister.'

Acknowledgments

There are a great many people without whom this book would not have been written, but also a great many without whom it would not have been read. So, first of all, I would to thank *you*, the reader. Whether this is your first experience of the DI Nick Dixon Crime Series or whether you have followed Nick, Jane and Monty through all seven books thus far, thank you and I hope you enjoyed the ride!

I would also like to thank my editorial team at Thomas & Mercer, whose patience has not yet run out despite my best efforts. And to my friends and unpaid editors, as always, and in no particular order, Alison Crowther Smith, Charlie Szechowski and Rod Glanville.

I should also like to express my particular thanks to Dr Harry Pugh MB ChB MRCOG FRCA and Mr Jonathan Bull MA MB BChir MD(Res) FRCSGlasg FRCSEng (Consultant Neurosurgeon) for their invaluable help with the medical aspects in this book. Needless to say, the surgical niceties involved went right over my head (if you'll pardon the pun!) and I am deeply grateful to them for sharing their knowledge and expertise.

I would also like to record my thanks to Beverley Milner Simonds for sharing her experiences of HM Coastguard operations and to the team at BARB Search & Rescue for the guided tour of their station and the hovercraft – for the record, they have two of them! And, once again, to Burnham-on-Sea RNLI who have been extraordinarily generous with their time. Thank you for the ride in the lifeboat too!

And lastly to my father, Michael. Thanks for everything, Dad. I'll see you on the other side.

Damien Boyd
Devon, UK
March 2017

About the Author

Damien Boyd is a solicitor by training and draws on his extensive experience of criminal law, along with a spell in the Crown Prosecution Service, to write fast-paced crime thrillers featuring Detective Inspector Nick Dixon.

Primary Teaching Assistants

Primary Teaching Assistants: Learners and Learning draws together ideas that are of central importance to teaching assistants and other support staff working in primary schools. It presents a rich variety of material written by teachers, teaching assistants, researchers and parents, that has been carefully chosen to offer a broad-based understanding of learning and the contexts in which learners can engage meaningfully with learning.

This second edition has been thoroughly updated and includes new chapters on effective communication, anti-cyber bullying, bullying amongst girls, higher level teaching assistants, restorative justice, and informal learning. Bringing together different perspectives it examines:

- the changing role of teaching assistants
- the nature of learning and assessment
- approaches to learning support and inclusive practice
- the relationships that are central to learning and children's social development.

Written for learning support staff and also their teaching colleagues, the book aims to enrich the contribution that adults can make to children's learning in schools.

Roger Hancock is an Educational Consultant and Researcher.

Janet Collins is a Staff Tutor at The Open University.

Mary Stacey is a Writer and an Educational Consultant.

Primary Teaching Assistants: Learners and learning

This Reader, and the companion volume *Primary Teaching Assistants: Curriculum in context* edited by Carrie Cable, Ian Eyres, Roger Hancock and Mary Stacey, form part of the Open University materials for modules about primary education.

Details of Open University modules can be obtained from the Student Registration and Enquiry Service, The Open University, PO Box 197, Milton Keynes MK7 6BJ, United Kingdom (tel. +44 (0)845 300 60 90, e-mail general-enquiries@open.ac.uk). www.open.ac.uk

Primary Teaching Assistants

Learners and learning
Second edition

Edited by
Roger Hancock,
Janet Collins
and Mary Stacey

LONDON AND NEW YORK

First published in 2005
by Routledge

This edition published in 2013
by Routledge
2 Park Square, Milton Park, Abingdon, Oxon OX14 4RN

Simultaneously published in the USA and Canada
by Routledge
711 Third Avenue, New York, NY 10017

Routledge is an imprint of the Taylor & Francis Group, an informa business

Published in association with The Open University, Walton Hall, Milton Keynes,
MK7 6AA, UK

British Library Cataloguing in Publication Data
A catalogue record for this book is available from the British Library

Library of Congress Cataloging in Publication Data
Primary teaching assistants: learners and learning / edited by Roger Hancock,
Janet Collins and Mary Stacey. — 2nd ed.
     p. cm. — (Published in association with the open university)
  1. Teachers' assistants—Great Britain.   2. Education, Elementary—Great Britain.
  I. Hancock, Roger.   II. Collins, Janet.
  III. Stacey, Mary, 1943–
  LB2844.1.A8P754 2012
  371.14'1240941—dc23

                                                                        2012007406

ISBN: 978–0–415–50430–0 (hbk)
ISBN: 978–0–415–50431–7 (pbk)
ISBN: 978–0–203–12838–1 (ebk)

Typeset in Bembo
by RefineCatch Limited, Bungay, Suffolk

MIX
Paper from
responsible sources
FSC www.fsc.org   FSC® C013056

Printed and bound in Great Britain by
TJ Books Limited, Padstow, Cornwall

Contents

Section 4
Learners' identities   **203**

Acknowledgements

We wish to thank those who have written chapters for this Reader or who have given their permission for us to edit and reprint writing from other publications. A special thanks to Kathy Simms for her invaluable secretarial support, and to Bharti Mistry and Gill Gowans for their ongoing involvement and preparation of the final manuscript for handover to the publishers.

Grateful acknowledgement is made to the following sources for permission to reproduce material in this book. Those chapters not listed below have been specially commissioned.

Hancock, R., Hall, T., Cable, C. and Eyres, I. (2010) '"They call me wonder woman": the job jurisdictions and workplace learning of higher level teaching assistants' *Cambridge Journal of Education*, *40*(2), 97–112. Reprinted by permission of Taylor & Francis Ltd, (http://www.tandf.co.uk/journals).

Mason, L. (1998) 'My history of helpers', *The Inclusion Assistant*, Alliance for Inclusive Education, London. For more information, please visit www.allfie.org.uk.

Wedell, K. (2001) 'Klaus' story: the experience of a retired professor of special needs education', in T. O'Brien and P. Garner (eds.) *Untold Stories: Learning Support Assistants and Their Work* (Stoke on Trent: Trentham Books Ltd).

Claxton, G. (2002) 'What is education for?', in *Building Learning Power* (Bristol: TLO Limited).

Burke, C. and Grosvenor, I., (2003) 'Learning: "Let us out . . .!"', in *The School I'd Like* (London: Routledge). Reprinted by permission of Taylor & Francis Ltd.

Thomas, A. (1998) 'Informal learning', in *Educating Children and Home* (London, Cassell). Reproduced with permission of CONTINUUM PUBLISHING COMPANY in the format Textbook via Copyright Clearance Center.

Dhillon, A. (2003) 'Net gains for "slum" children' *The Times* 17 July.

Crowley, S. and Richardson, M. (2004) 'Raising the bar: improving children's performance through information and communication technology', in C. Bold (ed.), *Supporting Learning and Teaching*, (London: David Fulton). In *Primary Teaching Assistants: Learners and Learning* (London: Routledge). Reprinted by permission of Taylor & Francis Ltd.

Kay, J. (2002) 'Assessment and recording', in *Teaching Assistant's Handbook*, Chapter 6, pp. 103–118, London, Continuum. Reproduced with permission of CONTINUUM PUBLISHING COMPANY in the format Textbook via Copyright Clearance Center.

Stern, J. (2003) 'Homework', Chapter 6, pp. 54–62 (London: Continuum). Reproduced with permission of CONTINUUM PUBLISHING COMPANY in the format Textbook via Copyright Clearance Center.

Alderson, P. (2003) *Institutional Rites and Rights: A Century of Childhood* (London: Institute of Education, University of London).

Collins, J. (1998) 'Hearing the silence in the classroom full of noise: empowering quiet pupils', *Topic: Practical Applications of Research in Education* issue 20, Autumn (Slough: National Foundation for Educational Research).

Royal College of Psychiatrists (2004) *Eating Disorders in Young People: Factsheet for Parents and Teachers* (London: Royal College of Psychiatrists).

Oliver, C. and Candappa, M. (2003) *Tackling Bullying – Listening to the Views of Children and Young People* Summary Report RB400, pp. 5–11, HMSO/Department for Education and Skills.

Anti-cyber bullying policy (East Herrington Primary School). This policy is reproduced by kind permission of East Herrington Primary School. The school in no way warrants that the policy is correct but has agreed to its reproduction as part of the larger work.

Johnson, P. (2004) 'Boys don't cry'. Copyright Guardian News & Media Ltd 2004.

Kay, J. (2002) 'Supporting children's learning and behaviour in school', in *Teaching Assistant's Handbook*, Chapter 7, pp. 119–139 (London: Continuum). Reproduced with permission of CONTINUUM PUBLISHING COMPANY in the format Textbook via Copyright Clearance Center.

Jameson, G. (1994) 'Three Billy Goats: six children and race, language and class', *Primary Teaching Studies*, *8*(2), pp. 27–31 (London: University of North London – now part of London Metropolitan University).

Gardiner, G. (2001) 'Life as a disabled head', *Primary Practice (Journal of the National Primary Trust)*, number 29, Autumn, pp. 20–22, National Primary Trust. Copyright Gina Gardiner 2001. For more information, please visit http://www.ginagardinerassociates.co.uk/

Watkins, C. (2009) 'Learners in the driving seat' *School Leadership Today*, *12*, 28–31, Teaching Times.

Kenner, C. (2003) 'An interactive pedagogy for bilingual children', in E. Bearne, H. Dombey, and T. Grainger (eds) *Classroom Interactions in Literacy* (Maidenhead: Open University Press/McGraw-Hill) pp. 90–102.

Cooley, R. (2003) 'Beyond pink and blue' *Rethinking Schools, 18*(2). (Milwaukee: Rethinking Schools).

Reay, D. (2003) 'Troubling, troubled and troublesome? Working with boys in primary classrooms', in C. Skelton and B. Francis (eds) *Boys and Girls in the Primary Classroom* (Maidenhead: Open University Press/ McGraw-Hill) pp. 151–166.

Disclaimer

Every effort has been made to contact all the copyright holders of material included in the book. If any material has been included without permission, the publishers offer their apologies. We would welcome correspondence from the individuals/companies whom we have been unable to trace and will be happy to make acknowledgement in any future edition of the book.

Introduction

In choosing chapters for this edited collection, *Primary Teaching Assistants: Learners and Learning*, two principles have been uppermost in our minds. First, the chapters have been chosen for their relevance to the knowledge and practices of teaching assistants in primary schools today. Second, the chapters have been chosen to meet the needs of students registered on Open University modules about primary education. (The companion book *Primary Teaching Assistants: Curriculum in Context* is also designed for this purpose.)

The book's sub-title Learners and Learning provides a further focus for its content. Our selections aim to bring together understandings about all learners in schools and this arises from the notion that a school contains a 'community of engaged learners' (Eckert et al. 1989). Children tend to be seen as the only learners in schools but we would argue that adults (teachers, teaching assistants, administrative staff, governors, and parents) are learners too. Adults need to learn about learning and its content, but also need to learn from children if they are effectively to support them in their learning. We believe education is an interactive process and feel uneasy with the idea of a curriculum being 'delivered' to children. This implies they are passive recipients of knowledge with little opportunity to impact upon it or make it their own. By comparison, in this book, we aim to reinforce the view that learners are active participants in their own learning. Our chapter selections also shed light on 'learning' as a whole school and life-wide process. There's a sense in which we are all experts on our own learning processes – whether we are adults or children.

Following their entry into classrooms in the 1960s as 'aides', 'helpers', and 'auxiliaries', teaching assistants have become essential to teachers and children. For many teachers it would be hard to contemplate running a classroom without the involvement of teaching assistants as team colleagues. Teaching assistant work ranges from classroom maintenance tasks, through to teaching-related activities and specialised learning support for children who 'provide the greatest challenge to the routine confidence and competence of teachers' (Nind and Cochrane 2002: 1). Given the way teaching assistants have increasingly taken on responsibilities that hitherto would only have been done by a qualified teacher, there is now a great deal of overlap between the training and study interests of teaching assistants and those of teachers.

Teaching assistants are immersed in the same professional world as teachers and they stand to benefit from reading what teachers read. However, teaching assistants have their own distinctive contribution to make to school life and children's learning. This arises from the way they are, to a large extent, positioned between teachers and children. This increases their opportunities for close contact with groups of children and with individuals. Their working 'place' gives them openings for shared, personalised exchanges with pupils, flexibility for moment-by-moment adaptations to learning tasks, and chances to gather 'inside understandings' about children's learning and to share these with teachers.

Until relatively recently, teaching assistants were dependent upon an educational literature written mainly for teachers. The last five years, however, have witnessed a growing number of publications aimed specifically at teaching assistants – particularly with regard to the practice of learning support. This is a welcome development because it does teaching assistants a disservice to see them simply as 'assistants' and an adjunct to a teacher's practice. The views, expectations, aspirations, beliefs, and values of learning support assistants themselves are beginning to be represented in the available literature.

In this book we aim to add to the existing knowledge arising from those well placed to describe learning support practice and analyse it. We have chosen pieces that we feel are authored in such a way as to communicate central ideas about learners and learning to a wide readership. We have therefore included pieces written by teaching assistants, teachers, academics, researchers, and others that reflect a broad-based understanding of learning, its many elements, and the abundant contexts in which learners can learn. We have also included chapters written by a parent and a pupil. Ideally, we would have liked to have included more 'insider' teaching assistant accounts than we have. We hope others will take this on as their work becomes better understood and theorised, and teaching assistants themselves become more confident at explaining and researching their own practice. Many are doing this through small-scale enquiries undertaken for degrees and through modules such as The Open University's 'Learning through enquiry in primary schools' (E101).

There is a sense, however, in which teaching assistants might now inherit a difficulty that teachers have yet to resolve – how to find the time and energy to write about classroom practice when the daily job is all consuming. Despite a 'teacher as researcher' movement dating back to the 1970s, most published work for teachers comes from those who have left the classroom as their main place of work, and, it needs to be said, from those who have little direct experience of it at all – apart from when they were children. Just as teachers need collaborative support to become writers and researchers, so it is true for teaching assistants. In order to further our understanding of school learning, and learning more generally, it is essential that all perspectives are heard in the educational literature (see, for instance, Dillow 2010, Collins et al. 2001; O'Brien and Garner 2001; Hancock 1997). In producing this book, it has been our aim to shed light on learning support in primary schools through bringing together a number of distinct voices that have significant things to say about learning and learners.

A note on titles

We are aware of the many titles that are used to describe adults who now work alongside qualified teachers in schools. As the UK government has expressed its preference for the term 'teaching assistants' we have used this in the book's title. (We note that this could be interpreted as 'assistants to the teacher's teaching' or 'assistants who themselves teach'. From our experience of talking to teaching assistants, observing them in classrooms, and our involvement in training, both interpretations ring true.) Within the 36 selected chapters, however, a variety of assistant titles will be found and this is important because it reflects the diversity of roles throughout the UK.

References

Collins, J., Insley, K., and Soler, J. (2001) *Developing Pedagogy: Researching Practice.* London: Paul Chapman.

Dillow, C. (2010) *Supporting Stories: Being a Teaching Assistant.* Stoke on Trent: Trentham Books.

Eckert, P., Goldman, S., and Wenger, E. (1989) *Jocks and Burnouts: Social Identity in the High School.* New York: Teachers College Press.

Hancock, R. (1997) 'Why are class teachers reluctant to become researchers?' *British Journal of In-Service Education, 23*(1), 85–99.

Nind, M., and Cochrane, S. (2002) 'Inclusive curricula? Pupils on the margins of special schools' *International Journal of Inclusive Education, 6*(2), 185–198.

O'Brien, T., and Garner, P. (eds.) (2001) *Untold Stories: Learning Support Assistants and Their Work.* Stoke on Trent: Trentham Books.

Section 1

Learning support

The practice of learning support as carried out by teaching assistants has developed considerably in recent times and has doubtless run ahead of conceptual and theoretical understanding. The eight chapters in this section have been selected because we feel they all contribute towards an understanding of the nature of support. Five of these are commissioned pieces and this reflects the shortage of published writing that captures, in detail, learning support practice.

In Chapter 1, through a review of ten learning supporters across the UK, Roger Hancock and Jennifer Colloby examine the variety of titles and roles and attribute significance to these differences. Nine higher level teaching assistants provide the focus for Chapter 2. A picture emerges of classroom involvements that, although willingly taken on by those in this study, appear to assume considerable teaching abilities and responsibilities. In Chapter 3, Belinda Shaw recalls significant support events in her life and sets the receiving and giving of support within a human rights framework. We need to know much more about how children experience learning support and particularly the inter-personal dimension of being supported. Lucy Mason, in Chapter 4, provides candid suggestions to supporters with regard to what may help and what may hinder. Chapter 5 provides an insider's view of providing support. Here, among other reflections on the practice of support, Klaus Wedell highlights the opportunities that learning supporters have for tuning into individual children's feelings.

In Chapter 6, Stephen Lunn writes of his involvement as a teaching assistant with a pupil who found it difficult to accept school norms and to engage easily with school learning. Stephen's experience is likely to resonate with many who provide support for children exhibiting behaviour difficulties. This chapter illustrates the way in which teaching assistants can be involved as a front-line resource for children who routinely challenge the skills of qualified teachers.

Chapter 7 was originally a conference presentation to a large audience of learning supporters at Manchester Metropolitan University by Katie Clarke and Pat Rangeley. Theirs is a first-hand account of inclusion in action during one day in the life of Nadia, Katie's daughter. It highlights the centrality of the contribution of Pat (and her learning support colleague Kath Williams) as Nadia's co-supporters. The final chapter in this section is a close description of the role of one teaching assistant as she works with a group of children in a mathematics lesson. In this chapter, Jennifer Colloby provides an insight into the way in which Caroline Higham shapes her 'intermediary' role, working directly with a small group of children, but also being very aware of the teacher's practice and wider developments within the classroom.

Chapter 1

Ten titles and roles

Roger Hancock and Jennifer Colloby

The roles and responsibilities of teaching assistants have become increasingly defined and stratified. In this chapter, Roger Hancock and Jennifer Colloby, from The Open University, document the wide ranging work of ten teaching assistants across the United Kingdom and consider the significant variations in their roles and responsibilities.

Learning support staff in the United Kingdom have many titles and many types of responsibilities. Preferences for job titles are to be found at both regional and local levels. Generic titles like 'classroom assistant', 'learning support assistant' and 'teaching assistant' are commonly used but there are many other terms by which support staff are known. There is too a tendency to combine roles so that someone who works generally with children in classrooms may also work specifically with an individual child with complex learning needs and be involved in after school provision. Also, given the possible range of duties, staff can find themselves doing significantly different work with varying levels of responsibility.

Job titles are important. Titles can be closely related to our sense of worth and status at work. Ideally, they should accurately describe the nature of work as an employer defines it, but also as employees themselves experience it. Titles that achieve this balance help people to feel good about themselves and the work they do. 'Non teaching staff' was once used in schools to refer to staff not qualified as teachers. Marland (2001) suggests this title is offensive. The use of the term 'assistant' can be questioned too, given that support staff are often doing much more than just assisting a teacher or a child.

In order to explore titles and roles, we obtained thumbnail sketches from ten classroom support staff from around the UK. Ten schools were selected

Source: A revised version of Hancock, R. and Colloby, J. (2004) 'Eight titles and roles', commissioned by The Open University for *Primary Teaching Assistants: Learners and Learning* (London: Routledge). Reprinted by permission of The Open University and Taylor & Francis Ltd.

with a degree of randomness through local authority website lists. Telephone contact was established with headteachers who helped with the identification of a support staff member from their school. The ten staff then collaborated with us to construct short accounts to capture what they saw as the main purpose of their work.

We make no claims for the representativeness of our findings. However, through the words of support staff themselves, we feel these accounts give a good sense of the nature of the work that is often termed 'learning support', and an indication of the variety of titles and roles that can be found across the UK.

A learning support assistant (LSA)

I give support in the classroom – especially with literacy and numeracy. I personally do a lot of craft, design technology and art. In fact, I run a lunchtime art club. I organise the staffroom, and when we have visitors I look after them. I'm the first-aider and I keep an eye on health and safety. I also stock-take art and audit the general use of materials, as well as having an involvement with our Book Fairs. I am team-leader for the other LSAs and I do quite a lot of clerical jobs. I accompany children and teachers when they go out on trips. I work the ICT equipment. I set up televisions, do photocopying and ensure the copier is running properly. I set up the overhead projectors and the listening centres. I have to make sure these machines are ready and available. I also take money and liaise with parents. I work with Years 1 and 2 but I'm all encompassing. We have LSAs who are attached to classes. However I divide my time between Years 1 and 2. This means I work with four teachers. I don't work in Reception. I'm therefore more wide-ranging than some colleagues who are based in single classrooms. I do a lot of display throughout the school as well as in classrooms. I'm there for the children but I support the staff as well. Everywhere in the school that I can be used, I'm used.

Jane Powell, St Francis RC Infant School, Cardiff South Wales

A classroom assistant

As a classroom assistant at Alexandra Parade Primary School I have lots of different duties assigned to me. I have responsibility for running the school tuck shop and children come to buy their tuck as school starts. I have to keep a check on stock levels and order more items, as they are needed.

Four days a week all the children receive a piece of fruit and it is my responsibility to distribute fruit throughout the school. After this is done I help out in the classrooms as needed. I work with small groups of children to develop their reading or help them with their writing. It depends on what the teacher asks me to do. I help to create displays by selecting and mounting children's work. Each day I work to a different timetable but I always undertake any administrative duties such as photocopying and filing for the teachers in Primary 4 to Primary 7 (8–12 years). I tidy up after art sessions and I particularly enjoy my work with individual children who are struggling with some aspect of mathematics. Every day I do playground duty and I share the role of first-aider with other assistants in the school. My husband runs the school football team and my duties include 1 hour each week to help organise the team and their equipment and transport them to away matches. At the moment there are just two girls in the football team and I hope that eventually more will want to play.

Margaret Verrecchie, Alexandra Parade Primary School, Glasgow, Scotland

A nursery assistant

I work in the pre-school with children who are 3 and 4 years of age. My main duties as a nursery assistant are to assist the teacher in both the planning of activities and the work with the children. I help to develop the yearly plan and, from this, the monthly plan which is then broken down into the daily plan. When I arrive at school I help to set out the resources that are first needed. The children arrive at 9.15 am and I settle them to various activities and help those who are painting to put on aprons and make sure names are written on paper so I can easily identify children's work. I am responsible for 'brek' for all the pre-school children. Brek is a healthy eating snack, which consists of milk, some fruit, and often toast. The supervision of this takes 1 hour as children come in groups of 6 at a time. After this I supervise class activities but if it is PE that day I go and set out the equipment in the hall. Some kind of physical activity takes place each day and I help the children with this. When we return to the classroom I help children change back into their shoes. The final 30 minutes of the morning is spent on reading or puzzle activities and making sure the children have all their belongings when parents collect them at 12 o'clock. After this I clear and tidy the classroom and update the teacher with any information I have been given by parents.

Together we also evaluate the morning's activities and consider our next day's plan.

Sheila McKnight, Strabane Primary School, County Tyrone, Northern Ireland

A nursery nurse

As a nursery nurse my main role is to assist the Nursery and Reception teachers with children in the early years, but I also help out generally throughout the school when necessary. I have a lot of direct involvement with children but I also oversee the classroom resources – I keep the art and craft areas running smoothly, for instance. I get involved in all parts of the curriculum, particularly supporting children's learning in literacy, numeracy, music, art, and IT. I am involved in planning learning activities with the teachers. At the moment, in the afternoon, we are taking steps to integrate the Nursery and Reception children and I find this enjoyable. I am a first aider, I assist children with toileting and washing, I take them to lunch and out into the playground, and I drive the school's minibus. I work with all children when in the classroom and I particularly enjoy working with those who sometimes struggle with their learning. I find it very satisfying to succeed with them, although I do have to work concertedly at achieving this success with some children.

I frequently attend one-day courses which I find very important for my development and knowledge. For instance, I recently went on an 'improving the classroom' workshop with the Reception teacher and an early years conference. I feel very fortunate to be employed as a nursery nurse because posts are not that easy to find in North Wales. When qualified nursery nurses get a nursery nurse post here they tend to stick with it.

Dawn Jones, Ysgol Cynfran Llysfaen, Colwyn Bay, North Wales

A learning mentor

I work with individual children who have barriers to learning. The overall aim is to improve attendance, reduce permanent and fixed term exclusions, and improve behaviour. I'm currently based in the Infants right through to Years 3 and 4. As the learning mentor, I observe them in the class to see how they are getting on. They might have targets they need to meet – for instance, to arrive on time or finish a task without being distracted. I liaise with parents early in the morning and they know that I am available at that time. Parents also know that they can ring me or ask to see me at other times. We run a breakfast club and that provides a good opportunity for me to talk informally to parents and children. There may be something that's on a child's mind – something that's troubling them. I have a room with resources where I can talk to children who are upset. I have regular planning meetings with teachers every Monday. I was a nursery nurse in the school for 15 years before I took on my current role. I had therefore developed relationships with most parents which are essential for my new role.

It's quite hard for me to draw the line between a classroom support role and a learning mentor's role, especially when you've done the former job for so many years. I am working with 13 children at the moment – the maximum is 15. When I'm in a class helping one of my children, if another child needs help of some kind and the teacher's busy I usually help out.

Alison Cundy, Alt Primary School, Oldham, England

A higher level teaching assistant (HLTA)

Becoming a HLTA has certainly presented me with a great many challenges. At present I support children in a Year 1 class every morning. I try to ensure a creative approach to my work and thrive on the challenges that I am given in preparing stimulating experiences for the children both indoors and out. I continually build on my specialism which has been in Early Years. By acquiring further knowledge of how children think and learn I feel more able to meet the many aspects of my role. I cover two classes twice a week for teachers on planning, preparation and assessment time (Years 1 and 3). I cover a Year 2 class for two afternoons per week. Curriculum subjects here range from design and technology, art, religious education, personal and social education, and physical education. I also support children who require language support, those with IEPs and those who need extra help in specific areas. As our school has extensive grounds, I develop areas into outdoor learning environments for the children. I am also passionate about playtimes in primary schools and have developed this aspect of school life for the children so that they engage in very positive experiences on a daily basis.

I feel my role as a HLTA demands a certain amount of self evaluation and reflection so although my day starts early, it also finishes late. I am continually seeking ways to present a stimulating lesson, one that above all ensures children enjoy their learning.

Karen Brownrigg, Percy Main Primary School, North Shields, Tyne & Wear

Behaviour support teaching assistant

My main role in the school is to support the behaviour of children so they can complete their education timetable. I do this in a number of ways. I'm on call all day, so if a teacher needs support with an incident I get a phone call and I go and withdraw that child and help them work through any issues as quickly as possible to get them back into class and on task. I can also go into a class and be an additional support whenever I'm needed. My biggest role is Diners Club, which is about placing children on individual behaviour plans. At the start of lunch they come to see me in my room and we go through their targets to see if they've been able to meet those for the day. Predominantly it's boys that I work with – I'd say they're ninety per cent of the children I see, particularly at the Diners Club. With girls, it tends to be that they're experiencing difficulties with friendships.

I took on my specialised teaching assistant role because it encompassed many aspects from my previous work. I've worked with the Youth Offending Service as a community panel member using Restorative Justice. I've also supported a lot of young people with complex needs who find it hard to fit into mainstream education. I felt my current role was exciting because it took all this previous experience into consideration and enabled me to feel I am utilising my skills.

James Galloway, Herbert Thompson Primary School, South Wales

A bilingual assistant and home–school link worker

I have two jobs – the first is a bilingual classroom assistant and the second a home–school link worker. In the first I work mainly with Turkish children, most of whom are new arrivals from Turkey. I am employed for thirteen hours a week. I usually work within the classroom with small groups, but sometimes I take one or two children outside the room. I also run a small class myself when I teach Turkish to Year 4 children. I find 8–9 years is the best age to teach Turkish because children have learnt to read and write English and this can be used to support their progress in another language. At this age they also seem to particularly enjoy learning Turkish – they appear 'ready'.

My second job arose out of the liaison work with parents that I did as part of the bilingual classroom assistant role. For this, I am employed for six hours a week. I work entirely with parents, supporting them as and when necessary. I help them with a range of tasks related to their children's schooling. I liaise with teachers, get involved in translations, help them with written English when, for instance, they need to register their children or fill out a school meals application form, take phone calls when parents find it hard to express themselves in English. I try to resolve any communication difficulties that may arise. I find I'm needed in many ways and that six hours is not enough time to meet the needs that parents have so I often give additional time that is voluntary.

Didem Celik, Whitmore Primary School, London, England

A parent helper (now classroom assistant)

When I was a teenager, I worked in a children's clothes shop, 'A and V Fashions', Lerwick, where there were always children coming in with parents. Some could have their tantrums and whatever else when they couldn't get things, but I'm a very patient person. Working in a clothes shop prepared me for working in schools. I kept a toy box and books in the corner. If the parents were looking a bit stressed then I would say to their children, 'Oh come and see this', and read them a story.

When my children went to school I started going on their school trips. I also volunteered to do the youth club as well as being a parent helper. It inspired me to do more. I just love working with children. As a parent volunteer I was flexible and would help with sale tables and raising money for charity. I would donate things to be sold. I'd go on school trips, any sort of trips with any age. I would get involved whenever I had the opportunity. I helped out for five years and it was fine because I could still be home for my three children.

At one time, I wasn't sure whether to work with children or older people, so I decided to go for K100 ('Understanding Health and Social Care') with The Open University. I got my certificate and ended up applying for a job here. My three children are fine about me getting involved. When I see them in school, two call me 'mam' and the other one calls me 'Louise'. I just treat them the same as the other bairns. They know I'm now a member of staff.

Louise Dix, Aith Junior High School, Shetland, Scotland

A teaching assistant

I work with small groups of pupils outside the classroom in a resource room. My work is part of the school's performance management programme and I am regularly observed by the head teacher. The majority of my working week is spent supporting a Year 4 class but for 30 minutes a day I withdraw a small group of Year 2 children to support their phonic awareness. I also withdraw a group of Year 4 children for literacy learning. I discuss and co-plan my input with the class teacher. We all return to the Year 4 classroom for the second half of the literacy lessons. During mathematics, I ensure my group are working well and offer support across the class.

I spend my lunchtimes preparing materials. In the afternoon I offer general support and thus build relationships with all the children. The school has a reading intervention programme and I spend the final 30 minutes of each school day working with Year 2 children who need this additional help. The school sent me on a 12-week training course for this. I also help children with their reading and each Tuesday afternoon I undertake pupil assessments. I liaise with parents and we work together to help children with their reading. I write reports for the SENCO and help create IEPs. As a school governor, I have responsibility for SEN provision.

I am the school's PE co-ordinator. I organise both PE lessons and the after-school sports clubs. As a qualified football and athletics coach, I run the football (for both boys and girls), run athletics clubs and assist with the clubs for skating and gymnastics.

Keith Eddyshaw, Warren Primary School, Nottingham, England

Discussion and conclusion

The ten roles and titles featured in this chapter are learning support assistant, classroom assistant, nursery assistant, nursery nurse, learning mentor, higher level teaching assistant, behaviour support teaching assistant, bilingual assistant, parent helper and teaching assistant, respectively. Analysis of these thumbnail accounts reveals the following main categories of involvement for those featured:

1. clerical and administrative duties (e.g. stock checking, photocopying and filing)
2. out-of-class involvements (e.g. liaising with parents, art club, support on trips)
3. setting up and maintaining equipment (e.g. IT support, reprographic maintenance)
4. health and safety (e.g. distributing fruit, overseeing children's snack time, first aid)

5.   curriculum and learning support (e.g. literacy and numeracy, art, teaching Turkish, encouraging appropriate behaviour)
6.   releasing teachers from classroom teaching
7.   management (e.g. leading other TAs)
8.   servicing (e.g. staffroom maintenance, tidying the classroom).

We note the wide-ranging nature of the duties highlighted in the above analysis but also the rich mix of involvements within each individual thumbnail sketch. We believe, however, that if we talked to the same group of people in a year's time we would pick up significant shifts in their duties and responsibilities. Moreover, if we had selected a different group of ten people with similar same titles, we would have found a slightly different set of duties being carried out. Lee (2003), in a review of the existing literature on learning support staff, suggests there is 'no common pattern to teaching assistants' work' (p. 25).

Although we identify eight types of work, Category 5 (direct support for children's curriculum learning) took, by far, the highest proportion of respondents' time. It is important to remember too, that other categories of work can result in support for children's curriculum-related learning – for instance, liaising with parents (Category 2) or distributing fruit (Category 4).

We suggest that the variation in titles, roles and responsibilities of learning support staff in this small enquiry arises because there is a great deal of negotiation about their roles and related deployment at the level of individual schools and, even, individual classrooms. Variation is also explained by the way in which support staff and teachers are working in locally negotiated 'interdependent ways' rather than clearly designated hierarchical relationships with watertight role boundaries (see Hancock & Eyres, 2004; Eyres et al, 2004).

Teachers and learning support staff, we believe, are involved in an on-the-spot process of decision-making whereby the totality of the work to be done is, in certain ways, shared with teachers. This means that learning support staff in this study are taking on some duties that once were done only by a qualified teacher but, we suggest, they are also doing work that teachers have not had sufficient time to do. Clearly this poses questions about where teacher professional boundaries should be drawn, but also what is to be done about the appropriate remuneration of support staff who are now very involved in teaching-related duties. However, that said, the variation in learning support staff roles seems to be a desirable workforce development. It offers a localised, creative way of utilising adult skills thus maximising support for teachers and for children's learning.

References

Eyres, I., Cable, C., Hancock, R., and Turner, J. (2004) 'Whoops I forgot David': children's perceptions of the adults who work in their classrooms, *Early Years*, Vol. 24, No. 2, pp. 149–162.

Hancock, R., and Eyres, I. (2004) Implementing a required curriculum reform: teachers at the core, teaching assistants on the periphery? *Westminster Studies in Education*, Vol. 27, No. 2, pp. 223–235.

Lee, B. (2003) 'Teaching assistants in schools', *Education Journal*, 68, 25–7.

Marland, M. (2001) 'Unsung heroes', Report (October), Magazine of the Association of Teachers and Lecturers, London.

Chapter 2

'They call me wonder woman'

Roger Hancock, Thelma Hall, Carrie Cable and Ian Eyres

The need for an advanced teaching assistant role – a 'higher level teaching assistant' (HLTA) – can be seen as a natural workforce development given the gradual extension of teaching-related roles reported by many research studies, and the developed contribution that some teaching assistants have made for many years. In this chapter, Roger Hancock and colleagues write about an interview study involving a small group of HLTAs from the north of England.

The impetus for higher level teaching assistants arose out of the English Government's response to an independent report which confirmed significant teacher work overload (Price Waterhouse Cooper, 2001). This overload, it can be argued, came about because successive governments had introduced a stream of curriculum reforms and bureaucratic requirements linked to accountability, testing, and competition between schools.

The Government's response was to establish a 'status' of higher level teaching assistant (HLTA). Teaching assistants with this status would cover classes so that teachers could be released for 'planning, preparation and assessment' (PPA). The creation of this HLTA role was set within a wider ambitious reform related to 'workforce remodelling' – in effect, a review of school staffing structures, revisions to teachers' performance management, and new professional standards. The HLTA cover role and workforce remodelling proposals were signed by all teacher unions (ATL et al., 2003) with the exception of the National Union of Teachers who saw the idea as undermining of a teacher's professional status.

Despite the opposition of the largest teacher professional body, the reform went ahead and many primary schools in England are now using HLTAs to release teachers from classes for PPA time and also to cover the short term

Source: An edited version of Hancock, R., Hall, T., Cable, C. and Eyres, I. (2010) '"They call me wonder woman": the job jurisdictions and workplace learning of higher level teaching assistants', *Cambridge Journal of Education*, *40* (2), 97–112. Reprinted by permission of Taylor & Francis Ltd, (http://www.tandf.co.uk/journals).

absences of teachers when they are on courses or unwell. HLTAs also relieve teachers of certain administrative duties, however, as with teaching assistants, HLTAs can also work with groups of children and individuals needing their specialised support and teaching. Given their teaching assistant backgrounds, such individualised work with children is an area of confidence and skill for all HLTAs. Covering classes, however, serves to take them away from this work. In some situations, HLTAs receive different payment levels depending on the type of role they are carrying out. HLTAs are formally assessed against 33 standards arising from the professional standards for teachers (TDA, 2007). In 2009, there were 21,000 HLTAs in England (Burgess & Shelton Mayes, 2009).

The research study

We report here on a small-scale interview study which aimed to obtain individualised data from HLTAs working in primary, first and middle schools in the north of England. The three principal objectives of the research were to investigate:

the specific responsibilities of HLTAs;
their ways of working;
the patterns of their deployment.

Our interviews were conducted in a semi-structured, conversational way. The interview schedule aimed to elicit responses related to the nine themes of: entry into support work; application for HLTA status; deployment, oversight by teachers, responsibilities, difference to teachers, parental contact, appraisal, and training. However, we encouraged the interviewees to develop their responses in ways that were meaningful to them. We were not able to triangulate this data with observations of the HLTAs in action or interviews with teachers, children, and parents, although the degree of consistency between interviewees does afford some confidence in our findings.

The HLTAs

Our study included nine HLTAs based in schools, and in a pupil referral unit (PRU – for pupils unable to attend school for various reasons e.g. pregnancy, medical needs, exclusion) in North Tyneside, Newcastle upon Tyne, Northumberland and Cleveland. Our selection arose out of a mixture of established school contacts (through previous association with

The Open University) and recommendation by local authority officers. Five HLTAs were interviewed face-to-face in their schools and four by telephone. Our fieldwork was undertaken between January and April 2007. The average age of the group was 48; the youngest person was 31 and the oldest 63. Overall, the group contained HLTAs with a range of formal qualifications. These included specific teaching assistant qualifications like the Specialist Teacher Assistant Certificate through to Foundation Degrees and a Post Graduate Certificate in Education (PGCE) – one means of obtaining qualified teacher status within England for holders of a first degree.

Interview analysis

Specific responsibilities

Given the traditional focus of assistant work on children's basic skills, all interviewees had a substantial involvement in English and mathematics in terms of support for children alongside teachers in classrooms and working with groups of children away from teachers outside the classroom. There was also mention of setting up special initiatives for identified groups of children. For instance, Erica (all names are pseudonyms) talked about starting a project with Year One (five to six year olds) children 'who were struggling with phonics'. This meant planning and implementing the proposed work and also doing pre and post project testing to evaluate the benefits for the children. As she states, there was little teacher involvement in this:

> 'Yes that's going to be my sort of baby and I've spoken to the Year One teachers and they're quite happy for me to just take it off them.'

In addition to teaching English and mathematics our HLTAs had involvements across the curriculum and this required a range of knowledge. Jill, for instance, explained that she was currently involved in teaching physical education, religious education, art and design technology, and personal, social and health education to Year Six children (10 to 11 year olds).

Given the way unexpected curriculum needs could arise, two interviewees mentioned that they could, sometimes quite suddenly, find themselves immersed in the deep end. Carol recounts such a situation and her solution:

'I'm teaching science. Now that is wonderful but my subject knowledge is kind of zilch so I've been on the internet and I've done research.'

Such resourcefulness and independence had resulted in the teachers giving her the name 'wonder woman.'

Parental contact

Our experience of training teaching assistants at The Open University suggests their contact with parents varies considerably from school to school. Some schools, recognising that many of their assistants are local parents themselves, encourage them to develop communications in an outreach way, feeding back important information to teachers when necessary. Others feel teachers, as the qualified professionals, are best positioned to do this. With the exception of Linda, all our HLTAs said they had contact and collaboration with parents and they all said that any difficulties they experienced were reported to a teacher.

Yolanda and Mollie said they often bring classes in at the start of the day and this enabled regular informal contact with parents. As Yolanda commented:

'. . . parents will come to you and give information if they have concerns or if they want further information about what's happening during that day . . .'

Mollie ran an after school literacy club for children and their parents. She planned the activities and often integrated IT. At the end of this club, children went on to another club whilst their parents stayed to talk to Mollie about their children's learning and any concerns that they might have.

Ways of working

Planning for children's educational experiences and, specifically, the curriculum in classrooms is assumed to be firmly within a teacher's job jurisdiction (Adamson, 1999). Advice from the eleven signatories to the HLTA agreement states: 'Cover supervision occurs when there is no active teaching taking place. Pupils would continue their learning by carrying out a pre-prepared exercise under supervision.' (TeacherNet, 2009). Although this situation might conceivably occur in some secondary classrooms, it seems both unrealistic and inappropriate for primary aged children and would surely severely limit their learning for a significant proportion of the week. Erica makes it clear that cover supervision is not as straightforward for her as policy makers assume:

'. . . occasionally I will just slip in and if the plans are there that's fine . . . some of the subjects that I do, it might be PE or IT, I will plan those . . . I deliver the teachers plans but they leave it very much up to me how I do it . . . so it's not cover supervision, I'm actually teaching the children.'

So, even when Erica uses a teacher's lesson plan, there is still the issue of 'how I do it'. She has to make a plan work for the children.

Our data contain much to suggest that all nine HLTAs were involved in planning at a number of levels. In some situations, for instance, it was clear that they might take full responsibility for planning certain activities.

Jill recounts her initial response to the fact that she would need to plan the detail of science lessons:

'So I thought how do I plan? It all sounds very well but how do I do it? So I went and got the science files. I found out what modules we were following. I printed off the specific areas. I found out from the teacher what they were looking into and as it happened it was electricity the first time round now it's something else . . .'

There is much here that questions the idea that a lesson planned by a teacher can be overseen by a HLTA without the HLTA doing something to make the lesson successful – and that something would seem appropriately described as teaching.

In open recognition of the amount of planning they did, head teachers in Jill and Carol's schools had given them their own PPA time.

Oversight

According to official guidelines, HLTAs 'work strictly under the direction and guidance of a teacher' (TDA, 2008). However, this assumed responsibility may not be straightforward in practice, especially given the unpredictable nature of life in schools. Additionally, children don't organise their learning needs according to adults' formal responsibilities or availability (Eyres et al., 2004). This means that teaching assistants can often find themselves having to respond to unexpected issues of learning or behaviour without ready access to teacher guidance.

None of our interviewees highlighted oversight as a strong feature in their relationship with teachers. One consideration was familiarity. Carol explains:

> 'I've worked there for so long they know my work they know that when they step out, I step in, and I do exactly the job as they would like it to be done and they know I can do it . . .'

Some interviewees gave the impression that oversight could operate informally and, in a context where people know each well, this could be an effective supervisory arrangement.'

A number of our HLTAs were involved in guiding and managing the work and the training of teaching assistants. This role extension relates to 'direct the work of other adults in supporting learning' which is HLTA Standard 33 (TDA, 2007). In former pre-HLTA times, this role might be taken on by a deputy or perhaps a teacher who is a SENCO (special educational needs co-ordinator).

Yolanda line-managed six teaching assistants and carried out their annual performance management. Mary, although not paid as a HLTA, had been asked by the head teacher to 'have a chat' with the teaching assistants in her school but she emphasised that it was not officially linked to their performance management.

Patterns of deployment

Each of the interviewees was asked to describe a typical day in terms of their deployment. For a number, this wasn't easy due to the fact that their days could vary considerably. Yolanda gives a sense of her various involvements in her First School (for children from five to nine years):

> 'I tend to only do four classes in a term because one of the classes has swimming during the term so we rotate . . . I'm doing Year One and Two at the moment. Year Two will go swimming next term but then I'll do Year Four . . . I'll do at least four classes each week.'

It seemed that each day carried a degree of unpredictability. There could be a need to cover for teacher sickness, teacher involvement in training, or even to stand in for a short while when a teacher needed to attend to something away from the classroom.

Erica mentioned that she sometimes even found herself covering for teachers who were unable to do cover lessons for other teachers. The demands of switching between classes and ages of children appear quite challenging in terms of adaptability and knowledge.

For most of the schools involved it seemed that the flexible use of HLTAs (and teaching assistants) meant that supply teachers were rarely used to cover classes. Mollie said in her school, in an emergency, two teaching assistants might cover the class of an absent teacher or if they weren't available she would cover it alone, sometimes supported by a teaching assistant.

Conclusion

Addressing the three main aims of our study, i.e. the HLTAs' specific responsibilities, ways of working and patterns of deployment, what can be concluded about their roles and job jurisdictions?

Each of our interviewees had quite wide ranging roles and involvements which were personally and socially constructed within their schools. They were also boundary crossers, frequently moving in and out of their own and teachers' roles within a day or a working week and this resulted in what Allen (2001, p. vii) refers to as 'fuzzy' occupational boundaries. It seemed too that head teachers were deploying these HLTAs as a flexible staffing resource that could be used with different aged children and to meet different curriculum needs as and when they arose. Linked to this was the use of the HLTAs as in-house supply teachers for absent teachers. This is an understandable development because the HLTAs were able to provide children with continuity – most had been working in their schools for between five and 20 years – and such deployment in an emergency saved schools the expense of recruiting supply teachers.

The overlap of role and jurisdiction with teachers made it hard for the HLTAs to give us a clear sense of the division of labour, apart from the fact that they cover classes for teachers' PPA release. When pressed, the HLTAs tended to refer to backstage factors like teachers' overall responsibility, especially for planning and this accords with Adamson's (1999) finding over ten years ago.

When they did cover for PPA time, it seemed that our HLTAs were releasing teachers to attend to the extensive record keeping and 'laptop work' that all public service professionals now do.

Because of their cover role (in reality, a class teaching role) our HLTAs were sharing in some of the whole class teaching work of teachers. Additionally, the HLTAs had colonised what Abbott (1988, p. 111) terms 'vacant jurisdictions'. Included here would be hands-on work with children that teachers might wish to do but have never had time to do, or work teachers have had to relinquish because of other demands on their time. Examples of the latter would be special projects of the sort that Erica mentions and supporting parent learning as with Mollie's after school literacy club. This, of course, runs counter to a policy discourse that HLTAs 'free teachers up to do what they do best: teach' (TDA, 2008).

Our data therefore reveal HLTAs entering into teachers' work and jurisdictions more as team-teaching colleagues rather than supervised para-professionals. Indeed, they confirmed that teacher oversight was, by and large, informal and sometimes, not provided at all when teachers were busy. We sensed that there was always deferment to teachers as the senior partners, however. Interestingly, we did not pick up any intra-occupational conflict as a result of what Abbott (1988) might describe as a HLTA 'assault' on teachers' work although, as we have said, we did not interview any teachers.

Despite their positive take on what they were doing, the degree of independence they were given and the status that came from working with whole classes, there was also perhaps a sense of isolation and a lack of support and oversight. A cover role separates HLTAs from teachers as team colleagues within a classroom – and reduces their opportunities to tune in to teachers' approaches. With the growth of support staff, teachers often have teaching assistants with them in their classrooms so teachers tend not to teach alone in this way.

Although they were doing their best to respond to the expectations of head teachers and teachers, our HLTAs seemed at times out of their depth. We therefore have to ask if, when covering a class, they were sometimes unavoidably diluting the practice of qualified and experienced teachers with implications for children's learning. For all their dedication and willingness to teach themselves new class teaching skills and the required curriculum knowledge, deploying HLTAs to cover classes in order to release teachers seemed not to be the best use of their training, abilities and time.

References

Abbott, A. (1988) *The System of Professions: An Essay on the Division of Expert Labour.* Chicago: University of Chicago Press.

Adamson, S. (1999) Review of published literature on teaching assistants. Report for the DFEE teaching assistant project. London: DFEE.

Allen, D. (2001) *The Changing Shape of Nursing Practice: The Role of Nurses in the Hospital Division of Labour.* London: Routledge.

ATL, DfES, GMB, NAHT, NASUWT, NEOST, PAT, SHA, TGWU, UNISON and WAG (2003) Raising Standards and Tackling Workload: a National Agreement. Time for Standards. London: DfES.

Burgess, H. and Shelton Mayes, A. (2009) An exploration of higher level teaching assistants' perceptions of their training and development in the context of school workforce reform. *Support for Learning*, 24, 19–25.

Eyres, I., Cable, C., Hancock, R. and Turner, J. (2004) 'Whoops I forgot David': children's perceptions of the adults who work in their classrooms. *Early Years*, 24, 149–162.

Price Waterhouse Cooper (2001) Teacher Workload Study. A Report of a Review commissioned by the DfES. London: Price Waterhouse Cooper.

Teachernet (2009) Guidance for schools on cover supervision. Retrieved from: http://www.tda.gov.uk/upload/resources/pdf/w/wamg_guidance_cover.pdf

TDA (Training and Development Agency) (2008) Higher level teaching assistant (HLTA) Retrieved from: http://www.tda.gov.uk/upload/resources/pdf/h/hltas_2008.pdf

TDA (Training and Development Agency) (2007) Professional standards for HLTA status. Retrieved from: http://www.tda.gov.uk/upload/resources/pdf/t/tda0426_the%20standards.pdf

Chapter 3

Supporting human rights

Belinda Shaw

Belinda Shaw, former co-director of the Centre for Studies on Inclusive Education and a trustee with the Alliance for Inclusive Education, has a long-standing commitment to human rights. Using memories from her childhood and previous work, she considers, in a heartfelt way, the nature of support and its potential to contribute towards a truly inclusive society.

Support has many aspects. I want to focus on the aspect often known as personal, emotional and spiritual support. To a greater or lesser extent, like fish in water, this kind of support is one of those funny things we are not aware of until it drains away or comes to revive us when our lives feels dry and barren. Support in this sense is not about money, or other material sustenance, but about how we human beings can help each other achieve what I can only call 'our hearts' desires' – to be the very best we can possibly be. Support in this sense is about helping people become their true selves. It is absolutely certain that, one way or another, giving and receiving support makes a difference.

Ironically, like many people, I like to think I don't need support. Independence is highly valued in our competitive, individualistic, consumerist culture and needing support exposes our vulnerabilities. Yet support, its nature, how to get it, how to give it, and why and how it's sought and given have been recurring considerations in my experience of growing up, education, work, and relationships.

Seeking support as a child

As a young girl, I felt unsafe when I started school having moved homes around the same time because of the sudden death of my mother. I

Source:. A revised version of Shaw, B. (2004) 'Supporting human rights', commissioned by The Open University for *Primary Teaching Assistants: Learners and Learning* (London: Routledge). Reprinted by permission of The Open University and Taylor & Francis Ltd.

remember it being a cause of great consternation that I couldn't learn to read and I was taken out of the classroom to have separate instruction in a room known as the 'sick room'. It was the room where children were taken when they were ill and contained various medical-looking materials. It was cold in there. I did not get better at reading in that sick room which only increased the consternation people expressed about me.

Then what seemed like a miracle happened. During the school week I sometimes stayed with my Nana. To me her house was a wonderful place, particularly the kitchen which had a cosy corner where the sofa met the open fire range. Here I was allowed to curl up at a little table and look at women's magazines. This is where I learned to read. Somewhere between looking at the magazines, talking with my Nana, and combing out her long grey hair, which I did whenever I stayed with her, I found I could read. I suppose my Nana was my first learning supporter and what a great job she did. I never forget it.

Support from my school teachers

Three teachers come to mind when thinking about support and education – all from my secondary school days where I had unpredictable swings in achievement, finishing very much on a down swing. I suppose I still felt unsafe at school and used to try and hide away at the back of the classroom. Mainly I got away with it, except in the classes run by Mrs Summer the English teacher. She would call me up to the front and ask me to tell the class what I had been reading and what I made of it (I was a vociferous reader by now). This I found easy because I loved books and because she made me feel good talking about them. English language and English literature were two of the four subjects where I got a GCE qualification. The other was art and the fourth was chemistry.

The physics teacher along with the music teacher were two people I remember for their distinct lack of support in the terms I am discussing it. The physics teacher did not like to talk and made us learn from books, which I was able to do. But one day I got stuck and asked a question and kept asking it because I so much wanted to understand, even though he kept referring me back to the book. This 'cheeky' act merited me a staff detention. As for the music teacher, his habit of flicking chalk at students who sang 'wrong' notes silenced the melody in many – permanently I fear. After all these years I am still practising my music and finding my voice with a wonderful singing teacher, conductor, pianist and choir, where everybody is made welcome.

Supporting human rights

Looking back, some events seem significant in arriving at my current understanding of supporting human rights.

I keenly remember Maureen, a woman of my age, whom I have not met since our school years. My last memory of her was as teenagers when occasionally, on my way to what was then a grammar school, I used to find her at the gate of her house with her mother. I used to say hello to her but she did not answer. Only her mother acknowledged me.

It was my feeling that Maureen did not use words. At that time she was no longer at school with us. It was when we were very young that I remember us being together in the classroom and it was then that an incident took place which had a profound effect on me. Something had happened to Maureen which I feared might happen to me. She had wet herself, and her shame was being made a target for bullying by a number of pupils. To my horror they forced her to sit down and stand up in ritualistic fashion along the length of an unvarnished wooden bench, leaving a trail of wet marks behind her. I remember feeling an absolute conviction that something was happening that should not be happening and I tried to stop it. I don't remember whether I had any effect but the overwhelming feeling that I felt then and which stays with me now is that this kind of behaviour, which I now recognise as stigmatising, is a threat to humanity and somebody must do something about it. It is what I now understand as part of a cycle of behaviours and attitudes which, if left unchallenged, perpetuate human rights abuse.

Supporting people with disabilities

I left school as soon as I could at 16 to begin a secretarial course. It was about this time that I had my first experience of disability. I was part of a youth group of disabled and able-bodied young people that held its meetings at a residential home for disabled people known as 'The Home for Incurables'. Here I met people who were not allowed out in the evening because the Home would be locked by the time they returned and no staff would be available to provide personal assistance. This was as much a pivotal experience for me as the experience of Maureen's personal torment in my early years.

Some of these people introduced me to the concepts of discrimination, social justice and civil rights for disabled people. I already knew that people can hurt others, although they might not mean to, and the disabled people I met taught me about the damage that social systems can do as well, also often unintentionally.

Media support for social justice

These issues of social justice came to play an increasingly important part in my working life, which began on a local newspaper. Although I trained as a secretary, I did not want to be one and I managed to persuade the editor of the local newspaper to give me a job. This was mainly because of a joint interest in the adventure books of John Buchan, and because being able to type and do shorthand meant I could be put to work immediately. This led to work on a regional newspaper and later on to a job on a radio station in Hong Kong where I arrived like many 'Westerners' before me after a year's travel in search of 'The East'.

During my time on newspapers it was customary for stories about disabled people to be directed to the Women's Page and for pictures of people with learning difficulties to be censored, although stories about them might also be allowed in that same section of the newspaper. Since I was for a period the only young woman on the local newspaper, it was often seen as one of my jobs, along with writing up the weddings, to provide material for the Women's Page. I took this as an opportunity to develop my understanding of disability as a human rights issue which I had been introduced to through my youth club and investigate and report on disability from that aspect. By the time I was working for the regional newspaper and on radio, 'care in the community' was increasingly being suggested as the preferred social policy for disabled people rather than institutional care. The human rights understanding of disability I provided was relevant to these developments and attracted a new status as important material for leading features and stories rather than Women's Page 'fillers'.

Although my work in radio in Hong Kong was different in many ways from that on newspapers in the UK, I still tried to bring human rights considerations to the fore in the stories I covered there in my role as a 'social welfare correspondent'. Ironically it was a matter of human rights which played a part in my eventually leaving journalism after more than 20 years. I felt I had to challenge an editor's approach to a story on human rights grounds. So, I returned to England and took up a job as a support worker for two women moving out of a long-stay mental handicap hospital to a home of their own.

Support, inclusion and human rights

The job as a support worker led me to work at the Centre for Studies on Inclusive Education (CSIE) where I was co-director from 1988 to 2007. CSIE is an independent education centre promoting inclusive education and challenging segregated schooling, part of a growing movement which wants to see the phasing out of segregated 'special' schools.

I remember a question at the interview about how being a support worker in community care was connected to what was then called integration in education. I said it was all part of the same human rights campaign. In many ways working at CSIE was an ideal job for me, combining writing, organising and lobbying about issues I care about. It was a worthwhile job and that is what I have always wanted from work. I can honestly say I have rarely felt bored or alienated in the work I have done. To me work is a foremost expression of who you are and of your relationship with life. To me it is a serious matter for a person to be made miserable at work and I resist it.

Supporting from the heart

Support work is a work of the heart and it is a work of relationships. It is an enduring concern of mine how the ground rules might be worked out to sustain a respectful, enabling and enhancing partnership all-round. This is something I find very complex when I am in a supporting role. Some of the complexity seems to me to be about how to resolve what feel like conflicting ideas. These are: support is about care and love and therefore should be 'free'. Most supporters, however, would not be able to support without pay. Supporters need to be held accountable, particularly regarding the way they handle differentials in status and power. Supporters deserve to be treated with respect and not as somebody's 'dogsbody'.

I would have been happy to remain a support worker but found the pay and conditions were not compatible with my personal life, especially financing a part share in a home of my own. The low status and recognition given to support work generally by society has changed little since then. It remains the general approach to career progression that managerial and specialist skills are rewarded more highly, and that the more expert and well-paid a person becomes the more distanced they are from giving personal support in the organisations where they work.

I stayed close friends with one of the women I supported until her death in 2010. That relationship fulfilled me in a way none of my other activities has done before or since.

Apart from pay and conditions, another element in relationships of support that causes tension is that people in the supporting role are not immune from the tendency to do more harm than good in taking action. The tendency to 'do something no matter what' is very strong in the Western tradition of individualism and independence (in Buddhist culture, for example, there are positive concepts of 'non-action' and 'no-thing'). We may forge ahead with changes without properly taking into account the wishes of those we seek to help or failing to envisage the possibility of unexpected consequences. 'The road to hell is paved with good intentions' is a saying which has been used to describe how the development of segregated services for disabled people proved counter-productive for many in terms of quality of life. It is a sobering reminder of how being well-intentioned is no guarantee of being helpful.

Supporting self worth and inclusion

In many ways support work in education is a new profession, a profession in the making with many issues to be addressed. The work of learning supporters, as I prefer to call them, or teaching assistants, which is the official term, to a large extent has been born of necessity. Mainstream schools, required to become more inclusive, are finding they need varied input from a team of adults with a wide range of skills and experiences in order to respond to the full diversity of pupils, whatever their needs and abilities. In short, teachers cannot do it alone.

It matters a lot to me that as supporters work out their new professional role, and their contribution to inclusive development, they can hold on to an understanding of support as being fundamentally connected with pupils' personal, emotional and spiritual development, and with justice and equality. Without a sense of dignity and self worth it's widely acknowledged that learning becomes more difficult and that if learning is difficult, dignity and self worth can be hurt. Supporters – as an integral part of schools and classrooms – can ease the way and help children and young people become the best possible learners they can be in the differing and often challenging circumstances in which they find themselves.

Chapter 4

My history of helpers

Lucy Mason

> Given the power of adults, pupils' voices are often at risk of not being heard. Pupils can provide valuable feedback, however, so we do need to invite them to tell us what they think. In this chapter, Lucy Mason, who has considerable experience of receiving support, reflects in a candid way on the helpers who have provided it.

Tracy

My first helper, as far as I can remember, was called Tracy. She was quite nice. She was the 'motherly' type but she wasn't OTT. She had a daughter at my school who was asthmatic. I think that gave her an understanding of how frustrating it was for young people when they couldn't always join in. She was my helper from nursery until Year 1, when she left because she hurt her back and could no longer lift me. Tracy always coped well when I hurt myself. She never seemed to feel guilty which was nice for me because so often when I'd hurt myself I spent more time reassuring helpers and calming them down than I did thinking about myself.

Mrs Marny

My next helper was Mrs Marny, and I can't remember ever liking her. She was strict and took it upon herself to scold me whenever she felt it necessary. So this meant all the little mischievous things young kids do had much bigger repercussions for me. She was a great believer that all children

Source: An edited version of Mason, L. (1998) 'My history of helpers', *The Inclusion Assistant*, Alliance for Inclusive Education, London. For more information, please visit www.allfie.org.uk.

told lies. I remember once, I'd told Mrs Marny you could buy goats milk at a shop near my house. Indeed this was a fib but the next day when Mrs Marny was unable to buy the milk she completely blew her lid. She wheeled me into the disabled toilet. 'You tell porkie pies don't you Lucy?', she yelled, her face inches away from mine. She paced up and down the toilet, 'blah blah blah blah blah', her face grew redder. This was somewhat comical to me. 'Are you laughing at me?' she roared. I shook my head. Unfortunately I do not have an inconspicuous laugh. My whole body tends to shake which in turn makes my chair squeak.

Mrs Marny was so nervous about leaving me that I had to accompany her to the loo! And when I first took my powered wheelchair to school in order to be more independent in the playground, she insisted on running along beside me, shooing away any friend who tried to come and play with me. She justified this by saying that it was to make sure I didn't injure any of their feet by rolling over them, because their mothers would come and blame her. By the age of 7 my mum and I were so fed up of Mrs Marny that we decided to leave the school. We had already tried numerous times to complain about her, but the head teacher saw nothing wrong with her routines and described her as the 'Salt of the Earth'. When I joined my next school Mrs Marny expected to transfer with me. She saw no reason why we had advertised the job at all and questioned it strongly when she applied for it. Luckily at my new school my headteacher was himself disabled, and he had already agreed that me and my mum could be part of the interview panel. There were three applicants – Flo, Mrs Pen, and Mrs Marny. At first glance Flo seemed to be quite nice but lost several Brownie Points by pinching me on the cheek and saying 'Aah, ain't she sweet'. Mrs Marny was a tyrant and in mid-interview blurted out 'She's a terrible liar, you know!' Funnily enough she was not reinstated.

Mrs Pen

Mrs Pen was great. Everyone picked her as their first choice. She didn't seem strict, but at the same time wasn't patronising. She had a son in my class who later came to be one of my good friends. Mum says she remembers the time he came to my house to teach me chess, a 'nice, quiet, civilised pastime', but instead we re-enacted World War Two. Mrs Pen seemed to have a good understanding of the oppression of disabled people. She was the most adventurous of all my helpers. So many of my helpers are so scared of 'Health and Safety' rules they do not let me do anything in the least bit risky, but Mrs Pen realised I had to learn for myself what was safe and what wasn't. I remember once I managed to climb two bars up a ladder by myself in P.E. which is something most of my helpers would never have let me have a go at. Unfortunately, two years on, Mrs Pen had to leave the job as she fell over a badly installed paving stone whilst chasing her cat and hurt her back. Indeed there were a few times I hurt myself whilst with Mrs Pen, like when on a school journey I broke my leg splashing around in the sea, but I would much rather have a few broken bones and an independent life than no broken bones and a sheltered life.

Flo

Funnily enough, my next helper was Flo. She had a job working in the school already, so we decided to give her a chance. I can't think of a better way to describe Flo than 'Fluffy'. She was the kind of person whose house you'd imagine to be pink and frilly and covered in posters of kittens and bunny rabbits. I always liked Flo. She never once shouted at me and we could have a good laugh. But Flo was not the kind of person you could call 'good in a crisis'. Mum told me that once she was called to the school because I had hurt my arm and when she asked 'Where's Flo?' I replied 'I don't know. She always gets upset when I hurt myself, so I didn't bother to tell her'. Flo stayed with me until I finished primary school. She could not transfer with me because my secondary school was too far, and she stayed on at my primary school to help another disabled child who had joined.

Ali

My first helper at secondary school was called Ali. She was only temporary which was a shame because we really got on. Ali was young and naughty and we had a great laugh. She had her nose pierced, which was a great ambition of mine, and was great around all my friends.

Rachel

My next helper was called Rachel. I liked her at first but found her a bit bossy. She was young and got scared if she didn't know exactly where I was. She showed this by getting angry at me. Rachel left because she was only temporary too.

Lauren

My next helper was Lauren. She started off quite timid but her confidence grew and so did her temper. Our friendship did not. Luckily Lauren was also temporary and left after three weeks.

Jade

After Lauren left, myself and the Head of the Inclusion Support Service decided to try a new set-up. I was to have two helpers, one for four days a week, one for one day a week. This meant I'd get to know two helpers so, theoretically, there'd be back-up if one was away. My main helper was Jade. She was great. All my friends liked her and she was a real laugh. There were times when we had problems with each other, but we sorted them out at fortnightly reviews with a mediator from learning support. Jade used to encourage me, especially in P.E. I remember doing badminton with her. It was not something I expected to be able to do, but we devised our own methods and it worked. I used to go swimming with her, the P.E. teacher and a friend. Jade and I used to do races and Jade would set me and my friends to do crazy things, like underwater ballet. With her help and the P.E. teachers, I managed my lifesavers badge, my survival badge, my 800 metres and my bronze. Jade and me were similar. We both hated insects. Once a huge cockroach crawled into the changing room. Jade picked me up, climbed up onto the changing bench and we both waited there screaming until a lifeguard came in and killed it. Jade left after 18 months because she was offered the same job in another borough, which paid over £2 an hour more. I found this hard because LSA work is so underpaid in some boroughs that you hardly can find someone who can do the job for a long time, which is disruptive to my education and my own personal feelings.

Clover

My other helper was called Clover. We never got on. I thought she was crazy. She never quite got the gist of the job. At first she wouldn't let my friends push me. When my mum had words with her she took them too literally and the next day at school she asked anyone who walked past, even if I'd never met them before, if they would like to push me! Something that really offended me about Clover was when one day in the corridor when it was very crowded, to make people aware that I needed room, she yelled

'Coming through, coming through!' I was not amused. Something that really embarrassed me about Clover was one day, when walking down the corridor we met Mr Tucker, a senior teacher whom Clover had never even seen before who happened to be eating a chocolate bar. Clover marched straight up to him and said, 'Ooh, can I have a bite?', and bit the end off his Twix! A little shocked, Mr Tucker looked down at his half-eaten Twix and gave it to Clover. It no longer looked so appetising. Clover not only lacked common sense, but was a bit religious too. I myself have nothing against Christians, I mean, I believe in God, but Clover went well over the top. Day after day she told me that if I went to church then God might cure me and make me walk. She told me that if I let Jesus into my life then I would go to Heaven. One day I replied, 'I won't go to Heaven'. 'Why?', she asked. 'Because as far as I know there are stairs up to Heaven and I haven't read anything in the Bible about a lift.' Clover did not see that I was being comical and told me not to worry, once I'd died God would raise me from my imperfect body and give me one like hers. She did not understand why I was not joyously relieved. Clover not only got on my nerves, but the nerves of all my friends too. Once, in a really important French exam she went round to everyone individually and introduced herself. 'Hello! I'm Clover, as in the butter, how do you do . . .' Clover was asked to leave four weeks later.

Karen

My next helper was called Karen. She was nice. We had a few arguments but got on most of the time. Karen was really helpful and my friends liked her. Karen was easy to talk to. She had two children of her own who she used to talk about a lot. After working with me for four months, Karen fell over playing volleyball and hurt her ankle. This meant she could not lift me for several months. Several people in my LEA started to question whether anyone should be lifting me at all. This would have caused great problems for me and other students, as our ability to cope in mainstream schools would have been jeopardised. I remember one thing which really upset me was when the whole of my year and the year below me went on a school trip to Chessington and I could not go because there was no one to lift me on and off the coach, and the school had forgotten about me. When I found out about this I was really angry and upset, feelings which often make me become stubborn. So in the following lesson I went on strike. My point was the school expected me to behave like everyone else in the sense that I had to do what they said, but they didn't offer me the same privileges.

Unfortunately my science teacher was not very sympathetic and threatened to put me on 'red report'. For the same financial reasons as Jade, Karen had to leave after eighteen months.

Mary

My next (short-term) helper was called Mary. She was claustrophobic and therefore would not go in the lift with me. Nor could she lift me as she had a bad arm. Mary spent most of her time working in a special school and talked to me like I was about three. In her time with me she decided that one of my friends was a schizophrenic and almost wrote to the school suggesting that she had counselling.

Sarah

My next helper was also short-term. She was called Sarah. She was nice a lot of the time and at the beginning I even recommended that she be given a full-time job at my school. But Sarah suffered from mood swings which put a heavy strain on our relationship.

Dotty

My current helper is called Dotty and her name says it all. The school seems to love her but I do not. She can often be rude. She is rarely on time to collect me for lessons and can appear to be quite selfish at times, e.g. my helpers are meant to buy lunch for me but unless I buy mine when she says, my friends have to buy it for me as she does not like to wait for her food. I could put up with Dotty's incapabilities but something which deeply offends me is that Dotty has said to me twice that I would not have a helper if I could make my own decisions, which I think is the biggest possible misunderstanding of the job.

I do not know where my 'history of helpers' will end as I cannot see into the future, but the stream of helpers will inevitably flow on and will never run smooth until the system is changed and LSAs are trained and paid properly.

(All names have been changed apart from the author's.)

Chapter 5

Klaus' story

Klaus Wedell

Klaus Wedell, emeritus professor at the Institute of Education, London, has made a major contribution to understanding and practice in the area of learning difficulties. His working week involves him as a volunteer helper in a small local village school whose 50 or so children are divided into two cross-age classes – infants and juniors. In this chapter, he analyses the role that he has taken on and his approach to supporting children and communicating with teachers.

It seems to me that support basically takes two forms. There is help, firstly, designed to enable children to take part in the normal curricular activity in the classroom – which already covers a range of levels – so that every child benefits from the teaching and learning going on in their group. This support is geared to help children to understand and respond, and so to bypass their particular learning difficulties as far as possible.

Secondly, help is aimed specifically at supporting children to overcome particular difficulties. Clearly, there is no hard and fast separation between these two forms of support. Even in our classes, which incorporate such diverse learning levels, however, there are a few children who teachers feel need additional help targeted specifically at their particular learning needs. There is considerable controversy about whether this kind of help should be given in the normal class group or by withdrawing children. In our school, children already experience a variety of subgroup and whole group learning, and so 'withdrawal' becomes a relative concept in terms of numbers, particularly as the school design is part open-plan.

Source: A revised version of Wedell, K. (2001) 'Klaus' story: the experience of a retired professor of special needs education', in T. O'Brien and P. Garner (eds.) *Untold Stories: Learning Support Assistants and Their Work* (Stoke on Trent: Trentham Books Ltd).

Working with individuals

I've usually been allocated to individual children whom the teaching staff feel need specifically targeted help. When I first started at the school, I was assigned children from one of the larger age cohorts at the upper infant level. Most only needed help for a year or less, until the teachers felt that they could continue to make progress with their age peers. In the last two years I have been assigned a couple of children in the top year who are still having difficulties. I've emphasised to the teachers that I'm working to them, and where relevant, also to our SENCO.

When I'm asked to work with a child, I ask the teacher to tell me as specifically as possible whatever he or she would like me to help the child achieve, which the child is not currently achieving. Similarly, with the SENCO, the question is how I can support a specific need as set out in the individual education plan (IEP). The SENCO and I share a notebook in which I write down each week what I have been trying to work on with the children, and the idea is that the teacher also reads this. In a small school like ours, it is usually possible also to talk briefly with the teacher during the course of the morning. My aim is to ensure that the children are not handed to me to carry out some supposedly beneficial activity which is not a part of the teacher's own day-to-day plans for the children.

I've been very concerned that working once a week with children lacks the intensity required to achieve an appropriate rate of progress. It has always struck me that it is unreasonable to suppose that, in most instances, this kind of drip-feed can be an effective way of helping children to progress. And yet it is probably still one of the most common ways in which help is offered, largely because of limitations in staffing. I've tried to devise arrangements by which this problem can be overcome – with greater or lesser success. One of the main ways of achieving some continuity is to devise activities which the child can continue in the current class work. In my work with the two children in the leaving class (Year 6), the teacher has asked me to support them in developing their narrative writing for SATS, so it has been relatively easy to link what they write with me with their writing in the classroom. Work with children in the infants class has usually involved me in devising activities which can be carried on as part of the current classroom work, which the children can share with other children. I've also tried to organise work children can do at home with their parents for a short period on three or four nights a week. This too has met with variable success.

Focusing on strengths and needs

All through my work, initially as an educational psychologist, and later in university posts, I've been trying to find ways to focus teaching on children's particular strengths and needs. I've tried to work out how one can achieve a progressive understanding of these by starting with activities which are as near as possible to the day-to-day learning problem. If teaching in this way doesn't work, I regard this as an indication for focusing more on underlying difficulties. Not surprisingly, I've sometimes been told a child I'm working with has indications of dyslexia. I've not found such descriptions more helpful than detailed information about exactly what difficulties the child is having in the classroom. When you are an LSA it can be quite hard to get specific information about what the teacher finds a child can and cannot do – and under what conditions. It is usually more difficult to obtain information about what a child can do than about where the child is failing. There is a similar problem about discovering the particular situations in which a child performs better than in others, so as to get an idea about likely teaching approaches. These values are a subject of the initial – and ongoing – conversations with the teachers and the other LSAs.

Two main strategies for support

There seem to me to be two main strategies for working with children who have particular learning difficulties. One is to start working at the level at which the children are achieving and work up from there. This usually seems to be effective with younger children. For older children, where building up self-esteem and confidence is crucial, such a strategy can seem rather demeaning. So it is better to find a way of enabling them to achieve as near as possible to the expected level, but providing all the cuing and support this requires. Progress then takes the form of systematically removing each of the forms of support, so marking steps in the children's progress.

One ten-year-old I was asked to help was one of those children who have difficulty in setting ideas down in writing. He also had some difficulties in sorting his ideas out. However, he was highly knowledgeable about sheep, and so we decided to write a booklet about what happened in the life-span of a sheep. He dictated this account into a tape recorder over several sessions and then played it back to both of us. Not surprisingly, the syntax and vocabulary of his oral account was infinitely more sophisticated than in his usual written work. We discussed the structure of his account stage by stage, making changes where necessary to improve the sense of what he was saying. He then wrote it out section by section, partly in the sessions and partly at home. I learned a great deal about sheep – for instance that barren sheep were termed 'empties', and that when you take your sheep to a show, you bring them in the night before to 'calm them down and tart them up'. The boy became increasingly impressed with his own account, so we were able gradually to omit the tape recording stage and proceed straight to writing. The complete account was finally printed out as a booklet and the headteacher helped him to incorporate pictures of sheep, so he could present it to his parents for Christmas.

The younger children I was asked to see were frequently those at the upper end of the infants class who were having difficulty in catching on to phonics. One problem was finding out exactly which spellings they were having difficulty with. It became apparent that we needed to derive a spelling progression and use it to check both those aspects they had already mastered and those which might be appropriate to learn as a next step. The errors the children made were usually of the plausible phonic alternative (PPA) type – which typically became apparent when they tried to spell words with vowel digraphs such as 'ou', 'ai'. Planning help for these difficulties pointed up an interesting difference of view between the teacher and myself. She thought it best to teach children digraphs by grouping words according to the various ways of spelling the same sound. My view was that the children's errors were already PPAs, and that one needed to start by teaching contrasting sounds. The contrasts needed to be highlighted by focusing attention on what the words looked like and also linking the spelling with the meaning of the words. So with respect to these particular children we agreed to differ.

Work on spelling at this level lent itself well to having children work in small groups or pairs so they could play phonics games. I had to devise tailor-made activities, adapting Happy Families games so that the families consisted of sets of relevant words with contrasting vowel digraphs the children had found difficult. The children could take these sets of cards back into their classroom, where they could teach others to play the game, and so gain kudos. I also used the computer so they could build up words with the relevant digraphs, and complete sentences using the words.

Checking progress

A crucial aspect of the 'building up skills' approach is recording progress over the short-term. The children – let alone I myself – needed to know that these approaches were in fact meeting their learning needs. Checking the accuracy of spelling words is relatively straightforward within the activities of giving individual or group help. Getting feedback about the children's performance in the classroom can be less precise – another instance where close collaboration with the teacher pays dividends. Checking progress on the work in the narrative writing task with the older children also has its problems. In one sense, the 'reducing cues' method can be self-validating. If the children can maintain the performance level when the cues and help are progressively withdrawn, there is reasonable evidence that learning has taken place. However, agreeing, for example, whether children have demarcated sentences appropriately, is more subjective. I worked with a boy and a girl who also still had limited spelling competence. We decided that the SENCO would tackle the spelling. The boy had difficulty using the given SAT title as a stimulus to start writing, but the girl wrote endlessly and with little relevance to the set title. We again used a cuing approach, largely to bypass the spelling limitations of the task. In this instance we used the Clicker software, which also spoke the written text back so the children could listen for where sentences might end. Because this work was closely geared to the work the children were doing in the classroom, the progress monitoring was largely taken on by the teacher, in the context of the assessments in the class. One could not fail to reflect on the fact that the national curriculum assessment procedure was pushing teaching into the SAT task as an end in itself.

Tuning in to children

The account of my work as an LSA shows what many of us find – that LSAs have the opportunity to tune in to individual children's feelings and attitudes to an extent which is often not open to teachers. Some children open up in conversation about their personal problems and about their family issues. Children's story writing also often reveals their preoccupations and concerns, so that one cannot help but become aware of the background to their problems. The dilemma then is in deciding how far one should allow these topics to open up, and when to make it clear that this kind of communication needs to be channelled back to the teacher. As an LSA, one at least has the opportunity to try to tune one's interaction and relationship with the children in a way which matches their needs. In some instances, children try to test the limits in terms of control; in others, one is faced with the task of defining the limits of personal interaction. Both situations can prove quite demanding for both male and female LSAs, and it is interesting to note how the perceptions of the relative roles of child and LSA gradually come to be established over time. This was brought home to me in a tangential way when it was decided one year to decorate the annual governors' report to parents with the infant children's pictures of the staff. My depiction featured me peering intently at a computer through my half-moon glasses.

Continuing to learn

During my jobs at universities, I also tried to keep my feet on the ground by learning from the experience of the teachers on our advanced courses and working with them on their assignments in schools. I used these opportunities to match the strategies for special needs teaching with the more theoretical issues which underpin one's actions. However, I feel the recent years of work as an LSA have taught me as much again – and I am continuing to learn. The experience has also brought home to me, even more, the superhuman intellectual demands made on individual teachers and LSAs faced with meeting the diversity of learning needs in class groups of children. It really is time we moved away from the rigidity which this organisation imposes on the education of our children. The contribution LSAs can make is slowly becoming recognised as part of the way in which the nature and levels of learning needs can be served by the nature and levels of expertise that a range of professional approaches can offer in schools. But as recent research into the function of LSAs has shown, it seems there is still a long way to go in many schools before the resource LSAs represent will be fully realised. Perhaps paradoxically, small village schools faced with finding ways to respond to the complex learning demands of their cross-age classes may well be indicating the way ahead.

Chapter 6

Calm, purposeful, happy

Stephen Lunn

This chapter, by Stephen Lunn, a teaching assistant, reveals how it is to be at the 'deep end' of classroom practice supporting a child who finds it extremely difficult to comply with the expectations of school. It also identifies some of the dilemmas that confront teaching assistants when they act as intermediaries building close relationships with children, but also working within the curriculum and behaviour framework which is required within a school.

Grant, a jazz aficionado, began singing 'There may be trouble ahead', as his recent friend Matthew went round the class selling 'Hope' ribbons in aid of Dr Barnardo's, at 50p each, during morning registration. What Grant knew that the rest of us didn't, was that Matthew was running a scam – the money was destined for his pocket rather than a good cause. There certainly was trouble ahead, and trouble behind, and the song became Grant's theme tune for much of the school year.

This chapter draws on a journal I kept whilst working as a teaching assistant in a middle school. My main role was to support Matthew, a low-attaining, statemented 11-year-old boy with a history of exclusions and violence. Matthew is the main focus but the story reveals much about the school and what it was like to work there through what may have been a turning point in Matthew's difficult young life. The title, *'Calm, Purposeful, Happy'*, was the school's motto, not a description of anyone's state of mind.

I joined the school in the middle of autumn term, working part-time, Monday to Wednesday. The school lay on the fringe of the inner city. Around 30% of pupils in the school were from homes where English was an additional language; a similar proportion were eligible for free school meals. The head teacher was a warm, friendly man with deep empathy for the

Source: A revised version of Lunn, S. (2004) 'Calm, purposeful, happy', commissioned by The Open University for *Primary Teaching Assistants: Learners and Learning*, (London: Routledge). Reprinted by permission of The Open University and Taylor & Francis Ltd.

children. He had no deputy because of budget cuts. Staffroom gossip hinted at inconsistency in the head's backing of his teaching staff in disciplinary matters. Some teachers seemed to struggle to maintain order, and no formal procedure for escalating problems was operated. The school was noisy and dirty, pupils were disobedient and disrespectful to staff and visitors, academic standards were low, and bullying and intimidation were widespread.

Support staff needing one-to-one time could resort to a 'quiet room' next to the library, which housed an ancient computer, a radio-cassette player, collections of reading schemes, workbooks, and games. This was where the Educational Psychologist and Educational Social Workers operated when they visited the school.

My first day

I started work at the school the day before Matthew arrived. Christine, the SENCO (Special Educational Needs Co-ordinator), gave me a brief sketch of Matthew's background, and explained my duties. Matthew had been assessed as violent, disruptive and of low ability when in Year 2, and in the subsequent four years had been excluded from six schools in five LEA areas, most recently for attacking a teacher with a chair, five months ago. He brought with him a statement of special educational needs (learning difficulties), made earlier in the term, at the time of his 11th birthday.

My duties included meeting Matthew at the school gates at 8.45 each morning, and conducting him through assembly and registration. Matthew would be at school for the mornings only, until he felt ready for more. Christine introduced me to some other support staff, and gave me copies of Matthew's statement and an IEP (Individual Education Plan) that she had drawn up for him. At the time I understood the words but not what they really meant: that would become clearer as the months passed.

Amongst many other things, this statement said that:

- his verbal skills were *low average . . . he may have difficulty in understanding age-appropriate instruction'*;
- his reading age was 6 years 10 months;
- his spelling age was 7 years 2 months;
- his numeracy skills were at the level expected for someone 8 years 7 months old.

The statement attributed his low attainment in part to *'past poor behaviour and poor attention to task and acceptance of teacher instruction'*, and suggested that there may be *'an element of specific literacy difficulty (dyslexia)'*. Tests carried out soon after his arrival produced consistent results in both literacy and numeracy. Two independent examinations in the following six months found no evidence of dyslexia, though his mother continued to believe that it lay behind his problems.

The statement concluded that Matthew had the following special educational needs:

- *to develop more age-appropriate basic skills of literacy (reading, writing, spelling) and numeracy;*
- *to consolidate age-appropriate skills of negotiation and conflict resolution in his peer relationships;*
- *to develop the skills of responding appropriately and acceptably in his relationships with adults in school.*

In the language of such statements, 'to consolidate' implies that there are some skills, albeit rudimentary, to build on; 'to develop' suggests that one is effectively starting from scratch.

The provision specified to meet these needs involved Matthew being taught in a mainstream setting with specified staffing arrangements, curriculum, programmes and teaching approaches.

Staffing arrangements included providing opportunities for small group work and discussion, to develop self-control in relationships with peers and adults; an identified individual member of staff for individually-focussed pastoral support, to help Matthew develop his self-esteem and behavioural skills; and adult support across the curriculum.

Curriculum, programmes and teaching approaches included access to the full National Curriculum; a small-step literacy programme; a structured maths programme; and access to *'age-appropriate models of acceptable behaviour'*. These programmes needed clear short-term goals of which Matthew was aware, built in to an IEP. Progress against this should be monitored and new objectives set, regularly. Progress should be reviewed 'with the parents' at annual reviews of the IEP.

Meeting Matthew

Christine and I met with Matthew and his mother in the quiet room. He was a slight, pale, blond boy with hooded grey eyes. He had chronic asthma, hunched posture and nails bitten to the quick. My first impression was of a small, cowed, frightened child, and a kind but exasperated parent whose resources were all but exhausted. Matthew avoided eye contact and conversation: he was soon ranging round the room looking into drawers and cupboards, but settled down and began to play absorbedly when he found a box of Lego. We discussed how he would get to school: his mother wanted transport provided, but he lived within three miles so would have to walk. He would not be allowed out of school during school hours without written permission.

His mother's plan was that he would leave home at about 7.30 a.m. in order to arrive for registration at 8.45. In practice he often arrived 30 to 60 minutes late, and spending two hours covering two miles gave ample opportunity for mischief en route.

Matthew, being 11, would join a Year 6 class. As Christine and his mother talked, I joined him with the Lego, and soon we were engrossed in a bridge-building project. From that point on we almost always worked together well on a one-to-one basis in the quiet room, which became a refuge in difficult times, and a daily reward for sustained effort on Matthew's part – on many occasions we gritted out the last twenty minutes of a maths lesson on the understanding that we would spend the half-hour before lunch there.

Trying to cope in the classroom

By the end of his second week Matthew was ready to start full-time. Unsurprisingly he made friends with 'the lads', three or four boys always in for a laugh or whatever distraction was on offer, with whom he would sit if given the chance. More surprisingly he also formed a friendship with the popular Laura, an academically able girl who played for the school soccer and netball teams.

The class teacher, Mr Trescotherick, known to all as Mr T., was firm and fair, and Matthew got on well with him. Year 6 was 'setted' for English, maths and science: Matthew joined the bottom set for each. This meant that for English he was in Mr T.'s group, which was fine: in maths and science he was with Miss Jakes, a semi-permanent supply teacher, which was not so good. It was in the first science lesson of his second week that we had our first real crisis. Up to this point I had applied gentle but absolutely firm pressure to keep him on task as long as seemed reasonable, negotiating units of work and periods of escape in the quiet room. On this occasion conflict arose between my duty to Matthew and my duty to the teacher.

Pupils were allowed to sit where they wanted, and Matthew gravitated to a table in the back corner, with three of 'the lads', Grant, Gareth and

Simon. Grant, the jazz lover, was bright, with a cruel streak. He was learning to play drums, but was not much interested in learning anything else. He had a great talent for stirring things up, dropping out of sight at the crucial moment, and coming up looking innocent. Gareth watched everything with a broad good-natured grin. He moved slowly, and was often the only one left to carry the can when authority arrived. He never engaged with any work other than the most simple and repetitive tasks. Simon was a bright middle-class boy who seemed to be trying to buy street cred with persistent mild naughtiness that never quite came off.

Matthew and I joined this group. The lesson was about nutrition, and the teacher handed out tracing paper and sheets containing pie charts showing what sources contributed what proportions of our energy, protein, calcium, iron, vitamin B1 and vitamin C requirements: for example the 'energy' chart showed that 29% of our energy comes from cereals, 16% from dietary fats, 16% from meat, 9% from sugars, etc. The pupils' task for the lesson was to trace these pie charts into their science books.

This task was right up Gareth's street, and his grin widened as he slowly adjusted his tracing paper over the worksheet, and slowly followed the lines underneath with his pencil. Though Matthew rolled his eyes heavenward at Grant, they all made a start. However, this task was anathema to Matthew, involving as it did reading, writing, and close control of eye, hand and pencil. Soon he complained that it was boring, and that he could not see the point of it. He kept making mistakes, rubbing out, starting again, and was getting frustrated. I tried to maintain my 'gentle but firm pressure' to keep him on task, but my heart was not in it. I could not help thinking that, as a Year 6 science activity, tracing pie charts left something to be desired – there was no discussion of the content, before or after the activity, and privately I shared Matthew's view that it was boring and pointless.

Eventually Matthew stood up, said: '*I ain't doing it!*', and headed for the door. Grant caught him on the back of the head with an eraser, which Miss Jakes did not see. However she did see Matthew pick it up and throw it back at Grant, before continuing towards the door. Miss Jakes bore down on him from the front of the room, shouting angrily for him to return to his place, and Matthew took one look and bolted. I apologised to Miss Jakes and went to find him and calm him down.

I found him hunched up at the bottom of the stair well, sobbing. I suggested a visit to the quiet room, but there was a meeting going on, so we climbed back up the stairs to our science lesson. We found the room in modest uproar. Miss Jakes was talking to a group of girls at the front, with her back to the rest of the class. Quite a few things were being thrown to and fro, no-one was working. Matthew and I returned to our table to join the three boys. I felt that I was in a difficult position. Did I ignore what was going on, thereby almost sanctioning it? Or did I intervene, thereby undermining the teacher's authority? In the event I did a bit of both: I intervened as far as our table was concerned, and ignored the rest of it.

On our table no-one had actually got as far as transferring any part of a pie chart into their science book, and I felt unequal to trying to force them to do so. Instead I tried asking them if they knew what nutrients did, and in particular what would happen to you if you did not get particular nutrients. The gory details of scurvy and rickets kept them interested and engaged until the end of the lesson. I emerged from it feeling confused, feeling that I had not dealt straight with any party, and feeling guilty in several ways: towards the teacher, a professional, for having subverted what I had judged to be a poor lesson, and for having communicated this judgement willy-nilly to the pupils, thus undermining what respect they had for her; and towards the pupils, for having appeared to take their side, whilst actually engaging them in what I thought was useful learning. Looking back on this now, I still feel guilty, still puzzle about what I could and should have done.

Hearing voices

On a Tuesday morning in early December Matthew arrived looking bruised and battered, with one very black eye. He had missed Monday because of a visit to a psychiatrist at a nearby children's hospital, following what Christine called as *'a psychotic episode'* over the weekend. As Matthew later described it, the voices that normally only whispered had started shouting and screaming at him about death. His bruises came from punching his head to try to stop the voices.

We spent most of Tuesday in the quiet room, playing games, listening to music on the radio, playing on the computer. At one point he stopped in the middle of a game and held out his hand, saying *'My hand is shaking'*. He seemed more puzzled than disturbed by this. He was very low, humble in his sadness and fear. I was afraid too, and felt that I was being asked to deal with something far beyond my competence.

Christine, the SENCO, joined us to help, later in the morning. She suggested we try to help Matthew develop a strategy for dealing with the screaming voices. Matthew was a Liverpool fan, and the plan we ended up with was that, when the voices threatened, he was to imagine that he was playing up front for Liverpool, at Anfield, in an end-of-season decider for the championship. The score was 1:1 and there were only minutes to go. Matthew received the ball and was through on goal. He ran in, scored in the top corner, and the crowd in the Kop roared. And the roar of the crowd was so loud that it drowned out the voices.

I do not know whether it worked; but the voices were not mentioned again.

Making progress

In our sessions in the quiet room we worked mostly on reading schemes and literacy workbooks. Playing on the computer was Matthew's favourite activity, and tended to be held back as a reward for some less enjoyable achievement. He liked playing games or using a 'paint' programme – until he discovered Logo (a programming language that can be used to control a floor-crawling 'turtle' robot, or to create patterns on screen). I had been a computer programmer in an earlier life, but had never used Logo or anything similar, so we explored together. We began by drawing simple geometric shapes – squares, triangles. Over several weeks we created more elaborate pictures – a house, a flower. Matthew enjoyed it, but crossed a threshold of enthusiasm when he discovered 'procedures'.

A procedure is a sub-program that a higher level program can 'call': e.g. a program building up a picture of a house and garden could call 'square' and 'flower' procedures to draw these things in appropriate places. A procedure can be called with 'parameters' that tailor its general purpose, e.g. that can say how big, what colour, where to start from. A procedure can call other procedures, to any number of levels. It is a simple, powerful, elegant concept that is tremendously liberating and empowering to the programmer, a bit like learning to fly. Matthew saw this and took off, soon producing magnificent swirling mandalas of colour that grew and morphed on the screen in front of us.

At about the same time, Matthew had a good run of punctuality and better focus in lessons, especially in maths. One morning he rattled through the two worksheets, with almost no help from me (on two questions I suggested 'Look at that again'). He was the first to finish, and proudly took his book out to Miss Jakes for marking. He had got them all right, and was awarded '1 Merit'.

One step forward, one step back

Later that term a boy called Darren arrived at the school and joined another Year 6 class. His history was not dissimilar to Matthew's, and he too had one-to-one support, from my colleague Martina. Darren's arrival coincided with the early retirement of the head and two new appointments. The head of the nearby comprehensive was appointed acting head while continuing in post at the upper school; and Catharine McGivan was appointed deputy head.

Darren was lawlessness personified. Matthew was fascinated and could not keep away. They would meet up on their way to school, and arrive an hour or more late, with an increasingly worrying daily addition to the items that they had 'found' – car keys, a briefcase, bicycle lights still in their packaging, knives, lighters. Martina and I confiscated anything dangerous, and started to keep a record of 'found' items, in case there was ever police involvement.

Darren and Matthew would get together and get involved in something almost every break-time. In one three-day spell, when they had an inexhaustible supply of cigarette lighters, they set fire to some waste ground; were seen smoking and setting bales of hay alight in a field beyond the school grounds; and were accused of trying to set fire to some smaller boys' ears.

The new deputy, Mrs McGivan, had just redefined the school rules and disciplinary procedures, and these began to bite with Matthew and Darren. Martina and I had to keep one or other in at break so they could not meet; lateness in returning from breaks was to be punished with detention; persistent problems were to be escalated from teaching assistant to class teacher to SENCO to deputy head to head.

One Wednesday morning Matthew arrived very early, before me. He left his bag in the quiet room and told the secretary he was going out to play. He came back half an hour later having 'found' some batteries, of a type kept in the science stock cupboard. This cupboard was usually kept locked, and was in a storage area that was also locked when not in use.

Later that morning we were working in the quiet room when Christine called me aside to say that the caretaker's keys had been taken from his coat in the staff cloakroom, earlier that morning, and asking me to keep a close eye on Matthew. For the rest of the week it was clear that something was going on between Darren and Matthew, which culminated on Friday with Darren threatening Matthew, and chasing him out of school, pursued by several of us until they were lost to sight. They did not return, and parents and police were informed.

The following Monday Matthew arrived on time, with his mother. Christine (the SENCO) and I met them in the quiet room. Matthew had 'as good as' told his mother that he had taken the keys to the science cupboard and given them to Darren, who had *'thrown them in a stream'*. She asked us if Matthew and Darren could be kept apart. Christine said we would try, and indeed had been trying for some time, but could not make guarantees.

Matthew seemed quite light-hearted that day, in lessons. He concentrated well during a maths test. In the library he selected a book and grinned at me as he showed me the title – 'Cops and Robbers'. In the afternoon his mother was back again, this time for a termly progress review. The main points were:

* his reading was improving;
* he had made *'excellent progress'* in maths;
* he was working at National Curriculum level 4 in science;
* his writing and spelling were still very poor;
* his behaviour was unpredictable.

His mother added that he liked coming to school, and Matthew's own contribution was: *'My behaviour is improving. I enjoy school. I am improving in reading and writing. I'm good at maths.'* It was decided to continue with full-time one-to-one support; to institute a formal rewards system, including rewards for time-keeping; to keep Matthew away from Darren; and to *'develop strategies to prevent him running away from school'*.

The following morning the disciplinary process caught up with Matthew. When we arrived in class for registration, Mr T. handed me a note from the deputy head, asking me to take Matthew down to see her immediately. Matthew gave an 'O-oh', and Grant accompanied us out of the door with *'There may be trouble ahead. . .'*

Mrs McGivan told him that it was known with certainty that he was responsible for stealing the caretaker's keys; that as a punishment for that and for running out of school, he would be kept in at break and lunchtime for the rest of the week; and that he was to spend the first lesson in the head's office, writing an account of why he ran away. He continued to deny taking the keys, refused to write anything, and *'exhibited a poor attitude'*. Mrs McGivan told him that he could not stay at school if he refused to do as he was asked, and phoned his mother to ask her to come and fetch him.

At that point Mrs McGivan had to teach. She asked me to meet Matthew's mother and explain that he was being sent home at least for the rest of today, and that he should not come back unless and until he undertook to do as he was told in school. Matthew listened in glum silence.

His mother arrived and I explained the position. Matthew continued to protest his innocence. His mother did not say much, but accepted that Matthew had to go home now, and that the school could not accept him back until he agreed to abide by instructions. Talking to his mother and me alone before they left, he agreed that he did not want to be excluded, and seemed genuinely contrite, apologising for his behaviour that morning, and agreeing that he would come back tomorrow with a genuine attempt to change his attitude to himself, his work, and other people, and an undertaking to do as he was told.

Later that day I phoned them at home. His mother said that he was genuinely sorry, and would come in tomorrow with a different attitude and would apologise all round. She had impressed on him that he would not only be expelled, but might also be taken from her into council care if he did not shape up.

Thus it was a subdued Matthew who arrived with his mother the following morning. They were asked to see the head and deputy, who re-iterated yesterday's messages. Matthew apologised and accepted the conditions of his return. The detentions were to start immediately: my job-share and I would sit with him in morning break while he worked through maths and English worksheets; the deputy head would look after him at lunchtime.

When we came out of the meeting, Matthew and I had a breather in the quiet room, then rejoined the class for the next lesson, maths. We sat at our table and Matthew got out his worksheet, then leapt up and ran out of the room, coming back moments later eating a large bread roll. I felt that this was a critical period, and told him firmly that he was not to go out without permission; that he was not to eat during lessons; and that he was to do as I asked immediately or he would be straight back down to Mrs McGivan. He shrugged, gave me a tiny smile, put away his lunch, turned to his maths worksheet, and started working intently. I was very relieved.

Later in that lesson the maths test from earlier in the week was handed out. It was a 'mock' SATs paper, and Matthew had achieved a good level 3: we agreed that he would begin his morning break detentions by working this paper again, with support, and that we would keep on doing it until he got it completely right – no-one in the year had achieved this first time round, and he seemed excited by the prospect.

Thus at break we were sitting outside the staff room, working through the maths test, at a table looking out over the main entrance to the school. We were surprised to see a computer monitor fall from a window on the upper floor, hitting the ground not far from us, soon followed by a cardboard box full of exercise books and other objects as a major disturbance passed through many classrooms and the library.

Darren had been scheduled for interviews with the head and deputy of a similar nature to Matthew's, and had reacted by running berserk through the school, causing widespread damage. Darren's mother and most of the staff were by now watching developments with us. Soon we saw a window of the quiet room open and Darren jump out. At the same time a police car drew up and two officers got out. They grabbed Darren and pushed him, struggling, into the back seat of the car. He scuttled across the seat and got out on the other side, running for the school field, pursued by the two policemen. He dodged and ducked, evading them for a while, until he was rugby-tackled and forcibly restrained. He was led back to the car in handcuffs, and driven away with his mother. That was the last we saw of him.

Matthew had watched all this open-mouthed. Afterwards he was subdued. It could easily have been him in the police car, but it wasn't. He was still in the school and had another chance.

A new beginning

Life as Matthew's one-to-one support was never going to be uniformly smooth, but from that time on he really did seem to change. He would do as he was told, albeit sometimes reluctantly. He did work hard, and he did keep out of trouble. By mid summer term, literacy tests were showing his reading age as 10 years, with writing and spelling around 9 years 6 months. He missed English KS2 SATs, but achieved level 3 in maths and level 4 in science. He no longer stood out as being conspicuously academically inferior to his peers, and this was enormously important to him.

I stayed in touch with Matthew's career when we both moved on at the end of the year. He had full-time one-to-one support through Year 7 and continued to progress well. The following year his support was reduced, and later withdrawn. At the time of writing he had completed his secondary education without any serious trouble, and was holding down a job on the ground staff of the local football team. He may not have become the 'calm, purposeful, happy' person of the school's motto, but he wasn't a bad kid.

Chapter 7

Nadia's education

Katie Clarke and Pat Rangeley

Katie Clarke is the mother of Nadia, and Pat Rangeley is a learning supporter working with Nadia at Savile Park Primary School, Halifax. They both talked about Nadia at a conference called 'Learning supporters and inclusion' run by the Centre for Studies on Inclusive Education in Manchester on 21 June 2002. What follows is an edited transcript of their presentation.

Katie: Nadia is a bright, happy and confident nine-year-old. She has, however, various diagnoses to put on her CV such as: she has severe athetoid cerebral palsy, severe communication difficulties and is *profoundly* deaf. Nadia uses sign language and various forms of communication, including low tech and high tech symbols. She's one of my six children. There's Sean who's ten, Nadia is nine, Nicky's seven, Ray is five and I've got twins, Jake and Samara, who are both two. So as you can imagine it's a rather hectic, chaotic, but very fun household. And Nadia is very much part of this household and we work very hard at making sure she's included, and it's not an easy job. We also work very hard at making sure she's included in the community.

Two years ago we lived in Northumberland, beautiful rural Northumberland. Nadia had gone to mainstream nursery and it was, in our eyes, very successful. She still talks about the learning support assistant, Margaret, who was the main force behind it being successful. However, getting Nadia into a local primary school was much more of a struggle. The LEA felt that Nadia's education couldn't be accommodated in a mainstream setting, and we felt we couldn't accommodate living in an area with an LEA who didn't want our daughter in a mainstream school—in the same

Source: An edited version of Clarke, K. and Rangeley, P. (2004) 'Nadia's education', commissioned by The Open University and based on an edited transcript of presentation at 'Learning supporters and inclusion' conference, Centre for Studies on Inclusive Education, 2002, for *Primary Teaching Assistants: Learners and Learning* (London: Routledge). Reprinted by permission of The Open University and Taylor & Francis Ltd.

school as her brothers and sisters. So we moved. It was pretty radical at the time and our decision attracted a lot of publicity. We moved to Calderdale, which was a hundred miles away, where we knew they had a more positive inclusion policy. We moved so that we could walk to our chosen school, Sevile Park Primary, with Nadia in the wheelchair with her siblings. Surely it's something that most parents do every single day with their children?

I want to introduce you to Pat who works at Savile Park and who's one of Nadia's two learning support assistants (Kath Williams is the other). They are part of a dedicated team ensuring that Nadia's education is meeting her needs.

Pat: This is just a snippet of my day with Nadia. I could have written a book, believe you me. At Savile Park we have seven hearing impaired children, six LSAs, one teacher of the deaf and one deaf instructor, and numerous other support staff. Nadia is one of the hearing impaired children, only Nadia has cerebral palsy as well. Nadia's day begins in the school yard. I have to fight my way through the many children coming into the school. They all want to come in and I'm trying to get out. So eventually, when I get out of the door, Nadia's waiting patiently in the yard. Once we get her into school we try, as quickly as possible, to take her either into assembly or into class. Three times a week she goes into a standing frame for assembly, which is quite difficult to get into. Kath, my learning support partner, helps with this. This is followed by the usual 'good mornings' with everyone, and 'did you have a good weekend' and so on. Once in the standing frame and secure, we scan through the home-school book which Katie brings in every day, and if there's anything we need to know it's in there. Off she goes into assembly. Every assembly has a signer.

During assembly, her cochlea implant sometimes falls out several times. (Obviously, a lot of people here today know about that particular problem.) Nadia's implant is low down on the side of her head so she can sometimes accidentally knock it off by moving her head from side to side. For some children it's above their ear. Even the collar on her coat can knock it off, and sometimes so can her hair.

After assembly is over Nadia is helped back into the electric wheelchair. Children are chit-chatting in class. They start to sign across the room as soon as Nadia comes. She's got lots of friends and some of them are excellent signers—better than me in fact.

I'll now talk about Nadia's school work. In literacy, we do need to modify the work. We might blow it up and put it onto A3, and sometimes prepare 'Clicker' for her. Clicker is a computer programme that offers children with communication impairment a grid containing words, phrases or pictures which are linked to a joystick. It can be programmed by LSAs or teachers to relate to the curriculum area being studied. Nadia loves it. I love Clicker too. It's been superb for Nadia. We've got so many different ways of approaching her work but, to me, Clicker is really good. When she starts working I can leave her and walk around the classroom and generally help some of the other children. If she wants me she either signals, or she comes and finds me.

The teacher comes over to look at Nadia's work, 'Well done Nadia, a sticker for you.' The bell goes and she stays in her electric wheelchair for playtime. Because there are six of us, one of us takes her out at playtime on a rota basis. Nadia wanders round playing games, perhaps tig, or just making conversation. A problem of summer playtime is that the children are allowed to play on an area of grass that we have and Nadia cannot access this. She has a buggy that will go on the grass with somebody pushing it, but the time it takes to change her over, she'd only be getting about five minutes.

So the bell rings and it's toilet time now. Now this is a scheduled toilet visit that we do every day. It may seem strange because we are supposed to take children when they want to go. But this is now a routine of Nadia's, and Kath and I take her to the toilet at about a quarter to eleven, so as not to miss any literacy or maths, or whatever subject she's doing. It's usually quickly done. Every adult and child in our school knows the sign for toilet. So if at any time Nadia's signing for the toilet they understand straight away.

I next go and work with two other hearing impaired children up to lunchtime and Nadia goes into maths. We have to be quick as maths has started. Kath takes her to the classroom and Nadia is excellent at maths, she's absolutely superb. It's a lot easier for Nadia to access maths because of the signing. You know, five times five and she's got it there in her hand. The answer's immediate to her.

It's usually all hands for maths, and of course Kath writes down anything that needs to be written down. Lunchtime arrives and we sometimes cover Nadia's lunchtimes as getting a lunchtime assistant for an hour a day isn't very easy. Not a lot of people want five hours' work a week in the middle of each day. The person that we've got at the moment is pregnant so she'll probably be leaving in September. Kath and I do lunchtime on a rota basis, and whoever takes Nadia for lunch will have their lunch after that. But, unfortunately, that means another child is missing out on support during that time.

So off Nadia goes with a group of helpers over to the canteen with a packed lunch. Everybody wants to sit next to Nadia. I mean, she's been at Savile Park School for three years and children are still fighting to get next to her at the dining table! Conversation is going on as Nadia's eating her dinner. At home she would eat a lot of it herself unaided, but there isn't the time in school because it's only a short time for lunch.

It's one o'clock and the bell has gone so it's back to work. Now the first twenty minutes is reading time and children look at a book with a friend. Nadia goes to the friend she wants to be with and takes them back to where she's working. We've got twins who have just started, Camilla and Antonia, and she likes them because they remind her of the twins in her family. So she goes and picks one of them and they look at a book together. At this time the teacher and I (or the teacher of the deaf) would be discussing the afternoon's work and how best we can put it to Nadia.

It's science today which is difficult, especially for me. We're doing force meters and I haven't got any idea of the sign for 'force meter'. So I have to sign a spring balance, which is the nearest I can think to a force meter. I use the word 'force meter' but I use the sign of a spring balance and this is a little difficult for Nadia. We do have an instructor for the deaf who sometimes comes in but it's not her day to come so I have to deal with the signs myself.

Clicker's now ready. It's so easy to add words to it, words I'm going to need like 'force meter'. So the teacher demonstrates the force meter, tells me how it works, and how it measures in 'Newtons'. None of the children know anything about Newtons at all. So the only way I can put it over to Nadia is to introduce Isaac Newton and how he discovered gravity.

We're lucky enough to have, in Halifax, 'Eureka' (an interactive museum for children) where there is a massive Isaac Newton ball which drops down into a bath every hour. Nadia understands the connection between 'a Newton' and Isaac Newton. But with signing you've got to put things over the best way that you can if you don't know the meaning of a word or the sign.

Mr Richards, the teacher, wants all the children to try out the force meters and asks Nadia if she'd like to have a go at trying to pull a force meter. We've had them for years and they're stiff so they don't actually work very well. We get down to the worksheet and Nadia's copying from Clicker the relevant words. When she's finished we print it off and there's a space to draw a force meter. On this occasion, she asks me to draw the hook that was attached to the force meter.

Then Nadia wants the toilet. So I rush off to the other side of the school, open all the doors so she can access the way out, straight into the disabled toilet. I have to tell you that this toilet is also for all staff. So, if there's somebody in there, we have to wait. We've got thirty five staff and we've got two toilets including the disabled toilet. I get a colleague to help me

and we're quickly in the toilet. It's then straight back into class. I ask
Mr Richards if we can spend a bit more time to finish the work. So, we
draw a force meter and Nadia concentrates extremely hard. Mr. Richards
comes over, has a word with Nadia and praises her work.

It's 3.10 pm and it's time to go home. Kath and I meet in the unit room.
Such is the electric wheelchair that one of us has to take her out and hold
her while the other one transfers the seat onto another, manual, wheelchair.

So that's the procedure that we go through. Every day has its ups and
downs for Nadia, some good some not so good. Perhaps she's had a restless
night after going several times to the toilet. All these things we try to take
into consideration. She works very hard and she's also very curious. She
always wants to know what's happening, 'Why's Jamalba crying?' or 'Why's
Mr. Richards cross with Keith?'

This has been a typical school day for Nadia. I've been working with her
for three years now and I'm still learning all about her. We're always trying
different methods of supporting her but, of course, we're no miracle
workers. We're trying our best and we're striving for a better education for
Nadia. We never turn any ideas down. Last week we had someone from
SCOPE and we thought she might suggest something that we hadn't tried,
but she didn't and strangely that made us all feel good. It did, you know,
because it made us feel nobody has all the answers but (*looking towards Katie*)
you read that bit because I might get upset.

Katie: It says, 'We're all working at Nadia having a happy and fulfilling life
and we all know we'll be a part of it'. So, this is how I see the role of Pat
and Kath (see Figure 7.1).

There are so many people involved with a child with such complex
needs. There are many people telling Pat and Kath what to do at school.
Some of the people actually don't value Pat and Kath. All these services
have to be co-ordinated and Nadia's needs change daily so the links have to
be there and the links of the family are absolutely vital. I'm so lucky I can
go into Savile Park whenever I want. I pop in, I write in the handbook, but
I'm there to help make sure that Nadia's education is working. There are
two or three meetings a week that I attend, some with the learning support
assistants, some with the various agencies.

There are a lot of services advising the LSAs but this is how I see Pat and
Kath. I see them as powerful and actually as the main persons involved.
They've got so many skills and there are more skills that I could have
mentioned. They've got to do all these things to make sure that Nadia's
education is working (see Figure 7.2).

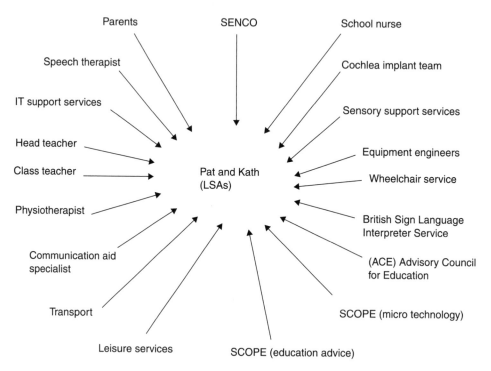

Parents SENCO School nurse

Speech therapist Cochlea implant team

IT support services Sensory support services

Head teacher Equipment engineers

Class teacher Pat and Kath Wheelchair service
(LSAs)

Physiotherapist British Sign Language
Interpreter Service

Communication aid (ACE) Advisory Council
specialist for Education

Transport SCOPE (micro technology)

Leisure services SCOPE (education advice)

Figure 7.1 Pat and Kath co-ordinating advice and services for Nadia

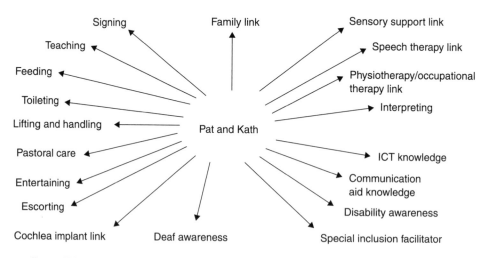

Signing Family link Sensory support link

Teaching Speech therapy link

Feeding Physiotherapy/occupational
therapy link

Toileting Interpreting

Lifting and handling Pat and Kath

Pastoral care ICT knowledge

Entertaining Communication
aid knowledge

Escorting Disability awareness

Cochlea implant link Deaf awareness Special inclusion facilitator

Figure 7.2 Roles performed by Pat and Kath

That's how we're going to end our presentation and it's with thanks to Pat and Kath and also Anne, who's Nadia's teacher of the deaf. Because they are the body, they are the team; they are the key workers behind making Nadia's inclusion work in a mainstream school.

Chapter 8

Support in a mathematics lesson

Jennifer Colloby

Ofsted, the school inspectorate for England, suggests that teaching assistants provide important support for up to one-in-four primary school children (Ofsted 2003). Jennifer Colloby, a Staff tutor with The Open University, provides a closely observed study of Caroline Higham, a teaching assistant working within the context of a mathematics lesson. Her chapter highlights the involved nature of learning support.

Caroline is employed in a small rural school with just over ninety pupils and four staff including the head teacher. She has worked as a teaching assistant for several years. She has two children who were previously educated at this school. She now works full time, i.e. 35 hours a week. She would eventually like to be a qualified teacher and is studying to complete her BA degree.

Since working at the school Caroline's role has grown, both in the number of hours she is employed and in the nature of her responsibilities. She has responded willingly to these developments. She has responsibility for organising and maintaining the school's reading programme and works closely with the head teacher on this. She enjoys the associated responsibility for children's progress and attainment. She keeps records of the individual children she supports and updates these at the end of each school day and shares them with staff. Caroline's experience has given her increased status in the school. She is invited to and participates in staff meetings.

Parents do seek her out for advice but Caroline knows when to pass them on to teachers. She is compassionate and fiercely loyal to the children. She has commitment, patience and determination.

Her own work area in the school is welcoming with interesting displays on the walls. Here, she sometimes supports small groups of children or

Source: An edited version of Colloby, J. (2004) 'Support in a mathematics lesson', commissioned by The Open University for *Primary Teaching Assistants: Learners and Learning* (London: Routledge). Reprinted by permission of The Open University and Taylor & Francis Ltd.

individuals. Her current timetable involves her supporting a group of Year 4 and 5 pupils (9–10-year-olds) each day for their mathematics lesson.

The mathematics lesson

Caroline makes her way to the classroom and greets the class teacher. A quick discussion between them confirms both the plan and objectives for the lesson. For numeracy the pupils are grouped according to ability and she will be supporting a group of four low-attaining pupils.

She counts out pencils and rulers, ensuring that the groups have sufficient supplies. Her preparation for the lesson involved meeting with the teacher earlier in the week (not always easy) so she was aware that the theme was 'pictograms'. From this planning session she knows which books are needed and hands them out. The pupils are in an extended assembly and arrive late for the lesson. She moves quickly, assisting the teacher in settling the children. She has thought about how she will prompt and encourage children by taking part in the mental warm-up activities. She knows she will need to explain, repeat, assist and encourage her group throughout the whole class activity and group work.

As the lesson begins, she positions herself near her group. Pupils are chanting two, five and ten times tables. This is an animated activity and she joins in. An exploration of mid-way points begins with the teacher asking, 'What number lies halfway between 20 and 30?' Caroline's group offer no answers but she shows an active interest in the lesson, which encourages them in their silent participation. The teacher moves onto the topic of pictograms and talks about conducting a survey on the colour of cars. Pupils volunteer colours such as red, blue, silver, white and gold and the class finds much amusement in the teacher's drawing of a car on the board. The teacher admits it looks like a submarine and then jokes with the class saying, 'Don't criticise and don't drive one of these particularly on a Thursday morning!' Caroline laughs and then her group does too.

After 15 minutes of whole class activity the pupils move back to their desks. Caroline goes round the class handing out worksheets. She settles them and then returns to sit with her group. She reminds them what they have to do and Amy is struggling to understand. Caroline explains this again while acknowledging that Beth has progressed to worksheet two. Caroline moves and crouches down beside her. Mistakes are found and Caroline suggests they count together. Beth chants along with Caroline. As Beth's confidence grows she returns enthusiastically to her work.

Caroline quickly moves back to Amy, collecting her own chair on the way. Amy is still experiencing difficulties so Caroline moves to the board to make use of the number line as a visual aid. Caroline demonstrates and repeats the activity the teacher did with the class. She checks that Amy now understands by posing questions for her to answer and encourages her to continue.

Caroline moves back to the group. Cassie is not perturbed that Caroline finds mistakes in her work. Caroline encourages her to have another go before shuffling her own chair next to Diana, the quietest member of the group. Diana has made little progress and Caroline explains the task. Cassie asks for help and Caroline moves to her but is aware that Diana is struggling again. Cassie is now trying to work out the quantities represented by the shapes on pictograms and Caroline explains this. Caroline moves back to Diana but is still questioning Cassie on the pictogram. 'I'll come back to you,' Caroline promises Cassie as she turns her attention to Diana and her troubles with the number line. Fifteen minutes have gone by and the teacher calls for the class's attention. Caroline moves back to her chair, positioning herself well to observe the whole class activity. The teacher wants to emphasise the need for accuracy with bar charts as well as explaining the challenge of extension work from the textbook.

It's back to her group for Caroline. She moves her chair to be with Amy, ticking answers and asking for Amy's explanations. Amy enjoys talking with Caroline and there is a natural bond between them. Caroline moves her chair next to Beth who hardly seems to notice. Have Beth and Cassie worked out question three? asks Caroline, and turns her attention to Beth's work.

The teacher passes by and Cassie is eager to tell him she has finished the first work sheet. Caroline does not confirm this but neither does she express surprise to Cassie. Amy and Diana are on their feet bringing their worksheets to be marked. Diana has her arm round Caroline as she marks her sheet. It's congratulations all round. Amy and Diana have done well and are told to get out their exercise books and find page 31. Cassie is now on her feet but Caroline asks her to sit down and moves close to her. Two boys have arrived and are asking Caroline about page 31. They are Peter and Jonathan whom Caroline has supported since Year 1 in a range of subjects. Caroline quietly explains that they should speak to the teacher today, and adds she is looking forward to working with them later. Off they go and Caroline returns her attention to Cassie. Cassie can now begin to work from the textbook and Caroline kneels by Diana who is looking at a bar chart in the textbook.

The teacher asks the class to listen to two boys at the board who want to conduct a quick survey on favourite subjects. Caroline remains kneeling and tells Diana to think of her favourite subject. Caroline expresses delight that it's maths. The pupils are voting and Caroline reminds Cassie to vote. Cassie won't be voting for maths or science! Amy is not listening and Caroline reminds her to do so. Diana claims she is now 'going slow' because she doesn't want to do any more of the bar chart. The teacher is explaining to the class about 'scaling the axis' on a bar chart but Caroline is absorbed with Diana who further claims not to have 'a Friday' on her chart. 'Friday' is found and Caroline moves on to Amy to discuss her answers to questions from page 31. Amy can explain her answers well and Caroline shows she is pleased with her understanding.

The door to the classroom opens and two men enter. They see Caroline and move to her thinking she is the teacher. They explain that they wish to test the electrical equipment in the classroom. Caroline quietly directs them to the teacher. She returns her attention to Amy and finishes discussing her work. She then moves to Beth who has done very little. The teacher tells the whole class to close their books and look his way. Caroline ensures her group does so and sits down.

The teacher is explaining on the board about labelling the axis for the bar chart on favourite lessons and Caroline is watching him. A mobile phone rings! It belongs to one of the men who are checking electrical equipment and the teacher comments on this. Caroline smiles but continues to watch the board and the interruption by the phone passes almost without notice.

All pupils are now finishing off their work. The group have to think of their own title for the 'favourite lesson' bar chart and this causes difficulty for Beth. Caroline offers assistance suggesting words that could be used. Diana asks her how to spell 'favourite' and Caroline asks, 'How does it start?' Diana begins to sound it out and Amy joins in. Caroline is encouraging Diana who is responding well when Amy recognises the word is already written on the board. Caroline congratulates them both—but for different reasons.

Caroline returns her attention to Beth who is having difficulty choosing a scale for the bar chart but she wants Beth to choose it. Together they start to count to ten in twos but the teacher now tells the whole class to close their books, as it's nearly the end of the lesson. Caroline quietly continues with Beth until ten is reached and then ensures the other three have packed away. Beth is talking to Caroline about today's work and Caroline asks both her and Cassie if it was hard. Cassie replies that she knew the work would be 'more serious' in this class. Caroline senses the enjoyment and achievement of this group of pupils (including Beth), tells them well done and they go off to playtime.

Over a cup of tea in the staffroom Caroline advises the teacher of her group's progress. She reports they worked well, concentrating and trying hard to complete the task. Caroline is pleased with their use of vocabulary and will update their individual records later. Together they decide that Caroline will support this group tomorrow to complete the week's work but now it's nearly time for the literacy hour.

Conclusion

What is it that teaching assistants do when they provide learning support to children and classroom support to teachers? Caroline's practice provides insights into the complex nature of the role. It is a many-sided mix of personal and professionally acquired skills. She has to be confident about her own subject knowledge to effectively support learning so enabling her to connect with the plan of the lesson and its stated objectives. Her links with individual children and groups—explaining, questioning, prompting and reminding them of what it is they are meant to do, keep them focused on the planned lesson. Caroline also links with the class as a whole, always aware and reacting to spontaneous changes to the lesson plan.

Caroline mediates between 'her' children and the demands of the teacher-led, larger classroom experience. She enables learners to engage with the learning objectives of the lesson by prompting children when they need to be involved in a whole class activity. She also mediates between learners and their sense of achievement by ensuring her children can access the tasks through her additional explanations, encouragement and support.

With regard to spontaneous requests from children, she reacts by reinforcing, redirecting and consolidating the links between knowledge and understanding. She also adjusts to unforeseen events in such a way that the classroom continues to be a productive learning environment. Finally, she supports the teacher's management of the teaching and learning within the classroom in such a way that children can model her attitude and behaviour.

This sweep of 'mediating' support skills exhibited by Caroline is part of a repertoire of skills that might be drawn upon by a teaching assistant. However, perhaps they tend to be taken for granted. This close description of practice suggests they are very important for the effective support of both children and teachers.

Reference

Ofsted (Office for Standards in Education) (2003) *The National Literacy and Numeracy Strategies and the Primary Curriculum*, HMI 1973. London: HMSO.

Section 2

Learners and learning

In this section the focus shifts from learning support per se to a consideration of what we mean by learning and what learners do when they learn. Chapter 9 reminds us that when we concentrate on the immediate details of school learning we also need to consider the purposes of education in a broader sense. Schools, Guy Claxton argues, need to prepare learners for a life-long involvement with learning.

Chapter 10 looks at learning through the eyes of children. When asked to imagine the school that they would like, children suggested that too much learning in classrooms is arid and de-contextualised. They emphasised the importance of having opportunities to learn outside school and the need for learning to be both active and enjoyable. Chapters 11 and 12 take up the related theme of informal learning but within the context of home education. Alan Thomas and Harriet Pattison, in Chapter 11, draw on their research with home educating parents to discuss informal learning and conversational learning. They highlight the importance of learning that takes place away from schools and make suggestions as to how informal learning can be enabled in classrooms. In Chapter 12, Claire Young writes of 'living and learning' with her three home educated sons. Claire reminds us that learners can have highly individual approaches to learning.

If children are provided with the appropriate resources, there is much that they, as self-directed learners, can learn for themselves. Chapter 13, written by Amrit Dhillon, provides an example from the streets of New Delhi where internet connections were provided in public spaces for children's use. This chapter illustrates the great promise of new technology in terms of its ability to stimulate and support the process of learning. Chapter 14 brings this discussion back to the classroom. Sue Crowley and Mike Richardson offer teaching assistants and teachers suggestions with regard to how they might work together with children to increase their ICT confidence and maximise the use of ICT in classrooms.

Chapters 15 and 16 address the theme of assessment from two different perspectives. The call for higher standards gives impetus to monitoring and assessment in schools and many teaching assistants have become involved in assessing children's learning – a task that hitherto was seen mainly as a teacher's responsibility. In Chapter 15 Janet Kay reviews assessment practice and identifies an expanding role for teaching assistants. Chapter 16, by Ian Eyres, describes a team approach to observation and assessment that is geared towards the justification of a play-based curriculum.

The last chapter in this section addresses the learning that can arise from homework. Julian Stern, in Chapter 17, considers the reasons behind certain kinds of homework and the implications that this can have for parental involvement. The chapter argues that schools need to take care when sending work home and for staff to recognise the variety of pupils' home circumstances.

Chapter 9

What is education for?

Guy Claxton

With the concerted focus on measured standards in education, it's important not to lose site of the deeper reasons why children attend school. Guy Claxton, Professor of the Learning Sciences, at the University of Winchester, has written extensively on creativity and learning. In this short chapter, he lays emphasis on the role of education in preparing pupils for a changing world and offers a rationale for lifelong learning.

At root, education is what societies provide for their young people to help them get ready to make the most of the world they are going to find themselves in. We want them to be able to make a living in a way that is fulfilling, enjoyable and responsible. We want them to be able to use their leisure productively: to have fun in a way that does not harm other people or the common resources of locality or planet. We want them to be able to make successful relationships, to be good parents, to be capable of being (and disposed to be) loving and kind.

We would like them to be naturally respectful of people of different beliefs, faiths and persuasions, especially those who are less fortunate. We would like them to feel able to take part in the public life of their community and nation. We would like them to have clear values and principles, and to live by them. We want them to live, as much as they can, without fear or insecurity. We would like them to be happy.

Different people and different societies might express their aspirations for the next generation in different terms, but all education rests on some such statements of hope.

The attitudes, beliefs and capacities young people will need in order to achieve those goals depend crucially on what their world is going to be like. And the education they will need therefore depends on the accuracy

Source: Claxton, G. (2002) 'What is education for?', in *Building Learning Power* (Bristol: TLO Limited).

with which the current generation, the designers and providers of education, anticipate what the major challenges and opportunities of the future are going to be. It is no use providing education that prepares young people, however effectively, for a world that they are not going to meet, perhaps one that no longer exists.

In stable times, where the culture is relatively homogeneous and the demands of the future relatively predictable, education can provide young people with the knowledge, skills, and ways of thinking that *we* know *they* are going to need. It is a truism that we do not live in such times: a truism because it is so obviously true.

For the vast majority of young people on the planet (and many of their parents), the world is confusing, complicated and rapidly changing – and likely to get more so over their lifetime.

Most people agree that the only thing we can say with any confidence about the year 2025 is that there is not much we can say about it with any confidence.

In this situation, education has to take a step back. Of course we want to give young people the knowledge and attitudes we value: the trouble is, most societies are now a jumble of different we's. Young people are subject to a welter of conflicting advice and images about what matters, and how to be. It's as if they were standing in the middle of a circle of street-lights, each casting their shadow in a different direction. In a world like this, the only sensible role for education is to get them ready, as much as it can, to cope well with complexity, uncertainty and ambiguity – and to handle the high level of responsibility for crafting their own version of a satisfying life that this challenge entails.

The way the world is going

It does not take an astrologer to know the way the world is going. Mobile phones, e-mail, satellite TV and video games, the internet, cheap international air travel . . . a host of technological innovations have changed the face of work, life and leisure in dozens of ways. Millions of people in the UK work at least part of the time from home. Many of them do daily business with people they have never met. Instead of a 'steady job', people are getting used to being employed for the life of a project: having to adapt quickly to the particular languages and worldviews of team members from diverse professional and cultural backgrounds, and then move on. Microelectronics companies come and go, chasing the best costs-to-skills ratios around the globe, leaving a legacy of deepened insecurity, middle as well as traditionally working class, in their wake. Business people look for security to their financial bonuses, pension funds and their fattening C.V., not to company loyalty.

The traditional heavy industries, and the community life which they supported, are things of the past. The gap between those consultants and 'knowledge workers' who are doing well out of globalisation, and the millions at the poor end of the service industries, packed into call centres, forced to smile on the minimum wage, is widening. As Doug Ross, Assistant Secretary for Employment and Training in the US Department of Labor, told an international conference a few years ago, 'the new poor and marginal in the societies of the developed world will be those who cannot or will not engage in lifelong learning.'

Chapter 10

Learning: 'Let us out. . .!'

Catherine Burke and Ian Grosvenor

This chapter arises from a Guardian newspaper competition asking children to describe 'The School I'd Like'. Catherine Burke, senior lecturer at the University of Cambridge, and Ian Grosvenor, Professor of Urban Educational History, University of Birmingham, consider what children said about their school learning. The children's responses highlight the importance of promoting learning which is active, engaging and fun.

Learning, like play, is a natural activity in childhood. There are biological and neurological impulses towards learning that children are not entirely conscious of but occur as part of growth and development. Early educators such as Pestalozzi, Montessori and Dewey believed strongly that one of the most important roles of a teacher is to create or adapt an environment which does not fetter this natural process and to know when to stand back and allow such natural activity to take place (Pestalozzi 1894; Montessori 1912). However, the routines of traditional schooling, and particularly the language of reward and punishment, indicate a belief that the child will only learn under certain imposed conditions. Children recognise this paradox and in their alternative visions remind the adult world of their natural proclivity to learn.

One commentary, describing an imagined school of the future, challenges the current assumption that children must be forced to learn.

> In this school, lessons are not strictly divided by subjects. Most of the time, lessons in Maths, English, Geography or Science can be taught as one. Students learn concepts by doing – seeing, smelling, hearing, touching, and tasting as well as thinking either creatively or logically. All their senses are utilized in all sorts of manners so that learning is

Source: An edited version of Burke, C. and Grosvenor, I. (2003) 'Learning: "Let us out . . .!"', in *The School I'd Like* (London: Routledge). Reprinted by permission of Taylor & Francis Ltd.

meaningful and practical — not something so alien that they have to be forced upon to do. When children find learning meaningful, they will naturally want to learn more and hence, they will be self-motivated and do not need to be pushed by adults to learn.

(Oliver, 13, Loughborough)

The school, as traditionally conceived, is only one possible site of learning. There has been a massive growth in the cultural and leisure industries in recent years which has spawned a new generation of 'interactive' learning environments visited by children with other family members outside of school time. Gardens, museums, nature reserves, galleries and ecological centres often employ education officers whose job it is to liaise with schools and to enhance the educational impact of the site. These developments have led some to consider what the experience of children and their families when visiting such sites can tell us about alternative contexts of learning.

The Eden Project in Cornwall, opened in 2001, is a garden theme park consisting of several bio domes containing representations of the world's eco zones. When school groups visit such sites, they can be observed to adapt classroom-style, task-oriented approaches which contrast with the 'natural learning behaviours' manifested by family groups visiting at weekends (Griffin and Symington 1997). Such behaviours tend to be less formally organised, more random and led by curiosity rather than design. It has been argued that school-imposed task structures inhibit the natural tendency to learn at such sites. 'Worksheets encouraged "tunnel vision", box-ticking and emphasis on literacy rather than environmental objectives' and surveys have indicated that 'most teachers and pupils felt that learning would have been more effective if there had been unstructured time for exploration, open-ended questioning and consolidation through structured discussion' (Peacock 2002:10).

The comments of children about their ideal learning environment unite across time with the cry 'Let us out!'. For some this means having more opportunity to learn outside of school boundaries, to see, touch, smell and feel real artefacts or nature. Many children dream of escaping the confines of the walled and windowless classroom to learn in the school grounds or in special open-air classrooms designed for the purpose. Blishen (1969) found that children were:

begging that they be allowed to *get out* of the dead air of the classroom — to be freed from that sterile and cramped learning situation in which the teacher, the text book and the examination-dominated syllabus have decided what should be learnt, and how it should be learnt, and that virtually everything should be presented as a hurried intellectual abstraction.

(Blishen 1969:55)

Once more, the tediousness of lessons, the failure of teachers to inspire and the boring methods to communicate facts are criticised. However, there is no doubt that children want to learn and they believe that changes in the organisation, design and structure of education can allow learning to happen more readily.

Learning will happen with ease when it is allowed to be fun and when children are regarded less as 'herds of identical animals', but as individuals who are made comfortable in mind, body and spirit. Part of the sense of comfort and stimulation will result from being granted some control, choice and direction in their learning. Children and young people long to be allowed more activity, experimentation and continuity in the task; once started, they want to be allowed to finish. A study comparing secondary school pupil experience of learning in three European countries, Denmark, France and England, found that the English children 'enjoyed school and lessons the least and were the most likely to want to leave school as soon as they could and to feel that school got in the way of their lives' (Osborn 2001:274). The same study found that an important cross cultural 'constant' among young people was the pupils' concern that learning should be active and that lessons should have an element of 'fun' or humour.

This is what some children had to say about schools and learning:

In the pretty, lively school there are lots of different classes. There are language lessons on French and German, also there are maths and history lessons. You can go to whatever class you feel like any day. The teachers are kind and interested in the children's ideas. . . The most important thing is learning is fun.

(Alix, 7, Oxford)

The School I'd like . . . could slow down a little occasionally. They all speak too fast. Some of the children can sign and all of the staff do but it's all usually too fast. Normal schooling is very heavily based on hearing and reading the English language. There are too many words and too many letters. I can understand key words and simple sentences. It is really helpful if I can see a photograph, an object of reference, a symbol and signs accompanied by hearing the sound of the word. The school I'd like could do more sensory things, more hands on, more touchy/feely. Everyone has loads of senses. We can feel with different parts of our body, we can see, hear, taste, smell. How many senses does the national curriculum focus on? Sometimes I find life in the classroom boring and sometimes the pace is too fast and I switch off. Well, who wouldn't – day in, day out, literacy hour, numeracy hour, registration. How about smelling hour, tactile hour, music hour and physical activity hour. What about employing Charlie Dimmock to fill the school with wonderful water features that we could see, hear, touch, smell and feel?

(Hugh, 6 (with help from his mum), Wellington)

One change that we would make would be to in summer have some lessons outside. In summer in a classroom you get hot and bored. Outside we would be a lot happier and work harder. There could be special outside areas in the school grounds with tables and chairs and the teacher could book lessons there.

(Alex, Jessica and Sarah, 12 and 13, Okehampton)

The place must be unafraid of kids staring out of windows and must not insist on 100% attention or even 100% attendance. . . It is a terrible pressure for kids to have to pay attention and think what they are told to think. I would encourage people to dream more and enjoy the sun and the sky, the growing grass and the bare boughed trees. I would encourage kids to look beyond the classroom, out of the classroom and see themselves doing different things.

(Hero Joy, home educated, 14, Kent)

The best thing about the maths classroom is that when our teacher enters, hundreds of sparkling numbers tumble down from the ceiling and then disappear as they hit the floor. And all of us scurry around clutching nets in our hands, trying to catch them. If you're quick enough, you might find you've caught the golden number which gives you the answer to that day's homework.

(Jade, 9, London)

When we were doing the Vikings in history, we didn't see any of their weapons up close we only saw them in pictures. It would be better if we were taken to a museum to see them. We should be taken on trips as part of our topics, it would help us understand more.

(Richard, 12, Glasgow)

Time to learn and see a task through to its completion is very important to children, suggesting that they may often be frustrated by the school timetable and its demands. Children recognise too that school is not the only place of learning. Many interactive and imaginative learning resources are now to be found outside schools. Also, the application of electronic devices such as televisions, computers and mobile phones gives community- and home-based learning distinct advantages over the seemingly restricted regime of the school. [Editors]

References

Blishen, E. (1969) *The School That I'd Like*, London: Penguin.

Dewey, J. (1916) *Democracy and Education. An Introduction to the Philosophy of Education* (1966 edn.), New York, NY: Free Press.

Griffin, J. and Symington, D. (1997) 'Moving from task-oriented to learning-oriented strategies on school excursions to museums', *Science Education*, 81, 763–79.

Montessori, M. (1912) *The Montessori Method*, New York, NY: F.A. Stokes Company Inc.

Osborn, M. (2001) 'Constants and contexts in pupil experience of learning and schooling: comparing learners in England, France and Denmark', *Comparative Education*, 37(3), 267–78.

Peacock, A. (2002) 'Making the environmental message more effective: working with children for ecological awareness at the Eden Project'. Paper presented at the 'Beyond Anthropocentrism' Conference at the University of Exeter, 16–17 July.

Pestalozzi, J.H. (1894) *How Gertrude Teaches Her Children*, translated by Lucy E. Holland and Frances C. Turner, London: Swan Sonnenschein.

Chapter 11

Home education and informal learning

Alan Thomas and Harriet Pattison

Alan Thomas and Harriet Pattison work at the Institute of Education, London. They have carried out research into methods used by parents who choose to educate their children at home rather than send them to school. In this chapter their focus is on informal learning which has implications for all adults who are regularly in contact with individual or very small groups of children. All parental quotes are taken from Thomas (1998).

Home education is a legal option for parents/carers in most, though not all countries throughout the world. There are no reliable figures apart from the United States where a minimum of a million children are being home educated. In the UK, estimates vary, though it is likely there are at least 50,000. Parents can generally be divided into those who choose to home educate from the outset and those who withdraw their children from school for a variety of reasons, both academic and socio-emotional, bullying for example. Some cite moral or religious reasons, especially in the USA.

Parents, certainly in England and Wales, are free to choose how to set about their task. At one end are those who use highly structured, formal teaching methods. At the other are those who are completely informal, unlike school in almost every way. The majority are probably somewhere in between, typically with some structure in the mornings with the rest of the day free for informal activity.

It is important to bear in mind that formal and informal learning have different meanings at home compared with school. Formal learning at home would probably be regarded as relatively informal by most teachers because it is child-centred and highly flexible with no requirement to follow a set curriculum. Informally home educated children learn entirely

Source: A revised version of Thomas, A. (1998) 'Informal learning', in *Educating Children and Home* (London: Cassell). Reproduced with permission of CONTINUUM PUBLISHING COMPANY in the format Textbook via Copyright Clearance Center.

through everyday living experiences and by following their own interests, simply a continuation of the way in which all children learn between birth and reaching school age.

While acknowledging that children certainly learn a great deal before reaching school age, few professional educators, or anyone else for that matter, would expect much of what is learnt in school to be learnt in the context of simply living at home, challenging the "classical assumption that children learn because they are taught" (Trevarthen, 1995: 97). There is little doubt however, that school children whose education is completely informal achieve most of what might be expected of them in school and do so without a curriculum, lessons, learning objectives or tests.

A continuation from early childhood

The best support for the proposal that school-age children can go on learning as they did in infancy comes from those parents who, when their children reach school age, just go on doing what they are already doing. Parents have certain unstated goals obviously, to facilitate their children's acquisition of literacy and numeracy as well as a wide range of general knowledge and development of emotional maturity and social competence. But these goals do not have to be spelt out as objectives any more than they did when their children were younger. There is no logical reason behind mainstream educational practice which assumes that children should submit to a radical change in the way they learn once they start school. Home educated children are simply continuing what Barbara Rogoff, in her research into early learning, has called their 'cultural apprenticeship' (Rogoff, 2003). After all, the culture surrounding children on an everyday basis contains countless opportunities to acquire much of what is taught in primary school: basic maths, literacy and a wide range of general knowledge.

Consider these reflections from home educating parents:

- At the start it was just a continuation of what had gone before . . . learning will take place anyway. I'm a trained teacher.
- We've gone on doing exactly the same things as when she was younger. It will be better for her than for [her older brother who was taken out of school at 13], less structure, more of an evolution.
- I was doing a lot with [him]. He's really bright. He takes in any information. We always talked when we were out. I thought then, if only I could I'd keep it like this . . .

One parent who saw education as a continuation, still wanted at least to mark what would have been the first day of 'school'. So, on the day, she and her daughter caught a bus and kept the ticket as a memento.

The lifestyle of these families attests to their reliance on informal learning, again being highly reminiscent of life in early childhood.

- There is very little that is organized . . . We start the week doing lots of things and get to Sainsbury's by Friday.
- Children can learn a lot at home, not by having school at home but just by living at home – learning happens naturally.

The parent's role

Although children who learn informally have a large measure of control over what they learn, there will be limits to what is learnt if they are entirely left to their own devices. Of course, this is not to say that children do not learn a great deal for themselves, observing and engaging in the world around them, following their own interests, reading for pleasure and through individual and social play. At the same time, parents and all the other adults and children they come into contact with, obviously have a crucial role, at least as much as they would if they were formally teaching their children. How do 'informal' parents do this? Partly by cottoning on to what the child is interested in and extending it and partly by suggesting things the child might be interested in and seeing if they are taken up.

- Basically, I supply resources, tap into my wealth of information, see opportunity where it arises, listen and observe . . .
- I follow them around. I try to be subtle and there when needed. Then they go on, on their own.
- [It's] a question of offer and respond. If you have an idea of what might be of interest you make a suggestion and see how it goes; alternatively you cotton on to something that has caught the child's attention or is otherwise of interest . . .

So, parents are nearly always on hand to extend their children's interests and to introduce topics, not planned, but in the course of everyday life. To a lesser extent this is also true of parents of school children. In cooking alone there is estimation, fractions, volume, weight, temperature and timing, not to mention biology, chemistry, health, environmental issues, etc. Then there is shopping (including price/weight comparisons), saving and spending pocket money, etc. In the car there is distance and speed and the relationship between them. These are just by way of example. The possibilities are endless. Even multiplication tables can be learned informally in unexpected contexts, just as learning the alphabet was, chanting them in the car, in bed, in the kitchen or out walking, and then related to practical questions that arise, measuring area for example. Finally, parents react to their children's observations, answer their questions, follow up some of their interests, constantly extending and building on what they already know. As one parent put it, unlike school 'there is no entity of knowledge, just learning how to learn'.

A very difficult lesson for parents to learn is not to insist on continuing with a topic if their child is uninterested or not listening. For many this came about when they first embarked on home education and tried to teach from a set curriculum. Many children simply resisted being taught. At home, where it is one-to-one, there can be nothing more pointless than trying to teach a child who is simply not paying attention! It was one of the reasons given by parents for becoming more informal. It seems that these children *do* want to learn, but as active participants rather than as passive receptacles for knowledge.

- We are getting less structured because they do much more for themselves. Once you learn to trust them it's amazing what they can do.

Conversational learning

If there is one aspect of the informal approach which, above all others, contributes to learning, it is conversation. Again, this is an extension of the kind of learning that occurs in early childhood, vividly described in the work of Tizard and Hughes (1984), who demonstrated the opportunities there were for learning through everyday conversation in their study of 3/4 year old children who attended school on a half day basis. They noted the rich opportunities for learning that arose at home through social conversation with parents compared with conversation with staff in the nursery classroom which was far more likely to be contrived and artificial or related to classroom management.

- During a visit to [a nature reserve] he asked me: How do they harvest the reeds? We talked about the water table, end of summer harvest, drying out of land, etc. He didn't have to write about it; he had the answer immediately he wanted to know. It was a real life situation, no books, just human interaction.

- Most of their education is talking to them. That's how I do most of it. If you answer questions truthfully and talk to them as adults . . . Their questions are often at great depth.
- We talk an awful lot, from the time they get up till the time they go to bed . . . It's constant, non-stop.
- Lots of questions come up especially at meal times. We talk about people and relationships and difficult people, interaction with older children, being spiteful, being excluded, how to cope. Also moral questions, how you should try and be with different people; otherwise anything from ethics to astrophysics.
- [She learns] from being next to me, asking questions, watching . . . What is important is me giving my time and not rushing off. We can take half an hour to walk down the street.

Informal learning need not be sequential

In keeping with the above, some parents came to realize their children learned a great deal in apparently unrelated bits and pieces.

- Teachers want things done sequentially. We don't learn to talk like that – not sequentially . . . Some things we may spend five minutes on now and then pick up two months later . . . I started with very little structure, but a sort of mental sense of what they should be doing. I had this big thick book. I wrote down what we did every day, for quite a while. I felt I had to prove I was good at what I was doing and I needed a record to show anyone. I found it really hard to keep a diary. We'd start on one subject and then go through a heap of things and end up 'somewhere'. They might read ten books in a day; we had tons of books. We went to the library book sales . . . For the school inspector I wrote down what we did in one hour: make a cake, do maths, flour, wheat, birds, flying, bird book, flight and feathers, timing the cake, heat, plan for evening, etc.

If there is one body of knowledge the learning of which requires structure and sequence, it would appear to be maths. Even so, the amount of maths that could be learned incidentally and informally, certainly at the primary level, attracted comment.

- We've used maths books, mainly to fill in the gaps with what they learn anyway, but lots of maths is with 'real things', practical rather than abstract . . . Recently they built a cardboard castle with some friends. It involved building turrets, working out floor space, how to cut a spiral . . . and no one mentioned the word 'maths'.

- A lot of maths occurs just through something cropping up . . . maths just crops up. The children are always more ahead than you expect them to be.

This is not as surprising as it at first appears if you consider that most children informally pick up basic concepts in maths before starting school, and that a great deal of maths at the primary level is what adults use on a day-to-day basis, capable of being assimilated informally along with other common cultural knowledge. Thomas (1998) used a mother's extremely detailed journal of her daughter's informal learning to show how she acquired most of the maths taught in primary school without having been taught a single lesson. The only exception was that her mother tried to teach her the multiplication tables, with very little success. However, she learned the 20 x table before many of the easier ones, as a result of collecting 20 cent coins from supermarket trolleys abandoned in car parks in inclement weather and enthusiastically totting up her takings. A spin off from being home educated was she could be there when other children were in school! There are echoes here of what has been called 'street learning' in which economically active children acquired mathematical skills, working in a market stall or selling goods in the street for example (Nunes *et al*, 1993).

We are continuing to explore informal learning in greater depth, both theoretically and in relation to literacy and numeracy (Thomas & Pattison, 2008, 2011). This follow up research has led to placing more emphasis on the proactive role of children in their learning and on the importance of play, certainly right through the primary years. We also argue that informal learning is of a very high quality even though it might appear haphazard to an outsider. This is because, without structure and planning, children have to wrestle with new understandings rather than have knowledge predigested for them as is the case of much learning in school.

Can children learn informally in school?

The school curriculum is tightly planned and taught so that children in school obviously have little opportunity for informal learning. They cannot choose what to learn or not to learn. And most of what they learn does not arise from or relate directly to their everyday life experiences.

Conversational learning of the kind described above, is not really feasible in the classroom. Most classroom talk, whether with teachers or teacher assistants, is necessarily directed at the task in hand. But teaching assistants do have more opportunities to converse informally with their pupils, simply because they often work with small groups or individual children. In such situations it is in the normal run of things to break from planned work from time to time and talk about other things, just as adults at work do. An important aspect of this informal chat will be just helping children to feel comfortable with themselves, enjoying a social relationship with an adult as well as a teacher-learner one. But what is, on the surface, simply social conversation, will almost certainly include opportunities for learning informally from someone who has a much wider knowledge of the world. Teaching assistants are also 'around' more than most teachers and able to extend interaction with children in the playground, over lunch and during school events, performances and visits outside school. Learning that occurs may be incidental, just in passing, related to news events in the wider world or some issue in school. Family and social life outside school also provide topics of conversation. Talk about your own life—well, up to a point anyway! The lives of school staff and their families are always of interest to children. There is also the opportunity to discuss children's interests and develop threads of conversation across days or weeks. But the main thing is to make the children feel comfortable about talking – topics will emerge anyway. And for the most part they will be everyday "real life" topics.

Summary

Informal learning within the context of home education has much in common with the kind of learning that nearly all children experience before starting school. A great deal of it occurs through everyday living and social conversation which, on closer analysis, contains many opportunities for learning. To an observer it might seem highly unstructured, chaotic even. But if a child educated informally at home can progress, even in a school subject as structured as maths tends to be, then informal learning is very powerful indeed. Moreover, it is as if the children themselves impose their own personal, sometimes idiosyncratic, sequence on what they learn. Of course, in school, teaching assistants do not spend as much time with pupils as do parents at home. Nevertheless, they do have opportunities both to understand each pupil and to further their knowledge in the course of naturally occurring social conversations, both during lessons and at other times. This painless kind of learning generally goes unnoticed but what pupils get out of it may have a positive influence throughout their school years and later lives.

References

Nunes, T., Carraher, D.W. & Schliemann, A.D. (1993) *Street Mathematics and School Mathematics: Learning in Doing: Social, Cognitive and Computational Perspectives*, Cambridge University Press.

Rogoff, B. (2003) *The Cultural Nature of Human Development*. New York, Oxford University Press.

Thomas, A. (1998) *Educating Children at Home*, London, Cassell.

Thomas, A. & Pattison, H. (2008) *How Children Learn at Home*, London, Continuum International Publishing Group.

Thomas, A & Pattison, H. (2011) "Informal home education: philosophical aspirations put into practice" Studies in Philosophy and Education (in press).

Tizard, B. & Hughes, M. (1984) *Children Learning at Home and in School*. London: Fontana.

Trevarthen, C. (1995) "The child's need to learn a culture" In: M. Woodhead, D. Faulkener & K. Littleton (eds.) *Cultural Worlds of Early Childhood*. London, Routledge.

Chapter 12

Living and learning

Claire Young

Claire Young has been home educating her three sons and keeping a diary about this experience for some eight years. In this chapter she looks back over what she and her three children have learned together. Her piece provides important insights into the process of learning and, particularly, the importance of children's interest and motivation.

Our learning took place as we lived life to the full; we are a family who love reading and talking and being out of doors. That just about sums up how we home educated. I know families who played musical instruments for hours each day, and others who painted, sewed and trailed through charity shops. Each has produced well socialised children who are active learners. Success comes when adults actively engage with children in whatever way comes naturally to both parties.

Learning memories

Remembering incidents from when my children were younger, it amazes me that so much learning took place in and around ordinary living. Some was planned, but more often it happened as we did chores, met friends and even while having arguments. At the time it felt as if they never stopped learning, it was 24 hours a day education. Actually, I think everyone home educates, like it or not. It's just that some people also send their children to school.

In January 1993, Tony was 6 years old, Michael 4, and Paul 1. One Sunday after church we went to a country park, running, hiding and watching motorised model boats. On returning I wanted to make a phone

Source: Young, C. (2004) 'Living and learning', commissioned by The Open University for *Primary Teaching Assistants: Learners and Learning* (London: Routledge). Reprinted by permission of The Open University and Taylor & Francis Ltd.

call to my brother in Canada. We used the atlas to look for date lines and time zones and ended up discussing pie charts and colour keys. Tony asked for us to sew a Canadian flag; we discussed the relationship between the words 'Canada and Canadian' and 'Britain and British'.

In November 1994, Tony got a Lego container ship for his birthday. We read books about ships, looked up our junior encyclopedia on ports and container ships, and then visited a container ship base in Gourock. This was how a lot of learning happened, by picking up on something happening in the family, and seeing what else linked in via newspapers, library books, conversations with friends. I wanted them to see the range of options for following an interest. This would probably constitute a 'project' at school, but ours only ran as long as it sustained the child's interest, the learning being the aim, not project presentation.

Michael and Tony wanted to collect a cereal box special offer; this resulted in much counting of pocket money and they very swiftly became competent with pounds and pence. When Paul was 6, he was given 5 pounds per person for Christmas presents, and by having to work out prices in shops, swiftly came to a similar understanding. Decimals were never a problem in maths.

In December 1995, Paul, aged 3, was inclined to fall asleep if we travelled in the car after 4.00 pm – not a good idea as he then stayed up late. To keep his interest, we started counting Christmas trees in people's houses. This became the way Michael, then 6 years, learned to count past 10. By Christmas he could count to 90.

The concept of learning subjects or concepts in a particular sequence didn't seem to apply at home. There would be spurts of interest and then a lull with no apparent learning, only to have them bound forward a month or so later. I had made myself a 'mind map' of the maths concepts for primary-aged children and about every six months I'd glance at it to see if there were any yawning gaps. For instance, if we hadn't done graphs we'd do a survey of birds coming to the feeding table and draw a relevant graph.

Travelling down to Grand-da at Christmas we looked at maps to help pass time. Enjoying maps has become a feature of our family life. We have used a world map pinned on a dining room wall to talk about news items or understand history books, road maps to plan holidays, and town maps to plan cycling trips to friends. Talking about scales and keys of maps came up naturally.

By this stage Tony and Michael had a small 'desk-work' programme which I put together. This would take about an hour each day and was fitted around chores and trips to the park and long, daily sessions of reading together.

Normally children develop speech and walking without being taught. However, I don't believe it happens in the same way with writing, reading or written maths. (There are, however, home educators who have proved me absolutely wrong!) I used a variety of exercises found in books at the Teachers Resource Centre, local stationers and ideas from friends. Maths was as practical as possible, reading and writing little and often.

In June 1996, the toy library was threatened with closure. The boys asked 'Why?' This resulted in a discussion which covered councils, their functions, their funding, decision making and democracy. This conversation ran for about three days, and, as I have no particular political interest, involved asking many other people for the answers.

That year, with Tony 9, Michael 7 and Paul 5, they each had their own piece of garden and grew plants of their own choice. Gardening has always been a great source of learning opportunities, for example organic versus chemical, different types of soil, root formations, and the need for light and nutrients.

There was a General Election May 1997, and the boys, taking note of this, decided to run their own soft toy elections. The Tyrannosaurus Rex Party won, on the promise that they would set up burger bars for the carnivores and investigate DNA storage to prevent extinction. I always enjoy sharing interesting things I've been reading with them so the week before had read them a brief article on DNA and cloning.

A week did not go by without us doing something together in the kitchen. Cooking is a rich area of learning; making a cake, we would discuss what made it rise. When melting chocolate, we would discuss reversible reactions. Recipes require reading, measuring gets learnt naturally, and discussions about nutrition would arise from why it wasn't a great idea to make toffee shortbread every week.

As they got older I found we did about two or three six-week sessions of 'homework', as we termed it, per year and for the rest just read copiously, covering every subject under the sun, in fiction or non-fiction. Book work included a variety of maths and English work and I'd add in science, geography or history, depending on the child's interests or lack of. One child was physically a little lazy, so he had exercise on his list.

I set a weekly quota from textbooks and work books and put up the social diary for the week so they could decide when to work. If we got to Thursday and they wanted to play out but had done no homework, as agreed, the answer was 'after work'. I have always told the boys 'School is optional, education is not.' Having said that, home education can only be done by mutual consent, which I think is one of its strengths. We have talked together using Edward de Bono's 'six hat thinking' and Tony Buzan's 'mind maps' to get the children to take responsibility for their learning.

In November 1999 Paul, aged 7, continued to collect bones and interesting rocks, and noticed on a walk the clear layers of different rock in a freshly eroded river bank. He still has an abiding interest in the out of doors – fishing, Scouting, hawking lessons, reading adult-level books on survival and fishing.

Ways of learning

Answering questions as they came up was one way they learned.

As a 6-year-old Paul asked, 'What does "hotel" mean?' I replied, 'You know what it means.' 'Yes,' he said, 'but what does it really mean?' Do you mean where does it come from? I asked. (Noise of possible agreement from him.) I said, 'Find me a dictionary.' (I was probably cooking dinner at the time.) Paul fetches me the big dictionary which he knows shows word origins, not just spelling, so I take it I have correctly guessed what his question meant. We look up 'hotel', read it out and he goes off with no further comment.

Aged 7, Paul came in holding a cardboard toilet roll with a mini rolling pin as the plunger and a plasticine 'cannon ball'. 'Look how far it can fire,' he said. I look. He says, 'Hmm not very far, but if I aim it higher.' He tries again with more success.

When 9 and cuddling up in bed in the early morning, Paul says, 'If we had a glass almost full of water, just air at the top. If we closed it and turned it over where would the air go?' After puzzling that through, he then moved on to ask 'What would happen if you had a metal box of air and you closed it and squashed it?' This led onto a discussion of how a pressure cooker works – there being a well known family story of when a pressure cooker blew beetroot all over the kitchen!

I have had to adapt to their ways of learning, otherwise it would have been just a waste of time. It took me till one child was four to realise he was scared of new things. I actually love new things and was making his life difficult by emphasising 'new' as we started anything, even swimming lessons. He needed to know he would be in the same pool and wearing the same costume and not that he had a new teacher and was in a new class. When I realised this tactic also worked academically I would approach a new step in learning saying it was a slightly different way of doing something that he already knew. So division was introduced as multiplication done backwards.

Our family has several of the learning types Howard Gardener has identified, and it's been a challenge to learn how to present the same thing differently. Tony learned to read easily with phonics. Michael wanted to be able to read at 5, but disliked being taught. I eventually gave up when he was 6, as it was causing such fights. A year later, I discovered he could read even complicated words like 'through'. Paul proved to be different again, much more a physical learner. So he has 'run' letter shapes out in the garden, laid rope out in their shapes and then written them on the patio in chalk. While learning to read he had to get up and run around the house between each few lines because his legs went 'funny'. He always came back to work, but found concentrating such hard work he needed to blow off steam. He finally learned to read at the age of 9, and by 10 was well up to his reading age, now happily immersing himself in books for hours.

I often felt the tension between letting a child discover for himself and actively teaching. On one occasion, Michael, of his own accord, made a set of traffic lights. I made several comments on how to improve the design, and he ended up crying because I had confused him with too many ideas. If I believed in self-discovery, why did I still want to butt-in?

What did not come naturally with any of our boys was writing. I found getting the boys to write was like pulling teeth and early on decided I was going to use our time to learn, not fight over pages of writing. Most 'creative writing' was done orally. I would type out stories they told, or just listen to their endless imaginative accounts. Michael would, of his own accord, draw a detailed picture and then come and tell me about it. Tony and Paul would make complicated clay models of an island, or a mine, and then tell me the story behind it.

I never worked out whether it was better to present a new concept practically or via a book at first. It was easier to read a book about estuaries when we had followed a river to the sea, but we discussed racism in reading books like Kim by Rudyard Kipling in a way we might not have done otherwise in our mainly white town.

We have often joined with other home educators for group events, numbers varying from eight to 28 children. These have included felt-making with a friend, a talk on Romans at a museum, a series of art lessons and a technology workshop. Paul loved rock and bone collecting, so a geology trip should have been his favourite. However the man who took us was newly graduated, enthusiastic to share with us his new-found knowledge and understanding, and that was over Paul's head. Children who were older, 14 years old, learnt a lot.

The drama workshops were taken by a home educating mother, who'd been a professional actor. She was brilliant in her ability to set a theme and then work in all the ideas the children came up with. With her interactive approach she totally hooked the children.

We found group learning benefited only a few in the group and seldom equalled one-to-one conversation, because the child tends to get talked at rather than with. However, the children remember the group events as happy times and so as socialising times they were useful.

The love of learning

I was pro-home not anti-school. I never wanted to teach, but I did want them to be hooked on learning. I home educated because I did not believe young children needed teachers. I think they need loving and enthusiastic companions in learning, and a normal environment. We eventually had to make a decision as to when, and if, to use the school system. I wanted them at home at least long enough for them to see learning as enabling and interesting, not 'boring' as I often hear children describe it around here.

Many home educators, in the USA and here in the UK, have continued right the way through to school-leaving age, not sitting exams, and found the children are actively welcomed into colleges and employment. Home education has been reported as producing mature, active learners who will give of their best.

We have chosen to put the boys into the last year of primary school, for a settling-in year, and then on to secondary in order to sit exams. I've been delighted, and relieved, to find our minimalist approach to written and formal work has, so far, resulted in two of the boys doing very well in all subjects. They found the first year in school a steep learning curve in terms of speed and quantity of writing expected, but did not struggle in any other way. With one son, I told the teacher, after the first month, he was very aware of how little he wrote compared with others. The teacher's reply was she'd rather have one paragraph of his writing than a page of the others because the quality of ideas and word use was so much better.

My third son, the one who takes book learning and writing like medicine, has struggled with his first year at school and has a long way to go before he realises his ability. He is bright, but I sense that school is never going to suit his interests and style of learning. He continues to have an enquiring mind with subjects he values; they just aren't in the school curriculum!

Watching children develop, mind, body and spirit, is a source of wonder for me. To be involved as an enabler and encourager, perhaps like a sports coach, has been hard work sometimes, but it's been great fun and so rewarding.

Chapter 13

Net gains for 'slum' children

Amrit Dhillon

There is time-honoured debate in education about how children should learn in school. On the one hand, it is said they learn best through a detailed curriculum that is planned and 'delivered' to them. On the other, there is a belief in their abilities to learn much from their own endeavours assisted and stimulated by teachers, teaching assistants and parents. Amrit Dhillon, a writer, provides an example of what children can learn for themselves when they are provided with the means to do so.

Go to a slum district of Delhi, put a computer with an internet connection into a public wall and leave it on. Wait and watch through a remote video camera rigged up on a nearby tree. Children who cannot read or write, with no English but blazing with curiosity, come along and start fiddling with the weird contraption that has surfaced out of nowhere.

Eight minutes later, children who do not know what a computer is are navigating the web. By evening more than 70 are surfing the net. Days later they are playing games, creating folders, cutting and pasting, creating short cuts.

A fluke? That is what Dr Sugata Mitra, who conducted the experiment three years ago, thought, too. So he repeated it. Even in remote wildernesses, where the only mouse that desperately deprived children knew was the furry kind, Mitra kept seeing the same extraordinary results: children learning basic computer literacy on their own, with no instruction.

They invented their own vocabulary to define terms, so the cursor is 'sui' (Hindi for needle) and the hourglass is the 'damru' after the hourglass-shaped drum that the Hindu god Shiva plays.

When Mitra, who heads the Centre for Research in Cognitive Systems at one of the world's largest computer-training institutions, the National

Source: Dhillon, A. (2003) 'Net gains for "slum" children' *The Times* 17 July.

Institute for Information Technology (Niit), added sound, the children discovered what MP3 was and began playing their favourite Hindi film songs. 'They didn't know what any of this was called,' Mitra says. 'But they would say, "if you take this little box, and you drag this file into this box, it plays music." They gain a functional literacy very fast.'

At Daksllinpuri, another slum district of the Indian capital, seven-year-old Rajendra cranes his neck to see the screen. 'I'm learning English by using it,' he says proudly. 'I know words like save, delete, folder. With him is ten-year-old Akansha, clutching a baby sister on her hip. Asked what the internet is, she replies: 'It's where we can do everything, even if we don't know anything?'

The computer kiosks are designed to exclude adults (they are set low in the wall, with a keyboard angled so that taller people find it awkward to access), and are engineered specially to endure India's searing heat, dust storms and monsoons. They are also designed to have a high fault tolerance; if some software is damaged, for example, the computer notices and restores it. There is also software to prevent Windows from hanging so that children do not have to know how to reboot.

The key insight from this hole-in-the-wall experiment is that if India's poorest children can become computer literate by learning on their own, or in groups, they do not need formal computer education.

The implications for India's primary education system are staggering. Starved of resources, schools lack books, paper, chalk, everything. Some have computers, but not enough for the 700 million Indians under 18. As the world lunges farther into the information age, the most socially fragmented society on Earth faces the emergence of yet another social divide – between the information haves and have-nots.

But if children need no formal training to use computers, it means that precious time and money can be freed up for teaching them what they cannot learn on their own. In the process, India might just succeed in bridging the knowledge gap that will otherwise condemn millions to exclusion from the modern world for ever. James Wolfensohn, the president of the World Bank, is taken by the experiment because it suggests a bold new way of tackling rural education. That is why the bank is giving $1.6 million (£966,000) to a joint venture – the Hole in the Wall Company – for setting up the project in 108 locations in India.

'If we can put in 100,000 kiosks, I reckon that we could get 500 million children computer literate in five years, at a cost of $2 billion. If you educated the same children using traditional methods it would cost twice as much,' says Mitra.

But the application of Mitra's findings is potentially much wider. What Niit and Mitra are now exploring is how far a computer in an urban or rural slum district can go in delivering a classical primary school curriculum to children who will never go to school.

This is an important question, and explains the World Bank's excitement. In India and the rest of the developing world, the economics of the classical bricks-and-mortar model do not work. There is not enough money to build and equip all the schools that are needed.

So maybe on-line education is the solution. 'I am not saying that if we put computers in all slums, children can become literate on their own,' Mitra says.

'I am saying that in situations where we cannot intervene frequently, you can multiply the effectiveness of ten teachers by 100 if you give children access to the internet.'

Chapter 14

Information and communication technology

Sue Crowley and Mike Richardson

In this chapter Sue Crowley and Mike Richardson, lecturers at Liverpool Hope University, review the role of ICT in school learning and highlight ways in which teaching assistants and teachers can further develop their ICT knowledge, skills and confidence – not least by supporting each other and learning alongside children.

Introduction

Information and Communication Technology (ICT) can be an extra, versatile tool for learning, which sits alongside books, pens, glue and other vital items in the primary and secondary teacher's toolbox. In the past, children were introduced, sometimes reluctantly, to many such tools from slates to slide rules, and Heppell points out in the Foreword to Loveless and Ellis (2001) that they have even had innovations such as the ballpoint pen and mobile phones confiscated. However, it is now time to embrace new technologies and use them to change and improve pedagogy. The desire of the teacher should not be to set a standard that all children must achieve, but rather to enable children to realise that ICT offers practical and fun ways to achieve more. The assistant in the classroom needs to be prepared to reinforce this ethos and support the use of ICT if it is to become firmly established as a learning resource in school. We believe our children need to know about the use of ICT in everyday life around them and its potential for the future, but more importantly they deserve opportunities to begin to realise the full potential of ICT as a tool to support and present their developing learning and creativity.

Source: A revised version of Crowley, S. and Richardson, M. (2004) 'Raising the bar: improving children's performance through information and communication technology', in C. Bold (ed.), *Supporting Learning and Teaching* (London: David Fulton). In *Primary Teaching Assistants: Learners and Learning* (London: Routledge). Reprinted by permission of Taylor & Francis Ltd.

One ultimate goal of the use of ICT in education is that the pupils are able to use the technology independently and appropriately. Moseley *et al.* (1999) found that successful teachers of ICT gave children choices rather than directing them. Teachers who were not confident users of ICT would employ another adult to help and direct the children with ICT and hence not use ICT in any way to change pedagogy. The teaching assistant can prepare specific resources and activities. In addition, the assistant will help the children learn how to use ICT for learning. Pupil empowerment is more desirable than receiving instruction or completing work from an adult's point of view. Naturally, children need to acquire certain skills, which need teaching. However, once basic skills have been learned, ICT offers a medium that is ripe for experimentation. Children show fewer inhibitions than adults and are more willing to try different icons and menus without fear of damaging the computer. They may not experiment if an over-zealous adult tells them what to do, or presses the keys for them.

Confidence and skills

Monteith (2002) suggests that teachers who are skilful in ICT are most likely to develop skilful pupils. It is important that the teacher and the assistant both feel confident that they can support their children with ICT skills and have sufficient knowledge to be able to plan appropriate ICT activities into the curriculum for all children. This chapter does not include guides to software but we hope that both the teacher and assistant are aware of areas for their own personal development. Remember that nobody needs to know everything about the appropriate software to be effective. It is important to stay open-minded as your learning continues, so that you will be able to support pupils' ICT work appropriately.

The teacher and the assistant should work in partnership to develop ICT capability for themselves and their pupils. If both adults have little experience, then it might be best to take different aspects of ICT to develop personally, then pool and share their knowledge and ideas. If the assistant is new to ICT, and the teacher has some knowledge, then they could spend some concentrated time, i.e. an in-service morning or afternoon, going through the core skills in relation to the ICT planned for the term/year. It is better to spend time learning, and teaching each other, away from the busy school day. Ideally, teachers will give the assistant time and opportunities to get to know all the ICT peripherals so that he or she will be able to do what is required with ICT. For example, the children will benefit from the assistant's ability to use a digital camera immediately when a situation arises. Too often, we miss the opportunity of catching children's smiles of satisfaction when they have recognised a significant achievement.

The general principle we are trying to promote here is that teachers and assistants should try, as much as possible, to pre-empt potential causes of frustration. You can promote a positive attitude to the subject by refusing to allow the computer or any ICT equipment to become a 'nuisance in the corner'. When all the adults in the room are prepared to cope with the difficulties and know when to refer difficulties to a technician, the more they will view the computer as a valuable learning and teaching tool. We need to be positive about ICT no matter how we feel! When unsure, we must seek help from a sympathetic technician, friend, colleague or relative and explain that we want to learn how to do things for ourselves (not just be shown). The secret of becoming a confident user of ICT is to use it a little and often at first and be prepared to ask for advice. We practise what we preach; we have been using computers for personal use and in our teaching for nearly 20 years, but we will still come into each other's rooms and say 'How can you do this?' or 'Is there another way to . . .?'

As a confident user of ICT, a teaching assistant can be invaluable to a school, as one assistant from Castlefield Infant School, Rastrick (DfES 2003a) stated:

> I advise, I teach ICT in small groups, I keep my own records, run parents and pupils sessions and a lunchtime ICT club, and by fair means or foul have encouraged the other staff to use e-mail. I used the children's enthusiasm for e-mail to influence the teachers.

The head teacher from Mission Primary School (DfES 2003b) has also praised his teaching assistant on her knowledge of the use of ICT:

> Julie exemplifies the progressive development of the TAs. In addition to her classroom support duties she has also become expert in training pupils in the use of ICT. Julie has a powerful influence in ICT. In partnership with the designated teacher, she has reviewed the QCA requirements for ICT. She has then selected the most appropriate software to deliver the curriculum. I have tried to promote the idea that each TA develops a specialist expertise such as literacy, numeracy or special needs, and that these skills are then practised across the curriculum. In this way the TAs develop two focuses to their work: one will be class-based but the other is related to the whole school curriculum. Like Julie with ICT, each TA then becomes an important additional resource in a specialist area. The response of the TAs has been overwhelmingly positive.

Many primary and secondary schools in the north-west of England are now employing assistants with particular ICT expertise to work in the classroom.

Making opportunities, planning and assessing

Whether it is a whole-staff or departmental approach, the ICT co-ordinator's or the class teacher's plan, the curriculum at all levels should include ICT for the whole year. In this way, ICT opportunities can be broad, balanced and progressive. Planning should start with the big picture: a table of topics in all taught subjects in the year with identified opportunities where ICT can support the subject. Obvious examples might be:

- a Key Stage 2 mathematical topic on 2-D shapes, involving work with a programmable toy
- a Foundation Stage topic on the seasons, using an art programme to show what a tree looks like at different times of the year, e.g. a picture could be pre-made by the teacher or assistant of the trunk and branches, and the children complete the picture.

Once all the obvious ICT is in place for the year, an audit needs to be made of the types of ICT used to ensure a balance. Auditing is a simple process of gathering information about ICT. As teachers are very busy, any lightening of administrative duties that help to inform their teaching is generally welcomed. Hence, the teaching assistant may find that he or she becomes involved in the auditing process. There needs to be some of each aspect of ICT across the curriculum, i.e. communication, information retrieval, information handling in the form of data collection and graphs, presentation, modelling, monitoring and control. If one type of ICT is lacking from the first scrutiny of the year plan, then teachers should seek opportunities to extend the range where it would be appropriate. At times, it may be relevant to plan a discrete ICT project in order that aspects such as control or modelling are taught as part of a specific ICT lesson. In addition to ensuring the ICT curriculum is taught, an audit will look at the resources needed to deliver the lessons. For example, some equipment may need servicing or need the batteries changed. Although the ICT co-ordinator, head of department or technician is the person who has primary responsibility for ensuring these resources are in place and working, he or she will rely heavily on other members of staff at the school to inform them when these maintenance or preparation tasks are required as well as help with suggestions on how to improve provision. A teaching assistant working closely with children using ICT will make a valuable addition to the team.

Using individual or small groups of computers

Individual or small groups of computers are often found in both primary and secondary school situations. The primary classroom might have a single standalone computer, or one linked to the Internet. In both primary and secondary schools, there is often one or more dedicated ICT suite. Teachers use these facilities in different ways to suit the curriculum and the situation in the school.

Teaching the skills

Inevitably, computer skills such as inserting and moving images need to be taught to most children at some time in order to carry out planned projects. For example, in making a poster/leaflet to advertise local amenities, in a geography project, the assistant and teacher will have to do the following preparatory work. First, they will need to discuss a list of skills required. These skills will include:

- the ability to use font sizes and colours appropriately
- the use of text editing features such as centring, underlining and **bold**
- the insertion, resizing and moving of images
- the use of digital camera
- the use of word art
- the use of three columns to make a fold-over leaflet.

Prior assessment of the children's knowledge and ability will need to be carried out and a plan of action drawn up as to who needs to be taught what. You should not need to teach the entire class all the skills. If the children are in small groups of similar ability, then the teacher or assistant can teach each small group the skill required for the project; this would move them forward from where they are in their computer knowledge. These small ICT ability groups may not fit in snugly with numeracy and literacy groups in a primary school situation. We suggest that at primary level the assistant can take them out of the subject lesson for 10–15 minutes and teach computer skills related to the planned subject ICT activity. It is quite feasible in many schools, as long as it fits in with the subject expectations. Once the project is underway, the children will learn from each other any particular skill they really want.

When children are learning from one another, some may see this as an opportunity for feeling superior or even carrying out minor bullying. We can prevent such bullying by establishing a good ethos in the school that leads to a clear etiquette for computer use. Peer tutoring principles can help. The key features are the selection of children as tutors, training in mentoring skills and clear expectations given of what was involved. Such a system needs to be a whole-school strategy.

Using the computer as a tool

Once the teacher or assistant has taught the skills of a project, then the children can use the classroom computer/s on a rota system for small groups or as individuals to produce and present their work. Ideally, no other adult should be required for this project; however, ideal situations and computers don't always mix! The children should know that if they have an important query either the teacher or the assistant is available. Therefore, only one of these adults should be working with concentration with a group of children while the other is available to ensure the computer project can progress, allowing the children to work independently. The children need to know who is on 'computer duty'; you could follow the example of a colleague of ours who used to put on an apron with a large cat on the front when she didn't want to be disturbed! A wall display containing 'prompts' is very useful for older children at Key Stages 2 and 3, especially if situated near the computer area. Such a display aids independence.

Some computer activities may require planned intervention in order to encourage thought and reflection. For example, when producing computer graphs from data collected from an investigation, there needs to be the prompt 'What does your graph tell you about your findings?' or, when using a modelling program that includes decisions, 'Why did you take that path?' This need not occur often but it is a good opportunity for speaking and listening skills to develop alongside reflective thought. However, the teacher and assistant need to discuss whatever is going on that day and decide on the teaching strategy and who will do what, whether it is teaching, planned intervention or waiting for invitations to help. This kind of approach works well in situations where there is less time pressure on the curriculum. For example, in Sweden where the compulsory element to the curriculum is approximately half that of our own, teaching assistants are able to provide support to children as they engage in independent learning activities.

Some more recent ideas for suitable projects where there is scope for support from another adult include:

- Podcasting – this is non specific to a curriculum area but has enormous potential for engaging children in speaking and listening activities. It also allows the wider school community to become engaged and develops children's sense of audience
- Animation – again non specific this allows reluctant writers to learn some of the basic elements of story telling through a digital medium.

As the story features can be worked on in a way the children are familiar with through their engagement with stories told in this fashion, it has been the authors' experience that these children benefit and are often then motivated to try and put their stories into more traditional formats (Brook, 2010). The authors would further recommend Bazalgette (2010) as a rich source of ideas and background information as to how to incorporate creative ICT in support of the Primary Curriculum.

Anyone seeking to set up projects of this nature must realise that both the class teacher and the teaching assistant need to spend some time carefully planning how this will be implemented around the resources they have available. One advantage is that whilst there is proprietary software to enable these activities, free and open source software such as Audacity, and software that often comes bundled with the computer's operating system, make this a possibility for any school to start this approach with a minimum degree of initial expenditure. There are also plenty of support guides available on the Internet that will help the beginner see how the technical aspects can be mastered.

Conclusion

Teaching assistants will need to work alongside teachers in preparing for the use of ICT in lessons by:

- ensuring they understand how to use equipment
- making resources and assisting with their use
- supervising computer use and assisting children with their developing ICT skills.

Although some people claim to be techno-phobic, with a little perseverance these technical skills are well within their reach. After all, much of the equipment, or in some cases software, is designed for use by children. Most problems come because things are done out of sequence, due to assumptions made by the user. The best advice is to spend some personal time with unfamiliar equipment or software so that you are aware of the pitfalls and dangers. All the best users of technical equipment can tell the tale of the time when they came unstuck because they didn't prepare themselves. If you don't like doing it on your own, then find others who will be prepared to join you in a practice session. Finally, children love having people who are prepared to learn with them and good teachers and teaching assistants have been doing it for years.

References

Bazalgette, C. (2010) "Teaching Media in Primary Schools" (ed.) Cary Bazalgette London: Sage.

Brook, T. (2010) "Digital Glue:Creative Media in the classroom" chapter in "Teaching Media in Primary Schools" (ed.) Cary Bazalgette London: Sage pp. 116–128.

DfES (2003a) "'Castlefield Infant School": a case study in support for the curriculum', at www.teachernet.gov.uk/management/teachingassistants/Management/casestudies/, accessed June 2003.

DfES (2003b) "'Mission Primary School": a case study in support for the curriculum, at www.teachernet.gov.uk./management/teachingassistants/Management/casestudies/, accessed June 2003.

Loveless, A. and Ellis, V. (2001) ICT, *Pedagogy and the Curriculum*, London: Routledge Falmer, pp.xv–xix.

Monteith, M. (ed.) (2002) *Teaching Primary Literacy with ICT*, Buckingham: Open University Press, pp. 1–29.

Moseley, D., Higgins, S. and Bramald, R. (1999) *Ways Forward with ICT: Effective Pedagogy Using ICT for Literacy and Numeracy in Primary Schools*, Newcastle upon Tyne: University of Newcastle upon Tyne.

Chapter 15

Assessment

Janet Kay

With an increased attention on measured standards, assessment and recording are very important school activities and many teaching assistants have a significant role in these teaching-related tasks. Janet Kay, principal lecturer at Sheffield Hallam University reviews some of the skills involved in assessment, feedback and recording and suggests ways in which teaching assistants might contribute to effective assessment in collaboration with teachers.

Introduction

Teaching assistants have a significant role to play in the monitoring and assessment of groups of children and individual children whom they are involved in supporting. Assessment is a more major part of the activities in primary classrooms, more so since the introduction of the National Curriculum formalized the curriculum in primary schools. The role of assessment in monitoring the performance of individual children, whole schools and the broader education system has been well established over many years.

But what is assessment for? O'Hara (2004) states that assessment is to ensure that classroom staff know:

- what children know at a particular point in time
- what they can do at a particular point in time
- where they need to go next and how to support them.

Assessment provides the basis on which the next round of planning for teaching and learning can take place. If assessment is ongoing and accurate,

Source: An edited version of Kay, J. (2002) 'Assessment and recording', in *Teaching Assistant's Handbook*, Chapter 6, pp. 103–118, London, Continuum. Reproduced with permission of CONTINUUM PUBLISHING COMPANY in the format Textbook via Copyright Clearance Center.

staff can plan teaching and learning from a baseline of knowledge as to where the children have already progressed. Assessment is also used to check children's progress against National Curriculum levels both as a group and as individuals.

Assessment is not a single process, nor does it all take place formally or at preset stages in the school year. Formal assessment has a role to play, but is only one part of the wide range of assessment processes which take place throughout each school year. Children are formally assessed at the end of each primary Key Stage through teacher assessment at KS1 and teacher assessment and National Curriculum Tests (commonly known as SATs) at KS2, which measure children's progress against a nationally determined range of criteria across particular parts of the curriculum. KS1 teacher assessment is based on a range of tasks and tests which cover reading, writing and maths. Children are also assessed on speaking and listening and science. SATs at the end of KS2 focus on English (reading, writing, spelling) and maths (including mental arithmetic). Teacher assessment at the end of KS2 covers English, maths and science also.

Both teacher assessment and SATs results give the teacher feedback on the child's progress and abilities. They also give the school feedback on the whole class achievement, which can be compared with previous classes at the end of each Key Stage. SATs results are compared with other schools' results within the local authority, and nationwide. Each school will have set targets for achievement and the SATs results will be judged against these targets. Parents are informed of their children's results through a written report which also includes results for all children in the age group at the school and national results for the previous year.

But formal end of stage assessments are only a small part of the assessment process in schools. These formal assessments rarely tell teachers and schools much they do not already know about the children in their care. While end of KS1 teacher assessments and SATs can be typified as 'summative' assessment—assessment that takes place at the end of a phase of the curriculum—schools are also involved in ongoing, formal and informal 'formative' assessment. This type of assessment is the day-to-day monitoring and judging of children's work, which informs staff of the ongoing progress of individuals and the whole class.

All assessment is vitally important in the teaching and learning process because:

- It gives feedback on the effectiveness of learning and teaching strategies.
- It helps staff to become aware of areas that the whole class needs to work on more or in a different way.

- It helps staff to recognise specific problems or areas of lack of progress a particular child may have.
- It helps staff to assess the rate of progress the class and individual children are making.
- It is the basis of feedback to children as a group or individuals and provides material for giving praise and acknowledging progress.
- It provides information which can be shared with parents.
- It can help teachers and heads to become aware of deficits in resources, both human and physical.
- It helps staff judge their own performance and planning and make adjustments as required.

All assessment is based on the process of judging children's progress and achievements against known criteria. When end of KS1 teacher assessments and SATs are taken, this is a more formal process based on clearly stated criteria. However, during the more informal processes of assessment, the criteria are not necessarily so clearly stated and the assessment is not usually achieved through tests.

Types of assessment

A number of different types of assessment are used with young children. It is important to note that the choice of type of assessment is not random. We choose the type depending on what we want to assess and for what purpose. The type of assessment used must match the outcomes required if it is to be effective. This does not mean that there are no choices to be made. Very often there will be different ways in which a particular assessment can be made. Choices may depend on the resources available and the forms of assessment that are most familiar and seem most effective to those involved. In some circumstances, it is helpful to draw information for assessment purposes from more than one source, to strengthen the judgments that may then take place.

Choices of assessment must also be geared to the needs of young children and the possible impact of different assessment methods on their confidence and progress. There have been some criticisms of formal testing of 7-year-olds because of the possible negative impact of this type of assessment on some young children's self-esteem and confidence and children of this age now no longer sit SATs tests. The type of assessment used must therefore both fit the purpose of the assessment process and meet the needs of the children involved. While some types of assessment are so 'feather light' the children are more or less unaware of them, others are more obvious and therefore have more impact.

Summative assessment

As discussed above, summative assessments take place at the end of a specific phase of learning. Summative assessment, such as the SATs described above, sum up what the child has achieved at a specific time or stage of learning. Summative assessment usually also takes place at the end of each school year, providing a basis for teachers to feedback to parents on their children's progress within the school year. This end-of-year assessment can also be used to inform the teacher of the next class up, in terms of his or her planning. It can be used to determine if special educational needs (SEN) are evident in respect of individual children, and what sort of support is required to assist the child to make progress. Not all summative assessment is based on a formal process. End-of-year assessment is often based on both informal and formal formative assessments that have taken place over a period of time. Summative assessment is important in checking each child's progress against expected levels of attainment (criteria), but has less use in helping teachers plan their teaching and learning or give regular feedback to children and their parents, because it only takes place periodically.

Formative assessment

Formative assessment is more ongoing, whether it is based on formal methods or informal methods. It is the constant feedback teachers use to decide what sort of teaching and learning, support and encouragement their pupils need, either as individuals or as part of the whole class. This feedback comes from a wide range of informal sources:

- daily examination of children's work
- feedback from reading records
- the answers children give to questions
- the questions children ask
- the mistakes children are making and the problems children are encountering with specific activities
- comments and concerns of parents
- comments and concerns of the children.

More formal sources include assessment that is planned beforehand such as:

- tests, e.g. spelling tests, maths tests
- criteria-based assessment (assessing children during tasks against pre-set lists of criteria)
- homework.

Formative assessment comes from a wide range of sources of information which are collated and seen as a whole by the class teacher. This type of assessment draws on the skills of all staff and volunteers in the classroom and the wider school, on the views and observations of parents and children, and on the expertise of specialist staff from outside the school. Formative assessment can help to diagnose particular difficulties children may have, as well as provide an ongoing record of the children's progress.

For example, Kerry, 6, had problems with her handwriting to the point where she actively avoided writing tasks and sometimes refused to write. In discussion with her parents, it became clear that they were concerned about aspects of Kerry's physical co-ordination as well as her performance at school. Kerry's parents arranged paediatric assessment for Kerry through the local children's hospital. The physiotherapist found that Kerry had poor strength and stability in her shoulders and upper body, which made writing a difficult task for her. In consultation with the teacher and the Special Educational Needs Co-ordinator (SENCO) and the direct involvement of two support workers, Kerry was supported with a programme of physiotherapy at home and at school in order to help her gain strength and stability in her upper body, and ultimately to help her make progress with her handwriting. She also received extra help in class and was encouraged to use the computer to develop literacy skills so that her writing delays had less general impact on her literacy development.

Approaches to assessment

There are a number of different measures against which a child's work can be judged, and it is important to know which is being used and why. They are:

- national criteria such as the National Curriculum level descriptors, which set general attainment standards against which work can be measured

- the average of the class, which may not reflect the above, but which can give information about the level of development in relation to the rest of the group
- the child's own progress rates in terms of his or her individual development.

The Assessment for Learning Strategy 2008–11 introduced the Assessing Pupil's Performance (APP) materials which aimed to provide guidance on assessing to National Curriculum levels more accurately in the classroom. The aim was to track pupils' progress against the levels more effectively to inform target-setting, curriculum planning and teaching. However, assessment against National Curriculum levels is only one useful measure of progress. Judging a child's progress against his or her previous achievements is a sound basis for giving praise and encouragement and helping unconfident children to recognise that they have progressed. Children with SEN have this process formalized through their Individual Education Plans (IEPs) which set targets for the child to progress towards their targets, reviewed on a regular basis. This helps the child, parents, teachers and support workers to recognize and praise areas where progress is being made, and review support in areas where progress is less evident.

Effective assessment is usually based on a range of different approaches to provide the assessors with a full picture of the child's abilities. One type of assessment may simply not give enough information or may not provide all we need to know about the child's ability to learn and progress to date. For example, when Dan was 6 his delays in learning to read and write seemed to dominate the view of his learning progress held by his parents, school and, sadly, himself. With the support of other types of assessment, however, Dan's oral skills became a much stronger focus for assessment, giving a broader and more encouraging picture of his progress and ability to learn. Dan's self-confidence and self-esteem benefited directly from this wider view of his abilities and this more positive view of self was reflected in his learning.

Using different approaches also means that different individuals involved in the child's learning can contribute to the assessment process. Different assessment methods may be effective with different children depending on a number of factors:

- gender
- culture and language

- particular skills and strengths
- response to different assessment methods.

Assessing to determine children's strengths as well as their areas for further development is an important basis for positive and encouraging feedback to both parents and children.

Feedback

Giving feedback is a crucial element in the assessment process. It is not much use to children to be assessed if the outcomes of that assessment cannot be or are not translated into information that will support and encourage the child's learning in the future.

Feedback comes in many forms, formal and informal, written and verbal, instant and delayed. Some feedback is associated with summative assessment, for example, annual reports and discussions at end-of-year parents' evenings, end-of-stage and SATs results. Some is associated with formative assessment, and can include feedback on written work or oral work, group work and individual work, projects and play. It can include written comments and verbal comments, grades and marks out of a total, for example spelling test results. Feedback appears as comments in a child's reading record, ticks and comments on written numeracy work, praise for the whole class or a particular group, a child being asked to show work to the class or even to the whole school. Feedback can come in the form of stickers ('Star of the Week'), certificates ('Super Speller') or comments to parents at home time.

Whatever the form feedback takes it should always be based on the following principles:

- Feedback should be positive as well as negative.
- It should be considered and pertinent to the particular achievement.
- It should link that achievement to the child's overall progress where possible.
- It should suggest areas for further development where appropriate.
- It should not be critical, overly negative or condemning.
- It should involve the child's views and opinions which should be actively sought.
- It should be shared with others where appropriate.
- It should never damage a child's self-esteem or confidence.
- Praise should be genuine and based on progress.

Feedback is often given at a high level in primary schools, based on the principle of supporting self-esteem and good levels of self-confidence. Children need to know they are doing well and progress is being made. They will benefit from being in an environment where praise and encouragement are the norm. However, there are a few pitfalls, which need to be considered alongside this positive approach. Children will not necessarily benefit from the 'that's nice, just pop it over there' syndrome, which can be found in some establishments. If children learn that standard praise comments will be issued for every piece of work they do, this may not promote high standards. Work needs to be properly examined and discussed, and the child's view on its quality sought, in order to give genuine and valuable feedback. Feedback has more meaning when it is focused on a few pieces of work or aspects of progress rather than being general. Over-use of praise can devalue it in the children's eyes, so although praise is very important, children should feel it is based on real progress or achievement. For example, Damien, 7, was so used to 'smiley faces' on his work, to encourage his slow progress, that he drew them on his work himself before completing it. Any value they had as a form of positive feedback had faded by this stage, and new methods of giving Damien praise had to be sought. Giving feedback that is carefully considered, immediate and based on a considered assessment of the child's work, however, can be a vital part of the learning process and central to the child's overall development.

The teaching assistant's role

The role of the teaching assistant in assessment will vary considerably depending on the specific work you are each involved in. All assessment activities will be agreed with the teacher and possibly other members of the school staff or other professionals involved with a particular child. The teaching assistant's role is to:

- Make assessments as agreed with the teacher and record these as planned.
- Report back to the teacher on the progress of individual children and groups of children as required.
- Identify learning points which will inform future planning, e.g. areas of a subject that the child or children needs to do more work on.
- Identify successes, achievements and breakthroughs and share these with the teacher.

- Give feedback to the child as required.
- Report back to any other professionals or parents as agreed.

Much of the assessment you do will contribute to the teacher's formative and summative reports. Some, however, will be the definitive record, particularly where you work directly with one child. The formative assessment you are involved in should contribute to the teacher's planning process and the teaching and learning which takes place in the classroom.

There are some key aspects of assessment and feedback that teaching assistants can contribute to in their individual and small group work with children. These include:

- making sure that children's learning is assessed through a range of strategies including written work, oral work and examination of products such as drawings
- checking that children understand what they need to do to achieve – what are the requirements? What is the standard?
- looking at patterns of success and difficulty for groups and individual children to feedback to the teacher – what is hard for them? What is not? Are other pedagogical approaches indicated?

In order to be successful in assessing work, teaching assistants need good listening skills and observational skills to 'capture' information which contributes to assessment.

The role of the teaching assistant also includes ensuring records are fair and open, and that they avoid subjective and possibly damaging comments about the child. It is very easy to develop a particular view of a child, which may then affect all our dealings with that child, especially if the child has difficult or demanding behaviour patterns. These fixed views or stereotypes can prevent us from seeing the child's progress and achievements clearly, as we tend to observe only the aspects of the child's behaviour that support our fixed view. Stereotyping children can limit the effective support they are given, it can reinforce negative self-esteem and poor self-confidence in the child, and it can mean the opportunity to build on areas of strength goes unnoticed.

Finally, it is important to remember that your role is not just as a human recording instrument, passing information on to the teacher. You bring your own skill and expertise, knowledge and understanding, to the process, enriching the assessment with your own evaluation and interpretation of what is observed or recorded. This is a very valuable aspect of the teaching assistant's role in assessment and recording and one that should be developed to the full. The sorts of knowledge and understanding which can be usefully brought to bear when evaluating assessment information are:

- how young children learn best
- child development and developmental delays
- your specific knowledge of individual children's learning needs
- your knowledge of the child or children's ongoing progress and achievements
- your knowledge and understanding of how best to support children sensitively and effectively
- your knowledge and understanding of effective verbal and written communication.

Conclusions

Teaching assistants have a major role to play in the assessment processes taking place in primary classrooms. Teachers need assessment information for planning and for tracking pupils' progress, yet often the logistics of assessing large classes are highly challenging. Teaching assistants have increasingly supported the assessment process in partnership with the teacher and other staff. Developing confidence in your ability to use assessment processes effectively and to understand the types and purposes of assessment is a key role for teaching assistants. Giving feedback to children and recording and evaluating assessment information are all tasks that are becoming more a part of that role. As teaching assistants continue to gain prominence in classrooms, this role seems likely to continue to expand, requiring the further development of the range of skills and abilities discussed above.

Further reading

O'Hara, M. (2004) *Teaching 3–8. 2nd ed.* London: Continuum.

Chapter 16

Fighting the fuzzies

Ian Eyres

How might play be justified in schools? This chapter describes a collaborative approach to observation which supports the use of a play-based curriculum. Ian Eyres, a senior lecturer in education at The Open University, considers the nature of observation in an educational setting, and highlights the way in which nursery-based staff take steps to ensure objectivity and rigour.

Located in central Cambridge, Brunswick Nursery school offers half-day places to 80 children. The diverse intake usually includes several with English as an additional language and a relatively high proportion with special educational needs. The staff comprises the headteacher, two teachers, (one part-time–50%), two nursery nurses and four learning support assistants attached to individual children.

Curriculum and play

The curriculum is planned according to the six areas of learning within the Early Years Foundation Stage. Play is central to the curriculum as the staff have always believed that 'well planned play is a key way in which children learn' (QCA 2000:7). On one afternoon, for example, children were to be seen engaged in playing with wet and dry sand, sharing picture books with an adult, making models from recycled materials, hammering nails into a section of tree trunk, looking at and drawing logs, using a computer programme to sort geometrical shapes and engaging in make-believe play in the 'house'. All these experiences had been carefully planned to provide opportunities for 'playing, talking, observing, planning, questioning, experimenting, testing, repeating, reflecting and responding to adults' (QCA 2000:6) as ways of deepening their understanding within areas of learning.

Source: An edited version of Eyres, I. (2004) 'Fighting the fuzzies', commissioned by The Open University for *Primary Teaching Assistants: Learners and Learning*, (London: Routledge). Reprinted by permission of The Open University and Taylor & Francis Ltd.

Children are not directed, but are free to follow their interests and become absorbed in activity and enquiry. Staff therefore need to be skilled in seizing opportunities to both assess and foster development towards particular curriculum aims on the basis of what the children actually do.

Key to the success of any early years setting, then, are the adults' understanding of how children learn and develop and of the curriculum and, based on these understandings, their ability to observe, respond and plan appropriately. This approach, according to an Ofsted visit to this nursery, has been judged to be effective.

The rest of this chapter is based on discussions with three staff members: Colette Williams (nursery nurse), Jane Holt (teacher) and Nicola Davies, learning support assistant (LSA) and special educational needs coordinator (SENCO). For an LSA to be a SENCO is perhaps unusual. It should, however, be noted that Nicola undertook substantial training for the SENCO role and was already a qualified (secondary maths) teacher. Her appointment offers additional evidence of the non-hierarchical nature of the school. Since the original draft of this chapter was written the picture has been further complicated by Nicola's appointment to a part-time teaching post in addition to her LSA post.

Observation at Brunswick

> By observation I managed to develop proper respect for what they're doing. Concentrating on one child does show you a much greater depth of understanding and powers of 'reasoning things out' than I would have credited young children with.
>
> (Jane Holt)

At Brunswick, all adults are actively involved in the observation process, most directly by watching carefully and noting details of what children do and say on Post-it notes. This may be done alongside a child or by writing up observations immediately afterwards. The information collected is sorted weekly by Jane, Nicola and the headteacher (Marian Funnell) who look for evidence of learning in each of the six areas. Gaps and uncertainties in this record influence future observations and support.

Observations provide particularly valuable information to inform the support given to children with special educational needs, both for the statementing process and as the basis for termly targets. The detail of the assessment means that very precise targets can be devised and progress towards them closely monitored and supported. Social development, a crucial factor in inclusion, is particularly closely monitored. Even for apparently sociable children, systematic observation (noting the number and nature of contacts with peers) can be revealing. They may be talking to other children without getting a response or simply talking to themselves. What looks like interaction may be parallel play, where two children play independently alongside each other.

Children of all kinds can suffer if they are 'labelled'. Continuous detailed observation helps shape the curriculum for individuals and the nursery by eliminating inappropriate expectations and overgeneralizations.

Although the curriculum is planned to provide for particular learning outcomes, sometimes surprising evidence emerges. One child, for example, faced with a set of objects which included a toy crocodile, spent some time using the crocodile's jaws to measure the other objects, and then arranged them according to their size. Another child used coloured blocks to make an elaborate symmetrical pattern. Without constant observation these aspects of the children's mathematical knowledge could have been overlooked, and opportunities to challenge and develop their understanding lost.

Children's achievements are assessed in a natural context and staff have access to evidence gathered in different contexts by a number of observers. One child was able to join in the counting of children before the distribution of mid-session fruit but had difficulties in counting the number of bean bags thrown into a hoop. Although on the face of it these are 'the same task', in the former example the child has the support of a well-rehearsed routine and of the arrangement of the children (sitting in a circle – a single curved line). This knowledge helped staff find ways of supporting more difficult forms of counting, for example by encouraging the child to arrange the bean bags in a single line. Continuous observation also enables staff to cope with the 'three steps forward and two steps back' nature of learning. It is also the basis for the planning of 'next steps' both for individuals and for the nursery as a whole.

At the end of their first week at the nursery, staff pool all their observations and construct a preliminary sketch of each child and formal reviews are conducted regularly throughout the year. In staff meetings towards the end of the first term, there is discussion of how well each child has settled, and of their strengths and needs in all areas. Similar meetings are held in the spring term shortly before Jane and Marian meet parents individually to discuss each child's progress and development.

Facts or fuzzies?

> . . . even though all observers are likely to be less than objective,
> objectivity can be aimed for.
>
> (Hurst and Joseph 1998)

While absolute objectivity is practically impossible, staff work towards it through an agreed approach to what is recorded, and through the way in which knowledge is shared.

Nicola introduced colleagues to the notion of fuzzies', imprecise comments which describe an interpretation of an event rather than what the observer has actually seen. For example, the note, 'Tom enjoyed this activity' is an interpretation, not hard evidence. Noting that 'Tom smiled', or that he 'remained at the activity for more than five minutes' provides facts which can be evaluated alongside other observations. Newcomers sometimes need to unlearn the skill of interpreting underlying emotions and motives, in order to develop the practice of reporting dispassionately on what they see. Enjoyment cannot be seen – a smile can. Some events are more easily reported, for example if they are quantifiable: how long did an activity take? How much of a puzzle was completed? ('50%' may convey more information than '5 pieces'). Noting children's talk (always the exact words) provides much evidence about their language and wider learning. A concentration on what can be observed also helps to separate the observer's (inevitable) bias from what is noted down.

The way assessment data is shared among the whole staff also supports objectivity. Often, the evidence accumulated on a particular child is mutually confirmatory, illustrating different facets of consistent behaviour. Fragments of dialogue noted in the context of home–corner play, painting and doing puzzles may all support the conclusion that a child is developing the ability to interact purposefully with peers, for example. Where discrepancies are identified they need to be investigated and sometimes existing evidence will have to be challenged. This process may begin in a staff meeting or in informal conversations. If different observers report a different dominant hand for a particular child, for example, everybody would be alert to the need to observe the child drawing, painting, building and so on; a flood of observations usually follows. In this example it may be that the child has not yet developed a preference for using a particular hand, or that one hand is preferred but not used exclusively. Further discussion would then focus on what intervention, if any, might support the development of appropriate motor skills.

Sometimes the nature of the area of learning calls for multiple assessments, as the 'counting' example demonstrated. Counting with correspondence cannot be 'ticked off' after a single sighting. It must be seen in a variety of contexts. Sometimes this means setting up a situation which repeats or re-presents what has been observed already, though never in a way which leaves a child feeling they have been tested.

Of course, sometimes multiple perspectives simply fit together like the pieces of a jigsaw. For example, someone might note that a particular child 'hasn't gone to the collage table today'. Others might add 'That's because he was very busy at the computer', 'But he took a model home last Friday' and so on. Not visiting the collage table then becomes part of a larger picture which shows the child's varied interests and perhaps a tendency to concentrate on one thing at a time. On the other hand, successive observations may show that he never visits the collage table. By working together, the team builds a picture of each child's learning.

Making individual assessments in context and basing conclusions on the totality of children's nursery experience means that this is an 'authentic assessment' approach (Pollard 1997:287) offering higher validity than one based on less frequent observations or specially devised activities.

Challenges

> We're always aware that we can improve.
>
> (Jane Holt)

Observation is something you have to keep doing all the time or the child's record can quickly develop gaps. However, it is important to strike the proper balance between the desire to record and the need to fulfil other roles.

> It can be difficult making time to get all the observations in, especially during a very physical or messy activity – you can be covered in clay or paint and in any event you want to be interacting with the children as well. Sometimes you can hold something in your head while you finish working with a child and then make notes afterwards. It can be difficult to know when to start writing something down; should you wait and see how the activity develops and then see if you can remember it to write it down later? If you do that, you have to hope nobody comes in with wet knickers in between!
>
> (Jane Holt)

'Saving an observation for later' is all the harder when recording something that a child has said, as it has to be memorized exactly. Sometimes the choice has to be made between collecting something for the record and using the observation as a starting point for supporting further learning.

Some children are very adept at drawing attention to what they are doing, while others simply don't want to interact with an adult, preferring to end an activity and move off. Staff know to make the time to observe the children who might otherwise be overlooked. It's obviously easier to make notes on the children who do verbalize their thoughts or who volunteer things at story time. The temptation to record many sayings of children who say 'the most fascinating things' has to be resisted. You must also remember to make observations of *how* children play as well as what they say, and that can be more difficult to record.

Staff also guard against following their own areas of interest exclusively, and against being influenced by preconceptions which might arise from discussions about a child; they must not fall into the trap of simply looking for evidence to prove a theory. Each practitioner records more about the children she knows best, but as every child's record has contributions from several adults this is no cause for concern. Although the team is aware of many pitfalls in the process, there are established strategies to deal with most of them, and an awareness that practice can always be improved.

Working with parents

> She hasn't brought much home – is she doing anything?
>
> (Brunswick parent)

Parents hold Brunswick in high esteem and they overwhelmingly want to work with the staff to support their children's learning. They often express surprise at how well nursery staff know the children. Observation data plays an important part in opening and developing the dialogue between home and school; through sharing observations, and through seeing how carefully they are made, parents appreciate the value of what the nursery has been doing.

Any parent's understanding of a child's behaviour may differ from the nursery's. Expressing different interpretations as 'conflicting' is not a good starting point for a dialogue, while sharing impressions and interpretations can provoke unhelpful responses. Fortunately, a record of things the child has actually done offers a basis for more dispassionate discussion. A practitioner might say, 'Your child really seems to finish the puzzles.'

Whether the parent replies, 'Yes, he plays with them a lot at home', or 'Does he really? I haven't seen him do that', a dialogue has begun. Parents who begin by thinking that they disagree with the nursery's view of their child usually come to see that apparently conflicting information is, in fact, complementary. Areas where parents do not recognize the picture painted of their child are explored in much the same way as contradictory observation evidence.

Parents find it easy to make sense of evidence of things that are practical and observable that they can easily relate to their own knowledge of their child. They may say s/he 'doesn't do that at home', or that the things which haven't been observed in the nursery are the things s/he spends hours doing at home. The nursery meets different needs for different individuals. An only child may look forward to the nursery session as a time for socializing, a child from a larger family might seek out quieter activities and opportunities for sustained concentration. Parents help staff build up a full picture of a child's interests and accomplishments and the dialogue can help parents understand how their children are learning. Of course, information flows two ways and a discussion may begin with some concern of the parent.

Working together

> Everyone's opinion is valued. That works against the setting up of a hierarchy and supports the ethos of working together; supporting each other.
>
> (Jane Holt)

> You can't run a nursery if you don't all get on; we are a team.
>
> (Colette Williams)

One important feature of the observation process is the way in which it reflects the ethos of the nursery. Just as every child is valued, so is the contribution of every member of staff, whatever their job title. All are actively involved, on the one hand in observing and recording children's learning in context, and on the other in interpreting observations and identifying 'next steps'. All are equally involved in talking and listening with children, supporting them physically and supporting and extending their learning; children rarely make a distinction between different kinds of adult they meet in the nursery. The observation strategy emphasizes the fact that everybody's views are valued equally. There is no sense of hierarchy during the nursery day, even though some staff may have special roles in respect of the analysis and presentation of observation data.

The pooling of information emphasizes the necessity of team working: colleagues take ideas from each other and give each other advice. There is no place for criticism, and differences of view are reconciled in a professional way. This cooperative *modus operandi* offers a good model to children, who also enjoy working together.

Observations can contribute more directly to the school's ethos too. Noting what children are doing gives them an explicit signal that their work is valued. Observing and recording what children *can* do has the potential to raise their self esteem and this can be especially valuable in respect of children exhibiting anti-social behaviour. Additionally, if a child with special educational needs has behaviour problems then the behaviour of other children around him or her would be noted too.

At Brunswick children never feel under pressure to demonstrate particular areas of learning. They may be encouraged to follow a certain activity, but never directed: a new skill is noted when a child is ready to use it. Because of this, play (by definition a self-motivated activity) can remain the principal medium through which the curriculum is taught.

All this emphasizes the view that the most important role of the nursery is in fostering the development of individual children. Close observation leads to a greater respect for a child.

> You understand, particularly with children who have special educational needs, the efforts they are actually making when there is no adult there to help them; you see how hard things are for them and how they cope by really struggling. The level of effort is something you need to remind yourself of time and time again.
>
> (Nicola Davies)

Final words

> Observations really do make you aware of what you're doing and what you're expecting the children to do.
>
> (Colette Williams)

> One of the things I enjoy very much. You always learn something about a child, you always learn something about the other people in the nursery.
>
> (Nicola Davies)

Everyone at Brunswick agrees about the value of observations and about the sense of satisfaction they give. Observation offers a way of ensuring that every child is considered as a whole person.

Observation enables a play-based curriculum to be implemented rigorously and in a way which fully supports the demands of the Foundation Stage. The assessment strategy supports inclusion by ensuring that all children receive the attention and support they are entitled to. As a bonus, every day, staff learn more about the children, more about successful planning and teaching strategies and more about making and interpreting observations.

The strategy has grown out of the underlying values of an established staff who have respect for each other and for children and for children's rights to receive a broad and balanced education which is stimulating and enjoyable. All at Brunswick are convinced that play is at the heart of early years education and that their assessment strategy is the key to making a play-based curriculum effective for all.

References

Hurst, V. and Joseph, J. (1998) *Supporting Early Learning: the way forward*. Buckingham: Open University Press.

Ofsted (1998) *Inspection Report: Brunswick Nursery School*. London: Ofsted.

Pollard, A. (1997) *Reflective Teaching in the Primary School: a handbook for the classroom*. London: Cassell Education.

Chapter 17

Homework

Julian Stern

Julian Stern, Dean of Education & Theology, York St John University, has a particular interest in ways of involving parents in schools. Here he considers the potential impact of children's homework on home life, and suggests ways of making it meaningful in order to promote closer home – school understanding.

A teacher friend of mine was burgled. When the police came around, they were tremendously sympathetic, as the burglar had not only stolen the video and jewellery, but had wrecked the house too, throwing things all over the place. The burglar had in fact been very tidy: it was teaching that had left no time for housework. Suppose that teacher decided to get a grip of the housework, and when there was no time to do the ironing at home, it was brought into the staffroom, and during staff meetings, the teacher stood at the back, doing the ironing. What would you, as a colleague, do? Whenever I have asked this question, incidentally, the respondents have said that they would ask the teacher if they would do their ironing as well. Nevertheless, most people recognize that school is not the best place for ironing. Housework is best done in the house and it disrupts the school to bring housework in and complete it there. Likewise, much of schoolwork is best done in school, and it disrupts the home to complete schoolwork there. Let us consider three kinds of homework that schools can set, each having different implications for the involvement of parents.

First we could use homework to 'expand' the 15,000 hours of schooling currently suffered by children, making parents into cheap and unqualified school staff, working in the worst possible conditions. This is perhaps based on the 'vanity' model of governments and schools, suggesting that no learning happens outside school without schools *making* it happen. The most

Source: A revised version of Stern, J. (2003) 'Homework', Chapter 6, pp. 54–62 (London: Continuum). Reproduced with permission of CONTINUUM PUBLISHING COMPANY in the format Textbook via Copyright Clearance Center.

common 'expansion' homework task is 'finishing off' – the most common homework task of all, and the one that most disadvantages slower workers who generally need most help from school staff. Other expansion tasks might be to complete lists of questions or general 'research' tasks (such as 'find out about the Second World War'). It is no wonder that expansion homework is rarely liked and is likely to have little impact on learning (as in Stern 1998). Involving parents means using parents as prison guards ('you're not going out until you finish your homework') or as pupils themselves ('I'll look it up for you'). Parents may welcome this, as homework can be a genuinely helpful means of control: a bargaining tool in the battle of the generations. And parents may really enjoy looking things up in encyclopedias, or completing maths questions – even if this means they will also get upset by low marks for their work. However, these ways of involving parents are not generally the best ways of exploiting what parents are good at, and can distance parents further from the whole schooling process (Stern 2009). Expansion homework is also one of the main reasons why parental support for their children's homework is so reduced as children move to secondary school – with 57 per cent of primary pupils getting regular help from parents, and only 17 per cent of secondary pupils getting regular help from parents (MacBeath and Turner 1990).

A *second* way of looking at homework would be to use it in such a way that the 15,000 hours of schooling could be applied to the rest of the child's world. 'Application' homework is based on the idea that school subjects need to be relevant, or that school learning consists of a set of 'apprenticeships' in the world:

- Food technology should help with food preparation in the home, and is about being an apprentice in catering.
- History should help pupils understand causes and implications of current local and national situations and the community's place in history, and is about being an apprentice historian.
- Science should help pupils understand how the physical world works and how to test this, and is about being an apprentice scientist.
- PE is about physical and sporting understanding and control, and is about being an apprentice sportsman or sportswoman.

These and similar ideas, more popular in secondary than primary schools, are often popular with members of subject-based professions and with governments concerned with the usefulness or value to the economy of schooling. When it comes to application homework, parents are more likely to be enablers than helpers. For example, parents might allow a child to shop for and make one meal a week, or investigate the home in order to find evidence of the age and original use of the building, or grow plants on a window sill. Similarly, pupils studying musical styles might analyse the music used in a range of adverts on the television, pupils studying French could choose a song they like and write some French lyrics for it, or pupils studying moral systems in different religions (such as the ten commandments and the five precepts) could see how many moral rules are broken in particular soap operas. Parents are invited, not assumed, to be enablers. For example, letters sent home from a primary school (quoted by the government in 2003 as examples of good practice) said:

> Today we have been learning about floating and sinking. You can help your child continue the experiments by putting some objects made of different materials in the bath to see which float and which sink. See if your child can guess what will happen!

And:

> Today we made some fruit salad. We used . . . You could ask your child to look at and name any fruit you have at home. Also, children could look at the fruit in the market and supermarket, and practise saying the names as often as possible.

The *third* way of looking at homework is based on the imbalance in time mentioned at the start of this book (Stern 2003a). There are 15,000 hours of schooling up to the age of sixteen, which leaves 125,000 hours spent by pupils with their families and friends, or on their own, outside school. Homework could be used to ensure that these 125,000 hours of childhood be made use of in school. The homework tasks capture the child's world for the schoolwork. 'Capture' homework sees school as largely derivative of non-school life, especially home life. It recognizes that schooling and subjects are primarily about humanity and the world, rather than being about subjects for their own sakes. Parents and other adults can be 'interviewed' by their children about their views or experiences of life, rather than their knowledge of subjects:

- How could the area best be developed (for geography)?
- What was school like when they were young (for history)?
- What sports do they enjoy watching or participating in most or least (for PE)?

- What do they think is the most important moral principle (for RE)?
- How do they choose a candidate, or choose whether or not to vote, when it comes to elections (for citizenship)?
- What were their favourite stories when they were young (for English and other languages spoken by parents)?
- What five pieces of music would they take to a desert island and why (for music)?

Parents and other adults can be sketched for art, measured to provide a set of data for work in statistics, asked to rank a set of statements about or pictures of types or styles of clothing (for technology), and so on. To involve parents with capture homework, means to capture the worlds of parents, including the languages of parents, and use them in school. Then, when parents visit classrooms or look at pupils' work, they will recognize a little bit of themselves, and will recognize aspects of the lives of other parents. There will be something familiar (as well as something unfamiliar) in the classroom, and school will be that much more inclusive. It is a puzzle that parents who themselves work in schools, and who are incessantly 'educational' with their children ('Ooh, look at that interesting cast-iron Victorian lamppost!' accompanying a walk to the park), still often feel stressed by the need to support homework. 'Homework is hell', a teacher-parent once wrote to me, and causes 'endless friction between concerned and caring parents and their teenage children'. If homework includes plenty of capture homework, grabbing hold of the world beyond the school, then parents can be involved more painlessly and imaginatively.

Whatever kind of homework is set, school staff should be aware of the variety of pupils' home circumstances:

- All pupils, and especially pupils who themselves have family responsibilities, may welcome breakfast, lunchtime or after-school homework clubs. This means that they are less stressed by multiple responsibilities around the home, and the family is less pressured.
- Pupils who split their time between two homes, for example of separated parents, may welcome a full week to complete homework tasks. This means they will be able to make use of people or facilities – such as computers or books – in either home.
- Pupils whose parents are less likely to be in a position to help with homework, for whatever reason, will welcome tasks being set that say 'ask an adult' or 'talk to a grown-up, such as a parent or someone who

works in the school'. Providing opportunities for pupils to ask other adults around the school – such as support staff of all kinds – has the advantage of bringing the whole school together to support learning. I remember a quiz set by a history teacher, where the pupils had to ask adults in the school what famous women they could name from history. This created a real 'buzz' around the school, as all through break and lunchtimes teachers and administrators and premises staff and supervisors were being quizzed by very competitive pupils.

- When there is homework about families or homes themselves, make sure that you do not make things difficult for the pupil by asking for information they may not want to share with you or other pupils, or may not know. Avoid questions such as 'draw your family tree' (who is who on the tree, and whom shall I call 'father'?), or 'count the number of rooms in your house' (which house, or if a local authority care home, how much of the house?). A simple alternative would be 'think about a family/house you know well – either your own family/house or the family/house of a friend or someone else you know', followed by the task. This allows pupils to put a little distance between themselves and their responses.

- Sleep is a good idea. Children and adults alike, these days, apparently get too little sleep. Homework should not mean that children get even less sleep. It is important to say to pupils and parents how long homework should take, overall, and to see this as a maximum rather than a minimum amount of time. Few adults welcome a work contract that says 'be at work for a certain number of hours, but the work may take much longer' (even if some contracts look like that), and few children would like a lesson that started 'this lesson may take an hour, or it may last for several hours'. Yet this is a common attitude to homework, which therefore seems endless and more stressful – and more likely to be completed at the expense of much-needed sleep. I recommend asking pupils to write at the end of each piece of homework how many minutes it took to complete. They then have an incentive to complete the task in good time, and to underestimate, if anything, how long the task took – as they do not want to appear too slow.

If there are to be breakfast, lunchtime or after-school homework clubs (popular in UK schools at least since the 1930s, as in Great Britain Board of Education 1936), then these will need financing and staffing – providing further opportunities for involving parents in school, either as fund-raisers or paid or unpaid helpers in the clubs. If there are effective family learning activities, then these will help parents become more confident in their dealings with their children and with the school, as well as supporting parents' own further learning (as described in Stern 2003b).

References

Great Britain Board of Education (1936) *Homework (Educational Pamphlets, No. 110)*, London: HMSO.

MacBeath, J. and Turner, M. (1990) *Learning out of school: Report of Research Study carried out at Jordanhill College*, Glasgow: Jordanhill College.

Stern, L.J. (1998) *The OoSHA Review: Out of School Hours Activities in Lambeth: Report for Lambeth LEA, Spring 1998*, Isleworth: Brunel University.

Stern, L.J. (2003a) *Involving Parents*, London: Continuum.

Stern, L.J. (2003b) *Progression from Family Learning*, LSC-funded research report for Hull CityLearning, April.

Stern, L.J. (2009) *Getting the . . . to Do Their Homework, 2nd edition*; London: Continuum.

Section 3

Learning relationships

This section is concerned with the relationships within which learning for children is often embedded. In Chapter 18, Priscilla Alderson argues that we should respect the opinions of children more than we do and involve them in our decision-making, not least so that we can learn from them. The theme of learning collaborations between adults and children is continued by Henry Maitles and Ross Deuchar in Chapter 19. They argue that teachers and teaching assistants should approach education for citizenship with enthusiasm and that it should not be unduly adult-led and controlled. Children, they suggest, need to be fully involved as participants. Chapter 20, by Janet Collins, recommends that some children may need focused support in order to fully participate as learners. Children who are habitually quiet in school, she suggests, may find it easier to express their feelings and ideas to teaching assistants and peers within the context of small group activities.

Eating disorders often make the headlines. However, although many children have individual preferences for food, even idiosyncrasies, most do not develop serious difficulties. Nevertheless, it is important that teachers, teaching assistants, and lunchtime supervisors have insights into the causes of potential difficulties and a sense of when a difficulty becomes a potential disorder. Chapter 21, by the Royal College of Psychiatrists, provides advice.

The next two chapters consider the needs of two distinct groups of children who may be at risk of not being included sufficiently in school learning. In Chapter 22, Gwynedd Lloyd and Gillean McCluskey provide information and challenge some commonly held stereotypes with regard to the children of Gypsies and Travellers. Chapter 23 addresses intra-personal communication and opportunities for us to learn from each other. Here, Mary Stacey discusses how best to communicate unambiguously and, where necessary, assertively.

Bullying is extremely upsetting for children who experience its effects and potentially very disruptive to their learning and their lives. We therefore felt it appropriate to include three chapters on bullying in this

Reader. Chapter 24 reports on the views of children. It is written by Christine Oliver and Mano Candappa and arises from a study involving nearly 1,200 primary and secondary pupils. The next chapter is an anti-cyber bullying policy compiled by staff, children, governors, and parents at East Herrington Primary School. It is a reminder of the way in which new technology can bring unwanted as well as exciting developments in schools. In Chapter 26, Pete Johnson examines the reason why many bullied boys feel they must hide their unhappy experiences.

The two final chapters in this section look at the relationship between children's learning and their behaviour. In Chapter 27, Norma Powell, in discussion with a safer schools officer, examines the way in which conflict resolution and distributive justice can be effectively used in schools. Chapter 28 reviews support practice with regard to learning and behaviour. Janet Kay highlights the potential contribution of teaching assistants to a 'positive' learning environment both in terms of supporting the teacher and also within their own remit, working with groups and individuals.

Chapter 18

Institutional rites and rights

Priscilla Alderson

Priscilla Alderson, professor of childhood studies at the Institute of Education, London, gave her inaugural lecture on 4 June 2003. This chapter draws together three extracts from that lecture. The first considers the 'institution of childhood' and the way adults define and organise this for children. The second considers how schools, places where adults have all the power, might feel through the eyes of children. In the third extract, the conclusion to the lecture, it is argued that even the youngest children can be helped to make informed, responsible decisions, and that children need to be more involved in planning and organising the institutions that exist for their benefit.

Institutions – childhood

Childhood itself is an institution with its established laws and formal customs. It is often thought of as a biological and inevitable stage of life. It is, however a social stage, lasting until around 7 to 12 years in some societies, or up to the mid-20s for some young adults in modern western societies. About 150 years ago in Britain, after a short infancy (infant meaning 'without speech') working-class children were very much treated as adults – and most adults were treated rather as children. They had few rights or possessions, heavy workloads, little leisure, the anxieties and hardships of poverty. As far as we can tell, many had strong ties of affection and loyalty. Childhood has since gradually been subdivided into babies, toddlers, pre-schoolers and so on, including adolescents – they were first officially classified in 1904 (Hall 1904).

Children are real living people. But childhood is a set of ideas about what children are and ought to be like, and how they should behave and relate to adults. These ideas change very much over time. Near our London school,

Source: An edited version of Alderson, P. (2003) *Institutional Rites and Rights: A Century of Childhood* (London: Institute of Education, University of London).

mosaics on the library walls recorded how Chaucer's pilgrims set out from that street over 600 years ago, with their highly educated young squire. Around 2,000 years ago, some local families lived in the newly imported Roman style. Today, pearly princes and princesses undertake regal duties in the area. Incidentally, the images record waves of immigration, from Italy, France and the Caribbean, each wave bringing new ideas about childhood and education.

Children are so confined today, that it is often assumed that they cannot, and should not, take an active part in their communities. Less than a century ago, their lives were far more closely woven in 'adult' society, and still are today in the poorer majority world. Children aged 4 or 5 years would go alone on errands across a busy city, use public transport, shop and barter, or ramble in the countryside (Ward 1994). Today, millions of young children ably help their parents, by working in homes, farms and streets. In war-torn, AIDS-torn Africa, children head households (Muscroft 1999:74), as 12-year-old Sophia Ingibire Tuyisenge's story tells. She is caring for her two sisters and despite many problems is 'coping just fine' (McFerran 2003:66). In Britain today, thousands of children aged from 3 years upwards help to care for a sick or disabled relative (Aldridge and Becker 2002). The point here is not whether this should happen, but that it does happen, and shows young children's strengths and competencies. Perhaps children are happier today, with more toys, books, games, clothes, comfortable homes, food, education and care services planned for them. We cannot know. Certainly they are lonelier, with so many fewer children per family and per street, and are far more confined. Fashions in childcare swing from harsh to indulgent, from fairly loose to tight control (Hardyment 1984). Today, alongside indulgence, children are often controlled more rigidly than ever before.

Just as women's views are largely missing from history, children's views are almost wholly absent. Instead we have adults' records, discussions and images of childhood (Hendrick 1997). What was it like for a 5-year-old to sit still hour after hour on cramped benches? How did those older boys and girls feel, who were beaten for being 'thick' and 'idle' but who could do fairly skilled work that would bring in money their family desperately needed? And what did older sisters in large families think about being 'taught' to do tasks they had been doing at home for years?

Local doors have closed, while virtual and global ones have opened throughout the past century for western childhood, more than ever before. Today, children may not know their next-door neighbours, partly because of current stranger-danger fears, but they may know lots about rain forests or space travel, and have perhaps been to Florida or Pakistan. In Derby in 1902, Margaret, aged 5 years, took a pushchair across the city to collect her sister Elizabeth, aged 3 years, who had been in hospital for weeks. The matron was annoyed that their mother had not come, but assumed that the girls were old enough to go home on their own. Cities were dangerous places then, with plenty of horses and other traffic, muddy cobbled roads and no zebra crossings or traffic lights. Myths have grown up that children cannot and should not do these things. Researchers ask to whom does childhood belong, when parents and teachers assume they must organise and oversee almost every moment of children's lives (Shamgar-Handelman 1994).

Adulthood is assumed to mean being strong and informed, reliable and wise, and childhood means being vulnerable and ignorant, unreliable and foolish. Schools are planned on this assumption and constantly reinforce it. A curriculum is 'delivered' to children, as letters are posted into letterboxes, until children turn into adults. These institutionalised 'laws and customs' seem too obvious and natural to be worth noting, but are they true?

How would adults react to being treated as many school students are?

We could review a typical secondary school day. Nowhere safe to leave your coat and belongings, which must be carried everywhere. Regular crowded mass treks from one part of the campus to another. Queuing to wait, sometimes in the rain, until a teacher arrives to unlock doors. Up to a quarter of your time taken up with silent queuing and marching (Griffith 1998). Much reduced break times. Petty rules about uniform, jewellery and hints of individual expression, that in turn stop freedom of speech: 'We cannot have a school council because all they want to talk about is uniform and they cannot do that,' some teachers reported (Alderson 2000a, 2000c). Britain and Malta are the only European countries to have uniforms (Hannam 1999), which indicates that they are not essential.

Would you care to arrive home and hear your partner say, 'Your boss has just phoned to tell me you broke that agreement I signed with her. You were late back from lunch and she says I must stop you watching television for a week.' You might reply, 'But I was helping a friend whose mobile was stolen.' 'Tough,' your partner will say, 'I don't want any more lame excuses. Now get on with that work you have to give in tomorrow.' And so you labour on through a 6- or 7-day week that far exceeds the European limits for adults' working hours. With breakfast clubs and after school clubs, even young children may spend 50 hours a week at school. Most children would prefer not to attend the clubs, if they had the choice (Smith 2000; Smith and Barker 2002). Many children are not happy about the growing alliances between home and school, and mothers being turned into teachers, and they would prefer there to be a clear gap (Alldred *et al.* 2002). By the way, you are not paid a penny, your pocket money may be stopped too sometimes, and your work, however skilful, complicated, hard, interesting, beautiful or original, does not count as 'work', but as mere practising or learning for your benefit (Morrow 1994). You cannot have the satisfaction of feeling that you are helping or benefiting others; adults insist that they help you.

Teachers can act as claimant, witness, judge and jury if students are accused of misdemeanours. Despite this complicated overlapping of roles that the justice system exists to separate, children may be punished and even excluded without routine means of appeal or fair arbitration (UNCRC 2003). Home-School Agreements are the reverse of a legal contract, which is an informed and unpressured agreement freely negotiated between equal partners. The Agreements appear to assume that any alleged misdemeanour will be entirely the child's fault, and not possibly be linked to mistakes or other problems in the school. Parents who support their child can be criminalised, fined and even sent to prison.

Mothers of 4-year-olds have told me about class teachers advising them to 'ground' their children to punish alleged inattention and misbehaviour. During small discussion groups about rights in schools (Alderson and Arnold 1999), some children mentioned their fear that when teachers call their parents into school to complain to them, 'my mum will beat me up'; 'my dad whacks me'. So although the 1993 Education Act banned physical punishment in state schools, this has been exported, in some cases, to the home, rather than abolished. Children are the only members of British society who can, by law, be hit, as if somehow they do not mind as much as adults would, or as if 'a smack is the only language they can understand'. Yet research shows that young children can feel deeply hurt and rejected (Willow and Hyder 1998). The dire state of the toilets in many schools is another sign of disrespect for bodies that adults' institutions would not tolerate. A colleague who read a draft of this paper commented:

> My daughter aged 9 has to sign a book whenever she goes to the toilet at school and then sign back in. The teachers want to find out who is vandalising the toilets. She won't go to the toilet in case she gets blamed and because they are unpleasant. She won't drink so she is dehydrated but longing to go to the loo. How can she learn?

Instead of making all the children suffer when a few offend, another approach is to involve everyone in planning and carrying out positive solutions. This often requires some funding, and effective school councils see budgets and have some share in deciding how certain funds are spent.

Despite all the discouragements in schools, most young people do work very hard and creatively. They enjoy at least some of their schoolwork, and they rate time at school to be with their friends very highly, especially as there are so few free public spaces where they are encouraged to meet outside school. As they become older and more competent, however, their enjoyment and interest fall (MacBeath and Mortimore 2001:85; Alderson 2000c; Pollard *et al.* 1997). Yet we treat all school students as if most of them, instead of only a relatively tiny minority, were potential truants, by making schooling compulsory and enforced with heavy sanctions.

Conclusion

At the end of his novel *Vanity Fair*, Thackeray says to his readers, 'Come, children, let us shut up the box and the puppets, for our play is played out' (1847:733). This lecture concerns trying to close away old ideas of children as puppets, to make space for children as persons. I began by asking:

* What can adults do that children cannot do?
* At what age can children start to do activities that are often seen as 'adult' ones?
* What is the difference between children and adults?

If you thought before hearing this lecture that there were clear and large differences between adulthood and childhood, I hope that now you believe there are considerable overlaps, and that many of the differences result from how we (mis)perceive and treat children rather than from children's actual capacities. Perhaps you will also agree that a rigid double standard, of respect and rights for adults, and compulsion and control for children, is neither principled nor productive. How can we possibly encourage children to be responsible agents, as many school brochures claim, by treating them as helpless dependants hemmed in by many rigid rules, often listed in the brochures? We might as well expect frogs to turn magically into princes, and drudges into princesses (Griffith 1998).

This is an 'inaugural' lecture, a rite that implies that a new, youngish professor inaugurates or institutes a programme of work for the next 20 to 30 years. I do not have that long time ahead of me, and so instead I will propose a programme that I hope the Institute will inaugurate – plan and develop – over the next century. As we have seen, dominant thinking in the Institute over the past century has sometimes mistaken the nature of childhood and education. Instead, in the twenty-first century, we could take more heed of Marion Richardson's faith in 'sincere free' relationships, and in those nineteenth-century working people's respect for education where the learners would 'go first and the master would follow' (Godwin 1797). These ideals are practised to some extent in some Italian early years centres, Rajasthan night schools, Colombian schools (Hart 2003), and in some schools in Britain and around the world (Apple and Beane 1999).

Surely universities are places for exploring new and alternative ideas carefully, instead of dismissing them. The philosopher Mary Midgley (1996) compares thinking with plumbing. Beliefs and pipes tend to be invisible and ignored until something goes obviously wrong, such as leaks or blockages. Then the importance of hidden pipes, or hidden assumptions, becomes clear, and the most practical thing to do is to sort out the (mental) plumbing. Instead of simply suggesting new techniques or practices to improve schools, at the level of patching leaks, it is time to look more deeply at what is going wrong and why. Unlike 1902, 2003 is a time when British adults assume that their rights, choices and responsibilities should be respected. Childhood has been left behind in a historical limbo and this has skewed relationships and double standards between the institutions of childhood and adulthood. It is as if a great dam has grown higher over the past century to exclude children and young people and direct them into separate channels away from mainstream society. Adults claim that this is to protect and cherish children, but the system can very much harm children, young people and adults while tending mainly to serve adults' economic and political interests.

Suppose we took seriously the hope that there are better ways for children and adults to work together in schools, such as in the words of the Danish law that schools must 'build on intellectual freedom, equality and democracy' (Davies and Kirkpatrick 2000:22). A logical step is that school attendance would become voluntary instead of compulsory. The vast majority of children and young people would attend school voluntarily for three reasons they value very highly besides learning: to gain necessary training and qualifications for the next stages of education and employment; to enjoy time with their friends; and to have opportunities and resources especially for the arts and sports (Alderson and Arnold 1999). Most children start school eager and able to learn. Black children, particularly, do very well at first and then fall behind (Gillborn and Youdell 2000). With the fall in interest in secondary schools already noted, this suggests that many problems may arise in schools rather than at home. The benefits of voluntary attendance would include respect for students as the informed 'consumers' or, far better, co-creators in their education, supported by their parents and carers, besides a creative, positive, welcoming school ethos. So much time, frustrated energy, and wasted resources could be re-channelled into working with the majority instead of trying to work against a resistant minority. That would release many teachers from administration and management back into teaching, with better teacher-student ratios, resulting in more personal and rewarding relationships. There would be more time to help the small minority who are unhappy, resistant or absent, and to work with them towards solutions, whether the difficulty is with reading or maths, bullying from children or adults, parents who keep them at home too much, or other problems (see, for example, Katz 2002).

There could be a programme of research and teaching to address the advantages and problems associated with voluntary school attendance, and to support the necessary new policies and practices. In the programme children, young people and adults would share the responsibility to:

- rethink the meaning and relevance of childhood and children's competencies and rights
- work to plan better curricula, real learning and teaching, and improved teacher training
- map new approaches to education itself and to schooling that can accommodate a new mutual respect and voluntary (willing) partnerships between learners and teachers
- plan how to prevent and resolve problems
- devise new effective systems of intrinsic rewards, credits, and paced flexible learning for core and optional subjects
- wrestle with the challenges of trying to combine liberty, equality and solidarity in schools
- recognise children as contributors and resources, instead of assuming that respecting their rights means increasing their expensive dependence
- seek to change society's treatment of and attitudes towards children and young people – the views of parents, 'experts', journalists, politicians and all others who influence public opinions and policies.

Children can see though the current hypocrisy of repressive schools and token school councils. 'We get played like fools,' they say (Morrow 2002). An

8-year-old girl succinctly summarised how rights are trivialised and distanced, in vain attempts to conceal how children's rights are disrespected in schools: 'It's so boring when they keep telling you that making the world a better place means picking up litter and not killing whales' (Alderson and Arnold 1999; Alderson 1999). The aim of changing the blocked plumbing of compulsion, and rigid though ineffectual control, into new channels of shared willing human agency would be that, whatever future forms schools take, all children and young people and adults will be able to flourish in civilised, respectful and caring communities. In the words of the UNCRC, respecting the inherent worth and dignity and the inalienable rights of all members of the human family promotes social progress and better standards of life in larger freedoms, and lays foundations for justice and peace in the world.

References

Alderson, P. (1999) 'Human rights and democracy in schools: Do they mean more than "picking up litter and not killing whales"?' *International Journal of Children's Rights*, **7**, 185–205.

—— (2000a) 'Practising democracy in inner city schools', in: A. Osler (ed.), *Democracy in Schools: Diversity, identity, equality*. Stoke on Trent: Trentham Books.

—— (2000b) *Young Children's Rights*. London: Jessica Kingsley/Save the Children.

—— (2000c) 'Citizenship in theory or practice: being or becoming citizens with rights', in: R. Gardner, D. Lawton and P. Walsh (eds.), *Citizenship and Education*. London: Continuum.

Alderson, P. and Arnold, S. (1999) 'Civil Rights in Schools'. *ESRC Children 5–16 Programme Briefing no. 1*. Swindon: ESRC.

Aldridge, J. and Becker, S. (2002) 'Children who care', in: B. Franklin (ed.), *The New Handbook of Children's Rights: Comparative policy and practice*. London: Routledge.

Alldred, P., David, M. and Edwards, E. (2002) 'Minding the gap: children and young people negotiating relations between home and school', in: R. Edwards (ed.), *Children, Home and School: Regulation, autonomy or connection?* London: Falmer/Routledge.

Apple, M. and Beane, J. (1999) *Democratic Schools*. Buckingham: Open University Press.

Davies, L. and Kirkpatrick, G. (2000) *The EURIDEM Project: A review of pupils' democracy in Europe*. London: Children's Rights Alliance for England.

Gillborn, D. and Youdell, D. (2000) *Rationing Education*. Buckingham: Open University Press.

Godwin, W. (1797/1976) *An Enquiry Concerning Political Justice and its Influence on General Virtue and Happiness*. Harmondsworth: Penguin. Quoted in Ward, C. (1991) *Influences*. Bideford: Green Books.

Griffith, R. (1998) *Educational Citizenship and Independent Learning*. London: Jessica Kingsley.

Hall, G.S. (1904) *Adolescence*. New York: Appleton.

Hannam, D. (1999) 'Biodiversity or monoculture – the need for alternatives and diversity in the school system'. Summerhill Conference: The Free Child. Summerhill School.

Hardyment, C. (1984) *Dream Babies: Child care from Locke to Spock*. Oxford: Oxford University Press.

Hart, R. (1997) *Children's Participation: The Theory and Practice of Involving Young Children in Community Development and Environmental Care*. London: Earthscan/UNESCO.

—— (2003) 'Children and youth on the cultural front line: the radical challenge of authentic participation in different settings'. Paper presented at ESRC Seminar Series: Challenging social inclusion: perspectives for and from young people, 2nd Seminar on Participation, Strathclyde University, Glasgow, 8–10 April.

Hendrick, H. (1997) 'Constructions and reconstructions of British childhood: An interpretive survey 1800 to the present', in: A. James and A. Prout (eds.), *Constructing and Reconstructing Childhood*. London: Falmer.

Katz, A. (ed.) (2002) *Parenting Under Pressure: Prison*. London: Young Voice.

MacBeath, J. and Mortimore, P. (eds.) (2001) *Improving School Effectiveness*. Buckingham: Open University Press.

McFerran, A. (2003) 'A life in the day'. *Sunday Times Magazine*, 6 April.

Midgley, M. (1996) *Utopias, Dolphins and Computers: Problems of philosophical plumbing*. London: Routledge.

Morrow, G. (1994) 'Responsible Children? Aspects of children's work and employment outside school in contemporary UK', in: B. Mayall (ed.), *Children's Childhoods: Observed and experienced*. London: Falmer.

—— (2002) '"We get played like fools": Young people's accounts of community and institutional participation', in: H. Ryan and J. Bull (eds.), *Changing Families, Changing Communities*. London: Health Development Agency.

Muscroft, S. (ed.), (1999) *Children's Rights: Equal rights? Diversity, difference and the issue of discrimination*. London: Save The Children.

Pollard, A., Thiessen, D. and Filer, A. (eds.) (1997) *Children and their Curriculum: The perspectives of primary and elementary school children*. London: Falmer.

Richardson, M. (1938) quoted in R. Aldrich (2002). *The Institute of Education 1902–2002: a centenary history*. London: Institute of Education.

Shamgar-Handelman, L. (1994) 'To whom does childhood belong?', in: J. Qvortrup, M. Bardy, G. Sgritta and H. Wintersberger (eds.), *Childhood Matters: Social theory. practice and politics*. Aldershot: Avebury.

Smith, F. (2000) *Child-Centred After School and Holiday Childcare*. Swindon: ESRC Research Briefing from the Children 5–16 Programme.

Smith, F. and Barker, J. (2002) 'School's out. Out of school clubs at the boundary of home and school', in: R. Edwards (ed.), *Children, Home and School: Regulation, autonomy or connection?* London: Falmer/Routledge.

Thackeray, W. (1847/1967) *Vanity Fair*. London: Pan Books.

UNCRC (United Nations Committee on the Rights of the Child) (1995, 2003) 'Consideration of Reports Submitted by States Parties Under Article 44 of the Convention, Concluding Observations: United Kingdom of Great Britain and Northern Ireland'. Geneva: United Nations.

Ward, C. (1994) 'Opportunities for childhood in late twentieth century Britain', in: B. Mayall (ed.), *Children's Childhoods: Observed and experienced*. London: Falmer.

Willow, C. and Hyder, T. (1998) *It Hurts You Inside: Children talk about smacking*. London: National Children's Bureau/Save the Children.

Chapter 19

'It's not fair – anyway, we've got rights!'

Henry Maitles and Ross Deuchar

Education for citizenship is now a national priority, and the creation of an open, trusting, and participative school ethos is essential. In this chapter, Henry Maitles and Ross Deuchar, both from the University of Strathclyde, provide practical illustrations of the way in which primary school pupils can become engaged in discussing controversial social and political issues as a means of enhancing their understanding of, and potential participation in, a democratic society.

There is increasing recognition that the general ethos within a school can have a profound impact on the teaching of citizenship education, and the full understanding of the principles underpinning democracy. Schools should ensure that their daily practices do not conflict with or undermine their perceived aims for democratisation. The exposure of pupils to the controversial issues of society is a vital step towards encouraging pupils to develop empathy with the interests, beliefs, and viewpoints of others; to value a respect for truth and evidence in forming or holding opinions; and to participate in decision-making, and value freedom and fairness as a basis for judging decisions. Such exposure is therefore vital for enabling pupils to fully understand what it means to live in a democratic society and behave with respect.

For classroom assistants and teachers, the creation of a positive classroom and school ethos is key. All research evidence (although limited at the moment) suggests that classroom assistants who understand the need for democracy and consultation can give the necessary impetus in the class to develop a better ethos; moreover, having additional adults in the room gives some teachers the confidence to effect that positive classroom ethos. Dobie

Source: Maitles, H. and Deuchar, R. (2004) 'It's not fair – anyway, we've got rights!', commissioned by The Open University for *Primary Teaching Assistants: Learners and Learning* (London: Routledge). Reprinted by permission of The Open University and Taylor & Francis Ltd.

(1998) argues that the way in which a school is run transmits messages to pupils about the nature of society, and cites pupil councils as having a huge role to play in the process of encouraging pupils to have a sense of ownership in the life of the school community.

There is no set way to form a pupil council. Most schools in Scotland now have them but they have been set up in different ways, usually due to a mixture of the school's individual circumstances and the thinking of the senior management. Most councils are elected and representative, either of classes or of year groups. They should be used to discuss issues of interest to the pupils; most common topics are toilets, school meals, and issues such as bullying. Some councils, however, have budgets and clear input into some quite major school issues. It is to be hoped that classroom assistants will become increasingly involved in school councils, providing, as they do, an important adult non-teacher perspective. This may be especially significant where classroom assistants are parents and/or members of the local community. We would welcome further research and the identification of positive examples here. Our investigation into best practice throws up a number of areas, best explained by the following example.

A pupil council in action

A large Scottish primary school in an area of socio-economic deprivation with a predominantly ethnically white pupil body has had a school council in place for almost 8 years. The school has routine weekly meetings in which representatives from Primary 1 to Primary 7 (5 to 12 years) get together with their headteacher to discuss the various points on their agenda, which is informed by class suggestion boxes and council representatives' own ideas. At one series of meetings, observed by one of the authors, items included the possibility of raising money for the local hospice, the development of a school newspaper, introduction of new features in the school dinner hall such as flavoured milk and fruit, and the ongoing difficulty of fighting on the football pitch between Primary 5 and Primary 7 boys. For each issue on the agenda, the headteacher acts as facilitator, encouraging pupils to think about and reflect upon the feasibility of the ideas or how to solve any difficulties. Where appropriate, she also makes suggestions or provides relevant information. The pupils take the lead in the discussion, and are able to speak up at any time. Decisions are made jointly and, where necessary, by means of a vote. At the end of their meeting, pupils decide to consult with classmates about the type of fundraising activities they would like to do for raising money for the local hospice, to name the school newspaper 'The Newsflash', to present ideas to the dinner ladies about new types of fruit that could be introduced, and to suggest to Primary 5 and Primary 7 boys that they might share the school football pitch at lunchtime through the use of mixed-aged teams.

Council members are reminded by the headteacher to report back on these decisions to classmates immediately following the meeting, and that members will announce the pupil council decisions at assembly on Friday. Teachers in the school, although sceptical in the beginning, now embrace the aims of the Pupil Council and see the benefits. They encourage pupils to report back from meetings immediately on their return to the classroom. Indeed, there may be a particular role for classroom assistants in supporting the reporting-back stage. Pupils are elected to the Council by democratic means: pupils in each class write down two people (a boy and a girl) who should be elected, and the most popular choice is elected. Children who are on the Council feel that it provides a forum to have an opinion listened to, and that they see change happening as a result. They feel proud when they are elected to the Council. Non-Council members also seem happy about the process; they know that they can come back and re-discuss ideas, if they are not happy with initial decisions. Many changes have come about as a result of the Pupil Council, apart from those outlined above, such as new equipment in the gym hall, different cakes in the dining hall, a 'Golden Bench' for children who are bullied, and a 'buddying' system for Primary 7 pupils to assist new Primary 1 children.

Even where there are functioning and well-organised pupil councils, there should be space in the classroom to discuss socially or politically sensitive issues, whether that be bullying, local issues, drugs, animal welfare, or international events, such as wars, conflict, or terrorism. There is evidence suggesting that although youngsters are turned off formal party and government politics, they are very interested in single issue campaigning politics (Roker et al. 1999). Again, a case study showing good practice follows.

Democracy in the classroom

In this large non-denominational primary school located within a prosperous section of a West of Scotland town, Primary 7 pupils are encouraged to bring in news stories that are of interest to them as part of their weekly 'international news day' session. The discussions provide a forum for pupils to express aspects of their political interest, and demonstrate their strong engagement in world affairs, often at a very mature level. The main philosophical view underpinning the class teacher's approach appears to be the need for openness and creating an ethos of encouragement for pupils to express their opinions, often in relation to quite controversial issues. Among many of the issues for which she has noted particular pupil interest in recent years, she highlights teenage pregnancy, the use and misuse of drugs, animal rights, and the debate about the teaching of religion in schools as being the most common. She noted a strong interest developing among pupils about issues surrounding terrorism and the Iraq War in the spring of 2003.

The media appear to play a large part in stimulating these particular pupils' interest and curiosity about the Iraq War, and the use of interactive sessions on international news issues provides a useful setting for them to share their curiosity, interest, and personal opinions and also for the teacher to address some particular misunderstandings. Although she clearly encourages pupils to express their opinions and sees the importance of demonstrating the value of these opinions to children, this teacher also takes up the stance as advocated by Ashton and Watson (1998) of 'critical affirmation' in allowing pupils to develop their arguments. The relationship, trust, and respect between the pupils and the teacher become central in such an approach. Although proven to be highly successful, this teacher feels that this approach is not as common among other teachers as it should be. Through her own experience, she has observed the reluctance of some teachers to value pupils' opinions because of their fear of 'losing control' of classroom discipline. Her view here is that teachers who have the confidence and courage to allow pupil participation and to value its worth can, in fact, minimise indiscipline because children will be less frustrated at school.

During their discussions about the Iraq War (Maitles and Deuchar 2004), these pupils displayed a rich knowledge of topical and contemporary issues at international levels, as well as an awareness of the nature of democracy through their views about the future of Iraq and how it could and should be decided. Their concern for humanitarian issues related to the war reflected their growing understanding of the nature of diversity, social conflict, and a concern for the common good. In addition, they were highly reflective about the underlying causes of the war, illustrating their ability to engage in a critical approach to the evidence presented via the mass media. The pupils displayed a strong concern for human dignity, equality, and the need to resolve conflict diplomatically, and are increasingly able to recognise forms of manipulation that may be used by political leaders in their attempts to justify the need for war. They appear to have a growing understanding of human cultures, political structures, human rights, and the underlying sources of conflict between communities.

They also appear to be developing a capacity to imagine alternative realities and futures for the people of Iraq through their discussions, and their ability to empathise with other communities and create reasoned argument in favour of democracy and against war is clearly providing the foundations for active citizenship, permeated by a sense of social and moral responsibility (Advisory Group on Citizenship 1998; LTS 2002). It is clear that there has to be a supportive atmosphere and a positive ethos for this to work effectively; classroom assistants (and, in particular in these kinds of issues, those from ethnic minority backgrounds) can be vital here.

It is evident that the particular class teacher involved here firmly believes that these children's interests in single-issue, environmental, and third-world issues are not untypical of the wider primary-aged pupil population. However, it is also clear that she feels that her intense valuing of pupil opinions is not so typical among teaching colleagues in the wider profession. The evidence of her positive results with pupils helps to confirm the view that, where there can be developed a respectful, trusting relationship between the teaching and support staff and the pupils, and the teacher encourages the pupils to develop their opinions, even the most controversial issues can be sensitively discussed in classrooms. The type of social empathy and tolerance that may emerge from such discussion combined with the ability to engage critically in the consideration of conflict resolution strategies may also assist pupils in dealing with more local controversial issues and incidents as they occur within their own lives in the school, playground, and at home.

Conclusion

We are still in the infancy of education for citizenship, although many of the ideas and practices described above flow from long established practice in schools. While there is evidence of much good practice and we describe some major examples, it is also true that education for citizenship can be boringly, routinely introduced so as to appease audit forms and inspectors. This is a shame as its enthusiastic introduction can lead to better relationships, better behaviour, less bullying, and better learning as the pupils feel some ownership of their work patterns. Hart (1997) outlines eight stages of participation from teacher-led, manipulated, and controlled to pupil-initiated and shared. He shows the importance for democracy and learning if education workers (and particularly senior managers) encourage less of the former and more of the latter. Our evidence endorses that.

References

Advisory Group on Citizenship (1998) *Education for Citizenship and the Teaching of Democracy in Schools*. London: DFEE.

Ashton, E., and Watson, B. (1998) 'Values education: a fresh look at procedural neutrality'. *Educational Studies*, *24*(2), 183–193.

Dobie, T. (1998) 'Pupil councils in primary and secondary schools', in D. Christie, H. Maitles, and J. Halliday (eds.) *Values Education for Democracy and Citizenship*. Glasgow: Gordon Cook Foundation/University of Strathclyde, pp 72–75.

Hart, R. (1997) *Children's Participation: The Theory and Practice of Involving Young Citizens in Community Development and Environmental Care*. London: Earthscan Publications.

LTS (Learning and Teaching Scotland) (2002) *Education for Citizenship in Scotland: A Paper for Discussion and Development*. Available at: http://www.ltscotland.org.uk/citizenship/files/ecsp.pdf

Maitles, H., and Deuchar, R. (2004) 'Why are they bombing innocent Iraqis? Encouraging the expression of political literacy among primary pupils as a vehicle for promoting education for active citizenship'. *Improving Schools*, *7*(1), 97–105.

Roker, D., Player, K., and Coleman, J. (1999) 'Young people's voluntary and campaigning activities as sources of political education'. *Oxford Review of Education*, *25*(1–2), 185–197.

Chapter 20

Hearing the silence

Janet Collins

This chapter argues that quiet children are sometimes too easily overlooked in school. Janet Collins, a staff tutor at The Open University, believes that teaching assistants can play an important role in identifying and supporting quiet learners. Teaching assistants often work with individuals and small groups. They also have excellent opportunities to observe children in a range of different situations in the classroom and outside in the playground.

For teaching assistants and teachers to support children they have to learn what these children already know and what is still to be learned. Much of this is achieved by talking them, and listening to what they have to say. Successful assessment and learning in school is therefore dependent on children being willing and able to talk freely to adults and children and to be active participants in the discourse of the classroom. Children who are unable or unwilling to talk freely to adults in school are at an acute disadvantage when compared with their more vocal peers. Similarly, students who are quiet in university tutorials may not be learning as much as those who ask questions and check with their tutor what they think they have learned.

Some time ago I carried out some research with children in primary schools (Collins, 1994, 1996). This research highlighted the fact that quiet children are often very anxious about talking with, or in front of, others, especially during whole class discussions. They can become extremely embarrassed when adults try to persuade them to talk against their will. This anxiety prevents quiet pupils from taking an active role in their learning. It can also make them feel inadequate, especially in comparison with their more confident peers.

For example, Mandy recalls how uncomfortable she feels when she is 'picked on' to answer a question in class when she does not have her hand

Source: A revised version of Collins, J. (1998) 'Hearing the silence in the classroom full of noise: empowering quiet pupils', *Topic: Practical Applications of Research in Education* issue 20, Autumn (Slough: National Foundation for Educational Research).

up, 'I feel horrible. I don't like it. Because I don't know the answer . . . I just sit there. Sometimes I gave him an answer . . . but sometimes not'. In situations like this, quiet pupils can appease the teacher by offering an answer, or they can satisfy their own need to be silent by refusing to speak. Mandy's obvious discomfort at being asked to speak suggests that neither response is easy or likely to enhance her self-esteem.

When quiet children do not join in class discussions it is extremely difficult for teachers and teaching assistants to assess the extent and depth of their understanding or to support further learning. This problem is compounded by the fact that quiet children find it very difficult to ask for help from adults even when they are experiencing serious difficulties. As the following example shows, a lack of contact with a teacher or another adult can have a detrimental effect on a pupil's learning and may lead to the development of a negative self-image.

Mandy decided to do extra homework in order to progress quickly through the school's individualised maths scheme. As the teacher was unaware of this decision he was not in a position to encourage this commitment to learning. Moreover, he was unaware that whilst Mandy was clearly well-motivated, she had not understood the work to be done. Working without guidance from the teacher both at home and at school, Mandy's mistakes were not identified for some time. Consequently, when her work was eventually marked she found that she had pages of corrections to do. For Mandy this was a blow to her perceptions of herself as an able mathematician. In order to avoid repeating this experience she simply stopped doing homework, thus potentially limiting her opportunities for improvement. This incident is not quoted here as an illustration of bad teaching, but rather to demonstrate how a lack of communication between pupils and adults in the classroom can disrupt learning.

When working with quiet pupils it is important to recognise that compliance does not necessarily equate with a commitment to learning. Justina's behaviour in a French lesson is an obvious example of this. Throughout the lesson, including during oral work, Justina worked hard, writing in her exercise book. Judging from the comments in this book the teacher was highly delighted with her progress. Page after page, she was complemented for the neat presentation of her written work.

However, since Justina did not speak a single word of French it would appear that she had missed the central point of the lesson. Her one interaction with the teacher was conducted in English and focused on the presentation of her work. The teacher seemed oblivious to her lack of participation in the oral part of the lesson. When I asked Justina to read what she had written she said, "I don't speak French because it confuses me". Justina's compliance with her teacher's expectations for her written work was matched by an equally stubborn refusal to share the language with anyone. What, I wondered, did Justina expect to learn during the French lesson? Clearly, this educational experience had not made an impression on her view of the world.

There is a view that quiet children are 'getting on with their work', and therefore must be learning. However, this research confirmed what I had suspected through decades of teaching, learners can be busy doing the wrong thing like Justina or, be seriously engaged in repeating the same mistakes like Mandy. An observant teaching assistant may well be able to talk with the child and put them 'back on the right track' so they can achieve the intended learning outcome.

In addition to inhibiting learning, quiet behaviour in school can also mask serious social and emotional needs. Whilst it is relatively easy to identify the emotional and behavioural difficulties of loud, potentially aggressive pupils (Lee, 2011), the special educational needs of quiet withdrawn pupils can be easily overlooked by teachers and teaching assistants alike.

Paul and Heather attended the same inner city primary school with a high proportion of pupils with special educational needs. Paul's violent, aggressive and often offensive behaviour drew attention to his emotional and behavioural needs, with the result that a variety of adults devoted a huge amount of time offering support. In sharp contrast, Heather's silent compliance meant that no one in the school was aware that she had suffered abuse at the hands of her father and step-father. Heather's story is an extreme case; clearly quiet behaviour does not, of itself, indicate either physical or sexual abuse. However, her experience serves as a useful signifier for the quiet, withdrawn pupils who can so easily be overlooked.

Whatever the cause, habitually quiet withdrawn behaviour should be regarded as potentially detrimental to learning. Such behaviour:

- prevents children from learning to express themselves (learning to talk);
- prevents children from asking questions and making the learning their own (learning through talk);
- prevents children from an active exploration of the subject being learned;
- prevents teachers and teaching assistants from finding out what children know and thus monitor and support learning;

- reinforces stereotypes. Girls, especially those with moderate learning difficulties, are more likely to exhibit quiet passive behaviour in the classroom than other groups of children;
- renders children invisible and can reinforce poor self-images;
- can be linked with social isolation and can make pupils vulnerable to bullying;
- can, in a minority of cases, mask serious emotional trauma such as bereavement, abuse, family separation.

As their roles continue to expand, teaching assistants might use their well developed interpersonal skills to support the learning of quiet children. Teaching assistants are perceived to have close relationships with children. They are also able to adopt more flexible roles within the school. As part of these roles teaching assistants may well be able to observe children in and out of the classroom and take note of what encourages the child to be more expressive. Individual children may, for example, talk freely in the dining room but become silent in the classroom. Similarly, some children might talk freely to people they know very well but not want to talk in front of relative strangers. Quiet children may be very talkative with younger children or children of the same gender but silent in the presence of older people or people of the opposite gender.

Based on my research and ongoing observations of children in school (and adult learners in a university) I have concluded that empowering quiet withdrawn learners essentially involves the following strategies. All of these strategies can be carried out by competent teaching assistants. Indeed, as identified above, the role of the teaching assistant may make them best placed to support the learning of quiet children by:

- emphasising the value of talk and making it the medium for learning rather than the precursor to the 'real' work of writing;
- rejecting whole class teacher-directed talk in favour of small group child-centred talk;
- identifying the rules of discussion and making them explicit to the pupils;
- increasing feelings of security by establishing friendship groups or 'talk partners' and using them as the basis for all initial discussions;
- providing activities which encouraged collaboration;
- allowing pupils opportunities to consider what they wanted to say before calling on them to speak in front of large groups;

- working with the pupils to devise ways of assessing talk and providing opportunities for pupils to reflect on what makes for effective talk.

In short, empowering quiet children involves recognising the importance of talk for learning and adopting collaborative small group learning strategies. Teaching assistants and learning support staff are often well placed to 'hear the silence' and can often play a crucial role in identifying and supporting children who may be reluctant to talk in school.

References

Collins, J. (1994) 'The Silent Minority: Developing Talk in the Primary Classroom', unpublished PhD thesis, Sheffield University.

Collins, J. (1996) *The Quiet Child*. London: Cassell.

Lee, C. (2011) *The Complete Guide to Behaviour for Teaching Assistants and Support Staff* London: Sage.

Chapter 21

Understanding eating disorders

Royal College of Psychiatrists

Most children enjoy eating and move through childhood and adolescence with very few difficulties. However, a few develop eating disorders which can give rise to considerable concern at home and in school. This chapter has been written for parents and schools by the Royal College of Psychiatrists. It reviews the signs, effects and causes of eating disorders and highlights when it may be necessary to seek professional help.

What are eating disorders?

Worries about weight, shape and eating are common, especially among teenage girls. Being very overweight or obese can cause a lot of problems, particularly with health. Quite often, someone who is overweight can lose weight simply by eating more healthily. It sounds easy, but they may need help to find a way of doing this.

A lot of young people, many of whom are not overweight in the first place, want to be thinner. They often try to lose weight by dieting or skipping meals. For some, worries about weight become an obsession. This can turn into a serious eating disorder. This article is about the most common eating disorders – anorexia nervosa and bulimia nervosa.

- Someone with anorexia nervosa worries all the time about being fat (even if they are skinny) and eats very little. They lose a lot of weight and, if they are female, their periods stop.
- Someone with bulimia nervosa also worries a lot about weight. They alternate between eating next to nothing and then having binges when

Source: Royal College of Psychiatrists (2004) *Eating Disorders in Young People: Factsheet for Parents and Teachers* (London: Royal College of Psychiatrists).

they gorge themselves. They vomit or take laxatives to control their weight.

Both of these eating disorders are more common in girls, but do occur in boys.

What are the signs of anorexia or bulimia

- weight loss or unusual weight changes
- in girls, periods being irregular or stopping
- missing meals, eating very little and avoiding 'fattening' foods
- avoiding eating in public, secret eating
- large amounts of food disappearing from the cupboards
- believing they are fat when underweight
- exercising excessively
- becoming preoccupied with food, cooking for other people
- going to the bathroom or toilet immediately after meals
- using laxatives and vomiting to control weight.

It may be difficult for parents or teachers to tell the difference between ordinary teenage dieting and a more serious problem. If you are concerned about your child's weight and how they are eating, consult your family doctor.

What effects can eating disorders have?

- tiredness and difficulty with normal activities
- damage to health, including stunting of growth and damage to bones and internal organs
- in girls, loss of periods and risk of infertility
- anxiety, depression, obsessive behaviour or perfectionism
- poor concentration, missing school, college or work
- lack of confidence, withdrawal from friends
- dependency or over-involvement with parents, instead of developing independence.

It is important to remember that, if allowed to continue unchecked, both anorexia and bulimia can be life-threatening conditions. Over time, they are harder to treat and the effects become more serious.

What causes eating disorders?

Eating disorders are caused by a number of different things:

- Worry or stress may lead to comfort eating. This may cause worries about getting fat.
- Dieting and missing meals lead to craving for food, loss of control and over-eating.
- Anorexia or bulimia can develop as a complication of more extreme dieting, perhaps triggered by an upsetting event, such as family breakdown, death or separation in the family, bullying at school or abuse.
- More ordinary events, such as the loss of a friend, a teasing remark or school exams, may also be the trigger in a vulnerable person.
- Sometimes, anorexia and bulimia may be a way of trying to feel in control if life feels stressful.

Some people are more at risk than others. Risk factors include being female, being previously overweight and lacking self-esteem. Sensitive or anxious individuals who are having difficulty becoming independent are also more at risk. The families of young people with eating disorders often find change or conflict particularly difficult and may be unusually close or over-protective.

If you think a young person may be developing an eating disorder, don't be afraid to ask them if they are worried about themselves. Some young people will not want you to interfere.

These simple suggestions are useful to help young people to maintain a healthy weight and avoid eating disorders:

- eat regular meals – breakfast, lunch and dinner
- try to eat a 'balanced' diet – one that contains all the types of food your body needs
- include carbohydrate foods such as bread, rice, pasta or cereals with every meal
- do not miss meals – long gaps encourage overeating
- avoid sugary or high-fat snacks (try eating a banana instead of a bar of chocolate)
- take regular exercise
- try not to be influenced by other people skipping meals or commenting on weight.

When professional help is needed

When eating problems make family meals stressful, it is important to seek professional advice. Your general practitioner will be able to advise you about what specialist help is available locally and will be able to arrange a referral. Working with the family is an important part of treatment.

If the eating disorder causes physical ill health it is essential to get medical help quickly. If the young person receives help from a specialist early on, admission to hospital is unlikely. If untreated, there is a risk of infertility, thin bones (osteoporosis), stunted growth and even death.

Sources of further information

The Eating Disorders Association provides information and advice. Youthline 0845 634 7650; Helpline 0845 634 1414; www.edauk.com. The YoungMinds Parent Information Service provides information and advice on child mental health issues. 102–108 Clerkenwell Road, London EClM 5SA. Telephone 0808 802 5544; www.youngminds.org.uk/ The Royal College of Psychiatrists' *Mental Health and Growing Up* series contains 36 factsheets on a range of common mental health problems. They can be downloaded from www.rcpsych.ac.uk.

Chapter 22

Gypsies and Travellers

Gwynedd Lloyd and Gillean McCluskey

In this chapter Gillean McCluskey, lecturer, and Gwynedd Lloyd, honorary lecturer, both from Edinburgh University, provide background information to the groups of Travellers currently living in Britain today, and consider what people think and say about them. They suggest that Traveller children are at risk of name calling and bullying at school as there is a widespread lack of understanding about their lifestyle and culture.

In this chapter we will look at some of the things that people often say or think about Gypsies and Travellers in this country. We will talk about some of the experiences that Gypsy and Traveller children have in school so that you can think about how their educational opportunities could be improved.

There are several different groups of Travellers living in Britain at the moment, and sometimes they call themselves different names, which can be confusing for settled people trying to understand. Gypsy Travellers in England and Wales are sometimes called Romanies or 'Romany chals'. In Scotland sometimes they are called Gypsy Travellers, Tinkers or 'Nawkens' or 'Nachins'. Irish Gypsy Travellers are also sometimes called Tinkers. Some of these words, like Gypsy or Tinker, may be used with pride by Travellers but can also be used as term of abuse by settled people.

All these groups have been in this country for generations. They are partly descended from some people who probably left India beginning hundreds of years ago and travelled through Asia and Europe. As they went they interacted with and sometimes settled for work or married the people who lived in the countries they passed through. The language known as Romani can be traced back along this route. Many of these Travellers

Source: A revised version of Lloyd, G. and McCluskey G. (2004) 'Gypsies and travellers', commissioned by The Open University for *Primary Teaching Assistants: Learners and Learning* (London: Routledge). Reprinted by permission of The Open University and Taylor & Francis Ltd.

settled and formed communities in these countries. In Europe they are now usually referred to as Roma, although in France they are known as Tsiganes and in Germany Sinti. The Roma communities in Europe were persecuted in many places over the centuries, culminating with their near destruction in the Holocaust, where probably around a million or more Gypsies were subjected to medical research and killed in the concentration camps.

In Britain groups of Romanies arrived over several centuries, meeting and mixing with groups of other Travellers on the roads. Although it is very difficult to get accurate figures some estimates suggest that there are around 25,000 to 30,000 Gypsies and Travellers in Britain today. The language of Gypsy Travellers in the different parts of the UK includes Romani words as well as words that reflect the cultures of the part of the country they have travelled in. For example Scottish 'cant' includes Gaelic words.

Other Gypsy groups in Britain include European Roma, many from Eastern Europe where since the Second World War they were often subject to forced settlement and where children were disproportionately educated in special schools. In recent years there has been a big increase in prejudice and violence in some European countries towards Roma.

Many people in Britain have strong, often negative, views about Gypsies and Travellers, sometimes based on direct experience with a few Travellers but often on folk tales, popular stories, myths or stereotypes about Gypsies. In the section of the chapter that follows we explore some views that are often expressed both by ordinary people and by professionals.

Gypsies in Britain aren't real Gypsies

Recent thinking in the field of race relations makes it clear that 'race' is a political rather than a biological term and that indeed it is racist to imply predictable personal qualities on the basis of some assumed biological basis. We all have ethnicity which means that we belong to communities with shared values and cultures. For most settled people this means that they may derive their habits of life and values from a diverse range of sources. Gypsy Travellers are still small groups with shared ethnicity, with clear historical status and traditions that they wish to protect and this recognition does not depend on discredited notions of racial purity. They, like everyone else, will also have different views and practices according to other factors such as age, gender and personal preference. Shared ethnicity does not mean that everyone is the same but that they agree on some important aspects of life style and values.

Gypsies live in caravans

Some British Gypsy Travellers live in caravans and still travel. However there has been a big reduction in the places where they can camp, so some find it difficult to travel. Some live in caravans all year round on permanent sites run by local authorities. Others live sometimes in houses and travel seasonally. Some live permanently in houses but still feel strongly part of the Traveller culture and community. Some live in houses on housing estates where they hide their Traveller identity out of fear of hostility from their neighbours.

Gypsies steal

Many people over the centuries grew up with stories of Gypsies stealing babies. There is still a widespread belief that Gypsies steal. This is very offensive to most Gypsies and Travellers who abide by the law. Many British Traveller families belong to recent Christian church movements and have clear moral views. Gypsy and Traveller communities are characterised by a strong commitment to the extended family and families often maintain much greater control over their adolescent children than in the settled community. Of course there may be a minority within Traveller communities who commit crimes as there are within settled communities, but we do not label all settled communities as criminal.

Gypsies don't want their children to be educated

Traveller communities often have rich oral histories. Scottish Travellers, for example, have a long history of music and storytelling. Most Traveller families today recognise the importance of literacy and numeracy; many wish their children to receive a full education in primary schools. However many Travellers attend primary school but drop out during secondary school years. Some parents are unhappy about the curriculum, which they see as irrelevant to their lifestyle and have anxieties about their children's safety in school (Wilkin, Derrington and Foster 2009). 'Many Traveller parents express anxieties about their children's moral, emotional and physical welfare in what they perceive to be a strange and hostile environment' (Derrington and Kendall 2004:4). Some local education authorities now provide some education out of school, for example on Traveller sites. However education support for Travellers is very patchy and

Traveller Support teachers sometimes feel overstretched and rather isolated (Derrington and Kendall 2004).

Gypsy children cause trouble in school

Research into the disciplinary exclusion of Gypsy Travellers from school found that often the exclusion occurred as a result of fighting or violence which stemmed from harassment and bullying of Travellers in school (Lloyd and Stead 2001). Racist name-calling and bullying is still clearly very common, permeating Travellers' experience at school (Archer and Francis 2007). Traveller families often say that schools fail to understand their lifestyle and culture. Ofsted (1999) in England argued that Gypsy Travellers were the group most at risk in the education system. Some schools are resistant to admitting Gypsies and Travellers.

So there is no evidence that Gypsies and Travellers are any more or less disruptive in school than other pupils. There is evidence that they are less likely to attend and that they may experience more difficulties both in their relationships with staff and pupils.

Conclusion

Many Gypsies and travellers in the UK experience major difficulties leading the kind of life they wish. They are more likely to suffer health problems and to die younger than the rest of the population. They are subject to regular prejudice and racial harassment. They find it difficult to access appropriate places to live. Many Travellers wish that their children could receive an education appropriate to their lives as part of Traveller communities and free from bullying. This is a challenge to our education system. You might like to think about how the system could be adapted to better respond to this.

References

Archer, L. and Francis, B. (2007) *Understanding Minority Ethnic Achievement in Schools.* Abingdon: Routledge.

Derrington, D. and Kendall, S. (2004) *Gypsy Traveller Students in Secondary Schools: Culture, Identity and Achievement* Stoke: Trentham.

Lloyd, G. and Stead, J. (2001) 'The Boys and Girls not calling me Names and the Teachers to Believe Me'. *Children and Society* 15 (5). 361–374.

Ofsted (1999) *Raising the Attainment of Minority Ethnic Pupils.* London: Ofsted.

Further reading

Wilkin, A., Derrington, C. and Foster, B. (2009) *Outcomes for Gypsy, Roma and Traveller Pupils: Literature Review.* RB077. London: Department for Children, Schools and Families.

DCSF (2008) *Raising the Achievement of Gypsy, Roma and Traveller pupils*, London: Department for Education and Skills.

SEED/STEP (2003) *Inclusive Educational Approaches for Gypsies and Travellers* Edinburgh: Learning and Teaching Scotland.

Kendrick, D. and Clark, C. (2002) *Moving On: The Gypsies and Travellers of Britain* Hatfield: University of Hertfordshire Press.

Chapter 23

Considering communication

Mary Stacey

In this chapter, Mary Stacey, an education consultant, looks at how important it is for staff to communicate openly and honestly with each other. As a trainer in assertive communication, she describes some of the issues people raise when attending her courses and suggests some approaches that can help. She recognises that we all have personal challenges to overcome if we are to communicate well with others.

Many teaching assistants get on well with the teachers they work with but this does not always mean that the communication between them is clear and effective. During a course I was running for teachers and teaching assistants, several teachers, particularly those who were much younger, said how hard they found it to ask teaching assistants to do things differently. The teaching assistants were surprised but agreed they could also find it hard to discuss difficult issues or ask for changes in classroom practice. Indeed, the more they liked the teacher, the harder some found this.

When asked what an assertive person is like, people often suggest that he or she radiates confidence and stays focused, getting what he or she wants and telling people clearly what to do. Certainly this describes someone who may be direct in the way he or she communicates but can be why assertiveness is often confused with aggressiveness. It misses out important factors: the importance of listening and respecting others as equals. It suggests that you can never be nervous or unconfident and must remain calm inside when putting a point of view across. But how many of us are confident all the time? Communicating assertively means expressing both negative and positive feelings clearly and directly without putting yourself or others down. There are strategies that help you do this but most important is to begin to understand yourself and your behaviour and realise

Source: Commissioned by The Open University for this volume.

that you may not be the only one finding it difficult to communicate. There are at least two people affecting the situation, and where and when the communication takes place can affect the outcome.

Learning to communicate assertively does not necessarily take away all the anxiety but it helps us to manage our feelings and to have a better understanding of how our own or others' behaviour affects the situation. Maria, for example, found it very difficult to communicate with her headteacher. Analysing why this was, she realised that most of their conversations took place in the head's office. As she knocked on the door, her memories of being a child at school came back. Thus, she entered feeling as if she were going to be told off. This feeling was affecting the way she responded and once she acknowledged this, she began to change her behaviour. She took some breaths before entering, began to concentrate more on what the headteacher was saying and to respond as an adult, asking questions when she was not clear, something she had never been able to do before. Despite the fact she still found the head a difficult person, she felt their communication improved and she felt much better about her role in their conversations.

The courses in assertive communication I have run have attracted people from all walks of life. I particularly like those where a range of educational personnel come together: governors, advisers, teaching assistants, teachers, administrative and other support staff; whatever their position, they are all interested in communicating more effectively. At the beginning of a course, there is always a sense of nervousness. What will happen? Will people be made to feel foolish? Some people have loads of qualifications and are high up in the hierarchy. That woman over there speaks so confidently. Surely a male deputy head doesn't need to come on this course? As I assure people, assertive communication is not about whether you are an extrovert, whether you have qualifications or how high up you are in the hierarchy. It is about developing clear and honest communication and improving your relationships with others. It is not something you learn on a day's course but involves lifelong learning.

Not long into the course, people are saying, 'I feel like that sometimes: I thought it was just me'. 'I'm OK when I talk to some people, but somehow, I lose all my confidence with others'. I have never yet come across anyone on a course who does not find some situation hard. As we have all had different experiences however, some people find a particular situation a challenge while others may find it easy. People may agree that some staff or parents are easier to talk to than others but have different ideas about what sort of people these are. Some have no difficulty talking in groups; others find this an ordeal. The specific situations may be different, but the reasons behind the difficulties are very similar. You may recognise some of these:

- the difficulty of managing nervousness, anxiety, or irritation;
- going off track when trying to express a point of view clearly;
- not wanting to upset someone, either because you like him or her or are in awe of him or her;
- wanting everyone to like you;
- questioning or making suggestions to someone who has more qualifications;
- feeling intimidated or stupid and getting flustered when talking;
- not wanting someone to disagree with you or say 'no'.

Assertiveness training shows people how to recognise different types of behaviour. It is not about judging the behaviour but demonstrating how the way we behave can affect the communication. We cannot change others' behaviour except by changing our own. Thus, when Maria began to behave as an adult leaving behind her childhood fears, the headteacher began to communicate with her as an adult.

When we behave passively, we avoid saying anything or communicate in such a way that others either do not hear us or don't take notice. Here are some examples of passive responses:

- I agree with you completely. I just thought we could do it another way.
- This is probably not very important but have you got a second?
- I know I'm only a teaching assistant but . . .

Notice the way these responses stop the communication or give mixed messages. For instance, if something is worth discussing, then it is important and will take longer than a second.

We may behave *manipulatively*, so others find it difficult to respond straightforwardly.

- You wouldn't mind if I go early today would you? I'm sure you don't need me with so many children away with chicken pox today.
- When I work in Bob's classroom, he always lets me do this.

It could be very hard for a new, young teacher to respond if Bob has been in the school for a long time and is a highly regarded teacher.

We may behave *aggressively* so as to control the situation and not allow others to respond.

- That won't work. We tried it lots of times before you came here.
- I don't see why I should do this. It's the teacher's job.

These kinds of responses do not encourage discussion. They may also lead to an aggressive response from the other person.

Staff need to discuss new ideas, improvements or difficulties and to be able to give 'constructive dissent' (Grint, 2005). When we behave *assertively*, we are open and honest but we also listen and respond to others in an equal relationship. We avoid putting them or ourselves down.

- I'm finding Ben's behaviour hard to manage. Could we arrange a time to talk about this?
- Jessie finds the work you planned for her very difficult. I suggest she has more practice in. . . . What do you think?

Behaving assertively means speaking up for yourself and giving others an opportunity to respond from their point of view. Using 'I' means you take responsibility for what you say.

During a course, I ask people to think about how they react and what they do in certain situations. Below are some examples. You may like to discuss these situations with someone else and see whether they respond in the same way as you and if not, why not.

- You find that you have not been given an important piece of information.
- People are discussing the children, parents, or other staff in a way that you do not like and find unprofessional.
- You don't understand what someone in a meeting is talking about.
- You ask someone you work with to do something and they take no notice.
- You believe there is a problem in the way you and another member of staff are working together. You need to discuss this with that person who is:

    1. in a more senior position
    2. a colleague who is a friend outside your workplace
    3. someone you have had difficulties with in the past

Take a moment to think about how you behave. Do you avoid situations? Do you blame others or moan to others? Do you find yourself behaving passively, manipulatively, aggressively, or assertively? You may find this depends on the situation. There is no right or wrong answer as we all find ourselves reacting in different ways depending on the circumstances.

Being assertive requires practice and it can take courage to say what we think straightforwardly and respectfully because of our fears or because we have got into the habit of behaving in a certain way. People may not do exactly what you want when you communicate more assertively, but if you become clearer in your communication they will probably begin to respect you, even if they do not necessarily agree with you, and you will begin to respect yourself more. You will also find that you are having more effective discussions as you share ideas.

You are likely to be more confident in some situations than others and understanding why will help you in your communication. The way you respond can depend on the following:

The nature of the situation

Do you find it easier to communicate one-to-one, in a group, in a formal or informal setting?

Strangely more formal settings can sometimes be easier forums for communicating than informal ones. For example, if staff meetings are run in a way that allows people to have their say, then the focus is on the business and avoids personal issues. People are encouraged to speak up and their ideas are listened to. There is, as one teacher described it, no need to 'battle to be heard' (Ofsted, 2009, p. 61).

Your pattern of behaviour

Have you got into the habit of behaving in a certain way? Are you clear about what your role is in the situation? Being clear about your role as teaching assistant and respecting this role will help you to speak up professionally. If you remember that the children are always at the centre of your discussions at school, then this will help you to focus on the issues you want to discuss.

The way others' behaviour affects us

During a course when we consider how we respond to others' behaviour, people are always surprised how passiveness often provokes irritation or even aggression. Some people may feel sorry for the person but, in any event, they are not seeing the person on an equal footing. It is frustrating when someone does not respond or always agrees. Grint (2005) suggests this is 'destructive consent' where nothing moves on or resentment grows.

People have different responses to aggression. It can be frightening and some people find themselves retreating into passiveness while others think about how to get their own back later. Others say they respond by becoming aggressive; again this stops any sort of communication because no-one listens.

Your feelings

For many, feelings such as nervousness, lack of confidence, frustration get in the way so that they find it difficult to concentrate on what they want to say. Although you may think you are the only one who feels like this, these are common and natural feelings. By acknowledging your feelings and not blaming yourself for having them you begin to manage them. For instance, you may say to yourself 'I know I'm going to be nervous but I would like to say it clearly so I'll focus on what I want to say rather than the fact that my hand will probably shake'. Or, 'I know I shall be so frustrated having to say this again and I'm likely to get quite aggressive so I'll think about what I want to say before I say it.' Much communication gets dispersed because it is muddled or not clear. So thinking about what you want to say and who is the right person to speak to is important. It may feel like a risk to speak up and some people find it helpful to imagine putting on a 'professional hat' beforehand.

A key skill is to be specific. You are not trying to win a debate, you are trying to communicate so try and be clear in your mind what you want to say. This can be easier said than done. Halvinder, for example, who managed the Breakfast Club was increasingly annoyed by another teaching assistant who constantly chatted and ignored the children. What she wanted to say was 'I would like you to talk to the children not to me', which sounds quite simple but that was hard for her because the teaching assistant was a very kind person and had worked in the school for a long time. Halvinder's relief when she actually did say it was enormous and although she had to remind the teaching assistant again later, this was easier because she believed in herself and the role she was in. You often have to repeat yourself because although you may have been thinking about what you want to say for a long time, the other person will not be prepared; it could come as a surprise or go over his or her head. Repeating what you have to say can help them and yourself to recognise that what you have to say is important.

If you have something important to communicate, preparing yourself beforehand helps. Here are some questions to think about:

1. What is the message that you want to get across? Try to be precise about this. When you are clear, how can you be specific?
2. Identify the ingredients in the situation that inhibit or help you (e.g., the people, never having said anything before, previous responses).
3. What negative messages are you giving yourself? (e.g. 'I'll look foolish. I'm sure they won't agree. She's going to be very upset).
4. How can you reverse this negative talk (e.g. 'the worst that could happen to me is . . .' 'it will grow into a big issues if I don't do anything about it').
5. Consider how you will feel: nervous, angry, resentful.
6. Now you have recognised your feelings, think how you can manage these so they don't get in the way of the communication. Managing is different from controlling. Here are some suggestions to help you.

   (a) Notice and acknowledge the feelings and recognise you may shake or blush then concentrate on what you have to say.
   (b) If appropriate, acknowledge verbally to others that you feel like this. 'I feel anxious . . .' 'I feel upset . . .' then concentrate on what you have to say. By using 'I', you show you are talking from your own point of view.
   (c) You may need to physically release these feelings afterwards by taking some deep breaths and relaxing or walking somewhere.

7. Think about what would be a satisfactory or realistic outcome for you:

   (a) You feel that the person has heard you even if he or she does not immediately act on it.
   (b) You have a discussion.
   (c) You both agree to do something about it.

   Just hearing yourself say it may be enough.
8. Think about how you will respond if others ask questions or do not immediately take on your suggestion?
9. If you are not totally successful this time in your communication, how will you learn from it?
10. If you are successful in your communication, how will you learn from it?

I have only touched on a few issues on how to communicate assertively and as I have said, it is not something that is learnt overnight. Sometimes when people have been on a course they say they become self-conscious; they forget the importance of listening as they think about what they want to say. In their anxiety to be heard, they find themselves being aggressive rather than assertive. Thus beginning to practise in situations that feel relatively easy will help you to develop your communication skills. When you give suggestions or are involved in discussions, try and think beforehand about the best way of communicating but also listen to what others have to say. Being clear about your role as teaching assistant and how you can support and contribute to the children's learning will help you in the first instance. Then, begin observing yourself, like Maria with her headteacher, and consider how you generally respond to people. Later, reflecting on how you handled a situation will help you to understand your own and others' behaviour without blaming yourself if the communication was not entirely successful and with satisfaction if it was.

After attending a course, Patsy thought about how she usually responded and practised being more assertive in her communication. She found it made a big difference:

'. . . it is not about acting; it is about believing in myself. I have learnt to put across my point of view though I still find it very difficult with some people. I am much more confident in speaking up now. Things that I thought were silly to worry about, I realise can grow into enormous issues. It is better to bring these into the open than leave them to fester. I am quite amazed at the way people treat me differently and I feel so much better about myself and am really enjoying my work with the children now. It's had a knock-on affect on my life outside too because I am so much happier.'

(Stacey, 2009. p. 47)

References

Grint, K. (2005) Public Opinion. The Times, 8 March, http://business.timesonline. co.uk/tol/business/industry_sectors/public_sector/article420933.ece

Ofsted (2009) *Twelve Outstanding Special Schools. Excelling through Inclusion.* Ofsted, http:// www.ofsted.gov.uk/Ofsted-home/Twelve-outstanding-special-schools-Excelling-through-inclusion

Stacey, M. (2009) *Teamwork and Collaboration in Early Years Settings.* Exeter: Learning Matters.

Chapter 24

Tackling bullying

Christine Oliver and Mano Candappa

> Children can help us towards a better understanding of the causes and the consequences of bullying. Christine Oliver and Mano Candappa from the Thomas Coram Research Unit, London, report on some of the findings of a study that asked children about their experiences of bullying and school responses to it.

Our research study involved twelve schools, six primary and six secondary, and we focused on the views and experiences of pupils from Years 5 and 8, respectively.

What is bullying?

In focus groups and in the questionnaire survey, pupils provided clear and comprehensive definitions of bullying. Their understanding of bullying was that it could include verbal and physical abuse, theft, threatening behaviour, and coercion. Bullying was also understood as behaviour intended to cause distress or harm. Pupils identified a broad spectrum of behaviours of varying severity that could be encompassed within a definition of bullying and the negative impact bullying could have on pupils' sense of well-being and personal safety. Their descriptions of bullying represented a narrative of vulnerability, inequality and abuse within a complex web of power relations between pupils. Vulnerability to bullying was described as the result of personal and individual characteristics, such as physical size or appearance, or the result of more structured inequalities (such as racism, sexism or homophobia). Typically, definitions of bullying included some or all of the following elements:

Source: Oliver, C. and Candappa, M. (2003) *Tackling Bullying – Listening to the Views of Children and Young People*, Summary Report RB400, pp. 5–11, HMSO/Department for Education and Skills.

Bullying is when someone picks on someone else because they are different—their race, height, weight, or looks. It's about prejudice and discrimination and when someone gets hurt physically or mentally, or when someone is not respected.

(Girl, Year 8)

Bullying is when people force others, usually smaller people, to do what they want.

(Boy, Year 5)

Bullying is intentionally causing physical or mental damage to others, like attacking them for no reason frequently, teasing them frequently, or even sexually, such as rape.

(Girl, Year 8)

How big a problem is bullying?

- Just over half of both primary (51%) and secondary school pupils (54%) thought that bullying was 'a big problem' or 'quite a problem' in their school.
- Just over half (51%) of Year 5 pupils reported that they had been bullied during the term, compared with just over a quarter (28%) of Year 8 pupils. Considerable variation was reported in the level of bullying between schools.
- Girls were almost as likely as boys to have been bullied in both age groups. In Year 8, a higher proportion of Black and Asian pupils (33%) reported that they had been bullied this term, compared with pupils of other ethnic groups (30%) or white pupils (26%).

What are the most common forms of bullying?

Name-calling was reported as the most prevalent form of bullying for pupils in Years 5 and 8. Bullying involving physical aggression was less common, but nevertheless was reported by a substantial proportion of pupils in both age groups. Behaviour resulting in social isolation (such as gossip, and the spreading of rumours) was also common for pupils in both years, but particularly for pupils in Year 5.

A minority of pupils reported sexist, racist and anti-gay abuse, although racist and sexist name-calling was more prevalent among primary than secondary school pupils: a fifth of pupils in Year 5 reported that they had been called racist names, compared with 6% of pupils in Year 8. 11% of pupils reported that they had been called anti-gay names. However, these forms of bullying were more prevalent in some schools than others.

Contrary to some research on gender and bullying, boys and girls in this study reported similar levels of physical bullying, name-calling, and social ostracism, although some forms of physical bullying were higher for boys in Year 8. Girls also reported a higher level of sexualised bullying than boys: 5% of pupils in Year 8 (mostly girls) reported that they had experienced unwanted sexual touching.

Although the numbers are small, it would appear that bullying by electronic communication is emerging as a new form of bullying: 4% of pupils in Year 8 reported that they had received nasty text messages and 2% had received nasty e-mail messages.

Responding to bullying

How good is your school at dealing with bullying?

According to pupils' memories and perceptions, the findings indicated that participating schools were more likely to approach bullying by introducing one-off initiatives, such as discussing the topic during assembly or lesson time, than by more targeted and on-going approaches, such as appointing anti-bullying counsellors or teachers designated with specific anti-bullying responsibilities.

In the questionnaire survey, a majority of pupils (over 60%) expressed positive views about their school's attempts to deal with bullying. However, secondary school pupils were less likely to give their school a glowing report: over a third of primary school pupils (36%) thought that their school was 'very good' at dealing with bullying, compared with just over 1 in 10 of secondary school students (12%).

Key elements in pupils' assessment of their school's effectiveness concerned the willingness of teachers to listen, to express empathy, and to act appropriately on the suggestions of pupils.

> The children suggest ways the playground could be made better and teachers and the Head, listen. They take notice. They change things.
>
> (Girl, Year 5)

> At this school it is OK. We talk about it at assembly and at the school council.
>
> (Boy, Year 8)

Conversely, schools that had a poor reputation appeared to be less likely to listen to pupils, and to take their complaints seriously or to take firm action:

> I don't think the school handles it very well. They say leave it for now, but if it happens again, come back. But when we do that and they say they are working on it, it never gets solved.
>
> (Boy, Year 8)

Setting a good example

With regard to the extent to which teachers might limit bullying behaviour by modeling pro-social behaviour, the majority of pupils of both age groups thought that teachers set a good example for how pupils should behave. However, pupils' views varied widely between schools. For example, in one primary school, 86% of pupils reported that teachers 'always' set a good example, compared with only 48% of pupils in a second primary school.

What are the most effective responses to bullying?

In exploring pupils' own responses in dealing with bullying, the findings indicated that the three most helpful factors in preventing, or helping pupils to deal with, bullying were friendships, avoidance strategies, and learning to 'stand up for yourself'. This section of the report discusses the costs and benefits of 'standing up for yourself', telling friends, telling teachers, telling parents and telling agencies outside the school.

Standing up for yourself

Being assertive

For pupils in Year 5, more confidence was expressed in the potential of 'talking back' and other, more assertive forms of direct verbal communication with the bully, than pupils in Year 8. Approximately a quarter of pupils in Year 5 thought that communicating verbally in an assertive way with the bully would 'always' or 'usually' work. Less than 10% of pupils in Year 8 shared this view.

Hitting back

Older pupils were more likely to believe that physical retaliation had a better chance of success: 23% of secondary school pupils and 15% of primary school pupils thought that 'hitting back' would 'always' or 'usually' work to stop bullying. Indeed, almost a third (31%) of pupils in Year 8 thought that learning a martial art might help to reduce the risk of bullying, although this was identified as a more long term strategy. However, in relation to gender, girls were less likely to support physical retaliation as an appropriate strategy. Black and Asian pupils expressed a higher degree of confidence in the positive potential of each of the strategies identified than white pupils, or pupils of other ethnic groups.

> You could learn self-defence, or Karate, but that might take some time.
>
> (Boy, Year 8)

> My mum says two wrongs don't make a right, but they bullied me so much my Mum said 'just fight back'.
>
> (Boy, Year 8)

> It might not work, because the person doing the hitting back might get into trouble.
>
> (Girl, Year 5)

Ignoring the bully

A higher proportion of pupils in Year 5 were optimistic about the potential effectiveness of ignoring the bully: 38% thought that such a strategy would 'always' or 'usually' work, compared with only 14% of pupils in Year 8. A number of potential risks and benefits were associated with this strategy:

> They bully you to get you annoyed. So if you show you're not annoyed, it will stop.
>
> (Girl, Year 5)

> It might not work because if you ignore them, the bully might do something worse.
>
> (Boy, Year 5)

Telling friends

A large majority of pupils in Years 5 (68%) and 8 (71%) reported that they would find it easy to talk to a friend if they were being bullied, although younger pupils were more likely to talk to their mothers. This suggests that anti-bullying initiatives that take friendship networks into account are likely to be of considerable value to pupils.

Having a group of friends was identified as an important protective factor in preventing, and helping pupils to cope with, bullying. Unlike teachers and other adults, friends were in a position to witness bullying in and outside school, and to provide support when needed.

> It's more comfortable talking to them. They're with you when you get picked on, so they know about it.
>
> (Boy, Year 8)

> They might go up to them and say 'why are you picking on X?' Because a friend is a friend. You want them to stick up for you, and they get involved.
>
> (Girl, Year 8)

However, the main risk of involving a friend was that they might also start to be bullied.

> Sometimes, if they know you're picked on, it might happen to them too.
>
> (Boy, Year 5)

Telling teachers

Just over half (51%) of pupils in Year 5, but less than a third (31%) of pupils in Year 8, reported that they would find it easy to speak to a teacher about bullying. Telling teachers was associated with a wide range of risks, particularly in relation to possible breaches of confidentiality, failure to act on reported incidents of bullying, and an inability to protect pupils from retaliatory behaviour on the part of perpetrators.

> Verbal bullying isn't taken seriously by teachers. If you have some bruises, they might take some notice.
>
> (Girl, Year 8)

> If you tell your tutor, they have to tell someone else, and then they tell someone else. It's like Chinese whispers.
>
> (Boy, Year 8)

> You get called a grass and a dobber, and you get beaten up.
>
> (Boy, Year 5)

On the other hand, some pupils reported that telling teachers could help to stop the bullying or that, armed with relevant information, teachers might be less likely to punish a pupil should they decide to take matters into their own hands.

> If you hit someone, and the teacher knows you've been bullied, they take that into consideration. If you don't tell, they might think you've hit someone for no reason.
>
> (Boy, Year 8)

Are some teachers better at dealing with bullying than others?

Most pupils could identify a teacher that they would be most likely to speak to if they were being bullied. Such teachers were reported by pupils to be demonstrably better at listening to pupils, more prepared to take pupils seriously, ready to take appropriate action (but not without the consent of the victim), and to be 'firm but fair'.

> She (the teacher) is strict. People say strict teachers are bad but really, strict teachers are better at sorting it out.
>
> (Boy, Year 8)

> Our teacher is good . . . she bothers to find out what really happened. She takes you seriously. She sorts it out with the Head, or she will tell the parents.
>
> (Girl, Year 8)

Telling parents

Parents were identified as offering a potentially valuable source of help, advice and moral support. In particular, pupils reported that parents who listened to them and took their experiences seriously, helped them to cope with bullying. However, pupils also reported that telling parents could make matters worse (for example, by taking inappropriate or unilateral action, or by disagreeing about the best course of action).

> Mums, dads, mates, can give advice.
>
> (Boy, Year 5)

> I know that if I tell my parents, they'll believe me. There would be no question. And I know that if I wanted them to come to the school, they would.
>
> (Boy, Year 8)

The risk of not being believed by a parent was identified as potentially very hurtful. Some were also concerned that, by talking about bullying, they might start a family argument. Other pupils also said that they would not tell a parent if they were being bullied, because they would not want to worry them or put them under pressure.

> I wouldn't tell my mum. She'd skin them.
>
> (Girl, Year 5)

> Your mum and dad might disagree about what to do, and then start arguing, and then they say it's your fault. Telling your parents is a serious step. They might take action you don't want.
>
> (Boy, Year 8)

Seeking outside help

Pupils were asked if they would seek outside help to deal with bullying, such as talking to the police or a confidential telephone helpline. Pupils were also asked if there were any other sources of help they had found useful.

ChildLine

Pupils were divided about whether they would contact a telephone helpline, such as ChildLine. Younger pupils (39%) were considerably more likely to consider such an option than pupils in Year 8 (14%). Some pupils expressed the view that ChildLine might not know about the local context, and might therefore not be in a position to give constructive advice.

The police

Only a small minority of pupils would consider talking to the police about bullying, although younger pupils (33%) were more likely than older pupils (11%) to consider such action. Nevertheless, in a small number of cases, pupils reported that they had been encouraged by their teachers to contact the police for help. A number of risks and benefits were associated with contacting the police:

> You might have to go to court.
>
> (Girl, Year 8)

> I'd tell PC Smith. She would probably talk to them, and talk to their parents.
>
> (Girl, Year 8)

Telling a counsellor

In focus group discussions, a minority of pupils suggested that external counselling organisations might assist pupils to deal with bullying. In one focus group, pupils identified Child and Mental Health Services (CAMHS) as a proven and effective source of help, while others mentioned counsellors and advice agencies targeted at children and young people. In another focus group, pupils reported that they were aware that the NSPCC might be able to help with bullying. However, others expressed surprise at this suggestion, as they thought that the NSPCC only dealt with adults who were cruel to children.

> A cousin of mine was being bullied and had a black eye and things They told the NSPCC and it worked. I don't know what they did.
>
> (Boy, Year 5)

Confidential sources of support were also valued for enabling pupils to control the pace of disclosure. Equally important, no risks were associated with this course of action. Further, in the context of pupils' concerns about breaches of confidentiality on the part of teachers and parents, the wider availability of confidential sources of help and advice may prove a valuable anti-bullying strategy.

> If you talk to a counsellor, it's someone you don't know. They don't know your life story and they don't tell no one nothing, unless you're

going to harm yourself or someone else. So it's completely confidential. They realise how you're feeling and it's a lot easier than talking to a parent or a teacher.

(Girl, Year 8)

Conclusions

The findings of this research project indicated that, when thinking about how to respond to bullying, children and young people engage in a complex process of risk assessment. Pupils identified a number of different ways of tackling bullying and explored the anticipated advantages and disadvantages of each option. No tidy solutions or easy remedies were identified. Consequently, pupils' discussions about 'what works' in tackling bullying might more accurately be re-framed as 'what might work'.

Although it is common for adults to encourage pupils to report bullying, pupils of both age groups expressed a preference for 'sorting it out' and 'standing up for themselves'. Alternative strategies necessarily involve pupils in the dilemmas and consequences associated with 'telling'. It appears that, even if pupils decide to 'tell' an adult, they are very aware of the gap between how teachers and parents should respond to bullying, and how they actually respond. A pupil in Year 5 had this insight to offer on 'telling' and its aftermath:

> If the dinner ladies don't help you, tell your teacher. If the teacher doesn't help you, tell your mum. Then your mum will tell the headmistress. Then the headmistress will go and tell the parents of the bully. And the parents of the bully (pause) . . . well, some of the parents don't care and just say 'don't do it again'.

(Boy, Year 5)

In listening to children and young people talk about bullying, it is clear that they receive a number of mixed messages from adults (teachers and parents). These mixed messages might be summarised as follows:

- Adults (teachers and parents) claimed that bullying is a serious or 'bad' thing, but pupils' experience is that bullying is often dismissed as 'child's play'.
- Pupils are encouraged to report incidents of bullying, but when they do, pupils frequently felt that they are not listened to or believed.

- Schools encouraged pupils to report bullying but are also perceived by pupils as unable to protect pupils from retaliatory action, particularly after school hours.
- Teaching involves working and forming relationships with pupils, yet often teachers were perceived as taking complaints made by parents more seriously than complaints made by pupils.
- Adults (teachers and parents) claimed that they could be trusted, but telling an adult about bullying was perceived as involving a risk that they would break promises of confidentiality.
- Adults often told pupils not to fight back, but pupils (particularly in Year 8) found that fighting back works sometimes.

These findings suggest that anti-bullying policies might be expected to have limited effect if they fail to take into account the realities of the child's social world. For this reason, it would seem appropriate for schools to consider more 'bottom up' (rather than 'top down') responses to bullying, that attempt to involve pupils in decision-making at an individual and school-wide level.

It is also clear that encouraging a child 'to tell' requires an adult willingness to listen. Often, pupils expressed a wish simply to speak to an adult in confidence, in order to unburden themselves, get advice and support, and to consider their options. Importantly, there were hardly any disadvantages and some considerable benefits associated with such a course of action, particularly in relation to pupils' emotional well-being.

Nevertheless, the findings indicate that anti-bullying policies provide a useful starting point for tackling bullying. Indeed, some pupils highlighted different approaches that were described as working at least some of the time (e.g. school councils, peer group initiatives, discussing bullying regularly during assemblies, and during class time). Pupils also recommended that anti-bullying initiatives should be sustained over the long term.

Chapter 25

Anti-cyber bullying policy

East Herrington Primary School

Many schools now recognise that digital media can be used by some children for malevolent purposes. East Herrington Primary School is a large mixed school for children aged 4–11 years. It is situated in the village of East Herrington on the southern outskirts of Sunderland city close to the A19. The school was built in 1964 and currently has 476 pupils with 60 in the nursery. Its website contains a succinct yet informative anti-cyber bullying policy which is made available to children, staff, parents and governors. We reproduce it here.

This school believes that all people in our community have the right to teach and learn in a supportive, caring and safe environment without fear of being bullied. We believe that every individual in school has a duty to report an incident of bullying whether it happens to themselves or another person.

What is cyber-bullying?

There are many types of cyber-bullying. Although there may be some of which we are unaware, here are the more common.

1. Text messages – that are threatening or cause discomfort – also included here is 'Blue-jacking' (the sending of anonymous text messages over short distances using 'Bluetooth' wireless technology.
2. Picture/video-clips via mobile phone cameras – images sent to others to make the victim feel threatened or embarrassed.
3. Mobile phone calls – silent calls or abusive messages: or stealing the victim's phone and using it to harass others, to make them believe the victim is responsible.

Source: *Anti-cyber bullying policy* (East Herrington Primary School). This policy is reproduced by kind permission of East Herrington Primary School. The school in no way warrants that the policy is correct but has agreed to its reproduction as part of the larger work.

4. Emails – threatening or bullying emails, often sent using a pseudonym or someone else's name.
5. Chat room bullying – menacing or upsetting responses to children or young people when they are in a web-based chat room.
6. Instant messaging (IM) – unpleasant messages sent while children conduct real-time conversations online using MSM (Microsoft Messenger) or Yahoo Chat – although there are others.
7. Bullying via websites – use of defamatory blogs (web logs), personal websites and online personal "own web space" sites such as Bebo (which works by signing on in one's school, therefore making it easy to find a victim) and Myspace – although there are others.

At East Herrington Primary School, we take this bullying as seriously as all other types of bullying and, therefore, will deal with each situation individually. An episode may result in a simple verbal warning. It might result in a parental discussion. Clearly, more serious cases will result in further sanctions. Technology allows the user to bully anonymously from an unknown location, 24 hours a day 7 days a week. Cyber-bullying leaves no physical scars so it is, perhaps, less evident to a parent or teacher, but it is highly intrusive and the hurt it causes can be very severe. Young people are particularly adept at adapting a new technology, an area that can seem a closed world to adults. For example, the numerous acronyms used by young people in chat rooms and in text messages (POS – 'Parents Over Shoulder', TUL – 'Tell you Later') make it difficult for adults to recognise potential threats.

At East Herrington Primary School, pupils are taught to:

• understand how to use these technologies safely and know about the risks and consequences of misusing them;
• know what to do if they or someone they know are being cyber bullied;
• report any problems with cyber bullying. If they do have a problem, they can talk to the school, parents, the police, the mobile network (for phone) or the Internet Service Provider (ISP) to do something about it.

East Herrington School has:

1. an Acceptable Use Policy (AUP) that includes clear statements about e-communications;

2. information for parents on: E-communication standards and practices in schools, what to do if problems arise, what's being taught in the curriculum;

3. support for parents and pupils if cyber bullying occurs by: assessing the harm caused, identifying those involved, taking steps to repair harm and to prevent recurrence.

Information for pupils if you're being bullied by phone or the Internet:

-   Remember, bullying is never your fault. It can be stopped and it can be traced.
-   Don't ignore bullying, tell someone you trust, such as a teacher or parent or call an advice line.
-   Try to keep calm. If you are frightened, try to show it as little as possible.
-   Don't get angry, it will only make the person bullying you more likely to continue.
-   Don't give out your personal details online – if you're in a chat room, watch what you say about where you live, the school you go to, your email address etc. All these things can help someone who wants to harm you build up a picture about you.
-   Keep and save any bullying emails, text messages or images. Then you can show them to a parent or teacher as evidence.
-   If you can, make a note of the time and date bullying messages or images were sent, and note any details about the sender.
-   There's plenty of online advice on how to react to cyber bullying. For example, www.kidscape.org and www.wiredsafety.org have some useful tips.

Text/video messaging

You can easily stop receiving text messages for a while by turning off incoming messages for a couple of days. This might stop the person texting you by making them believe you've changed your phone number. If the bullying persists, you can change your phone number. Ask your mobile service provider about this. Don't reply to abusive or worrying text or video messages. Your mobile service provider will have a number for you to ring or text to report phone bullying. Visit their website for details. Don't delete messages from cyber bullies. You don't have to read them, but you should keep them as evidence. Text harassment is a crime. If they are simply annoying, tell a teacher, parent or carer. If they are threatening or malicious and they persist, report them to the police, taking with you all the messages you've received.

Phone calls

If you get an abusive or silent phone call, don't hang up immediately. Instead, put the phone down and walk away for a few minutes. Then hang up and turn your phone off.

Once they realise they can't get you rattled, callers usually get bored and stop bothering you.

1. Always tell someone else: a teacher, youth worker, parent or carer. Get them to support you and monitor what's going on.
2. Don't give out personal details such as your phone number to just anyone. Never leave your phone lying around. When you answer your phone, just say 'hello', not your name. If they ask you to confirm your phone number, ask what number they want and then tell them if they've got the right number or not. You can use your voicemail to vet your calls. A lot of mobiles display the caller's number. See if you recognise it. If you don't, let it divert to voicemail instead of answering.

Don't leave your name on your voicemail greeting. You could get an adult to record your greeting. Their voice might stop the caller ringing again. Almost all calls nowadays can be traced. If the problem continues think about changing your phone number. If you receive calls that scare or trouble you, make a note of the times and dates and report them to the police. If your mobile can record calls, take the recording too.

Emails

Never reply to unpleasant or unwanted emails ('flames') – the sender wants a response, so don't give them that satisfaction. Keep the emails as evidence and tell an adult about them. Ask an adult to contact the sender's Internet Service Provider (ISP) by writing abuse @ and then the host, e.g. abuse@ hotmail.com. Never reply to someone you don't know, even if there's an option to 'unsubscribe'. Replying simply confirms your email address as a real one.

Web bullying

If the bullying is on a website (e.g. Bebo) tell a teacher or parent, just as you would if the bullying were face-to-face – even if you don't actually know the bully's identity. Serious bullying should be reported to the police – for example threats of a physical or sexual nature. Your parent or teacher will help you do this.

Chat rooms and instant messaging

Never give out your name, address, phone number, school name or password on line. It's a good idea to use a nickname and don't give out photos of yourself. Don't accept emails or open files from people you don't know. Remember it might not just be people of your own age in a chat room. Stick to the public areas in chat rooms and get out if you feel uncomfortable. Tell your parents or carers if you feel uncomfortable or worried about anything that happens in a chat room. Think carefully about what you write: don't leave yourself open to bullying. Don't ever give out passwords to your mobile or email account.

Three steps to stay out of harm's way

1. Respect other people – online and off. Don't spread rumours about people or share their secrets, including their phone numbers and passwords.
2. If someone insults you online or by phone, stay calm – and ignore them.
3. 'Do as you would be done by'. Think how you would feel if you were bullied. You're responsible for your own behaviour – make sure you don't distress other people or cause them to be bullied by someone else.

Chapter 26

Boys don't cry

Pete Johnson

Pete Johnson has written a number of story books about bullying. In this chapter, he discusses reasons why boys may be particularly vulnerable as victims. He cites two reasons: firstly, their tendency to keep things bottled up; and secondly, the concern of being 'shamed up' within their peer group if they draw attention to their plight.

'But why can't boys tell if they're being bullied?' This was the question a teacher asked during a recent class discussion of my novel, *Traitor*. The boys all looked at each other before answering, then one said, quietly. 'It's just too shaming, Miss.'

Another added. 'If he'd been punched in the face he could say something: but not if someone had just been nasty to him.'

In *Traitor*, Tom is regularly intimidated and picked on by a gang on the way home from school. Yet, he cannot bring himself to tell anyone. The overwhelming majority of boys agreed they wouldn't either.

In my new book, *Avenger*, I've explored this theme further. What I've written about here is psychological bullying, or, as boys dub it, 'trying to get inside your head'.

Of course, the myth is that only girls go in for this sort of thing. Boys will settle all their disputes with a swift punch. But that really isn't true. Certainly the boys I interviewed while researching Avenger had many stories to tell me of 'mind games'. For instance, how stories are spread about you. Everything from saying you've got fleas, to making up nasty comments about your mum. Others told me of how they'd been deliberately excluded from playing football at lunchtime, or from a party, or from an outing with a group of mates.

Source: Johnson, P. (2004) 'Boys don't cry'. Copyright Guardian News & Media Ltd 2004.

We tend to think of girls' friendships as being emotionally charged, while boys' relationships with each other are much more casual. Again, that isn't really true. Boys do have a much keener sense of who their 'best mates' are than might be commonly supposed. And a number spoke of attempts to 'break up' a friendship by 'making up stuff that I'd never actually said'. This aroused especial passion with one boy declaring: 'I swear on my life I never rubbished my mates like he said I did.'

Then there is the silent treatment. This actually happened to me when I started at a new school. A small group of boys decided I was 'big-headed' and all the boys in my year 'sent me to Coventry'. Even boys I'd been quite friendly with had to join in. Each day this went on seemed to last for about five years. Yet, I didn't tell anyone. I just put on a mask and acted as if I wasn't the least bit bothered. But inside, I was seething with hurt and anger. So much has changed since I was at school. Yet, boys still feel they have to suffer in silence and cannot open up about emotional problems.

In *Avenger*, Gareth upsets the charismatic new-boy, Jake. He tells Gareth: 'This is war now' and sets about playing a series of vicious mind games on him. Nevertheless, his form teacher never notices any of it. As Gareth writes: 'It was all smuggled past her. But every day more invisible blows rained down on me. There was never any let-up.'

In the end Gareth barricades himself inside his bedroom. In a blaze of frustration he started pounding his fist against the wall as hard as he could. 'But my anger didn't subside. It grew stronger. It was like some great tornado, whirling and raging about inside me which just had to be released.'

Later he slips under the cover of his bed. 'All I wanted now was to live in this bed forever. My anger was at last ebbing away but I didn't feel calm and peaceful – just totally, totally defeated.' Or, as one boy put it: 'You just want to hide away in your bedroom and never come out again.'

A few boys I interviewed did have a close mate they could completely trust. But the most common person boys seemed able to confide in was a grandparent. In Avenger, Gareth's grandfather becomes his only confidant.

Each night Gareth tells his grandfather what has happened. Only his grandfather is dead. But Gareth still feels he is close-by and says: 'Please come back properly. I need to talk to you urgently. You're my only hope.'

I've already had some interesting discussions in schools about Gareth's feeling of total isolation. 'It's sad,' said one boy, 'that he thinks he can only talk to a ghost about what's happened.' We also talked about Jake and his behaviour. One boy comments: 'People don't act the way he does unless they're feeling bad themselves.'

The really great thing about stories is they enable us to make connections with the characters. And we discover we're not on our own and share much more than we realise.

Can stories also change the culture? I believe they can. And I'd like to think Avenger will play a part in challenging the view that boys — if they are to keep their cred — must act as if they're detached from all human emotion. As one boy wrote to me. 'The worst thing of all was not telling anyone how I felt. So the pain inside me just grew and grew.'

Chapter 27

Police in schools

Norma Powell with PC Dave

In recent years paraprofessional teams working in schools in the UK have widened dramatically. In the London Borough of Barnet, as well as many other areas of the country, the police service has taken on roles within these teams. Safer schools officers (SSOs) and police community support officers (PCSOs) work in close partnership with schools in the Borough to present a structured programme for children related to discipline and measures taken to maintain good behaviour. Norma Powell is an associate lecturer with The Open University. In this chapter she discusses conflict resolution and restorative justice with an SSO.

'PC Dave', a safer schools officer (SSO), told me about the programme that begins in Year 1 with teaching around personal safety and stranger awareness and that continues twice yearly until Year 6. By the end of Year 5 'yes and no' feelings are introduced to allow appropriate discussion of physical and sexual abuse and how a child can bring any worries to the attention of school staff or the police. PC Dave explained,

> An example of this would be that I would ask the children to shake hands with the child sitting next to them. This they do. I then suggest they give each other a hug and mostly they are happy to do this with some giggling! I say 'now give them a kiss' and the children dissolve into giggles and cries of 'eeugh'. This I suggest is how they can judge whether a request or touch is appropriate. In the simplest terms, 'If it doesn't feel comfortable for you then don't do it'.

Source: Commissioned by The Open University for this volume.

He continued:

> The programme also includes teaching on child safety, 999 emergency and 'rules, laws and punishments'. In Year 6 the final talk includes discussions around drugs, internet safety, offensive weapons and safer routes to places to which children walk.

I asked PC Dave what roles he felt the police play in primary schools and what he felt was the importance of police carrying out these roles rather than the traditional school team.

In primary and secondary schools, he said, officers are involved in a number of different roles and activities including playground and after school support, teaching programmes, solving actual crime and supporting victims of crime, mentoring, organising sporting activities, governing body positions and attendance at parent meetings and staff development sessions. Several police officers have taken up teaching assistant positions in schools after their retirement from the police force.

PC Dave further explained:

> From a police point of view, working in schools leads to longer term relationships with the police and breaks down barriers giving young children a positive view of the police which they can keep for life. It is the only chance that young people have to build up a long term positive relationship with an officer. I often meet children in the street and in secondary school who have quite a tough reputation but who greet me with a 'hi PC Dave.' Educational psychologists have stated that it is very important for positive police contact in a child's formative years. It is crucial to reinforce the link to the community. The Northern Ireland Peace Process started through police going into schools and breaking down barriers in children's thinking. School is the key future link to community – it's the one place you can go where you can change the future where you can access every demographic including private schools and religious schools. Parents can actively be involved too, thus changing thinking and effectively communicating a message. Community groups can be effective but are quite splintered. School contact is the most efficient way of progressing attitudes.
>
> Some schools have attempted to follow this programme but this has generally been unsuccessful as the material needs an informed expert. The police add their experience and a slightly different point of view. Officers can give students authentic examples and answer questions

from personal experience and can deal with unexpected items arising. Children often want to know what actually happens, for example, if someone is found with a knife and the police can explain this accurately.

PC Dave commented:

> Officers in school might spend time over breaks and lunch with the children and the staff and develop a wider relationship over time giving advice and providing an unbiased opinion. For example, I am involved in mentoring children in school schemes and am a governor in a primary school I work in.

I asked him what skills he thinks are important for school-based police officers.

He thought it was important for them to be approachable and be able to listen carefully. He highlighted the importance of officers using positive body language and having a calming influence on people. He mentioned that officers needed to be impartial and to be perceived to be impartial by children. He felt officers should be able to give advice to teachers, pupils, and their families; and he thought showing the ability to care and 'give some of yourself' as very appropriate.

Other important skills include the ability to be able to sensitively deal with any actual crime in school and working closely with school staff, children, and parents. This might involve considering all options along a continuum from restorative justice [whereby the offender(s) thinks of ways of putting things right] to friendly advice, to no further action, to possible arrest, which is very rare in primary schools, PC Dave was pleased to add.

He highlighted that officers must not make false promises and must give honest answers to questions. He also valued the ability to think out of the box and to solve problems in order to meet police regulations but also address the needs of a school. Some officers, he said, can find this difficult and get somewhat stuck in police procedure.

As a result of the success of the schools programme it became apparent that many school staff were keen to use the SSO in conflict resolution. School officers were seen as a way to repair relationships and resolve conflicts between children and between children and adults in schools. 'Restorative justice' is an increasingly popular method used by schools. It reconceptualises the way that conflicts have traditionally been dealt with.

How does conflict resolution work?

Restorative justice conferencing was first used in its current form in New Zealand and taken up by police officers in Australia. Thames police developed a 'restorative cautioning' experiment in the 1990s. Marshall (1999) credits Barnett (1977) for the first use of the term. The roots of restorative justice can be seen in many early cultures and is particularly evident in Maori and Native American traditional culture. It requires a community focus and it is important that the offender takes responsibility and feels some ignominy and remorse for his or her actions. This reaction is generally absent when punishments are imposed without restorative justice principles being taken into account.

As yet, there is little research available on the outcomes of restorative justice in schools. However, Marshall and Merry (1990) and Marshall (1999) produced research that shows the majority of victims of crime generally would like to meet with their offender and that of those who were offered the opportunity 80%–100% looked back on the experience as worthwhile. They also showed that the completion rates for reparation were 70%–100% rather than the 40%–60% completion in standard reparation. There are people who consider restorative justice as 'soft' as the reparation is agreed rather than imposed. However, with restorative justice there is a demand on the offender to own up, apologise personally, and take active responsibility for putting things right that is not generally seen in standard punishment systems.

In schools there are conflicts that arise in many different forms. There may be bullying, stealing, fights and arguments, a sense of unfairness, and an inability to continue in a working relationship with staff and other pupils. Where there is a conflict between people, traditionally, schools have punished the person seen to be the perpetrator. This can leave the conflict unresolved and the deeper issues untouched, meaning that the conflict is likely to reoccur. Interestingly, most victims in schools do not particularly want to see the offender punished. They just want the behaviour to stop and to feel that it has been addressed and repaired.

Although some individuals may have instinctively used a restorative style approach, the main approach, for many years, has been reprimand and retribution. Restorative justice puts repairing the damage to people and relationships above the need to blame and punish. Restorative justice will try to put all those involved in a position where they can discuss and resolve the conflict. Roger Graef (2000: 11) summarises it as:

Restorative justice means just what it says: restoring the balance of a situation disturbed by crime or conflict, and making good the harm caused to the individuals concerned.

PC Dave describes it:

As a means of bringing victims and offenders together and actually resolving the issues, moving forward instead of leaving things unresolved even after retributive punishments have taken place, alleviating the potential for re-ignition and continued victim dissatisfaction.

Restorative justice empowers the victims and offenders to work towards their own solutions. A question asked during a restorative justice conference to the offender is 'How will you repair the harm?' This is a fundamental difference as the offender is asked to acknowledge having caused harm and has to consider a way to put things right with the help of a facilitator. This is where Police staff come in to their own due to the confrontational nature of policing; but this allows for a much more creative solution strategy.

An example is where two pupils have had a fight. The pupil who started it apologised to the victim having understood that it was unacceptable to use violence, the other party also accepting that he was partly to blame for winding up the situation. Both parties understand that the school community was involved as the fight was witnessed by younger students who now may well not feel safe. Both pupils therefore came up with visiting classes together with an anti-bullying poster to which they spoke and thus attempted to repair the harm done to the wider school population.

Can anyone facilitate restorative justice?

Anyone can be trained in restorative justice and there are several agencies offering training. Teaching assistants are often effective as they are often perceived to be fair by students. Some teachers also have good skills but because teachers sometimes need to reprimand students they can experience a conflict of role that may cause tension and restrict open discussion and the sharing of emotions. Police officers usually facilitate the more challenging restorative justice when there could even be an outstanding crime or a pupil–teacher dispute where parents are questioning the effectiveness of the school's intervention. Some Year 6 students have been trained in restorative justice, which works well in them dealing with younger pupils' disputes as they can relate well to each other.

With disputes, teachers often feel they are impartial when dealing with pupils. However due to the fact that they know them reasonably well it is very difficult to be impartial in the eyes of the pupils. If the relationship with the school staff has broken down then all parties need to feel that the person facilitating the conference is impartial and fair. Police staff are, in general, recognised by society as being impartial. Even when dealing with members of the public who are anti-police these people still expect the police to react in the correct manner, i.e. according to 'the rules'. Officers have the training, experience, and authority to make sure the victim is heard, there is no intimidation, and the conference is, as far as possible, fairly conducted.

Examples of successful restorative justice conferencing

PC Dave mentioned that a parent came to school with the intention of assaulting a pupil who was bullying their child. The children involved had a restorative justice conference where both parties were listened to. The victim explained how she felt about coming to school with the threat of the other child. The perpetrator was upset and ashamed, not having considered how her actions and words were being perceived. The children agreed on a plan to work together and left the conference in a positive frame of mind. The parent (who was not actually a part of the restorative justice procedure) was surprised to see pupils so happy afterwards, which prevented a further assault or even a possible arrest.

In the second example a pupil felt that he was always being punished by a particular teacher and the relationship between them had broken down. The teacher listened to the pupil's feelings with an impartial police officer facilitating. It takes a lot of courage as a teacher to admit that the child is right and you are wrong but this teacher went back into class and discarded his 'black book' that was the actual source of the conflict. The relationship between the teacher and pupil is now positive and healthy.

Many schools have now begun to build strong teams of people who have a variety of different skills to bring to the 'community of practice' (see Lave and Wenger 1998). With regard to police in schools, there are positive benefits for both the school and the police service in working together for the good of the children and their families. My discussion with PC Dave leads me to believe the role of the police is growing and that the introduction of SSOs and PCSOs in schools is a very important partnership development.

References

Barnett, R. (1977) Restitution: a new paradigm of criminal justice. *Ethics: An International Journal of Social, Political and Legal Philosophy,*87(4) 279–301.

Graef, R., with Liebermann, M. (2000) *Why Restorative Justice? Repairing the Harm Caused by Crime.* London: Calouste Gulbenkian Foundation.

Lave, J., and Wenger, E. (1998). *Communities of Practice: Learning, Meaning, and Identity*: Cambridge: Cambridge University Press.

Marshall, T. F. (1999) *Restorative Justice: An Overview. A Report by the Home Office Research Development and Statistics Directorate.* London: Crown Copyright.

Marshall, T. F., and Merry, S. E. (1990) *Crime and Accountability: Victim/Offender Mediation in Practice.* London: HMSO.

Chapter 28

Supporting learning and behaviour

Janet Kay

Given the numbers of children in schools there is always a need to maintain good standards of behaviour so that no one comes to any physical or emotional harm, and moreover, to enable education to proceed. In this chapter, Janet Kay, principal lecturer at Sheffield Hallam University, examines a sweep of themes of relevance to children's behaviour in classrooms and schools.

Introduction

Good standards of behaviour are not just about the actions of individual children or groups of children. Developing good standards of behaviour is part of children's learning, and how effectively this learning takes place depends very much on how behaviour is managed across the whole school.

In this chapter, we will explore the factors that contribute to problems with behaviour across the school, and the ways in which this might affect children's learning. The role of the teaching assistant in contributing to whole school development in this area is discussed. The teaching assistant's responsibilities are discussed in the context of their role within the school and their relationship with the class teacher. Behavioural factors influencing the effectiveness of work with individual children and groups are discussed. The development of a framework of rules and policies within school, which support and promote good standards of behaviour, is discussed. Strategies for dealing with potential and actual conflict are explored, along with limitations on the teaching assistant's role in managing behaviour in school. The various approaches to supporting children in difficulties, dealing with distressed children, and working with children to modify their behaviour are also examined.

Source: An edited version of Kay, J. (2002) 'Supporting children's learning and behaviour in school', in *Teaching Assistant's Handbook*, Chapter 7, pp. 119–139 (London: Continuum). Reproduced with permission of CONTINUUM PUBLISHING COMPANY in the format Textbook via Copyright Clearance Center.

A key theme is the development of interpersonal skills for supporting effective behaviour management. These include good communication, responsiveness, developing positive relationships with children and using disciplinary measures appropriately.

Policies and rules

Every school should have a policy on behaviour which clearly outlines the expectations placed on pupils within the school. This policy is drawn up and approved by the governing body, including the headteacher. Parents are usually asked to comment on the policy and contribute to developing it over time. School behaviour policies are important in terms of creating a common standard which can be worked towards by all sectors of the school community. However, like all policies, the value of a behaviour policy can only be measured by the extent to which it is implemented. Put simply, a policy is merely a piece of paper unless action is taken to make sure that the proposals within it are put into practice. Policies on behaviour tend to give an outline of expectations of children's behaviour and when and how disciplinary measures will be taken. These policies are supported by home-school agreements, which are contracts signed by parents and children, stating that they agree to abide by certain rules within school. These include, amongst other things, standards of expected behaviour. Home-school agreements are not compulsory, but are used as a method of stating what the school expects from parents and pupils, and what parents and pupils can expect from the school. Research into home-school agreements, which were introduced in all schools in 1999, has shown, however, that not all schools have found them helpful or influential in improving standards of behaviour (Parker-Jenkins et al. 2001). Because they are not compulsory, many do not get signed or returned to school, and the conditions within them are not binding. However, home-school agreements may fulfil an important function in raising the issue of standards and expectations within schools and between schools and parents.

Children need to know what is expected of them in order to behave well. Learning school rules can take time and children may be worried about breaking rules because they do not really know what the rules are. For young children just entering school, there is a need to explain rules patiently and repeatedly until they start to understand what is expected. Children may not have had previous experiences of having to be quiet and sit still for the length of time school sometimes demands of them. They may have to learn about turn taking, lining up and putting their hands up. They may not remember that it is a good idea to go to the toilet at break time.

School policies are an important starting point for developing a whole school approach to generating good standards of behaviour and positive social attitudes. However, they are not much use unless all school staff, parents and children are aware of the policies and are actively involved in developing them.

Dealing with conflict

Conflict between individuals or groups within the school community can be a major source of disruption to the smooth and harmonious atmosphere in which children learn best. Dealing with conflict either between children or between you and a child is one of the most important skills for managing behaviour in schools. Conflict is almost inevitable in any situation where there are a lot of children and adults together in an enclosed space. This is not peculiar to schools. Parents will often state that conflict between siblings is a major source of disruption in the home.

However, there are strategies for both reducing the chances of conflict developing, and dealing with conflict effectively when it arises, which can be learned and used with the children you work with. Conflict is not always a negative aspect of any group relationship. It can be used positively to air differing views and ideas and to create and promote debate. However, conflict can be damaging if it is mishandled or someone 'loses' or is hurt physically or emotionally.

What is conflict?

Conflict can be expressed verbally or physically, although sometimes it is not expressed at all. It is about the tension between two or more individuals, based on some form of disagreement. It can be temporary or long term and it can arise for all sorts of major or trivial reasons. Some children are more likely to be involved in open conflict than others. Some may appear never to get involved in conflict at all. The ways in which different children express conflict may depend on what they have learned from the adults around them and their own personality and characteristics. Conflict can be healthy, in terms of the expression of different viewpoints and the ability to express these. However, conflict can be damaging when it is expressed in personal terms, when it goes on over a period of time or when it involves harm to an individual.

Preventing conflict arising

We can never hope to eradicate conflict from the school altogether. However, it is possible to create an environment within school where conflict is reduced, where it is healthy, and where it is resolved quickly without harm to individuals. School development is crucial to this process, based on promoting positive relationships between adults and children, founded on mutual respect and consideration. This type of development does not take place overnight but is part of a more general ethos which needs to be constantly renewed and reviewed. Some elements of this whole school ethos could include:

- developing good relationships with children through communication, active listening and an interest in the individual child
- showing respect for all children and adults within the school
- taking action to reduce racism and discrimination within the school
- fostering a climate in which children are encouraged to help and support fellow pupils, and adults model this behaviour
- creating and promoting clearly defined standards of behaviour and ensuring that these are part of the high expectations of children in the school
- developing strategies to deal with unacceptable behaviour and applying these in a timely and consistent way
- involving parents in discussions and strategies to develop the whole school ethos.

It is vitally important that you model these types of behaviour in your work with the children, demonstrating good practice in your relationships with others and a calm, problem-solving approach to any difficulties which arise. Receiving respect from others is important in building young children's confidence and their belief in themselves as valued beings; therefore it is important to maintain respectful relationships with the children you work with.

It is also important to consider your self-presentation. Children will respond better to adults around them who behave in authoritative ways and who present themselves as confident and coping. It helps to be firm and calm in your dealings with children and to demonstrate that you do not need to get angry or shout to ensure the children pay attention and respond appropriately to you. Positive, confident body language and open, confident facial expressions can reinforce an effective personal presence. A calm tone and relaxed manner can help children to learn to trust you and to gain respect for your authority.

A positive, problem-solving environment in school, in which opportunities are taken to discuss and explore difficult issues, either one to one or in circle time or assembly, will contribute to reducing the incidence of conflict. However, children bring many worries, problems and difficulties to school, as well as those that develop at school, and inevitably some conflict will arise.

Dealing with conflict in school

Conflict most commonly arises between children, but can arise between teaching assistants and a child or children. Dealing with conflict between children needs patience, sensitivity and tact to ensure that positive solutions are found and implemented. Not all conflict requires adult intervention. Unless a child is becoming distressed or there is physical aggression it may be better on many occasions to let children work out their differences themselves. In this way, children learn about compromise and negotiation, controlling their stronger emotions and altruistic behaviour. It is important that young children have the opportunity to do this, as a significant contribution to their social development. Children of school age often have the skills and maturity to sort out short-term conflicts between themselves. However, adults should always intervene when:

- conflict between the same individuals persists
- there is bullying
- any child is becoming distressed or humiliated
- there is physical aggression
- other children are becoming involved or distressed.

Strategies for intervention will obviously vary, depending on the situation, the age of the children and the type of conflict. Power-assertion techniques, such as shouting at the children, may be successful in the short term, but do not solve the longer-term problems that have caused the conflict in the first place. In order to do this, it is important to consider causes and motivations and to ensure that the outcomes of conflict resolution are going to be positive for all involved. A good solution is one where there are no 'winners' and 'losers' but where all involved gain from behaving in different ways.

There are a number of stages to dealing with conflict, which may include:

- stopping aggressive verbal or physical behaviour and ensuring all children's safety as a priority
- communicating with the children about their behaviour and the reasons for it
- listening to the children and accepting their feelings about the situation
- looking for the underlying problems which are causing the conflict
- seeking solutions that help everyone involved to behave and feel better, and which reduce the chances of further conflict.

Children and adults may sometimes get into conflict and this may need dealing with in a similar way to conflict between children. If a child is angry or aggressive, it is important to:

- remain calm and in control, never become aggressive
- seek help if necessary
- talk to the child and listen to him/her
- acknowledge that the child is upset and try to encourage him/her to share his/her feelings
- try to remove oneself and the child to a quiet place
- try to get other children to move away.

It may be necessary to involve others in an incident to ensure that it does not escalate and that it is dealt with appropriately and within the law and policy guidelines. Teachers are permitted to restrain children physically in certain limited circumstances, to avoid harm to the child, other children or adults, or property. If a child becomes physically aggressive, it is very important to seek help immediately from the teacher and to ensure that other children are removed from the vicinity as quickly as possible. Any such incident should be recorded and discussed with the teacher and possibly the headteacher so that strategies to avoid a repetition can be developed, and parents informed.

Dealing with other types of unwanted behaviour

In this section we will explore effective responses to a range of more general unwanted behaviour in children. In order to provide children with an effective learning environment, there needs to be order and discipline in schools. Children should not be fearful or oppressed by rules and disciplinary measures, but should be taught to recognize the benefits of an orderly environment. Children learn positive social values such as self-discipline, concern for others, helpfulness and respect for others from being in a school where values are part of their wider learning. Discussions about values, what is expected and what is unacceptable, are part of the day-to-day learning about good behaviour which young children need.

Inevitably, there will be some unwanted behaviour among children in primary schools. Young children are still learning a great deal about accepted social behaviour at this age. There are many variations in the level of maturity among children in the infant stage. They may know what is expected of them but occasionally forget. They may be testing the boundaries to see if they are firm. They may he bored or tired, or upset about something at school or at home. They may be confused or uncertain about the activity they are supposed to be doing, or unable to understand what is expected of them. They may need help, but not feel confident about asking for it. Or they may want to attract more attention from other children or adults because they feel forgotten or ignored. The sorts of behaviour that are expected of children within the home also vary, So that there may be disparities between what is expected at home and school for some children.

There are many reasons why children behave in unwanted ways. There are also many different possible responses to unwanted behaviour, which may have different outcomes. It is important to recognize that most young children need support and help to behave well, rather than criticism, harsh discipline or condemnation. Some basic principles for dealing with unwanted behaviour include:

- Criticize the behaviour not the child.
- Explain to the child why the behaviour is not acceptable.
- Do not describe the child in negative terms e.g. 'silly girl'.
- Listen to the child's explanation.
- Use firm tones, but do not shout or raise your voice.
- Be clear about the behaviour that is expected.
- Praise and encourage desired behaviour to help children understand what is expected of them and to 'reward' them for meeting those expectations.
- Do not humiliate the child in front of others.
- Make sure the reprimand or punishment is proportionate to the level of unwanted behaviour, and not excessive or unkind.

- Be fair and consistent.
- Deal with the behaviour at the time, not later.

Types of unwanted behaviour

The sorts of behaviour which are unwanted in young children in school are those which:

- are disruptive to the learning process
- threaten the health and safety of children or adults
- distress, embarrass or upset other children or adults
- involve verbal or physical abuse of another child or adult.

Typical examples of some of these are:

- During 'carpet time', Ryan ties his shoelace to that of the child next to him, creating a domino effect so that after twenty minutes four children are shackled together.
- During whole class teaching Hannah leans forward and starts to twiddle with the hair of the child in front of her, distracting about five other children in the process.
- During silent reading, several boys gather at the shelves to 'change their books', and instead start to chat among themselves about toys.
- Kay and David reach for the same pencil at their table and then start a loud squabble about who should have it, culminating in pushing and shoving each other off their chairs.
- At dinnertime, Dan leaps out of the queue for lunches and entertains the other children by dancing round, pulling faces and blowing 'raspberries', until the queue collapses.
- Karen and Shiraz, both 7, rampage around the playground play-fighting with each other, shouting at the top of their voices, oblivious of others until they flatten a smaller child.
- Supposedly absorbed in completing drawings of different types of dwelling places, Mark entertains his table by drawing pictures of 'willies'.
- Cheryl asks Tom to pass her a rubber, instead he throws, she catches and tosses it back and so on.
- Harry refers to the child next to him as 'you prat'.
- Fauzia and Jane follow the lunchtime supervisor down the playground doing an exaggerated imitation of her walk.

Strategies for dealing with unwanted behaviour

Dealing with unwanted behaviour requires patience, tact, firmness and fairness. The object is to minimize the disruption caused by the behaviour and to discourage the child or children from repeating it. In some cases, the child or children may need to be made aware of the distress they have caused and to make reparation, usually apologies. Children respond best to disciplinary measures from adults who they respect and feel positive about. Possible strategies include:

- verbal reprimands, delivered in a calm, but very firm tone
- ignoring minor incidents of unwanted behaviour, in the context of praising unwanted behaviour
- explaining to the child why their behaviour is unacceptable, dangerous or hurtful to others
- suggesting alternative ways of behaving
- removing the child from an 'audience' or removing the 'audience' from the child
- giving the child additional responsibilities or tasks to do to occupy him/her more.

For more serious incidents, teaching assistants will need to report the behaviour to the teacher for consideration of further sanctions or punishments. However, it is important to be able to deal with incidents as they arise and to do this confidently and with authority.

Finally, it is important to remember that repeated and possibly escalating unwanted behaviour might be an indication of a deeper problem. Children who are abused or being bullied or who are worried or distressed may behave in unacceptable ways in order to draw attention to their plight. Children who have learning difficulties or special educational needs may be trying to distract others from recognizing their difficulties or gain the status they feel they cannot get through achievements in the classroom. Children going through changes at home, such as divorce or the birth of a new baby, may be expressing their uncertainty and anxiety. Any concerns about the possible causes of patterns of unwanted behaviour should be shared with a teacher who may then discuss these with parents.

Conclusions

Teaching assistants play an important role in whole school development towards a positive learning environment, both within and outside the classroom. The development of personal skills and strategies to promote good standards of behaviour and to deal with conflict, bullying and racism is important for anyone working within the school community. We know that children learn best in orderly, well-managed environments. Teaching assistants need to be able to support the teacher in creating and maintaining an appropriate learning environment within the classroom. They also need to create and manage a positive learning environment within their own particular remit, working with groups and individual children. Children not only learn best in such an environment, but they also learn about positive social behaviour, consideration and respect for others and anti-discriminatory behaviour. Developing skills to manage behaviour and learning effectively, without the use of power-assertion (shouting, threatening, frightening) techniques, is a significant part of the teaching assistant's learning requirements.

References

David, T. (ed.) (1993) *Educating our Youngest Children: European Perspectives*. London: Paul Chapman.

Kay, J. (2001) *Good Practice in Child Care*. London: Continuum.

Parker-Jenkins, M., Briggs, D., Taylor-Basil, V. and Hartas, D. (2001) *The Implementation and Impact of the Home-School Agreement in Derbyshire Primary Schools*. University of Derby, School of Education and Social Science, Research Centre for Education and Professional Practice Working Papers Series 1: No. 1.

Section 4

Learners' identities

The final section of this Reader contains eight chapters that link learning to issues of class, ethnicity, and ability. These chapters examine the identities of learners, the way in which individuals think about their own identities, and the ways they are viewed by others.

Rosalyn George, in Chapter 29, reports on her study into teenage girls' friendships. Her research involved observing them in the playground, speaking to their teachers and parents, and asking the girls to keep their own diaries. In Chapter 30, Graham Jameson describes a classroom project that served to bring unwarranted linguistic assumptions to the surface. The way children speak, he suggests, can cause adults to make inaccurate assumptions about their abilities and their potential to learn.

Chapters 31 and 32 both consider potential impairments to learning. Jonathan Rix, in Chapter 31, describes the work of a teaching assistant as she draws upon the available human and material resources in a classroom to enable Jared, a child diagnosed with autism, to be included in the life and learning of that classroom and the school. In Chapter 32, Gina Gardiner, a headteacher who needs to use a wheelchair, reviews the positive and negative sides of her work.

In Chapter 33, Chris Watkins argues that children should be encouraged to take greater responsibility for their own learning – that they, rather than adults, should be in the 'driving seat'. Developing a multicultural theme, in Chapter 34, Charmian Kenner outlines an approach to fostering a multilingual learning environment. Learning for bilingual children can be greatly enhanced when teaching assistants and teachers enable linguistic and cultural interaction to take place within the school.

Robin Cooley is particularly interested in promoting anti-bias understanding amongst the children she teaches. In Chapter 35 she provides an account of work in her classroom that highlights gender and family stereotypes. Lastly, in Chapter 36, Diane Reay notes a history of concern about boys' behaviour in primary classrooms. She feels that their achievement needs to be viewed against a background of race and class, but that boys (and girls) respond well to teaching that maintains good order but is also fun.

Chapter 29

Looking out for little miss popular

Rosalyn George

Rosalyn George is Professor of Education and Equality at Goldsmiths, University of London. She is particularly interested in exploring urban girls' friendship networks and schooling. In this chapter, adapted from her inaugural lecture presented on 10 May 2011, she reports on her study of the way the friendships of 12–14 year old girls are constructed and enacted and the bullying that can arise.

Grace is waiting there and Carol, and especially Cordelia. Once I am outside the house there is no getting away from them. They are on the school bus, where Cordelia stands close beside me and whispers into my ear: "Stand up straight! People are looking!" Carol is in my classroom, and it is her job to report to Cordelia what I do and say all day. They're there at recess and at lunchtime. They comment on the kind of lunch I have, how I hold my sandwich, how I chew. On the way home from school I have to walk in front of them, or behind. In front is worse because they talk about how I'm walking, how I looked from behind. 'Don't hunch over' says Cordelia. 'Don't move your arms like that.' They don't say any of the things they say to me in front of others, even other children; whatever is going on is going on in secret, among the four of us only. Secrecy is important, I know that to violate it will be the greatest, the irreparable sin, and if I tell I will be cast out forever. But Cordelia doesn't do these things to have power over me because she's my enemy. Far from it, I know about enemies. Cordelia is my friend. She likes me, she wants to help me, they all do. They are my friends, my girlfriends, my best friends. I never have had any before and I'm terrified of losing them.

(Atwood, 1988: 119–120)

Source: Commissioned by The Open University for this volume.

My own memories of a subordinated 'girlhood' in pursuance of friendship have been reawakened by observing the painful investments made by daughters and their young friends in attempting to belong and be accepted by others.

The kind of concern revealed by the quotation above from Margaret Atwood's novel *Cat's Eye*, illustrates the importance of relationships and connection in girls' lives, along with the fear of solitude, which leads many to hold onto destructive relationships, even at the expense of their emotional safety.

In *Cat's Eye*, Atwood describes how Elaine who is bullied by Cordelia, the 'popular' girl, knows that by staying friends with her she will be cared for at times and under circumstances beyond her control. Elaine's fear of losing her friends leads to her silent acceptance of what appears to be unacceptable behaviour. Such silence is woven into the fabric of the female experience and in the hidden culture of girl's friendship groups, the façade of intimacy often hides the anguish and psychological pain that friends may and often do inflict upon each other.

Girls' friendship groups have traditionally been characterised by teachers, other adults in classrooms, parents, and educational researchers as 'malicious, bitchy, catty and resentful' (Davies, 1979: 65), with boys' friendships being seen as far more straightforward (Nilan, 1991). In the secondary phase of schooling, we find that current work on girls' friendships challenges such stereotypes and is concerned with exploring the complex processes through which friendships are constructed and sustained. Valerie Hey's (1997) study on older girls' friendships dismissed these simplistic characterisations and instead highlighted a series of sophisticated practices, which underpin adolescent girls' friendship groupings and their social networks.

In contrast to the work on adolescent girls, existing work on primary-aged children has focused on collaborative working groups, adult–child relationships, and girls' willingness to conform to school structures and organisations, a construction that this research challenges. What my research does show is that girls' troubled friendships in their primary schools have warranted little serious attention from their teachers, support staff, and other adults who perceive the 'breaking' and 'making' of friendship as an inevitable and almost a 'natural' and routine part of their daily classroom experiences and, furthermore, over so quickly that intervention is unnecessary. It's just part of growing up!

Traditionally, the way educationalists and indeed psychologists have framed issues relating to children's friendships have allowed basic and commonly held views of masculinity and femininity to predominate. Girls are positioned as conforming, compliant, and responsive to an imposed moral and indeed ethical order.

As Adler and Adler observe:

> In contrast to the boys' defiance, girls become absorbed into the culture of compliance and conformity. They occupy themselves with games and social interactions where they practice and perfect established social roles, rules and relationships. Not only do they follow explicitly stated rules, but they extrapolate upon these, enforcing them onto others as well.
>
> (Adler and Adler, 2001: 209)

I would argue that these studies over simplify how young children construct their friendships and ignore the power of children's subcultures in which friendships are formed. Furthermore within these studies there is no acknowledgement that friendship is also subject to social change.

From the early 1970s to the present, Angela McRobbie (1978) has been one of the major protagonists in researching girls. Her work highlights the pressure exerted on girls 'to achieve idealised expectations of femininity', a theme that is very visible within the data of this study. Her research has been concerned with exploring the influence of popular culture on girls' behaviour at school and within their friendship group or subculture. These studies were prompted by the lack of attention paid to gender by male sociologists, which had led to an overestimation of the conformity of girls to the norms and values of the school and the wider society. There is a whole range of work on girlhood, in particular the work of Walkerdine (1990), Skeggs (1995), Allen and Mendick (2013) suggest that girls, by engaging in popular culture, internalise conceptions of what it is to be feminine and argue that such a construction plays out a message telling girls they have to be 'good' and 'selfless' putting others before themselves. Walkerdine's work illustrates that the practice of femininity through friendship comes at a social cost for being 'good' and 'selfless' is an impossible ideal that can only be resolved by projecting badness from the self onto others.

The research context

The data for the study were drawn from semi-structured interviews with the girls, their teachers, and their mothers. Through a detailed analysis of the girls' talk about themselves and their friends, it became apparent that the dynamics of their friendship networks were focused around a single leader with a set of girls forming an 'inner circle' and an additional pool of girls who were on the periphery.

The complex internal dynamics of the friendship groups meant that it wasn't easy to see how and why an individual emerged as a leader but it was possible to ascertain how once she was positioned, her leadership was maintained by the 'discursive' practices entered into with other friends, her teacher, and other adults.

The particular groups I am going to refer to in this Chapter consisted of:

Names	Position in Group	Characteristics of Group Membership
Isobel: Year 6 Jane: Year 2	Group leaders	As bright if not brighter than all the girls in their groups. Both girls were the most socially skilled and the most articulate amongst their friends.
Hafsa: Year 6 Shumi: Year 6 Chloe: Year 2	Inner circle members	Hafsa and Shumi were good friends with each other sharing the same interests in music, fashion; this did not detract from their main concern to keep Isobel happy. Chloe was friendly with both Jane and Tiffany
Lisa, Tan, and Lauren: Year 6 Tiffany: Year 2	Peripheral group members	Members of the peripheral group who moved in and out of the inner circle

I worked with the girls over a period of 4 years, interviewing them regularly, meeting their mothers, and in some cases their fathers, and asking them to keep a journal where they recorded incidents both good and bad in relation to their friendships.

The 'bleak side' of friendship

Working with the girls revealed that there was a very bleak side to their friendship and this was confirmed by a short clip of film *'Girls' friendships at primary school can be destructive'* made by the BBC (23/3/2011) following an article published in *The Education Guardian* (22/3/2011) reporting this research.

Each of the girls in the film clip articulated the minefield that characterised the dynamics operating around their friendships as well as resonating with the concerns expressed by the girls in this research. They described the whispering to the giggling; the moodiness and being touchy, and the way girls are positioned either 'inside' or 'outside' of their friendship group. They also showed how this positioning becomes one of constant negotiation amongst the girls and the uncertain dynamics it creates.

This negative side of girls' friendships resonates with the research of Bjoerkqvist and Niemela (1992) who found that girls were not averse to aggression but expressed it in different and more indirect ways than boys, for example, through social exclusion or passing nasty stories about someone behind their backs. These forms of aggression were more subtle and less easy to detect by teachers and other adults working in the classroom, but seen as being more effective in the tighter-knit friendship group of girls. Their findings suggest that the cultural rules by which girls relate to each other demand that they engage in non–physical aggression and that, far from being 'sweet' and 'good', the researchers described the girls in their study as at times 'ruthless', aggressive, and 'cruel.'

As suggested earlier, girls' internalised version of femininity requires them to be 'good' and 'selfless' and to put other wishes and desires before their own. This is an impossible ideal to maintain within any relationship and the only way girls can respond is to project 'badness' from the 'self' onto others. The implications of these dynamics suggest that girls' relationships to femininity and to each other can be fraught with difficulties and, as Mary Jane Kehily (2002) also observed, it is this 'badness' that manifests itself in the exclusionary practices operating within the girls' friendship groups.

This 'bleak side' of friendship is manifested by power struggles, exclusion, and betrayal and it was this exclusion and betrayal by friends that allowed what seems a contradictory position, that of friend and that of bully, to become conflated in the girls' talk about friends.

RG: Do you think having friends stops people bullying you?

Tiffany: It depends on the kind of friends you have, because like when you have friends and people want to bully you they like, well, they tend to like it if you are getting bullied by someone sometimes.

Jane: No! They say 'excuse me, what are you doing?'

RG: So was it your friends who were bullying you? Did you do what the people who were bullying you told you to do?

Jane: Umm, no.

Chloe: Not really.

RG: And Tiffany what about you?

Tiffany: I forgot the question.

In this extract Tiffany's experience of her friends, who sometimes like watching her getting bullied or bully her themselves, highlights an uncomfortable and contradictory position between understandings of friendship and understandings of bullying. Jane, the group leader, in glossing over her complicity in the bullying of Tiffany, does at one and the same time present herself as a good friend who challenges such behaviour, but silences Tiffany who conveniently forgets the question rather than revealing more. By revealing more, Tiffany risked the wrath of Jane, the group leader, resulting in her possible exclusion from the friendship group. Moreover, Jane maintains her power over Tiffany by controlling her version of events.

One of the major difficulties about bullying has been about understanding what bullying is and how to distinguish it from other forms of children's misbehaviour. Evidence from Childline is able to define teasing as bullying.

> What is often referred to as teasing sometimes appears indifferent to the feelings of the victim; it seems aimed at exciting the admiration or laughter of other children who, by providing an audience for the bully, participate albeit passively in the bullying.
>
> (La Fontaine, 1991: 12)

However, there is a danger in this kind of inclusive defining of bullying, leading to a view that almost every negative interaction that takes place could be perceived as bullying. Lauren's, a peripheral member of the friendship group led by Isobel, response to bullying in her school illustrates the dangers of such a broad and encompassing definition:

Lauren: I would always stick up for the person who is being bullied.

RG: Is there much of it going on?

Lauren: No, only the very odd occasion, and then it's not really bullying, only light bullying, more like teasing.

RG: Oh, teasing?

Lauren: Yes. There is actually physical bullying, but the emotional bullying it's so small I don't think it hurts them much . . . I don't think any class has no bullies.

In this extract Lauren, who maintains that she would always stick up for someone being bullied, also seems to show a fairly sophisticated understanding of how bullying can be both emotional and physical. However she fails to, or chooses not to, see the impact that 'light bullying' may have on 'them', and in doing so absolves herself of any responsibility for stopping the bullying and ultimately becoming complicit in its practice. There is a clear link between power and bullying and, within the structure and culture of the school, bullying can occur in seemingly socially acceptable forms, e.g. academic and sporting achievements. The girl leaders in this research displayed their power in several ways (firstly, through their academic ability; secondly, through the confidence they had in an unquestioning following from their peer group; and, lastly, also from the explicit support and admiration from their teachers they enjoyed.

Beneath the radar and hidden from view

In Margaret Atwood's *Cat's Eye*, Elaine the girl who is bullied by Cordelia is seated frozen in fear on a windowsill, where she has been forced to remain in silence by her friends as she waits to find out what she has done wrong. Elaine's father enters the room and asks if the girls are enjoying the parade they have been watching:

> Cordelia gets down off her windowsill and slides up onto mine, sitting close beside me.
> 'We're enjoying it extremely thank you very much,' she says in her voice for adults. My parents think she has beautiful manners. She puts her arm around me, gives me a little squeeze, a squeeze of complicity, of instruction. Everything will be all right as long as I sit still and say nothing, reveal nothing. . . . As soon as my father is out of the room, Cordelia turns to face me 'How could you?' she says. 'How could you be so impolite? You didn't even answer him.' 'You know what this means don't you? I'm afraid you'll have to be punished.'
> (Atwood, 1988: .119)

In *Cat's Eye*, Cordelia, like many girl bullies, invests as much time and energy in her good-girl image, presenting herself as nice and caring to adults, as she does in the destruction of Elaine's self esteem.

Some girls' bullying is either invisible to adults or not recognised as bullying. This research suggests that some girls retreat behind a surface of sweetness in order to hurt each other in secret. They engage in exclusionary tactics and acts that are difficult to detect by their teachers or other adults in the classroom.

In a society where the rules for girls deny them access to open conflict, battles take place in silence. The potency of the 'whisper, whisper, whisper' as described by the girls in the BBC film clip provides a good example of the less visible way girls manage disagreements that enables forms of bullying to take place that are designed to be kept out of the sight of teachers and other adults. This covert and emotional bullying is not just about evading getting caught, but looking like you would never mistreat someone in the first place. The current concerns with cyber bullying, a much more sophisticated form of communication, provides evidence that this less visible but equally pernicious form of bullying is alive and well (Kowalski et al., 2008).

In this research, the leaders managed to mediate and control the exclusionary practices and covert forms of bullying. Through their manipulation of interpersonal relationships they were able to maintain their central position as leaders and to dominate and direct the consensus amongst the group of friends.

Why the girls remained part of peer groups that caused such pain and frustration is hard to discern. None of the girls could articulate very clearly why she felt compelled to stay connected to her groups. For example Lisa who was in the friendship group that was dominated by Isobel, had her self-esteem so undermined that this had sapped any confidence she may have had to remove herself from a very disempowering relationship to join another group. 'If I'm not friends with Isobel then Lauren won't be my friend nor will Eve and I'll end up with no friends at all.' Lisa, by choosing to associate with Isobel, chose a damaged relationship over a perception that she would have no relationship with anyone. Such a tough choice highlights how Lisa was not prepared to risk either the emotional isolation of not staying within the friendship group led by Isobel, nor the social isolation of having no one to sit with, play with, or walk home with. It would seem that the girl leaders have a charismatic and a seductive quality that, as Simmons (2002: 62) has observed, resulted in them having an 'almost gravitational pull on their victims'. And as shown by Lisa, 'the friendship is mesmerizing, and often the victim is gripped by a dual desire to be consumed and released by her friend'.

The teachers and support staff

At the same time that this hidden aggression below the radar was being enacted by the girl leaders, these same girls were being celebrated by their teachers for being polite, caring, and clever. As Brown (2003: 108) observes 'the girls have learnt from experience that it is the impersonation of nice, perfect girls that is what adults are really interested in'.

This possibly lends credence to the fact that many teachers and classroom assistants see the fallings in and out of friendship as an everyday occurrence and over so quickly that it is not something they should spend too much time worrying about. For example Lisa's exclusion by Isobel, the leader, from her group of friends was read by the class teacher as a deficiency in Lisa, rather than in Isobel; for like Cordelia from *Cat's Eye*, Isobel's charming and engaging persona dupes the teacher into believing that it is Lisa who has created the problem – for wanting Isobel all to herself.

In the study, there were several examples of teachers who, wittingly or unwittingly, colluded with the powerful members of the friendship group and, in so doing, enhance their status and power further. Paul, the Year 2 teacher, confirms this when he said:

> Poor Jane is stuck in the middle. Chloe wants to take Jane away to play on her own, so does Tiffany and poor Jane just doesn't know which way to turn.

The classroom adults also failed to take a sufficiently serious account of the effect of changes in group composition of who was 'in' and who was 'out' and, instead, tended to trivialise the emotional impact it had on individual group members. It would seem that these teachers, drawing on the cultural ideal of 'real' friendship, discounted any ruptures to the girls' relationships, brushing aside their upset, assuming that the next day will see a restoration in the friendship. Despite their concern with their children's well being, teachers tended to view 'problems' with friends as no more than an inconvenient disruption to the school day rather than something that could significantly affect their performance: As Kevin a Year 6 teaching assistant said:

> If they've had an argument in the playground then we'll sort it out at lunch-time and not in the next session, because we've got work to do in the next session and they need to forget about their argument . . .

Indeed in the ubiquitous climate of targets relating to assessment, achievement, and performance, teachers are currently having to maintain a demanding 'pace and challenge' in the classroom and do not want to be distracted from the job in hand, as one teacher complained:

> Girls bullying each other, it's the farthest thing from our minds. I'm sorry but I wasn't looking for it. . . . I'm not focused on it . . . I don't have time for that.

Conclusion

When I started out on this research I wanted to take something that I knew to be complex but was understood and seen as nothing out of the ordinary, an everyday occurrence, and dismissed as unimportant, nothing to be concerned about. I wanted to challenge a 'reality' that either ignored or dismissed the complexities of young girls' friendship as simply 'girls will be girls', 'this has happened since time began', 'what's new about this?'

The danger is that what happens in schools and classrooms becomes a kind of inscription, a handed down assumption that this is how girls are, it's just part of growing up. Given the target driven educational climate with its emphasis on achievement and attainment, what are schools and teachers and teaching assistants to do? There is no shortage of professional development on behaviour management and there have also been national level initiatives undertaken in dealing with bullying, but these programmes have failed to address the everyday low level disruption caused by girls' behaviours. It is currently this invisibility of girls' behaviour that puts teachers on shaky ground, with many feeling unable and unwilling to challenge or discipline behaviour that they have not witnessed.

It is essential as a first step that the issues pertaining to downsides of friendship are accepted as a factor in generations of girls being unable to fully engage in the schooling process. The excluded girls become very withdrawn, their personalities change, their facial expressions alter, and they often withdraw from their teachers and their group of friends. I can reflect on my own experiences as a teacher and say without hesitation that I could have given this crucial area of the classroom economy greater attention and priority. As teachers and adults working with young children we do fail to see the signs and, consequently, only the child can be relied on to come forward and explain what is happening. But if she believes that her teacher or other adults will trivialise or ignore her pain or treat the problem insensitively she will remain silent for fear of making things worse.

References

Adler, A., and Adler, P. (1998) *Peer Power: Preadolescent Culture and Identity*. New Brunswick, NJ: Rutgers University Press.

Allen, K., and Mendick, H. (2013) Young people's use of celebrity: class, gender and 'improper' celebrity. *Discourse: Studies in the Cultural Politics of Education*.

Atwood, M. (1988) *Cat's Eye*. New York: Doubleday.

BBC (2011) *Girls Friendships at Primary School can be Destructive*. www.bbc.co.uk/news/entertainment-arts-12836019

Bjoerkqvist, K., and Niemela, P. (eds.) (1992) *Of Mice and Women: Aspects of Female Aggression*. San Diego, CA: Academic Press.

Brown, L. K. (2003) *Girlfighting: Betrayal and Rejection Among Girls*. New York: New York University Press.

Davies, L. (1979) Deadlier than the male? Girls conformity and deviance in schools. In L. Barton and R. Meighan (eds.) *Schools, Pupils and Deviance*. Driffield: Natfield Books, pp. 59–73.

The Guardian (2011) 'Schools must take account of girls precarious friendships', 22 March.

Hey, V. (1997) *The Company She Keeps*. Buckingham: Open University Press.

Kehily, M. (2002) Private girls and public worlds: producing femininities in the primary school. *Discourse*, *23*(2), 179–192.

Kowalski, R. M., Limber, S. and Agatston, P. (2008) Cyber bullying: Bullying in the digital age. *American Journal of Pyschiatry*, *165*(6), 780–781.

La Fontaine, J. (1991) *Bullying: The Child's View*. Gulbenkian Foundation.

McRobbie, A. (1978) 'Working class girls and the culture of femininity', in Women's Studies Group (eds), *Women Take Issue*. London: Hutchinson.

McRobbie, A. (1981) Just like a Jackie Story, in A. McRobbie and T. McCabe (eds.), *Feminism for Girls: An Adventure Story*. London: Routledge & Kegan Paul.

McRobbie, A. (1991) *Feminism and Youth Culture*, Basingstoke, Hampshire: Macmillan.

McRobbie, A., and Garber, G. (1982) Girls and subcultures, in S. Hall and T. Jefferson (eds.), *Resistance Through Rituals: Youth Subcultures in Post-War Britain*. London: Hutchinson.

Nilan, P. (1991) Exclusion, inclusion and moral ordering in two girls' friendship groups. *Gender and Education*, *3*(1).

Simmons, R. (2002) *Odd Girl Out*. New York: Harcourt.

Skeggs, B. (1995) *Feminist Cultural Theory: Process and Production*. Manchester: Manchester University Press.

Walkerdine, V. (1990) *Schoolgirl Fictions*. London: Verso.

Chapter 30

Language, culture and class

Graham Jameson

It is very easy to make unwarranted assumptions about people based on how their speech sounds rather than on what they actually say. Graham Jameson, headteacher at Edmund Waller Primary School, London, uses the story of 'The Three Billy Goats Gruff' to stimulate children's understanding about the relationship between the way we speak and the value of what we say.

About a year ago, one of our infant classes did an assembly based on the story of the *Three Billy Goats Gruff*. Like most fairy stories, the basic structure allows for 'caustic interpretation' and we certainly saw that in vivid and dramatic form – the fight between the Troll and the Great Big Billy Goat Gruff in particular being positively Wagnerian. In the week that followed I asked a group of older children (Year 5) that I was taking for a writing session to recast the story as a television programme. In deciding to call this 'Spotlight', they demonstrated straight away an understanding of the portentousness that attends so many news programmes and this level of sophistication continued throughout the programme. We recorded the final production and a group transcribed the result.

The programme started with suitably urgent and arresting music and then Sophia came to the microphone and said: 'Tonight on Spotlight we investigate the case of the three Billy Goats Gruff. They've got a problem. We ask are they entitled to cross the bridge and eat the green grass on the other side? Or do they have to put up with the crusty conditions in their own field? We talk to the Billy Goats. But what about the Troll? What is his opinion? The Billy Goats have a right to decent grass, but doesn't the Troll have a right to be left in peace in his own field? We talk to him as well.'

Source: An edited version of Jameson, G. (1994) 'Three Billy Goats: six children and race, language and class', *Primary Teaching Studies, 8* (2), pp. 27–31 (London: University of North London – now part of London Metropolitan University).

We went over to the goat field to talk to 'our woman on the spot,' Mary. She was interviewing Rebbekah as the middle-size Billy Goat Gruff who, when asked why the Billy Goats wanted to move fields, replied: 'Because when mi a wak di grass a juk up ina di battam a mi foot and when me eat di grass a eatch up ina mi throat. Dat is why mi waant fi move'. And later said of the Troll that: 'Him is a very selfish monster, mi a go tell fada Billy government an see whaat him a fo say about it.'

Then it was back to the studio for Sophia to say judiciously: 'Of course, there are always two sides to any question. We're going to go over now and talk to Mr Brian Troll'

The exchange between Mr Troll and the reporter casts an unusual light on the story:

'Mr Troll, why won't you let the goats cross the bridge to eat the grass?'

'Because it is my grass and if I let them eat my grass, then a whole family of goats will eat my grass and then there will be no grass for me.'

'But surely, more grass will grow.'

'It will take weeks for it to grow. Do you eat grass? You don't know nothing about eating grass!'

'But there is water and fish.'

'I know there is water and fish but I hate water and fish!'

'Mr Troll, be reasonable, give them a chance. The goats are living in disgusting conditions. What are you going to do about it?'

'Nothing!'

'I think you should let them eat your grass, think about it.'

'Listen mate, this is my grass and those goats have dirty grass because they made all the mess. I am not letting them come to eat my grass.'

'But don't you think they have rights?'

'Yes, I think they should have rights. But what about my rights!'

Then 'back to the studio' and from there to: 'Down here at the goat field things have really moved on. Apparently, the goats got really fed up with the situation and are now in Mr Troll's field. The whereabouts of Mr Troll himself are unknown. I've got two eye-witnesses here, Georgie Porgie and Dave Divhead who saw what happened and I'm going to talk to them.'

Messrs Divhead and Porgie turned out to be a *Brookside*-style Liverpudlian and a Racer-style Geordie who described the expulsion of the Troll from the field and his disappearance into the waters after which event the goats were perhaps a little unsuitably triumphalist:

'He danced about and his brothers came on the bridge with him and they danced about too.'

'Yeh, yeh and then they wrote "Goats Rule OK" on the side of the bridge and then they all went trip-trapping into the new field.'

'That's all we've got time for, terrar.'

The immediate drama over, we were back again to the studio for a summing-up by the presenter. The moral maze traversed. 'Viewers, what I would really like you to think about is what do you think would happen if it were you in such a situation? Would you 1) fight the battle out or 2) converse with your opponent? Please think positively; when the goats and Mr Troll were fighting it out, has it done them much good? Think to yourselves a moment, what do you think would have happened if they were to talk the matter through? Would they have such a problem? The big problem is – Who is right? Well the correct answer in one sense is that neither of the two sides is right. But in another sense, if one lot of people (or trolls) have too much and another lot of people (or goats) are on the edge of starvation, then I know where I stand on the matter. Personally, I think they should pack in the argument and share the grass between them all.'

A year later

A year elapsed before we went back to the project. This was not intentional, I just got overtaken by events. Anyway a year on, I got these now-Year 6 children to reflect on their programme.

Their reading of the title music and the images over it was that it was about 'News' because it was 'serious' but 'fast'. It was 'direct' and 'straightforward'. The images were 'moving' (in the sense of dynamic) and the people in them were 'action men'. The words and the music were saying to the viewer 'see this', 'hear this', 'this is serious', 'pay attention', 'stop the ironing and look at this'. The positive aspects of such presentation are that 'it gets people to watch the news'. On the other hand such presentation can try to pass off boring subjects as interesting. Following this a more general point was made about why some things were counted as news. They were very clear that it was not the viewers who decide what the news is. It was 'the people who make the programmes'.

I talked to the children about the opening of their programme being the first of many voices. I asked Sophia to read the opening sentences of her transcript as the anchor person/narrator of the piece. As in the original, she enunciated in measured, received pronunciation ('RP') vowels. Why, I wondered. Nobody had told her to talk like that as the presenter. She had chosen this voice in the interests of clarity and because the people who make the news and present it are often 'posh'.

I wondered if it were possible to read the same text in a different accent but with equal intelligibility. Mary read it with a West African accent and it was, to be sure, equally clear. However, the group thought that we don't ever hear that voice in that context because 'it isn't British' and the 'posh people' think that the audience won't understand it. They think African people are 'uneducated' and the way they speak is therefore redolent of 'stupidity'. The only way for a black person to become a presenter, like Moira Stuart or Trevor McDonald, is to sound like a posh white person – 'they have to train their voice'. At least two of the group thought this dynamic was an example of racism, but they all thought that the exclusion of all but the prestige dialect of RP from the narrating role in TV was to do with the workings of class. One of the group, for instance, with a now only vestigial Liverpool accent would be unsuitable as a newsreader, as would another white member of staff with a South London accent even though each speaks 'very clearly'. The group thought that programme-makers thought it slightly less important that the reporter should speak with a posh accent but she/he still had to make it sound official.

I wondered how young they were when they first would have known that it would be appropriate to speak like this. The consensus was that you developed this knowledge with the development of language itself. Rebbekah gave the example of her sister who from the age of three showed in her play that an official role was articulated in a 'posh' voice. They all gave examples of older relatives making their own speech 'more posh' in situations such as answering the telephone.

None of the group had been conned by the notion of RP as 'standard' or neutral. 'Everybody' had an accent, they thought. One of them said it beautifully, 'everybody who speaks English is standard English' and 'any language is standard language' and 'language is language'.

Language for them, however, is clearly to do with identity. Rebbekah chose to enunciate the voice of the Billy Goat in Jamaican South London because 'she doesn't really need to put on any accent, she's just herself'. She doesn't bother to change her speech because 'she's fine about the way she is'. Having said that, she can speak to her brothers and sisters in a way that would be unintelligible to the reporter. Jamaican people can, if they choose, have a 'private language'. The historical antecedents of this, they thought, are that the slave owners made the African slaves speak English so that 'they couldn't resist' in their own languages but they can still resist by adapting English to their own purposes and having a common, but 'private', language.

Brian's Troll is 'angry', 'fierce', 'smelly' and 'lower class'. He has a good point, but doesn't help himself by the way he articulates it. People are thus judged – as Mary puts it, 'people think that how you speak shows your character'. The poor Troll is judged as 'rough' and a 'nut-case'. He could make what he says more effective by seeming to be more reasonable but he would be 'less honest'.

George's 'Divhead' and Brian's 'Porgie', are 'dopey'. People believed that all 'scousers' are stupid, drink beer and smoke heavily. We rehearsed the same text using 'posh' accents. Exactly the same words were spoken but this time the two respondents would be judged as intelligent, they would not drink beer nor smoke. Equally, Sophia's final summing-up of the moral issues is attended by a gravitas that is to do with register, not content. If she said exactly the same things in 'an African accent' it wouldn't have anything like the same impact.

It is possible for a person who speaks with an accent like this to become a presenter but only at the price of 'changing who they are'. This was thought by all of the group to be a very high price to pay. I wondered how they thought things might change. They were not optimistic about change, but thought we should make a start in school by valuing the way real people speak, by not 'correcting' 'errors' of accent, only correcting when children 'get words wrong'.

A teacher's reflection

Like the man said, the isle is full of noises. It is the same as it ever was, only more so. This work reflects the multiplicity of voices that children hear, voices which reflect the plethora of cultures they consume. We see them trying to synthesize these voices into a coherent and critical understanding. My head is also full of voices, some of them frameworks or templates for understanding how the world works. It is interesting how much of the children's understanding fits within these. They know about a range of literacies, that different genres have their own grammars that encode weighted meanings. They know about the 'dialogistic' nature of cultures – that one culture feeds and is fed by another, that texts are social artefacts. They know that 'a speech genre is not a typical form of language, but a form of utterance' and that each such utterance has social (political) weight. That, as Bakhtin put it, 'any speaker is not the first speaker, the one who disturbs the eternal silence of the universe', that 'an utterance is filled with dialogic overtones' (Bakhtin 1986).

They know about the 'linguistic equivalence' that you can say the same thing in different registers and the meaning, linguistically, is the same. Equally, they know about the power of class. They are well towards the edge of what Vygotsky calls 'a zone of proximal development', they are on the verge of knowing that, as Labov puts it, 'the myth of verbal deprivation is particularly dangerous as it diverts attention from the real defects of our educational system to the imaginary defects of the child' (Labov 1972).

They nearly know that the 'twaddle' articulated by Ministers of Education about 'standard English' is a reflection of their own class positions rather than analysis.

To be sure, it could be said that I have been 'leading the witnesses', but then I am with Jerome Bruner (1986) in that I think it is part of our job as teachers to set up situations where students can extend and develop their own critical ideas, guided by structures and enthusiasms of teachers, occasions where they are led through 'zones of proximal development'.

I am emboldened by this work. In my gloomier moments I think that what Gramsci called 'hegemony' is getting more and more complete (Gramsci 1970). I think of the way that our lives are more and more structured and controlled so that ideas, consumption and education become all of a piece each reinforcing the other and all speaking with one controlling voice. Then I think to myself, what if someone had set up a similar situation for me and my classmates in 1957 and asked us similar questions? Almost certainly we would have said that standard English was that of the strangled, hernia vowels of the chappies who read the news on the radio. We would probably have 'known' that the social order, reflected in such articulation, was contingent with the moral order. That the class system was, in some way, 'natural'. What if. . .? – the idea is absurd. Nobody would have considered such a thing; in that sense hegemony then was even more complete.

When I hear this word hegemony an image floats into my head from the Eisenstein film, *Alexandr Nevsky*. I see the frozen lake, the ice forming a skin over the water, a smooth meniscus of normality. Later in the scene, the Teutonic knights ride confidently out across that surface but their combined weight is too much for it and it cracks and breaks and they slide desperately and ignominiously into the icy water.

In my gloomier moments, the world feels like the frozen lake. I wouldn't go so far as to wish the fate of the drowning knights on the present order. I lighten up, though, at the prospect of work like this, especially as I know that knowledge about language is being discussed and extended into 'meta-linguistic' and social awareness in classrooms all over the place. The ice may not be breaking up yet, but there are plenty of air-holes in it.

References

Bakhtin, M.N. (1986) *The Problem of Speech Genres.* Texas University Press.
Bruner, J. (1986) *Actual Minds, Possible Words.* Harvard University Press.
Gramsci, A. (1970) *Selections from the Prison Notebooks.* London: Lawrence and Wishart.
Labov, W. (1972) 'Language in the Inner City', in *Studies in the Black English Vernacular.* Philadelphia University Press.
Shakespeare, W. *The Tempest.*
Vygotsky, L.S. (1962) *Thought and Language.* MIT Press.
Vygotsky, L.S. (1978) *Mind and Society.* Harvard University Press.

Chapter 31

A balance of power

Jonathan Rix with Anna Tan and Susie Moden

Anna Tan is a Teaching Assistant at a primary school in West Sussex. This chapter, written by Jonathan Rix, a senior lecturer at The Open University, describes Anna's morning as she works to include Jared alongside his peers in their typical class activities. Anna shares this task with the class teacher, Susie, and a classroom assistant, Bridget, who works with groups of pupils as is required.

It is a sunny November morning. Anna arrives at 8.30 am, earlier than her contract requires. She checks the teaching resource boxes and what is happening today. Susie greets her warmly and says she needs to show her some information from Jared's Statement of Special Educational Needs. Jared is a child who has been diagnosed as experiencing autism. The information is at home, and Anna would not normally have access to it since she is not part of the formal assessment process. Officially, Anna has little to do with formally assessing Jared's work, although she sometimes passes important notes to Susie for assessment purposes.

Anna gathers together her visual timetable for the morning, and Susie asks Anna what she knows of Jared's holiday. They then talk about Jared's desire to do cutting and sticking, computer work, and drawing tractors. Anna explains that Jared turned the spiral that they were doing the day before into the wheels of a tractor. Everyone is impressed by some of the patterns that Jared was producing on cards by himself the day before.

Susie and Bridget tell Anna about the previous afternoon when Anna was not in class. They tell Anna about a disagreement that occurred in the afternoon between Jared and another boy. Jared kept distracting the boy when he wished to listen to the story. Anna feels it is important to find out

Source: An edited version of Rix, J. with Tan, A. and Moden, S. 'A balance of power: observing a teaching assistant', commissioned by The Open University for *Primary Teaching Assistants: Learners and Learning* (London: Routledge). Reprinted by permission of The Open University and Taylor & Francis Ltd.

how Jared gets on when she is not around. She worries that he is not independent enough to get the most out of the learning situation. She is also aware that there are times when he becomes anxious about her leaving. Susie tends to have more open activities when she is working on her own. She often draws upon strategies she has seen Anna using or has discussed with her. She sometimes struggles to cope without Anna there, but feels it is important for her relationship with Jared, so that she gets to see him as a whole person. She is aware that there is a danger of assuming that Anna is the expert on Jared and that she does not have the knowledge or experience to work with him. Susie also thinks that maybe when the sessions have more freedom the children get on better with Jared.

Susie takes Anna around the class running through the activity tables for the day. On one table is a cut and stick activity based around a Guy Fawkes storyline. On the other tables are sewing, drawing opportunities, leaves, picture sequences, alphabets, white boards, shapes, and numbers. They discuss the need to read the Guy Fawkes book again so that Jared knows what is going on, and is able to carry out the activity. They both agree that the bad photocopy will make it more difficult for him to relate to the story. This is Anna's first chance to be involved in the planning for the day's work. This is something that frustrates her. Anna explains that she will ask Jared to describe what he sees in the pictures, before cutting and pasting. Susie values Anna's ability to adapt to the situation as she finds it.

At 8.50 am the parents enter. Jared arrives and drops off his bag, crosses to Anna and is welcomed. Anna sits down with Jared and has a brief chat with his mum, then gets Jared involved in an activity so that the mother can leave with minimum disruption.

Susie claps for the children's attention and they sit on the carpet. She takes the register and Anna chats quietly at the back of the group with Jared. She is explaining the activity that will follow. The students are to go into singing practice. As they get up to leave for the hall Anna picks up the visual timetable.

Anna sits at the side of the hall, and then, at Susie's request, goes to check for an absent class. She returns with the class. She sits down again and then notices that there is a boy crying. She crosses to the boy to comfort him. He wants his mum so she gives him a hug and asks him what his favourite song is. The boy is suitably distracted and the singing begins.

Jared is happily positioned in the front row joining in with the singing to a certain degree and copying the hand movements of Susie, who is leading the practice. After a few minutes Jared turns, looking for Anna to ask a question. She slides forward from her position beside the boy who was crying. As the class stand up Anna focuses on Jared again with a reminder that soon they will return to class where he'll be able to blow bubbles before carpet time. Susie is not aware of Anna's intervention, but later says that if Jared had become too distracted, distressed, or anxious she would have asked a member of staff to take him out.

At 9.25 am the children return to their classrooms and Anna takes Jared into the adjoining room to re-read the story of Guy Fawkes and to blow a few bubbles. Before beginning, however, she gives Jared a choice of whether to join the others on the carpet or to have this one to one session. Jared wants to have this moment to himself, which Anna sees as a moment to calm and reorient himself after the stress of the singing practice. They agree too on an activity that they can carry out later. This is a tempting prize to keep him on target for the next couple of hours. She is aware though that she is separating him from the rest of the class. She feels that in a few weeks' time she will be able to take out some of the other children too, making this session less segregating and more of an opportunity for social learning.

After reading the story and after a few minutes of playing with the bubbles, Anna gives Jared advance warning that he has two minutes left before they will return to the carpet. When it is time, Jared runs into the classroom and throws himself into a corner, potentially disrupting the focus of the other children. Transition is often tricky. Susie checks with Anna that Jared is joining them and gives him some instructions about coming to join them on the carpet.

Anna feels that Jared usually responds well to instructions from Susie. She feels the buck stops with the teacher, but, on this occasion, Jared shouts at Susie that she can't tell him what to do and begins to talk about not being at home. Anna crosses to Jared with the egg timer and calms him. She and Susie both feel that he is aware that he has got away with behaviour that others in the class would not. But they do not make an issue out of it and neither do the other children. (At the end of the morning Susie wonders if Jared responds this way because he has been singled out and, unlike other children, would respond better to a class-wide request for silence.)

Susie explains to the children the different activities that they can carry out that day. She is aware that Jared and other pupils will benefit from simple language supported by strong visual cues and attempts to build this into her explanation. She points out that they have got some 'join the dots' sheets to do today, because one of the boys had expressed an interest, and a number of parents said children enjoyed doing them at home. On the table

Susie finds one of Jared's pictures. She picks it up and hands it to Bridget to file, congratulating Jared on a good piece of work. As Susie demonstrates the different activities, Anna repeats some of the questions that Susie is asking. Jared is too distracted and is not following Susie's description of the Guy Fawkes story. He gets up. Anna goes across to the visual timetable, takes this with her and leaves the class once again with Jared.

Outside they discuss the story of Guy Fawkes that Anna feels Jared only partially understands At 9.45 am the class split up. Susie will be working on the letter Y and spelling and handwriting with groups of children. Bridget will be working with groups on number. These are based on ability as defined by the teaching staff. Anna is not a fan of this system. She feels that the group Jared is in does not do him any favours. She feels that being in the bottom group means that he suffers more than most from their being distracted. She feels a more focussed group would help him.

Anna positions herself first of all at the cut-and-paste table with Jared but she is regularly approached by pupils from the other tables, particularly the sewing table, for her assistance and her opinions. Susie believes this demonstrates how important Anna is to the whole class, even though they know that she focuses on Jared.

Anna talks to all the pupils on a table, helping to focus them on the work, correcting mistakes, and encouraging Jared in his communication with them. Jared is not that taken with the task, but, by giving him small targets, she keeps him focused. After 20 minutes Jared decides he wants to go into the Post Office so Anna accompanies him after inviting another boy to join them. Some other children join them too. Anna has to gently reprimand one boy for his behaviour, and then Susie gives a stern reminder from her place at the literacy table.

A 10.15 am Jared leaves the Post Office and Anna goes to get the visual timetable again. She crosses to Jared and shows him that he has one activity to do before playtime. At this table a young boy begins to talk to Anna about a leaf that he has, but Anna notices that Jared is standing and spinning in the middle of the classroom and therefore likely to fall over. Anna apologises to this boy and quickly crosses to Jared who has now fallen over. She refocuses Jared, but it's break time, so sends him to get his coat, pointing out two boys who have got their coats. Jared returns with his coat having inspected his work file on route. When he comes back he pushes into line and is reminded by Anna that he really should have lined up properly like everyone else.

Once Jared has left, Susie apologises to Anna for not having given Jared specific instructions at the start of the day. They agree that something is bothering Jared. They wonder if it is the interruption of going out for the singing. They discuss whether it's more important for him to be involved in an activity and to understand what that activity is or whether it is better for him to be involved in carpet time. This encapsulates much of their concern about how they work with Jared. They are aware that many of Jared's difficulties in learning are due to the curriculum and teaching and learning environment, but that equally he does bring with him unusual sets of skills and ways of thinking that they cannot always be in tune with. They are aware that sharing their ideas at a planning stage may make it easier to overcome their concerns, but to do this they must make time out-of-work.

At 10.35 am, after a quick cup of coffee, Anna goes into the playground to see what Jared is doing. She is aware that Jared may become too dependent on her, so often leaves him alone at break or just goes to quickly check how things are going. Jared is in the large cubes with other children clamouring around. Anna turns to leave but suddenly Jared is behind her asking her to join him which she does for a few minutes. Anna sees dependency as a real risk. This is one of the reasons she believes that across the years Jared should work with a variety of support staff. She feels the transitions between staff and year groups need to be carefully handled.

At 10.45 am the class activities start again. Jared is busy doing the joining the dots activity, but using the visual timetable and the temptation of a train set activity Anna gets Jared to join Bridget at the numeracy table. While she's doing this she congratulates a boy on his strip story.

Bridget is aware that Jared is joining them, so moves a girl to sit next to her so that the two members of staff are not sat together. Jared focuses on the questions being asked of him by Bridget in relation to fireworks, shapes patterns and numbers. Anna encourages Jared with his answers. She is aware that at times he does not appreciate how much he is achieving. She sees it as important that she helps him to understand his capabilities. After 10 minutes Jared is distracted. Anna and Bridget allow him to make the contextually inappropriate noises for a couple of minutes, and then Anna brings Jared back to complete the task. Jared quickly finishes and then moves off, with Bridget congratulating him as he goes.

Jared wants to work on the computer but there are already other students working there. Anna negotiates the order of computer usage. Jared must wait, but through Anna he becomes involved with the discussion with three other boys about the game one of them is playing.

When Jared begins his activity, Anna discusses what he is doing with another boy. She helps this boy with his own work too, solving a computer problem. She gets him to comment on a picture that Jared has produced on the computer. Jared is enjoying his computer work. He does not wish to move on to the next task despite Anna's negotiation. She explains she will leave him to his work and wait at the next table. She waits for a few minutes and then returns. She reminds him of their agreed plan, and asks him if he wishes to have the computer turned off. Jared is annoyed. He pushes Anna away firmly, touching her on the side of the cheek. Anna repeats her threat after another patient explanation and this time Jared joins her at the sewing table.

Jared begins rocking his chair and is clearly distracted. Anna allows him this space. Susie says "sh!" automatically, then realises that it is Jared who is making this noise, looks across at Anna and decides to leave the control of the situation in her hands. A boy shows Anna his picture and she points it out to Jared. The boy makes some comments to Jared about the drawing he's just done, Jared makes comments himself and immediately starts to draw a picture. Much to Anna's relief something has come out of the everyday context of the class to help with her problem of how to focus Jared on the next task.

Susie asks Anna whether Jared is ready to do the literacy session. They agree that he will be a couple of moments, so Susie gathers the rest of the group together leisurely in order to give Jared the time to move on happily. It is in informal moments such as these that most of their communications about ideas and situations take place. It is important to both Susie and Anna that they can learn from each other in this way, but they are aware that they lack formal opportunities in the workday to have discussions. Anna would like more formal time allocated for this, but Susie feels that Anna's past experience with the class prepares her for whatever they do.

At 11.15 am Anna negotiates with Jared again about moving on to the next activity. She uses the visual timetable, once more pointing out that if he carries on with the timetable activities as agreed he can play with the train set. Jared joins Susie at the literacy table but once again argues with her about her instructions, saying that she can't tell him to sit and that he won't if she asks. He leaves the table but Anna gets him back. It is clear that Susie now feels awkward and undermined. Susie controls her own sense of frustration, but tells off another distracted boy with more firmness than she might typically. She then starts a story about yoghurts, and when she mimes the eating of yoghurts, and Anna and the other children join in, Jared's attention is grabbed.

Anna is able to leave the table to go to the other group on the ground. She has moved away from Jared but she is keeping her eye upon him, in case she can be of assistance. She is never sure what will happen next. She is always wondering if he is happy doing a task and wondering how she can change the situation to maintain his interest. She sees it as moment-to-moment, trying to work it out as she goes along.

Jared's interest in another boy's name and how it is spelt is evident. So is his desire to make the shape of letters with his hands and then with ribbons on sticks, and then in sand. At the end of the session Jared and a number of others in this group have received a house point for good work.

At 11.30 am Jared leaves the class and Anna follows. There is 15 minutes until the next carpet time. Anna has an egg timer and they go and collect a train set from the toy cupboard and set it up. Anna has also taken the visual timetable with them. Back in the class there's been a disturbance. Susie has to deal with one boy destroying the work of another and the refusal of children to co-operate with this disruptive boy. This is the group that Anna has left to go out with Jared.

At 11.45 am, through precise usage of her visual timetable and egg timer, Anna returns with Jared, discussing past activities with the toys he has spotted in the cupboard. Jared begins tidying-up. He spends quite some time examining what the other students have built. Susie puts on some music. Jared crosses to this music and begins to play with a car on the table. He does a little clearing up – one book – and then joins the other children on the carpet.

Bridget reads the class a poem and then leads a discussion about rhyme and the pictures in the book. The children leave the classroom and head out to get their lunchboxes. For the last 15 minutes there has been no contact between Anna and Jared.

It has been a good morning, but nothing out of the ordinary.

Watching Anna, Susie, and Bridget it is clear to see their awareness of the importance of each other in the creation of a learning and caring environment. Each of them gives way to the other at different times out of respect for their role and because of their different abilities to work with the children. There is considerable scope for role expansion and role overlap. Rather than clearly designated boundaries between three individuals, theirs is a team endeavour and a 'division of labour as an interaction' (Dewar and Clark, 1992, p. 119). At times too, they 'give way' to the pupils, fitting in with them, though it does not always make their professional role any easier. This chapter has been about a work in progress. It is not meant to be an ideal example of inclusive practice, but it serves as one example. It reveals differing views about ways of working and organising the class. What is clear, however, is that in attempting to make the most out of their situation, the staff and pupils find themselves constantly shifting their positions and related interactions within the classroom's balance of power.

Reference

Dewar, B., and Clark, J. (1992) The role of the paid professional nursing helper: a review of the literature. *Journal of Advanced Nursing, 17,* 113–120.

Chapter 32

Life as a disabled head

Gina Gardiner

In the last 30 years there has been a concerted move towards the inclusion of children with physical impairments in mainstream primary schools. However, the number of teaching assistants and teachers with such impairments remains conspicuously low. Inclusion, it seems, is not being promoted at the level of the primary school workforce. In this chapter, Gina Gardiner, a headteacher, reflects on the negative and positive aspects of her job in the light of her disability.

Manager, organiser, problem solver, are all attributes of successful headship. Being a disabled head teacher simply means you get a tremendous amount of extra practice in these skills. A sense of humour is an absolute necessity; a good staff a godsend, and a school site that is reasonably accessible makes it possible.

I have been a head teacher for 18 years, and have used a wheelchair for 14 years, being in it full-time for the last five. I run a large junior school on the outskirts of North East London. Headship is never easy; being disabled adds another dimension to the position, which has both negative and positive sides to it.

Positive aspects

In good educational style let me identify the positive things created through my disability first. My children have an opportunity to see disability in a constructive way. New pupils will often ask why I am in the chair and are quite satisfied with the explanation. Pupils who have a disability have a positive role model; disability need not mean you can't assume a management position. They know that being in a wheelchair does not mean

Source: An edited version of Gardiner, G. (2001) 'Life as a disabled head', *Primary Practice (Journal of the National Primary Trust)*, number 29, Autumn, pp. 20–22, National Primary Trust. Copyright Gina Gardiner 2001. For more information, please visit http://www. ginagardinerassociates.co.uk/

you are unable to speak for yourself. Not so the bar tender at a hotel entirely taken over by a head teacher conference who took the £20 note out of my hand and asked the person pushing me what I would like to drink!

I have learned to be super organised, to use my limited reserve of energy in a more productive way. I have learned to make the most of my time, and where possible give myself space before deadlines just in case. The plethora of Government initiatives make it much more difficult for us all to achieve this of course.

I think I have become more patient about some things, and less tolerant of others. I think being disabled has made me more sensitive to the needs of others.

My style of management has changed over the years and professional development of staff is a priority. We achieved Beacon Status on the strength of our programme. I believe that the school and the individual staff have gained much from the programme, and developing their skills, confidence and expertise has also ensured that things are covered (many of them outside my physical capacity).

The Education Authority and Manpower Services have been very supportive and the school has only two classrooms which are not accessible. For example electronic doors have been fitted onto the front door, so that I can now actually get into the building by myself. Many is the time I have sat in the car park waiting for someone to arrive in school, hear me beeping or the phone going. It would be untruthful to say that being disabled is easy. It remains a constant struggle to keep one step ahead, no sooner do you think you have things sussed and something else gets in the way. A bit like being an able bodied head when you think about it.

The downside

Daily life in school as a head in a wheelchair has a number of pitfalls. I cannot negotiate the wheelchair around the classrooms. No it isn't simply that I'm a bad driver, although the doorways have been remodelled somewhat. (I put the really big flakes of paint/plaster in the bin before they are noticed.) This means that monitoring has been organised in a rather different way; my deputy and coordinators have received training to enable them to undertake a range of monitoring. Contact with the children has to take a different form, as once through the classroom door furniture moving is the most pressing skill needed. Whilst the children are super about moving things and being helpful it is not conducive to slipping in and out without making a grand entrance.

When I became completely wheelchair bound I was unable to access any toilet within the school. It was a circus act trying to get into the loo until a wall could be knocked down. Discussing personal needs with education officers was not a comfortable experience – my problem not theirs; they were very sympathetic. I find no difficulty in fighting for my staff, pupils or their parents but fighting for yourself is a very different thing. Eventually a new building project included a loo suitable for me and the wheelchair. On one morning we played my version of 'how many people you can get into a Mini' as the site manager, caretaker, surveyor, builder, sanitary ware inspector and I were all squeezed into the new loo space discussing what height the loo needed to be.

When I first found my mobility getting difficult I delayed using a wheelchair longer than was good for me as I was very worried about the response from others, particularly parents. The school site is very large and spread out. I have nearly half the school in outside classrooms, which are situated right across a large playground. For a couple of years I struggled to manage movement around the site and had to plan my movements very carefully. When things deteriorated to the point that I really had no choice I broached the subject with my governors and the education authority first and I was extremely concerned about their reaction. There was no problem. The children took it in their stride; they are much better than adults I find in simply accepting you as you are. They were actually far less bothered about it than I was. The parents made very little comment to me, but I know the talk at the gate has given me most conditions found in a medical encyclopedia. At times I think it helps parents, particularly those who have children with special needs. Now as an established head it is accepted by everyone that I am in a wheelchair. New parents are occasionally surprised when they meet me for the first time but the school's reputation is the reason they have come so they seem confident to leave their children in our care.

Reliance on the wheelchair is fine until it goes wrong. My electric wheelchair has been known to die in the middle of the corridor much to the amusement of staff. I provide much opportunity for humour. Still when one or two staff have asked for a go in the chair their appreciation for my driving expands hugely; usually great squeals of mirth emitted as they make their higgledy piggledy way down the corridor. One lass has been banned since she ran my secretary over at speed! The children are happy to push me in the manual chair when necessary. (More chips in the paintwork.) Machines I believe are very sensitive to your mood and level of stress. It is quite apparent that computers always go wrong when you have the least time and temper to deal with their games. My electric chair is no exception: it has died on the first day of both the Ofsted Inspections, four years and a term apart! . . . creepy.

I now have a chair which rises until you are at standing height. It gave the children such a shock when I rose majestically in assembly the first time. Not quite so impressive when I failed to get it back down into the right position the first time. I use the facility sparingly but it has its uses.

School is actually the place where my disability has the least effect. I have a super staff, a deputy, secretary, site manager and chair of governors who are all very supportive and whose roles are somewhat modified so that each of us contributes the best of their skills and where the effect of my inability to walk is minimised. There are usually people about to lift things I find too heavy. School is where I feel most effective, in fact far more than when I am in a social capacity as I am very limited in those things I can access when I have no electric chair.

Off site

Life as a head becomes far more complicated and frustrating when I leave the site.

Local meetings require prior organisation. I have to arrange for someone to meet me in the car park as once I leave school I use a manual chair. Timing for head teachers meetings is critical, too early you cannot get into the playground of the school in question and you sit and wait, too late and the kind head teacher colleague you have asked to meet you is left standing – usually in the rain! I have arrived and beeped the horn to let people in the office know I am there and watched whilst they scratch their head, wondering who was making all that row. Mobile phones are a boon – until they go wrong.

Gatherings are complicated as once I'm in the manual chair I am dependent on people approaching me rather than being able to network. Neck ache usually follows from looking up at those standing. Some kneel as they are trying to be sensitive or perhaps their feet or their back are killing them. On one occasion I was on stage in front of several hundred people, being handed our Investors in People award, the dignitary in question knelt to present me ours. My then deputy was a little too keen to get out of the limelight and dragged the poor fellow right across the stage on his knees . . .

Accessibility is a word which means entirely different things to different people. The gap in the translation becomes greatest when attending courses and conferences. Please bear in mind that I always take great trouble to contact the providers to check how wheelchair friendly places are and only go if I'm told things are possible.

Some examples

Our local Education Offices are built on a nightmare site. The main corridor has a flight of steps half way along; if I have to visit both ends, or indeed wish to access the one disabled loo and am at the other side of the steps, I have to be pushed outside the entire length and width of half the building. On those days the weather always seems to be awful. The main hall has a flight of steps down into it that can be accessed from outside but I am unable to join colleagues at the coffee area. I tend to limit my intake of liquids on these occasions because I hate having to ask if someone will wheel me to the toilet but it also limits the opportunity for informal chat with colleagues. I have to wait for people to approach me in those situations, which is a pain. I have a super network of close friends who are brilliant about helping me. I still hate being dependent upon others. The building has an upstairs, in two halves. When the education authority moved to these premises it took them three years to have a lift fitted to one half of the building. I'm still waiting for them to make the curriculum side accessible. As they are now talking about moving again I expect the lift will remain as a plan on a drawing. No venue has been decided upon so it could be a long wait. I have to check that every meeting, course, workshop, etc has been sited in a room I can access. Occasionally I turn up and communications have broken down. I am allowed to know the combination for the security system as I can only access the side door. Fine until they change the number.

I attended a local course, run by Social Services. It was held at a site completely unknown to me. I phoned to check that it was accessible and was told, 'no problem.' When I arrived I was told that I would have to be carried up three flights of stairs, that it was all arranged. In these situations I have a real dilemma – do I make a scene, go straight home or put up with it. Particularly in the early years I didn't want to make a fuss or draw attention to myself so often put up with things, which made me cry inside. I was hauled up the stairs, an embarrassing and uncomfortable experience for me and positively dangerous for the two unfortunate volunteers. After the second session on the first day (Titled – 'Inclusion, all about dealing sensitively with people's needs') I was told I should not return for the second day as I constituted a fire risk. In those days I didn't want to make a fuss. Today I'm much less prepared to accept the indignity.

Last year I attended a training session where I sat downstairs whilst the other ninety-nine delegates ate upstairs.

Buildings are often said to be perfectly accessible – once you negotiate the steep flight of steps to the front door. I have been left in a busy London street whilst the taxi driver tried to sort things out and it was raining, of course.

I have been to hotels for training or a conference where access has been up a plank of wood through a window.

In another hotel last year, I was unable to get to the room where the introductory session was held, and probably more importantly, the bar. The same hotel required a journey through the car park, onto the road, along the pavement and in through another door every time I needed to get from the conference area or my bedroom to the restaurant. Guess what the weather did for the three days of the course? They offered to bring me a tray to the conference area, where I would have eaten in total isolation. This was a course run to train Threshold Assessors.

I was invited to speak at a conference. After a long drive I arrived to find the site quite impossible, flights of stairs between each of the rooms, some with temporary ramps which were so steep you needed crampons. Some rooms totally inaccessible including the room designated for me to give my talk.

I could go on . . . at length . . .

The teaching profession, which takes equal opportunities for its pupils very seriously, often pays far less attention to the needs of the adults who work within it. I feel strongly that all venues used by educational organisations putting on conferences and courses should only use appropriate venues. An added pressure is created because often the organisers both private and governmental are unprepared to take responsibility. As a disabled head it is left to me to check every time. It is common to be passed from person to person when trying to get information about the venue. The record stands at seventeen different phone calls for one event. That information is often incomplete or incorrect. When things don't go to plan people are always apologetic but that doesn't really help very much.

I get great satisfaction from my job but I have been determined that school should not be adversely affected by my disability. This has been an added pressure, entirely self inflicted but nevertheless uncomfortable. To run any school well takes enormous commitment and leaves little time for a life outside. Being a disabled head adds an extra dimension to planning and organisation.

Chapter 33

Learners in the driving seat

Chris Watkins

Who is responsible for children's learning in a primary school? Is it the headteacher, the governing body, teachers and teaching assistants, or an Education Secretary based in Westminster, perhaps? In Chapter 33, Chris Watkins, a Reader at the Institute of Education, University of London, suggests children should be much more involved and in control. He believes learning is usefully seen as a car journey and that children should be in the 'driving seat'.

School leadership today

Try this activity with a class you know. Ask them all to point an index finger at the ceiling. Tell them that you are going to ask them a question, and when they have come up with their answer to the question they should then point their finger at the answer. The question is: "Who is responsible for your learning?"

In many cases all fingers will point at the teacher. Sometimes pupils start to notice this and their fingers begin to waver. On one occasion I heard a class of 11-year-olds start to voice additional answers: "parents", "the governors", "the Government"! Whatever the immediate result, the ensuing conversation can lead to a few more learners quizzically pointing their fingers at themselves.

And who can blame them for being slow? After all, it's the school's performance that matters for league tables and it's the teacher's performance that all this management is about – so what do we suppose the learner actually does?

The picture in our classrooms is illuminated by recent evidence from interventions such as Assessment for Learning (AFL) and its later variants. When handled by the people who know its research base and understand the

Source: Watkins, C. (2009) 'Learners in the driving seat' *School Leadership Today, 12,* 28–31, Teaching Times.

rationale, a focus on learners' autonomy is a central theme (James *et al.*, 2006). Yet this same team of researchers finds that only one fifth of lessons in their project is characterised by such a spirit of AFL (Marshall and Drummond, 2006). It would be wrong to suggest that the reasons for low pupil autonomy are that teachers do not value it. Further Learning evidence shows that promoting learners' autonomy is where the gap is biggest between current classroom practice and teachers' values (James and Pedder, 2006). So we can gain optimism from knowing that teachers would wish the situation to be better, but doubtless feel significant tensions in the current climate.

So what do we want for learners in our classes (as well as for ourselves as learners)? Here's where the metaphor of 'driving' our learning can offer some valuable description. When driving we have an idea for a destination – perhaps a bit of a map of the territory; we have hands on the wheel, steering – making decisions as the journey unfolds; and all this is crucially related to the core process of noticing how it's going and how that relates to where we want to be. When it comes to learning, those core processes are the key to being an effective learner. They involve planning, monitoring, and reflecting.

Plenty of research demonstrates that when learners drive the learning it leads to:

- greater engagement and intrinsic motivation (Ryan and Deci, 2000)
- students setting higher challenge (Boggiano *et al.*, 1988)
- students evaluating their work (Boggiano and Katz, 1991)
- better problem-solving (Boggiano *et al.*, 1993).

If we continue the metaphor of learning as a journey then we can also reclaim something of value from the current overemphasis on end points and underemphasis on the journey to those ends. So how can we add some detail to this metaphor? Try reading the following sequence and see whether it describes some of your experience of a driving journey.

Before starting:

- Where do we want to get to?
- Which way should we go?
- Has someone got a map?
- Or shall we make up our own route?
- Is there anything to remember from previous journeys?
- Do we need to take any equipment?

On the road:

- How's it going?
- Are we on the right track?
- Do we need to change direction?
- Shall we check back on the map?
- Has anyone gone another way?
- Cor, look!

Journey's end:

- Where did we get to?
- Is this the place we planned? Maybe it's better!
- Shall we take a photo/send a postcard?
- Did anyone get here by another route?
- Where next?

Now read the sequence again and see whether it can describe some of your own experience of learning. If it does, you might agree that we can help any learner become more effective at the core skills of planning, monitoring and reflecting by using metaphors and prompts such as these. To do so is to help them notice more about the experience of learning and become more in charge of it. In any climate, it's the learners who are responsible for whatever achievements occur, so let's give them credit for it and improve from there.

No magic bullets

Classroom practices for promoting learner-driven learning (and there are no simple 'magic bullets') cluster around the themes of 'purpose and planning', 'choice', and 'voice and review'. If learners are to find purpose in classroom activities, we may need to revise some current practices which have squarely placed purpose in the voice of the teacher (as a ventriloquist for the QCA schemes of work). For example, Sonia is in a school where she is asked to put the 'learning objective' on the whiteboard. Fortunately she does not spend time getting learners to write it down, but instead asks them in pairs to discuss:

- What could it mean?
- Who uses that?

- What might I be able to do with it?
- How could we best learn that?

The discussions highlight important issues about understanding, and make key connections with pupils' real lives. And even a creative teacher like Sonia finds new ideas in the suggestions pupils make for how best to learn.

Learners also feel engagement with purpose when they feel they have made a choice. This point is sometimes responded to as though I was proposing the classroom suddenly becomes all 'free choice'. Not so. Indeed, children themselves do not seek this. Even young children express views along the lines of 'I want to make my own choices. . . sometimes.' Children can gain value from what adults choose as important. So even when pupils' choice is extended, it will be alongside another important aspect of learning – how they get themselves to do things they have not chosen.

Pupils might make classroom choices on what they learn, how they learn, how well they learn, and why they learn. Classroom approaches of the style of Philosophy for Children and 'intelligent learning' are salient here. When learners' questions are elicited in order to drive the agenda, teachers are often surprised. Sarah, a Reception class teacher, tried this at the start of a unit on forces, only to hear many high-level questions, including "How does a helicopter stay up?" In the same school Christie, a Year 6 teacher who is very practised in supporting learners' autonomy, was astounded at the questions that were generated after reading a short story: "What is real?", "How do we imagine?" and more.

For learners to 'drive' classroom activity we may have to review other current practices, especially those carrying the message that the teacher is driving the agenda (again sometimes as a ventriloquist for the latest package or the future test). Literacy is a domain where this is prevalent, and children continue to have to create text for the teacher, rather than write with their own purpose. A teacher, Maria, wrote to me recently about a colleague's experience with their Year 6 class as part of a school review of the curriculum: "They asked the children what they liked and what they would like to see more of (or less of). The children said that they would often just like to have a go at writing – they felt that the teachers modelled too much sometimes and it could take the fun out of writing. They felt that if they were given a chance to 'have a go' first, then any marking or feedback would make much more sense because they'd already know what they could do and what they needed to improve."

Maria herself is someone who also engages learners' voices in significant ways. Recently she was bored with starting the year on 'classroom codes' because they turn out to be focused on compliance. So she asked her class to decide some principles for how their classroom should be in order for their learning to be best. The class came up with four principles – listening to each other, active learning, sharing thoughts and ideas, and thinking of others – and created a large poster with the acronym 'We're LAST!' (a fun provocation for their teacher in a year which could be dominated by SATs!).

It's so much easier to review a journey when one has been aware of and in touch with it all along, and that is made easier if one has planned a direction at the start. So end-of-journey reviews are likely to be much more vibrant and rich than lots of the stilted conversations in current 'plenaries'. They may be prompted by asking: "How did the driving go?"

Promoting learner-driven learning

So how can we promote the development of more learner-driven learning? Here we may have to face the challenging insight from those who have studied the culture of schools and its impact on classroom pedagogy. As Seymour Sarason put it, teachers treat their pupils in the same way that they as teachers are treated by their managers. So has management in your school adopted the 'command and control' style favoured by government nowadays? Or does the management in your school recognise the facts of the school situation – that it's the classroom that makes the difference – and operate in a more distributed way to help the classroom be the best it can be?

Encouraging learner-driven learning needs several actions; one is *naming the problem*. We need to foster a widespread awareness that some aspects of the current climate may be having counter-productive effects in the classroom, as put by Maryellen Weimer:

- The more structured we make the environment, the more structure the students need.
- The more we decide for students, the more they expect us to decide.
- The more motivation we provide, the less they find within themselves.
- The more responsibility for learning we try to assume, the less they accept on their own.
- The more control we exert, the more restive their response (Weimer, 2002).

A second element of promoting learner-driven learning is *identifying the way ahead*. Here again, recent research points a direction. Out of many aspects of school conditions and their management that promote learner autonomy in the classroom, only one element has been shown to be Pedagogy Leading Learning influential: inquiry (Pedder, 2006). So here again there is a parallel between teachers' experience in school and learners' experience in the classroom. To turn this parallel into a proactive one for both parties, teachers need to inquire and thereby be treated as professional learners themselves.

Thirdly we must *recognise the tensions for teachers*. Without a supportive forum for experimentation to help them onwards, teachers are likely to fall back on archetypal judgements of their role. These old models have been repeated in modern times by the centralised strategies in which most of the practices are based on the idea that adults know best. This in turn reflects our society's deep underestimation of young people. So we will need to help colleagues talk about the tensions that arise when they start to operate in another way, promoting more autonomy for learners, and learn to judge themselves by another set of criteria. Did they help their learners learn how to drive?

Next there is *reviewing our planning*. Much of the current pattern of classroom life relates to the ways in which teachers are being pressured to plan. An experienced teacher said to me yesterday: "Effective learning happens in classrooms when freedom is planned for." This brilliant insight reminds us that it's not a matter of giving up planning, but more a process in which teachers avoid over-engineering through gradually released control of processes and objectives. It's about planning for what learners do rather than for what teachers do.

Finally it is necessary to *recognise the reservations*. There are likely to be several 'ah, buts' which may need to be addressed:

- "They haven't got the skills." Rather than talk about students in terms of deficits, can we think about their experience to date and whether we have helped them master it yet?
- "They're not mature enough yet!" So will we stand by and wait? Or will we offer the experiences that help them mature?
- "It's unrealistic to give kids absolute freedom!" That seems like an extreme suggestion – is there anything between the extremes?
- "We've got to get on with covering the curriculum." So what shall we do with the finding that learners who plan and reflect the most get 30 per cent better scores in public examination tasks?

In classroom life, learners can come to feel like either an origin or a pawn. An origin is someone who perceives their behaviour as determined by their own choosing, whereas a pawn is someone who perceives their behaviour as determined by external forces beyond their control. Students who have felt themselves to be pawns can be helped to become origins: they then catch up with the achievement norms of their age group, and succeed more in what school has to offer.

And just in case anyone was beginning to think that the theme of this article is a new-fangled way of handling classrooms, let's close with a reflection from nearly 400 years ago, which highlights a lot about classrooms today, and which could serve as a good motto for our management:

> *"Let the beginning and the end of our didactics be: seek and find the methods where the teacher teaches less but they who sit in the desks learn more. Let schools have less rush, less antipathy and less vain effort, but more well-being, convenience and permanent gain."*
>
> (Comenius, 1632)

References

Atkinson, S. (1999), 'Key factors influencing pupil motivation in design and technology', *Journal of Technology Education* 10:2, 4–2.

Boggiano, A.K., Flink, C., Shields, A. *et al.* (1993), 'Use of techniques promoting students' self-determination: effects on students' analytic problem-solving skills', *Motivation and Emotion* 17, 319–336.

Boggiano, A.K., Katz, P.A. (1991), 'Maladaptive achievement patterns in students: The role of teachers' controlling strategies', *Journal of Social Issues* 47:4, 35–51.

Boggiano, A.K., Main, D.S., Katz, P.A. (1988), 'Children's preference for challenge: the role of perceived competence and control', *Journal of Personality and Social Psychology*, 54:1, 134–141.

Comenius, Jan Amos (1632), *The Great Didactic*.

James, M., Black, P., McCormick, R., Pedder, D., Wiliam, D. (2006), 'Introduction: Learning How to Learn, in Classrooms, Schools and Networks: aims, design and analysis', *Research Papers in Education* 21:2, 101–118.

James, M., Pedder, D. (2006), 'Beyond method: assessment and learning practices and values', *The Curriculum Journal* 17:2, 109–138.

Marshall, B., Drummond, M.J. (2006), 'How teachers engage with Assessment for Learning: lessons from the classroom', *Research Papers in Education* 21:2, 133–149.

Pedder, D. (2006), 'Organizational conditions that foster successful classroom promotion of Learning How to Learn', *Research Papers in Education* 21:2, 171–200.

Ryan, R.M., Deci, E.L. (2000), 'Intrinsic and extrinsic motivations: classic definitions and new directions', *Contemporary Educational Psychology* 25, 54–67.

Weimer, M. (2002), *Learner Centered Teaching: Five Key Changes to Practice*, Jossey-Bass.

Chapter 34

An interactive pedagogy

Charmian Kenner

Many people in the world regard their ability to speak and understand more than one language to be an integral part of their cultural identity. In this chapter, Charmian Kenner examines the knowledge and understanding that bilingual children bring with them to school. She also explores the ways in which children can draw on their awareness of different languages in developing literacy and learning in more than one language.

Would you like to do more Gujarati at school?
Yes, write things in Gujarati, draw things and write the words, and make things.

(Meera, aged 7)

In this statement, Meera expresses her hope and belief that her home language, Gujarati, could be integrated into the everyday activities of her primary school class. For bilingual children, interaction between a rich variety of linguistic and cultural experiences is an ever present feature of their lives. If schools can build on these interactions, the potential contribution to children's learning is huge. To do so requires a commitment to developing education for a multilingual and multicultural society, with the all round benefits which this will entail for children from both monolingual and bilingual backgrounds. Whilst the need for a national educational policy is clear, practitioners also have a key part to play. This chapter will discuss how teachers and teaching assistants can enhance children's educational experiences by enabling linguistic and cultural interaction to take place within the classroom, and between school and community life.

Source: An edited version of Kenner, C. (2003) 'An interactive pedagogy for bilingual children', in E. Bearne, H. Dombey, and T. Grainger (eds) *Classroom Interactions in Literacy* (Maidenhead: Open University Press/McGraw-Hill) pp. 90–102.

As teachers and teaching assistants know, the quality of their relationships with children is key, and depends on a recognition of the 'whole child' as a complex and multifunctional person with an already established history in their home and community. In the case of bilingual children, an important element is the recognition of their bilingual and bicultural knowledge, which is a fundamental part of their identities as learners. I shall first look at what kind of knowledge children might have, based on the findings of research with young bilingual learners in London, England.

The next step is to make links with children's knowledge in curriculum activities, and I shall discuss how this might be accomplished, drawing on the experience of an action research project which created a multilingual literacy environment in a nursery classroom. While my own experience is with young learners, a stage when it is particularly possible – and crucially important – to build links with children and families, a multilingual approach can be used with any age group and I shall suggest how this can be done.

Bilingual children's knowledge and capabilities

The majority of children in the world are bilingual. Growing up with more than one language and literacy is part of life in many countries which operate multilingually (Datta 2000), and also occurs through the increasingly common experience of families moving to a new country. From birth, children have the potential to become proficient users of any language met within their daily environment (Baker 2000). By opening our minds to these possibilities, we can discover what children have already learned in the world outside the classroom.

By the age of 3 or 4, when they begin to enter the school system, many young bilingual children will have encountered literacy materials in different languages at home, ranging from a newspaper being read by a grandparent in Turkish, to an air letter being written by a parent in Gujarati, to a Chinese calendar on the kitchen wall. As part of their continual curiosity about graphic symbols, children start to interpret the potential meanings of these texts. In some cases, they are able to combine their interpretations with ideas derived from direct instruction in their home literacy, because family members may have begun teaching them some initial reading and writing.

For example, 4-year-old Mohammed, growing up in south London, was being taught by his mother how to recognize the letters of the Arabic alphabet in preparation for joining Qur'anic classes at the age of 5 (Kenner 2000). Mohammed's older siblings already had their own copy of the Qur'an, and Mohammed would receive his when he had learned sufficient

Arabic – a strong motive for literacy acquisition. When Mohammed's mother prepared a poster showing the Arabic alphabet for use in his nursery class at primary school, Mohammed proceeded to demonstrate his knowledge of the letters. As well as being able to name some of the letters for his nursery classmates, he worked by himself to produce his own version of his mother's poster in which each letter was accurately written. His mother was astonished to see Mohammed's work because she had so far only taught him to read: 'He's never written any Arabic before!' The detail of the letters was a considerable accomplishment for a 4-year-old, and showed Mohammed's desire to become a writer in Arabic.

In contrast, 3-year-old Meera (who attended the same nursery class) was being taught to write only in English by her mother because her parents thought it would be easier for her to learn one literacy first. However, Meera herself had other ideas. As well as speaking Gujarati at home, she had participated in literacy events involving Gujarati script, such as sitting next to her mother while letters were being written to her grandparents in India and writing her own 'letter', or observing her mother filling in crosswords in Gujarati newspapers. When she saw her mother writing in Gujarati for a multilingual display in the nursery, Meera climbed on a chair to do her own emergent writing underneath. She stated 'I want my Gujarati' and 'I write like my mum'. Meera's determination to find out more about Gujarati writing, fuelled by its significance in her home life, continued during the school year with a series of spontaneous versions of a poster made by her mother about Meera's favourite 'Bollywood' film video.

Comments by Meera as she was making these posters in the nursery showed how, at the age of 4, she was able to think about different aspects of literacy and enhance her learning by comparisons between her two writing systems. Like Mohammed, she looked closely at the detail of letters, noting that her mother's version of the English 'a' looked different, rather like an inverted 'p' ('my mummy done a "p" – never mind'), and considering in what order she produced the different elements of a Gujarati letter (asking herself as she wrote it for the second time 'Did I do the line first? Yes I did'). Noticing that her mother had written three groups of letters representing the names of the film heroes in Gujarati, but that only two groups of letters appeared in English underneath, she asked 'Why three?' She had realized that there should be a correspondence between equivalent items in the two languages, and indeed it turned out that Meera's mother had not been sure how to transliterate the third hero's name.

Some children, like Mohammed, begin to attend community language classes at the age of 5 or 6, while also learning to read and write in English at primary school. A research project (Kenner et al. 2004) showed that young children are very capable of dealing simultaneously with more than one language and script. Case studies of 6-year-olds attending Saturday school classes in Chinese, Arabic or Spanish produced striking evidence of their ideas about different writing systems. This knowledge was demonstrated when the children were engaged in 'peer teaching sessions', showing their primary school classmates how to write in their home literacy.

Selina, for example, who had been attending Chinese school since the age of 5, was already proficient at writing Chinese characters. A page from her first year exercise book showed the process of building up a character through the correct stroke sequence, and then practising it for several columns. Each stroke needed to be executed precisely, to achieve a character which was both correct and aesthetically pleasing. Selina was proud of her writing, demonstrating characters of considerable complexity to her primary school peers. She also understood that the Chinese writing system operated very differently from English. Chinese does not have an alphabet; rather, most Chinese characters correspond to an English word. Selina's mother was teaching her about the meaning of different elements within a character, for example, the symbol for 'fire' appears in a number of associated characters such as 'lamp'. Selina would point out the symbols she found within characters, such as 'fire' in 'autumn'.

Tala, learning Arabic, emphasized that her 'pupils' in peer teaching sessions must start from the right-hand side of the page when doing Arabic writing, and she provided a helpful arrow to remind them. She also commented on grammatical features of Arabic such as male and female verb endings, writing an explanation to emphasize (in case her audience was unsure) that 'femail is a girl' and 'mail is a boy'.

Brian showed his primary school class the typical way of learning to write in Spanish, by forming syllables which combined a consonant with a vowel. Using the example of the letter 'm', and translating his Spanish teacher's explanation into English, he told his classmates 'the M on her own doesn't say anything, just "mmm" – you have to put it together . . . with "a" it makes "ma" '. He also showed his 'pupils' how to write and pronounce the Spanish letter 'ñ' (as in the word 'España'), saying It's a different N'.

We can see that these children – all of whom were also making steady progress in English – were deriving considerable benefit from the experience of biliteracy. As a result of their participation in the research project, their knowledge became evident to their primary school teachers, just as Mohammed and Meera's understandings had become visible in the nursery class. I will now discuss how the teachers' responses enabled children's bilingual knowledge to become more closely woven into their primary school learning.

Developing multilingual learning environments in the classroom

An interactive pedagogy for bilingual children involves several elements. The first of these is a teacher who sees bilingualism as a resource rather than a problematic condition, and wishes to expand her knowledge about her pupils' home and community learning. It is not necessary to be an expert on what happens in children's homes – indeed, this is not even possible, given the huge variety of linguistic and cultural experiences which would be relevant to any multilingual group of pupils. What is important, and will be sensed by children and families, is a clearly stated support for bilingualism and an open-minded interest in how children are achieving this.

Support and interest are most strongly demonstrated by the second element of the pedagogy, which is a *direct engagement* with children's bilingual learning in the classroom. In the research project in Meera and Mohammed's nursery class, I worked collaboratively with the teacher to find out in what ways it was possible to create a multilingual literacy environment. We began by informally talking with parents about literacy materials and events in different languages which children enjoyed at home. In this way we found out that, for example, Mohammed liked listening to a tape of a children's song about the Arabic alphabet. We invited Mohammed to bring this tape into the nursery so that the whole nursery group could hear it, and asked his mother to make a poster showing the alphabet letters (with a transliteration in English) so that we could sing along with the tape.

The third step is to *integrate* bilingual material into curriculum activities. In the case of the Arabic tape and poster, these became part of the nursery's investigation of how graphic symbols relate to meaning – an essential building block for early literacy. As well as the English alphabet, we now had a new set of different looking symbols which related to a different set of sounds. The teacher talked about this with the whole class, and, whether bilingual or monolingual, the children were intrigued. Extra impetus was given to their understanding of the concept of sound–symbol relationships. Mohammed's own Arabic alphabet poster was displayed alongside an English poster, next to a cassette player into which children could place different tapes. Over the next few weeks, the children were observed to select the English alphabet song, or the Arabic one, and to dance to the music while pointing to various letters on the posters, showing that they were thinking about the possible connections. Children also made their own alphabet posters, using the English and Arabic posters as a resource. Again, this extended the range of their investigations into literacy.

The fourth element of the pedagogy is to give *institutional* support to children's home and community learning activities. In the nursery, this was happening directly through the important place being given to bilingual learning in the classroom. For Mohammed, it meant that he gained the opportunity to further explore and reflect on his home experiences of the Arabic alphabet. A few weeks after making his first poster, he decided to make a similar one, again based on his mother's example. He also wrote some of the Arabic alphabet letters as part of a text which included a drawing of 'a snake in the garden'. The interest of his teacher and classmates legitimized Mohammed's Arabic learning, which would otherwise have occurred at the margins of officially recognized education rather than in the mainstream, and this had a positive effect on his involvement at home; his mother reported that she heard him singing the Arabic alphabet song more often.

Over the school year, many bilingual texts were produced by children in the nursery, and, by engaging with material which interested them from home, the multilingual work proved motivating to several who otherwise seemed to be 'reluctant writers'. Billy's main enthusiasm for writing at home, according to his mother, was shown when he sat alongside her as she wrote letters to Thailand, talking about what she would say to the family and doing his own writing at the same time. When Billy's mother wrote an airletter in Thai in the nursery, this led him to write some symbols of which he said 'Mu-ang Thai' ('Thailand') and 'I write like my mum'. This was the gateway to a spate of texts produced by Billy at home, including both English and Thai symbols as well as drawings of people, and to an increase in his writing at nursery. When his mother brought a birthday card to Billy from his aunt in Thailand to show us, she placed it in the nursery book bag which was designed to carry his school reading books. Her action symbolized the links built between home and school literacy.

In the pedagogy just described, each element of the process interacts with the others, leading to the development of a 'virtuous circle' which recognizes, sustains and extends children's learning. When we engaged with Meera's home language in the nursery by asking her mother to join in a multilingual activity for parents, we discovered more about Meera's interest in home literacy events; while she did her emergent Gujarati below her mother's writing, Meera began to talk about films and TV. By asking her mother more about this, we discovered that Meera loved watching Indian films with her family. Thus the second step of the pedagogic process linked back to the first, expanding our knowledge about Meera's home experiences. The third step, integrating the film material into the curriculum, owed its success to the centrality of film watching in Meera's family life. When Meera brought her film video into the nursery, we showed one of her favourite extracts during the nursery's weekly 'video time'. Her mother's poster about the film, written rapidly at our request in the nursery one morning before she left to go to work, then provided Meera with a link between home and school which inspired her to create five related texts over the next three months adding to her learning in both English and Gujarati.

The third element of the pedagogy, integrating bilingual learning into curriculum activities, has a direct effect on the fourth, because it is the strongest form of support for bilingualism from an institution which ethnic minority families perceive as particularly powerful – the school. It also links back to the first and second elements, because as parents and children see that home literacy materials are being used as part of the curriculum, rather than as temporary decoration, they are motivated to bring more materials and to participate in writing events in the classroom. When Billy's mother and other parents were asked to write air letters in different languages in the nursery, as if they were writing to relatives at home, they agreed to participate in this role play activity because they knew that their texts would be used for the children's further learning.

Another way of taking the fourth step – giving institutional support to children's home learning activities – is to initiate direct contact with community language schools. During the research project with biliterate 6-year-olds, the children's primary school teachers began to see evidence of their community school learning. The teachers were keen to meet their pupils' Saturday school teachers to find out more about this other educational setting. At a specially organized seminar, the two groups met together, with the primary teachers expressly stating that they were coming in order to learn. As the community teachers explained how they went about their work each Saturday, the mainstream teachers realized that these were colleagues with professional knowledge, whose commitment to their pupils was total despite their low paid voluntary status.

The seminar had a profound effect on the primary teachers' understanding of bilingual learning, giving them a much fuller idea of how such learning was both possible and productive. When the biliterate children taught their whole primary school class as part of the research project, the teachers used this new information to support the activity. Ming's teacher decided to give him the opportunity to teach Chinese in one of the periods assigned daily to reading and writing work, the Literacy Hour, and drew on what she had learned from the seminar to make suggestions about the kind of issues he could talk about. These suggestions linked in with Ming's own ideas; he had spontaneously set about planning his lesson at home the night before, and arrived with a set of activities already on paper. The lesson lasted for an hour and a half, with Ming's classmates thoroughly engaged in the challenge of writing Chinese characters on their whiteboards. As soon as he arrived home from school that afternoon, Ming phoned me (I had also been present at the session) to ask 'Charmian, when can I teach Chinese again – the whole class?' He had already evaluated his lesson and decided which characters would be most appropriate to teach next time; the experience of teaching in mainstream school had thus validated and added to his Saturday school learning.

Maintaining an interactive pedagogy

Once having begun to make links with bilingual pupils' educational experiences outside the mainstream classroom, teachers can conduct an ongoing dialogue with children and families which enriches learning. This dialogue can include remaining aware of children's current home and community interests, and celebrating Saturday school work, for example, by making a photo display of children who attend community language classes and noting their achievements. In Britain, children can be encouraged to record their knowledge in the European Language Portfolio designed for use in schools (CILT 2002).

Where multilingual activities have been incorporated into the curriculum, teachers can direct parents' attention to the texts made by children and what has been learnt from them, and this discussion can take place with monolingual as well as bilingual parents. The learning may involve general issues about language, such as how alphabets work, or specific content, such as how to write particular Chinese characters. In either case, teachers do not need to know the languages involved in order to facilitate learning; in the nursery there were at least ten different languages, of which we only knew one. We were able to draw on the knowledge of children, their siblings and other family members.

This interactive pedagogy can also be pursued with children in the upper primary years and with young people in secondary school. They may have had the opportunity to further develop their biliteracy knowledge at community language school, or they may have come directly from another country where they have been educated in a different language. As well as demonstrating their knowledge in activities which raise language awareness for the whole class, pupils can make use of their other literacies to write subject-based material. A project in a London secondary school involved producing web pages in English and Bengali (Anderson 2001) with a potential worldwide audience; this experience enabled the pupils to extend their range of writing in both languages. In this kind of work, texts brought from home can again be a point of reference; newspapers in different languages, for example, provide a resource for a vast number of culturally related topics.

Expanding multilingual pedagogies

Multilingual work in schools can flourish more widely if there is institutional support. At the level of the individual school, this is aided by a whole-school language policy which states that home languages are an integral part of learning. This, in turn, is given weight if national policies take a similar view. Taking England as an example, it seems that the tide which has been running against multilingualism in education since the 1980s may be beginning to turn. Although bilingual children's knowledge has been little recognized in educational initiatives of recent years – the national curriculum of 1989 was set up on an entirely monolingual and monocultural basis – there are signs of change at a national policy level which can potentially support work in home languages in schools.

Both in England and elsewhere, as increasing numbers of children live multilingual lives, teachers need to engage with this variety of experience and explore its potential to enhance learning. A multilingual pedagogy engages children positively by integrating their home and community knowledge into mainstream classroom work. The impact on children's self-esteem is considerable and supports further learning both inside and outside school. Classrooms become sites where, as 7-year-old Meera envisaged, children can 'write things . . . draw things and write the words, and make things' in more than one language. Teachers and teaching assistants become the active facilitators of this linguistic and cultural creativity.

References

Anderson, J. (2001) 'Web publishing in non-Roman scripts: effects on the writing process', *Language and Education*, 15(4), 229–49.

Baker, C. (2000) *A Parents' and Teachers' Guide to Bilingualism*. Clevedon: Multilingual Matters.

CILT (Centre for Information on Language Teaching and Research) (2002) *European Language Portfolio*. London: CILT.

Datta, M. (2000) *Bilinguality and Literacy: Principles and Practice*. London: Continuum.

Kenner, C. (2000) *Home Pages: Literacy Links for Bilingual Children*. Stoke-on-Trent: Trentham Books.

Kenner, C., Kress, G., Al-Khatib, H., Kam, R. and Tsai, K-C. (2004) Finding the keys to biliteracy: how young children interpret different writing systems, *Language and Education*, 18(2), 124–44.

Reproduced from Kenner, C. (2003) 'An interactive pedagogy for bilingual children', in: E.Bearne, H.Dombey and T.Grainger (eds.), *Classroom Interactions in Literacy*, pages 90–102 with the kind permission of the Open University Press/McGraw-Hill Publishing Company.

Chapter 35

Beyond pink and blue

Robin Cooley

Robin Cooley, a teacher in Newton, Massachusetts, has worked to increase children's understanding of the way in which advertising and commercial products reinforce gender, race and family stereotypes. In this chapter she tells how she used stories to break gender stereotypes and how this led her fourth grade class (9-year-olds) to influence the advertising approach of a toy company.

'Pink, pink, pink! Everything for girls in this catalogue is pink' exclaimed Kate, one of my fourth graders, as she walked into the classroom one morning, angrily waving the latest 'Pottery Barn Kids' catalogue in the air. 'I hate the colour pink. This catalogue is reinforcing too many stereotypes, Ms Cooley, and we need to do something about it!'

I knew she was right. And I was glad to see that our classroom work on stereotypes resulted in my students taking action: As we finished up the school year, my students initiated a letter-writing campaign to Pottery Barn, one of the country's most popular home furnishings catalogues.

Newton Public Schools is actively working to create an anti-bias/anti-racist school environment. In fact, beginning in fourth grade, we teach all students about the cycle of oppression that creates and reinforces stereotypes. I wove discussion of the cycle of oppression throughout my curriculum to help my students understand how stereotypes are created and reinforced, and more important, how we can unlearn them.

Anti-bias literature

I began the year's anti-bias work in my multiracial classroom by looking at gender stereotypes. As a dialogue trigger, I read aloud the picture book

Source: An edited version of Cooley, R. (2003) 'Beyond pink and blue' *Rethinking Schools, 18* (2). (Milwaukee: Rethinking Schools).

William's Doll, by Charlotte Zolotow. This is a wonderful story about a little boy who is teased and misunderstood by his friends and family because he wants a doll. When I finished the book, I asked the students the following discussion questions: 'Why was William teased? What did William's father expect him to be good at because he was a boy?' I explained that the fact that William was expected to like sports and play with trains were examples of stereotypes, oversimplified pictures or opinions of a person or group that are not true.

Next, I asked the class, 'Why did William's family and friends tease him because he wanted a doll? Why should only girls play with dolls? Where did this idea come from?' The students immediately said, 'Family!' Through discussion, the students began to understand that they are surrounded by messages that reinforce these stereotypes. We brainstormed some ideas of where these messages come from, such as television shows, advertisements, and books.

Next, I asked the class, 'Why didn't William's father listen to his son when he said he wanted a doll?' One student exclaimed, 'Because William's father believed only girls played with dolls!' I explained that the father believed this stereotype was true.

One boy in my class complained, 'I don't get it. I like dolls and stuffed animals. Why did William's dad care? Why didn't he buy his son what he wanted? That doesn't seem fair. Someday, I'm going to buy my kid whatever he wants!'

Finally, I asked the class, 'In the story, who was William's ally? Who did not believe the stereotype and helped William get what he wanted?' The students knew that William's grandmother was the one who stood up for him. She was an example of an ally. William's grandmother bought William the doll, and she taught the father that it is okay for boys to want to hold dolls, the same way he held and cared for William when he was a baby.

Each week during the fall semester, I read a picture book that defied gender stereotypes, and we had discussions like the one on *William's Doll*. Tomie dePaola's *Oliver Button Is a Sissy* is another excellent book about a boy who wants to be accepted for who he is. Oliver really wanted to be a dancer, and all the kids at school teased him about this. Despite great adversity and risk, Oliver had the courage to do what he wanted to do, not what others expected him to do or be. After reading the book, students in my class were able to share personal stories of what their parents expected them to do, or when they were teased for doing something 'different'.

A few more tales that helped to break gender stereotypes were *Amazing Grace*, by Mary Hoffman and *Horace and Morris but Mostly Dolores*, by James Howe. In *Amazing Grace*, Grace loves to act in plays and has been taught that you can be anything you want if you put your mind to it. When she wants to audition for the part of Peter Pan, her classmates say she can't. But she pursues her dream and gets the part.

Horace and Morris, but Mostly Dolores is about three mice that are best friends. One day, the two boy mice decide to join the Mega-Mice Club, but no girls are allowed. Dolores pins the Cheese Puffs Club for girls. She is unhappy and bored because all the girls want to do is make crafts and discuss ways to 'get a fella using mozzarella'. One day, the three friends decide to quit their clubs and build a clubhouse of their own where everyone is allowed, and you can do whatever you want, whether you're a boy or a girl.

Looking at families

Next we explored stereotypes about families. The students were aware of the messages they've absorbed from our culture about what a family is supposed to look like. Ben, who is adopted, said he was upset when people asked him who his 'real' mom was. 'I hate that I have to explain that I have a birth mother who I don't know, and my mom lives with me at home!' he said. We discussed some different family structures and talked about how some families might have two moms or two dads, a single parent, or a guardian. *Heather Has Two Mommies*, by Leslie Newman, is a great picture book that illustrates this point.

After two months of eye-opening discussions, the last anti-bias picture book I read to my class was *King and King*, by Linda De Haan. This picture book does not have the typical Disney ending. In this story, the queen is tired and wants to marry off her son so he can become king and she can retire. One by one, princesses come, hoping the prince will fall in love with them. Each time, the prince tells his queen mother that he doesn't feel any connection. It's not until the last princess arrives with her brother that the prince feels something – but it's not for the princess. He falls in love with her brother. The queen approves, and they get married and become 'king and king'. My students loved this story because the ending is not what they expected at all! They also appreciated hearing a picture book that has gay characters because they know gay people exist. They wondered why there aren't more gays and lesbians in picture books.

Since my students were so excited about their anti-bias work, I decided we should do a project with our first-grade buddies and teach them about breaking stereotypes. We created a big book called 'What Everyone Needs to Know'. This became a coffee-table book that we left on the table at the school's entrance waiting area. The first and fourth graders brainstormed all the stereotypes that we knew about boys, girls, and families. Then each pair picked a stereotype to illustrate on two different pages. On one page, the heading was, 'Some people think that . . .' with a drawing portraying the stereotype. On the next page, the heading would say, 'but everyone needs to know that . . .' with a drawing breaking the stereotype. For example, one pair came up with, 'Some people think that all families have a mom and a dad, but everyone needs to know that all families are different. Some families have two moms or two dads. Some families have one grandparent. All families are different.'

Another pair came up with, 'Some people think that only girls wear jewellery but everyone needs to know that both boys and girls wear jewellery'.

I knew our work on stereotypes was sinking in because my students would continually share with the class examples of how they tried to speak up when they saw people acting on stereotypical beliefs. One day, a student told the class about how she spoke up to a nurse at the hospital where her baby brother was just born. 'I couldn't believe the nurses wrapped him in a blue blanket and the baby girls in pink!' she said. 'I asked the nurse why the hospital did that and she said it was their policy. I don't think I can change the hospital's policy, but maybe I at least made that nurse stop and think.'

Making a difference

The day my class decided that they wanted to write individual letters to 'Pottery Barn Kids' catalogue was the day I knew my students felt they could make a difference in this world. They wrote letters that told the truth about how they felt and why they thought the catalogue was so hurtful to them. I was so proud that my students were able to explain specific examples of gender stereotypes in the catalogue and why they thought the images should change. The students analysed the catalogue front to back, and picked out things I hadn't noticed. One student wrote:

Dear Pottery Barn Kids,
I do not like the way you put together your catalogue because it reinforces too many stereotypes about boys and girls. For instance, in a picture of the boys' room, there are only two books and the rest of the stuff are trophies. This shows boys and girls who look at your catalogue that boys should be good at sports and girls should be very smart. I am a boy and I love to read.

The boys in my classroom felt comfortable enough to admit out loud and in writing that they wished they saw more images of boys playing with dolls and stuffed animals. Another boy wrote:

Dear Pottery Barn Kids,
I am writing this letter because I am mad that you have so many stereotypes in your magazine. You're making me feel uncomfortable because I'm a boy and I like pink, reading, and stuffed animals. All I saw in the boys' pages were dinosaurs and a lot of blue and sports.
    Also, it's not just that your stereotypes make me mad but you're also sending messages to kids that this is what they should be. If it doesn't stop soon, then there will be a boys world and a girls world. I'd really like it if (and I bet other kids would too) you had girls playing sports stuff and boys playing with stuffed animals and dolls.
    Thank you for taking the time to read this letter. I hope I made you stop and think.
    – From a Newton student

The day we received a letter from the president of Pottery Barn, my students were ecstatic. The president, Laura Alber, thanked the students for 'taking time to write and express your opinions on our catalogue. We'll try to incorporate your feedback into the propping and staging of our future catalogues and we hope that you continue to see improvement in our depiction of boys and girls.'
    I knew the students would expect the next Pottery Barn Kids catalogue to be completely void of pink and blue and I reminded them that change is slow. The most important thing is that they made the president of a large corporation stop and think. I pointed to two of the quotes I have hanging in my classroom, and we read them out loud together:

Never doubt that a small group of thoughtful, committed citizens can change the world. Indeed, it's the only thing that ever has.
– Margaret Mead

Each of us influences someone else, often without realizing it. It is within our power to make a difference.
– Deval Patrick

Epilogue

The next Pottery Barn Kids catalogue arrived in my mailbox in late August, and the first thing I noticed was the cover. There's a picture of a boy, sitting at a desk, doing his homework. Another picture shows a boy talking on the phone, not just a girl, which was something one of my students had suggested. The boy is also looking at a *Power Puff* magazine, something that is typically targeted for girls. When I asked one of my former students what she thought, she said, 'Well, the catalogue sort of improved the boys, but not really the girls. They still have a lot of changes to make.'

One thing I know for sure is that my students now look at advertisements with a critical eye, and I hope they have learned that they do have the power to make a difference in this world.

References

De Haan, L. (2002) *King and King*. Berkeley: Tricycle Press.
dePaola, T. (1990) *Oliver Button Is a Sissy*. New York: Voyager Books.
Hoffman, M. (1991) *Amazing Grace*. New York: Scott Foreman.
Howe, J. (2003) *Horace and Morris, but Mostly Dolores*. New York: Aladdin Library.
Newman, L. (2000) *Heather Has Two Mommies*. Los Angeles: Alyson Publications.
Zolotow, C. (1985) *William's Doll*. New York: HarperTrophy.

Chapter 36

Working with boys

Diane Reay

Boys' achievement in schools is a cause for concern. In this chapter Diane Reay, professor of education at Cambridge University, looks back over her career and suggests that this is not a new phenomenon. Boys' achievement, she believes, cannot be separated from a discussion of class, race, or an understanding of how these different factors impact on boys' self perceptions and group identity.

Introduction

There is a long history of concern in relation to boys' behaviour in primary classrooms. My own career has been inextricably entangled with, and defined by, that concern. After becoming a Gender Equality Advisory Teacher in Ealing, London, even more of my energies went into boys. Despite my own desire to work on gender projects that involved girls, the pressing concerns of the primary school teachers I was working with dictated that the vast majority of the projects that I initiated focused on boys. As I wrote in the article describing my work on gender in Ealing:

> In the last two years over a dozen teachers, all female, have approached me to discuss boys in their class who were presenting problems by demanding an excessively high proportion of teacher time and attention; in terms of discipline in both the classroom and playground; and through lower levels of engagement with the English curriculum resulting in lower levels of achievement than the girls.
>
> (Reay 1993:13)

The inevitable consequence was that gender work became work with boys. So, in the mid-1990s, after 17 years as a primary practitioner whose main

Source: A revised version of Reay, D. (2003) 'Troubling, troubled and troublesome? Working with boys in primary classrooms', in C. Skelton and B. Francis (eds) *Boys and Girls in the Primary Classroom* (Maidenhead: Open University Press/McGraw-Hill) pp. 151–166.

tasks had been variously motivating, 'rescuing' and 'reforming' boys, I was amused by the allegedly new discovery of boys' underachievement and disaffection. Where had everyone been for the past two decades? Certainly not in any of the inner London schools that I had been working in. This concern about boys' disaffection has continued into the millennium.

The first key point to make is that it is primarily, although not exclusively, a class phenomenon. The research by Frosh et al. (2002) is very useful here. It demonstrates how challenging the teacher is an integral component of popularity among male peer groups across social class, although the middle-class boys, and particularly those attending private schools, also recognise the needs to work hard academically. The second key point to make about boys and disaffection is that it has a long history.

Classed and racialized masculinities

The educational context of boys' disaffection is very different now to what it was in the late 1980s. The tensions have both increased and intensified. There has been a widening of social class inequalities, an increasing privatisation of education, the implementation of the National Curriculum and an intensification of both selection and testing (Reay 2006). As David Jackson (1998:79) points out, these processes have resulted in many boys feeling 'brushed aside by dominant definitions of school knowledge – their home and community languages, their often raw but direct insights and their everyday, street knowledges have all been experienced as invalid' as a limited, exclusive definition of school knowledge has gained dominance.

Competitive grading, testing and streaming have instituted a steep academic hierarchy which has emphasised differences between masculinities and has widened the gap between 'failing and disruptive boys' (particularly white working-class and African Caribbean boys) and successful boys (predominantly white and middle class). Paul Connolly (2004) captures the radicalization of disaffection in his account of the over disciplining of Black boys in primary schools, a process which sets up a vicious cycle of stereotyping. Connolly describes how the over disciplining of 'the bad boys', four African Caribbean boys in the primary school he studied, generated a peer group context in which they were more likely to be physically and verbally abused. Connolly (1997:114) concludes that as a consequence they were more likely to be drawn into fights and to develop 'hardened' identities which then meant they were more likely to be noticed by teachers and disciplined for being aggressive.

The current educational climate has exacerbated an entrenched culture of winners and losers broadly along social class and ethnic lines, and in doing so, increased the already existing working-class and racialized alienation from schooling. Willis (1997) captured the powerful, and often explosive, combination of anger, fatalism, alienation and resistance that characterised white working-class male relationships to schooling in the 1970s but in the 2010s the conditions that generated such disaffection are even more pervasive. And, in primary classrooms across the UK, the resulting social exclusion and academic rejection that such conditions generate entice failing boys into a compensatory culture of aggressive laddism (Jackson 1998; Connolly 2007). Lucey and Walkerdine attribute this 'aggressive laddism' and the anti-reading and anti-school position that underpins it to 'a defence against fear. They act against study for fear of the loss of masculinity'; a masculinity that, they go on to argue, 'is already seriously under threat in terms of the disappearance of the jobs which require it' (Lucey and Walkerdine 2000:49). However, it is important to recognise that there are other losers from boys' disruptive behaviour – girls and teachers – and we need to explore how they are affected by boys' disaffection.

At the receiving end?: the impact of boys' behaviour on girls and women teachers

Women teachers, classroom assistants and female pupils can be dominated and oppressed by certain boys in primary classrooms. A classic study by Valerie Walkerdine (1981) describes the humiliation of a female nursery teacher by a 4-year-old boy. Almost all women teachers can recite low level incidents of rudeness and abuse by a small number of boys who have been in their charge.

In many classrooms I have worked and researched in, it is girls who are at the bottom of the male peer group hierarchies! It is easy to forget when responding to the pressure to change boys' behaviour, and the media hype that 'the future is female', that it is still necessary to engage in work that focuses on girls' learning as well. What boys and girls need are gender equality programmes which privilege both sexes rather than focus on the needs of one at the expense of the other (Skelton 2001b).

Practicalities: what can teachers and teaching assistants do?

So how can school staff work productively on changing peer group hierarchies rather than either challenging or accommodating them? And how do they improve the classroom environment for the girls and the majority of boys who, as Connell (2000:162) points out, 'learn to negotiate school discipline with only a little friction'? It is important to remember that in spite of popular scare stories about underachieving and uncontrollable boys, the majority of boys in primary schools relate perfectly well to their female teachers and girls. I still believe that paradoxically bringing the concerns of the pupil peer group into the classroom is important in reducing and addressing disaffection. There is an even greater temptation now with the National Curriculum and the relentless testing and auditing to leave those concerns at the classroom door but I strongly believe that they will flood in anyway, impacting on behaviour and learning, creating at best divisions amongst children, at worst major disruption. This is particularly so in relation to bullying.

A great deal of my work with boys in the 1980s focused on bullying because that was an issue that all the boys' groups identified as a major problem for them. Writing about the boys' group I ran in 1988/9 I stated:

> The sessions we had on bullying were amongst the most productive of the year. First there was genuine relief amongst the boys that the subject was being tackled directly. Everyone, including myself, recalled an incident in which they had been bullied, while just over a third of the boys admitted to having bullied on at least one occasion. It was obviously a very emotive issue, and one that for the year six boys was inextricably bound up with their fantasies and fears about moving on to secondary school. We spent two sessions attempting to work through such fears and fantasies, focusing on how to use humour, peer group support and adult authority to prevent bullying.
>
> (Reay 1990:276–7)

Of course now there would not be the space for such sessions among the contemporary preoccupation with Standardised Assessment Tasks (SATs) but perhaps what I did with the Year 5 (9–10-year-old) boys would be more of a possibility. I integrated a focus on bullying into their maths and information communication technology (ICT) curriculum. We designed a questionnaire for a whole school survey on bullying, worked out a representative sample and then the boys carried it out. An integral part of their task was to impart the strategies for dealing with bullying we had discussed and agreed in the group sessions to any younger child who disclosed that they had been bullied. As only two children in the sample claimed never to have been bullied, the boys had lots of opportunities to rehearse preventative strategies. Since this work on bullying, my own more recent research and that of others (Reay 2009a; Frosh *et al.* 2002) has revealed that working hard and being diligent at school can lead to boys being bullied. Frosh et al. (2002) found a polarisation of popularity and schoolwork in which popular masculinities are pervasively constructed as antithetical to being seen to work hard academically, leading to hardworking 'clever' boys being demonised within the male peer group.

Research has uncovered disturbingly high levels of bullying in primary schools. Whitney and Smith (1993) revealed that over 25 per cent of primary school pupils were being bullied in Sheffield, while according to MacLeod and Morris (1996) 50 per cent of primary pupils in London and the South-East reported being bullied in school during the previous year.

A further continuing concern for primary school teachers is boys' literacy practices. In my own work with boys I tried to combine 'doing' with writing activities through book making projects involving both mixed and boys only groups. Setting the groups the task of producing book proposals that appeal to the widest possible class readership both challenges and modifies existing stereotypes, and if supported by whole class surveys, generates useful information for the teachers as well as the children (Reay 1993). The subsequent process of designing layout, working out the graphics, producing publicity and marketing materials, as well as writing the text, meets the requirements of English, maths, art and ICT curricula at the same time as helping to change preconceived ideas about gendered preferences.

In addition to concerted work on bullying and literacy a lot of my time in the sessions was spent helping the boys to question conventional gendered characterisations. Any work with boys needs to recognise gender as relational elements (Francis 1998; Skelton 2001a) and focus on the images of femininity as well as those of masculinity that boys bring with them and construct in the context of schooling. Relatedly, I would argue that such work also needs to recognise the relationships between gender, class and ethnicity. The other curriculum interventions I developed were rooted in this belief that gender cannot be explored in isolation from other powerful aspects of identity. The anti-racist work on Black history was enjoyed by all the boys and even prompted the most writing phobic boys in the group to commit pen to paper. One of my main worries about the National Curriculum is that it has marginalised any notion of 'really useful knowledge' (Johnson 1979) for the working classes but anti-racist work that looks at the lives of 'ordinary but heroic' black people like Rosa Parks is clearly both useful and inspiring. So was the work on the franchise and working-class histories I covered. At the time I wrote that the primary-aged boys I was working with suffered the fate of all low status groups in society, be they black, female or working class: 'They had had no access to a meaningful history which explained why they and others like them came to be situated in a particular social location' (Reay 1990:279). Today the obsession with 'the basics' have left even less space for curriculum initiatives that I still see as vital in predominantly working-class schools like those I was working in.

Devolving power to pupils and instituting more collaborative, reflexive and democratic ways of working are also simultaneously ways of tackling disaffection. It is good to see the 'new-found' enthusiasm for formative assessment (Black et al. 2002) as that which underpinned learning in the boys' groups that I was teaching in the 1980s. The self and peer evaluation with its focus on pupil discussion and responsibility for learning that has become fashionable in the late 1990s was a pivotal part of the boys' groups I ran in the late 1980s:

> From the beginning I instituted a process of self-evaluation where boys evaluated their ability to work co-operatively on a scale of one to ten. They then made a group assessment which involved evaluating the input of other members of their group in addition to their own contribution. I fed back my own observations and we negotiated a final score. Initially, their contributions were brief to the point of curtness but by the summer term they seemed to have a much better grasp of what self and group evaluation entailed, giving far more detailed comments.
>
> (Reay 1990:273)

Black *et al.* (2002) argue that both self and peer assessment are valuable but that peer assessment is especially valuable because pupils accept from one another criticisms of their work – and I would add behaviour – which they would not take seriously from their teacher. As is implicit in the quote above, peer assessment also allows the teacher space to observe and reflect on what is happening and to frame useful interventions.

Implicit in all the above is the view that the issue of tackling boys' disaffection and disruption in primary classrooms needs to be intrinsically, irrevocably linked to a project of social class, gender and racial justice in education. This does not mean suspending the National Curriculum and instituting a series of boys-only discussion groups. Rather, the curriculum and attainment targets need to be creatively rethought. A good starting point is to find out 'the gender state-of-play' in your classroom and cover mathematics, ICT and English curricula at the same time by getting the children to research what ideas pupils hold about men and women and how they differ by sex (see Francis 1998). When I attempted something similar I was pleasantly surprised:

> I came to the boys' group with a set of preconceived ideas about boys not being able to express their feelings and expecting female servicing. I was not entirely wrong but like all stereotypes my preconceptions were far too simplistic. It transpired that I was drawing on more traditional notions of masculinity in the spheres of domestic labour and tears than were the boys.
>
> (Reay 1990:274)

However. as Christine Skelton (2001b) points out, work on the images of masculinity and femininity children bring with them into school and act out in the classroom and playground needs to be accompanied by parallel work on the dominant images of masculinity and femininity schools reflect to their pupils. Reflecting on and questioning dominant gender categories is something the staff need to do as much as the boys and girls in their classes.

The bigger picture: contextualizing boys' disaffection

In Shaun's story (Reay 2002) I write about a white, working-class boy, who, in spite of a contradictory, ambivalent relationship to schooling (that, I would argue, characterises almost all, and especially white, working-class relationships to education) desperately wants to achieve educationally. The article raises questions about the possibilities of bringing together white working-class masculinities with educational success in inner-city working-class schooling. Lucey and Walkerdine (2000:43) argue that 'to be both academically successful and acceptably male requires a considerable amount of careful negotiation on the part of working class boys'. I argue that to combine the two generates heavy psychic costs, involving boys and young men not only in an enormous amount of academic labour but also an intolerable burden of psychic reparative work. Shaun's situation reveals the tenuousness of working-class, and in particular male, working-class relationships to schooling. In the article I describe how he is caught between two untenable positions, continually engaged in a balancing act that requires superhuman effort; on the one hand ensuring his masculinity is kept intact and on the other endeavouring to maintain his academic success. Inner-city schools and their wider contexts are often spaces in which success is in short supply and, as a consequence, it is frequently resented and undermined in those who have it. Below we see both the enormous effort Shaun puts into reconciling two contradictory aspects of self, and also the ways in which they are beginning to come apart:

> It's getting harder because like some boys, like a couple of my friends, yeah, they go 'Oh, you are teacher's pet and all that'. Right? What? Am I a teacher's pet because I do my work and tell you lot to shut up when you are talking and miss is trying to talk? And they go, yeah so you're still a teacher's pet. Well, if you don't like it go away, innit.
>
> (Reay 2002:228)

Shaun's ambitions are created under and against conditions of adversity. Reputations in his school comes not through academic achievements but is the outcome of jockeying for position among a male peer group culture, in which boys are 'routinely reproducing versions of themselves and their peers as valued because of their hardness, appearance or capacity to subvert schooling' (Phoenix and Frosh 2001). Shaun's narrative suggests that the problem of 'failing boys' cannot be solved alone through school based initiatives. How can Shaun both set himself apart from and remain part of the wider working-class male collectivity? That is the task he has set himself and the dilemma it raises lies at the very heart of the class differentials in attainment within education. I conclude that until social processes of male gender socialization move away from the imperative of privileging the masculine and allow boys to stay in touch with their feminine qualities the problem of 'failing boys' will remain despite the best efforts of teachers, teaching assistants and researchers.

Working class boys like Shaun recognize that, unlike their middle class counterparts, working class students need to transform their identity in order to succeed. And transformation is a fraught, risky, and often painful struggle if you and your kind have historically been, and are currently positioned as 'other' to the educated, intelligent and cultured subject. For Shaun academic success is not normative and he has to literally think and enact himself as 'other' in order to attempt to do well. In her book on *Educational Failure and White Working Class Children in Britain* Gillian Evans highlights the need for research to help understand how white working class boys come to perceive troublesome, oppositional and resistant behaviour within schooling as a social good. However, I would suggest that confronted with a high risk of educational failure, a context in which they are seen to have little value, and a difficult, often impossible transition from failing to successful learner, such attitudes are understandable. Facing an educational competition they cannot win they construct peer group macho and physically aggressive competitions where some of them can and do win (Reay 2009b).

Frosh and his colleagues (2002) offer further helpful insights into male peer group cultures in school in their delineation of popular and unpopular masculinities and the classroom behaviours that underpin them. They found that 'an important part of being "cool" and popular entailed the resisting and challenging of adult authority in the classroom' (Frosh *et al.* 2002:200).

Popular boys were expected to 'backchat' teachers, while boys who were seen as too conscientious were made fun of. As Christine Skelton (2001b) demonstrates through her case study of Shane, primary school boys who consistently challenge the teacher's authority earn themselves not only significant amounts of teacher attention but also the attention and tacit approval of their male peers. Here we can see a frightening correlation between popularity among the male peer group and getting into trouble in primary classrooms.

So have I moved from a counsel of hope to a counsel of despair? At times the research and literature in the area appears overwhelming, giving the impression that the male peer group is so dominant there is little teachers can do. However, as I've tried to show in the section on practicalities, teachers can make a significant difference and not just in terms of curriculum offer which is the area I have concentrated on, but also in terms of ethos and culture. Boys (and girls) respond best to teachers who can keep order and have fun with pupils. All children have a keen sense of unfairness: for example, they resent being punished collectively when only one or two boys have misbehaved. Frosh *et al.* (2002) found in their interviews with boys that many reported that their teachers treated boys unfairly with some also saying that teachers particularly picked on black boys. They conclude that:

> While this does not necessarily indicate that most teachers are unfair in these ways – particularly since, from their own accounts boys can make life difficult for teachers – the pervasiveness of this narrative from boys is important to considerations of boys' educational attainment.
>
> (Frosh *et al.* 2002:224)

Conclusion

I am certainly not advocating my ways of working as the answer. What I have tried to do in this chapter is give some indication of which strategies worked best in the educational contexts that I was working in during the 1970s and 1980s. I have also tried to map out how 'the problem' of boys has changed since the late 1980s and suggested, through recounting some of Shaun's story, that only partial solutions can ever lie with teachers and schools. Wider constructions of both masculinities and femininities need to change and while teachers have a part to play, it is ultimately a challenge that the whole of society needs to face up to.

References

Black, P., Harrison, C., Lee, C., Marshall, B. and Wiliam, D. (2002) *Working Inside the Black Box: Assessment for Learning in the Classroom*. London: King's College Publications.

Connell, R.W. (2000) *The Men and the Boys*. Cambridge: Polity Press.

Connolly, P. (2004) *Boys and Schooling in the Early Years*. London: Routledge.

Connolly, P. (2007) "Boys Will Be Boys" but in what Ways? Social Class and the Development of Young Boys' Schooling Identities in International Handbook of Student Experience in Elementary and Secondary School. Section Two, 321–346.

Evan, G. (2006) *White Working class educational failure* London: Palgrave.

Francis, B. (1998) *Power Plays: Primary School Children's Constructions of Gender, Power and Adult Work*. Stoke-on-Trent: Trentham Books.

Frosh, S., Phoenix, A. and Pattman, R. (2002) *Young Masculinities*. London: Palgrave.

Jackson, D. (1998) 'Breaking out of the binary trap: boys' underachievement, schooling and gender relations', in: D.Epstein, J.Elwood, V.Hey and J.Maw (eds.), *Failing Boys: Issues in Gender and Achievement*. Buckingham: The Open University Press.

Johnson, R. (1979) 'Really useful knowledge: radical education and working–class culture 1790–1948', in: J. Clarke, C. Critcher and R. Johnson (eds.), *Working Class Culture: Studies in History and Theory*. New York: St Martin's Press.

Lucey, H. and Walkerdine, V. (2000) 'Boys' underachievement: social class and changing masculinities', in: T. Cox (ed.), *Combating Educational Disadvantage*. London: Falmer Press.

MacLeod, M. and Morris, S. (1996) *Why Me? Children Talking to ChildLine About Bullying*. London: ChildLine.

Phoenix, A. and Frosh, S. (2001) 'Positioned by "hegomonic" masculinities: a study of London boys' narratives of identity', *Australian Psychologist*, 36 (1):27–35.

Reay, D. (1990) 'Working with boys', *Gender and Education*, 12(3):269–82.

Reay, D. (1993) ' "Miss, he says he doesn't like you", working with boys in the infant classroom', in: H. Claire, J. Maybin and J. Swann (eds.), *Equality Matters: Case Studies from the Primary School*. Clevedon: Multilingual Matters.

Reay, D. (2002) 'Shaun's story: troubling discourses of white working class masculinities', *Gender and Education*, 14(3):221–34.

Reay, D. (2006) The Zombie stalking English Schools: Social Class and Educational Inequality *British Journal of Educational Studies* Special issue on Social Justice 54 (3) 288–307.

Reay, D. (2009a) Identity Making in Schools and Classrooms *The Sage Handbook of Identities* (eds.) M. Wetherell and C. Mohanty New York: Sage.

Reay, D. (2009b) Making Sense of White Working Class Educational Underachievement in K Sveinsson (ed.) Who Cares about the white Working Class? London: Runnymede Trust.

Skelton, C. (2001a) 'Typical boys? Theorising masculinity in educational settings', in: B. Francis and C. Skelton (eds.), *Investigating Gender: Contemporary Perspectives in Education*. Buckingham: Open University Press.

Skelton, C. (2001b) *Schooling the Boys: Masculinities and Primary Education*. Buckingham: Open University Press.

Walkerdine, V. (1981) 'Sex, power and pedagogy', *Screen Education*, 38:14–25.

Whitney, I. and Smith, P.K. (1993) 'A survey of the nature and extent of bullying in junior and secondary schools', *Educational Research*, 35(1):3–25.

Willis, P. (1977) *Learning to Labour*. Aldershot: Saxon House. adapted from Reay, D. (2003) 'Troubling, troubled and troublesome? Working with boys in the primary classroom', in: C. Skelton and B. Francis (eds.), *Boys and Girls in the Primary Classroom*, pages 151–166 with the kind permission of the Open University Press/McGraw-Hill Publishing company.

Index